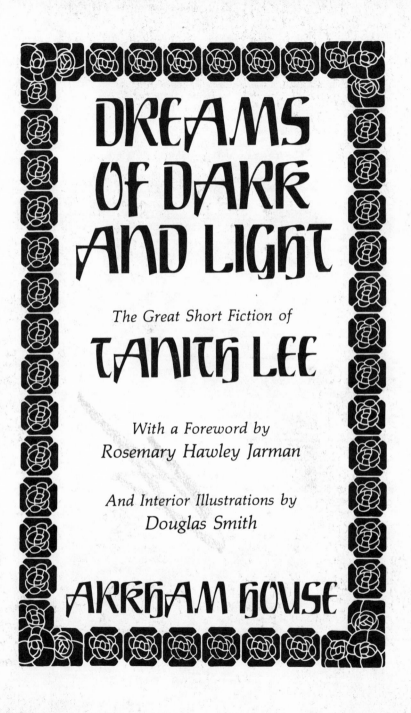

# DREAMS OF DARK AND LIGHT

The Great Short Fiction of

# TANITH LEE

With a Foreword by
Rosemary Hawley Jarman

And Interior Illustrations by
Douglas Smith

# ARKHAM HOUSE

Copyright © 1986 by Tanith Lee

Library of Congress Cataloging-in-Publication Data
Lee, Tanith.
    Dreams of dark and light.
    1. Fantastic fiction, English.   I. Title.
    PR6062.E4153D7   1986   823'.914   85-28571
    ISBN 0-87054-153-6 (alk. paper)

Printed in the United States of America
All rights reserved / First Edition

# CONTENTS

# FOREWORD

If anything can truly be attributed to chance, it was thus that, some years ago, I first encountered Tanith Lee's work and so experienced one of the most pleasurable surprises of my literary life. As a novelist who endeavours to dust off history and imbue its embalmed characters with motion and light, I acknowledged a very broad similarity between fantasy and SF and my own field, in which those who work must, by necessity, use a certain amount of imagination to blow life into long-dead protagonists and where, implicit in any reconstruction of yesterday, are worlds alien and fabulous. Despite this fragile bond, and excluding such great masters as Poe, Bradbury, and others, I found fantasy writers slightly sterile, often intimidating. One seemed to need a degree in physics to travel their esoteric landscapes, though doubtless the fault lay with my own dull wits. Or maybe the artist in me marched to a different drummer, who can say? And then I discovered Tanith Lee.

Here was no collection of rasping androids, no cosmic mathematics. Yet nonetheless, here were worlds apart, their denizens surrealistically proportioned but, by some intellectual sleight-of-hand, rendered totally viable, comprehensible, and relevant. I read epic hero-tales that could have been bred from bardic mythos or sung on antique Aegean waterfronts; from the magnificent debut of *The Birthgrave* to the cornucopia of subsequent novels and collections, finally surfacing stunned, delighted, and near to disbelief.

True, this was fantasy and SF, but it was something very much more than swords-and-sorcery or the grappling of planets. For Tanith Lee is a prose-poet of the highest calibre, and her writing would stand undiminished in any company. While she shifts and turns her multifaceted worlds about, she arrests the reader with a melodious metaphor or graceful irony. She sets and lights her stage with care. Like Flaubert, she attends lovingly to the smallest detail, mining new fields, hemispheres, and cultures as keenly as a scientist seeking a cure. A chameleon, she glides with uncanny ease into the mode and meter of each fresh theme, where nothing is ever remotely derivative, but subject to a continuous staggering flow of innovation.

As if this were not enough, the inexhaustible freshness of idea and melody of language is married to a profound philosophical awareness. Her themes are historical in their roundness and plausibility. All human (and inhuman) nobility and frailty are paraded in her pages. While her often bizarre concepts evoke a chain reaction of joy, terror, or both, her characters step from another dimension and find, in the reader's intellect, a magic mirror-image, tantalisingly akin yet alien to our own life-experience. Here, the mundane is made marvellous, the extraordinary exotic. Fish sing in trees, jewelled birds feed from the ocean floor. Creatures phantasmagoric and mythical, secret lights and ciphered darknesses—all move their timeless pattern across eastern deserts to the cold canyons of a star, from haunted islands to weird cities so convincingly drawn that they tempt one to seek them on a map of our world, and these are only the tip of the iceberg. The wonders of Lee's invention are absolute, her sorcery infinite. She can disturb, even terrify, but she is never gratuitously sadistic; *au fond*, there is a deep logic to her legends, and in the darkest soul-night comes tenderness. In her horrors there is often humour, and she is the only writer of her genre who can make me weep.

Also there are the games. Lee is a philologist and her lexicon is daunting; half-hidden allusions, paradoxes, classical figures rather wickedly disguised, inversions, contrasts, counterpoint, echoes, *trompes l'oeil*, and semantic doppelgängers dance to the measure of her wit. Yet there is always technical control, and self-indulgence is rare. Consciously or otherwise, she keeps a light hand on the pulse of the reader, so that again and again, even after an encounter with a man made of water, or time flowing backwards, comes the response: yes, I understand, I sympathise, I *know*. Or even . . . I remember. . . .

For while Lee conjures demons and saints from other spheres and clothes them in prisms, jewels, and changes, her creativity, like Mary Shelley's, is often subtly humanitarian, ever mindful of the fates and chances of the known, as well as the unknown, world. Her work has heart and spirit, and maybe herein lies her worldwide appeal. To create empathy within the fantastic is unusual, but she achieves it nonetheless. Although she works on several levels and in many colours and dimensions, there is, in her great talent, the demonstration of insights equal to any topflight storyteller, regardless of genre.

The breadth of Lee's imaginative spectrum and the power of her descriptions make her, above all, an entertainer. This is in no way an attempt to denigrate or patronise, rather a tribute to her readability. This rich trait goes hand in hand with a classical form wherein are structures, denouements, and humanities greatly transcending the mere fantastic. Her work is rooted in the best narrative traditions, and these are, quite often, strangely heightened by the boundlessness of her themes.

Therefore, in these pages, there is that which can be appreciated on several levels, as the ingenuity with which she limns her far horizons enhances and augments her profound power and control. To those countless Lee aficionados I need say no more by way of celebration. To those fortunate enough to be about to discover her: here is a banquet—tastes and textures vital with poignancy and piquancy—fit for the intellectual gourmet as well as the seeker after shudders. Even the legendary sultan who sought a thousand and one diversions could not, I fancy, fail to be enthralled by these dreams of dark and light. Without doubt, Tanith Lee is the Scheherazade of our time.

ROSEMARY HAWLEY JARMAN

# DREAMS OF DARK AND LIGHT

# BECAUSE OUR SKINS ARE FINER

I N THE EARLY WINTER, WHEN THE SEAS ARE STRONG, THE GREY seals come ashore among the islands. Their coats are like dull silver in the cold sunlight, and for these coats of theirs men kill them. It has always been so, one way and another. There were knives and clubs, now there are the guns, too. A man with his own gun and his own boat does well from the seals, and such a man was Huss Hullas. A grim and taciturn fellow he was, with no kin, and no kindness, living alone in his sea-grey croft on the sea rim of Dula, under the dark old hill. Huss Hullas had killed in his time maybe three hundred seals, and then, between one day and the next, he would not go sealing anymore, not for money and surely not for love.

Love had always been a stranger to him, that much was certain. He had no woman, and cared for himself as any man can in the islands. And once a month he would row to the town on the mainland, and drink whisky, and go upstairs with one of the paid girls. And row back to Dula in the sunrise, no change to be seen in him for better or worse. Then one time he went to the town and there was a new girl working at the bar. Morna was her name. Her hair was black as licorice, and her skin was rosy. As the evening drew to a close, Huss Hullas spoke to Morna, but not to order whisky. And Morna answered him, and he got to his feet and went out and banged the bar door behind him. It seemed she would not go with him as the other girls would. She had heard tell of him, it seemed.

Not that he was rough, or anything more than businesslike in bed, but he was no prince either, with no word to say and no laugh to laugh, and not even a grunt to show he had been gladdened. "I will not go upstairs with a lump of rock, then," she said. "There are true men enough who'll pay me."

Now love was a stranger to him but so was failure. And though this was a small prize to fail at the winning of, yet he did not like to fail. If he would eat a rabbit or bird for his meal, he would find and shoot one. If he baked bread, it would rise. If he broke a bone, he could set it himself, and it would mend. Only the sea had ever beaten him, and that not often, and he is a foolish man will not respect the sea, who lives among her isles. Even the Shealcé, the Seal People, dropped down before Huss Hullas's gun obediently. And since he had never yet asked a free woman to take him, he had never yet been refused, till Morna did it.

When he went again to town, he went before the month was up, and when Morna came by his table, he said she should sit down and drink whisky with him. But Morna stepped sharply away. "I will not do that, neither."

"What will you do then," said Huss Hullas, "will you be got the sack?"

"Not I," said she. "The rest like me. They have cause."

"I will give you a pound more," he said.

Morna smiled. "No."

"How much, then?"

"Nothing, then." And she was gone, and presently so was he.

When he came back the next month, he brought her a red lacquer comb that had been his mother's.

"What now," she said, "is it wooing me, you are?"

"Learning your price, then," he said.

"Well, I'll not go with you for an old comb."

"It's worth a bit."

"I have said."

"For what then?"

Morna frowned at him angrily. It must be made clear, he was not a bad-looking man for all the grim way he had with him, which had not altered, nor his stony face, even as he offered her the comb. And his eyes, dark as the hill of Dula, said only: *You will do it. This is just your game.* And so it was.

It was winter by then, and all along the shore the oil-lamps burned where the electricity had not yet been brought in, and the seals were swimming south like the waves, as they had swum for hundreds of years.

"Well," said Morna. "Bring me a sealskin for a coat, and I'll go upstairs with you. That is my promise. It shall keep me warm if you cannot, you cold pig of a man."

"Ah," said Huss Hullas, and he got up and went out of the bar to find another woman for the night, on Fish Street.

The seals came that month and beached on all the islands west of Dula. They lay under the pale winter sun and called to each other, lying on the rocks where the sea could find them. On some of these bleak places it might seem men had never lived yet in the whole world, but still men would come there.

One or another rowed over to Dula and hammered on Huss Hullas's door, and he opened it with a rod and a line he was making in one hand.

"The seals are in. Are you ready, man?"

"I am."

"We shall be out at dawn tomorrow, with the tide to help us."

"I'll be there."

"So you will, and your fine gun. How many will you get this winter?"

"Enough."

"And one for her on the mainland."

"We'll say nothing of that," said Huss Hullas, and the man looked at him and nodded. Grim and hard and black, the eyes in Huss Hullas's head could have put out fires, and his fists could kill a man, as well as a seal.

In the first stealth of the sunrise, Huss Hullas rowed away from Dula with his gun and his bullets by him. He rowed to where the ocean narrows and the rocks rise up to find the air. In the water over westward, dark buoys bobbed in the blushing water that were the heads of seals. Tarnished by wet they lay, too, on the ledges of the isles, shelf on shelf of them, and sang in their solemn inhuman way, not knowing death approached them.

There was some ice, and here and there a seal lay out on the plates of it. They watched the men in the shadowy boats from their round eyes. The Shealcé is their old name, and still they are named so, now and then, the Seal People, who have a great city down under the sea.

When the guns spoke first, the Shealcé looked about them, as if puzzled, those that did not flop and loll and bleed. When the guns spoke again, the rocks themselves seemed to move as shelf upon shelf slid over into the water and dived deep down. The guns shouted as if to call them back, the pink water smoked and blood ran on the ice. Men laughed. It is not the way, anymore, to know that what you kill is a living thing. It was different once, in the old times, very different then, when you would know and honour even the cut-down wheat. Men must live, like any other creatures, and it is not always a sin to kill, but to kill without knowledge may well be a sin, perhaps.

Huss Hullas had shipped his oars, and let the current move him through the channels. He knew the islands and their rocks as he knew his own body, their moods and their treacheries, and the way the water ran. He drifted gently in among the panic of the seals, and slew them as they hastened from the other men towards him, along the ice.

Each one he killed he knew, and would claim after. Every man marked his own.

Then, as Huss Hullas's boat nosed her way between the rocks, the sun stood up on the water. In the rays of it he saw before him, on a patch of ice, one lone seal, but it was larger by far than all the others, something larger than any seal Huss Hullas had ever seen. Plainly, it was a bull, but young, unscarred, and shining in the sunlight. It had a coat on it that, in the dawn, looked for sure more gold than grey. And even Huss Hullas could not resist a little grimace that was his smile, and he raised the gun.

As he did so the seal turned and looked at him with its circular eyes, blacker than his own.

*Yes, now, keep still*, the man thought. For to blunder in the shot and spoil such fur would be a grave pity.

Huss Hullas was aiming for one of the eyes, but at the last instant the great golden seal lowered its head, and the bullet, as it speared away, struck it in the brain. It seemed to launch itself forward, the seal, in the same instant, and the dull flame of its body hit the water beyond the ice. Huss Hullas cursed aloud and grabbed up one of his oars. Already dead, the seal clove the water in a lovely arching dive —and was dammed against Huss Hullas's wooden rower.

His strong arms cracking and his mouth uttering every blasphemy known among the islands—which is many and varied— Huss Hullas held the seal, first with the oar, next with his hands, and as the boat roiled and skewed and threatened to turn herself over in the freezing sea, he struggled and thrust for the nearest edge of rock. Here, by some miracle, he dragged the dead weight of the seal, the boat, himself, aground, his hands full of blood and fur, and the oar splintering.

He stood over the seal, until another boat came through the narrows. Frost had set the seal's dead eyes by then, as he towered over it, panting and cursing it, and the golden fur was like mud.

"That is a rare big beast, Huss Hullas. It should fetch a good price at the sheds."

"This is not for the sheds."

Taking out his knife then, he began to skin the great seal.

When he was done, he tossed the meat and fat and bones away, and took the heavy syrupy skin into the boat with him. After the other seals had been seen to, he left his share with the rest of the men. They saw the oar was ailing, and they knew better than try to cheat him.

He rowed back to Dula with the skin of the one seal piled round him, and the oar complaining.

The remainder of that day, with the skin pegged up in the outhouse, Huss Hullas sat fishing off Dula, like a man who has no care on earth, and no vast joy in it, either. If he looked forward to his next visit to the town, you could not have said from the manner of him. But he caught a basket of fish and went in as the sun was going out to clean and strip them and set them to cook on the stove.

The croft was like a dozen others, a single room with a fireplace in one wall and a big old bed on another. Aside from the stove there was a cupboard or two, and tackle for the boat or for the fishing stacked about, some carpentry tools, and some books that had been his father's that Huss Hullas never read. A couple of oil-lamps waited handy to be lit. Often he would make do with the light of the fire. What he did there in his loneliness, sitting in his chair all the nights of the months he did not go drinking and whoring, was small enough. He would clean his gun, and mend his clothing and his boots; he would repair the leg of a stool, cook his food and eat it, and throw the plate into a pan of water for the morning. He would brew tea. He would think of himself whatever thoughts came to him, and listen to the hiss and sigh of the sea on the rim of Dula. In the bed he would sleep early, and wake early. While he slept he kept his silence. There rose up no comfortable snoring from Huss Hullas, and if he dreamed at all, he held the dreaming to himself. And two hours before the sun began, or before that, he would be about. He could stride right across Dula in a day, and had often done so and come back in the evening, with the stars and the hares starting over the hill.

This night though, as the fish were seething and the sun going down into the water on a path of blood, he walked back to the outhouse, and took a stare at the sealskin drying on its pegs. In the last sunglare, the fur of the pelt was like new copper. It had a beautiful sheen to it, and no mistake. It was too good to be giving away. But there, he had made his bargain—not to the girl, but to himself. Set in his ways, he had not the tactics to go back on his word. So with a shrug, he banged shut the outhouse door, and went to eat his supper in the croft.

It was maybe an hour after the sunset that the wind began to lift along the sea.

In a while, Huss Hullas put aside the sleeve he was darning, and listened. He had lived all his life in sight and sound of the ocean, and the noise of water and weather was known to him. Even the winds had their own voices, but this wind had a voice like no other he had ever heard. At first he paid it heed, and then he went back to his darning. But then again he sat still and listened, and he could not make it out, so much any could tell, if they had seen him. At last, he got to his feet and took the one oil-lamp that was burning on the mantelpiece, and opened the door of the croft. He stood there, gazing out into the darkness, the lamp swinging its lilt of yellow over the sloping rock, and beyond it only the night and the waves. There was nothing to be found out there. The sea was not even rough, only a little choppy as it generally would be at this season of the year. The sky was open and stars hung from it, though the moon would not be over the hill for another hour or more.

So there was no excuse for the wind, or the way it sounded. No excuse at all. And what had caught Huss Hullas's attention in the croft was five times louder in the outer air.

It was full of crying, the wind was, like the keening of women around a grave. And yet, there was nothing human in the noise. It rose and fell and came and went, like breathing, now high and wild and lamenting, now low and choked and dire.

Huss Hullas was not a superstitious man, and he did not believe any of the old tales that get told around the fires on winter nights. He had not enough liking for his own kind to have caught their romancing. Yet he heard the wind, and finding nothing he went inside again and bolted the door.

And next he took a piece of wood and worked on it, sawing and hammering it, while the kettle sang on the hob and the fire spat from a dose of fresh peat. The wind was not so easily heard in this way. Nor anything much outside. Though when the knock came sharp on his bolted door, Huss Hullas heard it well enough.

In all the years he had lived on Dula, there had only been one other time someone had knocked on the door by night. There are some two hundred souls live there, and no phone and not even a vet. One summer dark, with a child of his ailing, a man came to ask Huss Hullas to row him over to the mainland for a doctor. Huss Hullas refused to row, but for three pounds he let the man hire his boat. That was his way. Later that night the doctor was operating for appendicitis over the hill on a scrubbed kitchen table. The child lived; the father said to Huss Hullas: "Three pounds is the worth you set on a child's life." "Be glad," was the answer, "I set it so cheap."

Money or no, Huss Hullas did not like to be disturbed, and perhaps it was this made him hesitate, now. Then the knocking came again, and a voice called to him out of the crying of the wind.

"Open your door," it said. "I see your light under it."

And the voice was a woman's.

Maybe he was curious and maybe not, but he went to the door at last and unbolted it and threw it wide.

The thick dull glow of the lamp left on the mantelpiece fell out around him on the rock. But directly where his shadow fell instead, the woman was standing. In this way he could not see her well, but he made a guess she was from one of the inland crofts. She seemed dressed as the women there were dressed, shabby and shawled, and her fashion of talking seemed enough like theirs.

"Well, what is it?" he said to her.

"It's a raw night," she said. "I would come in."

"That's no reason I should let you."

"You are the man hunts the seals," she said.

"I am."

"Then I would come in and speak of that."

"I've nothing to sell. The skins are in the sheds across the water."

"One skin you have here."

"Who told you so?"

"No matter who told me," said the woman. "I heard it was a fine one. Beautiful and strangely coloured, and the size of two seals together."

"Not for sale," said Huss Hullas, supposing sullenly one of the other sealers had jabbered, though how news had got to Dula he was not sure, unless he had been spied on.

"It is a love gift, then?" said the woman. "You are courting, and would give it to her?"

At this, his granite temper began to stir.

"This skin is mine, and no business of yours," he said. "Get home."

When he said this the wind seemed to swell and break on the island like a wave. Startled, he raised his head, and for a moment there seemed to be a kind of mist along the water, a mist that moved, swimming and sinuous, as if it were full of live things.

"*Get home,*" the woman repeated softly. "And where do you think my home to be?"

When he looked back at her, she had turned a little and come out of his shadow, so the lamp could reach her. She was not young, but neither was she old, and she was handsome, too, but this is not what he saw first. He saw that he had been mistaken in the matter of the shawl, for she was shawled only in her hair, which was very long, streaming round her, and of a pale ashy brown uncommon enough he had never before seen it. Her eyes, catching the lamp, were black and brilliant, but they were odd, too, in a way he could not make out, though he did not like them much. Otherwise she might have seemed normal, except her hair was wet, and her clothing, which was shapeless and looked torn, ran with water. Perhaps it had rained as she walked over the hill.

"Your home is nothing to me," he said. "And the skin is not for sale."

"We will speak of it," she said. And she put out her hand as if to touch him and he sprang backwards before he knew what he did. Next moment she came in after him, and the door fell shut on the night, closing them in the croft together.

In all his life Huss Hullas had never feared anything, save the ocean, which was more common sense than fear. Now he stood and stared at the woman with her wet dress and her wet hair, knowing that in some way fear her he did, but he had not the words or even the emotion in him to explain it to himself, or what else he felt, for fear was not nearly all of it.

He must have stood a long while, staring like that, and she a long while letting him do so. What nudged him at length was another thing altogether. A piece of coal barked on the fire, and in the silence after, he realised the wind had dropped, and its eerie wailing ceased.

"Your name is Huss Hullas," the woman said in the silence. "Do not ask me how I learned it. My name, so we shall know each other, is Saiuree."

When she told him her name, the hair rose on his neck. It did not sound human, but more like the hiss the spume would make, or the sea through a channel, or some creature of the sea.

"Well," he said harshly. "Well."

"It shall be well," she agreed, "for I'll have the skin from your shed. But I'll pay you fairly for it, whatever price you have set."

He laughed then, shortly and bitterly, for he was not given to laughter, he did it ill and it ill-became him.

"The price is one you would not like to pay, Missus."

"Tell it me, and I shall know."

"The price," he said brutishly, "is to spill between a woman's spread legs."

But she only looked at him.

"If that is what you wish, that is what I can give you."

"Ah," he said. "But you see, it's not you I want."

"So," she said, and she was quiet awhile. He felt an uneasy silly triumph while she was, standing there in his own croft with him, and he unable to show her the door. Then she said, "It is a black-haired girl on the mainland you would have. Her name is Morna."

His triumph went at that.

"Who told you?" he said.

"You," said she.

And he understood it was true. She smiled, slow and still, like a ripple spreading in a tide pool.

"Oh, Huss Hullas," said she, "I might have filled this room up with pearls, and not have missed them, or covered the floor with old green coins from the days before any man lived here. There is a ship sunk, far out, and none knows of it. There are old shields rotting black on the sides of it and a skeleton sits in the prow with a gold ring on his neck, and I might have brought you that ring. Or farther out there is another ship with golden money in boxes. Or I could bring you the stone head with stone snakes for hair, that was cast into the sea for luck, and make you rich. But you will have your bar girl and that is your price."

Huss Hullas sat down in his chair before the fire and wished he had some whisky by him. At the woman who called herself Saiuree, he snarled: "You're mad, then."

"Yes," she said. "Mad with grief. Like those you heard in the wind, crying for the sea they have lost and the bodies they have lost, so they may not swim anymore through the waterworld, or through the towered city under the ocean."

"I've no interest in stories," he said.

"Have you none."

"No. But you'll tell me next you are one of the Shealcé, and the skin you seek is your own."

"So I am," she said. "But the skin is not mine. It is the skin of my only son, Connuh, that you shot on the ice for his beauty and his strength as the dawn stood on the water."

Huss Hullas spat in the fire.

"My mother had a son, too. There's no great joy in sons."

"Ah," she said, "it's that you hate yourself so much you can never come to love another. Well, we are not all of your way. Long before men came here, the Seal People held this water and this land. And when men came they took the fish from us and drove us out. And when, in passing then, we paused to rest here, they killed us, because our skins are finer than their own. How many of this People have you slain, man? Many hundreds, is it not? And today with your gun you slew a prince of this People. For he was of the true Shealcé, from whom all the Shealcé now take their name. But still even we do not give hate for hate, greed for greed, injustice for injustice. I'll pay your price. Look in my eyes and see it."

"I'll not look in your eyes."

"So you will," she said.

She came close. No steam rose from her, nor was she dry. Her dress was seaweed, and nothing else. Her hair was like the sea itself. He saw why he had misliked her eyes. About their round bright blackness there was no white at all. Even so, he looked at them and into them and through them, out into the night.

Above, the night sea was black, but down, far down where the seal dives, it was not black at all. There was a kind of light, but it came from nothing in the sea. It came from the inside of the eyes of the ones who swam there, who had seen the depths of the water in their own way, and now showed it to the man. If Huss Hullas wished to see it, who can say? Probably he did not. A man with so little life-love in him he was like one without blood, to him maybe to see these things he saw was only wasted time. But if he had only walled himself in all these years against his own thought and his own dreams, then maybe there was a strange elation in the seeing, and a cold pain.

At first then, only the darkness through which he saw as he went down in it, like one drowning, but alive and keeping breath, as the seals did, on land or in ocean both. Then there began to be fish, like polished knives without their hafts, flashing this way and that way. And through the fish, Huss Hullas began to see the currents of the water, the milky strands like breezes going by. All around there were, too, the dim shadows of the Shealcé, each one graceful and lovely in that gentle shape of theirs, like dancers at their play, but moving ever down and down, and ever northwards.

They passed a wreck. It was so old it was like the skeleton of a leaf, and in the prow a human skeleton leaned. It had a gold torc round its bone throat, while the shields clung in black bits and flakes to the open sides of the vessel, just as Saiuree had said. It was a Wicing longboat of many, many hundred years before.

The seals swam over and about the wreck, and then away, and Huss Hullas followed them.

And it began to seem to him then that he felt the silk of the water on his flesh, and the power and grace of the seal whose body he seemed to have come to inhabit, but he was not sure.

Shortly beyond the wreck there was a space of sheer blackness, that might have been a wall of rock. But here and there were openings in the black, and one by one the seals ebbed through with the water, and Huss Hullas after them. On the farther side was the city of the Shealcé.

Now, there are many tales told of that spot, but this was how he saw it for himself.

It must in part have been a natural thing, and this is not to be wondered at, for the Shealcé have no hands in their water form with which to build, whatever figure they may conjure on the land. Above would be islets, no doubt, where they might bask in the sun of summer. But here the cold-sea coral had grown, pale greyish red and sombre blueish white, and rose in spines and funnels all about. It seemed to Huss Hullas like a city of chimneys, for the curious hollow formations twisted and humped and ascended over each other, but all went up—in places ten times the height of a man and more—and at their tops they smoked and bubbled, and that was from the air brought down into them by the Shealcé themselves, in their chests and in their fur, which gradually went up again and was lost in the water.

So he beheld these pastel spires, softly smoking, and glittering, too. For everywhere huge clusters of pearls had been set, or those shells which shine, or other ornaments of the sea, though nothing that had come from men, not silver or gold, nor jewels.

But strangest of all, deep in the city and far away, there were a host of faint lights, for all the world like vague-lit windows high in towers. And these yellow eyes beamed out through the water as if they watched who came and who departed, but if the Shealcé had made and lit them he did not know. Nor did he think of it then, perhaps.

For all the seals swam in amid the chimnied city and he with them, and suddenly he heard again that dreadful hopeless crying, but this time it was not in the wind he heard it, but in his own brain. And this time, too, he knew what it said. He saw, at last, the shapes about him were shadows for sure, were wraiths, the ghosts only of seals, who swam out this final journey before their lamenting memory should die as their bodies had already died from the bullets of men.

*Oh, to be no more, to be no more,* the seals were crying. *To be lost, to be lost. The hurt of the death was less, far less, than the hurt of the loss. Where now are we to go?*

If he felt the hurt they cried of, he did not know himself, most likely. But he was close to it as generally no man comes close to anything, and rarely to his own self.

And then one of the yellow-eyed towers was before him, and he swam up into the light and the light enclosed him—

—and he was in the corridor above the mainland bar with Morna opening a door.

Then they were in the bedroom, and she was not sulky or covetous, but smiling and glad. And she took her stockings off her white legs and bared her rosy breasts and combed her licorice hair with her hands. He forgot the seals that moment, and the water and the crying. "Lie down with me, sweetheart," said Morna, and took him to her like her only love. And he had something with her that hour he never had had with any woman before, and never would have again so long as he lived.

A while before dawn, just as the sky was turning grey under the hill, he woke up alone in his bed in the croft. That he thought he had been dreaming is made nothing of by the fact he came instantly from the covers, flung on his clothes, and went to the door. He meant to go and look in the outhouse, doubtless, but he had no need. What he sought lay on the rocky edge of Dula, less than twenty strides below him.

The whole sky was higher, with the darkness going fast. He had a chance to see what he was staring at.

There by the ocean's brink a woman knelt, mourning over a thing that lay along the rock and across her lap. Her showering hair covered what remained of this thing's face, and maybe Huss Hullas was thankful for it. But from her hair there ran away another stream of hair that was not hers, richer and more golden, even in the 'tween-light. And beyond the hair stretched the body of a young man, long-limbed and wide in the shoulder, and altogether very large and well-made, and altogether naked. At least, it would seem to be a body, but suddenly you noticed some two or three shallow cuts of a knife, and then you would see the body had no meat to it and no muscle and no bone—it was an empty skin.

There came some colour in the sky within the grey, and the woman, with a strange awkward turn, slipped over into the water and dragged the human skin with her, and both were gone.

And then again, as the sun came up over the hill of Dula, and Huss Hullas was still standing there, he saw the round head of a seal a half mile out on the water, with an odd wide wake behind it as if it bore something alongside itself. He did not go to fetch his gun. He never shot a seal from that day to this. Nor did he go drinking or to find women in the town. Indeed, he went inland, over the hill, to live where he might not heed the noise of the sea. He kept away from his own kind; that did not change.

Do you think it was guilt then that turned him from his outward ways, deeper into those inner ways of his? Perhaps only he saw the seal tracks on the rock and sand, or found a strip of seawrack in between the covers of the bed, and knew what he had lain with, even if it had passed for rosy Morna. The Shealcé are an elder people. It is said in the stories they can take each form as they will, the seal or the human, as it suits them, or some older form that maybe they have, which no one knows anymore who has not entered the heart of their city of coral and pearl, and remembered it.

But it is true they were in the islands long before men came there. And who knows but they will be there long after we are gone.

# BITE-ME-NOT
## OR, FLEUR DE FUR

### I

I N THE TRADITION OF YOUNG GIRLS AND WINDOWS, THE YOUNG
girl looks out of this one. It is difficult to see anything. The
panes of the window are heavily leaded, and secured by a lattice
of iron. The stained glass of lizard-green and storm-purple is
several inches thick. There is no red glass in the window. The
colour red is forbidden in the castle. Even the sun, behind the glass,
is a storm sun, a green-lizard sun.

The young girl wishes she had a gown of palest pastel rose—the
nearest affinity to red, which is never allowed. Already she has
long dark beautiful eyes, a long white neck. Her long dark hair is
however hidden in a dusty scarf, and she wears rags. She is a scullery maid. As she scours dishes and mops stone floors, she imagines
she is a princess floating through the upper corridors, gliding to the
dais in the Duke's hall. The Cursed Duke. She is sorry for him. If he
had been her father, she would have sympathised and consoled
him. His own daughter is dead, as his wife is dead, but these things,
being to do with the cursing, are never spoken of. Except, sometimes, obliquely.

*"Rohise!"* dim voices cry now, full of dim scolding soon to be
actualised.

The scullery maid turns from the window and runs to have her
ears boxed and a broom thrust into her hands.

Meanwhile, the Cursed Duke is prowling his chamber, high in the East Turret carved with swans and gargoyles. The room is lined with books, swords, lutes, scrolls, and has two eerie portraits, the larger of which represents his wife, and the smaller his daughter. Both ladies look much the same with their pale egg-shaped faces, polished eyes, clasped hands. They do not really look like his wife or daughter, nor really remind him of them.

There are no windows at all in the turret, they were long ago bricked up and covered with hangings. Candles burn steadily. It is always night in the turret. Save, of course, by night there are particular *sounds* all about it, to which the Duke is accustomed, but which he does not care for. By night, like most of his court, the Cursed Duke closes his ears with softened tallow. However, if he sleeps, he dreams, and hears in the dream the beating of wings. . . . Often, the court holds loud revel all night long.

The Duke does not know Rohise the scullery maid has been thinking of him. Perhaps he does not even know that a scullery maid is capable of thinking at all.

Soon the Duke descends from the turret and goes down, by various stairs and curving passages, into a large, walled garden on the east side of the castle.

It is a very pretty garden, mannered and manicured, which the gardeners keep in perfect order. Over the tops of the high, high walls, where delicate blooms bell the vines, it is just possible to glimpse the tips of sun-baked mountains. But by day the mountains are blue and spiritual to look at, and seem scarcely real. They might only be inked on the sky.

A portion of the Duke's court is wandering about in the garden, playing games or musical instruments, or admiring painted sculptures, or the flora, none of which is red. But the Cursed Duke's court seems vitiated this noon. Nights of revel take their toll.

As the Duke passes down the garden, his courtiers acknowledge him deferentially. He sees them, old and young alike, all doomed as he is, and the weight of his burden increases.

At the farthest, most eastern end of the garden, there is another garden, sunken and rather curious, beyond a wall with an iron door. Only the Duke possesses the key to this door. Now he unlocks it and goes through. His courtiers laugh and play and pretend not to see. He shuts the door behind him.

The sunken garden, which no gardener ever tends, is maintained by other, spontaneous, means. It is small and square, lacking the

hedges and the paths of the other, the sundials and statues and little pools. All the sunken garden contains is a broad paved border,
and at its centre a small plot of humid earth. Growing in the earth is
a slender bush with slender velvet leaves.

The Duke stands and looks at the bush only a short while.

He visits it every day. He has visited it every day for years. He is
waiting for the bush to flower. Everyone is waiting for this. Even
Rohise, the scullery maid, is waiting, though she does not, being
only sixteen, born in the castle and uneducated, properly understand why.

The light in the little garden is dull and strange, for the whole of
it is roofed over by a dome of thick smoky glass. It makes the
atmosphere somewhat depressing, although the bush itself gives off
a pleasant smell, rather resembling vanilla.

Something is cut into the stone rim of the earth-plot where the
bush grows. The Duke reads it for perhaps the thousandth time. *O,
fleur de feu—*

When the Duke returns from the little garden into the large
garden, locking the door behind him, no one seems truly to notice.
But their obeisances now are circumspect.

One day, he will perhaps emerge from the sunken garden leaving
the door wide, crying out in a great voice. But not yet. Not today.

The ladies bend to the bright fish in the pools, the knights pluck
for them blossoms, challenge each other to combat at chess, or
wrestling, discuss the menagerie lions; the minstrels sing of
unrequited love. The pleasure garden is full of one long and weary
sigh.

"Oh flurda fur

"Pourma souffrance—"

Sings Rohise as she scrubs the flags of the pantry floor.

"Ned ormey par,

"May say day mwar—"

"What are you singing, you slut?" someone shouts, and kicks
over her bucket.

Rohise does not weep. She tidies her bucket and soaks up the
spilled water with her cloths. She does not know what the song,
because of which she seems, apparently, to have been chastised,
means. She does not understand the words that somehow, somewhere—perhaps from her own dead mother—she learned by rote.

In the hour before sunset, the Duke's hall is lit by flambeaux. In
the high windows, the casements of oil-blue and lavender glass and

glass like storms and lizards, are fastened tight. The huge window by the dais was long ago obliterated, shut up, and a tapestry hung of gold and silver tissue with all the rubies pulled out and emeralds substituted. It describes the subjugation of a fearsome unicorn by a maiden, and huntsmen.

The court drifts in with its clothes of rainbow from which only the colour red is missing.

Music for dancing plays. The lean pale dogs pace about, alert for tidbits as dish on dish comes in. Roast birds in all their plumage glitter and die a second time under the eager knives. Pastry castles fall. Pink and amber fruits, and green fruits and black, glow beside the goblets of fine yellow wine.

The Cursed Duke eats with care and attention, not with enjoyment. Only the very young of the castle still eat in that way, and there are not so many of those.

The murky sun slides through the stained glass. The musicians strike up more wildly. The dances become boisterous. Once the day goes out, the hall will ring to *chanson*, to drum and viol and pipe. The dogs will bark, no language will be uttered except in a bellow. The lions will roar from the menagerie. On some nights the cannons are set off from the battlements, which are now all of them roofed in, fired out through narrow mouths just wide enough to accommodate them, the charge crashing away in thunder down the darkness.

By the time the moon comes up and the castle rocks to its own cacophony, exhausted Rohise has fallen fast asleep in her cupboard bed in the attic. For years, from sunset to rise, nothing has woken her. Once, as a child, when she had been especially badly beaten, the pain woke her and she heard a strange silken scratching, somewhere over her head. But she thought it a rat, or a bird. Yes, a bird, for later it seemed to her there were also wings. . . . But she forgot all this half a decade ago. Now she sleeps deeply and dreams of being a princess, forgetting, too, how the Duke's daughter died. Such a terrible death, it is better to forget.

"The sun shall not smite thee by day, neither the moon by night," intones the priest, eyes rolling, his voice like a bell behind the Duke's shoulder.

"Ne moi mords pas," whispers Rohise in her deep sleep. "Ne mwar mor par, ne par mor mwar. . . ."

And under its impenetrable dome, the slender bush has closed its fur leaves also to sleep. O flower of fire, oh fleur de fur. Its blooms, though it has not bloomed yet, bear the ancient name *Nona Mordica.* In light parlance they call it Bite-Me-Not. There is a reason for that.

# II

He is the Prince of a proud and savage people. The pride they acknowledge, perhaps they do not consider themselves to be savages, or at least believe that savagery is the proper order of things.

Feroluce, that is his name. It is one of the customary names his kind give their lords. It has connotations with diabolic royalty and, too, with a royal flower of long petals curved like scimitars. Also the name might be the partial anagram of another name. The bearer of that name was also winged.

For Feroluce and his people are winged beings. They are more like a nest of dark eagles than anything, mounted high among the rocky pilasters and pinnacles of the mountain. Cruel and magnificent, like eagles, the sombre sentries motionless as statuary on the ledge-edges, their sable wings folded about them.

They are very alike in appearance (less a race or tribe, more a flock, an unkindness of ravens). Feroluce also, black-winged, black-haired, aquiline of feature, standing on the brink of star-dashed space, his eyes burning through the night like all the eyes along the rocks, depthless red as claret.

They have their own traditions of art and science. They do not make or read books, fashion garments, discuss God or metaphysics or men. Their cries are mostly wordless and always mysterious, flung out like ribbons over the air as they wheel and swoop and hang in wicked cruciform, between the peaks. But they sing, long hours, for whole nights at a time, music that has a language only they know. All their wisdom and theosophy, and all their grasp of beauty, truth, or love, is in the singing.

They look unloving enough, and so they are. Pitiless fallen angels. A travelling people, they roam after sustenance. Their sustenance is blood. Finding a castle, they accepted it, every bastion and wall, as their prey. They have preyed on it and tried to prey on it for years.

In the beginning, their calls, their songs, could lure victims to the feast. In this way, the tribe or unkindness of Feroluce took the Duke's wife, somnambulist, from a midnight balcony. But the

Duke's daughter, the first victim, they found seventeen years ago, benighted on the mountainside. Her escort and herself they left to the sunrise, marble figures, the life drunk away.

Now the castle is shut, bolted and barred. They are even more attracted by its recalcitrance (a woman who says "No"). They do not intend to go away until the castle falls to them.

By night, they fly like huge black moths round and round the carved turrets, the dull-lit leaded windows, their wings invoking a cloudy tindery wind, pushing thunder against thundery glass.

They sense they are attributed to some sin, reckoned a punishing curse, a penance, and this amuses them at the level whereon they understand it.

They also sense something of the flower, the *Nona Mordica*. Vampires have their own legends.

But tonight Feroluce launches himself into the air, speeds down the sky on the black sails of his wings, calling, a call like laughter or derision. This morning, in the 'tween-time before the light began and the sun-to-be drove him away to his shadowed eyrie in the mountain-guts, he saw a chink in the armour of the beloved refusing-woman-prey. A window, high in an old neglected tower, a window with a small eyelet which was cracked.

Feroluce soon reaches the eyelet and breathes on it, as if he would melt it. (His breath is sweet. Vampires do not eat raw flesh, only blood, which is a perfect food and digests perfectly, while their teeth are sound of necessity.) The way the glass mists at breath intrigues Feroluce. But presently he taps at the cranky pane, taps, then claws. A piece breaks away, and now he sees how it should be done.

Over the rims and upthrusts of the castle, which is only really another mountain with caves to Feroluce, the rumble of the Duke's revel drones on.

Feroluce pays no heed. He does not need to reason, he merely knows, *that* noise masks *this*—as he smashes in the window. Its panes were all faulted and the lattice rusty. It is, of course, more than that. The magic of Purpose has protected the castle, and, as in all balances, there must be, or come to be, some balancing contradiction, some flaw. . . .

The people of Feroluce do not notice what he is at. In a way, the dance with their prey has debased to a ritual. They have lived almost two decades on the blood of local mountain beasts, and bird-creatures like themselves brought down on the wing. Patience is not, with them, a virtue. It is a sort of foreplay, and can go on, in pleasure, a long, long while.

Feroluce intrudes himself through the slender window. Muscularly slender himself, and agile, it is no feat. But the wings catch, are a trouble. They follow him because they must, like two separate entities. They have been cut a little on the glass, and bleed.

He stands in a stony small room, shaking bloody feathers from him, snarling, but without sound.

Then he finds the stairway and goes down.

There are dusty landings and neglected chambers. They have no smell of life. But then there comes to be a smell. It is the scent of a nest, a colony of things, wild creatures, in constant proximity. He recognises it. The light of his crimson eyes precedes him, deciphering blackness. And then other eyes, amber, green, and gold, spring out like stars all across his path.

Somewhere an old torch is burning out. To the human eye, only mounds and glows would be visible, but to Feroluce, the Prince of the vampires, all is suddenly revealed. There is a great stone area, barred with bronze and iron, and things stride and growl behind the bars, or chatter and flee, or only stare. And there, without bars, though bound by ropes of brass to rings of brass, three brazen beasts.

Feroluce, on the steps of the menagerie, looks into the gaze of the Duke's lions. Feroluce smiles, and the lions roar. One is the king, its mane like war-plumes. Feroluce recognises the king and the king's right to challenge, for this is the lions' domain, their territory.

Feroluce comes down the stair and meets the lion as it leaps the length of its chain. To Feroluce, the chain means nothing, and since he has come close enough, very little either to the lion.

To the vampire Prince the fight is wonderful, exhilarating and meaningful, intellectual even, for it is coloured by nuance, yet powerful as sex.

He holds fast with his talons, his strong limbs wrapping the beast which is almost stronger than he, just as its limbs wrap him in turn. He sinks his teeth in the lion's shoulder, and in fierce rage and bliss begins to draw out the nourishment. The lion kicks and claws at him in turn. Feroluce feels the gouges like fire along his shoulders, thighs, and hugs the lion more nearly as he throttles and drinks from it, loving it, jealous of it, killing it. Gradually the mighty feline body relaxes, still clinging to him, its cat teeth bedded in one beautiful swanlike wing, forgotten by both.

In a welter of feathers, stripped skin, spilled blood, the lion and the angel lie in embrace on the menagerie floor. The lion lifts its head, kisses the assassin, shudders, lets go.

Feroluce glides out from under the magnificent deadweight of the cat. He stands. And pain assaults him. His lover has severely wounded him.

Across the menagerie floor, the two lionesses are crouched. Beyond them, a man stands gaping in simple terror, behind the guttering torch. He had come to feed the beasts, and seen another feeding, and now is paralysed. He is deaf, the menagerie-keeper, previously an advantage saving him the horror of nocturnal vampire noises.

Feroluce starts towards the human animal swifter than a serpent, and checks. Agony envelops Feroluce and the stone room spins. Involuntarily, confused, he spreads his wings for flight, there in the confined chamber. But only one wing will open. The other, damaged and partly broken, hangs like a snapped fan. Feroluce cries out, a beautiful singing note of despair and anger. He drops fainting at the menagerie-keeper's feet.

The man does not wait for more. He runs away through the castle, screaming invective and prayer, and reaches the Duke's hall and makes the whole hall listen.

All this while, Feroluce lies in the ocean of almost-death that is sleep or swoon, while the smaller beasts in the cages discuss him, or seem to.

And when he is raised, Feroluce does not wake. Only the great drooping bloody wings quiver and are still. Those who carry him are more than ever revolted and frightened, for they have seldom seen blood. Even the food for the menagerie is cooked almost black. Two years ago, a gardener slashed his palm on a thorn. He was banished from the court for a week.

But Feroluce, the centre of so much attention, does not rouse. Not until the dregs of the night are stealing out through the walls. Then some nervous instinct invests him. The sun is coming and this is an open place, he struggles through unconsciousness and hurt, through the deepest most bladed waters, to awareness.

And finds himself in a huge bronze cage, the cage of some animal appropriated for the occasion. Bars, bars all about him, and not to be got rid of, for he reaches to tear them away and cannot. Beyond the bars, the Duke's hall, which is only a pointless cold glitter to him in the maze of pain and dying lights. Not an open place, in fact, but too open for his kind. Through the window-spaces of thick glass, muddy sunglare must come in. To Feroluce it will be like swords, acids, and burning fire—

Far off he hears wings beat and voices soaring. His people search for him, call and wheel and find nothing.

Feroluce cries out, a gravel shriek now, and the persons in the hall rush back from him, calling on God. But Feroluce does not see. He has tried to answer his own. Now he sinks down again under the coverlet of his broken wings, and the wine-red stars of his eyes go out.

# III

"And the Angel of Death," the priest intones, "shall surely pass over, but yet like the shadow, not substance—"

The smashed window in the old turret above the menagerie tower has been sealed with mortar and brick. It is a terrible thing that it was for so long overlooked. A miracle that only one of the creatures found and entered by it. God, the Protector, guarded the Cursed Duke and his court. And the magic that surrounds the castle, that too held fast. For from the possibility of a disaster was born a bloom of great value: now one of the monsters is in their possession. A prize beyond price.

Caged and helpless, the fiend is at their mercy. It is also weak from its battle with the noble lion, which gave its life for the castle's safety (and will be buried with honour in an ornamented grave at the foot of the Ducal family tomb). Just before the dawn came, the Duke's advisers advised him, and the bronze cage was wheeled away into the darkest area of the hall, close by the dais where once the huge window was but is no more. A barricade of great screens was brought, and set around the cage, and the top of it covered. No sunlight now can drip into the prison to harm the specimen. Only the Duke's ladies and gentlemen steal in around the screens and see, by the light of a candlebranch, the demon still lying in its trance of pain and bloodloss. The Duke's alchemist sits on a stool nearby, dictating many notes to a nervous apprentice. The alchemist, and the apothecary for that matter, are convinced the vampire, having drunk the lion almost dry, will recover from its wounds. Even the wings will mend.

The Duke's court painter also came. He was ashamed presently, and went away. The beauty of the demon affected him, making him wish to paint it, not as something wonderfully disgusting, but as a kind of superlative man, vital and innocent, or as Lucifer him-self, stricken in the sorrow of his colossal Fall. And all that has caused the painter to pity the fallen one, mere artisan that the painter is, so he slunk away. He knows, since the alchemist and the apothecary told him, what is to be done.

Of course much of the castle knows. Though scarcely anyone has slept or sought sleep, the whole place rings with excitement and vi-vacity. The Duke has decreed, too, that everyone who wishes shall be a witness. So he is having a progress through the castle, seeking every nook and cranny, while, let it be said, his architect takes the opportunity to check no other window-pane has cracked.

From room to room the Duke and his entourage pass, through corridors, along stairs, through dusty attics and musty storerooms he has never seen, or if seen has forgotten. Here and there some re-tainer is come on. Some elderly women are discovered spinning like spiders up under the eaves, half-blind and complacent. They curtsy to the Duke from a vague recollection of old habit. The Duke tells them the good news, or rather, his messenger, walking before, announces it. The ancient women sigh and whisper, are left, prob-ably forget. Then again, in a narrow courtyard, a simple boy, who looks after a dovecote, is magnificently told. He has a fit from alarm, grasping nothing, and the doves who love and understand him (by not trying to) fly down and cover him with their soft wings as the Duke goes away. The boy comes to under the doves as if in a heap of warm snow, comforted.

It is on one of the dark staircases above the kitchen that the gleaming entourage sweeps round a bend and comes on Rohise the scullery maid, scrubbing. In these days, when there are so few children and young servants, labour is scarce, and the scullerers are not confined to the scullery.

Rohise stands up, pale with shock, and for a wild instant thinks that, for some heinous crime she has committed in ignorance, the Duke has come in person to behead her.

"Hear then, by the Duke's will," cries the messenger. "One of Satan's night-demons, which do torment us, has been captured and lies penned in the Duke's hall. At sunrise tomorrow, this thing will be taken to that sacred spot where grows the bush of the Flower of the Fire, and here its foul blood shall be shed. Who then can doubt the bush will blossom, and save us all, by the Grace of God."

"And the Angel of Death," intones the priest, on no account to be omitted, "shall surely—"

"Wait," says the Duke. He is as white as Rohise. "Who is this?" he asks. "Is it a ghost?"

The court stare at Rohise, who nearly sinks in dread, her scrubbing rag in her hand.

Gradually, despite the rag, the rags, the rough hands, the court too begins to see.

"Why, it is a marvel."

The Duke moves forward. He looks down at Rohise and starts to cry. Rohise thinks he weeps in compassion at the awful sentence he is here to visit on her, and drops back on her knees.

"No, no," says the Duke tenderly. "Get up. Rise. You are so like my child, my daughter—"

Then Rohise, who knows few prayers, begins in panic to sing her little song as an orison:

"Oh fleur de feu
"Pour ma souffrance—"

"Ah!" says the Duke. "Where did you learn that song?"

"From my mother," says Rohise. And, all instinct now, she sings again:

"O flurda fur,
"Pourma souffrance
"Ned ormey par
"May say day mwar—"

It is the song of the fire-flower bush, the *Nona Mordica*, called Bite-Me-Not. It begins, and continues: *O flower of fire, For my misery's sake, Do not sleep but aid me; wake!* The Duke's daughter sang it very often. In those days the shrub was not needed, being just a rarity of the castle. Invoked as an amulet, on a mountain road, the rhyme itself had besides proved useless.

The Duke takes the dirty scarf from Rohise's hair. She is very, very like his lost daughter, the same pale smooth oval face, the long white neck and long dark polished eyes, and the long dark hair. (Or is it that she is very, very like the painting?)

The Duke gives instructions, and Rohise is borne away.

In a beautiful chamber, the door of which has for seventeen years been locked, Rohise is bathed and her hair is washed. Oils and scents are rubbed into her skin. She is dressed in a gown of palest most pastel rose, with a girdle sewn with pearls. Her hair is combed, and on it is set a chaplet of stars and little golden leaves. "Oh, your poor hands," say the maids, as they trim her nails. Rohise has realised she is not to be executed. She has realised the

Duke has seen her and wants to love her like his dead daughter. Slowly, an uneasy stir of something, not quite happiness, moves through Rohise. Now she will wear her pink gown, now she will sympathise with and console the Duke. Her daze lifts suddenly.

The dream has come true. She dreamed of it so often it seems quite normal. The scullery was the thing which never seemed real.

She glides down through the castle, and the ladies are astonished by her grace. The carriage of her head under the starry coronet is exquisite. Her voice is quiet and clear and musical, and the foreign tone of her mother, long unremembered, is quite gone from it. Only the roughened hands give her away, but smoothed by unguents, soon they will be soft and white.

"Can it be she is truly the princess returned to flesh?"

"Her life was taken so early—yes, as they believe in the Spice-Lands, by some holy dispensation, she might return."

"She would be about the age to have been conceived the very night the Duke's daughter d—— That is, the very night the bane began—"

Theosophical discussion ensues. Songs are composed.

Rohise sits for a while with her adoptive father in the East Turret, and he tells her about the books and swords and lutes and scrolls, but not about the two portraits. Then they walk out together, in the lovely garden in the sunlight. They sit under a peach tree, and discuss many things, or the Duke discusses them. That Rohise is ignorant and uneducated does not matter at this point. She can always be trained. She has the basic requirements: docility, sweetness. There are many royal maidens in many places who know as little as she.

The Duke falls asleep under the peach tree. Rohise listens to the love-songs her own (her very own) courtiers bring her.

When the monster in the cage is mentioned, she nods as if she knows what they mean. She supposes it is something hideous, a scaring treat to be shown at dinnertime, when the sun has gone down.

When the sun moves towards the western line of mountains just visible over the high walls, the court streams into the castle and all the doors are bolted and barred. There is an eagerness tonight in the concourse.

As the light dies out behind the coloured windows that have no red in them, covers and screens are dragged away from a bronze cage. It is wheeled out into the centre of the great hall.

Cannons begin almost at once to blast and bang from the roof-holes. The cannoneers have had strict instructions to keep up the barrage all night without a second's pause.

Drums pound in the hall. The dogs start to bark. Rohise is not surprised by the noise, for she has often heard it from far up, in her attic, like a sea-wave breaking over and over through the lower house.

She looks at the cage cautiously, wondering what she will see. But she sees only a heap of blackness like ravens, and then a tawny dazzle, torchlight on something like human skin. "You must not go down to look," says the Duke protectively, as his court pours about the cage. Someone pokes between the bars with a gemmed cane, trying to rouse the nightmare which lies quiescent there. But Rohise must be spared this.

So the Duke calls his actors, and a slight, pretty play is put on throughout dinner, before the dais, shutting off from the sight of Rohise the rest of the hall, where the barbaric gloating and goading of the court, unchecked, increases.

# IV

The Prince Feroluce becomes aware between one second and the next. It is the sound—heard beyond all others—of the wings of his people beating at the stones of the castle. It is the wings which speak to him, more than their wild orchestral voices. Besides these sensations, the anguish of healing and the sadism of humankind are not much.

Feroluce opens his eyes. His human audience, pleased, but afraid and squeamish, backs away, and asks each other for the two thousandth time if the cage is quite secure. In the torchlight the eyes of Feroluce are more black than red. He stares about. He is, though captive, imperious. If he were a lion or a bull, they would admire this "nobility." But the fact is, he is too much like a man, which serves to point up his supernatural differences unbearably.

Obviously Feroluce understands the gist of his plight. Enemies have him penned. He is a show for now, but ultimately to be killed, for with the intuition of the raptor he divines everything. He had thought the sunlight would kill him, but that is a distant matter, now. And beyond all, the voices and the voices of the wings of his kindred beat the air outside this room-caved mountain of stone.

And so Feroluce commences to sing, or at least, this is how it seems to the rabid court and all the people gathered in the hall. It seems he sings. It is the great communing call of his kind, the art and science and religion of the winged vampires, his means of telling them, or attempting to tell them, what they must be told before he dies. So the sire of Feroluce sang, and the grandsire, and each of his ancestors. Generally they died in flight, falling angels spun down the gulches and enormous stairs of distant peaks, singing. Feroluce, immured, believes that his cry is somehow audible.

To the crowd in the Duke's hall the song is merely that, a song, but how glorious. The dark silver voice, turning to bronze or gold, whitening in the higher registers. There seem to be words, but in some other tongue. This is how the planets sing, surely, or mysterious creatures of the sea.

Everyone is bemused. They listen, astonished.

No one now remonstrates with Rohise when she rises and steals down from the dais. There is an enchantment which prevents movement and coherent thought. Of all the roomful, only she is drawn forward. So she comes close, unhindered, and between the bars of the cage, she sees the vampire for the first time.

She has no notion what he can be. She imagined it was a monster or a monstrous beast. But it is neither. Rohise, starved for so long of beauty and always dreaming of it, recognises Feroluce inevitably as part of the dream-come-true. She loves him instantly. Because she loves him, she is not afraid of him.

She attends while he goes on and on with his glorious song. He does not see her at all, or any of them. They are only things, like mist, or pain. They have no character or personality or worth; abstracts.

Finally, Feroluce stops singing. Beyond the stone and the thick glass of the siege, the wing-beats, too, eddy into silence.

Finding itself mesmerised, silent by night, the court comes to with a terrible joint start, shrilling and shouting, bursting, exploding into a compensation of sound. Music flares again. And the cannons in the roof, which have also fallen quiet, resume with a tremendous roar.

Feroluce shuts his eyes and seems to sleep. It is his preparation for death.

Hands grasp Rohise. "Lady—step back, come away. So close! It may harm you—"

The Duke clasps her in a father's embrace. Rohise, unused to this sort of physical expression, is unmoved. She pats him absently.

"My lord, what will be done?"

"Hush, child. Best you do not know."

Rohise persists.

The Duke persists in not saying.

But she remembers the words of the herald on the stair, and knows they mean to butcher the winged man. She attends thereafter more carefully to snatches of the bizarre talk about the hall, and learns all she needs. At earliest sunrise, as soon as the enemy retreat from the walls, their captive will be taken to the lovely garden with the peach trees. And so to the sunken garden of the magic bush, the fire-flower. And there they will hang him up in the sun through the dome of smoky glass, which will be slow murder to him, but they will cut him, too, so his blood, the stolen blood of the vampire, runs down to water the roots of the fleur de feu. And who can doubt that, from such nourishment, the bush will bloom? The blooms are salvation. Wherever they grow it is a safe place. Whoever wears them is safe from the draining bite of demons. Bite-Me-Not, they call it; vampire-repellent.

Rohise sits the rest of the night on her cushions, with folded hands, resembling the portrait of the princess, which is not like her.

Eventually the sky outside alters. Silence comes down beyond the wall, and so within the wall, and the court lifts its head, a corporate animal scenting day.

At the intimation of sunrise the black plague has lifted and gone away, and might never have been. The Duke, and almost all his castle full of men, women, children, emerge from the doors. The sky is measureless and bluely grey, with one cherry rift in the east that the court refers to as "mauve," since dawns and sunsets are never any sort of red here.

They move through the dimly lightening garden as the last stars melt. The cage is dragged in their midst.

They are too tired, too concentrated now, the Duke's people, to continue baiting their captive. They have had all the long night to do that, and to drink and opine, and now their stamina is sharpened for the final act.

Reaching the sunken garden, the Duke unlocks the iron door. There is no room for everyone within, so mostly they must stand outside, crammed in the gate, or teetering on erections of benches that have been placed around, and peering in over the walls through the glass of the dome. The places in the doorway are the best, of course; no one else will get so good a view. The servants and lower persons must stand back under the trees and only imagine what goes on. But they are used to that.

Into the sunken garden itself there are allowed to go the alchemist and the apothecary, and the priest, and certain sturdy soldiers attendant on the Duke, and the Duke. And Feroluce in the cage.

The east is all "mauve" now. The alchemist has prepared sorcerous safeguards which are being put into operation, and the priest, never to be left out, intones prayers. The bulge-thewed soldiers open the cage and seize the monster before it can stir. But drugged smoke has already been wafted into the prison, and besides, the monster has prepared itself for hopeless death and makes no demur.

Feroluce hangs in the arms of his loathing guards, dimly aware the sun is near. But death is nearer, and already one may hear the alchemist's apprentice sharpening the knife an ultimate time.

The leaves of the *Nona Mordica* are trembling, too, at the commencement of the light, and beginning to unfurl. Although this happens every dawn, the court points to it with optimistic cries. Rohise, who has claimed a position in the doorway, watches it too, but only for an instant. Though she has sung of the fleur de fur since childhood, she had never known what the song was all about. And in just this way, though she has dreamed of being the Duke's daughter most of her life, such an event was never really comprehended either, and so means very little.

As the guards haul the demon forward to the plot of humid earth where the bush is growing, Rohise darts into the sunken garden, and lightning leaps in her hands. Women scream and well they might. Rohise has stolen one of the swords from the East Turret, and now she flourishes it, and now she has swung it and a soldier falls, bleeding red, red, *red*, before them all.

Chaos enters, as in yesterday's play, shaking its tattered sleeves. The men who hold the demon rear back in horror at the dashing blade and the blasphemous gore, and the mad girl in her princess's gown. The Duke makes a pitiful bleating noise, but no one pays him any attention.

The east glows in and like the liquid on the ground.

Meanwhile, the ironically combined sense of impending day and spilled hot blood have penetrated the stunned brain of the vampire. His eyes open, and he sees the girl wielding her sword in a spray of crimson as the last guard lets go. Then the girl has run to Feroluce.

Though, or because, her face is insane, it communicates her purpose, as she thrusts the sword's hilt into his hands.

No one has dared approach either the demon or the girl. Now they look on in horror and in horror grasp what Feroluce has grasped.

In that moment the vampire springs, and the great swanlike wings are reborn at his back, healed and whole. As the doctors predicted, he has mended perfectly, and prodigiously fast. He takes to the air like an arrow, unhindered, as if gravity does not anymore exist. As he does so, the girl grips him about the waist, and slender and light, she is drawn upward too. He does not glance at her. He veers towards the gateway, and tears through it, the sword, his talons, his wings, his very shadow, beating men and bricks from his path.

And now he is in the sky above them, a black star which has not been put out. They see the wings flare and beat, and the swirling of a girl's dress and unbound hair, and then the image dives and is gone into the shade under the mountains, as the sun rises.

## V

It is fortunate, the mountain shade in the sunrise. Lion's blood and enforced quiescence have worked wonders, but the sun could undo it all. Luckily the shadow, deep and cold as a pool, envelops the vampire, and in it there is a cave, deeper and colder. Here he alights and sinks down, sloughing the girl, whom he has almost forgotten. Certainly he fears no harm from her. She is like a pet animal, maybe, like the hunting dogs or wolves or lammergeyers that occasionally the unkindness of vampires have kept by them for a while. That she helped him is all he needs to know. She will help again. So when, stumbling in the blackness, she brings him in her cupped hands water from a cascade at the poolcave's back, he is not surprised. He drinks the water, which is the only other substance his kind imbibe. Then he smooths her hair, absently, as he would pat or stroke the pet she seems to have become. He is not grateful, as he is not suspicious. The complexities of his intellect are reserved for other things. Since he is exhausted he falls asleep, and since Rohise is exhausted she falls asleep beside him, pressed to his warmth in the freezing dark. Like those of Feroluce, as it turns out, her thoughts are simple. She is sorry for distressing the Cursed Duke. But she has no regrets, for she could no more have left

Feroluce to die than she could have refused to leave the scullery for the court.

The day, which had only just begun, passes swiftly in sleep.

Feroluce wakes as the sun sets, without seeing anything of it. He unfolds himself and goes to the cave's entrance, which now looks out on a whole sky of stars above a landscape of mountains. The castle is far below, and to the eyes of Rohise as she follows him, invisible. She does not even look for it, for there is something else to be seen.

The great dark shapes of angels are wheeling against the peaks, the stars. And their song begins, up in the starlit spaces. It is a lament, their mourning, pitiless and strong, for Feroluce, who has died in the stone heart of the thing they prey upon.

The tribe of Feroluce do not laugh, but, like a bird or wild beast, they have a kind of equivalent to laughter. This Feroluce now utters, and like a flung lance he launches himself into the air.

Rohise at the cave mouth, abandoned, forgotten, unnoted even by the mass of vampires, watches the winged man as he flies towards his people. She supposes for a moment that she may be able to climb down the tortuous ways of the mountain, undetected. Where then should she go? She does not spend much time on these ideas. They do not interest or involve her. She watches Feroluce, and because she learned long ago the uselessness of weeping, she does not shed tears, though her heart begins to break.

As Feroluce glides, body held motionless, wings outspread on a down-draught, into the midst of the storm of black wings, the red stars of eyes ignite all about him. The great lament dies. The air is very still.

Feroluce waits then. He waits, for the aura of his people is not as he has always known it. It is as if he had come among emptiness. From the silence, therefore, and from nothing else, he learns it all. In the stone he lay and he sang of his death, as the Prince must, dying. And the ritual was completed, and now there is the threnody, the grief, and thereafter the choosing of a new Prince. And none of this is alterable. He is dead. Dead. It cannot and will not be changed.

There is a moment of protest, then, from Feroluce. Perhaps his brief sojourn among men has taught him some of their futility. But as the cry leaves him, all about the huge wings are raised like swords. Talons and teeth and eyes burn against the stars. To protest is to be torn in shreds. He is not of their people now. They can attack and slaughter him as they would any other intruding thing. *Go*, the talons and the teeth and the eyes say to him. *Go far off.*

He is dead. There is nothing left him but to die.

Feroluce retreats. He soars. Bewildered, he feels the power and energy of his strength and the joy of flight, and cannot understand how this is, if he is dead. Yet he *is* dead. He knows it now.

So he closes his eyelids, and his wings. Spear-swift he falls. And something shrieks, interrupting the reverie of nihilism. Disturbed, he opens his wings, shudders, turns like a swimmer, finds a ledge against his side and two hands outstretched, holding him by one shoulder, and by his hair.

"No," says Rohise. (The vampire cloud, wheeling away, have not heard her; she does not think of them.) His eyes stay shut. Holding him, she kisses these eyelids, his forehead, his lips, gently, as she drives her nails into his skin to hold him. The black wings beat, tearing to be free and fall and die. "No," says Rohise. "I love you," she says. "My life is your life." These are the words of the court and of courtly love-songs. No matter, she means them. And though he cannot understand her language or her sentiments, yet her passion, purely that, communicates itself, strong and burning as the passions of his kind, who generally love only one thing, which is scarlet. For a second her intensity fills the void which now contains him. But then he dashes himself away from the ledge, to fall again, to seek death again.

Like a ribbon, clinging to him still, Rohise is drawn from the rock and falls with him.

Afraid, she buries her head against his breast, in the shadow of wings and hair. She no longer asks him to reconsider. This is how it must be. *Love* she thinks again, in the instant before they strike the earth. Then that instant comes, and is gone.

Astonished, she finds herself still alive, still in the air. Touching so close, feathers have been left on the rocks, Feroluce has swerved away and upward. Now, conversely, they are whirling towards the very stars. The world seems miles below. Perhaps they will fly into space itself. Perhaps he means to break their bones instead on the cold face of the moon.

He does not attempt to dislodge her, he does not attempt anymore to fall and die. But as he flies, he suddenly cries out, terrible lost lunatic cries.

They do not hit the moon. They do not pass through the stars like static rain.

But when the air grows thin and pure there is a peak like a dagger standing in their path. Here, he alights. As Rohise lets go of him, he turns away. He stations himself, sentry-fashion, in the manner of his tribe, at the edge of the pinnacle. But watching for nothing. He has not been able to choose death. His strength and the strong will of another, these have hampered him. His brain has become formless darkness. His eyes glare, seeing nothing.

Rohise, gasping a little in the thin atmosphere, sits at his back, watching for him, in case any harm may come near him.

At last, harm does come. There is a lightening in the east. The frozen, choppy sea of the mountains below, and all about, grows visible. It is a marvellous sight, but holds no marvel for Rohise. She averts her eyes from the exquisitely pencilled shapes, looking thin and translucent as paper, the rivers of mist between, the glimmer of nacreous ice. She searches for a blind hold to hide in.

There is a pale yellow wound in the sky when she returns. She grasps Feroluce by the wrist and tugs at him. "Come," she says. He looks at her vaguely, as if seeing her from the shore of another country. "The sun," she says. "Quickly."

The edge of the light runs along his body like a razor. He moves by instinct now, following her down the slippery dagger of the peak, and so eventually into a shallow cave. It is so small it holds him like a coffin. Rohise closes the entrance with her own body. It is the best she can do. She sits facing the sun as it rises, as if prepared to fight. She hates the sun for his sake. Even as the light warms her chilled body, she curses it. Till light and cold and breathlessness fade together.

When she wakes, she looks up into twilight and endless stars, two of which are red. She is lying on the rock by the cave. Feroluce leans over her, and behind Feroluce his quiescent wings fill the sky.

She has never properly understood his nature: Vampire. Yet her own nature, which tells her so much, tells her some vital part of herself is needful to him, and that he is danger, and death. But she loves him, and is not afraid. She would have fallen to die with him. To help him by her death does not seem wrong to her. Thus, she lies still, and smiles at him to reassure him she will not struggle. From lassitude, not fear, she closes her eyes. Presently she feels the soft weight of hair brush by her cheek, and then his cool mouth rests against her throat. But nothing more happens. For some while they continue in this fashion, she yielding, he kneeling over her, his lips on her skin. Then he moves a little away. He sits, regarding her. She, knowing the unknown act has not been completed, sits up in turn. She beckons to him mutely, telling him with her gestures and her expression *I consent. Whatever is necessary.* But he does not stir. His eyes blaze, but even of these she has no fear. In the end he looks away from her, out across the spaces of the darkness.

He himself does not understand. It is permissible to drink from the body of a pet, the wolf, the eagle. Even to kill the pet, if need demands. Can it be, outlawed from his people, he has lost their composite soul? Therefore, is he soulless now? It does not seem to him he is. Weakened and famished though he is, the vampire is aware of a wild tingling of life. When he stares at the creature which is his food, he finds he sees her differently. He has borne her through the sky, he has avoided death, by some intuitive process, for her sake, and she has led him to safety, guarded him from the blade of the sun. In the beginning it was she who rescued him from the human things which had taken him. She cannot be human, then. Not pet, and not prey. For no, he could not drain her of blood, as he would not seize upon his own kind, even in combat, to drink and feed. He starts to see her as beautiful, not in the way a man beholds a woman, certainly, but as his kind revere the sheen of water in dusk, or flight, or song. There are no words for this. But the life goes on tingling through him. Though he is dead, life.

In the end, the moon does rise, and across the open face of it something wheels by. Feroluce is less swift than was his wont, yet he starts in pursuit, and catches and brings down, killing on the wing, a great night bird. Turning in the air, Feroluce absorbs its liquors. The heat of life now, as well as its assertion, courses through him. He returns to the rock perch, the glorious flaccid bird dangling from his hand. Carefully, he tears the glory of the bird in pieces, plucks the feathers, splits the bones. He wakes the companion (asleep again from weakness) who is not pet or prey, and feeds her morsels of flesh. At first she is unwilling. But her hunger is so enormous and her nature so untamed that quite soon she accepts the slivers of raw fowl.

Strengthened by blood, Feroluce lifts Rohise and bears her gliding down the moon-slit quill-backed land of the mountains, until there is a rocky cistern full of cold, old rains. Here they drink together. Pale white primroses grow in the fissures where the black moss drips. Rohise makes a garland and throws it about the head of her beloved when he does not expect it. Bewildered but disdainful, he touches at the wreath of primroses to see if it is likely to threaten or hamper him. When it does not, he leaves it in place.

Long before dawn this time, they have found a crevice. Because it is so cold, he folds his wings about her. She speaks of her love to him, but he does not hear, only the murmur of her voice, which is musical and does not displease him. And later, she sings him sleepily the little song of the fleur de fur.

# VI

There comes a time then, brief, undated, chartless time, when they are together, these two creatures. Not together in any accepted sense, of course, but together in the strange feeling or emotion, instinct or ritual, that can burst to life in an instant or flow to life gradually across half a century, and which men call *Love*.

They are not alike. No, not at all. Their differences are legion and should be unpalatable. He is a supernatural thing and she a human thing, he was a lord and she a scullery sloven. He can fly, she cannot fly. And he is male, she female. What other items are required to make them enemies? Yet they are bound, not merely by love, they are bound by all they are, the very stumbling blocks. Bound, too, because they are doomed. Because the stumbling blocks have doomed them; everything has. Each has been exiled out of their own kind. Together, they cannot even communicate with each other, save by looks, touches, sometimes by sounds, and by songs neither understands, but which each comes to value since the other appears to value them, and since they give expression to that other. Nevertheless, the binding of the doom, the greatest binding, grows, as it holds them fast to each other, mightier and stronger.

Although they do not know it, or not fully, it is the awareness of doom that keeps them there, among the platforms and steps up and down, and the inner cups, of the mountains.

Here it is possible to pursue the airborne hunt, and Feroluce may now and then bring down a bird to sustain them both. But birds are scarce. The richer lower slopes, pastured with goats, wild sheep, and men—they lie far off and far down from this place as a deep of the sea. And Feroluce does not conduct her there, nor does Rohise ask that he should, or try to lead the way, or even dream of such a plan.

But yes, birds are scarce, and the pastures far away, and winter is coming. There are only two seasons in these mountains. High summer, which dies, and the high cold which already treads over the tips of the air and the rock, numbing the sky, making all brittle, as though the whole landscape might snap in pieces, shatter.

How beautiful it is to wake with the dusk, when the silver webs of night begin to form, frost and ice, on everything. Even the ragged dress—once that of a princess—is tinselled and shining with this magic substance, even the mighty wings—once those of a prince—each feather is drawn glittering with thin rime. And oh, the sky, thick as a daisy-field with the white stars. Up there, when they have fed and have strength, they fly, or, Feroluce flies and Rohise flies in his arms, carried by his wings. Up there in the biting chill like a pane of ghostly vitreous, they have become lovers, true blind lovers, embraced and linked, their bodies a bow, coupling on the wing. By the hour that this first happened the girl had forgotten all she had been, and he had forgotten too that she was anything but the essential mate. Sometimes, borne in this way, by wings and by fire, she cries out as she hangs in the ether. These sounds, transmitted through the flawless silence and amplification of the peaks, scatter over tiny half-buried villages countless miles away, where they are heard in fright and taken for the shrieks of malign invisible devils, tiny as bats, and armed with the barbed stings of scorpions. There are always misunderstandings.

After a while, the icy prologues and the stunning starry fields of winter nights give way to the main argument of winter.

The liquid of the pool, where the flowers made garlands, has clouded and closed to stone. Even the volatile waterfalls are stilled, broken cascades of glass. The wind tears through the skin and hair to gnaw the bones. To weep with cold earns no compassion of the cold.

There is no means to make fire. Besides, the one who was Rohise is an animal now, or a bird, and beasts and birds do not make fire, save for the phoenix in the Duke's bestiary. Also, the sun is fire, and the sun is a foe. Eschew fire.

There begin the calendar months of hibernation. The demon lovers too must prepare for just such a measureless winter sleep, that gives no hunger, asks no action. There is a deep cave they have lined with feathers and withered grass. But there are no more flying things to feed them. Long, long ago, the last warm frugal feast, long, long ago the last flight, joining, ecstasy and song. So, they turn to their cave, to stasis, to sleep. Which each understands, wordlessly, thoughtlessly, is death.

What else? He might drain her of blood, he could persist some while on that, might even escape the mountains, the doom. Or she herself might leave him, attempt to make her way to the places below, and perhaps she could reach them, even now. Others, lost here, have done so. But neither considers these alternatives. The moment for all that is past. Even the death-lament does not need to be voiced again.

Installed, they curl together in their bloodless icy nest, murmuring a little to each other, but finally still.

Outside, the snow begins to come down. It falls like a curtain. Then the winds take it. Then the night is full of the lashing of whips, and when the sun rises it is white as the snow itself, its flame very distant, giving nothing. The cave mouth is blocked up with snow. In the winter, it seems possible that never again will there be a summer in the world.

Behind the modest door of snow, hidden and secret, sleep is quiet as stars, dense as hardening resin. Feroluce and Rohise turn pure and pale in the amber, in the frigid nest, and the great wings lie like a curious articulated machinery that will not move. And the withered grass and the flowers are crystallised, until the snows shall melt.

At length, the sun deigns to come closer to the earth, and the miracle occurs. The snow shifts, crumbles, crashes off the mountains in rage. The waters hurry after the snow, the air is wrung and racked by splittings and splinterings, by rushes and booms. It is half a year, or it might be a hundred years, later.

Open now, the entry to the cave. Nothing emerges. Then, a flutter, a whisper. Something does emerge. One black feather, and caught in it, the petal of a flower, crumbling like dark charcoal and white, drifting away into the voids below. Gone. Vanished. It might never have been.

But there comes another time (half a year, a hundred years), when an adventurous traveller comes down from the mountains to the pocketed villages the other side of them. He is a swarthy cheerful fellow, you would not take him for herbalist or mystic, but he has in a pot a plant he found high up in the staring crags, which might after all contain anything or nothing. And he shows the plant, which is an unusual one, having slender, dark, and velvety leaves, and giving off a pleasant smell like vanilla. "See, the *Nona Mordica*," he says. "The Bite-Me-Not. The flower that repels vampires."

Then the villagers tell him an odd story, about a castle in another country, besieged by a huge flock, a menace of winged vampires, and how the Duke waited in vain for the magic bush that was in his garden, the Bite-Me-Not, to flower and save them all. But it seems there was a curse on this Duke, who on the very night his daughter was lost, had raped a serving woman, as he had raped others before. But this woman conceived. And bearing the fruit, or flower, of this rape, damaged her, so she lived only a year or two after it. The child grew up unknowing, and in the end betrayed her own father by running away to the vampires, leaving the Duke demoralised. And soon after he went mad, and himself stole out one night, and let the winged fiends into his castle, so all there perished.

"Now if only the bush had flowered in time, as your bush flowers, all would have been well," the villagers cry.

The traveller smiles. He in turn does not tell them of the heap of peculiar bones, like parts of eagles mingled with those of a woman and a man. Out of the bones, from the heart of them, the bush was rising, but the traveller untangled the roots of it with care; it looks sound enough now in its sturdy pot, all of it twining together. It seems as if two separate plants are growing from a single stem, one with blooms almost black, and one pink-flowered, like a young sunset.

"Flur de fur," says the traveller, beaming at the marvel, and his luck.

Fleur de feu. Oh flower of fire. That fire is not hate or fear, which makes flowers come, not terror or anger or lust, it is love that is the fire of the Bite-Me-Not, love which cannot abandon, love which cannot harm. Love which never dies.

# BLACK AS INK

THE CHÂTEAU, DOVE-GREY, NESTED AMONG DARK GREEN trees. Lawns like marzipan sloped to a huge lake like a silver spoon, the farther end of which held up an anchored fleet of islands. Pines and willows framed the watery vistas. There were swans. It was hopelessly idyllic and very quickly bored him.

"Paris," he occasionally said, a kind of comma to everything. And now and then, in desperation, "Oslo. Stockholm."

His mother and his uncle glanced up from their interminable games of chess or cards, under the brims of their summer walking-hats, through the china and the crystal-ware, astonished.

"He is scarcely here," Ilena said, "and he wishes to depart."

"I was the same at his age," said Janov. "Nineteen. Oh, my God, I was just the same."

"Twenty," said Viktor.

"What would you do in the city, except idle?" said Ilena.

"Exactly as I do here."

"And get drunk," said Janov. "And gamble."

"I told you about the business venture I—"

"And lose money. My God, I was just the same."

"I—"

"Hush, Viktor," said Ilena. "You should be sketching. This is what you're good at, and what you should do."

"Or take one of the horses. Ride it somewhere, for God's sake."

"Where?"

"Or the boat. Exercise."

Fat Janov beamed upon his slender nephew, flexing the bolster muscles of his arms, his coat-seams creaking.

Viktor remembered the long white car left behind in the town, cafés, theatre, discourse far into the night. The summer was being wasted, ten days of it were already gone forever.

He thought he understood their delight in the château, the home of childhood lost, suddenly returned into their possession. Seeing his elegant mother, a fragile fashion-plate with a hidden framework of steel, drift through these rooms exclaiming, recapturing, he had been indulgent— "Do you recall, Jani, when we were here, and here, and did this, and did that?" And the gales of laughter, and the teasing, somewhat embarrassing to watch. Yes, indulgent, but already nervous at intimations of ennui, Viktor had planned a wild escape. Then all at once the plan had failed. And as the short sweet summer clasped the land, here he found himself, after all, trapped like a fly in honey.

"Just the place," Janov said, "for you to decide what you mean to do with yourself. Six months out of the university. Time to look about, get your bearings."

He had, dutifully, sketched the lake. He had ridden the beautiful horses, annoyed at his own clumsiness in the saddle, for he was graceful in other things. The boat he ignored. No doubt it let water. He observed Janov, snoring gently under a cherry tree, his straw hat tilted to his nose.

"I could, of course," said Viktor, "drown myself in the damn lake."

"Such language before your mother," said Ilena, ruffling his hair in a way that pleased or irritated him, depending on the weather of his mood, and which now maddened so that he grit his teeth. "Ah, so like me," she murmured with a callous, selfish pride. "Such impatience." And then she told him again how, as a girl, she had danced by the shore of the lake, the coloured lamps bright in the
. trees above, trembling in the water below. They had owned the land in those days. Even the islands had belonged to her father. And now, there were alien houses built there. She could see the roofs of them and pointed them out to him with contempt. *"Les Nouveaux,"* she called them. In winter, when the trees lost their leaves, the houses of the Invader would be more apparent yet. Only the pines would shield her then from the uncivilised present.

Viktor imagined a great gun poised on the lawn, shells blasting the bold aliens into powder. He himself, with no comparative former image to guide him, could not even make them out.

Presently she reverted to her French novel, and he left her.

He walked down into a grove of dripping willows and began to make fresh plans to escape—a make-believe attack of appendicitis, possibly, was the only answer. . . .

When he awoke, the sun was down in the lake, a faded-golden upturned bowl. Through the willow curtains, the lawns were cool with shadows, and deserted.

Yes, he supposed it was truly beautiful. Something in the strange light informed him, the long northern sunset that separated day from dark, beginning now slowly to envelop everything in the palest, thinnest amber ambience, occluding foliage, liquid, and air. One broad arrow of jasper-coloured water flared away from the sun, and four swans, black on the glow, embarked like ships from the shelter of the islands. The islands were black, too, banks and spurs of black, and even as he looked at them he heard, with disbelief, a cloud of music rise from one of them and echo to him all the way across the lake. An orchestra was playing over there. Viktor heard rhythm and melody for the briefest second. Not the formal mosaic of Beethoven or Mozart, nor some ghost mazurka from Ilena's memory—this was contemporary dance music, racy and strong, spice on the wind, then blown away.

Just as he had instantly imagined the gun shelling the island, so another vision occurred to him, in its own manner equally preposterous.

As he rose, loafed into the enormous house, found his way upstairs unmolested, and dressed sloppily for dinner, so the idea went with him, haunting him. Before the sonorous gong sounded, he leaned a long while at his window, watching the last of the afterglow, now the colour of a dry sherry, still infinitesimally diminishing. A white moon had risen to make a crossbow with a picturesque branch: how typical. Yet the phantom movements of the swans far out on the sherry lake had begun to fascinate him. The music, clearly, had disturbed them. Or were they always nocturnally active? Viktor recalled one of Janov's stories, which concerned a swan in savage flight landing with a tremendous thud on the roof of their father's study. The swans were supposed to be eccentric. They fled with summer, always returning with the spring, like clockwork things. Ilena said they sang when they died and she had heard one do so. Viktor did not really believe her, though as a child, first learning the tale, he had conjured a swan, lying in the rushes, haranguing with a coloratura voice.

The gong resounded, and with sour contempt he went downstairs to the china and crystal, the food half the time lukewarm from its long journey out of the kitchen, and the presiding undead of old suppers, banquets. "Do you remember, Jani, when—?" "Do you recall, Vena, the night—?"

The idea of the boat stayed with him there. He took soup and wine and a tepid roast and some kind of preserve and a fruit pastry and coffee, and over the low cries of their voices he distinguished the lake water slapping the oars, felt the dark buoyancy of it, and all the while the music on the island came closer.

Of course, it was a stupid notion. Some inane provincial party or other, and he himself bursting in on it through the bushes. We owned this island once, he could say, erupting into the midst of *Les Nouveaux*. Yet, the boat rowed on in his thoughts, the swans drifting by, turning their snakelike necks away from him. The music had stopped in his fancy because he was no longer sure what he had heard at all. Maybe he had imagined everything.

"How silent Viktor is," said Ilena.

"Sulking," said Janov. "When I was eighteen, I was just the same."

"Yes," said Viktor, "I'm sulking. Pass the brandy."

"Pass the brandy," said Janov. "Eighteen and pass the brandy."

"Twenty and I'm going upstairs to read. Good night, Maman. Uncle."

Ilena kissed his cheek. Her exquisite perfume surrounded her, embraced him, and was gone.

"Do we play?" said Ilena.

"A couple of games," said Janov.

As Viktor went out there came the click of cards.

He waited in his room for an hour, reading the same paragraph carefully over and over. Once he got up and hurried towards the door. Then the absurdity swept him under again. He paced, found the window, stared out into the dark which had finally covered everything.

The moon had begun to touch the lake to a polished surface, like a waxed table. Nothing marred its sheen. There were no lights discernible, save the sparse lights of the château round about.

Viktor took his book downstairs and sat brooding on it in a corner of the salon, so he could feel superior as his mother and his uncle squabbled over their cards.

At midnight, he woke to find the salon empty. From an adjacent room the notes of the piano softly came for a while, then ceased. "Go to bed, *mon fils*," she called to him, followed by invisible rustlings of her garments as she went away. Tied to the brandy decanter, with the velvet ribbon she had worn at her throat, was a scrap of paper which read: *Un peu*. Viktor grimaced and poured himself one very large glass.

Presently he went out with the brandy onto the lawn before the house, and scanned again across the lake for pinpricks of light in the darkness. Nothing was to be seen. He thought of the boat, and wandered down the incline, between the willows, to the water's edge, thinking of it, knowing he would not use it.

"Paris," he said to his mother in his head. "Next year," she said. "Perhaps." A wave of sorrow washed over him. Even if he should ever get there, the world, too, might prove a disappointment, a crashing bore.

The brandy made him dizzy, heavy, and sad.

He turned to go in, defeated. And at that moment, he saw the white movement in the water, troubling and beautiful. About ten boat-lengths away, a girl was swimming, slowly on her back, towards him. With each swanlike stroke of her arms, there came a white flash of flesh. It seemed she was naked. Amazed, Viktor stepped up into the black recess of the hanging trees. It was an instinct, not a wish to spy so much as a wish not to be discovered and reckoned spying. She had not seen him, could not have seen him. As the water shallowed towards the shore, she swung aside like a fish. Amongst the fronded trailers of the willows, not ten yards from him now, she raised her arms and effortlessly rose upright.

Her hair was blonde, darkened and separated by water, and streaked across her body so her slender whiteness was concealed in hair, in leaves, in shadows. The water itself ringed her hips. She was naked, as he had thought. She parted the willow fronds with her hands, gazing between them, up the lawn towards the château, or so it seemed. It was pure luck she had beached exactly where he stood.

He was afraid she would hear his breathing. But she seemed wrapped in her own silence, so sure she was alone, she had remained alone, even with his eyes upon her.

Another whiteness flashed, and Viktor jumped upsetting the

brandy, certain now she had heard him, his heart in his mouth. But she gave no sign of it. A swan cruised by her and between the willows, vanishing. A second bird, like a lily, floated far off.

A white girl swimming among the swans.

The water broke in silver rings. She had dived beneath the shallows, and he had not seen it. He stared and beheld her head, like a drowned moon, bob to the surface some distance off, then the dagger-cast of her slim back.

Without sound, she swam away towards the islands of invasion.

"My God," he whispered. But it was not until he was in his room again that he dared to laugh, congratulating himself, unnerved. Lying down, he slept uneasily.

He was already in the grip, as Ilena would have said, of one of his obsessions.

A day like any other day spread over the lake and the château, plaiting the willow trees with gold. Before noon, Viktor had one of the horses out and was riding on it around the lake, trying to find if the islands—her island—was accessible from shore. But it was not.

From a stand of birch trees it was just possible, however, to see the roofs of a house, and a little pavilion like white matchsticks near the water.

Viktor sat looking at it, in a sort of mindless reverie.

When he was thirteen years old, he had fallen wildly in love with one of the actresses in a minor production of *The Lady from the Sea*. This infatuation, tinged by tremors of earliest sexuality, but no more than tinged by them, was more a languid desperate ecstasy of the emotional parts, drenching him in a sort of rain—through which he saw the people he knew, and over the murmur of which he heard their voices, yet everything remote, none of it as real as the pale rouged face, the cochineal gown and thunderous hair. Never since had he felt such a thing for anyone. Not even that hoard of young women he had gazed after, then forgotten. Certainly not in the few, merely physical, pleasures he had experienced with the carefully selected paid women his walk of life gave access to.

But preposterously this—this was like that first soaring love. It was the artist in him, he supposed helplessly. For however poor his work, his soul was still that of the artist. The dazzle of pure whiteness on the dark lake, accented by swans, the sinking moon. He had been put in mind of a *rusalka*, the spirit of a drowned girl haunting water in a greed for male victims. And in this way, to his seemingly asexual desire was added a bizarre twist of dread, not asexual in the least.

"Been riding?" said Uncle Janov on his return. "Good, good."

"I thought I might try the boat this afternoon," said Viktor, with a malicious sense of the joy of implicit and unspoken things.

But he did not take the boat. He lay on the grass of the lawn, now, staring through the willows, over the bright water, towards the islands, all afternoon. In his head he attempted to compose a poem. White as snow, she moves among the swans . . . the snow of her hands, falling. . . . Disgusted with it, he would not even commit it to paper. Nor did he dare to make a drawing. His mother's parasoled shadow falling over him at intervals as she patrolled the lawns, made any enterprise save thought far too conspicuous. Even to take the boat could be a disaster. "Where is that boy going? He's too far out—"

Sugaring her conversation, as ever, fashionably with French, Ilena somehow made constant references to love throughout dinner. By a sort of telepathic means, she had lit on something to make Viktor suddenly as excruciatingly uncomfortable as a boy of thirteen. Finally she sought the piano, and played there, with Chopinesque melancholy and Mozartian frills, the old ballads of romance: *Désirée, Hélas, J'ai Perdu*. She could, of course, in fact know nothing. He himself scarcely knew. What on earth had got hold of him?

It was inevitable. To be so bored, so entrapped. There must be something to be interested in. He sprawled in a chair as Ilena plunged into *Lied*, trying longingly to remember the features of the girl's face.

When the house was quiet, save for some unaccountable vague noise the servants were making below, Viktor came downstairs and went out. He dragged the boat from its shed, pushed through the reeds, and started to row with a fine defiance.

There was no moon, which was excellent, even though he could not see where he was going.

An extraordinary scent lay over the lake, a smell of sheer openness. At first it went to his head. He felt exhilarated and completely in command of everything, himself, the night. He rowed powerfully, and the château, a dark wash of trees against the star-tipped sky, drew away and away. Then, unused to this particular form of labour, his arms and his back began to ache and burn. He suddenly became physically strained to the point of nausea, and collapsed on the oars, only too aware he would have to return by this modus operandi, and already certain he could not make another stroke in any direction.

But the rim of the island was now much closer than the far shore. He could distinguish the matchstick pavilion. Something white in the water shot blood through him like a charge of electricity, but it was only one of the swans mysteriously feeding or drinking from the lake.

Cursing softly, his teeth clenched, Viktor resumed work with the oars and pulled his way through the water until the boat bumped softly into the side of the island.

There was a post there among the reeds, sodden and rotted, but he tied the boat to it. The swan drifted away, weightless as if hollow.

Viktor scrambled up the incline. He stood beside the little pavilion, back broken, and full of a sinister excitement, trespassing and foolish and amused, and dimly afraid.

There was no music now, only the sound the lake made, and a soft intermittent susurrus of the leaves. Viktor glanced into the summerhouse, which was romantically neglected, conceivably even dangerous. Then, without hesitation, he began to make a way between the stalks of pine trees, and over the mounds of the grass, passing into the utter blankness of moonless overgrowth which had somehow seemed to make this venture permissible.

Beyond the trees was a house, surrounded by a wild lawn and a clutter of outbuildings. Viktor took a sudden notion of dogs, and checked, appalled, but nothing barked or scrabbled to get out at him.

There was something reassuringly ramshackle about the place. Even the house, far younger than the château, had a weird air of desuetude and decline. Viktor walked nearer and nearer through the rogue grass, passed under a rose-vine unravelling on a shed. A few feet from the veranda, in a clump of bushes, he came on a small china animal of indistinct species lying on its side as if dead, beside a wooden pole stuck in the ground. The purpose of the pole was moot. For the running up of a flag, perhaps?

Viktor laughed aloud, unable to prevent himself. To his outraged horror there came an echo, a feminine laughter that pealed out instantly upon his own.

"Good God," he said.

"Good God," said the voice.

Viktor, struck dumb, pulled himself together with an effort at the moment the echo voice said clearly: "Why don't you come here?"

"Where?" said Viktor.

"Wait," said the voice.

It seemed it was above him, and throwing back his head in a gesture of unnecessary violence, he noted a pale thing like tissue-paper in the act of turning away from a window. A moment later, he saw a light spring up and go travelling across the house. The impulse to flee was very strong. A lack of social etiquette had brought him here, but now the trauma of good manners, of all things, restrained him from flight. He felt a perfect fool. What would he say when the door opened? I was shipwrecked on your island by this terrible storm that has been silently and invisibly happening for the past hour?

Then the door opened and the light of a small oil-lamp opened likewise, a large pale yellow chrysanthemum across the wooden veranda. There was a hammock strung there, and a little table, and in the dark oblong of the doorway, the lamp in her hand, the girl he had seen swimming, naked as a swan, in the lake.

Of course he had known the second he heard her voice that it was she, no other.

"My God," he said again. He had an insane impulse to tell her how he had looked on her before, and choked it back with the utmost difficulty.

"Won't you come in?" said the girl.

He stared.

She wore a white frock, white stockings and shoes, her blonde hair pinned on her head in an old-fashioned rather charming way, and in the thick yellow light she glowed. Her face was not pretty, but had an exquisite otherworldliness.

"I was looking for—that is, I think I have the wrong house—" he blurted.

"Well, never mind. Since you're here, why don't you come in?" And when he still hesitated, she said with the most winning innocence, devoid of all its implications, "There's no one here but myself. My uncle is in town on business."

Viktor discovered himself walking towards her. She smiled encouragement. There was not a trace of artifice about her, not even a hint of the powder he had learned to recognise, on her eggshell face.

She led him inside, and he had the impression of one space tumbling over into another in a mélange of panellings and furnishings, and huge crazed shadows flung by the lamp. Then he was himself falling over a little card table, righting it, glimpsing the open window framed in the wings of opened shutters, the tassel of the blind swinging idly in the night air. He saw the lawn he had stood upon, the flagpole and the dead china animal. It was uncanny, surreal almost to him in that moment, to see from her viewpoint the spot he had only just vacated. She was saying something.

"—Russian tea," she finished. He turned too quickly, and observed a samovar. "Will you take some?" And he thought of Circe. He would drink the tea and change into a pig.

"Thank you."

And beyond the samovar, a beast with a monstrous horn. He noted the source of yesterday's music with another small shock. Not an orchestra at all. Of course not.

She had set the oil-lamp on the card table, and the light had steadied. Presently they sat down and drank the dark sweet tea, looking at each other neatly over the rims of the cups. There was nothing special about the room. He had seen many rooms like it. It was rather untidy, that was all, and the paper on the walls was distressfully peeling, due to damp he supposed. But the room smelled of water, not dampness, and of the tea, and of some elusive perfume which he wondered about, for it did not seem to be hers.

They did not speak again for a long while. It was so absurd, the whole thing. He did not know what to say. And was afraid besides of letting slip some reference to her nocturnal swim.

But he must say *something*—

"The château—" he said.

She smiled at him, polite and friendly, hanging graciously on his words.

"My mother," he said. "She owns—we live at the château."

"Yes?" she said. "How nice."

"And you," he fumbled.

"I live here," she said.

This was quite inane.

"It's very beautiful here," he said, inanely.

"Oh, yes."

"You must be wondering," he said, oddly aware she was not, "why I came up here."

"You said you thought it was another house. Someone you were looking for."

"Did I say that?" Yes, he had said it. "I'm afraid it was a lie. I came here out of curiosity. We used to own this land." Oh God, how pompous. "I say 'we.' I mean my mother's family. And I was . . . curious."

She smiled enigmatically. He finished the scalding tea at a gulp that seared his throat and stomach. Oink?

"Well," she said, standing up as if at a signal. "It was kind of you to call." She held out her hand, and disbelievingly, he rose and took it. Was she dismissing him?

"Well . . . " he repeated. Unsure, he felt in that instant another very strong urge to escape. "I suppose I should go back. Thank you for being so hospitable to a lawless trespasser." The words, gallant, buccaneering, pleased him. Cheered, he allowed her to lead him out to the veranda. "I heard your gramophone," he said, "the other night. Sound carries sometimes over the lake."

"Good-bye," she said.

He was on the lawn, and she stood above him on the veranda steps, white against the dark. He wanted to say: Do you often swim? And a vague wave of desire curled through him, making him tingle, and with it a strange aversion, drawing him away. But he said, without thinking, suddenly, "May I come back tomorrow?"

"Oh, no," she said. Nothing else. He stood waiting for almost a minute, waiting for there to *be* something else, some explanation, excuse, equivocation, or some softening reversal: Well, perhaps . . . But there was nothing. She stood there kindly smiling upon him, and presently he said, like a fool, "Good night, then." And walked off across the lawn.

When he came to the trees, he looked back. She had gone in, and the door was shut on the lamp, the peeling paper. It occurred to him for the first time that, before he had been seen, she had sat there in that large decaying house in the darkness. As if his arrival alone had woken her, brought her to life along with the bubbling samovar.

He was disgusted with it all, himself, her. She was that vile and typically bourgeois combination of the nondescript and the obscure. He climbed in the boat, loosed it, and pushed away from shore.

As he rowed, inflamed muscles complaining, he cursed over and over. What on earth had happened? What had it been for? She bored him.

By the time he reached the willow banks of the château he was exhausted. He dragged the boat into its shed with an embarrassed need to hide his escapade, and went in through one of the unlocked little side entrances of his mother's ancestral house. He threw himself on his bed fully clothed and began in sheer bewilderment to read a novel.

He fell asleep with his cheek on the open book, dissatisfied and disappointed.

The dawn woke him, stiff and cramped from the night's exercise. The long resinous light filled him with a terrible religious hunger for unspecified things. He thought of the nameless girl and how she had bored him, and her peculiar demeanour, and her slender pallor, and the moment of stupid desire. And realised in astonishment that it was the depression of jail he was feeling. He was certainly in love with her.

Halfway through the afternoon, as Viktor was lying encushioned on the lawn in an anguish of stiffness, dreading movement of any kind, a strange man appeared, walking around the château from the pine trees with a determined air.

Viktor sensed imminence at once. He hauled himself painfully into a sitting position. Ilena and her parasol, an odd creature from another planet, its second stalk-necked head twirling so far above the first, was parading gracefully up and down a long way off. Janov was indoors, engaged in billiards.

The stranger approached.

He towered over Viktor on the grass, an awful figure incongruously done up, even in the summer heat, in a black greatcoat caped like wings, and a tall black hat. A red beard streaked with darker red frothed between the two blacknesses, and a set of beautiless features, beaklike nose, small cold eyes of a yellowish, weaselish tinge.

"What do you want?" Viktor inquired haughtily.

The stranger considered.

"You, I think. I think I want you."

"What do you mean?"

"Get up, if you please. We must have words, you and I."

Viktor flushed with nerves.

"I don't think so."

"*I* think so."

"And who the hell are you," Viktor cried, "to think anything?"

The man's gelid face did not alter. Only the mouth moved, as if the rest of the countenance were a mask. But he pointed inexorably out across the lake.

"Over there," he said. "The house on the island. You know it?"

"Do I?"

"Yes, you know it. In the night, a visitor. You."

Viktor sneered. He was still sitting, helpless from the stiffness of that illicit row which now loomed above him, it seemed, in the retributive person of the red-bearded man.

"I will say this," said the man, "I do not like my niece disturbed when I am away. I do not like it. You hear me?"

Viktor stared arrogantly into the distance, blind. He could not bring himself to any more fruitless denials, or to argue.

"No further visits," said the man. "You will leave my niece alone. You hear me?"

Viktor stared. He was appalled but not entirely astonished when the ghastly black thing swooped on him like a bird of prey, close to his ear, hissing, "You *hear* me?"

"I hear," said Viktor, coldly, feeling an inner trembling start.

"Otherwise," said the man, "I shall not be responsible for anything I may do."

Miles off, in some other country, Ilena had turned, her parasol tilting like a fainting flower. "Viktor!" she called.

"You hear me?" the man said again.

"Yes."

"Good," said the man. He rose up and his shadow withdrew. He moved in short powerful strides, across the lawn, away into the pine trees.

Viktor, crouched in an agony of muscles and inarticulate fury, watched him go. The mystery of the whole momentary episode added to its horror. That the man was uncle to the white girl in the house—very well, one could accept that. That he had reached the shore, rowing an unseen boat himself in his heavy unsuitable garments—this seemed unlikely. But how else had he come here, save by flight? And the threats, out of all proportion to anything— Viktor became aware he should have stood up, threatened in turn, gone for one of the servants. That the very activity for which he was accused—yes, *accused*—had kept him riveted to the earth, seemed damning.

And the girl. She must have reported his coming to the island.

Said she did not care for it, was afraid. Ridiculous horrid little bourgeoise. Since dawn, he had been thinking of her, wondering if he could bear to woo her, and how it might be done, tactfully and pleasantly. Wondering too with romantic dread if she were a ghost, brought to quickness only by his arrival, swirling into a tomb at his retreat. A vampire who would drink his blood, a *rusalka* who would drown him. . . . And then, hammered flat across these sexually charged, yearning images, this beastly ordinary evil thing, the uncle like an indelible black stamp.

"Who was that man?" Ilena said, manifesting abruptly at his side.

"I don't know, Maman." Not quite a lie. No name had been given.

"Viktor, you are white as death. What did he say? Is it something you've done? Tell me. Some gambling debt—*Viktor!*"

"No, Maman. He was looking for another house, and asked the way."

"Then why," she said, "are you so pale?"

"I feel rather sick." That was sure enough.

"You drank too much at dinner," she said.

"Yes, Maman. Probably."

"What am I to do with you?" she asked.

"Send me back to the city?" he cried imploringly, the perpetual pleading shooting out of him when he least expected it to do so, had not even been thinking of it at all.

"Don't be foolish," she said. "In the city you would drink twice as much, gamble, do all manner of profligate idiotic things." She was smiling, teasing, yet in earnest. It was all true. Under her fragile cynicism her fear for him lurked like a wolf. She was afraid he would destroy himself as his father had done. And he caught her fear suddenly, fear of some lightless vortex; he did not even know its name.

"All right," he said, "all right, Maman. I'll stay here. I'll be good."

"There's my sensible darling."

When she had gone, he flopped on his face. Images of his father, a drunken man who died in Viktor's childhood, rose and faded. He recalled the lamps burning low on a winter's afternoon, and being told to play very quietly. And later, men in black at the door, and a white wax face in a long box that did not look remotely like anyone Viktor had ever seen before in his life.

But he was not his father. And abruptly there came an awful suspicion. That he had been brought here for no other reason than to be protected from the city, from all cities, to be *protected* from the long animated discussions and card games that ran into the early hours, from the theatres, the cafés, the pure excitement that a city symbolised. A prisoner. In that moment he thought of the girl again, and a strange revelation swept over him with a maddening sense of relief. Could it be she too was kept as a prisoner? That the loathsome man had brought her there and shut her up there, keeping all company away from her. Perhaps she had mentioned Viktor innocently, hoping for a repetition, and the devilish uncle had flown at her, battering her with the vulture's wings of his cape— No, no, you must go nowhere, see no one. I shall make sure he never comes here again.

But Viktor was powerless to alleviate her destiny. Powerless to alleviate his own.

He wondered which wine would be served with luncheon.

By the time the sun set on the lake he was very drunk. Somehow, he had contrived to be drinking all day. He did not know why this had seemed necessary, had not even thought about it. His mother's fear for him had begun it, and his fear for himself. As if by dipping into the vortex now and then, he could accustom himself to it, make it natural and mundane.

When the gong sounded for dinner he did not go down. He was afraid of Ilena seeing him as he was. But of course she came up, touched his forehead to see if he had a fever, gazed at him with her deep remorseless eyes. If she smelled the wine on his breath he was not certain, he tried not to let her, muffling himself in the counterpane from the bed, protesting he had a slight cold, wanted only to sleep—finally she left him. He lay and giggled, curled on his side, laughed at her a long while, then found himself crying.

He was surprised and shocked. He knew he was going to do something stupid, then, and such was his mental confusion that it was only two glasses of wine later that he realised what.

Rowing this drunk was much easier. He scarcely felt it at all, the grisly labouring drags and thrustings. Nor did he feel any anticipatory unease.

It was quite late, overcast, and a wind rising and falling. This would account perhaps for his only suddenly hearing the music that came from the island, when he was about a hundred yards from the reeds and the summerhouse. The gramophone. So near, it was obviously no orchestra, tinny and hesitant, cognisant of the little box that held it, and the big horn that let it out. Did the fact that the gramophone was playing mean the man was away? The man in the hat and greatcoat, the man like a black vulture? Or home?

What would Viktor do if he met the man?

Call his hand, of course. Just what he should have done before.

But really there was no need, if Viktor was careful, if he used the qualities of cunning and omnipotence he now felt stirring within himself, no need to meet the man.

Gently now. The reeds moved about him in a wave, and the boat jumped jarringly against the rotted post. With the drunkard's lack of coordination and contrastingly acute assessment, he had seen landfall and planned for it and messed it up, all in a space of seconds. With an oath and some mirth, he tethered the boat and got ashore on the island.

No swans. Just the music. And, as he passed the pavilion, the music ran down and went out. He had reached the edge of the lawn before it started up again, a cheerful frivolous syncopation that sounded macabre, suddenly, in the dark.

But there were lights in the house, two windows a thick deep amber behind drawn blinds. They were on the other side of the veranda from the window she had called him from, the window of the room into which she had subsequently led him for a few minutes of reasonless dialogue, and a burning mouthful of tea.

The outbuildings loomed. He ducked under the rose-vine, stepped over the china animal still lying there, and beneath the flagpole. He went towards the lighted windows, and paused, pressed against the veranda rail. Through the music he could hear the murmur of voices, or of a single voice. And now he could see that one of the blinds was not quite level with the sill. A trio of inches gaped, a deeper gold, showing slyly into the nakedness of the house.

Viktor advanced onto the veranda, crossed to the window and kneeled down, putting his face close to the pane. It was as simple as that. He saw directly into the room.

It was an amazing sight, a scene from a farce. He had no urge to laugh.

To the jolting beat of a dance melody, a couple moved about between the furniture. A huge oil-lamp threw light upon them, leaving the corners of the room in a magenta vignette. The girl was white, white hair, white dress; the man a black creature, clutching her close. The tall hat was gone from his head, which was covered with a snarled bush of reddish hair similar to that which sprang from the face. This face, that was for one instant in view on a turn, vanished on another, came in view again, was steeled in concentration, looking blindly away with its weasel eyes. Now and then the mouth spoke. Viktor found himself able to lip-read, with the slight aid of muffled sounds through the glass, and realised his adversary was counting out the beats. The girl's face was blank. Neither danced with pleasure or interest, and yet, oddly, they danced quite well, the man surprisingly fluid, the girl following like a doll.

Like a doll, yes, that was exactly what she was like.

Abruptly the dance ended. The man let go and stood back, and the gramophone ran down. In the silence, the voice spoke, quite audible now.

"Better. You are better. But you must smile while you dance."

The girl was facing in Viktor's direction. He saw her face at once break into a soulless grimace.

"No, no." The man was displeased. "A smile. Soft, flexible. Like this."

He turned away, and any smile that face could conjure, how could it be at all appealing? And yet the girl presumably copied his expression. And now, agitated, Viktor saw her smile limpidly and beautifully. He was charmed by her smile, mimicked incredibly from the monster.

"Better," the monster said again. There was a trace of accent, had been when he spoke to Viktor earlier in the day, unnoticed then in the alarm of the interview. What was it? Germanic, perhaps. "Now, sit down. Walk to that chair and sit on it. As I have shown you."

The girl, still with a trace of the magical smile on her lips, went to the chair, and seated herself, ladylike and graceful.

"Good, that is good. Now we will talk."

The girl waited obediently, her eggshell face uplifted.

"The gardens. A bench," said the man. Viktor noted, all at once, that along with everything else incongruous, the foreigner still wore his greatcoat, securely fastened. "It is late in the morning. I have sat beside you. Good day, m'mselle."

"Good day," she replied aloofly, turning her head a little away.

"I hope I do not disturb you?"

"No. Not at all."

"Have I seen you here before, m'mselle?"

"It's possible. Sometimes I walk my dog here."

"Ah, yes. Your dog. A delightful little fellow."

"I am training him to shake hands. He loves to show off to strangers. Perhaps you would be so kind—"

"But of course. Ah! How clever he is."

"Thank you. I should be very lonely without him."

"But are you alone, m'mselle? A lady like yourself . . . "

"Quite alone." The girl sighed softly. Her eyes were lowered. The extraordinary playacting went on and on. "My uncle, you understand, has business affairs which take him often from home."

"Then, you spend all day in an empty flat?"

"Just so. It is very tiresome, I'm afraid."

"But then, m'mselle, might I ask you to take luncheon with me?"

"Why—" the girl hesitated. Her eyes fluttered upward, and stayed, their attention distracted. It took Viktor several moments, so objective had he become, to understand it was on him her gaze had faltered and then adhered. She had seen him peering in under the blind.

Stricken with dismay, he seemed changed to stone. But the man, with a flap of his black wings, paid no heed to the *direction* of her eyes.

"Continue," he barked sharply. "Go on, go on!"

The white girl only gazed into Viktor's horrified stare. Then suddenly she began to laugh, rocking herself, clasping her hands —delighted wild laughter.

"On! On!" she cried. She bubbled, almost enchanting, somehow not. "On!"

The man reached her in two strides, and shook her.

"Be quiet. Quiet!" The girl stopped laughing. She became composed, and so remained as he coldly and intently ranted at her. "Was it for this I bought you in that slum, sores and verminous bites all over you, for this? You will be still. You will attend. You will *learn*. You hear me?"

The effect of those repeated words upon Viktor was awful. They seemed to deprive him of all the strength of his inebriation. Stunned and totally unnerved, he came noiselessly to his feet. He crossed the veranda, praying she would say nothing of having seen him. But she would not, surely. She was not quite normal, not even quite sane— He reached the veranda step and misjudged it, saw his misjudgement in the moment he made it, could alter nothing, and fell heavily against the railing.

The clamour seemed to throb through every wooden board and timber of the house. Before he could regain enough balance to break into a run, something crashed over in the lighted room, and then the main door flew open and a black beast came out of it.

He had known this would happen. Somehow he had come here for this—this goal of self-destruction.

"What are you doing?" the thing demanded. It caught hold of him, and he was brought about to face it again. All the rich light was behind the man now, full on Viktor. There were no excuses to be made. He flinched from the man's odourless cold breath. "You are here? You dared to come back?"

Viktor pulled some part of himself together.

"Of course I dared. Why shouldn't I?"

"You trespass."

"No. I came to see you."

"Why? This island is private. You were told to keep away."

"You have no right to—"

"Every right. It is mine. I warned you."

"Go to hell," said Viktor. He was afraid. Could not control his limbs, barely his voice and the slurred movements of his mouth.

"No," said the man. "It is you who will go there. I will send you there." And with no further preliminary, he punched Viktor in the arm and, as he stumbled away grunting with shocked pain, on the side of the jaw. Viktor fell backwards in the grass, and saw through a sliding haze, the man coming on at him.

As he rolled bonelessly against the legs of the veranda, the man kicked him in the side. The impact was vicious, filling him now with terror more than pain. Somehow, Viktor came to his feet.

"No," he said, and put up his arm. Like a big black bear the man lunged at him, bringing down both his fists together, sweeping away the protective arm as if it were a rag. The pain was awful this time, and the blow had been meant, clearly, for his head. Viktor had an impulse to curl up on the turf, allowing the man to beat him until he wearied himself and left his victim alone. Instead, Viktor's own fist lashed out. He caught the man on the nose, which began at once to bleed dark runnels of blood. But the madman scarcely hesitated. He flung his whole body after Viktor and caught him round the waist.

For a moment then Viktor felt himself trapped, and envisaged dying. To be weary would not be enough for his enemy. Only death could turn him aside. The man was squeezing him, choking him; stars burst in Viktor's brain.

"I warned you," said the man.

Some remnant of self-preservation—actually a story told him once by a prostitute—caused Viktor spontaneously to knee the hugging bear in its groin.

There was a dreadful sound, a sort of implosion, and the paws let him go. Staggering, Viktor ran.

There followed a nightmare sequence during which the china animal in the bushes tried to trip him, the grass and tree roots likewise. Then he plunged into water, found a rope, tore it free, and collapsed into the boat, crying for mercy to the darkness.

Somehow he made the oars work, and somehow the man did not come after him. Yet it was with the utmost fear that Viktor thrashed his way towards the midst of the lake. There, sobbing for breath, he lay still on the oars, and the great night grew still about him.

It seemed to be a long while afterwards that he began to row for the château. And by then he seemed, too, to be quite sober, but perhaps he was not, his feelings a slow chilled turmoil where nothing anymore made sense. *My little dog does tricks— Ah, what a clever fellow—better, m'mselle, better—* And in the middle of it all, something came over the last stretch of water from the shore, from the lawns where the château stood, serene and dislocated from reality.

It was a white something, and for a demented moment he thought the girl had jumped into the lake and swum out ahead of him. But no, it was a swan.

Feeling ill, he leaned on the oars, drifting, watching the swan come towards him. He became aware he must have disturbed it. It did not move like a ship but ran at him standing up on the water, flapping its wings which suddenly seemed enormous, like two white sheets. And abruptly the swan was beside him, hissing like a snake, smiting the boat, the air, his flesh—

He tried frantically to beat it off, to make for shore. This second nightmare sequence had no logic, and afterwards he did not properly remember it. All at once the boat slewed, and he was in the water. It was colder than before, and an agonising something had happened to his arm. He no longer had any control at all.

The first time he sank into the lake he shouted in terror, but the water was so very cold he could not shout again. And then he was falling down through it, knowing he was about to die, in absolute horror and despair, unable to save himself.

A month later he learned a servant, smoking a cigarette on the lawn near the water, had seen the swan attack, and the accident with the boat. The man had leapt heroically into the lake and saved Viktor, while the swan faded away into the dark.

The broken arm and the fever had debilitated Viktor, and as soon as he was well enough his mother returned them all to the city.

"A terrible thing," Ilena said. "You might well have been drowned. I remember a story of a boy drowned in that lake. Whatever possessed you?"

"I don't know," Viktor said listlessly, propped up in bed, surrounded by the depressing medicines, the dreary novels.

Ilena said nothing at all, but weeks after, apropos another matter, Janov mentioned a man who had kept his mistress on one of the islands, a young girl reckoned to be simple. It seemed they had packed up suddenly and gone away, and the house was in a nasty state, full of damp and mice.

It was half a year before any of them thought Viktor fully recovered. He had begun to play cards with Uncle Janov, and next, billiards. Viktor had stopped drinking beyond the merest glass at dinner; he had taken a dislike for light and noise, painting and discussion. And so Ilena sent him to Paris, when he no longer wanted to go.

It was more than fifteen years later that he saw the girl again.

In the winter of the northern city, the ice lay in blue rifts upon the sea, and a copper sun bled seven degrees above the horizon. He had been to visit his mother, cranky and bemused, in the house on Stork Street. Such visits, as the years went by, had become increasingly bizarre. Something was happening to Ilena. Arthritis, for one thing, had crippled her, twisting her elegant figure like the stem of a slender blasted tree. Betrayed by her bones, her sensibilities gave way. She made demands on Viktor and on everyone, calling the servants constantly: Bring me that pomander, that box of cigarettes. I want tea. I want my book of cuttings. She drove them mad, and she drove Viktor mad, also. Uncle Janov was dead. He had died ten months before, sitting bolt upright at the card table, without a sound. No one realised he had absented himself until he refused to play his hand.

There had been a war, too, setting the whole world on its ear. Somehow, some had escaped the worst of that.

To Viktor himself, time had offered a few patronising gifts. He had published four novels with reasonable success. More than anything, writing, which he performed indifferently now, and no longer with any pleasure, gave him an excuse for doing nothing else. He had become, he was afraid, the perfect archetype of what the masses reckoned an author to be: one too lazy to attempt anything more valuable. The family meanwhile remained wealthy; he really had no need to do anything at all, except, possibly, to marry, which he had idly been considering. A much-removed cousin had been presented as a candidate, a lushly attractive young woman, with indeed some look of Viktor himself. She was a nice girl, quite intelligent and entertaining, and maternally adequate, being ten years his junior. An ideal match. It would soothe Ilena, giving her the sense that the family continued, giving her, too, something fresh to criticise. For himself, the proposed liaison was rather like his "work." Something to give him an excuse to attempt nothing else. His libido, having reached a peak in his early twenties, was already diminishing. Sex had already lost all its alluring novelty. He had ceased to fall in love, and beyond a very occasional evening with one of the city's hetaeras, he had put all that away, as it were, in some cabinet of his physical emotions.

And then, he saw the girl again.

It would not have been true to say he had often thought of her. He had scarcely thought of her at all as the years went by. And despite a fleeting reference to the peculiar events on the island inserted into his first book, he had never really reexamined the case. It had seemed to him very quickly that nothing much had happened at all. It had been merely a series of coincidental occurrences, made dramatic only by his state of mind and the ultimate plunge into the lake. The fact that he had never returned to the château did not strike him as particularly ominous. He had been bored there. Just as he had mostly been bored in Paris and was now bored almost all the time and almost everywhere. The only difference was that his fear of boredom had gone away. He was accustomed to it now and expected nothing else. It had come to fit him, suit him quite comfortably, like a well-worn dressing gown.

He was walking through one of the sets of gardens that bordered the museum and art gallery, on his way to a luncheon engagement at the literary club. And suddenly he saw a small black shape, rather like an animated sausage, trotting across the whiteness of the snow. It was a little dog, seemingly impervious to the cold, a very black, very purposeful little dog, that he followed with his eyes intuitively. And then a woman came out between the white trees, against an oval of brown sky. She was fashionably dressed, at the height of fashion indeed, and maybe not warmly enough for the season. Yet like the dog, which was obviously hers, she seemed untroubled by the cold. Like the dog too, she wore black—jet black—save for the tall scarlet feather in her hat and a pair of blinding scarlet gloves, and the scarlet on her lips.

Perhaps it was the maquillage on her face that prevented his immediately knowing her, or maybe only the fifteen years that had separated those three brief glimpses he had formerly had of her from this. Then something, the turn of her head, her gesture to the dog as it bounced up to her, jogged his memory.

For a full minute he stared at her, unable to say a word. She did not seem to see him at all, and yet something in her manner told him she knew quite well a man stood watching her, as she picked up and petted the dog. And then, irresistibly, he found he had gone over.

And he heard himself saying, as if by rote, for all at once he remembered the words: "Good day, m'mselle."

And aloofly she replied, "Good day," just as on the island, through the window.

"Forgive me for disturbing you. But I was intrigued by your little dog."

"Oh, yes. I am training him to do tricks, to shake hands. He loves to show off to strangers. Look at him! He's trying to attract your attention."

And Viktor found himself pulling off one glove and extending his hand to take the icy little paw, shaking it.

"How clever he is," said Viktor.

"Thank you." The smiling face, pretty in its makeup, lowered mascaraed lids. No wonder she looked different. The dark lashes, the black eyebrows. "I should be very lonely without him."

Viktor almost choked, but he managed the words: "I find it hard to believe you're alone."

"Quite alone," she said. She sighed, petting the black little dog with scarlet fingers.

"Your uncle is often away from home," said Viktor, between sneering and joking and embarrassment.

"Why, yes," she said. She looked at him wonderingly. "Do you know my uncle?"

"I met him, once," said Viktor. "Perhaps that gives me the right to presume. Will you have lunch with me?"

"Why—" she said. She lifted her pale eyes and looked at him. "Why, of course."

She put her red hand through his arm as they walked, holding the dog with the other. He felt hilarious, and had already dismissed the other lunch engagement from his mind.

In the restaurant he talked to her randomly, hypnotised by the perfection of her answers. She replied to all, elaborated sometimes, giving the impression of an utterly charming negative neutrality, restful and obliging. And the little dog was a model of decorum, even when she awarded it a spoonful of the hot chocolate sauce. He marvelled at its training, and hers.

Framed in the black bell of her hat, her face fascinated him with its changes, but he longed for her to remove the hat, to show him if her hair, now obviously very short, was still blonde. As blonde as when she had swum in the lake among the swans.

After lunch he escorted her, naturally, to her flat. It was on a quiet street, between the ordinary and the modish. Flowerpots stood on the window-sills, winter bald. There was a plush carpet when, just as naturally, she invited him to enter and he did so.

They went upstairs to the second floor. She opened a door. It was much unlike the wild house with its peeling walls and oil-lamps. The paper on the wall was a subtle cream and beige brocade, quite dry. At the touch of a switch the warmth of electricity flooded the rosy chairs, the deep blue rugs.

At this point, supposedly, the true meaning of their adventure would drift to the surface. It did so. Putting down the dog, she returned to Viktor across the pleasant room. Her gloves were gone, and she laid the smooth skin of her hand on his lapel.

"You've been very kind," she said. Her eyes were brimming with invitation. From now on her clients would, probably, become more businesslike. And he remembered how she had dismissed him the first time, on the island, trained also to that.

With a strange sensation, Viktor lowered his head towards her. Her mouth was cool and perfumed with lip paint, curiously uninvolved as it yielded first to the caress and then to the invasion. What did she feel? Nothing? And he, what did he feel? He was unsure. He had persuaded himself to love her, once, the love of the unknown thing. He remembered her white body in the water, and a sudden pang of sexuality shot through him, startling him.

The girl drew gently away. "Come with me," she said secretively. And led him into her bedroom.

It was an ordinary chamber, in good taste, nothing lewd or even merely garish, no pictures of frolics intended to arouse or amuse, none of the bric-a-brac of the whore, except a heap of silken cushions.

"Take off your hat," he said to her. "Take off all your clothes. I want to watch you."

The girl laughed, and flirted with her eyes. The correct response. No doubt, his request was not unusual.

She stood then at the centre of a red and black autumn of falling garments, and mesmerised, he did watch her, his heart ludicrously in his mouth as once before so long ago, and still the bell-shaped hat was left in place, even now she stood in her slip—he gestured to the hat, unable to vocalise, and she smiled and drew it upward from her head.

Her hair was black. Black as ink. He had not expected such a thing, it stunned him, and he felt again the water of the lake filling his nostrils, his throat; and the old break in his arm, which for years had promised the ultimate penance of Ilena's arthritis, burned and ached.

"Your hair," he said, forcing out the words, his excitement quite dead.

It was smooth and short and black, so black, as if a cupful of paint had been poured over her skull. Fashionable, and horrible.

She did not seem disturbed by his reaction, but went on archly smiling at him, trained as she was—this outcry of his was too far removed from her training to facilitate one of her closet-full of suitable responses.

It was only then, glaring at her, the cameo of black silk and blonde flesh, that he saw she had not changed at all, was just as he recalled, the ink blackness only an overlay. There was not a line that he could see in her smooth face, on her neck, her breast—these fifteen years, which had touched everything, had not touched her at all.

He went forward, and she, thinking equilibrium restored, invited with eyes and lips. But he did not take her to him, only stared at her. It was true. She was unmarked. He put one finger to her cheek, running it across her flesh that was as smooth as wax— And the bedroom door opened behind him.

Her hand flew to her scarlet mouth. It was another learned

response, not real. Viktor could see that quite clearly. And he himself turned without any surprise and saw a man in a black greatcoat filling the doorway, his small eyes widened with outrage.

"What is this? I must ask you, sir—"

The voice was less foreign, the accent polished and succinct. The coat was of more recent cut, the face shaven, only a little red moustache and red hairs glinting in the flared nostrils. Nothing had faded, there was no grey. But the lines had deepened, quite normally.

Viktor felt a surge of relief. Yes, relief, that he would not have to go on with this absurd play, that he did not have to have her, the unobtainable, now ruined, thing.

He walked towards the man, who barked at her: "Get dressed!" And retreated out into the sitting room of the flat.

The bedroom door clipped shut. The black figure loomed before the mantelpiece.

"What am I to think?" the man said. "I come home unexpectedly, and I find my niece, and I find you, sir—and she is in her underwear—"

"What indeed," said Viktor. He knew the game, who would not? Once in Paris, he had almost been caught in such a way, if a chance acquaintance had not warned him: the flighty young woman, her husband bursting in—

"And she is a little—how shall I say this?—a little naïve in her wits, sir."

"An idiot," said Viktor.

"And you, taking advantage of such a thing, her plight—I see you are a man of substance, sir. What would your associates think, should they learn what you did this afternoon, how you tried to abuse a young girl of less than average mental capacity. Making her drunk, bringing her to her own home, with the purpose of satisfying your desires."

The voice went on. Now and then, almost smothered, Viktor noted the hint of the foreignness, still extant. He had known, probably, at some level of consciousness, from the moment he saw her in the garden. On an armchair, the little black dog slept, unperturbed by this rehearsal of fierce anger it had no doubt heard a hundred times.

Viktor sighed. He felt nothing anymore, not even satisfaction. Where was the island, the darkness? Where was twenty, now?

"Shut up," he broke in, loudly, but without emphasis.

The monstrous beaked thing did indeed fall silent.

"I do know your intention," said Viktor, calmly. "And I have a piece of news for you. I intend to pay you nothing. Nothing. Do you hear?" But not even this parody of the man's speech pleased him. Viktor went on, replacing his gloves as he did so. "If you wish, you may tell the world at large that you found me in the bedroom with your undressed niece, who is not your niece, but who you—let me get it right—bought in a slum, covered with sores and bites. And whom you taught to behave as she does, in gardens, ballrooms, and God knows where else, on an island, fifteen years ago."

The man's face had set, drawing in about itself, becoming unreadable, and most attentive.

"All of which," Viktor said, "I too am willing to reveal in my turn. Rather a blight on a profitable trade, I would think. And now," he found himself at the door, "good afternoon."

No move was made to stop him. He passed into the lobby and down the stairs, and on to the street.

Standing before the apartment house, Viktor paused and lit a cigarette, as if permitting pursuit to catch him up. But no one came, no window was flung wide, not even a flowerpot hurled. He wondered if the man even remembered him.

With a little shrug, Viktor turned to walk away. He felt a sullen disappointment which soon faded, slipping back into the worn dressing gown of boredom.

It was three nights later, strolling home alone from a dinner party, that someone came behind him on a deserted street, and brutally beat him, leaving him unconscious in the snow. It might only have been a coincidence.

He was presently found and taken home, but the episode resulted in a bout of pneumonia.

"My dear, you are so young, so young," said Ilena, holding his hand. She seemed quite her old self, dressed in inspiring pastel colours, somehow here and seated by the bed, not demanding, not complaining at all, only coaxing him. He smiled at her, to show her he was pleased she had come. He felt a remote tenderness, but somehow could not summon the strength to say one word to her. She spoke of his cousin, the one he was to marry. "She will be here directly. But the trains are so slow. The weather—"

Across from the bed, the wall went on slowly dissolving, as it had been doing now for almost an hour, a soft sweet dissolution, like melting snow.

The doctor shook his head at Ilena, gently. She stopped speaking and only held the hand of her son, who at thirty-six, it seemed, was about to die. Some fundamental weakness in his constitution had finished him. His lungs were filled by fluid, he was drowning, there was no hope at all. Ilena, who had railed and wept in the corridor, was now calm and tactful in the face of another's agony. Her own, like the pain of her crippling disease, she would ignore for the present. Janov had spared her this. Even now, she did not quite believe that Janov had died, or that Viktor was dying. The whole world had paid with death for its dreams, its youthful mistakes, and was not done paying yet. But not her son, her son.

Somewhere a clock ticked. One of Viktor's clocks. A miracle would happen soon, and he would get better.

Viktor watched the melting of the wall, and saw the long lawns of the château appear. Three years ago, the château had been sold again, lost again, but that did not matter now. The house was dim beyond the wall, vanishing. A thick mist lay everywhere, swathing the great stretch of water that must be the lake, a surface of dark silver, with one blank tear of soft white light across it. Beautiful, serene and melancholy, the light, the lake, and then a dark movement far away, something a mile out on the glacial water.

"Your last book," Ilena said, unable to restrain her words despite herself. "I was reading it again, just yesterday. What a curious, clever book it is. High time you wrote another, my dear. Perhaps, in the spring—"

Yes, Maman, he said. But he said nothing. He stared away beyond the wall and saw the shape of the darkness on the water drifting nearer. He could see what it was, now. A swan, a black swan, floating like a ship towards him over the utter silence of the winter lake.

"Do you remember," Ilena said, "when we were at the château and that silly thing happened with the boat?" It was the way she had been used to speak to Janov: *Do you recall, Jani, when we were here, and did this and did that?* Viktor smiled at her, but he did not smile.

The black swan came nearer and nearer, black as night, black as ink, and it seemed to him he heard it sing.

"You mustn't leave me," Ilena whispered, knowing he no longer heard her. "What shall I do, alone?"

But the shadow of the black swan had filled the room. She was alone already.

# BRIGHT BURNING TIGER

**L**ONG, LONG AGO IN LONDON A GIRL OF MY ACQUAINTANCE, finding her ginger feline asleep by the gas fire, struck a pose, one foot lightly on the cat's back, announcing: "Shot it in Injuh, y'know," and she had so perfectly caught, in voice and stance, the pompous waking dream of the British raj, that it became a game often repeated; only ended at last by the intolerance of the cat to playing tiger's skin. As for me, the joke summed up a basic personal attitude. I had then an allergic indifference to a type of man and his pursuits, as unlike myself and mine as those of an alien species. Later, when I learned more of the facts, some of the glibness of the joke had to be rethought. There are occasionally among tigers man-eaters, which can prey on the remoter villages of the jungle-forest, cruel, maddened things that seem to hate, killing from lust rather than hunger, leaving the half-devoured bodies of women among the stalks of the fields at sunrise; by night a nightmare shadow, so a man will be afraid to go out of his hut to make water in case death has him. There is sometimes a need for a bullet, which the sneer and the attitude had formerly cloaked. Much later again, when I met Pettersun, I came to understand, unwillingly at first, maybe always unwillingly, something of what drives one hunter, something actually of the uncanny bond which can come to obtain between one who hunts, one who is hunted. Certainly to perceive the slender division that exists, always interchangeable. For the man may misfire, the weapon stall, the beaters run away, and the dark come down which is the tiger's country, the land of night. And in the forests of the night, the golden beast with his nocturnal sight, the unalloyed weapons of his mouth, the blades of his feet, his great strength—the creature capable of eating men—that is no mean adversary. It isn't in me to enter, to want to enter, the magic circle of any of this. Not merely that I lack the courage, though I do lack it, but because I could never kill anything either ritually or callously that I absolutely did not have to. And luckily, I never have had to kill anything, beast or man. For this reason, perhaps, I can tell my story, safe by a sort of mitigating accident. I wonder.

It was just outside the Victoria Memorial in Calcutta that I met the fat man. Part of my living comes from carrying out paid research for others, and my mind was still idling somewhere between here and the Jadu Ghar, my feet already turning towards the hotel. Softening the slums and palaces, an orange sun bled low over the Maidan. The fat man blocked the view, halting before me on the steps and introducing himself. I can't recall who he said he was, but he knew me from an article that had carried my photograph. I was thinking with annoyance he would now engage me in argument over something I had written and forgotten, when he told me Pettersun was dead.

"How?" I was shocked by aptness, not surprise, and the query was half-rhetorical. It was fairly obvious what must have occurred, nor was I mistaken.

"A tiger killed him. Funny business. Damn funny. I've given myself the responsibility, you might say, to let people know, people who knew him."

"I never knew him well."

"Didn't you? That's all right then. But still, a funny business." I looked at the blankness of his dark silhouette with the amber sunset crackling around the fat edges of it. He wanted to say some more. "Funny," he said.

"You mean amusing, or peculiar?"

"Oh, not amusing. Not at all. Peculiar. Yes, that's it."

"Why?" I said.

"Well, he wasn't off hunting it, you know. He was in bed."

"In—*bed*—"

"Exactly. And the thing came in, right into the bungalow, and tore him to pieces. Pretty horrible, I gather. Yes, pretty damn horrible."

It certainly sounded odd. Monkeys, rats, snakes, these come into houses, not tigers that I ever heard of. The fat man stood, gloating over his own dismay, mine. I was compelled to go on, ask questions.

"Where did this happen?"

"North," he said, and named a small town. "About ten miles from there. A couple of villages. One of the old rangers' bungalows. He was living there, out in the jungle. Just drinking a lot, not doing anything. Then there was a scare apparently, a man-eater. They'd heard about Pettersun and came and asked him if he'd take it on, and Pettersun said, No, he was through with all that. But he started cleaning his gun—you remember that gun of his with ivory—"

"Yes, I remember."

"Then there's a panic, you know how they are. The tiger's everywhere. In the village. In the other village. Up a tree, in the fields, down the well— He was going out the next night, or that's how I heard it, torches and beaters, the whole bloody show. A little before dawn he was lying there with the gin bottle for company and —whap! One of his beaters found him and ran out screaming. It was mucky."

"How do you know all this?"

"Doctor at Chadhur was called in to look at the body. I know Hari pretty well. Second-hand news, but reliable."

"It sounds unbelievable."

The fat man didn't take offence. He shrugged.

"It does, doesn't it. But the Bombay papers had it, you know, a paragraph or two."

"How long ago was all this?"

"A couple of months. Well, that's life. I could do with something cool."

The dim wild cry of sunset worship was beginning to rise from distant mosques. I excused myself to the fat man and went away to get a drink alone.

I digested Pettersun's death slowly in the shadow of the turning fans, like huge insects in the ceiling. How else must a hunter die, but logically under the hoof or claw or fang of the entity he has so long himself stood over, his foot on its neck, the rifle smoking. Shot it in India. Though he had not been one for tiger-skin rugs.

I hadn't, as I said, known him well. I hadn't liked him, God forbid, or admired him, except possibly for his bravery, for there had been stories of that I had heard from other sources. I suppose to some extent he fascinated me, the forbidden fruit of what our own ethic tells us is wrong, which to another is only an ordinary facet of existence. I'd met him at a sprawling English party in Bombay, full of men in penguin costume and women in gold lamé dresses, all of them brown as tanned leather, which made the coffee flesh of the waiters look almost blue. We spoke generally for a while, part of a group, which gradually drifted away, leaving Pettersun alone with me. He then said, smiling, as if he'd been waiting the chance, "You don't like me much, do you." No question, no aggression; a statement. I said nothing. He swirled the last of his drink, drank it and said, "Or rather, you don't like what I do. Orion the Hunter. The wicked man who kills the nice animals."

I shrugged, considering the neatest way of escaping, which hadn't yet suggested itself. One of the waiters came by with more drinks, and Pettersun took off four, the fourth of which he handed to me.

"Thanks," I said.

"Yes," he said. He drank the first of his new drinks straight down, and said, "Call me names, if you like. I don't shoot men."

"Just tigers," I said, before I could stop myself.

"Just tigers? A tiger is never *just* tiger."

"For sport," I said.

"No," he said. Still the smile, throwing me, enjoying it? "I'd never call it that."

This was becoming boring and uncomfortable.

"Well," I said, helpfully, "a man-eater obviously—"

"So you won't stand up for your principles," he said, and drank that second drink. "You think I'm an offence on God's green earth, but you're not about to tell me so."

"Mr. Pettersun," I said, "what you do is your problem."

"Afraid I'll hit you if you speak up, break the chiselled nose, is that it? I won't. I'm a peaceable man. I like booze, preferably free. I kill tigers. Note, I didn't say I *liked* killing them. That's it. The sum of my parts."

"Excuse me," I said. As I turned, he put the third glass into my other hand, which duly stayed me, because he had obviously wanted it himself. "Have a drink?" he said.

I stood there with a glass in either hand, looking at him, wondering.

"What do you want?" I said.

"I think," he said, "I want to talk to you, tell you—about the very thing you don't want to hear about."

"In other words, you want to be a nuisance."

"No."

"Convert me? Not a chance."

"Well, of course not," Pettersun said. "There's no pleasure in conversion. And debate is normally pointless, isn't it?" I stayed where I was, caught despite myself because he had said something I myself believed. "So, what can it be?"

I started to sip the drink he had given me. I said: "Drunken egomania needing to find a voice?"

He laughed. "This affair stinks," he said. "I know a place on the waterfront where a girl dances with cobras on all the tables. You like that kind of thing?"

"Yes, I sometimes like that kind of thing."

In the "place" where the barefoot girl did her dance every two hours, swishing her black hair like a horse's tail, the milked snakes knotted on her arms, at her waist, we drank something alcoholic curdled in *lassi*. I wasn't even then sure what had made me go there with him. It would be easy enough, with hindsight, to say I sensed he needed to confess, last rites before execution. As someone I once knew said, there is something of the priest about me, somehow, somewhere, apparent both to myself and, under particular circumstances, to others.

The preliminary conversation rambled; I don't recollect much of it, but when he began to *talk* to me, as he had said he wished to, there came a kind of clarity which I do remember and maybe always shall. No sentences are left, but I retain their kernel. For this was when the free-masonry of the hunt was made known to me, and I was just drunk enough that it came in over or under the barriers of my mind and ethics, and I understood, and I still understand, though I won't condone. Condone it less, probably, since I saw the attraction, the religious element, the extraordinary bonding that might occur (at least in the human's mind), which must then be sought after like a drug. While it was some bloody old duffer with his rifle and his notions of sport it stayed safely and obscenely remote. But the sorcerous quality of the ritual of the hunt, arcane and special, and there, I suspect, in many of us, had a seductive frisson that had to be resisted—which in fact made it all the more repulsive—the Venus's-flytrap.

I recall too, well into the night, staggering back along by the seashore, the black water and the towering ghosts of apartment buildings, and the moon like ivory, like the ivory inlay on the rifle, of which he carried a snapshot, just as other men carry photos of their women or their children, or lacking those, their dogs.

In the morning, waking with a hangover, I thought it had been a waste of time, ridiculous. But very soon the teachings—for he had taught me his philosophy, under the wild fig tree of the dancing girl's shade—came back. Hunter and hunted, the stalker and the prey, woven by reeds, by leaves, by shadows, by bloodthirst and fear, and by desire. And which was which? Then getting up to put my head in the basin full of lukewarm water, I thought angrily: Rubbish. A man with a gun. What chance had the wretched tiger? Who did Pettersun think he was fooling? But he hadn't been trying to fool me. He had only been saying, This is how it is, for some, for me. Right or wrong. This. I had never had much patience with Hemingway, but I reread *The Old Man and the Sea* a week later, in the blazing Indian veranda. The relationship between the fisherman and the great beautiful hooked fish—aside from necessity, thickheaded, wanton, unaware—anything its detractors will prove it—but powerfully illustrative, in its way, of the mystique Pettersun had revealed to me. But if it is possible to murder with honour and love and pity, then all the more reason to stop.

I never met Pettersun again. A few months later, the fat man met me instead on the Memorial steps in Calcutta and said, "A tiger killed him. Funny business."

So, then. Just over twelve months later, doing this time some research on my own behalf, I ended up more or less randomly in Chadhur.

Once I had my own professional affairs in hand, I went over to the hospital building. Here I loitered, pondering if I really wanted or intended to chase the matter. But someone asked me, as they do Europeans, whom I was looking for. I replied with the name of the doctor the fat man had called familiarly, "Hari."

Graceful and gregarious, Doctor Hari invited me into his office for very good coffee, and I broached my subject tentatively. The response was not tentative at all. Doctor Hari had had for Pettersun all the rage of the good physician for the intransigent patient. "If the tiger had not done for him, his alcoholism would have seen to it. His system was in revolt. On the path he had chosen he had a year or less."

"But it's true, then. I heard the animal got into—"

"—the bungalow and attacked him in bed? Quite true. Do you have a strong stomach?"

Pettersun had been disembowelled, the heart and throat torn out—the rest of the corpse had been bitten, rent, virtually slit like a sack. "It was quite a mess. The villagers are used to death and mishap, but they were terribly afraid and superstitious. I too have seen a number of men killed by tigers or panthers. Never a body exactly in this condition, and all uneaten."

"Then it wasn't the tiger he was out to get?"

"Well, perhaps. The second village trapped a tiger about ten days after—an old tiger turned to man-flesh, as they sometimes do, because men are easier game. I should say this tiger was not strong enough to have done to the body what had been done. Naturally, sometimes they will kill and not eat, but then not maul so savagely, splitting open, almost a dissection. While the room was untouched."

"How did it get in?"

"The door was open. He had left it open—wide, like an invitation, one might almost say. Very strange. Very unpleasant. And sad. There are other villages in the area with cause to be grateful to Pettersun."

I had a dead feeling, the letdown of anticlimax. I didn't know what I had expected to hear. Then, as I was leaving, Doctor Hari said, "Of course, the drinking had made him do curious things. On the wall of the bungalow, for example, he had written something in big letters. A poem of some sort, some modern English or American verse, unrhyming. About a tiger, naturally. The villagers still refuse to go near the house at night."

To go out to the bungalow was the next thing to do, so I put off doing it. Pettersun's death was stale a year now, and nothing to me or to do with me. My interest did not seem purely ghoulish, but probably was. Against that, I knew I couldn't leave without follow-ing events to their proper conclusion. Finally I got a car and took to the new highway, which bore me all the way to the town of the fat man's tale. From there the wisest course was horseback, colonial style, along the dusty road and into the blistered, streaked, striped heart of the jungle. Here I almost gave myself entirely to the spirit of the place, the intense enclosure of the massive trees skirted with broad leaves and thickets of bamboo. A few times women passed me on the track, walking what I call the sari-walk, wound in their jewel-bright garments, basket or pot on head. They were lean and proud and sometimes beautiful beyond measure. Presently I saw a village, downhill in a valley, where the jungle broke and scattered. Grain stood straight up at the sky, children ran about, a herd of buffalo wallowed in summer mud.

The sky had turned briefly to a wall of glowing maroon beyond the trees, when I reached the bungalow—and nearly missed it. The jungle, as in Kipling, had been let in, vines and high grass all over everything, barely the glint of dirty-white veranda posts to show me. There was a cookhouse round at the back and a couple of huts, but these also were overgrown; the roofs had fallen in.

I stirred about for a while, the horse cropping the grass, uncon-cerned. The doors to the house had been boarded up by authority, and I had no intention of forcing them in the dark. There seemed nothing dangerous abroad, but as the night smoked through the forest, I remounted and made my way back to the village. Here I was greeted with curiosity amounting to joy. I didn't mention my errand or that I had been to the bungalow, merely did a little trad-ing over the rice and spiced vegetables. Later a child of five appeared, who spoke to the men in Hindi of his wife and family, the family cow and goat, the ailment of his youngest daughter. It was the memory of the recent past life. Such things are not uncom-mon in India. The child's mother presently came in and comforted him, telling him all would be well. He would soon forget prior responsibilities, as this life and its obligations claimed him. When the child had been taken off, I mentioned tigers, and at once a deep silence fell. The men looked at one another. Eventually someone told me, "There are no tigers here. They have all gone away."

"But surely," I said, "someone was attacked by a tiger in these parts, about a year ago . . . quite a well-known hunter—Porter, Potter—some name like that."

"Yes," said another gravely. "That tiger was killed. There are no more."

I looked at their gaunt, passionless faces, so handsome some of them, enduring all. Outside, across the space of nighttime earth, the forlorn child, burdened by obligations he could no longer uphold, slept on his mother's breast. They had shared food with me and would shelter me, and I could force no more of my own wants on them. I didn't sleep that night behind their safe stockade, lying listening to the rustle of leaves and stars. At first light I left, walking the horse through endless-seeming ranks of goats being arranged for milking, and girls walking to the well.

Up in the jungle-heart the bungalow had not altered, still locked up in its boards and creepers. Leaving the tethered horse I forced one of the windows, and climbed through into what had been Pettersun's sleeping room. The low Indian bed, its lacquer peeling and webbing broken, still stood dutifully at one wall, the rotted netting hanging down about it like cobwebs. Some shelves, a desk, a chair, these things remained, but no niceties, if there had ever been any. There was no idiosyncratic odour in the room. Becoming one with the invading jungle, it had the jungle smell, tinders and juices. Lianas had come through the foundations even, and covered the floor, so that any stains there were hidden.

The verse Doctor Hari had told me of was on the wall facing the bed, written in paint with long letters that leaned in all directions. It was dark enough, I had trouble making any of it out. When I did, an unnerving pang of recognition went through me, still displaced. Pettersun had written this:

> Symmetry fearful thy frame could
> Eye? Or Hand Immortal—What?
> Night—the; of forests. The in—
> Bright burning Tiger! Tiger!

I stood there, breathing audibly, startled, hearing the birds and the monkeys calling through the jungle, silently reading the words over, until suddenly, of course, that *Tiger! Tiger!* gave me the key. It was nothing else but Blake's poem, but all bizarrely reversed, the last line first, the second to last second, second line third, first line last. And each word in each line also reversed, first word last, last first, and so on. Gibberish. No astonishment Hari had thought it some avant-garde piece coined in Greenwich Village. The punctuation, too, was scarcely Blake's.

"Madman," I said aloud, jolted to an abrupt disgust and compassion neither of which had I thought to feel so forcibly, if at all. "Poor bloody drunken murdering madman." And, having spoken,

I read the nonsense on the wall also aloud, to the quiet box of bungalow held in noisy jungle.

Something clicked in my brain as I did so. I stumbled mentally after it. Elusive, it was gone. In some preposterous manner, the lunatic reversal of the fragment of poem—made sense. As if, blind-folded, one touched a cat's fur in darkness, not knowing, yet instinct to say: Ah, but *this* is—before the acceptable name came or light to disclose.

Then, letting in the jungle, something else was let in. Standing there with a shaft of olive green sunlight on the vine-carpet, I visual-ised the tawny shadow of death-by-night shouldering through the opened doorway. Every hair stood up on my body and my loins were cold and empty with horror. It was imperative to escape. I fled through the window, tearing skin and clothing, pursued by demons of the mind. Pettersun's mind.

When I had calmed down, I got on the horse and rode in the direction of the other village the fat man, and Doctor Hari, had informed me of.

The simple explanation of what happened next is that I mis-judged my road, got off the track, blundered about and made things worse for myself, ending up the proverbial panic-stricken lost traveller of song and story. I suppose that is what happened, though generally I rarely lose my way, or if I do I regain it fairly quickly. Not so in this instance. The track all at once dissolved, and carefully retracing my way for some distance, or trying to, I failed to rediscover it. Various formations of trees, angles of illumination, which I had noted and which might have provided guidance, seemed mysteriously changed, though the greenish jungle sun streamed through and the shadows massed and the monkeys screamed to each other, all as they had been doing minutes before. If anything, something was at fault in my own perception.

I fell into the pit of compounding my error by then defiantly pressing on. I was sure I would soon pick up the path again, discover a fresh one, or merely ride through a break in the foliage and so into the village, by a sort of serendipity. None of these things happened. In the end sheer heat and exhaustion forced me to halt, dismount in the shade, and drink water. Here I very fool-ishly went to sleep for almost an hour, an idiotic thing to do. As a rule, the beasts of the forest do not attack sleeping creatures, but Pettersun had probably been asleep when so attacked—what price

faith? Besides, snakes haunt the wilderness, and sometimes itin-
erant human beings, the worst predators of all.

When I woke, irritated by everything, mostly myself, I had given
up on my quest. The second village was plainly enchanted, and had
vanished. Using the compass, and occasionally aided by glimpses
of afternoon sun marking the west, I turned back towards the first
village, which was real. Although I had been floundering for some
while and my bearings were hopelessly out, that group of huts and
persons, and the reincarnated child, lay directly over to the east,
and the tracks which led to and from the place were good. I had no
doubts I should get there well before sunset.

Hours later, bathed in sweat, the horse shambling, the hollows
bowing into shadow and the glimpsed sky throwing hot bars
against the trees, I began to be dully afraid. It seemed I had now
lost my clue to anywhere. The jungle had me, bound me in its veils
and towering stems. There was no way back, no way out. I stopped
then, and tried not to lose my nerve too. It was difficult.

The red flame died and the greyness came in a rush, and in
another rush the black of night. I sat the horse, as the sounds of day
receded and the choruses of the frogs grew loud, mocking me, for
this black fearful interior was home to them. And to others.

The *Rāmāyana*, which speaks of the roaring of wild animals, the
tangled walks, the fatigue and privation of this landscape of trees,
says the forest is the realm of the wind, darkness, hunger, and great
terrors.

There was nothing now to be done till morning. I had water and
some crumbs to make my magnificent evening *khana*. I possessed
no weapon, save the means of starting fire, which I would arrange
at once. My sleep I had had. I would watch tonight.

I kept my vigil well. Maybe tiredness came to assist me, for I passed
swiftly into that Benzedrine state where sleep seems superficial anyway, an invention of time-wasters. Slight fear was here, too, a constant. Slight fear like a condiment sprinkled on the enormous
lulling beauty of the night. Not that I could see very much, beyond
the sharp gold splashings of my fire. The beauty was in the blackness, and only the blackness lay out there, fold on fold of it, vision
coming solely through the ears. Everywhere was the steady burring
of frogs and nocturnal insects, which frequently fell death-still, as it
does, not for any sinister reason, at least no reason that might be

sinister for me. A couple of times, too, came the pandemonic uproar of monkeys disturbed, bursting adrenalin through my bloodstream, after each of which alarums I relapsed, smiling a little. The forests, "realm of terrors," are essentially and potentially dangerous, but there will seldom be actual violence. The venomous serpent, dropping on the neck like coiled rope from the ceiling of boughs, the big cat, famished and rearing from the bushes, these are the stuff of the book and film industry.

Periodically I looked at my watch, pleased at the timelessness I had achieved, where minutes passed like hours, and where two hours could go in what seemed only minutes. That sacerdotalism I've mentioned perhaps lay behind the sense I had of the peace of contemplation the *sadhu* pursues to such spots. For yes, here you might feel the depth and shallowness of created things, their oneness, the bottomless, endless, blissful nothing that is everything, and which contains the vibrating root of the soul. I was delighted also that I had avoided the cliché of supposing I had been brought there by fate. The idea of silly accident sustained me. At length, I could say it would be dawn in scarcely more than an hour, and with the new day I should find my way wherever I wished.

I had no thought of Pettersun, who inadvertently had caused me to be where now I was. He seemed far off from my contemplations. As if I were forgetting him.

The light came when the dawn remained most of an hour away. This was not sunrise.

It was separated light, like that of my own fire. I formed the opinion at once, with mingled hope and distrust, that mankind had arrived with torches, and whether friend or foe I had no means of telling. I sat on with my spine to the tree, my hearth before me, trying to make out figures round the alien glare.

Presently my uneasiness increased. I had realised whoever carried the torches was playing some sort of puzzling game. First of all, they did not approach, but seemed to be circling me to the left, the flame flashing on and off as stands of fern or trunks interposed. Secondly, unless small children or midgets were concerned, whoever flourished the brands must be crawling on their knees.

My blood was undiluted adrenalin by now, and rising, I moved away from my fire as quietly as I could, taking up a position against a neighbouring tree. My anticipation was of robbers, even some revival of the stranglers of Kali Ma. My horse, tethered nearby, was snorting and prancing in the undergrowth. Perhaps the answer would be to slash the tether with the knife I had picked up and now defensively cradled, leap on the horse's back and make a wild dash through the pitch-black jungle. But such a headlong course was precarious, and I was not sure I preferred it. Bluff, lies, and a gift of rupees might be handier.

I had reached this partial decision when something else struck me about the circling, low-down blaze of torchlight. And now I was rather stunned, completely disinclined to attempt or plan escape because everything seemed inappropriate, faced by the fact that, though the light stayed all together—some thirteen or fourteen feet of it—it reflected on nothing, lit up nothing, could not therefore be *light* at all.

Just then the vegetable strands of the darkness parted, and the lightless light flamed through.

I remember I said, "Oh, God," quietly, as if I were expected to. That was all. It was pointless to say or do anything.

There is a kind of terror that is no longer truly terror, but some type of refined and developed emotion that terror has bred—a sort of ecstasy in which fear, actually, has no part, nor the will to resist that fear usually supplies. I had heard it once or twice described. Now I felt it.

I could make excuses at this juncture, or alternately could pile the expletives up to mountain height and let off fireworks from the top—both methods resorted to out of nervousness. Because what I must put down now will, of course, not be believed. I didn't imagine it, or dream it. I do believe in it myself, but only because I saw it.

What had appeared in front of me was a tiger; it was Pettersun's tiger, and I choose that possessive with care. It had a tiger's shape, and a tiger's aura, from the canine swagger of the hindquarters found always in the greater felines, to the sculpted, almost toylike, modelling of the head. The blazon of the tiger it had too; it was the colour of apricots laced with zebra stripes, as if the scars of a beating had been inlaid with jet. It stood longer and higher than any tiger I had seen or heard of; if it came closer, as undoubtedly it would, its head might nearly level with my own. But freaks occur in nature, men or beasts mightier, larger, than their fellows. The light was inexplicable. For the tiger, Pettersun's tiger, burned bright, bright as the fire I had mistaken it for, and on this conflagration which shed no gleam to either side, or anywhere, the black stripes seemed like the bars of a furnace, holding the power of it barely contained.

The eyes were also fire, or apertures into the fire which composed it, not green as the lenses of cats become by night, but golden like the rest. The eyes saw me, perhaps not my flesh, but piercing like an X-ray through to my bones. In my ecstasy of terror I understood this much: I was no prey to it. To kill me would be incidental—how it had killed Pettersun—death a by-product of the thing it was. And yet, this was not so, not the truth—even in that extremity I knew I had made a mistake and if I died, would die without the extreme unction of an answer. And then the tiger moved. It moved like a forest fire, plunging in a straight igniting line, right at me. My heart stopped. Started again as the gush of gold veered and crossed my path. At the last, its eyes avoided mine, uninterested. Its dog's ears were pricked, listening, but not to me, the trembling of my body and my mind. The unstrung bow of its tail brushed through the grasses that should have exploded into arson, that only dipped aside, falling over to lave my hands with coolest dew, not sparks.

Having seen everything, I then covered my eyes with my hands.

When I looked again, the forests were stirring; a subtle pencilling in of forms hinted at dawn; all other fires were out.

I put down the beginning of Blake's poem, though so well known, to facilitate this final act, as one sets out each stage meticulously, when solving a mathematical problem. It runs:

> Tyger! Tyger! Burning bright,
> In the forests of the night,
> What immortal hand or eye
> Dare frame thy fearful symmetry?

When the scald of morning lifted the black rind off the jungle, I started to walk, leading the horse, due east. If I had needed proof, which I did not, that something out of the ordinary had touched the vicinity, the horse would have furnished it. Sweating, shivering, and skittish, trying to kick at me, frothing, rolling its eyes—this was what my docile mount of yesterday had become. I led it with the utmost difficulty. It was clearly not afraid of anything that lay ahead, only unhinged; my own state, relegated to the primal.

After about fifteen minutes, I came into the clearing where a hint of dirty whiteness—a veranda rail and posts—announced the bungalow. This was how near I had been to it all night. I don't think the knowledge would have enhanced my pleasure. To find it now merely added a suitable footnote to what had gone before.

I skirted the building with pedantic caution. I wanted no part of it, and once it was behind me, the urge to bolt was almost irresistible. Somehow I controlled it, just as, somehow, I controlled the horse. When we reached the village, we were welcomed with courtesy and without comment. No doubt, the wound of the supernatural was raw for all to see, but I was not theirs, and they did not try to pry or comfort me.

A week later, when I had got back to Chadhur, I hung about in the hotel, waiting for myself to go off the boil like a kettle removed from the scene of the heat. My nerves were jarred in such a way that I could not put my finger on what the disorder was, or how it should be cured. I had accepted that I had brushed with things occult, but they had done me no physical harm. Reasonably elastic and rational as it generally was, my intellect would surely learn to cope with this; already I had perspective. Time would resolve the rest. Yet so far time had only made me worse. It was nothing so mundane as loss of appetite or sleep. I slept perhaps rather more readily than was my wont. And if my dreams were hectic, they were not about tigers, rather about a multitude of unimportant stupid items, that awake one would dismiss—a fly in the room, a dull, unidentified noise, trying to recall the name of someone never met. Awake, I ate and took healthy exercise, was no longer jittery; sudden sounds did not bring me to my feet with a wail. No, it was nothing I could lay my hand on, pick up and examine and so be done with. And yet it was as if my balance on the tightrope of life were gone. I could do all I should, could even be relaxed about it. Yet I knew I had fallen and somehow was suspended in midair.

After two days, I walked across to the hospital and located Doctor Hari's office and good coffee. He knew, without being informed, where I had been, and said nothing of it, only remarking as he poured the second cup, "You look a little not yourself. Can I do anything for you?"

"Only if you have a prescription for psychic whiplash."

"Ah ha! The phantom tiger of the forests."

I was not amazed he'd heard of it. I had come to believe that gaudy beast of golden fire was often sighted, and word passed on to credible and sceptic alike.

"Yes," I said. "And there really is one."

"Well," he said. "And why not?"

"You haven't said: Did you see it? Does that mean you've seen it yourself?" He only smiled. I thought perhaps he had not. I said, "What you can do for me, if you would, is ask your resident scholar if he'd consider letting me have a translation of this."

Hari accepted the sheet of paper mildly. The "resident scholar," his pet patient, was convalescing in an unusual condition of hermitage.

"I realise I'm being a damn nuisance," I said. "But I would be very grateful, and naturally I'd compensate him for his time in whatever way he felt was suitable."

"I am not hesitating for that. Your Hindi is fine, and I know from what you have written that you can read the language perfectly well."

"In this case, though, shall I say I need a second opinion?"

Hari glanced at the brief array of words. He may have recognised my own script, or some essence of text. He raised one long curved eyebrow, a dramatic gesture I respected, grinned and told me he would do what he could. Next evening, as the flying-foxes stormed the moon, he found me on the hotel roof and gave me the translation, its price an iced coconut juice. The scholar, it seemed, refused all payment.

I didn't read the translation then. I waited until I was alone, and then I waited until the hotel was noiseless, and the streets noiseless, and then until the streets and the hotel began to sound again with dawn. Then I chided myself, and opened the paper and read it through and put it away, and took it out again and read it again, and sat a long while as the window flooded with light, hearing goats and coughing cars, and bicycles and bullock carts, and the relentless drumming of my own heart, as my balance came back to me.

When I had said it aloud, that writing on the wall of Pettersun's bungalow, the phonetics had stolen in on me, and after gestation, offered themselves. They were basic enough; to replace "eye" with that which resembles it: "I." And in the vernacular that employs the word "thy" to guess that maybe the word "the" might become the word "thee." And primed by that, I had written out the back-to-front verse again, with its alterations, thus: *Symmetry fearful thy frame could I? Or Hand Immortal—What? Night—thee; of forests. Thee in—Bright burning Tiger! Tiger!* And again, a fraction closer, that *click* of intuitive knowledge—cat's fur touched blind-folded—yet not enough. And then I hit upon the obvious. I translated the bizarre sentences, as they stood, flatly into Hindi, and gave them to a bilingual scholar for free and profound translation back into our native tongue, Blake's, mine, and Pettersun's. And so I received my answer. It wasn't, I think, an invocation. Although Pettersun knew, he did *not* know. Although he wanted, he had no notion of wanting. Or at least of what the wanting was and how it might be satisfied. It had to tear him in pieces to get out, that monstrous and fantastical birth—the beast within, the glittering core of what he had tried to possess through pursuing, to become through destroying, the alter image, the bond, the magic circle, hunter and hunted—the place where the margin wears so thin that one may become the other. To the villages perhaps, it is the transmigration principle. He died and returned to pay *Karma* as a tiger. But no, he is the tiger's child, as surely as he gave birth to it—to *himself*. The Id foresaw, if Pettersun did not. The Id always foresees. And that was why, stumbling through the medium of Blake, knowing no other, he wrote on his wall what the kindly Brahman translated for me, this prayer to the infinite Possibility:

*Flawless and fearful One, could I assume thy form?*
*Or, Immortal moving Fate, what is my portion?*
*Thou art Night, thou art the forests' night. Thou art within—*
*Bright burning Tiger! Tiger!*

# CYRION IN WAX

"CYRION, BE WARY OF THAT MAN."

Cyrion raised guileless eyes.

"Why, and whom?"

Mareme, the beautiful courtesan, lowered her own eyes swiftly beneath turquoise lids. She was young, lovely, wealthy, and accordingly difficult to obtain. Being only for a few, she had learned something of the habits of those few, both in the bedchamber and out of it. This one she believed she knew well enough to judge that the thing he appeared unaware of was frequently what had gained his utmost attention. Besides, their game of lotus-and-wasp on the painted ivory board was beginning, she thought, to veer too readily in her favour.

In addition, the behaviour and appearance of the man in question were difficult to ignore.

Dark of hair and with the silken olive complexion common in the region, his forehead was bound with gold and his scarlet robe, long as that of a scholar or physician, stitched with bizarre golden talismans. Three pale purple amethysts trickled from his left ear. Satanically glamorous as an eagle, he had stalked into the cool garden of the expensive inn, two human jackals coming after, plainly a bodyguard, a pair of leering sadists, scarred and welted from ancient battles, and clearly keen for more as they smashed forward through the tubs of flowers and the unlucky patrons. Their hands rested ready to their swords and their fingers were coated with spikes. And nobody challenged them.

They mounted the steps beside their master, and stood over him as he seated himself. The seat was on the upper terrace nearest the kitchen wing, among the mosaic pillars and under the scented shade of the orange and cinnamon trees, not ten feet from where Cyrion bent his silver sun of a head and Mareme her coal-black one over their intellectual game. Below, from the open court with its flowers and the palm tree which made a necessary umbrella against the noon sky, men and women had broken off their talk uneasily, and rescued it only in whispers. Those who had been pushed flat arose and resumed their seats in silence. And, strange in this great coastal city of Jebba, where to stare was as natural as to breathe, eyes slid narrowly sideways and no more.

Presently, the inn's proprietor himself came hurrying. You could note, from a deal less than ten paces, the sweat making a mirror of his suddenly greenish face. He bowed to the dark man.

"What can I serve you with, Lord Hasmun?"

The dark man smiled.

"Eels fried in butter, some quince-bread. A jug of the black, very cold."

The innkeeper took a quarter step back, or tried to, on shaking, unreliable legs.

"We have no—eels, Lord Hasmun."

One of the jackals stirred eagerly, but Hasmun checked him with an idle finger.

"Then," said Hasmun softly, "get some eels in, my host."

The innkeeper fled as fast as jelly would permit, into the kitchen wing behind the house. A minute later, some boys crept from thence into the garden with quince-bread, Black Jebba wine packed in ice, and the news that others scoured the fish-market.

Hasmun sampled the wine. The jackals fidgeted.

Hasmun laughed, mellowly.

"Fine living is not for you, lads, eh? Well, go out and play in the streets for a while, my honeys."

The bodyguard went, but, in the garden, the conversation grew no louder, and not a head was raised.

Till Cyrion raised his to ask across the board of lotus-and-wasp: "Why, and whom?"

"I should have held my tongue, I perceive," said Mareme, very low, "but I thought you had marked him."

"The innkeeper? Oh, we are old friends," murmured Cyrion. He seemed to have remembered the game, and annexed two of Mareme's pieces neatly before she could fathom the move. When she had fathomed it, she said, "Beautiful as the angels you may be, my soul, but transparent, to a cunning lady of the night. Leave it alone, beloved."

Cyrion, having won the lotus-and-wasp, decided to let Mareme win the other game they were playing.

"I have already caught a rumour here of Hasmun. But not why I must beware of him."

"Not only you, my darling. All of us. They call him the doll-maker. Did you know?"

"He makes dolls then. No doubt a charming trade, the toy business."

"Not those dolls that children play with," huskily mouthed Mareme, as if her voice were trying to reach the very nadir of her throat. "The kind of doll a magus constructs of one he would slay, and then sticks a needle in its liver."

"Hasmun is an apothecary, though the rumour says magus. Does the trick work?"

"Trick!" squeaked Mareme as if her voice, having reached the nadir, had there changed into her own pet dove-rat. "There are three dead already, and others who have crossed him have gone blind, or their limbs pain them and they cannot walk— Ah, God bless me. *He is looking at us.*"

Cyrion leaned back in his chair, and slowly turned his head. The noon sun, raying through the orange trees, fired his elegant silk clothes, and revealed his hair as pure light. It was a fitting halo for the marvellous face Mareme had compared to an angel's—though whether of the heavenly variety or one of the descended sort, it was somehow hard to be sure. Hasmun was indeed looking in their direction, openly, and with amusement. Now he met this face full on and next Cyrion's dazzling smile. Hasmun's eyes half closed, enjoying it all, just as Cyrion seemed to be doing.

"I heard my name mentioned," said Hasmun. His words carried throughout the garden, and were meant to. Faces greyed further among the flower tubs. "Can it be my humble person is known to you?"

"Everyone knows Hasmun the doll-maker," said Cyrion courteously. Kindly, he added, "But take heart, no man can help his smell."

The sensuous enjoyment snapped off Hasmun's face. It became perfectly still. Perhaps this too was enjoyment; a different form of enjoyment.

"I think you must be tipsy," said Hasmun.

"I think I must be entirely sober," corrected Cyrion, rising, "for what I am about to do requires a steady hand."

Cyrion crossed the not quite ten paces with a mercurial speed that stunned the eye, and all in the fluid motion of it, as he reached Hasmun's table, the jug of Black Jebba seemed to soar up of its own accord into Cyrion's hands, contriving next to up-end itself over the magus's head.

Bathed in a black-red ichor of the vine, Hasmun yelped once like a trodden-on dog. Then stumbling up, sent the table and its contents flying.

Cyrion was distressed, incredulous.

"How can I have been so clumsy—"

A crash resounded hard on the table's crashing. Hasmun's bodyguard were returning through the garden. They had apparently got no farther than the intimidating of a girl in the doorway of the inn, and hearing the row, had come running, with prayers of thanks to the Fiend, no doubt.

Cyrion waited until the two were careering up the steps, then lobbed the wine jar, slippery with wine and ice, casually amid their feet. One bellowed, lost footing, and thudded backwards among the scented shrubs. The second went down on one knee, righted himself, and, sword dragged bare, leapt for the terrace.

Cyrion's sword was at his hip. He had seemingly forgotten it. He ducked under the first ham-fist blow, spun negligently, and kicked into the base of the bully's spine. The man screamed and plunged forward to land writhing on the terrace in the spreading pool of liquor.

The other thug had meanwhile extricated himself from the shrubs. As he bounded back up the stair, sword and one spiked fist much in evidence, the innkeeper emerged ingratiatingly from the opposite kitchen end of the terrace, bearing a spluttering dish of fried eels. Cyrion turned on his heel as if bored with the whole matter, skimmed the dish of scalding sea-worms and bubbling butter, and cast it unerringly over his shoulder into the face of the bodyguard. Buttered and blinded, dropping the sword with a clatter, the fellow again left the terrace in a backward manner. In passing, his skull met the rim of one of the stone tubs. He did not now get up.

Cyrion smoothed his finery with ringed left hand and ringless right one. For a man who had been hurling liquor and fried seafood about, he was surprisingly unspotted. As if resenting the fact, the writhing kicked bully on the terrace made a final token grab at Cyrion's ankle. Cyrion kicked once more, this time into the grab. A bone snapped somewhere, followed by a thin howling.

Cyrion glanced at Hasmun.

"A great uproar, master apothecary, over a little spilled wine."

Hasmun, soaked and perfumed with Black Jebba, had had the space to string his nerves and his wits together. He straightened himself, startlingly the same height and build as Cyrion himself, but otherwise as opposed as shadow and light.

"Choose," Hasmun said to the bodyguard with the broken wrist. "Be quiet or die." The howling ceased. "You, on the other hand," Hasmun continued, "will die in any case."

"As the priests lesson us, life is but the briefest kindling of sweet light doused in the darkness of eternity," quoted Cyrion philosophically.

"You are wrong," said Hasmun. As the wine dripped in his eyes, he actually managed a smile. "Your dousing will be rather prolonged and definitely not sweet. It will begin tonight. If you would see for yourself how I can break you, come to my Apothecarium and look. Your whore will tell you where."

And he nodded to Mareme, who had covered her painted face with her powdered hands.

The white daylight gradually reddened. The sun went bathing in the ocean. Jebba became an amber city at the edge of a sea of golden coins. Then the dusk filtered shorewards from the desert, and blue-dyed the windows of Mareme's exquisite apartment.

On the silken bed Cyrion was stretched, the flawless model for a young god, naked, beautiful, and mildly drunk. Mareme sat upright beside him, nervously plucking at the silks.

"Are you not afraid?" she suddenly blurted.

"Oh, I thought I had made you forget Hasmun."

Certainly, he could generally make her forget anything for a while. Even the touch of his hand on her face had the power to do that. The moment she had seen him, a year before, a casual meeting, by chance, Cyrion had possessed her thoughts, dominated not merely heart but also mind. She was slyly cool-headed enough with others, had had to be. But never with Cyrion. She had refused his money always. Instead, meticulously, he always sent her gifts. His scrupulous fairness disturbed her. She wanted Cyrion to love her, not pay her. Once, stupidly, she had sought to procure a love potion, but this venture had had none of the desired results.

"How could I forget Hasmun?" she said now. "Listen, my lord, I have not told you everything. His Apothecarium is in the Street of the Three Walls. Those who pass by sometimes see a small man-formed doll inside the front of the shop, set out as if to display its craftsmanship. And in the doll are stuck jewelled pins. Presently there is a pin in the heart, someone is buried, and the doll vanishes from the shop."

"I heard as much," said Cyrion. "Does no one ever go there, effect entry, appropriate the doll, extract the pins?"

"How could they, when the magus keeps watch? Even when he vacates the premises to sleep, ten of those human beasts of his guard the place."

Cyrion reached for the cup of blue crystal at his side, while the stars, as apparently impervious as he, evolved in the window.

"Tell me," said Cyrion, "do you know how the dolls are fashioned?"

"Who in Jebba does not? Hasmun boasts of his art. He requires nothing from his victim, only to have seen him once. He constructs the doll in the image of the one he would harm, then casts a foul spell on it to link doll and man together. While the spell is active, he tortures the doll with his pins. Then removes the spell. Without the spell, the doll is passive, only a doll. The man ceases to feel his hurts, rejoices, thinks Hasmun has forgiven him. Then Hasmun makes the spell again, and hurts him more, till he is crippled or dies screaming. And this, my wise master, you chose to pick a quarrel with. Why did you *do* it?"

"I am," said Cyrion humbly, "a masochist."

The window was now radiant with its stars. From a gilt cage, the little dove-rat cheeped imperiously to be let out. Softly albescent as any dove, round-eared, delicate of feature and with two large golden eyes, the dove-rat was the second love of Mareme. Minute though it was, she would sometimes lead it about the upper thoroughfares of Jebba on a long gilt leash. It had a habit of thieving bright objects, which might have proved embarrassing had not Mareme, versatile in many modes, turned trouble to advantage. Often, in former less-exalted days, she had let the dove-rat steal from the tumbled and discarded clothes of her patrons—earrings, buttons, coins. Next, herself running daintily after the client in the street, to return the items with a charming apology for her pet. Thus, she gained her not entirely founded reputation for honesty.

Mareme arose from the bed and let the dove-rat from its cage. It scampered instantly to her cosmetics table, to sit among the tall onyx pots of powder, coloured unguents, and black kohl, sometimes staring at itself in the mirror of rare silver-framed glass— Cyrion's latest gift. The crystal bottles and the tiny shiny paring knife had been shut away from the dove-rat's greedy gaze. Once, Cyrion had watched the miniscule animal drag an emerald torque, twice its size, from Mareme's jewel box to its nest in the cage, then come back for the pearls.

Mareme knelt by Cyrion.

"What will you do, Cyrion?"

The light was going fast, and the lamps not yet lit. At first she did not see the whiteness around his mouth, the fixed unblinking emphasis of his eyes. Then he said, offhandedly:

"Half a minute ago, I should have said I was going to wait, to see if Hasmun could make good his threats. I no longer need to wait, however. He can."

Mareme shuddered.

"What is it?" she hissed. "Do you suffer pain?"

"Somewhat. I assume he has one of his damned pins in my wax ankle."

He shut his eyes and opened them. His face had paled under its light fair tan, but his features were composed. Suddenly he drew a deep breath and said, with indifference: "A demonstration. He forgoes the pin. He will give me the briefest respite before demonstrating further. But not too much tonight, I hazard. He means me to— to visit his toyshop tomorrow. He wants me to beg his pardon and his—mercy."

On this occasion, beyond the slight stumble in his words, he gave no sign.

"How can I help you?" Mareme cried.

"Not in the usual way, I think," he murmured. "Take your lyre from its peg, and play to me instead. Music soothes all pain, they say. Let us try if it does."

Over the three white walls for which the street was named, fig, palm, and flower trees shook their fragrance and their piecemeal shadows. In the noon heat, the street was empty and innocent, and halfway down it, between the courts of the gold workers and the sellers of silk, gaped the hole of Hasmun's Apothecarium.

The door was open, and strings of blue ceramic beads hung over the entrance. Inside, incense rose in streamers on a shade that was infernal even by day.

As the bead curtain rattled, and a silhouette brushed by into the shop from the sun-drenched street, two of Hasmun's bullies surged from the interior to intercept.

"Peace, my cherubs," said a friendly and musical voice. "I am here to gratify your master's sweet tooth. Leave the damage to him, or he will make dollies for you, too."

The guard fell back, grunting, and Cyrion passed on into the depth of the shop.

In the gloom, black flagons on shelves were just discernible, and black caskets, and bottles of leaden green stoppered with parchment and cobwebs. A lustreless cobra, stuffed and placed on a stand in the attitude of striking, barred the way through a curtain of lion-skin. Beyond, a cell, similarly stacked, but picked out in the reddish light of a depending lamp.

Under the lamp's glow, Hasmun sat in a chair of ebony. On a lacquer table at his elbow lay Cyrion, in miniature, naked, blond, and with two fiery-glinting red-jewelled pins thrust one through the right ankle and the second through the lobe of the left ear.

"Not on display at the shop front, as I was told," said Cyrion blandly. "I had hoped to be the spectacle of Jebba."

"That is for later," said Hasmun, exactly as bland. "Did you enjoy your night?"

"I have had some dealings with the desert nomads. They teach a method of converting pain into delicious pleasure."

Hasmun, unruffled, called the bluff.

"I am glad that you reckoned it pleasant. Tonight should be more pleasant still. The jaw-bone—I have a topaz pin for that. The wrist and shin—sapphire. I keep the diamonds for your eyes, my beautiful. But blindness is not yet. Nor death. This will be a long game. Revel in it, my dear."

Cyrion had bent to examine the doll. He seemed to find its cunning likeness appealing, though he could see now it was not a perfect replica. Without the activation of the relevant spell, the pins caused no pain to him, even when he twisted them himself in the lightly pigmented wax flesh.

"Of course," Cyrion remarked, "I could steal the doll from you. Or kill you, perhaps."

"Try," invited Hasmun the magus. "I should like you to. Please."

Cyrion had already glimpsed four thugs, rippling the lion-skin as they lurked the other side of it. He had seen also the solitary narrow window high up among the shelves of the cell, wide enough to admit a man's hand, but no more. For Hasmun, psychic sparks played round his fingers.

"Try," Hasmun said again, winningly. "It will discomfort you a good deal, but not so much as these pretty pins, whose hurt you can turn to ecstasy."

Cyrion abandoned the doll. His face was unreadable.

"How if I ask for clemency?"

"How if you do."

Cyrion turned and walked out again through the lion-skin. The thugs, attempting a little idle bruising as they jokingly saw him from the shop, found him somehow too quick for them. One, kicked on the thigh by another who had expected to kick Cyrion, abruptly no longer between them, must console himself that, at least, Cyrion could not be quick enough for the magus.

Dusk came again, the constant and reliable night. Many in Jebba who had fallen foul of Hasmun had had cause to dread that reliable return, darkness which brought jewelled stars and jewelled pins and pain jewelled with tears and sweat.

In the hours of that night, white-faced, Mareme paced and prowled her exquisite apartment. She could not rest, and sometimes, in an instinctive memory of her primitive beginnings on the waterfront, she tore her hair.

Two hours before dawn, a cat's-paw rap on the door galvanised her. She flew to the door and, pulling it open, admitted Cyrion, whiter than she and gaunt as a man after a month of fever, who smiled at her companionably. He was closely wrapped in his cloak; in one hand, a couple of slender clay wine jars that were sold at all hours along the harbour.

"I cannot bear this—" Mareme cried out.

"Softly," he said, and shut the door. "I have had an interesting sojourn in a ship-shed and scared the rats with my writhings. The apothecary has finished with me for another night."

"I will kill myself," said Mareme. "You hid in a ship-shed so I should not see your agony. But your suffering is mine—"

"Not quite," said Cyrion. "Be glad."

"Have you no plan?" she wept.

"I plan to drink some harbour wine."

Still cloaked, he unstoppered a jar, poured liquor into the two blue crystal cups, handing her one. The girl drank unwillingly and reflexively, then, with a sigh, dropped the cup on the rugs and dropped full length beside it. A faint scent rose from the spilled wine, the perfume of the drug pellet Cyrion had crushed in it. He lifted Mareme and laid her on the bed. Then stepped noiselessly over to the cosmetics table, above which the dove-rat chirruped in its cage.

Hasmun's ten shop guards sat dicing in the murky room between the shelves of potions and poisons, presided over by the stuffed cobra. Three or four lamps burned fitfully to show the players their casts. In another hour, the sun would bound up from the desert at Jebba's back and the daylight guard would replace them. There had been some more fun tonight. The muttering of the spell, the drone of unseen pipes, the hot rushing of the air that betokened the arousal of unwholesome forces. Then the strategic interested silence of the magus beyond the lion-skin curtain, twisting the pins. None of Hasmun's thugs had ever witnessed his sorcery. They knew better than to spy, and indeed had no ambitions in that area. They made the odd jest concerning Cyrion's fate, but their eyes grew fixed when they spoke of it, and the dice clattered more loudly.

It was a nasty complex dicing they were having, with money and probably a fight resting on its outcome. Now there was quiet, as one nursed the dice and entreated some ratty noxious personal demon to be generous.

And in the quiet, a vast commotion began. It seemed fantastically to originate inside the shop, and to the rear. A smashing of pottery and a shouting and roaring, in which the name of Hasmun had mixed itself with imprecations.

The guards ran to the lion-skin and through into the cell, which crunched underfoot but gave no other evidence of an intruder. Soon the depending lamp was lit, to reveal the floor carpeted in sharded clay pottery from a jar which had apparently been flung through the window into the cell. The shouting had meanwhile ceased. Before any of the guards could hoist themselves via the shelves to the narrow window, a sharp and alarming report went off, from the front of the Apothecarium. As a single organism, the ten guards veered from the red-lit cell and plunged once more through the shop and thence through bead strings to the door. The door, unbarred and flung wide, revealed a second vessel, this one filled with burning tar, which had just now exploded it into a thousand bits in all directions. As the guards kicked hot debris, swearing, an apparition appeared, dancing wildly along the street.

It was the thin and wretched figure of the poorest sort of sailor. Head bound in the sailor's striped head-cloth—optionally filthy, as this one was—clad otherwise in revolting disarray and copious flapping pockets, all of it reeking of bitumen and corn spirits, and with a dark brown, black-stubbled face contorting insanely, the sailor cursed Hasmun with a multitude of curses.

Three guards sought to detain the apparition, but it danced aside.

"Upon Hasmun, the Swine of Rancid Smell, be vomited the manifold punishments of the Fiend!" wailed the sailor. "And you, his reeking minions, rolled from the dung of pigs and quickened by dog urine, may you be pickled in your own rottenness till the sea requites its salt!"

Five guards chased the sailor, who promptly fled, though encouraging them to pursuit with further elaboration upon their merits. Half down the street, all but two halted, recalling their duties to the magus's shop. The two who thundered on in the sailor's wake galloped about a corner and into an unlit alley. Next second, both were spun, gagging and half-strangled, to the ground, their gullets having made horrible connection with the thin cord which some minutes before the sailor had tied across the way, and subsequently ducked himself on his return.

When, yet choking and blaspheming, the failed rearguard action had reentered the Apothecarium, having lost their quarry, a violent discussion was in progress regarding the sailor's identity. Presently, they thought to douse the depending lamp in the magus's cell.

Bleary as they were, involved in rampaging anger to boot, the chances were they might not even have noticed. But one, blundering into the lacquer table, looked down. And beheld an empty space where previously the wax effigy of Cyrion had lain, impaled by its pins.

Cyrion had come on the sailor in the ship-shed, one of the scores dotted here and there about the port, sleeping off the night's drink and drugs before weaving shipwards at sun-up.

Now, however, this frightful spirit-stinking vision of a sailor was not heading, weaving or otherwise, towards the harbour, but along one of the comelier streets of Jebba. Presently, reaching a stair, the sailor went agilely up it, unlocking a door with a key taken from a girl's creamy neck, and pushed through into the apartment of Mareme, the beautiful courtesan. Arrived, and having kindled a lamp with some familiarity, the sailor dragged the striped head-rag off and wiped his face with a cloth, thereby revealing the blond hair, stubble, and skin of Cyrion.

The drunk sailor in the ship-shed, who would awake in the finery Cyrion had exchanged him for his own antisocial garb, could have few complaints. Perhaps he might miss his nearly empty wine jars, though, one having been tossed through the window of the magus's shop, the other exploded by a stick of fired bitumen outside.

Mareme, still sleeping, had not observed the transformation Cyrion had worked on himself, partly with the aid of her own cosmetics. Nor did she now observe Cyrion take from the left flapping sailor's pocket a velvet bag, which squirmed, and from the bag the reason for the squirming—the incensed dove-rat.

Having stroked the creature into a better humour, Cyrion removed the gilt leash and replaced the rat in its cage. Then, from the sailor's dexter pocket, he lifted the wax doll.

He had carried the rat to the wall of the gold workers which neighboured Hasmun's cell window. There, he snapped the end of the rat's long leash shut on a convenient overhanging tree bough. His first clamour and smashing of pottery brought the guard to the cell and caused the lighting of the lamp. Next, the jar he had already primed with a red-hot coal burst at the shop's front. The dove-rat had found itself elevated to the window of the cell, and put through onto a shelf. Cyrion meanwhile bolted to distract the guard about the doorway. Having lost and half-throttled his followers, Cyrion sped by a circular route back into the Street of the Three Walls. Quieter than a leaf, this time, he alighted against the cell window.

The dove-rat, which could be relied on to steal anything bright, had already completed its mission. Illuminated sparklingly by the depending lamp, the jewelled pins through the doll's body had attracted the rat immediately. It had climbed down to the lacquer table, and the length of its chain. Having tried to pull the pins free and failed, the rat had gripped the whole doll in its predacious teeth, and climbed up again to the window embrasure. Its chain, secured to the bough, prevented its wandering. Then, as always happened, someone, currently Cyrion, took away its hard-won prize.

It had been a long night, and it was not yet done.

Cyrion placed the lamp on the cosmetics table and stood there, turning the wax image, of such a near-likeness to himself, over in his ringed left hand, his bare right hand.

Mareme woke, her body soothed and comforted, her head clear, her heart like lead.

She understood what had been in her wine. Sometimes she had used it on others, or in the slight quantities that produced euphoria, for her own enjoyment. If she had not been distrait, its perfume would have warned her from drinking—yet, Cyrion had been kind to her, ensuring her forgetful sleep. Her eyes flooded again with tears, and through the tears she saw him gazing at her from beside the window. He was immaculate in the way that only he was capable of, like new-minted silver. Shaved, bathed, combed, unique, and magical—and clad in the dark nomadic robe of the desert he affected when travelling. The garment which meant he was going away.

"Yes," she said, "that is clever. For once, I am glad to see you leave me. In the desert, perhaps, you will be safe. When do you go?"

"Soon," he said quietly, "but there is something to do first. You had better rise, my love. Hasmun will be here, shortly."

Her eyes widened, then flicked across the cosmetics table. The pots of unguents were not as she had left them. The tall pot of kohl lay on its side. And, as he moved, she beheld the ornamental brazier had been lit, the smoke rising against the blue-skied window. There was the smell of tar, distinct and unusual in the luxurious room.

"What have you done?"

"Guess," said Cyrion.

She was knotting the robe of pearly-embroidered silk together about herself, when blows hammered into the door. No permit for admittance was asked. A few moments the door was a barrier. Then it burst inwards on shattered bars. Five of Hasmun's thugs edged grinningly aside, and Hasmun, the doll-maker, strolled into the chamber.

To Mareme he nodded politely. At Cyrion he smiled with love.

"As a rule," said Hasmun, "I have had to deal with cowards and idiots. To meet a sheep that bites the butcher's blade is fresh. I like your novelty. I almost feel inclined to spare you. But still, on the whole, I think I should prefer you dead. To snuff a candle is pleasing. But to finish you, my dear, is to blot out a sun. How can I resist it?" Cyrion, poised in an attitude of nearly sublime indifference, was expressionless. "And now, Sir Beautiful," said Hasmun, "where is the wax doll?"

"Look," said Cyrion gently, "up your arse."

Hasmun shrugged. He waved his guard forward, then stayed them with the precise checking finger by which he demonstrated the power of his brain over their brawn.

"Mareme," said Hasmun, "possibly you would prefer to tell me where your client has hidden the doll. It would save the rude handling of your furniture and person by these ruffians. It is difficult for me, you are aware, to control them."

Mareme shrank.

"Please—" she said, but no more, which left the single impotent word to drop between them like a slain pigeon.

"Oh, come now, Mareme," said Hasmun. He appealed to Cyrion. "This seductive night-lady of yours is not always so squeamish. But, of course, she loves you. I should know, having been privy to the secret. She once came to me for a love potion, when my reputation in Jebba was young and spotless. She did not get her potion. Such silly muck is not my trade. Though she did get something. She got, in fact, more than she yearned for. Did you not, my darling? Shall *I* tell," Hasmun inquired, "or shall *you* tell *me*?"

Mareme buried her face in her hands.

"I always considered it rather too opportune," said Cyrion, "that Hasmun the Apothecary arrived at the inn in conjunction with my own visit."

"Opportune and planned. She told me you would be there. And she made sure you would tangle with me, too. You could not resist the bait, this reputation of mine. It inflamed your vanity, Cyrion. As your reputation inflames mine. Jealousy. You must destroy wicked Hasmun and his wax, and rule alone in the cities of the coast. Eh, my honey? As I must, and will, destroy Cyrion."

Mareme shrieked through her hands at Cyrion: "He threatened me, to make my effigy in wax and torture me too—I was afraid. I could not master my fear. Oh, Cyrion—I love you as my life, but I could not die for you. And I swear I trusted you would outwit him. On God's name, I swear that I did!"

"But you did not trust me enough to offer me the truth," said Cyrion, soft as arsenic through a fine gauze.

Mareme took up the weeping she had set aside.

Hasmun said: "Cry tears of emerald if you must, beloved. But inform me where he has hidden the doll. Remember, I can still make your image. If I have seen Cyrion, I have seen you. One sight is sufficient. I need nothing else. The sight, the wax, the spell, the pin."

"The pot of kohl!" Mareme cried, then threw herself down before both men, the dark and the fair, her face in the rug.

Hasmun walked, as if he savoured each footfall, to the cosmetics table. He took up the pot of kohl.

"Such exceedingly dark kohl," said Hasmun. "Yet not so black, for I see a speck of white here." He scraped at the stuff. "And so hard, for kohl, so sticky, so gritty to smear about the doe-eyes of a lovely woman. And it does not smell like kohl, either. Perhaps it is not? Could it be tar from the ship-sheds, I wonder? The kohl scooped out, the tar heated and poured in the pot. Then the wax figure thrust home into the cooking substance—just the speck of a white wax sole left showing. This pot, now, is the exact size for such a doll—"

Hasmun dashed the pot suddenly onto the piece of bare stone floor beside the smoking brazier. The thin onyx, already weakened by heat, cracked. Hasmun retrieved from the two portions of the pot the solid lump of bitumen, and held it tenderly.

"Oh, my Cyrion. How miraculously sage you had been—if I had missed it. But as I have not missed, you have not been sage. Can you imagine, when I activate the spell—everything the bitumen has done to your image, you yourself will feel—burned, asphyxiated, blinded. Death in your nostrils and your mouth. I could almost experience compassion. A worse end even than I had devised for you. Do you wish to pray?"

Still expressionless, Cyrion said: "How long will I have for my prayers?"

"I have decided to be lenient," said Hasmun. "Rather than leave you in a nausea of dread all day, I will make the spell this instant. You shall die now."

Cyrion looked away. He stared into the blue sky beyond the window. He said nothing.

On the rugs, Mareme did not lift her head. At the door, the five bodyguards had excised their grins and were retreating in evident unease.

Hasmun raised his arms. He began to chant, in a voice far deeper and more vibrant than that he utilised during speech, the phrases of the spell. Sulfurous and bitter, these phrases splashed in searing drops about the room. The gleams of silk and sun faded; the window itself darkened as if with a premature dusk. In its cage, the dove-rat effaced itself in a quivering ball of fur. The atmosphere of the chamber shook, warmed drily and terribly. The notes of pipes were heard, withering the eardrum. The air surged, gushed, became the air of the desert where no shade had ever been.

A wind blew through the chamber.

Chaos touched the chamber, and the hot breath of Hell.

Then all was still.

The spell was set on the doll. No need for more. Hasmun gave a crow of triumph, irrepressible. A crow that snapped, was amalgamated and disintegrated in a scream of anguish, which in its turn was stifled.

Hasmun fell to his knees. He clawed at his eyes, his nostrils, and his mouth. His face congested; his hands seemed to freeze against his face. On his knees he staggered, and as he staggered, a desperate whining came from his lips. It might have been a resumption of the scream. Only Cyrion deciphered the fatal noise as a reversal of the spell, somehow got out through the jaws of clamped stone, by sheer will alone. And Cyrion, a lightning bolt, was first in one spot, then another. In a split second he had wrenched from the magus's grasp the lump of bitumen with the wax doll inside it. A split second further, and Cyrion had hurled the black cake into the brazier. An eruption of fire leaped at the impact. At once the tar began to melt. Within, the wax was melting too. His spell was lost to Hasmun now. He floundered some way across the rugs in his attempts to scream, and tiny squeakings came from his throat. Till finally, all movement and all sound deserted him, and he reeled backwards against the table of cosmetics, sending its exotic load into motion. As a rain of powder and rouge descended on him, Hasmun did not stir. The unguents spilled upon his blackened breathless face. The silver mirror slithered slowly from its stand and crashed to fragments at his shoulder.

He lay dead, and as the last atoms of wax and tar swirled together in the brazier, a dim smoke rose from his pristine clothing and from his unmarked flesh.

In the doorway the guards grovelled, saw Cyrion paid no attention, reversed themselves and ran. They no longer had a master.
They had a story, of Cyrion the Magus.

Cyrion glanced at the girl. Through fingers and the fringe of the
rug, she had watched. Falling rose powders had smudged her. With
one rose cheek and one plaster white, she now watched Cyrion.

"You are a sorcerer, too," she muttered. "Will you kill me, as
well?"

"No sorcerer," said Cyrion. There was the most fleeting trace of
tiredness in his eyes.

"But—" said Mareme, emerging a fraction more from her prone
position, "but how else—"

"I had the doll," said Cyrion. "He had formed the wax so it
should resemble me. I re-formed it with heat and a woman's paring
knife, and coloured the skin and hair with pigments from her jars.
When I had finished, it resembled Hasmun as much as it had ever
resembled me. By the nature of his spell, that was enough. He was
meant to find the thing. You made my task easier. So he worked his
magic, and discovered himself asphyxiated, burned and blind
inside a chunk of bitumen."

She sat up.

"I had faith," she said, "you would destroy him."

"My faithful Mareme," said Cyrion.

She trembled suddenly at his caressing tone. "But you forgive me
—it was my fear—"

"I forgive you," said Cyrion. He glanced now at the smashed
glass by the dead magus. Taking coins from his nomad's robe, he
flung them across Hasmun's corpse, lightly and pitilessly into her
lap. "Buy yourself another mirror," he said.

Her tears were silent in the silence that followed his departure.
She knew he was gone for good.

# A DAY IN THE SKIN
## (OR, THE CENTURY WE WERE OUT OF THEM)

A ND THE FIRST THING YOU MORE OR LESS THINK WHEN you get Back is: God, where's everything gone? (Just as, similarly, when you get Out you more or less think, Hey, where's all this coming from?) Neither thought is rational, simply outraged instinct. The same as, coming Back, it seems for a moment stone silent, blind dark, and ice cold. It's none of those. It's nothing. In a joking mood, some of us have been known to refer to it, this—what shall I call it? this *place*—as Sens-D (sensory deprivation). It isn't though, because when your Outward senses—vision, hearing, smell, taste, touch—when they go off, other things come on. The *alter*-senses. Hard to describe. For a time, you reckon them as compensation, stand-ins, like eating, out in the skin world, a cut of sausage when you hankered for a steak. Only in a while it stops being that. It becomes steak. The equivalent senses are just fine, although the only nontechnical way I can come up with to express them *is* in terms of equivalents, alternatives. And time itself is a problem, in here, or down there, or where the hell ever. Yes, it passes. One can judge it. But one rarely does, after the first months. In the first months you're constantly pacing, like some guy looking at his watch: Is it time yet? Is it time now? Then that cools off. Something happens, in here, down there. . . . So that when at last the impulse comes through *Time to get up* (or *Out*), you turn lazily, like a fish in a pool (equivalents), and you equivalently say, Oh really? Do I have to?

"Sure, Scay. You do have to. It's in the Company contract. And if I let you lie, there'd be all hell and hereafter to pay H.Q. Not to mention from you, when you finally get Out for keeps."

So I alter-said, in the way the impulse can assimilate and send on, "How long, and what is it?"

"One day. One huge and perfect High Summer day. Forty-two hours. And you got a good one, Scay, listen, a real beauty."

"Male or female?"

"A *fee*-male."

"All right. I can about remember being female."

"First female for you for ten years, ah? *Exciting*."

"Go knit yourself a brain."

Dydoo, who manages the machines, snuffled and whined, which I alter-heard now clearly, as he set up my ride. I tried to pull myself together for the Big Wrench. But you never manage it. Suddenly you are whirling down a tunnel full of fireworks, at the end of which you explode inside a mass of stiff jelly. And there I was, flailing and shrieking, just as we all flail and shriek, in the middle of a support couch in the middle of Transfer.

"Husha hush," said the machines, and gentle firm mechanical arms held me and held me down.

Presently I relapsed panting—yes, panting. *Air.*

"Look up," said Dydoo. I looked. Things flashed and tickered. "Everything's fine. You can hear me? see me?"

"I can even smell you," I gasped, tears streaming down my face, my heart crashing like surf on the rocks. There was a dull booming pain in my head I cared for about as much as Dydoo cared for my last remark. "Dydoo," I continued, speech not coming easy, "who had this one last? I think they gave it a cranial fracture."

"Nah, nah. 'S all right. Mike tied one on with the wine and brandy-pop. It's pumped full of vitamins and de-tox. Should take about a hundred and fifteen seconds more, and you'll feel just dandy, you rat."

I lay there, waiting for Mike Plir's hangover to go away, and watched, with my borrowed eyes, Dydoo bustling round the shiny bright room. He is either a saint or a masochist (or are they the same?). Since one of us has to oversee these particular machines, he agreed to be it, and so he took the only living quarters permanently available. The most highly developed local fauna is a kind of dog-like creature, spinally adapted for walking upright, like the Terran ape, and with articulated forepaws and jaw. With a little surgery,

this nut-brown woolly beast, with its floppy ears and huge soulful eyes, was all ready for work, and thus for Dydoo.

"My, Dydoo," I said, "you look real sweet today. Come on over, I'll give you a bone."

"Shurrup," growled Dydoo. No doubt, these tired old jests get on his furry nerves.

Once my skull stopped booming, I got up and went to look at myself in the unlikely pier-glass at one end of the antiseptic room.

"Well, I remember this one. This used to be Miranda."

There she stood, twenty-five, small, curvy, a little heavy but nice creamy gold, with long fair hair down to her second cluster of dimples.

"Yeah. Good stuff," said Dydoo, deciding yet again; he doesn't or can't afford to hold a grudge more than a minute.

"How long, I wonder, before I get a go at my own—"

"Now you know it doesn't work like that, Scay. Don't you? Hah?"

"Yes, I know it doesn't. Just lamenting, Dydoo. Tell me, who had me Out last time?"

"Vundar Cope. And he broke off a bit."

"*What?* Hexos Christ! Which bit?"

"Just kidding," said Dydoo. "If you're worried, I'll take you over to the Store, and let yah look."

"No thanks, for Chrissake. I don't like seeing myself that way."

"Okay. And try to talk like a lady, can't you?"

"Walkies, Dydoo," I snarled. "*Fetch!*"

"Ah, get salted."

It took me a couple of quivery hours to grow accustomed to being in Miranda's body; correction, Fem. Sub. 68. I bruised my hips a lot, trying to get between and by furniture that was no longer wide enough for me. The scented bath and the lingerie were exciting, all right. But not in the right way. I'd been male in the beginning and much of the time after, and I'd had a run of being male for every one of my fifty-one days a year Out for ten, eleven years. That's generally how it's designated, unless an adventurous preference is stated. Stick with what you're used to. But sometimes you must take what you can get. I allowed a while before I left Transfer, to see to a couple of things. The lingerie and the mirrors helped. It was a safe bet, I probably wouldn't be up (to miscoin a phrase) to any straight sex this holiday. Besides, I didn't know who else was Out, and Dydoo had gotten so grouchy in the end, I hadn't bothered to ask. Normally there are around forty to fifty people in the skin on any given day. Amounts of time vary, depending on how the work programs pan out and the "holiday" schedules have built up. My day, I now recalled, was a free diurnal owing to me from last year, that the Company had never made up. Perfect to the letter, our Company. After all, who wants to get sued? Not that anyone who sues ever wins, but it's messy.

I wondered, as the moving ramp carried me out into town, just what Dydoo was getting paid to keep him woofing along in there.

The first body I passed on Mainstreet was Fedalin's, and it gave me the creeps, the way it still sometimes does, because naturally it wasn't Fedalin inside. Whoever was, was giving it a heck of a time. Red-rimmed eyes, drug-smoked irises, shaking hands, and faltering feet. To make matters worse, the wreck blew a bleary whistle after Miranda's stacking. I didn't stop to belt him. My lady's stature and her soft fists were of use only in one sort of brawl. I could see, I thought, nor for the first, why the Company rules keep your own personal body in the Store whenever you yourself are Out. It means you never get into your own skin, but then too, there are never any overlaps, during which you might meet yourself on the sidewalk with some other bastard driving. Pandemonium that would be, trying to throttle them, no doubt, for the lack of care they were taking with your precious goods—and only, of course, ending up throttling yourself. In a manner. Although I didn't like looking at my own battered old (thirty-five) skin lying there, in ice, like a fish dummy, in the Store, I had once or twice gone over and compulsively peeked. The second occasion not only gave me the shivers, but I'd flown into a wow of a rage because someone had taken me Out for a week's leave and put ten pounds on my gut. Obviously, the machines would get that off in a few days. (The same as lesions, black eyes, and stomach ulcers get got rid of. The worst I ever heard tell of was a cancerous lung that required one whole month of cancer-antibodies, which is twice as long as it takes to cure it in a body that's occupied.) But there, even so, you get upset, you can't help it. So it's on the whole better not to go and look, though H.Q. says it's okay for you to go and look—which is to prove to us all our skins are still around in the public lending library. Goddamn it.

The contract says (and we all have a contract), that as soon as the Bank is open for Business (five years it's supposed to be now, but five years ago they said that, too) we all go Back into our own bodies. Or into new improved bodies, or into new improved versions of our old bodies, or—you name it. A real party, and we all get a prize. When it all started, around eighty years ago, that is, once everybody had settled after the initial squalling matches, Violent Scenes, hysteria, etc., some of us got a wild thrill out of the novelty. Pebka-Sol, for example, has it on record always, where possible, to come Out as a lady. And when he finally gets a skin of his own again, that is due to be a lady, also. But Pebka-Sol lost his own skin, the true, masculine one, so he's entitled. I guess we're the lucky ones, me, Fedalin, Miranda, Christof, Haro—those of us that didn't lose anything as a result of the Accident. Except, our rights . . .

I try to be conscientious myself, I really do. But handling Miranda was going to be a drag. She's a lot littler than me, or than I'm used to, and her capacity is less. I'm used to drinking fairly hard, but hard was the word it was going to be on her, if I tried that; plus she'd already been doused by some jack, yesterday. I walked into the bar on Mainstreet, the bar we used to hit in gabbling droves long, long ago under the glitter-kissed green dusk, when we were our own men and women. No one was there now, though Fedalin's haunt had just walked him out the door. I dialled a large pink Angel and put it, a sip at a time, into Miranda's insides, to get her accustomed. "Here's not looking at you, kid," I toasted her.

I had that weird feeling I recollect I had when I first scooped a female body from the draw forty-odd years ago. Shock and disorientation, firstly. Then a turn-on, racy, kinky, great. I'd got to the stage now of feeling I was on a date, dating Miranda, only I *was* Miranda. My first lady had been Qwainie, and Qwainie wasn't my type, which in the long run made things easier faster. But Miranda is my type. Oh, my yes. (Which is odd in a way as the only woman I ever was really serious with—well, she wasn't like Miranda at all.) So I dialled Miranda another Angel, and we drank it down.

As this was happening, a tall dark man with a tawny tan, the right weight, and nothing forcing steam out of his nose and eyeballs, came into the bar. He dialled a Coalwater, the most lethal beer and alcohol mix in the galaxy (they say); one of my own preferred tipples, and sauntered over.

"Nice day, Scay."

"He knows me," said Miranda's soft cute voice with the slight lisp.

"The way you drink, feller," he said.

I had emptied the glass, and Miranda's ears were faintly ringing. I'd have to wait awhile for the girl to catch up.

"Well, if he knows me that well, then I'll hazard on who he is."

"Win, and he'll stand you a Coalwater."

"The lady wouldn't like that. Anyway. Let's try Haro Fielding."

"Hole in one."

"Well, fancy that. They let us Out the same time again."

Haro, whom I thought was in the skin of one of the tech. people whose name I had mislaid, grinned mildly.

"I've been Out a couple of weeks. Tin and irradium traces over south. Due Back In tomorrow noon. You?"

"Forty-two hours."

"Hard bread."

"Yeah."

We stared into our glasses, mine empty, and I wished sweet Miranda would buck up and stop ringing so I could drink some more. Haro's rig had been auspicious, a tall dark man just like Haro's own body. But he'd treated it with respect. That was Haro Fielding all over, if you see what I mean. A really nice guy, super-intelligent, intellectual, all that, and sound, as about nothing but people ever are, and that rarely, let me add. We had been working together on the asti-manganese traces the other side of the rockies when the Accident happened, back here in town. That was how we two kept our skins. I remember we were down a tunnel scraping away, with the analysis robot-pack clunking about in the debris, when the explosion ripped through the planet's bowels. It was a low thrumming vibration, where we were, more than a bang. We were both a pair of tall guys, but Haro taller than me, with one of the best brains I ever came across. And he stood up and crashed this brain against the tunnel-ceiling and nearly knocked himself out. "What the F was that?" I asked, after we'd gotten ourselves together. "It sounded," said Haro to me, "like the whole Base Town just blew up, hit the troposphere, and fell back down again." He wasn't far out.

We made it back through the rock hills in the air-buggy inside twenty minutes. When we came over the top and saw the valley full of red haze and smoke and jets of steam, I was scared as hell. You could hear alarm bells and sirens going, but the smog was too thick to work out what kind of rescue went on and what was just automatic noise and useless. I sat in the driver's seat, gunning the buggy forward, and swearing and half crying. And Haro said, "It's okay."

"Of course it's not bloody okay. Look at it—there's no goddamn thing left—"

"Hey," he said, "calm down."

"Calm *down!* You're crazy. No, I'm not just shaken up over who may have just died in that soup. I'm pissing myself that if it's all gone, we'll never get off this guck-heeled planet alive."

The point being that planet NX 5 (whereon we are) is sufficient distance from H.Q. that it had taken our team, the "pioneer squad" every expert Company sends in ahead of itself, to explore, to test, to annotate, to break open for the use of Man, had taken us, I started to say, around thirty Terran years to arrive. We'd travelled cryogenically, of course, deep-frozen in our neat little cells, and that was how we'd get back when it was time. Only if Base had blown up, then maybe the ship had blown up, too, plus all the life supports, the S.O.S.'s—every darling thing. Naturally, if reports suddenly stopped coming in, the Company would investigate. But it would take thirty years before anything concrete got here. Though NX 5 is a gallant sight, with its pyramidal rocks rich in hidden ores, its dry forests and cold pastel deserts busy with interesting flora and fauna, and its purling pale lemon skies . . . it doesn't offer a human much damn anything to get by on. While the quaint doggies that roam the lands, barking and walking upright, joy of the naturalist, had a few times tried to tear some of us to pieces. Marooned without proper supplies, shelter, or defence: with nothing—that was a fate and three-quarters.

"We'll be dead in half a month," I said.

"To die—to sleep, no more," Haro muttered, and I began to think the blow on the head had knocked him silly, so it'd be a half month shared with a lunatic at that.

However. We careered down into the smoke, and the first thing, a robot machine came up and ordered us off to a safety point. Events, it seemed, weren't so bad as they looked. Matters were in (metal) hand.

The short High Winter day drew to its end under cover of the murk, and we sat in the swimpool building on the outskirts, which had escaped the blast. Other survivors had come streaming and racketing in. There were about ninety of us crammed round the pool, eating potato chips and nuts and drinking cold coffee, which were all the rations the pool machines, on quarter-power, would give us. Most of the survivors had been away on recon., or various digs, or other stuff, like Haro and me. A handful with minor injuries, caught around the periphery of Base Town, were in the underground medical sanitorium which, situated northside, was unscathed. There were some others, too, a third of the planet away on field studies, who had yet to find out. It seemed that the core in the third quadrant of Base's energy plant had destabilised, gone critical, and—wham. The blast was of course "clean," but that was all you could say for it. The third quadrant (Westtown) had gone down a molten crater, and most of the rest of the place had reacted the way a pile of loose bricks might do in a scale-nine earthquake. That means, too, people die.

By dawn the next chill day, we had the figures. There had been around five thousand of us on-world, what with the primary team, and the back-up personnel—shipmen, ground crew, service, mechanics, and techies. Out of those men and women, one thousand nine hundred and seventy-three were now dead. What we felt and said about that I won't repeat now; there's nothing worse than a bad case of requiemitis. Some of them were pals, you see. And a couple of them, well. Well, one of them was once practically my wife, only we never made it that far, parted, stayed friends (cliché). Yep. Requiemitis. Let's get on.

Aside from the dead, there were a lot of gruesomely injured down in the San., nearly three thousand of them. While the hospital machineries could keep them out of pain and adequately alive, the mess they were in required one form of surgery only. The form that's discreetly known on Earth as Rebo, and is normally only for the blazing rich. Rebo, or the transfer of the ego, with all its memories, foibles, shining virtues, and fascinating defects, from one body (for some reason a wash-out—crippled, pan-cancerous— what you will) to another, is only carried out in extreme cases. And indeed the business was hushed up for years, then said not to work, then said not to be in use. It happened though, that our Very Own Company was one of the sponsors of the most advanced Rebo (rebodying) techniques. Again, on Earth and the Earth Worlds, there are laws that limit transfer strictly. (And, naturally, there are religious sects who block the Sunday news, abhorring the measure.) In our case, though . . . we were different, weren't we? A heroic advance guard on a remote planet, needed to carry out vital work, etc.; and all that.

Those were the first tidings of comfort and joy; figures of death and injury and rumours of Rebo. It threw us about somewhat. I noticed that the machines started to serve us hot food and alcohol about this juncture. Then Haro and I got plastered to the plaster, and I stopped noticing. The second gospel came on about an hour later.

Now, an ego that's transferred, where doth it go? It goeth into another body, natch. Fine. Generally it's a grown body—android —tissue and cells. That can take anything from a trio of months to a year, dependent on format and specifications, and, let it be whispered, on the amount of butter you can spread. Sometimes, too, there have allegedly been transfers into the recently dead bodies of others (there is supposed to be a gal in Appeline, New Earth, who bought her way into the pumped-out body of a movie star, dead of an overdose. Apocryphal perhaps.) Or even of animals. (There's a poem about that one: Please, God, make of me a panther / A pretty panther, to please me / Pretty please, Hexos or Javeh or Pan / There is no God but the god who can— / Make me a panther, please.)

That—I mean, grown androids—is what should have happened here. Approaching three thousand bodies for those that, alive only on support systems, needed them. Trouble was—you guessed it— the tissue banks that would have begun the project were over in Westtown and blown to tomorrow. It would take thirty years to get us some more.

The only facilities they had were the remains of the cryogenic storage (the ship had caught the blast), whole if depleted berths for about two hundred, into which three thousand persons were not going to fit. And another outfit, of which we knew little, but which would act, apparently, as the interim point of the transferral operation, a kind of waiting room between bodies. Mostly, a transfer flashes the subject through that *place* so fast it's just a nonstop station on the way. Yet this area, too, was it seemed capable of storing. Storing an ego. And its capacity was *unlimited*.

Just as requiems can be tedious, rehashing old action replays of panic and mayhem can get one down. So, I'll just spin the outline for those of us who like it in the big bold type.

The Company, who had gotten word of the latest position via the beacon intercom, had a proposition to offer us. And for proposition, read Fact. For we who are Company Persons know we belong to our Company, body and—yes, let's hear it for laughs— *soul.*

The Company would like us to stay on, and hang in there. This was how: the survivors of the Accident (and isn't that a lovesome name for it?), about one hundred and fifty people of both sexes, would donate their bodies to a common fund. Now, and let me stress this, around one hundred and fifty bodies put out like pairs of pants and dresses for the use of—one deep breath—over three thousand footloose egos. For the life supports would be switched off and the liberated bodiless egos of the mortally wounded taken into the wonderful—what shall I call it?—*place*—that stored unlimited egos within its unlimited capacity. And into that *place*, also, would go the liberated egos of those whose "skins" had not been damaged, those skins now the property of All. And here in the *place* we would all live, not crowded, for the disembodied are not crowded, lords and ladies of infinite space, inside a nutshell. Then, when it was our allotted time physically to work or play, Out we would come and get in a body. Not our own. That would hardly be fair, would it? Make those who had lost their own bodies for good feel jealous. (For that reason, no one gets finally supplied from the Bank or the Store until *everyone* gets supplied. Suits for all or none at all.) Anyway, there might be a slip-up. Yes, slips-up happen, like cores destabilising. Grey vibes to meet oneself on the street in thrall to another. And in thirty years the androids would start growing like beautiful orchids in their tanks. And in maybe sixty years (or a bit longer, we're starting from scratch, remember, and not geared in the first place to do it) there'll be suits for all, bodies for everyone. New bodies, old familiar bodies, loved ones, forgotten ones—ah, the compost with it. It stank. And we shrilled and howled and argued and screamed. And we ended up in it to our eyebrows.

I recall wandering in a long drunk, and Haro, tall and dark and tawny, then as now, and drunk as me, said to me: "Calm down, Scay. They may blow it and kill us."

"But I don't want to be killed, pal."

"Nothing to it," said Haro. "Something to look forward to."

"My God, you still remember that," said Haro, draining his Coal-water.

Miranda's ears had stopped dinging.

"Say, Miranda, would you care for another?" I asked her in her own honeyed voice. "Of course I remember, you turkey. Get killed. Boy."

"Although Sens-D is a sort of death. You realise that, Scay?"

"Yes. Surely. Only I'm not dead in there. In there stops me getting dead. You know, I was thinking, it's funny—" ("You thinking is funny? You're right there," interpolates Haro) "—you get in a skin and you come Out and you feel wrong, and you feel okay, all at the same moment. And if you stay with the skin awhile, weeks, a month at a time, especially if you're working in it—it starts to feel natural. As if you always had it. Or something very like it, even if it isn't like it. Take Miranda here, I could get used to Miranda. Seems unlikely now, but I know from past experience I could, and would. Meanwhile, the—*place*—that starts to seem alien and frightening all over. So you can hardly stand to go Back there. And now and then, you need their drugs to stop you kicking and screaming on the way to Transfer, as if you were going off to get shot in the skull. And yet—"

"And yet?" said Haro, looking at me quietly with the other man's dark eyes.

"And yet, no one mentions it, but we all know, I suppose. When you come Out, there's the Big Wrench. It's yellow murder coming through into a new body. But when you go Back *In*—"

"No Wrench."

"No Wrench. Just like slipping into cool water and drifting there. I know there's sometimes a disorientation—it's cold, I've gone blind —that stuff. But it happens less and less, doesn't it? The last time I went Back. Hell, Haro. It was like gliding out of a lump of lead."

"And how do you feel about working, in Sens-D?"

I narrowed Miranda's gorgeous sherry eyes. Haro called it by the slang name, always, and I knew Haro. He was doing that just because, to him, "sensory deprivation" meant nothing of the sort, and he'd acknowledged it.

"I work fine down, up, In there. I do. When they started asking us to work that way, assessments, work-ups, lay-outs—the ideas stuff we used to do prowling round a desk—I thought it'd be a farce. But it's—stimulating, right? And then the assimilator passes on what you do, puts it in words Outside. I sometimes wonder how much talent gets lost just fumbling around in the physical after words—"

"And did you know," said Haro, "that some of the best work any of us ever did is coming out of our disembodied egos in Sens-D?"

I swore. "Ger-eat. That means we'll be stuck in there more and more. If the sweetheart Company found *that* out, they'll fix our contracts and—"

"But you just said, Scay, it's good In there."

"Devil's advocate. Come on. Where's the Coalwater you promised Miranda?"

He got the drinks and we drank them, and the conversation turned, because Company manoeuvres and all the Company Likes and Wants can be disquieting. There have been nights in the skin I have lain and wondered, there, if the Company might not have arranged it all, even the Accident, just to see how we make out, what happens to us, in the *place*, or in the skin of another guy. Which is crazy, crazy. Sure it is.

Anyhow, Haro was due Back tomorrow, and I had only thirty-seven more hours left.

Rebuilt, and glamorised to make us happy, once we were stuck here for a century or so, Base Town was a strange sight, white as meringue against NX 5's lemon sky. Made in the beginning for the accommodation, researches, and pleasures of a floating population of two thousand, you now seldom saw more than twenty people on the streets at a time. For whom now did the bright lights sparkle, and the musics play, the eateries beckon, the labs invite, and the libraries yawn? Who races the freeway, swims the pool? Who rides the carousel? And, baby, ask not for whom the bell tolls. With the desert blowing beyond the dust traps on all sides, the sand-blown craters of the west, the rockies over there, frowning down, where weird whippy birds go flying in the final spasms of sunset—Base has the look of an elegant surreal ghost town. It's as if everyone has died, after all. The ones you see are only ghosts out for a day in the skin.

A new road goes west, off to that ship the machines are still working on. Haro and I walked out to the road, paused, looked up it into distance, but made no move to do more. Once, years ago, we all went to see what progress they were making on the getting-home stakes. So the road had occasional traffic, some buggy or jetcar puttering or zooming along, like a dragonfly with wings of silver dust. Not anymore. Oh, they'll get the ship ready in time, it's in the contracts, in time for the new bodies, so we can all go to sleep for thirty years and wake up home in H.Q., which isn't home. Who cares, anyway. What's home, *who's* home, to hurry for? Thirty years older, sixty years, one hundred and sixty. And we, the Children of the Ice, are the same as always. Live forever, and sell your soul to the Company Store.

"Hey, Haro, what do we do now?"

We discussed possibles. We could take a jeep out into the desert and track a pack of doggies, bring back a lady doggy and give it to

Dydoo (who'd not smile). We could swim, eat curry, nap in the Furlough, walkabout, eat pizza, go to a movie. We did those. The film was *Jiarmennon*, sent out to our photo-tape receptors inside a year of its release on the Earth Worlds, by the kindly Company. A terrific epic, huge screen, come-at-you effects, sound that goes through the back of the cerebellum and ends up cranking the pelvis. One of those marvellous entertainments that exactly combine action, spectacle, and profound thought. I admit, some of the profound thought I didn't quite latch onto. But the overall was something plus. Five hours, with intervals. Three other people in the theatre. One of them, the one in Fedalin, was asleep or passed out.

When we came forth, the afternoon bloomed full across the town, a primrose sunshade for two suns, and it was sad enough to make you spit.

"Miranda's hormones are starting to pick up. Did she have crying jags, do you know?"

We walked across to the Indoor Jardin, the one place we hadn't yet reseen. In the ornamental pond, the bright fish live and die and are taken away, and new-bred bright fish put in. Maybe it was the last Coalwater taken in the Sand Bar on East, but I, or Miranda's body, began suddenly to weep.

"Goddamn it, Miranda, leave it out, will you? I've only got you for another ten hours, and you do this to me. *Quit*, Miranda."

"Why does it have to be Miranda who's crying?" said Haro in his damn nice, damn clever way."

"Well, who's it look like?"

"Looks like Miranda. Sounds like you, feller."

"Falsetto? Yeah. Well. I didn't cry since—Christ, when did I last?"

"You want me to tell you."

Belligerent, I glared at him through massed wet cilia thick as bushes. "So tell me, tell me, turkey."

"When the core blew, and took Mary with it."

"Ah. Oh, yes. Okay. Shit."

The pain of that, coming back when I hadn't expected it, stopped me crying, the way a kick in the ear can stop hiccups. You preferred the hiccups, all right?

"I'm sorry, Scay," Haro said presently. "But I think you needed to know."

"Know how I felt about—I *know*. It doesn't help."

"Sometime, it may. You wanted to be with her. And Company

red tape on marriage liability got in your way and you both chickened out. But your insides didn't."

"I used to dream about it," I said sullenly. "The Accident. And her, and what it must've—"

There was a long pause, and the fish, who lived and died, burned there in the pond like votive candles.

"It's over now," said Haro. "It isn't happening to her anymore, except inside your head."

We sat on the stone terrace, and he put his arm over my Miranda's shoulders, and Miranda responded, the length of her spine.

"Miranda," I said, slightly ashamed, "wants you."

"And I notice the guy I'm wearing today fancies the heck out of Miranda."

He turned me, carefully, because I was a woman and he was much larger in build than I, and he kissed me. It was good. It got to me how good it was.

"We've never been in this position before," I muttered, in Miranda's husky voice. As the space-captain said to the wombat.

"Never been male and female together, I mean." I elaborated, as our hands mutually travelled, and our mouths, and our bodies warmed and melded together like wax, and the flame lights up about the usual way, about the usual part, but, oh brother, not quite. "What I mean is, kid. If you'd tried this on when we were both male, I'd have knocked you into a cocked cuckoo-clock."

"The lady," said Haro, "doth protest too much."

So I shut up, and we enjoyed it, Haro, Miranda, and I.

The lemon light was going to the acid of limes and the birds were tearing round the sky when we started back along Mainstreet. I hadn't gotten Miranda too drunk, but I had got her well-laid, and that was healthful for her. She had nothing to reproach me with.

"You're not, by any chance, walking me home, Haro Fielding?"

"Nope."

"Well, good. Because, when I see you again, I don't know how I'm going to live this down."

Heck, yes, I could hear myself, even the sentence-constructs were getting to be like Miranda's. That's how you grow used to what you are. I suppose it was inevitable, the other scene, he and me, sometimes. Buddies. Yip.

"Don't worry too much about that," said Haro.

I shrugged. "I'll be Back In. I won't be worrying at all. That *place* is a real desexer, too. Genderless we go. And get Out . . . confused."

"That *place*," he repeated. "*In*. All that labour and all that machinery, to keep alive. When all the time, being *In* is, I'd take a bet, almost what death is."

"You said that already."

"I did, didn't I? So if that's what death is like, where's the difference?"

"The difference is, there's a guaranty on this one. You *get* there. You go on. Not like—not like Mary, blown into a million grains of sugar."

"Mary's body."

"Okay. Her *body*. I liked her body."

Haro stopped, looking up over the town at the glowing dying sky.

"Don't fool yourself. You loved Mary, not just Mary's skin. And though Miranda and this guy here were making love, you and I were making it, too."

"Oh, now look—I've got nothing against—but I'm not—"

"Forget that. You're missing the doorway and coming in the garbage-shoot with catsup in your hair. What I'm saying is this, and I want you to listen to me, Scay, or you won't understand."

"What do I have to understand, buster? Hah?"

"Just listen. Sens-D is—Christ, it's a zoo, an enclosure full of egos —of psychic, noncorporeal, unspecified, unclassified, inexplicable, and *unexplained* matter, that persists out of, and detached from, the flesh. Got it?"

"I got it. So?"

"Death, Scay, is being that same psychic, noncorporeal, etc., etc., material—only Out of the skin *and* Out of the box."

"Yes?" I said politely, to see if he'd hit me. He didn't.

"The *place*, as you call it, is a bird-cage. But look up there. That's where the birds want to be. The free wide sky."

I watched the birds in spite of myself. I thought about our extended peculiar lives in the slave gangs of the Company. Of going to sleep on ice. Of sliding into the *place*. Of days in the skin.

"That's it?" I said eventually. "All you want to tell me?"

"That's it, that's all."

We said our good-byes near the Transfer ramp.

"See you next skin," I said.

And Haro grinned and walked away.

Dydoo waved an ear at me as I strolled in. "Had a nice day?"

"Divine."

Poor mutt. He'd been smoking, two trays full, and spilling over. I refrained from cracks about dog ends. What a life the man led, held in that overcoat of fur and fume. It was a young specimen that died up on the ridge, and the robots found it, cleaned out the disease, did the articulation surgery, and popped in Dydoo. Sometimes, when he gets crazy-mad enough, he'll bark. I know, I used to help make him. And you know, it isn't really funny. Bird-cage. Dog-cage.

I got ready for going Back, and Dydoo gave me my shot. I wasn't bothered today, not fighting or wanting to. I guess I haven't really been like that for years. The anguish, that had also gone, just a sort of melancholy left, almost nostalgia, for something or other. Beyond the high windows the night was coming, reflecting on instruments and panels and in the pier-glass, till the lights came up.

"You ready now?" Dydoo peered down at me.

"Go on, lick my face, why don't you?"

"And put myself off my nice meaty bone? You should be so honoured. Say, Scay? Yah know what I'm coming Out as at the end, the new body? Heh? The Hound of the Baskervilles. And I'm gonna get every last one of you half-eyed creeps and—"

Then the switches went over.

One minute you are here, and then you are—*there*—

I glided free of the lump of lead into the other world.

Three days later (that's the time they tell me it was) I made history. I spent two hours in my own skin. Yes. My very own battered thirty-five-year-old me. Hey!

My body was due, you see, for someone else, and because of what happened, they dumped me into it first. So they could thump all those questions out at me like a machine-gun. The Big Wrench. Then Dydoo yelping and growling, techies from C Block, some schmode I didn't know yelling, and a whole caboodle full of machines. I couldn't help much, and I didn't. In the end, after all the lie-check tests and print-outs and threats and the apologies for the threats, I reckon they believed me that it was nothing to do with me. And then they left me to calm down in a little cubicle, to get over my own anger and my grief.

He was a knight, Haro Fielding. A good guy. He could have messed it up with muck, that borrowed skin, or thrown it off a rock or into one in a jeep, and smashed it up, unusable. Instead, he donated it, one surplus body, back to the homeless ones, the Rest of Us. All they had to do was fill it up with nice new blood, which is easy with the technology in town here.

He'd gone up into the rockies, sat down, and opened every important vein. The blood went out like the sea and left the dry beach of Haro lying under the sky, where the searchers found him—it. They searched because he was missing. He hadn't turned up at Transfer next day. They thought they had another battling hysteric on their hands. No use to try transfer now, obviously. The body had been dead long enough the ego and all the other incorporeal, etc., were gone. Though the body was there, Haro was not.

The slightest plastic surgery would take care of the knifecuts. One fine, bonus, vacant skin. He was a gentleman, that louse.

God knows how long he'd been planning it, preparing for it in that dedicated, clear-vision crusader sort of way of his. Quite a while. And I know, if I hadn't met him Out that day, the first I'd ever have heard of it would have been from some drunk sprawled in the Star Bar: Hey, you hear? Fielding took himself out.

As it was, obliquely but for sure, Haro'd told me all of it. I should have cottoned on and tried to— Or why should I have? Each to his own. In, or is it Out? For keeps.

And I guess it's grief and anger made me laugh so hard in the calm-down cubicle. God bless the Company, and let's hear it for the one that got away. As the line says, *flying to other ills*—but flying. Home free.

Free as a bird.

# THE DRY SEASON

## I

T WAS HIGH SUMMER WHEN HE CAME TO THRAISTUM. THERE HAD been something of a ride, fifty miles of it, at a parade walk. The column of men and horses had marched its inexorable way through the opaque light of afternoon, the yellow dust going up like powdered biscuit. And along with the dust, the column carried its own weary clanking, the rumble of feet and wheels, the bitter reek of hot metal, raw leather stink and sweat stink. The baked clay road looked close to catching fire; the poplars at the roadside wafted an unslaked parchment smell. The kind of ride where you wanted water, not wine, at the end of it.

And Thraistum looked as if it had never seen water in all its days. The terra-cotta walls, flame-ringed by fields of tindery grain, the wretched red dwellings packed like cells in a hive. The fortress, built from rufus stone.

And he himself, Marsus Seteva, scorched bronze, shut in the armour of gilded iron, the lion's-blood cloak, thirty years old, and all his life a burning, of years, of hopes, of thought, of quietness. Never alone. Yet alone. Buckled into an iron shell and lost in a desert. His whole life, maybe, had been a ride like this ride to Thraistum. Predetermined, slow, without surprise. Without water.

"Does it never rain in this godforsaken place?" he asked the adjutant riding beside him.

"Oh yes, sir," said the adjutant, who was afraid of him, launching into a travelogue of the region. Which gods obtained where. When the harvest was. How the rain never fell till Novemia.

Of course, there was water in the water bottles, warm gritty slosh tasting of leather.

The other water, the waters of life, like that same tepid filthy stuff? Plenty of wine, naturally. Smoky taverns, red whores, smart army orgies, decorous dinners, wine and women cooled by snow, melted, the shade of furnaces. But no water. Not before. Not now.

And then.

Water.

The sombre papery trees had gathered themselves about a well. At the well a girl drawing up a vessel by a rope. Her arms were white, and her neck, amazingly white in the sun-glare. Her hair was loosely knotted on her head. Fine hair, the colour of—

Of water.

No colour, in fact, just sheen, burnish, reflection. And texture— it looked like spun silk. No. Spun water.

Back along the line a couple of men called to the girl at the well. Scorpius's voice came next, yammering them into muteness and awarding god knew what penalty for breach of discipline, marching as they were into Thraistum, the velvet-sheathed axe-blade of Remusa in this far-flung province.

But the girl seemed not to hear. She unbound the rope. She walked away from the well quietly, the vessel on her shoulder. The young girls here carried jars that way. The right shoulder. It meant they were virgin. He waited for the adjutant to tell him so, but the adjutant was silent.

Seteva turned his head slightly to watch her go down the slope carrying the virgin vessel. The poplar umbra splashed off her body like a wave. Suddenly she too turned and gazed straight at him, as if she felt his stare (the covert, leering stare, more likely, of half the column behind him). But she seemed to be looking at him. She had a strange expression. Almost of shock, but as if the shock had not yet reached her eyes, her lips, her physical surface. Her face was like the face of some alien creature, from another plane of existence. As though he had never seen a human face before.

So he recognised her. Infallibly. And equally infallibly, he, the leader of the column, was pushed onward by the column. Remorselessly on to the distant, redly bleeding town.

His oasis slid away. There had been no time to drink.

"I saw a girl I fancied, when I was riding in," he said idly over the sour wine to Cailo. "What are the local taboos like?"

"Variable. Where did you see her?"

"On the hill. By a well."

"There are always girls by wells," Cailo said, a bizarre apposition; but perhaps all he had intended was the domestic reference. "However, as it's the hill well. . . . There's a temple precinct a quarter of a mile down from the road. She'd probably be one of the girls from there."

Seteva smiled. The smile was arid. He was glad, and sickened. He'd been recalling only how she had carried the vessel, on the right shoulder.

"No," Cailo said, catching the smile, "the temple girls here aren't that kind. That's Tynt you're thinking of, and Eshtira, in the south. All sorts there. Girls on their backs, boys on their faces. Fun all around. But here. Didn't they tell you at Mareuna?"

"They didn't tell me much. One major god. Puberty rites for males. Monogamy. And—what is it?—the doves are sacred to the temple, so don't let the men take slingshots at them, despite descending guano."

Cailo nodded.

"There's more. There's the sacrifice."

"Sacrifice?" Seteva repeated softly. He tried to go on grinning— doves spotting the valour of Remusa—but he saw flames curling out of a well.

"In five days' time. To make the rain come end-of-season."

"You mean an ox, or do these barbarians use horses?"

"Worse. I mean a girl. A temple girl, a virgin."

The fire ran into his mouth and through his belly.

"That's needlessly primitive, isn't it?" he said calmly. "Under Remusan rule, surely it gets stopped?"

"Hardly that. Come now, Marsus. You should know. The only thing that gets stopped under Remusan rule is failure to pay taxes. And insurrection. Remusa will tolerate anything else. Why not? Let the children play with their toys, as long as they're good children. And the Thraistians are models. Docile, friendly, courteous, hardworking. No problems here in twenty years. Their religion is the least we can let them have in return, if it keeps them so sweet. Come, it's not much to remember. Don't shoot the doves or shaft the temple girls. Sacrifice day is a festival. You'll probably be entertained by it. The town goes wild at sundown."

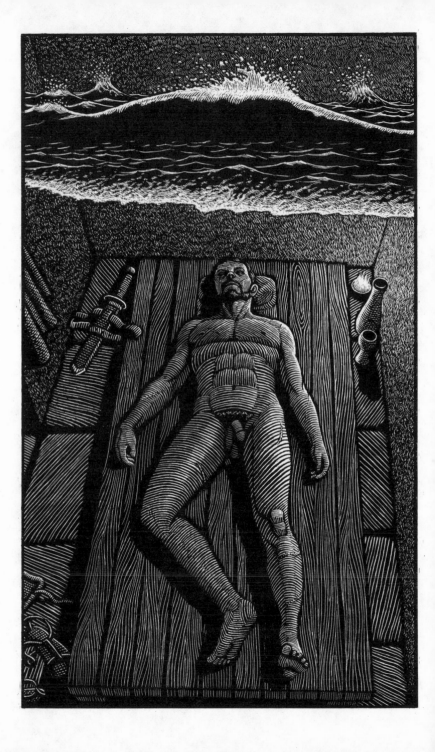

"And the girl? How do they choose? The shortest grass stem?"

"Not quite. It's an honour for her, actually, Marsus. That's how they see it. Die like this, and she's sure of her place in paradise. The same thing applies to their men who die in battle. Luckily they don't go in for battles anymore. That sort of incentive makes men hell to fight, hell to kill. Fanatics. I'd rather combat wolves."

"When?" Seteva asked.

"When what? Oh, that. The girl—they choose her today, near sunset. Probably about the time you brought your men into the fort. They'd have been doing it then."

Seteva drank the last mouthful of liquid bitumen called wine.

He knew they had chosen the girl. Her life was going to be poured away on their altar, for their god.

It didn't matter.

Some slut.

Some dirty, foreign slut. Possibly a whore, for all the ritual chat. Virgin—what was that anymore? They'd sew them up again in half the markets of the world for two silver Remusan capitas.

Stupid slut.

"Have some more wine," said Cailo.

In the dark, crickets, and through the slit of window the dry stars flickered in the brazen black of the sky.

Soaked in heat, too parched even to sweat, he lay on his back on the straight hard pallet, thinking of fountains, lakes, oceans. Water.

Cailo rode out in the morning with his six hundred, going west to Mareuna.

The business of the fort was simple enough. Outside, the town was peculiarly tensed. Moving, working, going about its parochial affairs, but yet somehow poised and waiting. These were the Days of Salt, the period of purification before the sacrifice.

In four days' time they would give her to their god on the end of a knife.

Cailo had been definite:

"You'd be advised to post men round the temple square. Not that they'll be necessary, but it's protocol. The temple building is to the north of the town; the square opens off three ways, closed on the temple side. A rotten area to contain in a skirmish, but fortunately you won't need to. They'll be gentle as lambs, and afterwards they get drunk, and the girls are generous to a fault. No taboos at all. Take my counsel and let the men off the leash. It does no harm, and they like babies here. You won't get recriminations."

"And if there are recriminations, you'll be in Remusa."

"Trouble at Thraistum is like the rain falling before Novemia. It never does. Just leave their religion alone, Marsus. The rest takes care of itself. This is going to be the nicest year of your army life. You'll go soft. Enjoy it."

The heat had drawn over like a curtain behind Cailo and the line of marching men and horses. Inside the curtain Thraistum cooked, and the dust lay like cinnamon on the air. The grainfields seemed to be smoking beneath the flat purple fresco of the hills, the blatant sky.

Days of salt. Salt in the wound. (A sword cut at Samaia, salt rubbed in at a makeshift hospital post, to staunch the bleeding; the smart searing to the bone, the backs of the ears, the groin, making him vomit with pain.)

The crickets had a different sound by day.

"Don't drink any water unless you mix it one-third with wine. It's not bad water exactly. Just native water. Full of red clay from the hills."

Cailo's imparted information had been comradely, endless.

He had a homily for every event.

The crickets tortured the grass.

The fortress should have been cool, its walls ten feet thick, in spots more. But the walls sweated and were not cool.

In the middle of the afternoon they brought the girl into the town from the hill precinct.

There were twenty priests, white linen and shaved heads, like the avatars of Aigum. There were subsidiary girls, too. They wore their hair long and unbound. In the middle of the procession two white she-asses pulled a little gilded car. The girl was in the car, motionless, and a child held a fringed sunshade over her head. The girl's hair too was unbound, plaited with flowers. Her wrists were ringed with silver, reminiscent of shackles.

Standing on the gate tower, he watched them pass through. People stood noiselessly in the street. The stillness had become symbolic.

He had the urge to shout.

Beneath the parasol, darkened, her hair appeared almost blue. She looked only before her. She did not seem afraid. Of course, she had been promised paradise.

Salt in the wound. It didn't matter.

## II

"But I thought you spoke the language well," he said to the adjutant.

"Sufficient to barter, sir. To make myself plain. But not good enough for this, sir."

"Good enough? Where do you imagine we're going? The plaster-and-lathe temple of some crackpot god. Gloria Remusa, soldier. Remusans go where they wish and speak to whom they wish, in whatever manner they wish. It devolves on our subject peoples to learn our tongue; we do not learn theirs. Do you see?"

Seteva spoke in mockery of an attitude. The adjutant, missing, naturally, the mockery, tried to reason with him.

"Yes, sir. The priests do have an adequate command of Remine, sir. But for this—"

"*This?* What is so special?"

"There could be—misunderstandings."

"And so?"

"I took the liberty—"

"Did you," Seteva said.

The adjutant flushed. He said, "A caravaneer from Mareuna, versed in many languages. A rogue, but reliable if well paid. He's been supplying the garrison at Thraistum for years with—different commodities."

"I know the sort. All right. Where is he?"

The adjutant hurried out and came back with the caravaneer. Cailo had mentioned him, too, a tall, wiry swarthy man with a gold nugget in his left ear and oiled black curls springing across his shoulders under the wound head-cloth. He had bought Remusan citizenship and had donned a Remusan name to match.

"So you're Nylerus."

Nylerus bowed. His face held all the loving, compassionate wickedness of six generations of desert nomads commingled five generations more with the serpentine city folk of the East.

"The Kastor requires an interpreter. I am his servant."

"The Kastor is not certain he requires an interpreter."

Nylerus smiled, resting, as he did so, one long umber finger across his mouth, a parody of concealment.

"The Kastor knows best. Gloria Remusa. But I speak Trasint as fluently as Remine. As my own tongue."

"Trasint?" Seteva inquired.

"The native name, sir, for Thraistum," the adjutant broke in nervously.

"What business brings you to Thraistum?" Seteva asked the Easterner casually.

Nylerus kept smiling. The smile said: *Illegal and barely legal business. But you will comprehend that, and pardon me. Remusans always comprehend how we second-class riffraff must scuff out our livings in this erroneous world. And we are quite useful to you, are we not?*

"Goods to sell, as ever, noble Kastor. My party leaves in three days—the morning of the sacrifice, to be exact. I dare not risk my men in the town longer. On sacrifice night there is a festival, a riot. Thus for three days, a portion less, my talents are at the worthy Kastor's disposal."

The temple was not as his mockery had fashioned it but a box of stone, older than the town, two or three centuries older than the fortress. A labyrinth of square courts opened into and out of each other. Daylight streamed in through high blue-painted walls, falling in spotlights, like static rain pools. It was actually cold, icy almost, coming in from the baked town.

Scorpius and ten polished privates kicked their heels in an anteroom. Seteva stood, helmet under arm, shivering slightly in the dank shade, politely waiting for the High Priest of Thraistum-Trasint to advance through the curtain. And at Seteva's side, Nylerus, the decorous servitor.

Religion had always been a focal point for danger and dissent. More focal than the subdued potentates, the petty kings. The princes of the temples had the bit of spiritual power between their teeth, and all over the Remusan-conquered world, High Priests were reckoned a cipher for trouble. Save this one, apparently, in the backwoods of Thraistum. *So why in the gods' name am I here, seeking to stir the dregs at the bottom of the cask?*

The curtain moved on its rings.

The High Priest entered.

He looked immediately at his visitor. The priest seemed to know Seteva, to recognise him. In late middle years, a heavy, rambling decline of manhood beside the fine-honed soldier, the High Priest of Trasint, like the temple itself, had built, nevertheless, upon the foundation of his age.

The priest bowed to Seteva. It was pure courtesy, neither fawning nor ironic. The bow accepted Remusa as master, accepted and ignored it. It was no matter. The sun still rose, the moon waxed and waned.

Seteva stood there, not acknowledging the bow. He addressed himself to Nylerus. "Tell him."

Nylerus spoke in Thraistian to the priest, conveying the thanks of the garrison's commander, Marsus Seteva, for the interview. This being also a device: formal words in one mode, the arrogance of the Remusan standing by, stone-faced, in another, as if disowning them.

Seteva watched the priest closely. To Nylerus, Seteva said, "Now tell him I want the sacrifice stopped."

Nylerus blinked. He made no remonstrance; the blink said it all. Delicately Nylerus translated for the High Priest.

The High Priest, too, looked nowhere but at Seteva. His face unchanged, he enunciated levelly to Seteva in the outlandish tongue. Seteva grasped a couple of fragments he could identify. The phrase that meant a betrayal, and the phrase that likened a man to a dog.

There was a brief lacuna.

"Well?" Seteva said, looking at the priest, addressing Nylerus.

"The Patriarch says the ceremony has always been permitted in the past."

"That's not what he said. Explain to the Patriarch that I don't allow any man to call me a scavenging cur. Even a priest."

The High Priest spoke mildly, in a sudden hesitant Remine: "That was not—decidedly—my meaning, Commander. My speech indicated—that even dogs cannot always obey their masters. We are—your dogs, Commander. But we cannot obey."

"You handle Remine excellently," said Seteva. "You should be able, therefore, to absorb my decision first-hand. I don't intend this rite to occur while I am in Thraistum. Offer your god a pig or a sheep. Your women have other uses."

Still mild, the priest said, "You do not know our ways, Commander. You must not expect to see sense in what you do not know. Under Remusa we have been allowed to follow our religion, always."

"As far as I am concerned," Seteva said, "to kill a woman on an altar is not merely barbarous, it poses a threat to law and order. While I am in command of the garrison, you will either suspend or discontinue the enterprise. That's my last word."

Now the priest stared. He uttered rapidly, once more in Trasint. Nylerus said, "The Patriarch vows the rite cannot be put aside. That it is unavoidable. That he must risk Remusa's displeasure."

"Remind the priest that Remusa, displeased, has been known to nail men on crosses. And no priesthood was ever exempt."

Seteva turned; one stride would take him back through the outer doorway. The priest said behind him, clear as a drop of water falling onto stone, "Commander, the girl is willing."

Seteva halted. "What did you say to me?"

"The girl is willing to die. I surmise this is what disturbs you, Commander. If you wish—with her own lips, she will assure you of the fact."

Seteva swallowed. Like an expert marksman the old man had pierced through officialdom, rage, Remusan arrogance, and struck the vital nerve. *I want to see the girl again. I want to hear her voice, touch her. I want to argue with her for her life, even though I can't do it in her own language. But. This is absurd.*

"The girl is nothing to me. Only a facet of your apparent refusal to abide by my order."

The priest spoke in Trasint.

"What does he say now?"

"Only that he is sorry, mighty Kastor, to offend you. And that the girl is in the adjacent courtyard."

It was becoming suggestive of a brothel, this insistence on the proximity of what he truly wanted. Except that, save in a very general way, that was not what he wanted. Nor what was offered.

Seteva's mouth was dry. A little breeze ruffled the linen curtain and he saw a pale shadow pass over it, outside. The girl?

As if mesmerised, he found himself crossing the room, drawing aside the curtain.

The court was half-open to the sky, white with sun to its centre, beyond that dyed blue by shade. There was a basin with static, transparent water in it. Doves were shooting up from about it like flung spears. The girl was seated on the lip of the basin.

She was combing her hair, slow shining motions, like waves running in over a smooth shore. There was no mark of death on her. Her stance conveyed a serenity of youth, gazing upon the endless vista of its future. That false dream of youth, which she, undeniably, could no longer possess.

Nylerus had reached him.

"No," Seteva said to him.

He moved out into the white sunlit half of the court and drove the curtain to with his fist as he passed, shutting the room into some other dimension that could neither see nor hear nor realise where he had gone, nor why.

The girl did not turn, but her hand with the comb sank away. Her hair was very long, covering her shoulders, falling like a silvery fringe almost into the water of the basin. Waterfall.

He walked towards her, around the basin. Her head was lowered, as if she examined the comb she held in her lap. The comb was ivory, bone, a mark of death after all. He could not see her face. He was the length of his arm from her when he spoke.

"Look up," he said. Perforce he used Remine, and she could not guess its meaning. But she did guess—the tone, perhaps—and raised her head.

Her eyes were wide and intent. Without modesty and without invitation, they explored him. He saw again that curious expression of amazement below the surface of her eyes. He could not explain to himself what she represented. His heart hitting his breastbone, the sound of blood in his ears like the sea, he thought, *Why did I never meet you on some marble avenue in Remusa, why did I never see you in some litter on the shoulders of slaves, going by, easy to follow? Why did I never meet you in the whorehouse at Tynt, easy to buy? Why not on the road to Mareuna, all those months kicking my heels, waiting for transport? Twenty, thirty girls, not one of them you. Why not that officer's wife at Samaia—I could have killed him. Easy, easy. But this. Why now?*

She said something to him, softly, in Trasint.

"What?" he said, as softly. "I don't understand you."

She had risen. She held up her hand before him, palm open. It was the semantic tribal sign, current the whole earth over: I am here without weapons. Suddenly he fathomed what she meant, and, appalling him, his eyes stung with tears.

In Remine, concisely, a declaration she had learned, she murmured, "I have consented. To die. I will it."

"No." He caught himself struggling with the few bits of Thraistian he had acquired. "We—I—can prevent—this."

She only looked at him. Probably he had not said what he believed he had at all. Once more she said, gently, "But I consent."

"In gods' name," he said in Remine. In Trasint he sought and found the crucial word: "Why?"

Her eyes never left his face. She answered in Trasint, then in Remine she said: "There is no alternate way."

He could not offer the truth to her, gagged as he was, but he saw he did not need to. She knew, and in spite of the truth, she had said: *There is no alternate way.*

He turned only his head, and shouted across the court.

"Nylerus!"

The doves swirled up again, white wings like segments of the white stone of the courtyard exploded by friction. Nylerus came from the curtained door mouth, through the swirling of the doves.

"Kastor?"

"Say to her that she is under the protection of Remusa. That no one is going to kill her."

Nylerus bowed and translated the sentences to the girl.

A veil seemed to slip down across her face.

She spoke in Trasint.

Nylerus said, "She replies that she is grateful; but it is not within your power to promise her this. She is not afraid, and she asks that you leave her in peace."

Nylerus did not smile now, too clever to smile at this ludicrous spectacle, the Remusan commander sent packing by the foreign child-woman. The gaze of Nylerus slid silkenly beneath its antimony, simply observing, as the Remusan swung abruptly about and walked out of the court. Quiet as sand or snake, Nylerus poured himself in the conqueror's wake.

Sentries patrolled along the ramparts of the fortress. Periodically the challenge rang out, isolated by the hot blue-black darkness, over the never-ceasing dazzle of the crickets. The stars burned inexhaustibly, and in the huddled, heat-swilled mass of dwellings below, the muddy lamps. Sometimes, from the northern end of the town, a dull vibratory chanting. The temple.

"Nylerus is outside, Commander."

Seteva glanced up. A pile of parchments lay on the table before him, brown withered leaves, the business of the fort, unread. "All right."

Nylerus slipped into the room.

"I thought we'd paid for your services as interpreter."

"So you have, noble Kastor." Nylerus did not seem to note the parchments on the table, nor the wine jug. "I wonder if the Kastor will indulge me."

"I gather Cailo did. But I'm not Cailo."

"Indeed not, Commander. You must not suppose I expect a welcome at your fortress. Though I have been welcome."

"What do you want?"

"In the East . . . " Nylerus said. He had assumed a storyteller's voice. He looked a second at Seteva, to gauge his reaction. Seteva did not move. Nylerus rested his hands on the air, lightly, expressively. "In the East our holy books inform us that when the first man had been made, the god breathed the divine breath into him, which became his soul, and caused him to become quick. It was then necessary to create woman. But the god did not breathe life directly into the woman. Instead he opened the man's body and removed from it a piece of the soul, and this he gave to the woman. Since then, for every man created, a piece of his soul is subtracted to quicken a woman. In memory of this deed the seed also passes from male to female. But if a man finds by chance the woman who contains that fraction of his own soul, he will know her, as he knows his own image in a mirror."

Outside something had caused the crickets to fall startlingly dumb.

"You gamble I have a weakness," Seteva said quietly. "You presume you can profit by it, just as you have profited here by Cailo's weaknesses."

"The Kastor misjudges me. Let me offer him the end of the story of the first man and the first woman who drew life from the same soul. Another god, jealous of the god who had quickened life in the bodies of men, seduced the woman. He put on the form of a serpent and persuaded her away by his beauty. They fashioned a second race between them, half-human and half-snake."

"From which, no doubt, you can claim descent."

"The Kastor is too generous. With my people the snake is revered for its wisdom."

"Then be wise, Nylerus. Get out."

"Before I go, Kastor, my caravan. It leaves on the morning of the sacrifice, one hour before the woman dies on the altar."

"You forget. The temple will forego the sacrifice, by my order."

"Oh, mighty Kastor—" Nylerus laughed, musically and low. "These barbarians . . . Do you think they will obey you? In preference to their *god?*"

"They will if they decide to keep their liberty."

"They are not civilised enough to put liberty before religion. This is your stumbling block."

The crickets had started up again, like flints perpetually striking on the peppery flanks of the hills.

Seteva poured himself wine. The jug was almost empty, and the liquor had the sour stale taste of repetition.

"You'd better finish what you started to say to me."

"As the noble Kastor desires. I was about to postulate a theory. The men of my caravan—what are they? Villains, no more. The rubbish of the alleyways. And when they are in drink, gracious Kastor, neither god nor demon will deter them. Maybe they have seen a girl they fancy. What do they do? They abduct her, Kastor. They drag the poor wretch away with them, careless of whom she might belong to. And such a girl, once lost, is rarely recovered. For this cause I remove my caravan from Thraistum before the riotous celebration of the sacrifice is due. But possibly I am not quick enough. Possibly these dogs of mine have already espied some girl. Abductions can always be managed. Even a temple is not impregnable. And the priests. No match for jackals of the desert. There are a thousand crannies in these hills where such a theft might be hidden. I might detail for the noble Kastor the most likely concealments."

Seteva drained the cup and set it down among the parchments. "And the price?"

Nylerus touched one hand fleetingly to his brow, his heart. "To have the Kastor's friendship would be sufficient reward."

"I'm sorry to disappoint you," Seteva said. "I don't mean to be in your debt throughout the remainder of my time here. You've mistaken your man, Nylerus. Now, I can only reiterate my earlier proposal: Get out."

Nylerus bowed and moved towards the door. At the threshold he said, "On the day of the sacrifice, Kastor, I will leave thirteen men near the gate. They will be dressed in the manner of my people. You could not miss them, should you wish any service."

In the dark the crickets stopped again and again, for no obvious cause. Like a heart suddenly faltering. He remembered how his brother had died at Samaia, sliced in two, body bloodless, skin white as salt.

Salt in the wound.

Days of salt.

They had burned the dead at Samaia on one great pyre. The heat of it had spread like the heat of a summer day.

And the crickets began again. And again.

## III

There was a woman in the town. She, or her Remusan clients, called her Pulcra, but she was ugly as forty years of whoring could make her. Her girls, younger, were a different matter.

In a minute cell of the scalding house, its walls painted with blue lotuses and red fruits, a girl the colour of amber took the wooden combs from her hair and the garish clothes from her body. They lay down on the pallet and made something, not love, between them. Fire, perhaps.

When he had had her, she offered him wine, politely lingering, eager to please. The wine was local, honeyed and thick, like syrup.

She spoke Remine haltingly but correctly. Anytime, she said, he would like her—or another girl, though she hoped it might be herself—they could come to him at the fort. There was a secret stair. Nylerus the Easterner knew the way. Jezit, the girl was named. The madam had told him. She would gladly come to him. Any night, save tonight.

"Why not tonight?" he asked her. He wasn't interested, but the sight of her eased him, the small fluttery trained movements she gave, like those of a caged bird. Her accented, hesitant voice.

The light of day was already thickening like the wine. The dense coppery glare which preceded sunset.

"Tonight is the night of the Passage of Sin. She who is to die will sit before the temple. All who need may go by, touching her. Through the touch we receive blessing. She takes our sins upon herself. I have many sins."

"The men you couple with," he said noncommittally.

But she merely lowered her lids. "No. They are not my sins. It is no sin to couple."

"You'll have to find another formula, in any case. Has no one told you? There will be no sacrifice."

The girl looked afraid. She whispered something in Trasint and brushed at an amulet that had been glued between them on her breast all the time he lay over her.

In the narrow street the red rays of latter-day stained the clay houses. The commander of the garrison stood, partially anonymous in the casual wear of the fort, just a Remusan officer, his army cloak wrapped loosely about him against the heat.

His feet walked him northward, through the sweet stenches of dust, dung, and spice, the odour of the town at this hour.

*What am I doing?*

He waited for the sun to set, under the shadow of a wall, across the temple square and facing towards the temple building. There was a matte blot on the light between him and the temple. It had not registered with him before. A stone slab about the height of a man, steps up to it, level across its surface.

*No. This won't answer. I must have a reason for what I do. I have no reason. Nothing that has the guise of reason.*

He had seen a man in one of the eastern villages five years ago. The man had run screaming through the village; he had eaten stones and drunk urine. When he uttered, it was gibberish. He was reckoned to be possessed by demons. That was, he had been motivated, without the power of his own will or sense, to perform acts injurious to himself and to others.

The sky altered from a wing of blood to a wing of indigo, and as the sky altered a crowd gathered along the edges of the square, as if the going of the sun had called it up.

Torches were flowing from the temple gate, droplets of fire running over the dusk.

There was no sound, no chanting. Voicelessly the crowd began to surge in on the gate, fulvously lit, then sinking forward into shadow.

The movements were such that he could not define their purpose.

Presently he also, muffled in the dark and in the cloak, joined the patient, slowly advancing crowd that pressed towards the gate.

Possessed.

By what?

A bit of his soul in her body. He had no soul; that was a dream of the East. The gods cared for a man simply while he was living. If there were gods.

Nobody stared at him or shrank aside disconcerted by this apparition of the Conqueror in their midst. They did not seem to notice.

Where the torches glared, he could see nothing. Only the silhouetted black shapes of men and women, shuffling, pausing, eddying away.

Then, like a curtain, the crowd parted. He beheld the light, and in the centre of the light, a creature in white robes, with a silver casque of hair; a blanched face, as if carved. A man knelt to her, contacting, with his fingertips, the hem of the robe, the silver-corded wrist. And next a woman, reaching to find the shoulder of the image. Sliding off into the shadow as the man had done, helplessly drawn to and thrust from the magnetic aura of the light.

It was the Remusan's turn now.

*Take my sins. No. You are my sin, my stumble from the road of honour and duty. From sanity.*

Did she remember him? The bleached face, white lips slightly parted, the eyes discs of jet, was raised to him like a mirror. But in the mirror nothing stirred.

There was a scent of incense and of drugs in the air.

He stood like a stone, a fold of his cloak over his head, hidden and unnamed.

The moment dissolved. Like a man stepping from a frieze, returned to flesh, he moved on into the shadow. Without touching her.

The girl, Jezit, sought him in the coal-black hour before dawn. Unsleeping, midway in the act of kindling the dish of oil, he heard a man laugh and a woman's protest. The sentry rapped on the door.

"One of Pulcra's daughters is here, Commander. She came in by the back stair and scratched at the postern." The man could barely restrain his amusement. Worse than Cailo, this new Kastor of the fort who could not leave the harlots alone.

Jezit poised in the dim yellow smudge of the lamp. Her head bowed, she extended to Seteva, mutely, a cloth-bound package.

"What's this?"

"It was sent to me, but for you, Kastor."

"And Nylerus reminded you of the way in? Don't use that stair again without my leave."

She did not reply, and he unwrapped the package, and there was the ivory comb the girl had plied in the temple courtyard, and wound about it, trapped in its teeth, a slender rivulet of colourless, shining hair.

His heart seemed to congeal. She had sent to him the symbol of her death. No speech could be so final or so essentially pathetic.

Like men drowning in some galley, casting their jewels from them, signets of their lives and office, to be swallowed by fish, perhaps, and discovered again a year later at the dinner table. His mother, when he was six years old, had recounted how his father's seal-ring had come back to her that way, from the sea battle at Mentum. But even then, somehow, he had known she lied, that the ring was a copy. That nothing, not even the glory of a name, could absolutely survive death.

The little whore drooped her head.

*Let it end,* he thought. *I'm far from land, but still the harbour is in sight. Turn back. She's nothing to you. Pretend, as her priests do, that you never ordered them to forego their sacrifice.* These fools believed she died for them, their scapegoat. Too much hung on her death. She was condemned, for if she lived, their sins remained. Probably even the might of Remusa could not contain their spiritual panic and fury if they were cheated of their purging. He could not save her. But then, she was happy to die. Let her be happy. *One more death, what's that?* One more cup spilled on the ground.

He glanced at Jezit. "Well," he said. "Since you're here."

The hot shadows flared on the walls and sank, unappeased.

"It is a passing trouble," she said to him, consolingly, as if to a child. Doubtless she had seen men ashamed at their inability to fill her. He looked at the lamp glow and the quiescent shadows. The drought was not only in the world now, but within him. Dehydrated of water and of seed.

*Die for me too, then,* he thought. *Die for my sins, and give me back the rain, the water in the cup, my manhood and my soul.*

# IV

"At noon," the adjutant said. "That's when they do it. To appease the sun, I think. Or to attract storms."

The hills seemed to be smoking. A brush of haze blurred the perimeter of the hard sky. Already the dust, momentarily laid by the flat black palm of night, was flouring the air, the ledges, the sills of the town, the sockets of the nostrils, eyes, and lips of men and beasts. Just another feverish day. This fifth day.

"I won't risk this mob getting out of hand," Seteva said. "Whatever precautions Cailo took, I want them doubled. Trebled, if necessary. A century deployed in blocks of ten, thirty men on each of the three open sides of the square, and ten across the gate."

"Yes, sir."

Scorpius cleared his throat. "That's extravagant, Commander."

"Not quite. Cailo treated this place as a combined brothel and sanctuary. It's neither."

Scorpius and the adjutant skimmed a glance between them, a memento of the harlot who had come in by the secret stair.

"And who's to take charge of this modest deployment, Commander?"

"I'll see to it myself."

*And I'll see her die.* But he was ready for that. He was balanced, beyond the trivia of his emotion, his superstition. Beyond the reach of her and the effluvia of this compost heap of barbarism and self-blindness. He walked at his own elbow. Inflexible, and objective. Guiding, indifferent.

"Where's that Easterner? Away yet?"

"Nylerus?" Scorpius spat economically through the window. "He rode out early. Though I hear he's left thirteen of his pack rats near the gate. Selling, or trying to sell, horses. No one'll buy anything so close to the sacrifice. But, my god, who devised this system? A young, healthy girl to be butchered. Some decent farmer could have got sons on her. A waste, and no mistake."

"Pulcra could have found a use for her, at the very least," Seteva said.

They grinned, glad he would admit his weakness, reduce it thereby to the unimportant vice it was. The vice they thought it was.

Let from their cages, streamers of doves tangled across the cloudless sky.

The hundred men stood, sweating in their leather and iron. Scorpius, on the roan horse he had brought from Mareuna, sat by the temple gate.

The crowd pressed against the wall of shields and of Remusan soldiery. But hardly a sound came from the crowd. Once or twice a child, crying, was miraculously hushed. The dust was settling on the rims and folds and creases of the crowd, as if on statuary in a desert.

On his own face Seteva felt the pollen of the dust, while the black horse he rode became a grey dust horse.

He was tired, as if after a day's march. He ached, shut in the iron oven of heat and metal. His shadow lay on the ground under the hoofs of the horse. He wanted this to be over.

Inside the box of the temple a ram's horn moaned.

The gates swung open. From the well of shade into the bowl of sun, changing colour and texture as the sun struck them, the linen-robed priests, shaved like the avatars of Aigum, flickered black to white, black to white. A sharp perfume of myrrh fanned from their censers, penetrating the nasal passages, seeming to pierce the dome of the brain.

Like high tide they washed in about the stone slab in the square, the slab that was the height of a man, steps up to it, level across its surface.

And now a girl came from the temple, also changing from black to white until, exposed in the force of noon, she too appeared to catch alight and to burn. She walked slowly, heavily, and observing her face, he saw that she was drugged, some poppy drink, to kill fear or to numb pain or simply to destroy the last vestige of the life-wish. She was very young. Life must be strong in her, despite her abnegation and her surrender to her god. She would need that drink.

He watched her face and felt nothing. She was a stranger, foreign-looking, not even actually beautiful. He could perceive now, as if from a high tower or across a vast distance, the gulf between them. She meant nothing. He was sorry for her, for her stupidity, for her death.

He had acted irrationally in this venture, and it could have become a worse irrationality if the more determined idiocy of these priests had not prevented it. He had been within an arm's length of losing everything. And gaining what? Some provincial doxy who could not even speak to him coherently in his own tongue.

Her eyes were entirely darkened by the drug, and nearly closed. Her heavy movements were graceful, sensual almost, as she moved towards the stone. As though she swam through a glaucous river.

Two priests drew her up the steps tenderly. Yes, most certainly, with tenderness.

Through the mask of the dust Seteva's mouth fixed itself in a sneer, and he was aware of the dust cracking to form new lines.

She lay on the slab, against the sky, the slight profile—head, breast, the curious addendum of the up-pointed, naked feet.

(He had seen enough of those feet, upturned, corpses in ranks, piled on each other, ready for burning after the battle.)

The ram's horn groaned again from the temple.

The fat High Priest was emerging now, and before him a girl about thirteen years old with a bough of greenery across her hands and something flashing white on that green, like a long blade of water.

Seteva was thirsty. The local wine wasn't bad, once you were used to it. And it would have to be wine. The local water had a foul taste.

The High Priest mounted the steps. He was on the other side of the slab, confronting Seteva over the profiled body of the girl. The thirteen-year-old offered the green bough to the priest, and he raised from it a honed and burnished knife, holding it aloft for the crowd to see, and perhaps for his god to see it, too.

It would require two cups of wine, more, to wash this dust-dryness out of the throat. *When I get to the fortress—*

He found, with a sort of unsurprised bewilderment, that he had kneed the horse and was riding forward. Not fast, in fact rather leisurely. The High Priest had seen him and had paused, the knife still pointed towards the sky. The priest's face was blank. Seteva felt the same blankness on his own face.

Now all the priests were in his way.

Suddenly he was no longer riding leisurely but with a headlong violence. The linen-wrapped figures were toppling sideways, dividing, the slab loomed, horizontally spread with white, the fat middle-aged man beyond it, and the silver blade abruptly tearing the sky with its motion.

The blade in his own hand, which he had not been conscious of till that instant, sheared through the High Priest.

The man's face was red now with his own blood, bloodily washed of its blankness, whirling backwards—

Seteva pulled the white shape from the altar effortlessly. It was the first time he had touched her, but he did not think of it then, for she did not seem human, or real.

It was not quiet anymore.

He turned the horse, pulling on the bit to set the hoofs lashing, and plunged straight through the crowd. Women were screaming, and far off he heard, almost with nostalgia, the yammering yell of Scorpius. The soldiers had broken their formation. Seteva glimpsed three youths brawling over an armoured man on his knees in the dust, and the army sword spitting guts before the soldier went down. And he saw a woman scratching her cheeks and tugging out handfuls of her hair. And another soldier crawling in circles. And another dead. But these things seemed removed, at a vast distance, or perceived from a high tower.

He did not question his direction until he noticed the way unhindered before him, the town gate standing unbarred, a scoop of ochre light in the clay-red wall.

A sentry shouted from the wall as he clattered through, the white swath, which was a woman, clasped before him.

As the horse hit the wall of light beyond the wall of clay, men on horseback foamed around him.

"With us, Kastor!"

A second called in the eastern language, and Seteva identified the thirteen men Nylerus had left for his "service."

The striped head-cloths flapped over the black fleeces of hair, and the gems seared, a perfect component of this madness.

Seteva laughed, and all about the jackal teeth answered him, and the narrow eyes evaluated. They rode together, galloping for the hills.

The town sank in their wake.

He sat the part-dead horse, the senseless woman a leaden weight now on his arm. The sun had set, a sky the colour of apricots going out behind the land.

"Nylerus, I said," he repeated.

Despite their prologue of cries and the ride through the hills, they did not speak Remine, or would not. Nor did they appear to realise that their own leader was the man he sought in the encampment. Of course, he himself had no authority left with them, or with anyone. The insignia of Remusa all over him, the gilded armour, the lion's-blood cloak, the crested helmet, the bronze-hilted blade—each had become the silliest and most unsavoury kind of joke.

Yet he was not mad. It seemed quite reasonable, after all, that he should be here, with nothing, everything he had been reduced to a disaster and left behind him. Men he had known, whose lives were subject to his command, were scattered dead in that past. Reborn into chaos, only thus Marsus Seteva had entered the encampment in the hills. He had put himself into Nylerus's power as neatly as if Nylerus, some fictitious sorcerer of the East, had led him here. And now Nylerus was absent, the final tile left out of the wall. A chink in the reinvented, appalling structure of things as they had come to be. Strangely it was this, more than all else, which disturbed Seteva, provoking him to rage, so he shouted at the men about him: *Nylerus—Nylerus*—the only word they might logically be expected to grasp, but to which they refused to react.

Indeed, they had withdrawn from him, clearing a wide space

about him as he sat there on the sodden horse, the white body of the girl leaden against his arm.

The sky faded, but the encampment fires rekindled the colour of the afterglow.

Nylerus stood by the horse.

His hands were raised as if to receive some burden from the soldier on his exhausted beast.

"Your men professed not to remember you, Nylerus."

"It was not that, Kastor. You made them uneasy."

"No longer 'Kastor,' Nylerus."

"No longer 'Kastor.' Dismount now; the ride is over. I will take the girl."

Seteva sat on the horse, looking at him. Seteva did not move.

"Are there any women in your camp, Nylerus? I think she'll need women to tend her. Women who speak her own tongue. I can still pay for the service, Nylerus. Remusan capitas."

"No, Kastor. That is no matter. This was not the service I offered, Kastor."

"Damn you, stop calling me that."

"As you wish, Marsus Seteva. But still it was not this service."

"What are you talking about?"

"I am saying to you, Marsus Seteva, that I offered you a method whereby you might bring your girl from Trasint before the sacrifice."

"Split hairs, Nylerus."

"Not so. Examine what you have brought from the town, Marsus Seteva. Closely."

The space had widened farther. Nylerus and the soldier and the horse and the limp form of the girl, ringed by fire-wash and shadow, by the settling canopy of darkness, by the men and their animals, but all a great way off.

He held her stiffly, like a heavy wooden bolster.

"They gave her a drug, to make her compliant," Seteva muttered. His arm no longer ached, holding her. His arm had grown into her body, become wooden as her body had become.

"She was compliant enough. Examine, Kastor. Examine."

Seteva glanced down.

Her face was tilted back, the bright hair gushing forth from the skull like spilling water from a tilted urn. Her eyes were open, dulled, opaque. Her lips did not meet. She stared at him as if about to speak.

A chill wind blew across the slopes, and the grass ran like the rollers of an ocean.

"Slow poison," Nylerus said softly, reciting to the lyre of the grass wind. "No harm in it, when they are to die anyway, their blood freed for the god. And it affords them a fair crossing from this earth into their paradise."

"She's dead," Seteva said.

"Yes, Kastor. From the moment she drank it. Dying even as she walked towards the stone. You cheated Trasint of her blood, but not of her death. Oh, they will not forgive it, Kastor. They will rebel and throw off the shackles Remusa put on them. Fresh soldiery will have to be sent to Thraistum. Men will need to be hanged, and crucified. Women raped. The temple burned. The fields salted. Afterwards, peace again. The peace of Remusa; quiescence beneath the booted heel. And you, Kastor, your own kind will hunt you like a dog. But all this is, ultimately, very little. Their god has what he desires. If he loves them, the rain will fall. The sun will rise. The moon will wax and wane. I am sorry, Marsus Seteva. I am sorry for you."

Seteva lowered the girl. Her bare feet met the grass of the hillside, and he let her go. She flopped like an emptied water sack, unhuman and spent, soulless, to the ground.

His arm, reprieved, began to pain him, prolonged runnels of pain flowing from the joints and sinews. He massaged the arm absently.

"What now?" Nylerus whispered to him.

"The end of the world," Seteva said. He pulled off the helmet of gilded iron, with its raw red comb, and dropped it by the white sack on the grass.

"Your world, Kastor."

"My world."

Seteva touched the horse, and tiredly, resignedly, it resumed the trained parade walk of the march.

"Wait," said Nylerus. "Where are you going?"

But horse and rider went by him, between the fires, and through the circle of firelit men, up the spine of one hill, descending from sight over another.

"The Remusan is going to Tophiteth, the place of burning," one of the men said malevolently. He spoke in the eastern language, his words striking on the quiet of the young night, scoring it like writing on a wall. "The Remusan is going to Hell."

# ELLE EST TROIS. (LA MORT)

CROSS THE RIVER, THE CLOCK OF NOTRE DAME AUX LUMI-
nères was striking seven. How deep the river, and how
dark, and how many bones lying under it that the
strokes of the great gilded clock upon the Gothic tower,
winged with its lace-work, did not rouse. Down there,
all those who had thrown themselves from the bridges, off the
quays of the city: the starving, the sick and the drugged, the desperate and the insane.

Armand looked down in the water, black as the night, looked
down and searched for them—and there, a pale hand waved from
the flowing darkness, a drift of drowning hair, now passed under
the parapet—a girl had flung herself into the river, and should he
rescue her, was it morally right that he should save her from whatever horror had driven her to this?

The young man, a poet, rushed across the bridge and stared over
from the other parapet. This time there was help. A lamp globe at
the bridge's far end caught the suicide as she glided out again into
view. The poet, Armand, sighed with relief and a curious disappointment. The thing in the water was only a string of rags and
garbage woven together by the current.

Straightening, Armand pulled his threadbare coat about him. It
was spring, but the city was cold in spring. There was no stirring in
its stones, or in his blood. He glanced now, with familiar depres-

sion, at the cathedral towers on the far bank of the river, the tenements on the nearer bank, towards which, returning, he was bound. Above, the stars, and here and there below a greenish lamp. So little light in the darkness.

He had not eaten in two days, but there had come to be enough money to buy cheap wine in the café on the Rue Mort. And for the other thing, purchased—was it yesterday?

He had been walking all afternoon until purpose ended in a leaden sunset. As flakes of the day sank in the river, Notre Dame aux Luminères towered up before him, as if out of the water itself, an edifice from a myth. Compelled as any knight, he had entered her vast drum of incense and shadow. Standing beyond the ghostly rainbow bubbles that were cast from the stained-glass windows to the ground, he lit one of her candles.

(My name is Armand Valier. I announce myself, since I think you don't remember me, God. As why should you? Why am I lighting the candle? For a dead work, a dead poem. She died in my arms today. I burned her.)

When night had wiped away the coloured windows, Armand left and began to walk back across the bridge.

He walked slowly, lost not in thought but in some inner country that faintly resembled the bridge, the river, the dimming banks—one drawing away, one drawing nearer, both equally unreal—a country nourished by facts of surrounding and atmosphere, yet denying them. So that halfway across the bridge, the young man paused in the clinging chill, his dark head bowed. (Where am I, then, if not here? Is it some place I recall from a dream? Have I crossed some barrier in time and latitude? And is this some world so like the world I have just vacated I may be deceived for a while, as though I had moved through the surface of a mirror?)

The impression of change, or of strangeness, became then so sharp a galvanic sensation ran through his nerves. In that instant, seeing no apparent alteration, he looked over the bridge and beheld the dead girl in the water who, a moment later, from the other parapet, became a chain of flotsam. Which convinced Armand, the poet, that merely by crossing from one parapet of the bridge to the other, he had recrossed the boundaries of normality.

But it was very cold. Shuddering in the inadequate coat, he began to stride briskly on, towards the pallid globe of the lamp that swam there against the uninviting homeward bank.

Mist was rising from the river, fraying out the poor light mysteriously, like a gauzy scarf. As Armand hurried closer, the impulse

came to him that he should once more cross to the opposite parapet, and pass by the mysterious lamp in, as it were, that other
partly different world where rags became drowned girls.

Presently, he obeyed the impulse; it was easy enough to accommodate, merely the matter of a briefly diagonal path. He found,
unaccountably, his heart—but perhaps only from lack of food, and
tiredness—beating urgently now. He gazed into the misty ambience
of the light as it approached nearer and nearer.

Until, suddenly, he saw a figure at the end of the bridge beneath
the lamp.

Armand checked, continuing to move forward, yet much more
slowly now. He heard his footsteps very keenly, over the counterpoint of the river, over the remote whisperings of the city. Louder
than both, his own breathing. He could already see clearly the figure was that of a woman.

She was dressed in a wave of black velvet. It was a cloak such as
those worn by the rich and the fashionable to the Opéra. But it
wrapped her within itself as if it, too, were alive, some organic
creature, folding her as if in the petals of a black orchid. Behind her
head, one petal was raised, a hood like the hood of a striking cobra,
framing a face smudged by the mist. He made out an impression of
her features. They were aristocratic and quite fixed, perhaps incapable of expression. All but the eyes, which were overlined by long
black sloping brows, and which had an indecipherable blueness
about the upper lids that was neither paint nor shadow, but suggested the translucent wings of two irislike insects, pasted there.
. . . Her mouth was hardly generous, yet it was soft, and seemed
disposed to smile. Yet this might have been, as so much else, a trick
of the mist. But now there was a turn of the whole head. Against
the cameo cheek a tendril of night-coloured hair, the twenty simul-
taneous struck sparks of jewel-drops fringing the hood. A gloved
hand pierced the cloak like a knife. The material of the glove was a
curious mauvish-blue, pearly and luminescent, insubstantial as a
new-born gas flame. The gloved hand made the unmistakable
mime of drawing closed a curtain.

Understanding, before understanding reached him, Armand
quickened his pace again, to match his heartbeats, but already it
was too late. The apparition had vanished.

Gaining the lamp, he quested about for her, vainly. He even
called to her once, his voice echoing mournfully, mockingly: "Ma-
demoiselle Fantôme—"

He did not search very long. The nausea of hunger was coming over him, prompting him to seek, not food, but wine, warmth, the company of others.

Ten strides off the bridge, beyond the lamp, he swiftly glanced back—only the mist, the unravelling gauze of light, the darkness emptied on the water.

The Café Vule on the Rue Mort was crowded, a raucous cave, its walls springing with black-stockinged dancers, its tables scattered by cards, papers, dice, and red wine. The drinkers sprawled, talked, pounded woodwork and each other, all washed by a shrill gamboge illumination, or else in the terra-cotta twilight to be found under the barrel-vaulting to the rear.

In this twilight Etiens Corbeau-Marc, half blinded by his fair hair and by the drizzle of one dull candle, sat sketching anything in the café. The strokes of the charcoal were spare and penetrating, with a slight distortion that tended to aid rather than dismiss reality.

(One day, such sketches will sell for hundreds of American dollars. But Corbeau-Marc will be safely shut in the earth by then.)

"I receive your shadow on my paper, Armand, without thanks. Please sit down or go away. Simply get out of my light."

"My shadow and the shadow of a wine bottle. An improvement?"

"Oh, we are rich tonight?"

"Oh, we are poor. But we can also be drunk. And here the bottle comes."

"But yes. Sit, generous friend. You see that woman? She has the face of a horse-fly. Do you think she would come and pose for me in my room?"

"Why not? All the other flies do." Armand poured wine in two murky glasses and drank from one thirstily, closing his eyes. He seemed to wait a moment, as if for some rush of sensation that did not arrive. His voice was melancholy and listless when he spoke again. "I saw a woman by the river tonight that you really should paint, Etiens."

"Give her my address, provided she doesn't want to be paid."

"I think—" Armand raised his lids, found the world, the glass, and drank again— "she would want to be paid in blood."

"A vampire. Excellent."

Etiens left his sketches and drank.

"Armand, you're very irritating. Are you going to elaborate or not? Or is this some dream you've been having? When did you last eat?"

"Yesterday, I think. Or the day before. A dream? I don't dream anymore, asleep or awake." Armand put his arms on the table and laid his head on them. He said something inaudible.

"I can't hear you. You've stopped me working; at least you can entertain me."

"I said I burned my latest disaster this morning. A moment before noon. The clock struck just after, and then I went out and over the river. When I came back, it was dark. The lamp was alight at the end of the bridge, and there was a woman standing there in black velvet and gas-colour gloves, with the face of the virgin mother of Monsieur."

"What? Oh, you mean the Devil. Did you speak to her?"

"No."

"Afraid of disillusion? No doubt wise. She was probably some luckless little whore."

Armand refilled his yawning glass from habit. It seemed to him he might have been drinking water. Only a distant throbbing in his temples conveyed the idea that it might be wine.

"It's strange. At first she surprised me. But then—I think I saw her once before. Or twice. She vanished, Etiens. Like a blown-out flame."

"There was, perhaps, a mist."

"Not in the mist."

"Tonight," said Etiens, "I will buy some cheese and a loaf. I shall sit sternly over you while you eat."

"Food makes me ill," said Armand.

"Of course it does. Your stomach's forgotten what food is for. You eat every tenth day and your inside cries: Help! What is this alien substance? I am poisoned."

"The woman," said Armand. "I know who she must be."

Etiens Corbeau-Marc had produced another scrap of paper and begun to draw again. This, at last, was nothing in the Café Vule. Armand, turning to him abruptly, hesitated.

An urchin girl stood on the paper, slender as a pen, wafted by hair blonde as the hair of Etiens, perhaps more blonde. Her eyes became white streaks in the cinnamon paper as he delicately scratched it away with his fingernail, as if he would blind her, or uncover her true eyes.

"And who is that?"

"Dear Armand, I can scarcely remember. A small wraith of my childhood. For some reason I just now recollected her—"

"One day, such sketches will be worth sheafs of francs, boxes full of American dollars. When you are safely dead, Etiens, in a pauper's grave."

Armand looked up, although Etiens did not, and found between them both, red-haired in the heavy reddish shadow, like the dusk of Mars, the occasional third member of this table in the Café Vule.

"Little bird," said Etiens, "sweet France, you are in my light. Move the candle, move yourself, move the earth—but do it quickly."

"The earth has been moved," said France, taking a seat around the table and pouring himself a glass of wine. He had already been drinking, and the long upper lids of his eyes were partly lowered like fine white blinds. "Well, well, I'm here for refuge, not earthquakes. I have had earthquakes enough in my room."

"What trouble are you in now, beloved angel? Can it be Jeannette has at last come to her senses and abandoned you?"

"Jeannette has been gone a month. She was becoming like a wife, a mother. Eat this, sit here, be home by such. Everything mended, the place horribly clean and so showing every wretched item of its meanness. And ragoût. All she would cook for me—ragoût. And two glasses of wine, no more. And tears. Who were you with? Where have you been? Say that you love me. Why *don't* you love me? And my piano— Oh God, God, God. What did she do?"

"Well, what?" exclaimed Etiens.

"Armand, you are not listening to me."

"I am listening."

"My piano—she brought in a man to value it."

Etiens clapped one hand on the rickety table. Armand let out a stilted snarl of amusement.

"Well, it would fetch some money, I suppose."

"Her own words. You never play it, she said to me. Where are the concertos, the preludes. . . .You make music only in the beds of other women. While we starve." France drank wine, directly from the bottle now. He stared at them. "I threw her clothes from the window. And her damnable flowers in pots. I very nearly threw her after them, but she ran out shrieking."

"Poor little girl," said Etiens. "But then, she was a fool to live with you. You use your women like rags."

"There's another rag now."

Armand retrieved the bottle. The wine was gone. He shut his eyes again, the length of the lashes on his cheeks making him look like an exhausted child.

"This latest one," said France, "she seemed to understand, and she had a little money. Now she says to me: 'I'm not jealous of your women. I am jealous of the music in your head. I'm jealous of your Negro mistress, the piano. You sit and fondle her, but you're tired of me.' Which is true. She's dreary. I threw her out."

"From the window?" said Etiens. "I do hope not."

"No, no, in God's name. Who has money for more wine?"

"Wine and bread," said Etiens.

"You are rich now?" France demanded.

"Someone bought a painting. Oh, a very modest sale. A couple of francs."

France turned to Armand.

"Drink, food. Wake up. Be happy! Dance on the table."

"Be happy? When I can't write anymore?"

"What rubbish."

"I can't, I tell you."

"Nor can I write a note," said France. "Jeannette's whining did that to me. And Clairisse, with her craziness. A melody comes—it's another man's melody. The development limps, falls down, expires. But do you see me? Look. I'll go on. It will come back."

"Wine used to help me," Armand muttered. "Before that—I can hardly believe it when I think back—just to be alone, and to walk somewhere—anywhere. The visions would rise and flow, like breathing. I could barely restrain the ideas, barely stop myself shouting aloud in the street with pure ecstasy. Now, nothing. A void. I need something more than drink, or solitude. I need something, some sort of searing acid, to release what's inside me. It's there. I can feel it, tapping on the inside of my mind like a bird in a cage. My God. What will become of me?"

"Be quiet," France grumbled. "You're annoying me now. You begin to sound like Jeannette."

The wine came, the bread and cheese.

Etiens moved his sketches. That of the strange urchin girl slid to the floor under the table, where feet, unknowingly, scuffed it.

The group itself had become one of Etiens's paintings. Theatrically dashed by light and shade, highlighted by a gem of candle-fire in the wine bottle, the three young men ripping bread savagely in pieces.

How alike each of them was to the others, in some uncoordinated, extraordinary way. Not a likeness of the flesh, though in some respects they were alike, slender in their squalid clothing, which in France was also garish, like his hair; their faces hollowed and desperate, leaning inwards like three aspects of one whole. Poverty, anger, tenacity, despair, and possibly genius. But who, at this hour, could be sure of that? The Artist, the Composer, the Poet. Blond, auburn, dark—like chess pieces of some three-handed game.

"Where's your sketch?" France asked suddenly.

They looked for it, the white-eyed gamine. . . .Some boot had borne her away on the sole. France swore. Armand offered to search the packed and riotous café.

"No matter," Etiens waved them down. "I'm glad it has gone. It wasn't as I wanted it. Or else, too much as I wanted it."

"It put me in mind of that old rhyme," said France, drinking from the second bottle. "I've no notion why. But you recall the one I mean? A sort of game. A circle and three figures, and should you come against them at the end of the saw, you're out of the play. How is it? *Elle est trois— Soit! Soit! Soit!*"

Armand glanced at him:

"*Mais La Voleuse, La Séductrice—*"

"That's it!" France shouted, a pale flush on his white cheekbones. "*La Séductrice et Madame Tueuse—*"

"*Ne cherchez pas,*" Etiens finished.

France rose, graceful and barbaric, raising the bottle, now his alone. He bellowed through the café, sporadically cursed, while here and there a woman giggled, or a voice joined him.

> "*Elle est trois.*
> *Soit! Soit! Soit!*
> *Mais La Voleuse,*
> *La Séductrice*
> *Et Madame Tueuse*
> *Ne cherchez pas!*
> *Ne cherchez pas!*"

France slid back into his seat. He pressed the empty wine bottle lovingly on Armand.

"What in hell does it mean?"

Etiens, who was not drunk, said sadly, "It means death."

*Elle est trois. . . . She is three.*
  *Fine!* (One.) *Fine!* (Two.) *Fine!* (Three.)
  *But the Thief—*
  The Thief.

The spring rain, cold as the city's glasslike blood, was falling viciously in splinters on the streets, and Etiens walked towards his lodging. His fair hair, rat-coloured now, plastered itself to his eyes; his shoes were full of water. It was midnight, the clock of the cathedral was striking, a wolf's howl across the river. Our Lady of Lights, with the little candles fluttering out and dying in her stony womb.

It was a lie about the sale of the picture. But it had seemed necessary to make a contribution of food. What did it matter? Etiens considered the beautiful words jammed behind the dam of Armand's fear, the sonatas trapped by France's appetites and lack of human-feeling. But yet, Armand saw visions on the bridge, France touched the battered piano and notes leapt in the air.

(And I, I can build pictures on leaves of paper and canvas, pictures good or bad, but ceaseless, responsive, nourishing. Life. *Life.*)

Yes, but he could still remember La Voleuse.

How old had he been then? Perhaps six, or seven. Probably seven. And he had been ill; this was a vivid yet curiously disjointed memory. He recollected the onset of the illness—some childish fever—as a bizarre uninterest in everything about him and a bewildered lack of comprehension in himself as to why this should be. Then came a patchy area of monochromes, shadows limned by light, and light too bright to be borne, a murmur of voices, and his mother's harried irritability that, in the midst of penury, filth, and hopelessness, she must also nurse an ailing child. He recaptured the most, for some reason, definite incident of all: that of being given water in a little spoon because he was too weak to lift his head. He had not been afraid, of course. The self-absorption of childhood, its blind reliance, obviated any qualms. He had not been aware of mortality, though mortality in some form must surely have come hovering about the attic, with its odours of garlic and rotten wood. Mortality at this time, perhaps, in the shape of a huge brown moth, had visited him by night, peering over into his unconscious face with its glittering pins of eyes.

Beyond the narrow attic windows, at the back of the house, was an unusual feature, a balcony with a balustrade of wrought iron, like a black spiderweb. Here a cracked pot or two with dead geraniums vied with blown washing tied across the rail. The dirty, uninspiring roofs and skylights clustered close, and five floors below stared a cobbled yard of an uncompromising hardness and lack of beauty.

His first awareness of the other child came, in some way, from this meagre balcony beyond the window.

Who is she? How did she get in? For here she sat in the pane of moonlight that sometimes evolved on the floor between the window and his bed. The stove was alight, but now it was out. Behind a screen across the room the mother and father snored and sighed.

The female child sat unblinkingly on in the flat container of moonlight, watching him.

He saw her only a moment. Then he slept again.

In the morning she was gone, and when he spoke of her he was told he had been dreaming.

The attic was often full also of the smell of cabbage soup, which Etiens recalled with slight loathing, aware that as a child of seven it had not offended him.

Adult head down against the rain, he crossed a square. He thought of La Voleuse, the Thief.

He saw her many times after that.

At first, she remained near to the window, and was expressionless. Then she came somewhat closer and she began to have an expression. Suddenly she smiled at him, and he became alert to her. Her skin was brownish, her hair a bleached rag. Her clothes, too, were bleached of colour, and ragged, but in a most formal way, as if holes had been carefully cut in them rather than torn or worn. In some respects she was like a tiny scandalised version of a Pierrette, and indeed now she was actually clowning. She scampered about the attic noiselessly, balanced on her hands, cartwheeled, turned a somersault, all with an astonished insouciance, so he had to stifle his laughter with an edge of the blanket. It was only when she was very close that he noticed her eyes were almost all white, except for the two small black dots of the pupils. Her eyes frightened him for a moment, making him think of those of a blind dog on the Rue Dantine. But, as she could obviously see perfectly well, his fear soon vanished.

After a long time of performing for him, she laughed soundlessly and ran away straight through the attic window and was gone. This did not seem peculiar. He would assume, if it were essential for him to assume anything, that she had a rope, and by means of this climbed down from the balcony. She was so agile that, even in adult recollection, it appeared partly feasible.

The convalescent child was disappointed. He had wanted to join in the play. Will she come back?

As if to tantalise him, she failed to return for a number of nights. He was by now at that stage of convalescence where he was horribly bored, still rather too weak to be about and occupy himself, but mentally fretful, anxious for diversion. And tonight his parents had left him alone, for he was thought well enough now to fend for himself. It was a wedding they had gone to. There would be gâteaux and wine. His mother had promised to bring him home a bag of pastries, but he had come to distrust her promises.

He had been dozing when he heard the clock strike from across the river: nine o'clock. The stove was unlit and it was cold as well as dark. The child Etiens prepared to huddle more deeply in the blankets, when he saw the other child, the pale Pierrette, step through the window. And for the first time he realised that now, as in all other instances, the window had been, was, closed.

He wanted to ask her what she meant by it, but she forestalled him, dancing towards him in her neatly punctured rags. He was so amused, so captivated, he said nothing. The reward was immediate. She capered. She performed incredible tricks. She bent backwards in a white hoop, then elevated herself, balancing first on her hands, next only on her fingertips. Coming down she sprang—her spring was like a cat's—and landed on the table-top. She spun, whirled over the edge, arrived on the back of a chair and ran along it—sprang again, and came to rest, on the ball of one foot, standing on the stove like a statue on a pedestal, her arms outflung. And from this position, motionless and in total equilibrium, she offered him the second reward. She beckoned.

He could hardly believe it. He had been invited to join in the fun. He knew she would teach him her tricks. They looked so easy that, although so far, practising alone and without strength in a corner, he had not mastered them, he was certain that with her guidance, her mere approval, he would learn them all.

As he emerged from the bed and stepped out on the floor of the attic, his friend smiled rapturously at him. Then, when he went to her, she flew from the stove and melted out again through the window.

He was dismayed. Was she deserting him, at the very moment when he looked for involvement, enlightenment?

Then he saw she was still there, on the balcony now, beyond the wing of the broken shutter and the grimy glass, her whiteness like a lamp against the dark winter sky and the army of darkly marching roofs. And again, urgently now, she beckoned to him.

He managed to open the window. Stepping out beside her, he felt the cold strike him like a hand, the hand of his father in rage. Pierrette laughed, without a sound. She darted upward, and suddenly she was standing on the thin curving rail of the wrought-iron balustrade. Soundlessly laughing, she ran up and down it, up and down, and despite the cold, he was entranced. Behind her flying hair like clawed string, the stars shrieked with frosty light. They seemed to snag on her hair, become caught in it, and two white stars had become her eyes.

At the far end of the rail, where one piece of forgotten washing still hung, she poised. With her outflung hand she showed him what she wanted him to do.

Climb up, climb up, follow me along the balustrade. This was what her hand, her face—tensed and nodding—the spikes of her hair, the stick of her body, were prompting him to do. Even her rags leaned out towards him, beckoning, explaining how simple it was.

He hesitated. Not out of caution, exactly; out of a sort of wonderment. As in miraculous dreams, it never occurred to him before how facile such an act could be. Of course it was simple, straightforward.

As if to prove it to him, she ran back along the balustrade. The rail was perhaps an inch wide, and where it curved it had buckled slightly. Her feet skimmed over it, sure and prehensile, and he knew that whatever she did he would be able, presently, to do.

But he was careful as he climbed over the flowerpots and up onto the balustrade, concerned, not of falling into the yard five floors below, but of tumbling back onto the balcony.

With the same care, he stood upright, his bare feet gripping the iron, which was icy and burned them, and pressed into them like a wire, but this did not bother him.

Pierrette was in ecstasy. She clapped her hands, she dazzled. Come, do as I do.

He heard, from a long way away, an agonised gasp from the room behind him. Initially it did not concern him, but then he understood, in some surprise, that he was already losing his balance.

He looked at Pierrette to see what he should do, but Pierrette was smiling, smiling at him. Could it be she had failed to note what was happening?

There ensued a long, long inexplicable second as he felt the rail of the balustrade turning under his foot, and the whole world tilting sideways. Automatically he was floundering now, his arms thrown wide, but this was a reflex. In fact he was bemused still as to what had taken place.

Even the stars were falling like rain away from him, and Pierrette going with them.

And then there was a fearsome crash, an awful concussion. Stunned, he found himself in the midst of a burst of pressure and shouting.

His father, too drunk to reason—for reason would have informed him he could not possibly reach the toppling child in time —had lunged towards the open window, half-fallen into space himself, and grabbed his son back out of it. Both had plunged thereafter to the floor of the balcony in a welter of pots.

The unique stink of wine on his father's breath and the sound of his mother's wailing, now released, demolished the child, who began to cry.

"We should never have left him—never, *never*. He was walking in his sleep—"

Etiens saw, through his tears, she had forgotten to bring the pastries. Venturing to glance at the balcony, he found the white child had gone.

Gone for good. He never saw her afterwards. But what, he might ask himself, and had done so from time to time, had she been, that apparition? Some dream of fever? Some ghostly thing inhabiting the attic, perhaps a child who had died there in similar circumstances, eager to see another fare as she had fared? Or a conjuration of the Devil, of Monsieur le Prince?

The rhyme had told him. The rhyme knew, apparently. Lady Death, in her three modes— *Elle est trois. Soit! Soit! Soit! Mais La Voleuse*— Yes, what had Pierrette been but a thief, dressed like one, too, or the stagelike presentation of one. A thief of life who would have stolen existence from him by means of a trick.

Etiens, turning a corner, caught himself saying the rhyme once more aloud, the rain entering his mouth with each sentence.

She was three. Fine! Fine! Fine! But the Thief, the Seductress, and Madame Slaughterer— *Ne cherchez pas.*

"Don't seek them out," he said again. Why had he never repeated his macabre story to Armand? "Once, when I was seven . . ." Armand, though probably discrediting the truth of it, might well have been able to use such an idea. Or he himself, the painter—why had he never attempted to depict that terrifying child with her eyes of snow? Nothing but a sketch, tonight, and that swept away.

Etiens checked, raising his head into the shattering tumult of the rain. He swore, but ritually. He had taken a wrong street and brought himself, not to his own lodging, but to that sprawling quarter of steps and crouching shops where France lived with his piano and whatever woman was foolish enough to indulge his parasitism. Looking about, Etiens beheld an alley, and along it the steep stair and the overhanging storey above, which housed the composer. There were lights burning.

(Why am I here? What am I doing here? I feel no amazement at having come here. Do I intend to visit him at this hour of the night? He may not even be there—true, he left the café before me, but most likely he's drinking elsewhere, or with a woman other than whichever woman is up there now, lamenting over his uninterest.)

From the core of the rain and the dark, coincidentally from the overhanging storey that shelled in France's room, a woman began frenziedly to scream.

Leaving the Café Vule before the others, France had not immediately returned to his room above the alley. He had loitered for a few free drinks with a woman he knew, the draper's widow, who lived behind the bourse. By keeping up a romantic fiction that he was almost inclined to go to bed with her—she was a plain, unappetising woman—France had gained many things for nothing, including a selection of astonishing neckties.

Perhaps fifteen minutes before the gilded clock of Notre Dame aux Luminères struck midnight, however, he was toiling up the rickety stairs to the room Jeannette had struggled so thanklessly and ill-advisedly to maintain. He was very drunk, in a fog of drunkenness that frankly did not wish to see beyond itself. So, finding the door unlocked, he did not consider it very much. He himself, storming forth in an angry mood, had most probably left it so. What, after all, might it be anybody's fortune to steal from him? Save the piano, too large and cumbersome for a common thief to shift down the vile staircase.

The piano. His "Negro mistress."

A drunken sneering laugh burst from him. Quite so. His mistress. His cold amour who would render him only the music of others.

He did not pause to light a lamp. Having slammed the door, he careened across the room and plunged his hands down on the keyboard in a blow. The discord jarred his ears, his very brain, and he let loose a string of oaths at her. (At *her*, why not? Why not?) This one female entity who did not court him or help him, and whom he could not dismiss as he had dismissed legions of women, even the submissive Jeannette, clinging like a wretched creeper. Even that bitch Clairisse, who understood him so well and used her understanding to prey on him—she too had been shown the door, and run out of it, weeping and threatening him. And here alone stood his real devil, on her four legs, bestially grinning her discoloured teeth.

France sat down before her, a furious penitent in the darkness. There was only a glimmer, seeping in from a lighted window left unshuttered across the alley, whereby to find his way over the keys. Well then, a piece of bad-tempered Monsieur Beethoven would suit the occasion.

As the chords crashed forth, he thought of neighbours wakened alongside and below, and grinned with malice.

"Wake, wake, *mes enfants!* It is the crack of bloody doom."

Then, halfway through the Beethoven, he lost patience with it and left off.

He squinted down at the keys and his hands clenched on them, and a trickle of notes went through his head. He started upright, listening, avid to follow the insistent impulse—and something distracted him, something at which he gazed, puzzled, mislaying the thread of melodic harmony, trying to detain it, trying also to make sense of what he saw, failing at both.

The inadequate second-hand illumination falling in his room from the window had been describing one panel of the piano, a dim flush of light, which he himself sporadically shut out through the movements of his body. But now the light on the panel, undisturbed by him, was curiously dividing itself in two portions about an area of darkness.

It was a singular, abstract darkness, a kind of hump, that slowly, incongruously—and quite formlessly—was rising upward, upward—

France turned and came to his feet clumsily, upsetting the chair as he did so.

There was really something there, across the room, a darkness darker than the darkness, and the open window behind it making it darker yet. It continued to rise up. He was peculiarly put in mind of dough rising in an oven.

"Who is it?" France demanded. Possibilities, laughable or unpleasant, suggested themselves. Instead of blundering forward to seize the intruder, he fumbled for a match. He considered perhaps Jeannette had come back to plead with him, or conceivably some creditor had lain in wait.

The shape had reached its required elevation and was now in stasis. What was that? There had been a muddy flash, an indoor lightning against the rainy window.

Then France had the match and struck it wildly.

The flame exploded like the detonation of a bomb, then fell through the air, a blazing leaf, and went out. France was speechless. He had seen something he did not believe in, and his terror could not cry out. Nevertheless he was stumbling backwards, attempting to reach the door.

He did not reach it.

The screaming had stopped almost as soon as it began, but people had flung open windows and were glaring out into the night. At the end of the alley loomed a vehicle, shrouded in rain. And at the foot of the stairs leading to France's room were two police, who refused to let Etiens by. A small crowd, others who inhabited the building, had gathered on the landing above, and eventually Etiens heard a ghastly moaning noise break out among these people overhead, and then the tramp of persons coming down.

As he stood there, nauseated by apprehension and distress, Etiens was soon able to watch a white-faced young woman, rigid with an unnatural, maniacal composure, escorted by police out into the rain. He would learn from the newspapers in the morning that this had been Clairisse Gabrol, the former mistress of an impoverished composer who had ceased to care for her despite her gifts of money, and whom she had subsequently murdered. Her choice of weapon would cause some comment. In the gloom by the stair-foot, Etiens had not seen how her dress and her coat were patterned, here and there. But shortly the body was brought down on the first stage of its journey to the morgue. Even through the covering, Etiens could not fail to remark the quantities of blood. In the doorway one of the policemen, who had been in the room above, doubled over and vomited helplessly into a puddle.

The scene in the room would later be described as resembling a butcher's shop. Etiens would read this sentence coldly. He would not paint for several months.

*Et Madame Tueuse—*

The neighbour whose cries had alerted Etiens as she entered for the first into France's room had summoned the police. The insane piano recital had woken her; she had been on the very landing outside the pianist's door, gathering herself to knock, and upbraid him —when a succession of unidentifiable yet strangely disturbing noises sent her instead to seek aid. She had not been able to explain her conviction that something evil had taken place. It was retentive though unconscious memory that had informed her. The analogy of the butcher's shop had not been random, and she, who had had cause to frequent such establishments often, recognised, unknowingly, the familiar, unmistakable sound that had no business in a human dwelling by night.

There was no other clue. France himself had not cried out, even when the meat cleaver, which Clairisse had cunningly stolen some hours before, severed his left hand at the wrist, his right hand midway between the wrist and the knuckles. Possibly he had peered after them, his pianist's hands, in the darkness, perturbed by such sudden and absolute loss. But then the cleaver passed through his neck, efficient as any guillotine, and the moment for all perturbation was done.

So it had been only Clairisse, one of so many abused and silly women who had loved or thought they loved, and suffered for it. One, nevertheless, who was different, who wished that France should suffer, too. Only Clairisse, then, who with the colossal strength of the maddened had hacked her lover into segments and strewn these about the floor. Only Clairisse who had been, for these minutes, Madame Tueuse—the Slaughterer.

But it had not, in the fractional ignition of his match, been Clairisse that France saw posed before him.

She was very tall, at least, one might assume, two metres in height. In the best tradition of her trade, a tradition adopted more by the military than the civilian branch of her fraternity, she was clothed in pulsing madder. Splashed by life-blood, after the merest moment, she would again appear immaculate. It would seem her long-sleeped gown was dyed in blood to begin with. Her head, naturally, was also fastidiously covered. The scarlet headdress called to mind the starched winged wimple of a nun of some unusual order. Held in this frame her face was shrivelled, blanched, and sightless. Genuinely sightless, for the eyelids were firmly sealed, sealed in a way that implied they could not, for whatever reason, be uplifted. The hands were also white, they would show the blood when it splashed. They were sensitive, the hands, long-fingered and slim, in fact quite beautiful: the hands of an artist. For one could tell from the implements hanging at her sash that her method was not always as brutish as on this occasion. There were many knives of varying scope; some daggers; an awl; even a solitary, though very elongated, needle; a cut-throat razor, scissors; a shard of mirror; a hat-pin—and much more, not all of it instantly to be named. Everything was finely honed and highly polished. Cared for. In perfect working order.

He saw her come towards him, but only as a shadow. There was not enough light in the room after the match had fallen to show how, at the first slicing stroke, the eyes of the woman opened wide after all. Each is a transparent void, shaped like a little bowl, and like a little bowl each one begins to fill with a pure and scintillant red.

And somehow, even without light, he did see, did see, did—
Until all seeing stopped.

As the clock of Our Lady of Lights struck one, beginning the new day in its blackness, Armand woke from a comfortless doze. The room, his own, was veiled over rather than revealed by its low-burning lamp. The bed, a stale shambles on which he had thrown himself, now repelled him, forcing him to sit, and next to stand up. On the table no manuscript lay to exalt or reproach him. There was, however, something.

Armand looked, his eyes enlarged, as if he had never before seen such an array, though he himself had bought and amalgamated these articles yesterday. Or the day before that.

It was stupid, then, to regard them with such misgiving. Indeed, the arrangement was rather attractive, something Etiens might have liked to paint. The utensils themselves were beautiful.

The preparation was not even very complex. To achieve what he wished would take a modicum of time.

Armand moved to the window and flung it wide on the black and rainy night. In the rain, the city itself might seem to lie beneath the river. (We are then, the drowned, already lost, yet measuring out our schemes, our prayers, as if they might be valid even now.)

Across the city, the bloody corpse that had been France was being trundled on its route to the morgue. Armand did not know this, nor that, some minutes before, bemused and soaking wet, Etiens had passed below, looking up at the poet's drearily lighted window—and finding himself completely unable to proceed to Armand's door, had gone away again.

The poet stared into the external dark. Roofs and chimneys held back the sky. Here and there a ghost of light, like a flaw in vision, evidenced some other vigil, its purpose concealed.

Armand did not know of the death of France, nor of Etiens's white child. Possessed of these things, coupling them with his own oppression, his own knowledge of where the night, like a phantom barge, was taking him, the poet would have presented this history quite differently. It would have been essential, for example, to provide some linking device, some cause, a romantic mathematic as to why such elements had fused within those hours sloughed from the great clock between the striking of seven and of three in the morning that was yet to come. What should it have been? A ring, possibly, with a curse upon it, given to Etiens in his infancy, inducing thereafter the first image of death: the white-eyed Pierrette; passed to France in disbelief or spite, summoning the second, the monstrous nun in her wimple of blood. While Armand, drawing the ring from the portioned body of France, would thereby unwittingly or in despair arouse the final aspect of the appalling triad.

But Armand, a character entangled by events, and not their reporter, had no say in the structure, apparently random—though immensely terrible—of what is taking place.

What then should one say? Merely perhaps that most children will, at some point, behave with dangerous foolishness, as if led on by imps, but it is only that they know no better. And that the Pierrette was an analogy for this which Etiens had fabricated for himself from a feverish dream and a patch of moonlight through a dirty window. And then, that France had suffered an hallucination invoked by drunken horror—if he had even seen the thing which was described. No proof of this is offered. Maybe he saw nothing but Clairisse, the stolen cleaver in her hand. There was a gruesome murder, a crime of cold passion. That was enough. And for Armand, the poet, he had perceived a shadow in the half-lit mist at the end of the bridge, a shadow of malnutrition and self-doubt and inner yearning. And in a moment he would have every reason to see her again, as he would see many things that thereafter would leave his work like a riot of jewels, inextinguishable, profound, terrifying, indisputable, cast in the wake of his own wreckage.

La Mort, Lady Death, La Voleuse, La Tueuse. The trick, the violent blade. And then the third means to destruction, the seductive death who visited poets in her irresistible caressing silence, with the petals of blue flowers or the blue wings of insects pasted on the lids of her eyes, and: See, your flesh also, taken to mine, can never decay. And this will be true, for the flesh of Armand, becoming paper written over by words, will endure as long as men can read.

And so he left the window. He prepared, carefully, the opium that would melt away within him the iron barrier that no longer yielded to thought or solitude or wine. And when the drug began to live within its glass, for an instant he thought he saw a drowned girl floating there, her hair swirling in the smoke. . . . Far away, in another universe, the clock of Notre Dame aux Luminères struck twice.

After a little while, he opened the door, and looked out at the landing beyond. There in the nothing of the dark he sensed her, and moved aside, welcoming her with an ironic courtesy into his room, his bones.

She was even more beautiful, now he saw her closely, than when he noted her at the end of the bridge.

Her skin was so pale he could gaze through it to a sort of tender, softly blooming radiance. Her eyes were mysteriously sombre. As her cloak unfurled, he observed the ice-blue flowers on her breast, and the corsetting of her bodice where La Danse Macabre was depicted in sable embroidery.

She seated herself with a smile before him, and he, his hand already moving of its own volition, as if possessed, began to write.

La Séductrice was his death. The drug would kill him in a year, having burned out his brain, nervous system, and marrow. But his spirit would be left behind him in the words he had now begun to find. We are not given life to cast it aside, but neither is life to be lived for life's sake only. What cries aloud within us must be allowed its voice. Or so it seemed to him, dimly, as the seascapes of the opium overwhelmed him, and the caverns of stars, and the towering crystal cities higher than heaven.

She is three: Thief, Butcher, Seducer. Do not seek her out. She is all around you, in the blowing leaves, the cloud across the moon, the sweet sigh behind your ear, the scent of earth, the whisper of a sleeve. If she is to be yours, she will come to you.

Across the river the clock sounded again.

Un, deux, trois.

# FOREIGN SKINS

**A**FTER THE SUMMER RAINS, THE ROAD UP TO THE BUNGA-low was for a while a river of red mud. As the mud dried, drowned things came to light; rats, a long-tailed bird, a mongoose.

"There was also the body of an old woman," said the man, uncaringly at his breakfast in the veranda. "A corpse some of them made a whole lot of fuss about."

"David," said the woman.

The man, her husband, glanced at her in slight though exaggerated inquiry. "What about David?"

"He's listening, dear."

"Let him listen."

"But Chaver, dear—"

"Death's a fact. Isn't it, old chap?" Across the table, the eight-year-old boy, pale still despite the heat of a mighty sun, nodded. "That's right," said the man. "My God, Evelyn. He's got to get used to it. He'll see it all round him in this place."

"Yes," said Evelyn, and she touched her napkin to her lips.

"What was I saying?" the man she had called Chaver asked them. When they could not or would not tell him, he shook out his paper, somewhat late as it always was up here, and began to read, dismissing them.

That evening, as the stars were lit across the sky and grass-hoppers whirred in the bushes, a woman came up the garden's impeccable path, between the orange trees, and halted by the rho-dodendron under the veranda. Dark as the dusk, making no move-ment, she stood there for some while, until the doors of the dining room were opened. Then the thick amber lamplight fell on her and there was shouting.

"What in God's name is all this noise?" demanded Chaver Finlay, striding up to the doors in his punctilious dinner jacket.

"A beggar woman," said the house servant who had shouted. "I tell her, she must go."

The man looked. He saw the woman by the ghostly rhododen-dron tree, in the light a creature of darkness, which folded its hands and bowed to him, and said in perfect English, "Lord, I seek shelter. I lost my home in the rains, and all I possess. I have been wandering a great time." She was clad, he saw, in a piece of filthy sackcloth, probably come on at the wayside. Under the rag, she appeared sup-ple and beautiful. Her hair was plaited into a black snake-tail that fell behind her. Her face was a fine one, with a delicately rimmed Asiatic mouth, the nose somewhat long but slenderly shaped, her eyes large and wide-spaced. On her wide low forehead, suggestive of intelligence and calm, there was no mark of caste. Nor did she have any jewelry, even to a glass bangle or a silver stud in the nos-tril.

"Well," said Chaver Finlay, who was rather fascinated by these women. "Well. Go to the kitchen. Tell them I said you get food. And see if Asha can't find you something to wear."

"The lord is very kind."

He liked, the man, to be called "lord," as they so often called him, in their own tongue or his. Tall and well-made, deeply tanned, hair and eyes black as the hair and eyes of any native, he found himself now, as often, stimulated by the contact of this world, so unlike his beginnings, so appealing to his spirit—or what he took to be his spirit. His work, which had to do with local gov-ernment, was dry and uninspiring. He saw little connection be-tween the work and the people, who continually intrigued him, that the work was ideally meant to serve.

Sitting at dinner, too, he compared Evelyn irresistibly and with-out quite knowing he did so, to the indigenous womanhood. Alas, poor Evelyn. How utterly unlike. Unlike to such an extent that it was almost a joke. Thin, but without any of the angular heroic grace of the village woman. Fair, and suffering for her fairness, burned a dreadful pink that was not becoming, even when heavily powdered. The alien sun was not kind to Evelyn. It seemed to have bled out the colour of her eyes which once, in a cooler clime, had enchanted him for two whole months. And the boy . . . the boy seemed set to go the same way. "Eat up your meat, David," the man said absently. Milksop. Could he have bred a milksop? Little and thin and pale, if not yet burnt. The blue eyes were so rarely raised to meet his father's, the father did not quite remember how they looked. Of course, Evelyn had spent a lot of time with the boy, and there were no other boys nearby for him to play with, to get some sense and some backbone thumped into him. Except the native children. But that was out of the question.

When the meal was over, the servant brought the decanter and glass and a box of cigarettes. Applying the lighter deftly, the servant said, "That woman is outside. She wishes to come in and speak to the Sahib, but I have said—"

"Whatever you said, go and tell her she may."

Evelyn lifted her sandy eyebrows. She got a word of explanation, before the vagabond entered.

Finlay had a desire to draw in a great breath of pleasure at her apparition. Asha had obviously given of her best, an outfit of singing green and saffron, which the stranger wore as if it were her own. Even the black, black hair had been oiled before rebraiding, and the oil's sombre perfume seemed to glow inside his nostrils like the whisky on his palate.

She gave him again the obeisance, her eyes unlowered, huge black coals with all the lamplight held in them in two little golden beads.

"I have come only to thank you," she said.

Finlay lounged a fraction. "But you'd thank me more if you could stay."

She said nothing, and the other woman in the room gave a quick sharp rustle, like something in undergrowth. Finlay did not look at either of them. He refilled his glass.

"I assume you'd like to, because you told me you lost everything in the flood. Even your . . . mother, would it have been?" There was a silence. When he looked up again, the dark ghost shook her head slowly. "It's just," he said, "an old woman was found about half a mile down the road, dead in the mud. Without clothing. The body was badly decomposed," Evelyn made a verbal noise this time, "and rather curiously—but of course, the kites had got there, too, by then—" Evelyn's noise was louder. "I merely thought, two strangers in these parts might have been travelling together."

"No, lord."

Finlay smiled, basking in that word.

"Well then, if we kept you, what could you do?"

"Really," said Evelyn. "I don't think—"

"Now, now," he said, all velvet, "we can't turn the homeless away, can we?" And she became once more dumb, only a pity it wasn't permanent. His dark ghost meanwhile had turned her eyes aside. She had fixed them, those lenses of coal and gold, on his son. Ah, yes. The surest way to the father's good graces, through his male offspring. As for David, he looked quite mesmerised, the little brute. "My son," said Chaver Finlay to the woman, "is something of a dunce. At languages, particularly. Our dialects round here fox him, don't they, old chap? On the other hand, your English is excellent, and I heard you exchanging words with my man, out there, in a splendid version of local lingo. Perhaps you might be helpful in this way. Do you think you could teach the boy something?" (*And I'm sure you could teach him a great deal. Only he's a touch young for that. I, though . . .* ) He only felt Evelyn on this occasion, her loud protests were mute, a sort of vibration. Evelyn did not like the new schoolteacher. But David did. His small pallid face was full of expectation. And Chaver liked her a lot.

"If you wish," she said, "I will try." She went on looking at David, and then slowly she smiled at him. Chaver Finlay would have preferred to have that smile himself, instead of its being wasted on the brat. But never mind. She would smile at the man soon enough. He offered her board and lodging now, and a small sum in *annas*, which she accepted as if it neither insulted nor amazed her, nor mattered; part of the Eastern Act, as he sometimes termed it.

"Come up to the house after breakfast, about nine o'clock. All right? My wife will see David's in proper order for you. What are we to call you?"

That brought her eyes back to him. She regarded him for some moments, as if considering. *Why, she's inventing a name for herself*, he thought. *Are you that notorious, my beauty?* And he resolved to check this tomorrow in the official offices, which was an oddly exciting idea, and would make a nice change from memoranda on irrigation and outbreaks of fever.

Then she said the name, and he missed it and had to ask her to repeat what she had said, as if testing her.

"Agnini," she told him, with no trace of reluctance.

"Oh," he said, teasingly, "then will you keep lightning from striking the house, O Daughter of Fire? That should be worth a *pa'i* or so more."

# II

He was a lonely child, lonely not so much for companionship as for peace. His mother was alternately irritated by him, or fussing him, calling him "Davy" when they were alone together, a strange intimacy he had come to find repellent. But then, she also referred to his father as "Daddy." He was afraid of his father, of course. Mostly, these feelings were instinctive. Only when he had got out onto the withered lawn, able to lie hidden in a bush and watch a bird or small animal, or just the sky, did he discover quietness. Sometimes, taken up for a ride on his father's horse (terrified), he had noticed the native children herding cattle, fighting or playing in the floury dust. They seemed as unlike himself as the free things which darted through the trees. Although he had left it less than a year before, he was forgetting Europe. The spot it occupied in his memory was a sort of sheet of whiteness, foggy, like an English winter sky. His mother sheltered him from this other sky as if it would hurt him, as, sure enough, once or twice it had hurt her, making her very sick so he was frightened and cried. "For heaven's sake, David, don't snivel!" his father said. The big tanned hand had caught itself back from a hard slap. It was clearly wrong to thrash one's son for concern at his mother's health. Punishment was reserved for deserving causes, failure at lessons, or lies to cover such failures or others that promised trouble. David was not a clever liar. He was not clever at anything. He had never asked as yet, What am I? Where do I fit in this unwieldy, unfriendly scheme of things? But because he did not seem cut out for life, obscurely he blamed himself. Everyone else managed. The fault must be in him.

When he saw sinuous motion coming through the orange trees, he watched it surreptitiously. Since it is possible to be in love at any age, David was in love with the adult person who had named herself Agnini. And since he loved her, he was rather afraid of her, and afraid, intuitively, of being disappointed in her.

Evelyn, who had left him there after breakfast, had admonished her child in various ways. She herself did not want to confront the native woman. To Evelyn's eyes, Agnini was equally ugly and a threat. Thus the white wife ran to organise a bridge afternoon, abandoning matters to the wishes of the husband now already gone off to the male world of work, and to his allotted governess. Over the cards, Evelyn was prepared to say, gaily, "Guess what, suddenly we have an *ayah!* Oh, of course it's silly, so we know whose notion it is, don't we? Chaver's. You know what he is." And they did know what he was, too, some of them. The ladies of the area much admired Mr. Chaver Finlay, who, stray as he would, was still Evelyn's lawful property. Not that he had strayed much with his own kind, she thought. No, it was elsewhere that Chaver's black eyes turned, after the black-eyed foreign women of this other planet, India.

The little boy looked up as Agnini's cool shade fell upon him. "Greetings," she said to him in Hindi. Pleased that he understood, he said in English, shyly, "Hallo." And then Agnini laughed. Her teeth were as white as forgotten English snow. Entranced, David let her take his hand and lead him off the veranda, away to the shrubs and trees of the garden. Here, in his domain, which had long spelled release and relief, which he did not mind sharing with her since it seemed hers already, they sat down. In English, without preliminary, Agnini began to tell him a story. David listened, and as he listened he watched her. In the slanting sunlight she was like a shadow, and as she spoke she made lovely, luminous gesticulations with her hands and neck and head, swaying slightly like a flower on a stalk. Now and then, in the way of the story, she would say, "Attend, O Beloved." And each time he would start very slightly, as if his mind had wandered, though it had not. It was grand to be told stories, though how it would help him master the ghastly chaos of another language he did not know.

"Attend, O Beloved," Agnini said.

David attended.

His blue eyes were wide. These eyes were so far the only beauty he had, the only sign he might grow up into a handsome man, his mother's lightness of complexion and his father's coarse, effective looks, refined into something much better.

"'Come,' said the god," said Agnini, "'come, be valorous, and descend into the city of the wise and wicked ones. Who shall hurt thee there, seeing thou hast my protection? Thou shalt behold marvels. And maybe thou mayest recover what the shape-changer stole.'"

Evelyn, who had sneaked out after all, in spurious search of a dead rosebush, paused to eavesdrop. *Useless,* she thought with satisfaction. *What good is it to sit there like a monkey and chatter at the boy in Hindi, when he can't speak three words of it?*

"Two weeks. She's not teaching him anything. She simply lives off our fare, like a parasite. Like they all do, given an ha'p'orth of encouragement."

"What does she do with him all day, then?" Finlay inquired lazily.

"She tells him fairy stories, I believe. Or rather, heathen myths. Only yesterday I heard him singing—howling is more like it—some perfectly grim sort of chant about Krishna, or Vishnu. Or somebody."

"Oh? Singing it in English, do you mean?"

"No, of course—" Evelyn paused, "not," she added lamely. "Oh, it was in some dialect or other, but he'd learnt it off parrot fashion. He didn't understand it, which was probably just as well. You know, dear, I'm very concerned about David's religious—"

"Just a minute," Finlay said. He got up from his desk, where Evelyn had disturbed him over a hunting journal and a pile of untouched paperwork lugged home for show from the offices. He walked past his wife, one and a quarter feet the taller, and went out onto the veranda. David, a small uncamouflaged white figure in his shirt and shorts, was pottering among the tamarisks. At his father's shout, the boy jumped as if at a shot, and turned a frightened face towards the house. The man beckoned vigorously, and the child came quickly with the forced speed of total helpless unwillingness. When he had almost reached the steps, Finlay barked at him: *"Jaldi, bebkuf! Bhagio!"*

*"Jee, Pitaji, mai bhagta hu—"* said David, and broke into a trot. Then faltered and stopped dead.

"Well, I'll be damned," said Chaver Finlay. He stood staring at his son, an evil grin splitting his face and revealing the unattractive teeth less strong than the rest of him. "What did you just say?"

"You—you told me to run, and I said I would—"

"In Hindi."

"Y-yes. I-I think . . . so."

"Don't think so, you did. Accent quite decent, too. Well done," said Finlay, delighted at it all. In Hindi once more, plus a heavy dose of the local dialect, he added to David, "And did she teach it thee?"

"Yes, Father," David said in English. It was a fact, he was never more uncertain than when his father seemed pleased by him. It happened so seldom.

And sure enough, Finlay scowled. "God damn you, boy! Answer as you're supposed to."

Evelyn shuddered at the blasphemies, retreating to the wall of the house. David replied again, rapidly, in the other words and syntax which were coming to seem quite familiar.

Chaver laughed. He turned on Evelyn, laughing in her face. "You see, Cold Comfort, our Aggi's worth her weight in rupees. If she can get the little owl to learn something—my God. I'll go over to their quarters and tell her she's done a good job. By God, I will."

Evelyn had continued to shrink away and had now shrunk right back into her husband's study. She watched him stride off through the brassy film of late day and into the dark of the *peepul* trees that hid the servants' dwellings from the bungalow.

The other side of those trees, almost instantly, he came on her who had named herself Agnini. She sat by a brown wall on a little faded mat of Asha's, cleaning her hair in the old way, by rubbing it with rice, then combing it through and through. He stood and watched her, leaning on a tree and hidden from the house, feeling his own power course through him, his blood stirring in the broad light and open as it rarely did now in an airless night bedroom.

Although she had acknowledged him politely, Agnini continued with her task. He took this as a kind of flirting.

"I came to congratulate you," he said at last. "We'd better give you a raise, Lady of Fires. David starts to speak tolerable native talk."

She nodded, a small bow, replied otherwise not at all. Finlay inhaled the scents of the earth and the tree, and the wholesome savage aroma of her hair with the rice rubbed through it. His investigations had offered no clue. There were no rumours of a female criminal at large in the area, or anywhere near it. Maybe they would come. Then he might say to her, Ah, Agnini-who-is-not. Now I know you. That game could be fun to play. For the moment he contented himself with, "But your husband, surely, must be pining for you."

She did stop her combing then, looking at him stilly. It was an odd look, and he was not sure he cared for it. Presently she said something that did not really sound like Hindi, and which he could not understand.

He guessed. "Dead? Is he? But he'll be back, won't he? He'll reincarnate, and fast, I'd think, to get with you again. Or are you a musulman woman, only one life and away to paradise? No, you're not that. Thank God. The times I've come out on a fine evening and been confronted by a row of their men's holy bums stuck up, faces at the other end to Mecca—"

Agnini rose. The movement was remarkable, like a dancer's, yet even more fluid—the word mellifluous came to mind. Even to Chaver Finlay's mind. Yes, flowing honey. But she had given him the obeisance, turned and gone in, flowingly stooping at the low doorway. Dismissed, the man stood and wondered, angry and tickled. Yes, yes, honey and fire, it would be a pleasure to have a rough wooing with this one, who seemed not to notice him as male flesh. And he had the sudden image of a darkness before him, redolent with the perfumes of night, and eyes and lips and strong hands on him holding him to insistent deeds of darkness, all awash with smoky hair and the elixir of a foreign skin.

# III

"Is it dead?" asked David, staring at the little rumpled creature on the lawn.

"*Yes.* Oh, come away at once. I'll send them to clear it. Don't be so ghoulish, Davy."

David did not know what this English word "ghoulish" meant, but knew better than to ask at such a moment. Obviously it was bad, obviously he was guilty of it. He walked quickly off to escape culpability and his mother as one, and sat down under a tamarisk. He watched Evelyn emit an exasperated sigh, and scurry in the other direction to find a servant. David was close to tears. The little animal was so beautifully made, so complex, the tiny pointed face, and the wonderful squirrelish tail, and all these marvels wasted now in death. It was of a category he had been inclined to call, in the plural, mongeese, since it was mongoose in the singular, and a plural goose became geese not gooses. The error had last summer earned him a light stinging cuff from his father's riding glove.

Soon, sitting under the tamarisk, he was able to watch one of the men come and sweep up and take away the mongoose who did not become geese in the plural, and would now become nothing at all except compost. David, unseen, gave in and wept. He wept with a breaking heart for all the sadness and cruelty of a world he scarcely knew, this land of giants.

Then, relaxed, lying facedown on the grass, he fell asleep. He woke once to hear the muttering of servants close by in a tongue he could now follow by means that were so simple they were inexplicable. What did these people say? Talk of the mongoose. Young and glossy, it had had no mark upon it. Of what had it died? No, not a touch, or an ill-wish, even, but the mere concentration of inimical presence. A presence not to be fought with, only to be bowed down to, and so, nature in revolt, an ultimate bowing down in death. After all, even the cobras kept out of the garden now, overawed, though of course they would come, if desired. But there was no need. One was careful. One did what was wanted. Even the Goan cook, a Catholic to the tips of his moustache, was courteous. And in turn, courtesy was given. Her purposes were otherwise; the male child. It seemed the lawless magic of the very young, or the bewildered anguish of the very young, this had drawn her here.

*Me? Are they talking about me? But about who else then? Is it—?*

The noon sun beat on the drumskin of the garden, dark-red behind his eyelids, and the voices melted away and he curled on his side and slept again, dreamless, which might mean only that he did not recall his dreams.

When he woke the sun had moved a little, burning on the linked arms of the *peepul* trees. A yard off Agnini sat, braiding her hair. David rolled over and lay watching her, smiling sleepily, for she had come to find him and she was beautiful and he loved her much.

"Beloved," said Agnini, "tonight I must leave thee."

David's entire body altered with distress.

"When wilt thou return?" he asked her, using the fluent fast speech, the inner tongue that was the core of her teaching.

"Return I do not," said Agnini.

"Not come back? Not ever?" he whispered, in English now.

"No, Beloved. Never to thee."

"Why must you go?" he cried, his pain too large yet for further crying, the adult pain of loss. "Did I do something to make you angry with—"

"The doing is not thine, Beloved. Nor yet. This night, another than thee will anger me. Then shall I go away."

In English still, though she had kept to the other tongue, he cried out: "Can't I—couldn't I—please *don't*—" and fell silent. For neither did English have, it seemed, the sentences he needed. To tell her the nameless hell that was his existence, and which she had filled in moments with motes of light and notes of joy. That if the motes and notes of light were to be taken from him, now he had touched them, he could not bear it. That, though he knew none of those mighty emotive phrases by which poets describe the deepest human despair, and the self-annihilation the deepest human despair invites humanity to embrace, yet that was all which remained of him if she were gone. He gazed at her, and though he did not realise it, his eyes told her everything that he or words could not. If perhaps even she had needed to be told such things.

In the garden there was now no noise at all. Beasts and birds slept in the last of the great heat of midday, and men slept or lay vanquished. The grass itself, the leaves on the trees, did not move. Even the wind slept somewhere, high in the hills, under the river, under a stone. There came then the great coolness of that great heat, which is not coolness but only the accepting of the heat, and therefore comfort in it. This David felt, and he sighed. There had come to him also the acceptance of pain, the finish of that business the doctrine of Jesus Christ conceives of as a kicking against tearing barbs, and the doctrine of the *Bhagavad-Gītā* as the blown and scattered ships of broken thought.

"Yes," said Agnini, as though she had read such sensations from him, "thou art brave, and thou shalt be wise, strong, and blessed. Come, I will show thee truths."

When she rose, David got up. She held out to him her beautiful hand that was like a sombre articulated flower. She led him away.

It seemed they went out of the garden, and onto the road, white and iron-hard now, and then they walked towards the open uplands, where David was forbidden ever to go alone. But David made no protest, did not even worry over this departure. The comforting envelopment of the heat was so intense, time itself seemed to have stopped. They might travel as they pleased, he and this woman that he loved as a mother and as an abstract dream of future love, and as a spirit. No one would come after them, or could find them. No one would ever know.

And a considerable distance seemed to hurry by them, under his enclosed shoes that he must wear against snakes, and under her bare feet, their darkness powdered with white dust.

So they were up in the hills where all was unfamiliar, being rocks and pitiless brown slopes, and an endless blue horizon beyond.

"Dost thou recall," Agnini said, "the story I told thee first, of the young student, and the serpent that stole from him, vanishing into the earth, and of how the man pursued the serpent, when Indra had opened for him the way?"

David nodded. Glancing down, he saw a slender rupture in the ground.

"See," she said, "the serpent's way to the city of his kind."

"But snakes don't have cities!"

"Thou hast forgotten the story, O Beloved."

He looked up at her, and watched her, the gentle movements of her hands, her body swaying like a stem in water. He remembered then the story, which was of the *Nagas*, that fabulous race of Serpent-People, demons; nearly gods, and of their tricks upon men, and their several cities underground.

David kneeled down by the hole. "Does it really go all the way into a city, Agnini?"

She smiled, and touched his blond skull.

"I have said, I will show thee truths. Thou art not afraid?"

"Not—if you'll be there too."

"I am here and shall be there. And now," she said, "I open the way."

And she spat. Her spit, like a bright star, went shooting straight as an arrow into the hole. At which, the rockside crumbled and fell inwards to a yawning nothingness, and he was drawn softly down with it.

## IV

He had not slept, or lost consciousness, yet he seemed to be waking up. There was a darkness, but not as one thinks of blindness; he was not afraid. He was standing, too, so he had not actually fallen, though he had thought he fell, slowly and easily, down into this place. And he was alone. Nevertheless, he believed he knew exactly what he must do next, and this, in a life of uncertainties, was such a reassuring conviction he obeyed it.

As he walked forward, another conviction began to come. *If I go on*, he thought, thinking in English still, *something will happen*. But he was not alarmed. It was only right and proper to go on. To go on was essential, like breathing. He went on, and the thing duly happened. At first he did not know what it was. It was as if he began to stretch, very pleasant and natural, and then as he stretched he threw off and cast something away from him, like the sheet on the bed. And then it was more as if he broke through water. *Ah*, he thought. *That's better. Much.* But then the feeling started once more, more imperative and more pleasant and more urgent, and he began to run through the serene darkness, his arms spread out, with no notion of obstacles, and met the feeling head-on and ran through it, and this time it was like jumping through a hoop of crackling paper.

*Now I shall be free of bonds*, he thought. *They will drop behind me.*

And once again he passed through the invisible barriers, and then once again, and again, and again, and there was almost a pain each time now, but a pain that was good and clean.

"Thus," he thought, "thou art no more, and yet thou art." He thought in Hindi now, or in the older language that was Hindi and was not, which Agnini had taught him. He raised his arms over his head and felt strength and fiery courage, and laughed aloud. And it was no longer the laughter of a child. He looked about him then, and by the light of a vague warm glow that was coming in ahead of him, he glimpsed the pale sloughed garments that he had shed, five or six or seven times, on the rocky floor. They were the skins he had cast, the empty bodies of boyhood, adolescence, and youth. All these deaths that are the sum of life, the endless reincarnation of self.

As he advanced towards the light, the one who had been David Finlay, eight years of age, was a man. And the man was tall and strong as though from two decades of faultless exercise, repose, and nourishment, beneath the mighty sun which had deeply tanned him and bleached his fair hair to a golden banner. While under the crown of the golden hair the man's brain, innocent and educated, understood everything, and was made by it amused, and reverent. So he walked out of the tunnel into the light.

The opening was the shore of a lake, or an enormous cistern, under arching rock like a dove-grey sky. Light came from the rock, and from the water, which was crystalline, and out of which grew huge crimson lotuses, standing on their stalks well clear of the surface, like inverted parasols. Across the water, through the lotus forest, he saw the flash and glitter of the towers and walls of the underground city.

Though he had no intermediary memories of his own life after the age of eight, for he had *had* no life, yet his adult brain was equipped with adult knowledge. He was able to gauge the distance from shore to city as a little less than half a mile, and to predict he could swim it, too. He knew his stamina and abilities, none of which he had himself built up or learned, but which had evolved for him in the casting of the skins—making him what he could be, would be. With a joyous, reckless control, qualities never his till now, he dived in a graceful powerful swoop into the water, cleaving it, passing through its silken undertones, and coming up again with the crimson lotuses brushing his forehead and eyelids.

He swam, without effort, along the natural lanes among the flowers. The water gleamed, and seemed to do him good, like that of a mineral spring. The shining city of the *Nagas* came nearer and nearer through sparkling showers of water-drops. Presently, his fingers brushed a flight of great steps, brilliant with coloured painting, which went up to a platform. Here there was a wall, crowded with exquisite and complex carvings. In the wall there was an opening crowned by a horseshoe shape, and without doors. The way was barred only by pillars of red sandstone.

He drew himself from the lake, shook away the water, and was instantly dry. As he climbed the marble towards the walls and their opening, he heard the sound of the city for the first time. It was a wonderful sound, of music mingled with action, and seemed imbued by energy and interest. Cities of men did not have this sound.

When he reached the platform, he saw that the seven sandstone pillars rose far up over his head, and each was roped by a serpent, living and golden, every one of which stared at him from its topaz eyes.

He made an obeisance to each of the seven. He had no right here, save the right of invitation, the rights of love and magic. The serpents were each large enough to crush him, but none had made a hostile move, only watched him as he approached.

He was perhaps nine strides from the opening they guarded, able to glimpse through it the extraordinary masonry of the city, when the serpents altered their positions on the pillars. Then each came sliding down. As they touched the marble of the platform they were changed. So he saw the *Nagas* as the carvings often show them. Upright on their tails of golden plates, sinuous as rope, they were from the waist upward almost men. The man-part was dark-

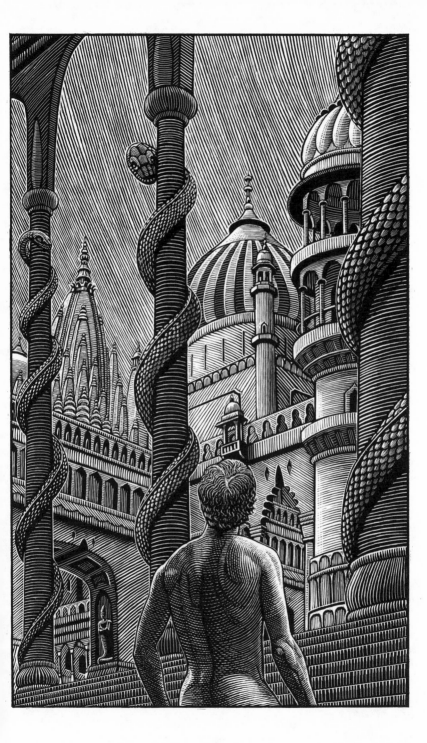

complexioned, the musculature formidable, and hung at breast and arms with gold and huge polished gems. The dark faces smiled, as in the carvings they do, but cruelly, stilly, the long mouths closed. And the large eyes, black and bright as certain of the jewels they wore, were without any white. Each head was cased in a diadem or helmet of gold, and behind head and shoulders there rose, like phantom wings or the plumed lily of the fleur-de-lis, a triplex black and gold formation of serpents, hoods spread wide in the rage display of a striking cobra.

It was the snake-man of the central seventh pillar who spoke, and as he did so his double tongue, slick black as a sloe, flickered in his mouth.

"Thou standst by a city of the Serpent-People, of the limitless realm of the Great King Takshak. Thy kind is unwelcome here. What seekest thou?"

"A woman of thy people, known to me."

The snake-men glared from their wicked eyes.

"Art a fool, thou. What is thy name, Fool, and who thy fool's protector, that thou darest so seek one of our race, naked and unarmed, among the thrice-weaponed, the crushers, the venomtoothed, the shape-changers, *we?*"

He now knew that the name "Agnini" would be of no use here—it was a game she had played, an English anagram of her merely racial name, *Nagini*. He knew also that his own English name was useless, as the English concept of God was useless. But who in the Indian Pantheon could he claim?

Before he could speak and maybe blunder, a woman's voice came from within the gateway.

"Canst thou not see, Cunning Ones, which Guardian he has? He is the Lord Darvinda, of the Kashatriya. His Patron is therefore Indra Vajri, whose wrath we have felt before. Let him by, my gentle brothers. He is here at my request."

Then the man-snakes turned away and flung themselves in corkscrews round the pillars, and became all snake again. There, between the seventh and sixth of them, stood the *Nagini* who had been hired for *annas* to teach a white child dialects.

She wore a crimson drapery sewn with gold discs. Her arms and throat and ankles were ringed with silver and soft gold, and clasps of gold and red coral and redder rubies were woven like fires in her hair. On her forehead was a star that seemed to have fallen out of heaven, and in her ears two more. Her breasts were bare, but for two white flowers. The palms of her hands were hennaed, and her fingernails paler than pearls.

She was so beautiful he could not immediately speak to her, but he greeted her with respect. He was not ashamed to stand before her naked. He had never learned that shame, though in his other life his mother had tried hard to teach it to him.

Inside the gate were two litters draped with gorgeous fabrics. It seemed men, her servants, bore them. But these too would be capable of the forms of snakes, or half-snakes, just as they were capable of putting on the form of mortals. His *Nagini*, also, was a serpent.

They rode side by side through the strange, busy, musical streets of the snake city.

"Why didst thou place me among the Kashatriya?" he asked. "I have no caste."

"All men have caste," she said, "of the soul, which never changes. And thou art Kashatriya. A Warrior."

"But I was a coward," he said.

"Who knows better than the warrior," she said, smiling, "the terror of battle, the loss of comrades, pain of wounds and death. This may make afraid, after many lives; thou hast lived often. Yet also thou art and shall be brave."

On every side there went up narrow painted towers and wide painted porticos, and pillars, and ascending, diminishing pyramidal slopes of stone, all blossomed with sculptures and burning with precious metal and enamel. Although there was a natural light throughout the city, every palace and temple seemed lit by lamps, and the colours of the windows and the colossal porches fell over them in slow and glorious lightings. Now and then a chariot would fly by, drawn by white horses, or red or black, with jewelry hoofs, and the charioteer braced forward, some lord standing and proud behind him. Palankeens also passed, hung with bells, and elegant pedestrians walked in a dance of gesture and conversation. In one place there was a smooth turf where riders played a fierce match with curved sticks and a golden ball. All these had taken human shape to suit their activities. But elsewhere snakes lay coiled along the ledges like heavy syrup, communing with each other mysteriously.

A river cut through the city. On its banks the steep *ghats*, lit by torches that shone in the water, climbed to the doors of magnificent houses. To one of these the litters were taken.

At the threshold, the *Nagini* kneeled, bidding her visitor be welcome, her hair sweeping the petals strewn on the floor.

He became in her house a prince. Bathed and anointed, he was dressed in the finest muslin and silk, garments such as the masters of the serpent race put on when they had taken the shape of men. There were ornaments, too, like the jewels he had once seen in a museum, behind thick glass. These things felt curious to him, yet not unfitting. All the rooms through which he was conducted were sumptuous, but it was in a chamber of golden walls and screens of pierced marble, that he sat down on cushions and ate wild and delicious foods, lightly spiced and pretty as mosaic.

Behind a curtain clear as thin smoke, musicians coaxed the strings of the *sarod*, and the *bilancojel* fluted like a bird. Then his hostess returned and seemed to light the room more brightly. They sat and drank wine, and played chess, which in his former life he had never learned, but which his adult brain knew well. When each had beaten the other once, the board was removed and they played a lighter contest, which was appropriately the business of snakes and ladders.

But though he had gained a name, that her servants used and that she used as if it had always been his, her name he did not hear. And so perforce fell back on calling her Agnini.

The city, too, was nameless. It had neither night nor day, and Darvinda sensed that time was of a different order on the earth, miles up over their heads. At last he stayed Agnini's hand on the board, and said to her, "Why then am I here?"

"As my guest," she said, "if thou wilt. But there is another matter, also, a thing of choice which I shall tell thee of, and which thou mayest then accept or decline to undertake."

"And if declined?"

"Then thou shall depart when rested, an honoured traveller who has rejoiced my house."

"And if accepted?"

"To accept is to aid me."

"Then where is my choice?"

"Hush, my lord. Promise nothing till you are informed."

Then she did tell him, and if not everything, enough.

It was an edict of their Great King that sometimes some of his people must leave their cities, and wander the world of men above. So with Agnini and the prince who was her husband. And whether in punishment for some fault, or due only to the Inescapable, they were separated, these two, and their guests became different, and of different duration, so that when Agnini's tasks were done and she might return to her own country, her lord had some while yet to spend in exile. Thus she returned alone to wait for him. And she was content to wait, for she loved him—they had been created for each other—and in the manner of the supernatural beings they were, for hundreds of mortal years they had remained together. This small absence of, perhaps, a century, could be borne. But then, another in the city claimed her, by the rights only of lust and vacancy. And since he was a prince, and since the *Nagas* were as they were, and her lord far off, and no kindred to intervene, she could not deny this unwanted companion. Her only recourse had been to escape once more above, and to wander the alien earth, homeless and desolate.

She did not have to tell him, Darvinda saw what he had been chosen to do. At once his mind, his senses, laid before him a panorama of skills which he perceived as his own. His surprise was mild, as was his excitement at them. Like the new clothes, his man's body had come to fit him swiftly and well; the cast skins of his childhood and his weakness were foreign to him now he had outstripped them. So, he understood also that he had courage and confidence and need no longer be afraid of his fear.

Nevertheless, he considered. To be used by Agnini flattered him, and pleased him. She had given him a great deal, when he was a terrified little boy. The chance to repay her gifts was to be wished for. Yet he was aware of other things, shadows moving inside the substance of what she had said.

"It seems to me now," he said then, "that I am strong and versed in combat. In any battle thine enemy may suggest, it appears I may attempt to match him. But it seems to me too, he is mighty. Can I prevail? If I go down before thy foe, what of thee thereafter? Will it go worse for thee?"

Agnini kneeled by him, smiling up at him, black-eyed as the nights of earth.

"Yes, thou mayest fall in the battle, dear lord. But if I swear that, even falling, even slain, he cannot triumph over thee, nor then over myself, wilt thou heed my words?"

"But thou sayest I may die in this."

"This I do say. Thou mayest die. Yet shalt thou be the victor, and I through thee."

What man of the world of men would not have flung her gifts and her words together back in her face? He said, "Die, yet prevail? Well, I trust thee. Through thee I know the soul does not perish, and through thee I know love exists, lessons no other gave me. So then, I will do it. When will he come?"

Agnini touched his hands with her forehead; then rose.

"Already, Darvinda, he is here."

He felt no alarm even at that. Rather he felt a surge of power and ferocity, the sword edge of the many-faceted *Kshatram*, the essence of the Warrior caste of which he now—bemusedly, humbly, and gladly—reckoned himself an adjunct.

It was as if he had cried out: *Let him come in!*

The doors were pulled wide and the enemy strode through.

He had come as a demon, maybe to appal, or else it was merely his jest. For though he wore a man's form, yet he had kept the scales of the snake as his armouring, and in his wide mouth the white serpents' teeth showed like tusks, gilded by ready venom. His eyes were not a man's eyes, but blood-red and terrible. Only his hair was truly that of a man, long and black, falling far below his waist. Behind him walked an albino ape with cold pink eyes of its own, simpering with malice, that carried its master's arms with a showy and martyred struggle.

"Yes," said the enemy, "look thou long at me, O mortal thing. Look at my skin which thou canst not pierce, and at my fangs which shall rend and poison thee. Stare into my eyes, red as the fire which shall burn thy corpse on the *ghats*, and my hair black as the River of the City which shall drink thine ashes. I am Rupanag. Or, thou mayest name me only Death, since I am thine."

"Greetings," said Darvinda. "Where wilt thou fight?"

"Below, on the bank above the water, where all may see. Or art bashful? Shall we set to in some dark place where none may witness thee?"

"Let me get arms, and we will meet below, where thou desirest, on the bank."

"She will arm thee," said Rupanag. "And arm thee well. Which is good. For soon everything of thine shall be everything of mine. And it is good too that we fight on the bank, the handier for the place where thy dead body shall be burned."

"Dost thou fence always thus," asked Darvinda, "with thy tongue?"

But Rupanag laughed, and was gone, and on the platforms

below, beside the river, there was a noise of gathering and eagerness.

As Darvinda left the doors of Agnini's palace, a beggar-woman plucked at his wrist. Her eyes were bright as the lamps and torches that flamed in the river below: this city had no true beggars. "Do not fight," she said. "Thou shalt be sorely harmed."

"Greater harm to another, if I do not."

Massed crowds stood on the *ghats*, their finery ablaze. As he went down between them to the platform Rupanag had selected, a sneering youth caught at Darvinda's elbow. "Do not fight. Thou shalt be put to shame."

"Thou shamest thyself to boast of it."

And as he reached the broad platform and stepped out onto it, a little girl child, no older than he had been before, ran to Darvinda holding in both hands garlands of marigolds, and pointed at his heart. And the child said, in a woman's voice, "Fight not, Darvinda. For thou shalt die."

But, "There is no death," he said, and took one of the garlands and put it on his neck with the collar of gold and precious stones. The child smiled and vanished in the crowd.

And then Rupanag came and filled the horizon.

At once the platform of marble was altered. It had grown as wide as a desert, and the crowd was no longer to be seen, nor the palaces of their lights, nor the reflecting river. Even Rupanag was miles off, although his immanence made him perfectly visible still.

Darvinda beheld Rupanag take from the pale ape with the pale eyes a colossal bow, bend and string it, and set to its lip an arrow large as a spear, which suddenly the bow spat out. The arrow came like a bird of prey, high and sheer, and the air was filled by the sound of its cry. At the last instant Darvinda leapt aside, flinging up his shield to deflect the missile. But the great arrow carried half the shield away with it, plunging on into the platform until only the quivering flight remained above ground. Then Darvinda took up the bow Agnini had given him, strung it, set an arrow to the string, and let it fly. No sooner was the arrow in the air than it too, swollen with the warrior power of the *Kshatram*, grew great and terrible. But Rupanag had snatched another arrow and discharged it. Like a falcon on a pigeon this second arrow stooped, and met Darvinda's arrow at the centre of the marble plain. There was a crash like thunder and a flash of fire, and splinters hurtled downward in a rain. Neither arrow had survived the impact.

As the last smouldering fragments hit the plain, the surface of it shook. Rupanag was running, his bounds eating up the illusory or actual miles in seconds. He loomed like an angry cloud, blotting out the light. But Darvinda moved to meet him, and either his own state enlarged, or the image of his enemy shrank. They met as two lions meet, springing forward, and the sword that each had drawn rang on the other's with a searing moan.

"Why," said Rupanag, "thou fightest as one crippled, but thy crippling is to come."

But for all that, Darvinda's blows made him skip and spin and keep busy to get out of the way of them. There seemed no hope of penetrating the scaly dermis; Darvinda's aim, then, was to bruise and stun, and to break if possible. So his sword smote down and down again. And all the while the blade of Rupanag hurtled towards him and away. Sometimes the impact was accepted on the half of Darvinda's ruined shield, all the arrow had left him. Sometimes the impact was avoided. But now and again, the point of the sword ripped home. Darvinda's red blood lay on his golden flesh and mingled with the red jewels of Agnini's gift.

"Thou hast garnets under thy skin, and rubies," cried Rupanag. "I find gems for thee brighter than those she gave thee. Yet alas, thou findest none for me."

But on and on they strove, and there came at length a blow between the swords that broke them, and they burst in pieces, like a firework, just as the arrows had been burst.

Rupanag fell back, and flung away his sword hilt with a snarl. Then he jumped straight upward, turned in the air, came down upon his hands, and so folded into a reeling living wheel, which rolled itself at Darvinda and caught him fast.

They fought then only with their bodies' strength, with hands and limbs and feet. And as they wrestled, all the time Rupanag grinned and gnashed his serpent's fangs, striving to bring them where they could close and inject a poison richer than that of seventy cobras into his adversary's veins.

But Darvinda had not loosed hold of the hilt of his own wrecked sword. Presently, as they struggled, he dashed this hilt with all his might against the beautiful ghastly teeth of Rupanag, and smashed the uppermost of the great biting fangs.

Rupanag screamed, and in that moment of his anguish, galvanised by enormous agony, he thrust his foot against Darvinda's breast and seizing the yellow hair in his hands he whirled him high. And as Darvinda fell down again across Rupanag's shoulders, Rupanag snapped his spine like a reed.

So the combat ended, and the city came back, and the *ghats* with the torches burning, and the palaces and crowds beside the river. And all who looked saw Darvinda lying on the marble among the blood and the marigolds, slain in the way that men most often kill snakes.

The Serpent-People did this much for Darvinda; they wrapped him in a white shroud and left him ready on the platform for Agnini to honour with the death-fire. He had fought well and given them a show, for though they seemed far off, they had stood close and watching all the while. But he was a foreigner, neither of their race nor their kind, and mortal.

Rupanag went away to be cleansed and tended, to pray and sacrifice, and change his shape. He came back as a bridegroom behind a concourse of chariots and horses and musicians and coloured lamps, though the ape-slave did not go with him; it was a female, and jealous, and had run to chatter on the tops of the city, like one mad. The conqueror stalked into Agnini's palace. After which the doors were closed.

So he sat down in the room of golden walls and Agnini's handmaidens served him. He frowned at her, for she too wore white, as if to indicate a widow's death. As a man, Rupanag was tall and well-made, his eyes and hair black as ebony. But when he smiled now, he kept his mouth shut, for his teeth, in whatever form he took, had been forever spoiled.

"Well, I will eat, and drink wine," said Rupanag.

"Do so, lord," said Agnini.

"Then I will go with thee to some chamber where thou shalt pleasure me."

"Perhaps not so."

"Why, who is there to prevent me now?"

"Listen," said Agnini, "thou shalt hear the doors fly open before him."

All this Darvinda saw and heard, in a detached way, as he drifted about in the air. Incorporeal, it seemed, he could see and hear anything he wished, and more than one thing at once. Nor did he see with eyes, nor did he hear with ears. Nor did he, exactly, see *or* hear.

There had been a time of quietness after death. Then curiosity had made him voyage through the atmosphere. Now some other thing drew him back to the platform. His death had not been a death, but only one more shedding of a skin. And returning, he was drawn down and in, and was once more clothed in body, thrusting his way from an envelope of torn flesh and severed spine, and lastly from the polite shroud, to stand upright and whole on the *ghats* above the river.

This, it seemed, was Agnini's magic still, but it was true and sure as she had told him. Carelessly he stripped from the flaccid skin and the rattling bones, which had been himself, the garments she had given him, and put them on. If any observed him now they made no sign. And when he turned towards the palace, no one came to warn or mock at him.

Every door flew open with a bang in front of Darvinda. When he reached the golden room and entered it, Rupanag, who had been sitting upright with a look of horror, started to his feet. On this occasion no words were exchanged. The serpent prince grasped platters from the tables and hurled them, and as they came they seemed altered to knives and lances, but Darvinda stepped from their path, and they passed him by, each with a rushing shriek.

When he reached Rupanag, Darvinda had only to put out his hands and lay hold on him. Rupanag had by this time drawn a long dagger, but in striking it turned on a jewel at Darvinda's hip. It was no longer the hour of Rupanag's triumph. And Darvinda took the dagger from his enemy's hand as a man takes a leaf from a bush, and drove it through Rupanag's armourless skin into the furious heart.

So Rupanag ended, and his man's body sprawled among the feast and the flowers.

"But even an immortal has a soul which cannot die," said Agnini. "See."

And at his foot Darvinda saw lying a serpent's egg, and out of the egg at that instant came frantically wriggling a little brown venomless snake, newborn and bewildered, and it crawled away over the floor.

"So he must remain awhile," said Agnini. "A little brown snake, dwelling in the lowliest crevices of the *Naga* city. For he died in lust and rage, and lust and rage were the cause. And they that die so deluded descend to the lowest way. But thou, lord, who died in the action of nobleness for another, aspiring to nothing more, thou art a man again, thy daylight path before thee."

Then she murmured softly, "And thou hast freed me."

There were other rooms to which her servants conducted him. Here he underwent a second time rituals of bathing and purification, and then, in a silent courtyard before a shrine of the god Indra, the Wielder of the Thunderbolt, Darvinda made his offerings, as was proper. And only in hanging the garland about the throat of the god did Darvinda pause a moment, a little embarrassed that once, long ago, he had thought him only a disreputable idol (his mother's term) before realising all gods were one and one many, and that they have a multitude of names. He begged Indra's pardon, but from courtesy and gratitude, which are not fear.

And then there was yet one more room, hung with silks like running rivers, perfumed with incenses, with blue collyrium and smoky sandalwood, with oils and flowers. The light there was low and subtle. When Agnini had entered the golden room she had brought a kind of sunrise into it. But here, entering the dark, she was like a moon of darkness, furled in a night of blackest hair.

He kneeled to her, and placed his hand upon her foot, where the rings glimmered. His body was a man's, and his desires also were those of a man. He knew quite well that he had won her, and better yet, that she would give herself. For there was love between them.

But when he drew her to him, her smiling eyes were sad. And he remembered all the rest of what she had told him. Of her husband, the prince for whom she had been created, her lord who was bound to wander still, and for whose sake—rather than accept another— she had returned to the bitter exile of the human earth.

So he stepped away from her, though his whole body burned and reviled him. And then the fires passed into a wonderful coolness, a sort of joy, because such a look of happiness had been borne in her face. She seemed younger than the youngest child. Her soul was dancing, and took his dancing with it. And there came in those moments, after all, a communion of love, if not of the love of the flesh.

When the summit of that marvelling shared tumult had passed with no words at all, she spoke to him.

"Because of this final benefit thou hast rendered me, I may greet my lord, running to meet him at the first sound of his footstep, without debasement or deception. And for this, I promise thee one further gift. Valour and strength thou shalt have, beauty and favour, fortune and sweetness all thy days, but also a perfect and enduring love shall be thine, a love even as the love of demons and gods. Remember me, lord, but once, when thou hast found her."

The darkness moved and flickered. It was so real it could not be possible it should pass. But the lovely moon, the sombre moon of the woman's face, swam on its night of hair. The walls of the room were fading. The towers and the lights beyond had lost their shape and shine.

Already the dream was ebbing away. It would soon be forgotten. There was a coldness at his back. Throat too dry, and eyes gritty from sleep, and feet sore from walking, raising his head, confused—to see the trees over the distant garden wall— The small boy stumbled down the dusty road, and through the swarming dusk, without music. . . .

# V

Evelyn was hysterical, to the point of madness. Chaver Finlay stood and poured himself scotch, waiting until the cries had died, or paused for breath.

"And that's why dinner is late, I take it?" he then said.

"Oh, Chaver!" she wailed, reminiscent of the jackals he had heard on the road. But one threw a stone at them, and Evelyn was not so easy to be rid of. She wilted before him, soiled by hours of tears and squawking in broiling weather, her hair practically on end and her faded eyes starting from her head. "All morning, all afternoon! All day, and not a trace of him. The servants looked everywhere. I had them all out—and then he came wandering in after sunset. I couldn't get a thing out of him. Just something about falling asleep in the hills. Oh, Chaver, he can't have got all that way by himself."

"No, of course he can't. Not on foot." The man drank. He said, "A surprising sort of adventure for our delicate little pet." His air of contemptuous approval did nothing to help.

Evelyn began to sob. "It's that woman," she snivelled. "That—that—" No epithet was both vile and polite enough to be utilised. "She took him off somewhere. I know it. You know what they are. Extraordinary things happen here in this awful country. Anything might have been done to him."

"But I take it, it wasn't?" Chaver finished the whisky. "Where is he now?"

"I sent him straight to bed."

"I see. Well, he'll keep, then. I'll go and have a word with Agnini."

"Oh, no—Chaver—no—"

"Why not? You seem to think she's at the bottom of the mystery."

"No, you mustn't—"

"Don't tell me," said Chaver, casting after all the stone, and unerringly, "what I may and must not do."

As he crossed the night garden with quick eager strides, between bushes that flickered tonight with fireflies, he saw his quarry almost by instinct, shadow in shade, under an orange tree near the wall. The spot was secluded, an invitation. He walked up to her, quite hidden from the bungalow and the servants' area, and said, "What's been going on, then? Thinking of abducting my son, maybe, and your accomplices never turned up? Too scared. As you should have been." She said nothing, and even in the dark her eyes glowed, as if they too held fireflies, or stars. He chuckled, roughly, to demonstrate it might all be a joke. "That's what the memsahib thinks, anyway. Taking my son and heir away to sell for immoral practices. But I don't think you'd do that, Aggi. Murdering an old woman now, that's more your line." Again he waited, and she said nothing. He put out one hand and let it fall on her shoulder, which was bare. He palmed her shoulder, liking the texture of her, as he had known he would. What she had on was a little puzzling. It was nothing of Asha's lending anymore, rather some piece of cloth taken up from somewhere and casually wound on her, and as casually, perhaps, unwound. "You did kill her, did you? The men said there was something wrong with the body. They said, it was hollow, like an empty sack, but full of mud that had been washed in and then hardened. It looked like an ordinary corpse to me." He moved his hand downward. "But you're all alive, aren't you? No, don't move away. After all, I could give you some trouble, Aggi, if I wanted to. If I reported that corpse to the authorities, and mentioned we'd had a stray wandering around here. Come on, Aggi. I'll talk Hindi-cindy to you, if you like." He had both hands on her now, and pressed close to her, to let her learn his readiness. "You know you want to, Aggi. You pray doing it, don't you, everywhere, on every bloody temple. You're full of it, you darkies—"
The sound came from her mouth, close by his ear, and turned his pounding heart to stone and the heat in his groin to ice. Before he could think, Finlay had jumped away from her, and gone on

stumbling backwards until he collided with another of the orange trees. His reaction was out of all proportion to what she had done. Yet it had not seemed to be: she had hissed at him. There was nothing catlike in it, nor anything human. It was the exhalation of the hunting cobra. And the sinuous shape of her against him, the weave of her head scarcely seen in the night gloom, these things had seemed snakelike too. In that split second, there between his hands and grappled to his torso—something cool and evil and untender rustled and swayed, and the great jaws gaped, the long teeth glinted, readying to deliver the paralysing and deadly bite. . . .

"For God's sake," he said hoarsely. But out of the black of his invisible foreign garden, her woman's voice came back at him, speaking rapidly in English, and then in Hindi, so he did not quite follow it all.

"Do what you wish," she said. "Tell whom you wish. My wandering is done. I go elsewhere. Thou canst not harm me, thou *man*. And that which thy slaves found on the road, that was only mine, no other's. The shed skin of my mortal youth and age, gone from me now I am young again, and free. But *thou*. Go woo thy pink-eyed wife. And for thy son—go thou and lie in the dirt at his feet, for that is thy place. Thou shalt see the sun rise in him, soul and body, while thy tiny strengths wither like old leaves. Thy way is darkness. Remember me, once, in the long and lampless night of thy life."

With his shoulders to the slender orange tree, his ears ringing and his intestines crawling, Chaver Finlay heard then something that made it seem as if a bundle of light material had been thrown down into the grass. It would take him months to erase the impression he had that the shadow of the woman vanished, while, about the height of his boot top, something whispered away like a river through the bushes, and all the fireflies winked out.

However, it took only half an hour to push the matter temporarily from his forebrain, with the admitted help of the whisky decanter and cigarette box. And only three minutes more to reach his son's bedroom.

"Get up, David," the man said in a cold, penetrating, and level voice, as his hand shook like a terrier at the scruff of the boy's neck. "Get up. We have some business."

In the semidark, a drift of light coming in from beyond, where Evelyn stood whimpering, the boy seemed luminous in his pale pyjamas.

"You've been damned disobedient," said the man. "You know that, don't you? Going off and scaring your mother. Telling lies. All right. You'll take your punishment. Drop your trousers and lean over the chair."

And then, after a moment, over the noise the woman was making, came the noise of a leather belt being applied to naked eight-year-old flesh. And the man panting at the work. But no other sound.

Outside, the woman wrung her hands, suffering every pain that the boy received, as if she herself bore it for him. Such chastisements drew them closer, a mother and son, both victims of the man. And it was a dreadful beating for a little boy. She was concerned he did not scream or weep. The former, lighter beatings had always caused him to cry out—would Chaver be able to stop, without this signal of acknowledgement?

In the end the man did stop, tiring, and abruptly aware he had gone too far. Defensively he said, "All right. You've been brave, I'll give you that. Lie down now. Go on, lie down." And then, loudly, violently, as if to a savage dog, *"Lie down!"*

Not properly grasping what was amiss, the woman heard fear in her husband's voice. Startled, on a reflex, she ran forward and pushed the bedroom door fully open, so the light sluiced in and filled the room.

Her son, David, stood at the centre of the room, the light, clad merely in the unbuttoned pyjama top and the blood that trickled down his legs. His fair hair was plastered to his forehead with sweat, but from the unfathomed day's exposure to the sun, she saw his body had acquired at last a deepening tan. He was less than half the height of the man, his father, yet the child seemed to dominate the entire scene. His mouth was firmly closed, his eyes tearless and wide.

"Davy," the woman said, under her breath. "Oh, do as Daddy tells you, Davy."

But it did not matter anymore that she called him "Davy." The dream had ebbed away, he had forgotten it. Nonetheless, brain and heart and spirit, it had bathed him through; nameless and unremembered, yet it had recoloured everything, and the dye was permanent. Now he knew himself, and what he might become, nor would he ever doubt, nor doubt the daylight path stretched before him and could not be missed. Whatever shadows scattered that path, he would pay them no heed. They were nothing now, compared to what would be his, in the golden future only years, days, moments away. And though the blood ran and the man panted and though "Davy, Davy," the woman muttered, there was even another name, a secret name, nothing would ever touch.

Less than half the man's height, the boy looked up. Chaver Finlay, who had not recalled the aspect of his child's eyes, now met it, blue as a jewel and falling like the blow of a seven-foot sword across his recoiling adult mind.

Pushing past his wife, the man went away, laughing coarsely. There was nothing to do save laugh, since his consciousness could not admit what all the rest of him already saw and shouted at. Though he did sense he had beaten his son for the very last time in his life.

# THE GORGON

THE SMALL ISLAND, WHICH LAY OFF THE LARGER ISLAND OF Daphaeu, obviously contained a secret of some sort, and, day by day, and particularly night by night, began to exert an influence on me, so that I must find it out.

Daphaeu itself (or more correctly herself, for she was a female country, voluptuous and cruel by turns in the true antique fashion of the Goddess) was hardly enormous. A couple of roads, a tangle of sheep tracks, a precarious, escalating village, rocks and hillsides thatched by blistered grass. All of which overhung an extraordinary sea, unlike any sea which I have encountered elsewhere in Greece. Water which might be mistaken for blueness from a distance, but which, from the harbour or the multitude of caves and coves that undermined the island, revealed itself a clear and succulent green, like milky limes or the bottle glass of certain spirits.

On my first morning, having come onto the natural terrace (the only recommendation of the hovellike accommodation) to look over this strange green ocean, I saw the smaller island, lying like a little boat of land moored just wide of Daphaeu's three hills. The day was clear, the water frilled with white where it hit the fangs in the interstices below the terrace. About the smaller island, barely a ruffle showed. It seemed to glide up from the sea, smooth as mirror. The little island was verdant, also. Unlike Daphaeu's limited stands of stone pine, cypress, and cedar, the smaller sister was clouded by a still, lambent haze of foliage that looked to be woods. Visions of groves, springs, a ruined temple, a statue of Pan playing the panpipes forever in some glade—where only yesterday, it might seem, a thin column of aromatic smoke had gone up—these images were enough, fancifully, to draw me into inquiries about how the small island might be reached. And when my inquiries met first with a polite bevy of excuses, next with a refusal, last with a blank wall of silence, as if whomever I mentioned the little island to had gone temporarily deaf or mad, I became, of course, insatiable to get to it, to find out what odd superstitious thing kept these people away. Naturally, the Daphaeui were not friendly to me at any time beyond the false friendship one anticipates extended to a man of another nationality and clime, who can be relied on to pay his bills, perhaps allow himself to be overcharged, even made a downright monkey of in order to preserve goodwill. In the normal run of things, I could have had anything I wanted in exchange for a pack of local lies, a broad local smile, and a broader local price. That I could not get to the little island puzzled me. I tried money and I tried barter. I even, in a reckless moment, probably knowing I would not succeed, offered Pitos, one of the younger fishermen, the gold and onyx ring he coveted. My sister had made it for me, the faithful copy of an intaglio belonging to the House of Borgia, no less. Generally, Pitos could not pass the time of day with me without mentioning the ring, adding something in the nature of: "If ever you want a great service, any great service, I will do it for that ring." I half believe he would have stolen or murdered for it, certainly shared the bed with me. But he would not, apparently, even for the Borgia ring, take me to the little island.

"You think too much of foolish things," he said to me. "For a big writer, that is not good."

I ignored the humorous aspect of "big," equally inappropriate in the sense of height, girth, or fame. Pitos's English was fine, and when he slipped into mild inaccuracies, it was likely to be a decoy.

"You're wrong, Pitos. That island has a story in it somewhere. I'd take a bet on it."

"No fish today," said Pitos. "Why you think that is?"

I refrained from inventively telling him I had seen giant swordfish leaping from the shallows by the smaller island.

I found I was prowling Daphaeu, but only on the one side, the side where I would get a view—or views—of her sister. I would climb down into the welter of coves and smashed emerald water to look across at her. I would climb up and stand, leaning on the sun-blasted walls of a crumbling church, and look at the small island. At night, crouched over a bottle of wine, a scatter of manuscript, moths falling like rain in the oil-lamp, my stare stayed fixed on the small island, which, as the moon came up, would seem turned to silver or to some older metal, Nemean metal perhaps, sloughed from the moon herself.

Curiosity accounts for much of this, and contrasuggestiveness. But the influence I presently began to feel, that I cannot account for exactly. Maybe it was only the writer's desire to fantasise rather than to work. But each time I reached for the manuscript I would experience a sort of distraction, a sort of calling—uncanny, poignant, like nostalgia, though for a place I had never visited.

I am very bad at recollecting my dreams, but once or twice, just before sunrise, I had a suspicion I had dreamed of the island. Of walking there, hearing its inner waters, the leaves brushing my hands and face.

Two weeks went by, and precious little had been done in the line of work. And I had come to Daphaeu with the sole intention of working. The year before, I had accomplished so much in a month of similar islands—or had they been similar?—that I had looked for results of some magnitude. In all of fourteen days I must have squeezed out two thousand words, and most of those dreary enough that the only covers they would ever get between would be those of the trash-can. And yet it was not that I could not produce work, it was that I knew, with blind and damnable certainty, that the work I needed to be doing sprang from that spoonful of island.

The first day of the third week I had been swimming in the calm stretch of sea west of the harbour and had emerged to sun myself and smoke on the parched hot shore. Presently Pitos appeared, having scented my cigarettes. Surgical and government health warnings have not yet penetrated to spots like Daphaeu, where filtered tobacco continues to symbolise Hollywood or some other amorphous, anachronistic surrealism still hankered after and long vanished from the real world beyond. Once Pitos had acquired his cigarette, he sprawled down on the dry grass, grinned, indicated the Borgia ring, and mentioned a beautiful cousin of his, whether male or female I cannot be sure. After this had been cleared out of the way, I said to him, "You know how the currents run. I was thinking of a slightly more adventurous swim. But I'd like your advice."

Pitos glanced at me warily. I had had the plan as I lazed in the velvet water. Pitos was already starting to guess it.

"Currents are very dangerous. Not to be trusted, except by harbour."

"How about between Daphaeu and the other island? It can't be more than a quarter mile. The sea looks smooth enough, once you break away from the shoreline here."

"No," said Pitos. I waited for him to say there were no fish, or a lot of fish, or that his brother had gotten a broken thumb, or something of the sort. But Pitos did not resort to this. Troubled and angry, he stabbed my cigarette, half-smoked, into the turf. "Why do you want to go to the island so much?"

"Why does nobody else want me to go there?"

He looked up then, and into my eyes. His own were very black, sensuous, carnal earthbound eyes, full of orthodox sins, and extremely young in a sense that had nothing to do with physical age, but with race, I suppose, the youngness of ancient things, like Pan himself, quite possibly.

"Well," I said at last, "are you going to tell me or not? Because believe me, I intend to swim over there today or tomorrow."

"No," he said again. And then: "You should not go. On the island there is a . . ." and he said a word in some tongue neither Greek nor Turkish, not even the corrupt Spanish that sometimes peregrinates from Malta.

"A *what*?"

Pitos shrugged helplessly. He gazed out to sea, a safe sea without islands. He seemed to be putting something together in his mind and I let him do it, very curious now, pleasantly unnerved by this waft of the occult I had already suspected to be the root cause of the ban.

Eventually he turned back to me, treated me once more to the primordial innocence of his stare, and announced:

"The cunning one."

"Ah," I said. Both irked and amused, I found myself smiling. At this, Pitos's face grew savage with pure rage, an expression I had never witnessed before—the façade kept for foreigners had well and truly come down.

"Pitos," I said, "I don't understand."

"*Meda*," he said then, the Greek word, old Greek.

"Wait," I said. I caught at the name, which was wrong, trying to fit it to a memory. Then the list came back to me, actually from

Graves, the names which meant "the cunning": Meda, Medea, Medusa.

"Oh," I said. I hardly wanted to offend him further by bursting into loud mirth. At the same time, even while I was trying not to laugh, I was aware of the hair standing up on my scalp and neck. "You're telling me there is a gorgon on the island."

Pitos grumbled unintelligibly, stabbing the dead cigarette over and over into the ground.

"I'm sorry, Pitos, but it can't be Medusa. Someone cut her head off quite a few years ago. A guy called Perseus."

His face erupted into that awful expression again, mouth in a rictus, tongue starting to protrude, eyes flaring at me—quite abruptly I realised he wasn't raging, but imitating the visual panic-contortions of a man turning inexorably to stone. Since that is what the gorgon is credited with, literally petrifying men by the sheer horror of her countenance, it now seemed almost pragmatic of Pitos to be demonstrating. It was, too, a creditable facsimile of the sculpted gorgon's face sometimes used to seal ovens and jars. I wondered where he had seen one to copy it so well.

"All right," I said. "Okay, Pitos, fine." I fished in my shirt, which was lying on the ground, and took out some money to give him, but he recoiled. "I'm sorry," I said, "I don't think it merits the ring. Unless you'd care to row me over there after all."

The boy rose. He looked at me with utter contempt, and without another word, before striding off up the shore. The mashed cigarette protruded from the grass and I lay and watched it, the tiny strands of tobacco slowly crisping in the heat of the sun, as I plotted my route from Daphaeu.

Dawn seemed an amiable hour. No one in particular about on that side of the island, the water chill but flushing quickly with warmth as the sun reached over it. And the tide in the right place to navigate the rocks. . . .

Yes, dawn would be an excellent time to swim out to the gorgon's island.

The gods were on my side, I concluded as I eased myself into the open sea the following morning. Getting clear of the rocks was no problem, their channels only half filled by the returning tide. While just beyond Daphaeu's coast I picked up one of those contrary currents that lace the island's edges and which, tide or no, would funnel me away from shore.

The swim was ideal, the sea limpid and no longer any more than cool. Sunlight filled in the waves and touched Daphaeu's retreating face with gold. Barely altered in thousands of years, either rock or sea or sun. And yet one knew that against all the claims of romantic fiction, this place did not look now as once it had. Some element in the air or in time itself changes things. A young man of the Bronze Age, falling asleep at sunset in his own era, waking at sunrise in mine, looking about him, would not have known where he was. I would swear to that.

Such thoughts I had leisure for in my facile swim across to the wooded island moored off Daphaeu.

As I had detected, the approach was smooth, virtually inviting. I cruised in as if sliding along butter. A rowboat would have had no more difficulty. The shallows were clear, empty of rocks, and, if anything, greener than the water off Daphaeu.

I had not looked much at Medusa's Island (I had begun jokingly to call it this) as I crossed, knowing I would have all the space on my arrival. So I found myself wading in on a seamless beach of rare glycerine sand and, looking up, saw the mass of trees spilling from the sky.

The effect was incredibly lush—so much heavy green, and seemingly quite impenetrable, while the sun struck in glistening shafts, lodging like arrows in the foliage, which reminded me very intensely of huge clusters of grapes on a vine. Anything might lie behind such a barricade.

It was already beginning to get hot. Dry, I put on the loose cotton shirt and ate breakfast packed in the same waterproof wrapper, standing on the beach impatient to get on.

As I moved forward, a bird shrilled somewhere in its cage of boughs, sounding an alarm of invasion. But surely the birds, too, would be stone on Medusa's Island, if the legends were correct. And when I stumbled across the remarkable stone carving of a man in the forest, I would pause in shocked amazement at its verisimilitude to life. . . .

Five minutes into the thickets of the wood, I did indeed stumble on a carving, but it was of a moss-grown little faun. My pleasure in the discovery was considerably lessened, however, when investigation told me it was scarcely classical in origin. Circa 1920 would be nearer the mark.

A further minute and I had put the faun from my mind. The riot of waterfalling plants through which I had been picking my way

broke open suddenly on an inner vista much wider than I had anticipated. While the focal point of the vista threw me completely, I
cannot say what I had really been expecting. The grey-white stalks
of pillars, some temple shrine, the spring with its votary of greenish
rotted bronze, none of these would have surprised me. On the
other hand, to find a house before me took me completely by surprise. I stood and looked at it in abject dismay, cursing its wretched
normality until I gradually began to see the house was not normal
in the accepted sense.

It had been erected probably at the turn of the century, when
such things were done. An eccentric two-storeyed building, intransigently European—that is, the Europe of the north—with its dark
walls and arched roofing. Long windows, smothered by the proximity of the wood, received and refracted no light. The one unique
and startling feature—startling because of its beauty—was the
parade of columns that ran along the terrace, in form and choreog-
raphy for all the world like the columns of Knossos, differing only
in colour. For these stems of the gloomy house were of a luminous
sea-green marble, and shone as the windows did not.

Before the house was a stretch of rough-cut lawn, tamarisk, and
one lost dying olive tree. As I was staring, an apparition seemed to
manifest out of the centre of the tree. For a second we peered at
each other before he came from the bushes with a clashing of
gnarled brown forearms. He might have been an elderly satyr; I,
patently, was only a swimmer, with my pale foreigner's tan, my
bathing trunks, the loose shirt. It occurred to me at last that I was
conceivably trespassing. I wished my Greek were better.

He planted himself before me and shouted intolerantly, and anyone's Greek was good enough to get his drift. "Go! Go!" He was
ranting, and he began to wave a knife with which, presumably, he
had been pruning or mutilating something. "Go. You *go!*"

I said I had been unaware anybody lived on the island. He took
no notice. He went on waving the knife, and his attitude provoked
me. I told him sternly to put the knife down, that I would leave
when I was ready, that I had seen no notice to the effect that the
island was private property. Generally I would never take a chance
like this with someone so obviously qualified to be a lunatic, but
my position was so vulnerable, so ludicrous, so entirely indefensi-
ble, that I felt bound to act firmly. Besides which, having reached
the magic grotto and found it was not as I had visualised, I was still

very reluctant to abscond with only a memory of dark windows and sea-green columns to brood upon.

The maniac was by now quite literally foaming, due most likely to a shortage of teeth, but the effect was alarming, not to mention unaesthetic. As I was deciding which fresh course to take and if there might be one, a woman's figure came out onto the terrace. I had the impression of a white frock, before an odd muffled voice called out a rapid—too rapid for my translation—stream of peculiarly accented Greek. The old man swung around, gazed at the figure, raised his arms, and bawled another foaming torrent to the effect that I was a bandit or some other kind of malcontent. While he did so, agitated as I was becoming, I nevertheless took in what I could of the woman standing between the columns. She was mostly in shadow, just the faded white dress with a white scarf at the neck marking her position. And then there was an abrupt flash of warmer pallor that was her hair. A blonde Greek, or maybe just a peroxided Greek. At any rate, no snakes.

The drama went on, from his side, from hers. I finally got tired of it, went by him, and walked towards the terrace, pondering, rather too late, if I might not be awarded the knife in my back. But almost as soon as I started to move, she leaned forward a little and she called another phrase to him, which this time I made out, telling him to let me come on.

When I reached the foot of the steps, I halted, really involuntarily, struck by something strange about her. Just as the strangeness of the house had begun to strike me, not its evident strangeness, the ill-marriage to location, the green pillars, but a strangeness of atmosphere, items the unconscious eye notices, where the physical eye is blind and will not explain. And so with her. What was it? Still in shadow, I had the impression she might be in her early thirties, from her figure, her movements, but she had turned away as I approached, adjusting some papers on a wicker table.

"Excuse me," I said. I stopped and spoke in English. For some reason I guessed she would be familiar with the language, perhaps only since it was current on Daphaeu. "Excuse me. I had no idea the island was private. No one gave me the slightest hint—"

"You are English," she broke in, in the vernacular, proving the guess to be correct.

"Near enough. I find it easier to handle than Greek, I confess."

"Your Greek is very good," she said with the indifferent patronage of one who is multilingual. I stood there under the steps, already fascinated. Her voice was the weirdest I had ever heard, muffled, almost unattractive, and with the most incredible accent, not Greek at all. The nearest approximation I could come up with was Russian, but I could not be sure.

"Well," I said. I glanced over my shoulder and registered that the frothy satyr had retired into his shrubbery; the knife glinted as it slashed tamarisk in lieu of me. "Well, I suppose I should retreat to Daphaeu. Or am I permitted to stay?"

"Go, stay," she said. "I do not care at all."

She turned then, abruptly, and my heart slammed into the base of my throat. A childish silly reaction, yet I was quite unnerved, for now I saw what it was that had seemed vaguely peculiar from a distance. The lady on Medusa's Island was masked.

She remained totally still and let me have my reaction, neither helping nor hindering me.

It was an unusual mask, or usual—I am unfamiliar with the norm of such things. It was made of some matte-light substance that toned well with the skin of her arms and hands, possibly not so well with that of her neck, where the scarf provided camouflage. Besides which, the chin of the mask—this certainly an extra to any mask I had ever seen—continued under her own. The mask's physiognomy was bland, nondescriptly pretty in a way that was somehow grossly insulting to her. Before confronting the mask, if I had tried to judge the sort of face she would have, I would have suspected a coarse, rather heavy beauty, probably redeemed by one chiselled feature—a small slender nose, perhaps. The mask, however, was vacuous. It did not suit her, was not true to her. Even after three minutes I could tell as much, or thought I could, which amounts to the same thing.

The blonde hair, seeming natural as the mask was not, cascaded down, lush as the foliage of the island. A blonde Greek, then, like the golden Greeks of Homer's time, when gods walked the earth in disguise.

In the end, without any help or hindrance from her, as I have said, I pulled myself together. As she had mentioned no aspect of her state, neither did I. I simply repeated what I had said before: "Am I permitted to stay?"

The mask went on looking at me. The astonishing voice said: "You wish to stay so much. What do you mean to do here?"

Talk to you, oblique lady, and wonder what lies behind the painted veil.

"Look at the island, if you'll let me. I found the statue of a faun near the beach." Elaboration implied I should lie: "Someone told me there was an old shrine here."

"Ah!" She barked. It was apparently a laugh. "No one," she said, "*told* you anything about this place."

I was at a loss. Did she know what was said? "Frankly, then, I romantically hoped there might be."

"Unromantically, there is not. No shrine. No temple. My father bought the faun in a shop in Athens. A tourist shop. He had vulgar tastes but he knew it, and that has a certain charm, does it not?"

"Yes, I suppose it does. Your father—"

She cut me short again.

"The woods cover all the island. Except for an area behind the house. We grow things there, and we keep goats and chickens. We are very domesticated. Very sufficient for ourselves. There is a spring of fresh water, but no votary. No *genius loci*. I am *so* sorry to dash your dreams to pieces."

It suggested itself to me, from her tone of amusement, from little inflections that were coming and going in her shoulders now, that she might be enjoying this, enjoying, if you like, putting me down as an idiot. Presumably visitors were rare. Perhaps it was even fun for her to talk to a man, youngish and unknown, though admittedly never likely to qualify for anyone's centrefold.

"But you have no objections to my being here," I pursued. "And your father?"

"My parents are dead," she informed me. "When I employed the plural, I referred to him," she gestured with a broad sweep of her hand to the monster on the lawn, "and a woman who attends to the house. My servants, my unpaid servants. I have no money anymore. Do you see this dress? It is my mother's dress. How lucky I am the same fitting as my mother, do you not think?"

"Yes . . ."

I was put in mind, suddenly, of myself as an ambassador at the court of some notorious female potentate, Cleopatra, say, or Catherine de Medici.

"You are very polite," she said, as if telepathically privy to my fantasies.

"I have every reason to be."

"What reason?"

"I'm trespassing. You treat me like a guest."

"And how," she said, vainglorious all at once, "do you rate my English?"

"It's wonderful."

"I speak eleven languages fluently," she said with offhanded boastfulness. "Three more I can read very well."

I liked her. This display, touching and magnificent at once, her angular theatrical gesturings, which now came more and more often, her hair, her flat-waisted figure in its 1940s dress, her large well-made hands, and her challenging me with the mask, saying nothing to explain it, all this hypnotised me.

I said something to express admiration and she barked again, throwing back her blonde head and irresistibly, though only for a moment, conjuring Garbo's Queen Christina.

Then she walked down the steps straight to me, demonstrating something else I had deduced, that she was only about an inch shorter than I.

"I," she said, "will show you the island. Come."

She showed me the island. Unsurprisingly, it was small. To go directly around it would maybe have taken less than thirty minutes. But we lingered, over a particular tree, a view, and once we sat down on the ground near the gushing milk-white spring. The basin under the spring, she informed me, had been added in 1910. A little bronze nymph presided over the spot, dating from the same year, which you could tell in any case from the way her classical costume and her filleted hair had been adapted to the fashions of hobble skirt and Edwardian coiffeur. Each age imposes its own overlay on the past.

Behind the house was a scatter of the meagre white dwellings that make up such places as the village on Daphaeu, now plainly unoccupied and put to other uses. Sheltered from the sun by a colossal cypress, six goats played about in the grass. Chickens and an assortment of other fowl strutted up and down, while a pig—or pigs—grunted somewhere out of sight. Things grew in strips and patches, and fruit trees and vines ended the miniature plantation before the woods resumed. Self-sufficiency of a tolerable kind, I supposed. But there seemed, from what she said, no contact maintained with any other area, as if the world did not exist. Postulate that a blight or harsh weather intervened, what then? And the old satyr, how long would he last to tend the plots? He looked two hundred now, which on the islands probably meant sixty. I did not ask her what contingency plans she had for these emergencies and inevitabilities. What good, after all, are most plans? We could be invaded from Andromeda tomorrow, and what help for us all then? Either it is in your nature to survive—somehow, anyhow—or it is not.

She had well and truly hooked me, of course. If I had met her in Athens, some sun-baked afternoon, I would have felt decidedly out of my depth, taken her for cocktails, and foundered before we had even reached the dinner hour. But here, in this pulsing green bubble of light and leaves straight out of one's most irrational visions of the glades of Arcadia, conversation, however erratic, communication, however eccentric, was happening. The most inexplicable thing of all was that the mask had ceased almost immediately to bother me. I cannot, as I look back, properly account for this, for to spend a morning, a noon, an afternoon, allowing yourself to become fundamentally engaged by a woman whose face you have not seen, whose face you are actively being prevented from seeing, seems now incongruous to the point of perversity. But there it is. We discussed Ibsen, Dickens, Euripides, and Jung. I remembered trawling anecdotes of a grandfather, mentioned my sister's jewelry store in St. Louis, listened to an astonishing description of wild birds flying in across a desert from a sea. I assisted her over rocky turf, flirted with her, felt excited by and familiar with her, all this with her masked face before me. As if the mask, rather than being a part of her, meant no more than the frock she had elected to wear or the narrow-heeled vanilla shoes she had chosen to put on. As if I knew her face totally and had no need to be shown it, the face of her movements and her ridiculous voice.

But in fact, I could not even make out her eyes, only the shine in them when they caught the light, flecks of luminescence but not colour, for the eyeholes of the mask were long-lidded and rather small. I must have noticed, too, that there was no aperture in the lips, and this may have informed me that the mask must be removed for purposes of eating or drinking. I really do not know. I can neither excuse nor quite understand myself, seen in the distance there with her on her island. Hartley tells us that the past is another country. Perhaps we also were other people—strangers—yesterday. But when I think of this, I remember, too, the sense of drawing I had had, of being magnetised to that shore, those trees, the nostalgia for a place I had never been to. For she, it may be true to say, was a figment of that nostalgia, as if I had known her and come back to her. Some enchantment, then. Not Medusa's Island, but Circe's.

The afternoon, even through the dapple *L'Après-midi d'un Faune* effect of the leaves, was a viridian furnace when we regained the house. I sat in one of the wicker chairs on the terrace and woke with a start of embarrassment to hear her laughing at me.

"You are tired and hungry. I must go into the house for a while. I will send Kleia to you with some wine and food."

It made a bleary sense, and when I woke again it was to find an old fat woman in the ubiquitous Grecian island black—demonstrably Kleia—setting down a tray of pale red wine, amber cheese, and dark bread.

"Where is—" I realised I did not know the enchantress's name.

In any event, the woman only shook her head, saying brusquely in Greek: "No English. No English."

And when I attempted to ask again in Greek where my hostess had gone, Kleia waddled away, leaving me unanswered. So I ate the food, which was passable, and drank the wine, which was very good, imagining her faun-buying father putting down an enormous patrician cellar, then fell asleep again, sprawled in the chair.

When I awoke, the sun was setting and the clearing was swimming in red light and rusty violet shadows. The columns burned as if they were internally on fire, holding the core of the sunset, it appeared, some while after the sky had cooled and the stars became visible, a trick of architectural positioning that won my awe and envy. I was making a mental note to ask her who had been responsible for the columns, and jumped when she spoke to me, softly and hoarsely, almost seductively, from just behind my chair—thereby promptly making me forget to ask any such thing.

"Come into the house now. We will dine soon."

I got up, saying something lame about imposing on her, though we were far beyond that stage.

"Always," she said to me, "you apologise. There is no imposition. You will be gone tomorrow."

How do you know? I nearly inquired, but prevented myself. What guaranty? Even if the magic food did not change me into a swine, perhaps my poisoned dead body would be carried from the feast and cast into the sea, gone, well and truly, to Poseidon's fishes. You see, I did not trust her, even though I was somewhat in love with her. The element of her danger—for she *was* dangerous in some obscure way—may well have contributed to her attraction.

We went into the house, which in itself alerted me. I had forgotten the great curiosity I had had to look inside it. There was a shadowy, unlit entrance hall, a sort of Roman atrium of a thing. Then we passed, she leading, into a small salon that took my breath away. It was lined all over—floor, ceiling, walls—with the sea-green marble the columns were made of. Whether in good taste or bad I am not qualified to say, but the effect, instantaneous and utter, was of being beneath the sea. Smoky oil-lamps of a very beautiful Art Nouveau design hung from the profundity of the green ceiling, lighting the dreamlike swirls and oceanic variations of the marble so they seemed to breathe, definitely to move, like nothing else but waves. Shoes on that floor would have squeaked or clattered unbearably, but I was barefoot and so now was she.

A mahogany table with a modest placing for eight stood centrally. Only one place was laid.

I looked at it and she said, "I do not dine, but that will not prevent you."

An order. I considered vampires idly, but mainly I was subject to an infantile annoyance. Without quite realising it, I had looked for the subtraction of the mask when she ate and now this made me very conscious of the mask for the first time since I had originally seen it.

We seated ourselves, she two places away from me. And I began to feel nervous. To eat this meal while she watched me did not appeal. And now the idea of the mask, unconsidered all morning, all afternoon, stole over me like an incoming tide.

Inevitably, I had not dressed for dinner, having no means, but she had changed her clothes and was now wearing a high-collared long grey gown, her mother's again, no doubt. It had the fragile look of age, but was very feminine and appealing for all that. Above it, the mask now reared, stuck out like the proverbial sore thumb.

The mask. What on earth was I going to do, leered at by that myopic, soulless face which had suddenly assumed such disastrous importance?

Kleia waddled in with the dishes. I cannot recall the meal, save that it was spicy and mostly vegetable. The wine came too, and I drank it. And as I drank the wine, I began to consider seriously, for the first time (which seems very curious indeed to me now), the reason for the mask. What did it hide? A scar, a birthmark? I drank her wine and I saw myself snatch off the mask, take in the disfigurement, unquelled, and behold the painful gratitude in her eyes as she watched me. I would inform her of the genius of surgeons. She would repeat she had no money. I would promise to pay for the operation.

Suddenly she startled me by saying: "Do you believe that we have lived before?"

I looked in my glass, that fount of wisdom and possibility, and said, "It seems as sensible a proposition as any of the others I've ever heard."

I fancied she smiled to herself and do not know why I thought that; I know now I was wrong.

Her accent had thickened and distorted further when she said, "I rather hope that I have lived before. I could wish to think I may live again."

"To compensate for this life?" I said brutishly. I had not needed to be so obvious when already I had been given the implication on a salver.

"Yes. To compensate for this."

I downed all the wisdom and possibility left in my glass, swallowed an extra couple of times, and said, "Are you going to tell me why you wear a mask?"

As soon as I had said it, I grasped that I was drunk. Nor was it a pleasant drunkenness. I did not like the demanding tone I had taken with her, but I was angry at having allowed the game to go on for so long. I had no knowledge of the rules, or pretended I had not. And I could not stop myself. When she did not reply, I added a note of ghastly banter, "Or shall I guess?"

She was still, seeming very composed. Had this scene been enacted before? Finally she said, "I would suppose you do guess it is to conceal something that I wear it."

"Something you imagine worth concealing, which, perhaps, isn't."

That was the stilted fanfare of bravado. I had braced myself, flushed with such stupid confidence.

"Why not," I said, and I grow cold when I remember how I spoke to her, "take the damn thing off. Take off the mask and drink a glass of wine with me."

A pause. Then, "No," she said.

Her voice was level and calm. There was neither eagerness nor fear in it.

"Go on," I said, the drunk not getting his way, aware (oh, God) he could get it by the power of his intention alone, "please. You're an astounding woman. You're like this island. A fascinating mystery. But I've seen the island. Let me see you."

"No," she said.

I started to feel, even through the wine, that I had made an indecent suggestion to her, and this, along with the awful clichés I was bringing out, increased my anger and my discomfort.

"For heaven's sake," I said, "do you know what they call you on Daphaeu?"

"Yes."

"This is absurd. You're frightened—"

"No. I am not afraid."

"Afraid. Afraid to let me see. But maybe I can help you."

"No. You cannot help me."

"How can you be sure?"

She turned in her chair, and all the way to face me with the mask. Behind her, everywhere about her, the green marble dazzled.

"If you know," she said, "what I am called on Daphaeu, are you not uneasy as to what you may see?"

"Jesus. Mythology and superstition and ignorance. I assure you, I won't turn to stone."

"It is I," she said quietly, "who have done that."

Something about the phrase, the way in which she said it, chilled me. I put down my glass, and in that instant, her hands went to the sides of the mask and her fingers worked at some complicated strap arrangement which her hair had covered.

"Good," I said, "good. I'm glad—"

But I faltered over it. The cold night sea seemed to fill my veins where the warm red wine had been. I had been heroic and sure and bold, the stuff of celluloid. But now that I had my way, with hardly any preliminary, what *would* I see? And then she drew the plastic away and I saw.

I sat there, and then I stood up. The reflex was violent, and the chair scraped over the marble with an unbearable noise. There are occasions, though rare, when the human mind grows blank of all thought. I had no thought as I looked at her. Even now, I can evoke those long, long, empty seconds, that lapse of time. I recollect only the briefest confusion, when I believed she still played some kind of hideous game, that what I witnessed was a product of her decision and her will, a gesture—

After all, Pitos had done this very thing to illustrate and endorse his argument, produced this very expression, the eyes bursting from the head, the jaw rigidly outthrust, the tendons in the neck straining, the mouth in the grimace of a frozen, agonised scream, the teeth visible, the tongue slightly protruding. The gorgon's face on the jar or the oven. The face so ugly, so demented, so terrible, it could petrify.

The awful mouth writhed.

"You have seen," she said. Somehow the stretched and distorted lips brought out these words. There was even that nuance of humour I had heard before, the smile, although physically a smile would have been out of the question. "You have seen."

She picked up the mask again, gently, and put it on, easing the underpart of the plastic beneath her chin to hide the convulsed tendons in her throat. I stood there, motionless. Childishly I informed myself that now I comprehended the reason for her peculiar accent, which was caused, not by some exotic foreign extraction, but by the atrocious malformation of jaw, tongue, and lips, which somehow must be fought against for every sound she made.

I went on standing there, and now the mask was back in place.

"When I was very young," she said, "I suffered, without warning, from a form of fit or stroke. Various nerve-centres were paralysed. My father took me to the very best of surgeons, you may comfort yourself with that. Unfortunately, any effort to correct the damage entailed a penetration of my brain so uncompromisingly delicate that it was reckoned impossible, for it would surely render me an idiot. Since my senses, faculties, and intelligence were otherwise unaffected, it was decided not to risk this dire surgery, and my doctors resorted instead to alternate therapies, which, patently, were unsuccessful. As the months passed, my body adjusted to the unnatural physical tensions resulting from my facial paralysis. The pain of the rictus faded, or grew acceptable. I learned both how to eat, and how to converse, although the former activity is not attractive and I attend to it in private. The mask was made for me in Athens. I am quite fond of it. The man who designed it had worked a great many years in the theatre and could have made me a face of enormous beauty or character, but this seemed pointless, even wasteful."

There was a silence, and I realised her explanation was finished. Not once had she stumbled. There was neither hurt nor madness in her inflection. There *was* something . . . at the time I missed it, though it came to me after. Then I knew only that she was far beyond my pity or my anguish, far away indeed from my terror.

"And now," she said, rising gracefully, "I will leave you to eat your meal in peace. Good night."

I wanted, or rather I felt impelled, to stay her with actions or sentences, but I was incapable of either. She walked out of the green marble room and left me there. It is a fact that for a considerable space of time I did not move.

I did not engage the swim back to Daphaeu that night; I judged myself too drunk and slept on the beach at the edge of the trees, where at sunrise the tidal water woke me with a strange low hissing. Green sea, green sunlight through leaves. I swam away and found my course through the warming ocean and fetched up, exhausted and swearing, bruising myself on Daphaeu's fangs that had not harmed me when I left her. I did not see Pitos anywhere about, and that evening I caught the boat which would take me to the mainland.

There is a curious thing which can happen with human beings. It is the ability to perform for days or weeks like balanced and cheerful automata, when some substrata, something upon which our codes or our hopes had firmly rested, has given way. Men who lose their wives or their God are quite capable of behaving in this manner for an indefinite season. After which the collapse is brilliant and total. Something of this sort had happened to me. Yet to fathom what I had lost, what she had deprived me of, is hard to say. I found its symptoms, but not the sickness which it was.

Medusa (I must call her that, she has no other name I know), struck by the extraordinary arrow of her misfortune, condemned to her relentless, uncanny, horrible isolation, her tragedy most deeply rooted in the fact that she was not a myth, not a fabulous and glamorous monster. . . . For it came to me one night in a bar in Corinth, to consider if the first Medusa might have been also such a victim, felled by some awesome fit, not petrifying but petrified, so appalling to the eyes and, more significantly, to the brooding aesthetic spirit that lives in man that she too was shunned and hated and slain by a murderer who would observe her only in a polished surface.

I spent some while in bars that summer. And later, much later, when the cold climate of the year's end closed the prospect of travel and adventure, I became afraid for myself, that dreadful writer's fear which has to do with the death of the idea, with the inertia of hand and heart and mind. Like one of the broken leaves, the summer's withered plants, I had dried. My block was sheer. I had expected a multitude of pages from the island, but instead I saw those unborn pages die on the horizon, where the beach met the sea.

And this, merely a record of marble, water, a plastic shell strapped across a woman's face, this is the last thing, it seems, which I shall commit to paper. Why? Perhaps only because she was to me such a lesson in the futility of things, the waiting fist of chance, the random despair we name the World.

And yet, now and then, I hear that voice of hers, I hear the way she spoke to me. I know now what I heard in her voice, which had neither pain nor shame in it, nor pleading, nor whining, nor even a hint of the tragedy—the Greek tragedy—of her life. And what I heard was not dignity either, or acceptance, or nobleness. It was *contempt.* She despised me. She despised all of us who live without her odds, who struggle with our small struggles, incomparable to hers. "Your Greek is very good," she said to me with the patronage of one who is multilingual. And in that same disdain she says over and over to me: "That you live is very good." Compared to her life, her existence, her multilingual endurance, what are my life or my ambitions worth? Or anything.

It did not occur immediately, but still it occurred. In its way, the myth is perfectly accurate. I see it in myself, scent it, taste it, like the onset of inescapable disease. What they say about the gorgon is true. She has turned me to stone.

# LA REINE BLANCHE

HE WHITE QUEEN LIVED IN A PALE TOWER, HIGH IN A SHADOWY garden. She had been shut in there three days after the death of her husband, the king. Such a fate was traditional for certain of the royal widows. All about, between the dark verdures of the dark garden, there stared up similar pale towers in which similar white queens had, for centuries, been immured. Most of the prisoners were by now deceased. Occasionally, travellers on the road beneath claimed to have glimpsed—or to have thought that they glimpsed—a dim skeletal shape or two, in senile disarray, peering blindly from the tall narrow windows, which were all the windows these towers possessed, over the heads of the trees, towards the distant spires of the city.

The latest white queen, however, was young. She was just twenty on the day she wed the king, who was one hundred and two years of age. He had been expected to thrive at least for a further decade, and he had left off marrying until absolutely necessary. But he had gone livid merely on seeing her. Then, on the night of the nuptial, stumbling on his wife's pearl-sewn slippers lying discarded in the boudoir—symbol of joys to come—the king was over-whelmed. He expired an hour later, not even at the nude feet of his wife, only at the foot of the bridal bed. Virgin, wife, and widow, the young queen was adorned in a gown whiter than milk, and on her head, milk-white-coiffed like that of a nun, was placed the Alabaster Crown of mourning. With a long-stemmed white rose in her hand, she was permitted to follow her husband's bier to the mausoleum. Afterwards, she was taken by torchlight to the shadowy garden beyond the city, and conducted into a vacant tower. It contained a suite of rooms, unmistakably regal, but nevertheless bare. She was to commune with no one, and would be served invisibly. Such things as she might need—food and wine, fuel, clean linen—were to be brought by hidden ways and left for her in caskets and baskets that a pulley device would raise and lower at a touch of her fingers.

Here then, and in this way, she would now live until she died.

A year passed. It might have been fifty. Spring and summer and autumn eschewed the garden, scarcely dusting it with their colours. The shadow trees did not change. The only cold stone blossoms the garden had ever put forth were the towers themselves. When winter began, not even then did the trees alter. But eventually the snow came. Finding the unaltered garden, the snow at last covered it and made it as white as the gown of the young queen.

She stood in her window, watching the snow. Nothing else was to be seen, save the low mauvened sky. Then a black snow-flake fell out of the sky. It came down in the embrasure of the window. A raven looked at the young queen through the glass of her casement. He was blacker than midnight, so vividly different that he startled her and she took half a step away.

"Gentle Blanche," said the raven, "have pity, and let me come in."

The white queen closed her eyes.

"How is it you can speak?" she cried.

"How is it," said the raven, "you can understand what I say?"

The white queen opened her eyes. She went back to the narrow window-pane.

"The winter is my enemy," said the raven. "He pursues me like death or old age, a murderer with a sword. Fair Blanche, shelter me."

Half afraid, half unable to help herself, the white queen undid the window-catch and the terrible cold thrust through and breathed on the room. Then the raven flew in, and the window was shut.

The raven seated himself before the hearth like a fire-dog of jet.

"My thanks," he said.

The white queen brought him a dish of wine and some cold meat left on the bone.

"My thanks again," said the raven. He ate and drank tidily.

The white queen, seated in her chair, watched him in awe and in silence.

When the raven had finished his meal, he arranged his feathers. His eyes were black, and his beak like a black dagger. He was altogether so black, the white queen imagined he must be as black inside as out, even his bones and blood of ebony and ink.

"And now," said the raven, "tell me, if you will, about yourself."

So the white queen—she had no one else to talk to—told the raven how she came to be there, of her wedding, and her husband one hundred and two years old, and of following his cadaver with her white rose, and the torchlit journey here by night, and how it was since the torches went away. It had been so long. Fifty years, or one interminable year, unending.

"As I supposed," said the raven, "your story is sad, sinister, and interesting. Shall I tell you, in turn, what I know of the city?"

The white queen nodded slowly, trembling.

The raven said, "There is still a king in the palace. He has had the walls dyed and the turrets carved with dragons and gryphons and swans. He loves music, dancing, and all beautiful things. He himself is young and handsome. He has been many months looking for a wife. Portraits and descriptions were brought from neighbouring kingdoms. None will do. The girls are too plump or too thin, too tall, too short, not serious enough, too serious. He sends back slighting messages and breaks hearts. There have been suicides among the rejects. He himself painted an image of the girl he wants. Slender and pale, with a mouth made to smile and eyes that have held sorrow in them like rain in the cups of two cool flowers. I have seen this portrait," said the raven. "It is yourself."

The queen laughed. She tossed a pinch of incense on the fire to make the room sweet, and so console herself.

"How cruel you are," she said, "when I have tried to be kind."

"Not at all. In seven hours it will be midnight. Do you not guess I am the cousin of midnight? It can therefore sometimes be made to do things for me. And you, as you say, have been kind. I am warmed and fed. May I sleep now by your hearth, fair Blanche?"

The white queen sighed her assent.

Beyond the casement the snow-dusk deepened, and on the hearth the fire turned dense and gave off great heat. The raven seemed to melt into a shadow there. Soon his hostess thought she had dreamed it all, though the empty dishes still stood, dull-shining in the twilight.

At midnight she woke, perhaps from sleep, and she was no longer in the tower. For a year of years it had contained her, all the world she knew. Now she was free—but how?

She walked over the snow but did not feel the cold through her slim thin shoes. A moon, the condemned white widow-queen of heaven, blazed in the west, and lit the way beyond the walls of the garden, on to the straight road that led to the city. Although the gates were obscured, Blanche passed directly through the mortared stones of the wall. So she knew. "This is only a dream." And bitterly, wistfully, she laughed again. "All things are possible to a dreamer. If this is the raven's gift, let me be glad of it."

Even at these words, she made out a vehicle on the road, which seemed waiting—and for whom but herself? As she stepped closer, she saw it was a beautiful charrette, draped with white satin, and with silver crests on the doors that were like lilies or maybe curved plumes or feathers. White horses in gilded caparison with bells and tassels drew the carriage, but there was no man to drive or escort it.

Nevertheless, the white queen entered and sat down. At once the carriage started off.

Presently, shyly, she glanced at herself. Her mourning garments were gone. The white silk of her gown was figured and fringed by palest rose and sapphire. Her slippers were sewn with pearls. Her hair flowed about her, maiden's hair, heavy, curled, and perfumed with musk and oleander. A chaplet of pastel orchids replaced the Alabaster Crown of widowhood and living death.

"And there are moonstones at my throat, silver bands on my fingers. And how the bells ring and sing in the cold night air."

They came into the city, through the gates, unchallenged, through dark slight streets, and broad boulevards where torches flashed and lamps hung like golden fruit from wide windows and bird-cage balconies.

Along this same route Blanche had been driven to her marriage. They had warned her from the beginning the king was old, and not easy, but even that had not put out her pride or pleasure. Until she met him on the mountainous stair and gave up her hand to his of gnarled wood and dry paper. He had glared at her in terrified lust, fumbling at his throat to breathe. But now she wished to forget and she forgot. Everything was novel, and fresh.

In the courtyard, the charrette stopped still. Blanche left the carriage. She looked and saw the wonderful gryphons and swans and dragons new-made on the turrets where the banners of the king floated out like soft ribbons. Every window was bright, an orchard of windows, peach and cherry and mulberry.

The guards on the stair blinked but did not check or salute her as she went up between them. Some gasped, some gazed, some did not see her. And some crossed themselves.

The doors glanced open without a sound. Or else she thought that they did. She came across several lamplit rooms into a moon-tinctured walk where only glow-worms and fountains flickered, and nightingales made music like the notes of the stars. At the end of the walk, Blanche the white queen saw a golden salon where candle flames burned low. She had known the way.

As she entered, she found the young king of whom the raven had told her. He was dark as she was pale, his own hair black as the branch of a tree against the snow. He was handsome, too. And she felt a pang of love, and another of dismay, though not surprise.

He caught sight of her at once, and started to his feet.

"Are you real?" he said. His voice was musical and tensed between delight and anger.

"No," said Blanche. "I am a dream. Mine, or yours."

"You are a painting come to life."

Blanche smiled. The raven, who surely was to be her tormentor, had spoken the truth to her. Or else, for now, it was the truth.

"I would," he said, "have waited all my life for you. And since you may not be real, I may have to wait, still. Having seen you, I can hardly do otherwise. Unless you consent to stay."

"I think I may be permitted to stay until sunrise. It seems to me I am in league with darkness. Until dawn, then."

"Because you are a ghost."

Blanche went to him across the golden gloom and put her hand in his outstretched hand.

"You are living flesh," said the king. He leaned forward and kissed her lips, quietly. "Warm and douce and live. Even though a dream."

For an hour, they talked together. Musicians were summoned, and if they saw or feared her, or whatever they thought, they played, and the young queen and the young king danced over the chequered floor. And they drank wine, and walked among roses and sculptures and clocks and mysteries, and so came eventually to a private place, a beautiful bedroom. And here they lay down and were lovers together, splendidly and fiercely and in rapture, and in regret, for it was a dream, however sweet, however true.

"Will you return to me?" he said.

"My heart would wish it. I do not think I shall return, to you."

"I will nevertheless wait for you. In case it chances you put on mortal shape. For this is too lovely to believe in."

"Do not," said Blanche, "wait long. Waiting is a prison." But she knew these words were futile.

Just then a bird sang far away across the palace gardens. It was not a nightingale.

"Let me go now, my beloved," said Blanche. "I must leave instantly. I am partly afraid of what the sun may do to me before your eyes."

"Alas," he said.

He did not hinder her.

Blanche quickly drew on her garments, even the chaplet of orchids which showed no sign of withering. She clasped her jewels about her throat. A frosty sheen lay on the window-panes that the stars and the sinking moon had not put there. "Adieu," she said. "Live well. Do not, do not remember me."

Blanche fled from the chamber and away through the palace, the rooms all darkling now, the silent fountain walk, the outer salons, the stair. In the courtyard the charrette and its horses remained, but it was half-transparent. This time, none of the guards had seen her pass. As she hastened on she realised that she had after all forgotten her pearl-sewn slippers. She felt only smooth cobblestones under her feet—there was no snow, and now it came to her that there had been none, in any corner of the city or the palace that she had visited.

The carriage started off. It flew like the wind, or a bell-hung bird, into the face of the dawn. And when the dawn smote through, the carriage fell apart like silver ashes. The sun's lilting blade pierced her heart. And she woke alone, seated in her chair before the cold hearth, in the pale tower, in the shadowy garden. As she had known she would.

"Cruel raven," said the white queen, as she sprinkled crumbs of meat and bread along the embrasure of her window. She was full of pain and stiffness, and even to do so much made her anxious. Nor did she think he would come back. The winter day had passed, or

had it been the whole of the winter which was gone? The snow faded between the shadow trees. The white queen looked from her narrow window and pulled her breath into her body without ease. "Spring will come," she said. "But not any spring for me."

She turned and went back to her chair. Within the white coif, under the Alabaster Crown, her face was like a carved bone, the eyes sunk deep, the cheeks and lips. Her hands were like slender bundles of pale twisted twigs. As she sat, her limbs creaked and crackled, hurting her. Tears welled in the sunken pools of her eyes. They were no longer two flowers holding rain.

"I am old," said the white queen. "In one night, I grew to be so. Or were they fifty nights, or a hundred nights, that seemed only one?" She recalled the young king, and his hair black as a raven. She wept a little, where once she would have laughed at the bitter joke. "He would despise me. No magic now and no demoiselle of dream. I should revolt him now. He would wish me dead, to be free of me." She closed her eyes. "As I wished my own aged husband dead, for I thought even this pale tower could be no worse than marriage to such a creature."

When the white queen opened her eyes, the raven stood in the opened window like a blot of ink.

"Gentle Blanche," said the raven. "Let me come in."

"You are in," she said. "My heart is full of you, you evil magician. I gave you food and drink and shelter and you did harm to me, and perhaps to another. Of course you did."

"Also you, my lady, told me a story. Now I," said the raven, "will tell one to you."

"Long ago," said the raven, "there was a maiden of high birth. Her name was Blanche. She might have made a good marriage among several of the great houses, to young men who were her peers. But it was told to her that she might also make a marriage with the king and rule the whole kingdom. He was old, decaying, and foolish, she was warned of this. But Blanche did not care. Let me agree; he will die soon, thought Blanche. Then I will be regent to any who come after, and still I will rule the land."

"Oh," said the white queen, "I remember."

"However," said the raven, sitting on the hearth like a gargoyle of black coal, "when Blanche was given to the king and saw and touched him, her courage failed her. By then it was too late. They were lighted to their bed and priests blessed it. As he had come from his disrobing, the king had stumbled on Blanche's discarded slippers, and called out, and fallen. As he was revived by his servitors, the aged monarch muttered. He had dreamed of a girl like Blanche eighty years before. Or else it was a spirit who visited him. The girl of his dreams had been his wife for one night, and he had worshipped her ever since, refusing to marry, looking only for his lover to return to him. In his youth he had been mad, ten whole years, following the uncanny visitation, wandering the earth in search of his ghost-bride. He had even unearthed tombs and dug up embalmed corpses, to see if any of them might be she. All his life, even when the madness left him, he waited. And it seemed that Blanche, whom he had now wedded, was the image of the ghost-bride and, like her, had left her pearl-sewn slippers lying behind her."

"Yes," said the white queen, "I recall." She leaned her head on her hand, on her sore wrist thin as a stick.

"However," said the raven again, "Blanche barely listened to these ramblings of her senile husband. She lay in the silk covers shrinking and in horror. She thought, he is decrepit and weak and easily distressed, and so easily destroyed. When the servants and the priests were gone, she kneeled upon the bridal couch and taunted her old husband and railed at him. Her tongue was sharp with ambition and loathing. She broke his heart. He died at the foot of the bed."

"I called at once for help," said Blanche. "I thought they would judge me blameless. But it seems someone had stayed to listen and had overheard. For a certain kind of murder, the murder of a king by his queen without the brewing of a draught, the striking of a blow, this is the punishment. Confined alive until death in a tower in a cemetery garden. A white queen, a murderess. I am punished. Why," said the old white queen, "is fate so malicious, and are you fate? If I had met him as he was that night, young and strong, handsome and wise, how could I not have loved him? Yet I was sent back eighty years to harm him, as I would harm him eighty years in the future. And as he has harmed me."

"You were his punishment," said the raven. "His pride and his own malign tongue had broken hearts, as his would break. He would brook only perfection, a single sort of perfection, and was intolerant of all others. So this perfection came to him and was lost to him. He might have relinquished the dream still, and would not. He waited until he was a hundred and two years of age to claim a girl of twenty, such, even then, was his overbearing blind pride. It cost him dear."

"While I was punished for my wickedness, willing and casting his life away when I might have been happy elsewhere, and he left in peace."

"Each the other's sentence and downfall," said the raven. "As perhaps each knew it must be."

"And you," she said, "are an angel of chastising God. Or the Devil."

"Neither," said the raven. "Should we not chastise ourselves, that we learn?" He flew to the embrasure of the window. Beyond the tower, the trees were dark as always, the tops of the other dreary towers pushed up. But the sky was blushed with blue. Over the wall it would be spring.

"Despite all sins and stupidities," said the raven, "I love you yet and yet have waited for you, gentle, fair Blanche. And you, whether you wished it or no, waited for me in your bone tower, and at the last as at the first, you were kind."

The white queen wept. Her tears were like pearls.

"Let us," said the raven, "be together a little while, in freedom and innocence."

"Oh, how can you speak?" she cried.

"Oh, how can you understand what I say?"

Then the white queen left her chair. She left her body and bones and old pale blood, for she was white now inside and out. She flew up into the window embrasure. From the prison towers only the souls of dreamers or the wings of birds could get out. Up like arrows flew two ravens, one black as pitch, one white as snow, and away together over the trees, the wall, the road, the city, the world, into the sky of spring.

# A LYNX WITH LIONS

**A**T MIDDAY, BEATEN ALMOST FLAT BY THE HAMMER OF THE sun, the desert lay in the perfect imitation of one near death. A deception. Life lurked and thrived in its own way just beneath the skin of the desert. Husks, buried shards, lost treasures, veins of water, and magic. While at dusk, the dying thing would rise and shake itself, and stretch to receive the cold balm of the stars.

Karuil-Ysem turned a black-hooded head, and seemed to listen more attentively to what the scout was saying. The black eyes of Karuil-Ysem, old, cruel, and intransigently wise, half closed. It was a sign reminiscent of the prostration of the desert, a deception of lifelessness and quiescence.

"And you say he has followed us since yesterday's sunrise?"

"Just so, Karuil."

"And on foot, and alone. And garbed as our people are garbed for the desert."

"And so, Karuil."

"And he is white-haired?"

"Or very fair. A Westerner. Neither of the cities, nor of our own people. Yet he walks the sands with the sure step of the nomads, as careless and as cunning. He wears a sword, yet this morning a viper came from the stones by his hand, where he had lain sleeping. It rose up to strike him, but he struck first. He threw a knife that parted its head from its body before it or I caught breath. He found the hidden watering-place, also, that only our people know of. Who can it be, Father, who understands our ways yet is neither ours nor our land's?"

Karuil, slowly blinking his eagle's eyes at the King's title: "Father," as he always did now, as if surprised still to be so addressed, turned his head back again, to regard the recent erection of black tents among the pillared trees of the oasis. Life moved sluggishly there, paying homage to the desert's temporary death.

"I believe I know who he is," said Karuil-Ysem. "I shall return with you. Let us see if I am wise, still, or have become a fool."

The scout kicked his horse so it leapt about and raced away, the reddish sand splashing up from its unshod feet. Karuil's horse moved no less willingly. They were gone.

Some of the nomads, tall men, all dressed alike in the long black robe, the hoods mostly up against the sun, sat under the soaked-out shadows of the palms, watching Karuil and the scout vanish.

"What causes that?" one asked.

The son of Karuil-Ysem, Ysemid, made the nomadic gesture equivalent to a wink.

"Someone has been following us, the scouts say. One of the Angel knights, perhaps, a Dove who has mislaid his nest."

"Who pursues the Lions of the Desert should be more careful of his meat," quoted another man.

Ysemid acknowledged this. He was handsome, young, and proud, one ear pierced by a knob of sapphire. Across the shadow-patched sand, more of his riches were observable. One of his three beautiful wives, black-clad but with girdle, wrists, ears, and forehead dripping with jewelry, the veil which covered her lips and chin sewn with sequins of polished gold, was bringing him a drink in a cup of fluted glass, on a tray of chased silver.

"My father, the Father," said Ysemid, "will give us the carcass if it is an enemy. If not, we shall see."

On a rise among the dunes, Karuil and the scout sat their horses, seeing for themselves.

The pursuer, now in sight, climbed steadily and unerringly towards them. He had probably seen them also, but as yet gave no sign of it.

"Behold how he treads, Father. He knows the sand."

"So he does."

"And the hair."

"Just so."

A minute more and the object of their scrutiny lifted his white-blond head. Without pausing, he looked straight at them. Coming on in this way, he was soon near enough that they could discern the features of a face lightly tanned but otherwise entirely remarkable.

"A Jewel of God," declared the scout, with contemptuous awe. The term denoted great beauty and was usually employed in scorn. The nomads, relentless travellers, ruthless warriors, and holding to a rigid and sometimes bloody code indigenous to themselves, tended to believe the truly beautiful were also the truly useless.

"A Jewel," the old man agreed. "But set in steel. Yes, it is the one I reckoned it must be."

Karuil-Ysem swung himself from the back of his horse—he was surprisingly limber. He stood, in obvious waiting as the un-stranger, his glamorous face composed and expressionless, came up the last of the rising ground.

When the young man was twenty paces off, Karuil said, still in the nomadic tongue, "The desert flowers at the footstep of the desired guest."

At this the arrival halted, and replied, in the same tongue, fault-lessly: "And water springs from the rock at the refinding of a friend."

His voice was beautiful as the rest of him, and the scout listened with offended amazement. Which increased, as with no great show Karuil opened his arms, and the blond Westerner completed the distance and walked into them. Embrace was calmly and strongly given and returned.

"Welcome, Cyrion," said Karuil.

"Your welcome is welcome," answered the Jewel of God who was called Cyrion.

"How did you happen on us?" inquired Karuil.

"In the usual manner. By following those signs the People of Karuil leave, for those who seek them in brotherhood."

"My scout is astonished."

Cyrion glanced at the scout, and smiled at him with appalling charm. "There are many roads to wisdom, of which astonishment is one," said Cyrion, demurely quoting a nomadic proverb.

Karuil laughed. It was rare, that dry crackle of amusement.

"Cyrion has spent time among us. He is also a swordsman and adventurer famous in the coastal cities and in yellow-walled Heruzala itself, which is now the Westerners' playground."

"And does he also," asked the scout, "heed the teachings of the Prophet Hesuf, as we do, and as the Westerners pretend to do?"

"I note astuteness and virtue in the teachings of Hesuf," said Cyrion, amiably. "Like yourself, perhaps, I sometimes stumble over that particular one which says I should enjoy being struck twice in the face."

The scout's eyes widened, then he grinned.

"You will go back with us to the tents?" Karuil asked.

"My intention, if allowed."

"It is allowed."

Karuil did not remount, and Cyrion himself took the tasselled reins of the desert king's horse, leading it. The scout trotted on a little ahead of them.

For a while there was silence, separated only by the hushed, blistering shifts, as the sand eased itself. Finally, as they descended from the last upgrade, and the oasis came in view, Karuil said: "And you live well, Cyrion?"

"Not so well as I have."

"Some reversal in fortunes."

"A reversal," the musical voice hesitated, "of a kind. I have come back into the desert in sore need of the disciplines I once learned here, things which fail me from lack of practice."

"The muscles of the spirit—you were adept. What is your need?"

Again, a pause. The man who rode ahead was not so far off he could not overhear, through the still, roasted air.

"My scout is to be trusted," said Karuil. "But yet. We will speak in my tent."

Cyrion murmured, "Father, I have no cause to mistrust any of your people. Better I tell you now. I fear it will become necessary in any case, very shortly." Again, a hesitation. Then, coolly and firmly: "There is an affliction of the brain and eyes, in itself unfatal and spasmodic. It begins with a slight disturbance of the vision, progresses to a period of blindness, and ends with a pain that inhabits half the skull for any number of hours, like a roosting axe-blade. The causes are numerous and unknown. Drugs will generally relieve the pain, and to those of a quiet disposition, the ailment is negotiable if unpleasing. However, you can judge, Father, its dangers to a man known to have lived by use of a sword."

Karuil stood immobile. Below, the drinking cup of the oasis glittered its water. The scout had reined in his horse nearby. He looked away, down into the encampment, frankly listening to what was said at his back.

"You?" said Karuil-Ysem to Cyrion.

"Very unluckily, I. You never heard of such a disability? The

Cassian emperors of Remusa were afflicted by it. Noble company, it would seem. But you tell my predicament."

"The cause?"

Cyrion shrugged, smiling, as if he spoke of nothing much. "I have no idea. A blow to the head, maybe, of which I have been gifted a few. Or some form of witchcraft—I have also come in the way of one or two of these. . . . My dissolute life. Whatever opened the door, the guest has come in. And while I can wield a blade through most sorts of pain, it may prove difficult to fight a man I cannot see."

The tent of Karuil-Ysem was set by itself, very close to the water, in a green net of shade. Inside, an incense lamp of bronze latticework depended low from a complex arrangement of chains stretched between the tent poles. The complexity of these chains resulted from the fact that they must avoid forming a cross. Hundreds of years before, the Prophet Hesuf had almost died on such an instrument, before being saved by popular outcry. For this reason, anything resembling a cross was abhorrent to the nomads. Their dislike they demonstrated even in the matter of their swords, the blades of which, in order to escape the accursed shape, were curved like a new moon.

Karuil-Ysem sat under the lamp, among the silk pillows, facing the opened entrance of the tent where the sun fell, Cyrion beside him. They had been served wine and date-juice, and a variety of candies. These sweets and the wine, Karuil remarked, were the product of his son's generosity. Ysemid spent much profitable time now in the cities. Across the glimmer of the water, Ysemid's tent was visible. As the heat of noon died down, black-robed men were indulging in violent horse races there, dust and cries splintering up into the bleached sky.

After the courtesies of eating and drinking the fare of Daskiriom and Heshbel, Cyrion sat at apparent indolent ease, his chin resting on his ringed left hand, as Karuil, with unexpected appetite, quaffed and chewed on.

At length Cyrion said, casually, "I take it, we shall no longer be overheard, here?"

"No," said Karuil, selecting a pastry.

"While your busy scout is already spreading the news of my sad affliction."

Karuil blinked. The snake-skin lids hovered. It was a signal of decided attention.

"The scout? I told you he would say nothing."

"Then what was the purpose of your invitation to speak in front of him?"

Karuil set down the pastry. The old face grew wickedly intent. Very slowly, his long teeth appeared. "What I told you, and what is true, may not be one and the same."

"You do delight me. The thought of engineering more rumours seemed unexciting, not to say heavy-handed."

"You also then play with truth. Your illness is a lie."

Cyrion looked at Karuil for some moments, then glanced towards the seethe of dust and action sixty feet off, over the water.

"The illness," said Cyrion quietly, "was a useful coincidence. I was instructed, was I not, to arrive armed with an excuse?"

"Then it is a fact—this blindness—"

"The thing is normally occasional. What disciplines I learnt among your people I have not forgotten, and do not need to relearn. You may imagine, if I was sick I would have tried them. Perhaps they would not be of help."

"Then," said Karuil, "you are here solely—" there was a distended pause. At last—"because I sent for you."

"Which is rather odd of me, I see, since you appear to trust me very little."

"That I should send for you at all demonstrates I trust no other so well. How did you come on my message?"

"In one of the places that I frequent and that you left it. How else? If I deciphered it correctly, you meant me to understand you were in danger."

Karuil, who had taken up the pastry again, set it down. His eyes sank into their deceptive dozing position.

"Ah. I thought you would interpret it in this way."

"I was mistaken."

"No. He is my enemy." Now the words came swiftly, with an edge to them, sere and bitter. "He cleaves to city ways. He revels in their decadence and luxury. He hangs his women with gold and his tent with gems, and sends this much of the bakeries to draw my strong teeth—" Karuil struck out suddenly, and sent the sweetmeats rolling like coloured dice. "Ysemid would make a dotard of me. Like an old lion, he thinks to lull me, then spring the trap."

Cyrion waited a moment before saying, "Among the People, patricide is the worst of all crimes, and receives the worst punishment. Will Ysemid risk that?"

"I do not know. Yes, I believe he will. Oh, not yet. But soon. He has those among us who love him, those who admire his dreams. He would pitch the tents beside the city walls and make a bazaar and show of us, and loll on his bed with his women while the bones of our sons turn to sticks and our daughters are made into whores —" Karuil broke off. His voice had not risen. The phrases were a fury, the rest of him stayed still as an eagle watching from a high rock. "Only I," he said, "stand in the beast's way. Yes. He will kill me. So I sent for you. You, that once lived among my people, and were like my son to me. You remember this?"

Softly Cyrion answered, "I remember. Without Karuil-Ysem, I should be far less than I am. What would you have me do, Father of your People?"

"For the moment, nothing. Linger here, and wait, as I do."

The old man drank Ysemid's wine, savouring it as if it were the blood of a foe, which like the demons, the nomads of ancient days had sometimes swallowed.

"Then," said Cyrion, "I will wait."

"They shall prepare you a tent. You shall be one of us again. But this affliction of your eyes, it troubles me."

"No. It is me that it troubles. When you require it, I shall be at your command."

A shadow fell across the threshold. Both Cyrion and Karuil-Ysem fixed their gaze on it. Abruptly, the man that the shadow had preceded stalked from around the tent. It was unlikely, even had he been listening, that he would have heard much. Their voices had been low, and the noise across the water, only now dying down, would have masked a good deal.

The man bowed in the nomadic way to Karuil. At Cyrion he stared.

"The Prince Ysemid begs you, Father, to grant him also the happiness of greeting your guest."

Cyrion rose, and observed the hanging lamp, now level with his forehead, as Karuil said to him: "Yes, go to my son, Cyrion. The young lion must have his way."

Cyrion politely agreed.

As he walked with Ysemid's messenger around the oasis, the man tried to conduct a stilted, partly scathing interrogation.

"The prince wonders what you can be, clad in our attire, yet of the pale foreign blood. It is said you lived among us. Why do we not recall you?"

"Either we did not meet at the time, or I am humiliatingly unmemorable."

"Hah! To live with us—did your own mother, revolted by you, slough you in the desert and run away?"

"Mothers are notoriously partial. They will put up with almost anything. Such a small number of us would otherwise survive."

They moved among the flock of black shelters. Lazy fires had been lit where meat already broiled. Where the water gathered in a pool, women idled over their pitchers, gossiping. At the approach of the two men they glanced, and giggled. On Cyrion, their eyes grew large, and often melting. Kept close among the tents, they had not frequently seen a Westerner. He, with his hair like the sky of earliest sunrise, his fair complexion, his eyes gilded by lashes longer than their own, was like a being from another world.

On the far side of the oasis the races had finished. Ysemid sat before his tent on a carpet, sipping from a glass cup. About him, his favourites sat or stood, joking and drinking. The three beautiful wives were in glinting evidence. As the sun touched their faces, one saw their black face-veils were thin as smoke, in violation of tradition.

Noting Cyrion, Ysemid rose, lifting his arms in a gesture of welcome and pleasure. The scout was nowhere to be seen, but no doubt had been here, before returning to his watch beyond the camp.

"Behold," announced Ysemid, "the white cat is a friend, or surely my father the Father would have slain him. Come, friend of Karuil's People."

Cyrion went forward and suffered himself to be embraced. Ysemid's entourage in their turn fell to patting him and smoothing his blond hair. Earrings and teeth flashed, and the slanting sun hit the scene with blows of tilted, steady light.

Ysemid pressed on Cyrion a cup of wine. Cyrion graciously sampled it and set it aside. Another of the men graciously pressed it on him again.

"It is not to your liking?" Ysemid was concerned.

"A little stony. The wine of Andriok is better, since you are prepared to pay such prices for it."

"A merchant! He knows and prices my wine. What else wonderful can you do, friend of the People of Karuil?"

Cyrion smiled dazzlingly.

"You should not overvalue me."

"But I divine genius. Come," said Ysemid once more, throwing an arm over Cyrion's shoulders, "we have brought horses out of Heshbel. Come and see. Tell us how they seem to you."

In a surge, the laughing young men thrust forward, Cyrion borne with them. As he passed, two of Ysemid's wives modestly lowered their eyes. The third looked after him with a strange deliberation.

In Ysemid's ear, the knob of sapphire sparkled, fired. Again and again the shattered brilliancies of the sun shot from it. It seemed both to attract and repel the eyes of Cyrion.

The horses stood in the shade of five palm trees, all but one stallion which, held by several boys, plunged and stamped, tossing his head.

"Now what," said Ysemid, "do you suppose is wrong with this animal? He has unseated two of my best horsemen. No sooner up— than down."

Cyrion said nothing amid the laughter of the entourage. The horse shook his head as if to loosen it from his body.

"Perhaps," said Ysemid, "you, illustrious guest of my father, would care to test your ability."

"No," said Cyrion, "I regret I should not."

All the gladsome faces, as if rubbed by a single cloth, were cleaned of their merriment.

"But am I to think you afraid?"

"Think me rather aware the horse is ungelded and there are nubile mares in the vicinity."

Ysemid cried out joyfully.

"Did I not commend him as a genius? Wine, horses . . ."

The voice of a boy piped through from beyond the crowd.

"A dwelling has been set for the stranger, under the stunted palm tree, a short distance from the tents."

Cyrion offered Ysemid the proud obeisance of the East, and asked leave to depart for the tent.

All fondness, Ysemid waved him off.

"Go, blessed Jewel of God."

He doubtless noticed the Westerner walked slowly, going back around the oasis. He did not seem inclined to look about, and reaching the segregated tent Karuil had allotted him, went directly inside, letting down the flap behind him.

Ysemid spat on the sand, a rare act among those who learned early to respect water.

The red flower of sunset opened, bloomed, and faded. In the black night the clustered stars of the desert blazed. When the stars of the fires died in the nomadic encampment, Ysemid walked from his tent, stretching himself, smiling as, within, the sleepy voice of a woman murmured. Presently Ysemid moved silently through the camp and around the water, responding, en route, to two brief challenges, with a muffled jest that caused the camp's sentries to chuckle. Just before he came to the tent of Karuil, the prince palmed up a handful of glisten from the oasis, and drank it.

At the entrance, where the flap hung closed, the young man stopped and called, very low, "My father?"

After a moment, from inside the tent, the old voice stirred in answer.

"What is it?"

"Do I disturb you? It is your son, Ysemid. Something weighs on my mind. May I come in?"

"Old men sleep shallowly. Enter."

Ysemid slipped inside the tent.

What greeted his eyes was perhaps a very curious sight. Seated on the pillows under the dully burning bronze lamp, Karuil-Ysem, Father of his People, sat ravenously devouring sweet jellies, gulping sherbets and redolent wines. Many trays and many cups stood about him, the clawlike fingers reaching for them eagerly, nor did the meal cease at the arrival of his son.

Smiling still, and still very low, Ysemid said:

"What a disgusting creature, the pig."

Karuil, even now not hesitating at his feast, replied: "Bondage and hire. I take my wages."

"You are owed no wages, foulness, being a slave."

"And how much longer must I be your slave?"

"Till I am done with you."

"Till you are sure?" The old eyes glittered like knife-points. "But can you ever be sure, dear son? Having played with us, how shall you ever be forgotten?"

"You forget already. You forget I have a security."

"One day, your security may be lost."

"I think not. And now. Tell me what the Westerner said to you in this tent."

Karuil-Ysem crushed a powdered slab of lakoum into his mouth and ate it, while the young man scowled and fretted. Eventually Karuil was done and rejoined, "He said what you expected, having been sent for as you expected. He said he knew me endangered by you and that he would aid me against you. So I bade him bide for my word. But there is another thing."

"Which is?"

Karuil raised nougatine to his lips, and Ysemid, with an oath, strode forward. Karuil lowered the sweet, beaming twistedly up at him. "Which is that the declared sickness is a true sickness, for he admitted it to me."

Ysemid, distracted from annoyance, nodded.

"So I thought it, though it sounds so curious. He crept to his tent. It is on him now. One I sent before me found this Cyrion sleeping like the dead—or the drugged. Nevertheless, this white house cat, I never feared him."

"Did you not, pretty son?"

Ysemid moved abruptly. He slashed the old man violently across the face, so he was flung back among the sweets and the cushions. Lying there, Karuil hissed, "Be careful of me. I am brittle and may break. That would not suit your plan."

"And you, vileness, you be wary. The sweetmeats may do as much harm as my fist."

"It is only for a little while," the felled king said. "I crave the novelty. I am your slave. You must allow me something."

"You shall have what you truly crave, very soon."

Karuil manoeuvred himself upright. The movement was oddly fluid and serpentine.

"Do you mean freedom? Yes, I crave that. As does my sister. To bind such as we, O brat, is to build fire in a vessel of dry reeds."

"Is it? We shall see."

Ysemid returned to the door-flap of the tent. Emerging, he looked upward at the stars, then back again at the weird figure on the pillows. Loudly: "The blessing of God upon you, my father."

With a terrible grimace, Karuil responded: "And the light of heaven gild *you*, Ysemid."

Ysemid did not move directly towards his own tent. He strolled to the edge of the oasis where the nomadic shelters ended under the palms. One final tree, warped and dying, rose on the outskirt, with one final tent beneath. Quietly Ysemid approached, raised the flap, and looked within. Starlight vaguely revealed the sleeping man, huddled in his nomad's black, a strand of white-blond hair frayed out like silk from under the hood, across a handful of shining rings. And, under that, the sheathed sword set handy. But Cyrion, it seemed, slept like the moon tonight. It would be easy to kill him so, but his death would not, in these circumstances, look well. There were more attractive ways.

Ysemid let fall the flap and went away. From the shade woven between two nearby palms, Cyrion watched him go.

Cyrion, with fire-soot rubbed in his hair—one skein of which he had previously lopped—dressed in the western garb of black silk he had affected beneath his nomad's robe, was barely to be seen in the moonless dark. Even the rings did not gleam on his left hand; for once he had removed them, and left them on five pared reeds, under the lopped hair, over the sword, beside the bolster-packed bundle of the robe. Only the knife had come out with him. These elaborate precautions had proved, however, an enchanting success. About an hour before, one of Ysemid's courtiers, coming to visit Cyrion, had been completely convinced, as Cyrion witnessed. The muffled sleeper's groan Cyrion had also generously supplied may, of course, have aided in the matter.

Across the water of the oasis, Ysemid might be heard cracking another joke with one of the watchmen. Cyrion, a vagrant shadow, moved soundlessly between trees and tents, gained that of Karuil-Ysem, and entered it without preliminary.

The Father was gormandising, as he had been previously to judge by the earlier—overheard—conversation. Now the old man stared, wine cup in one hand, candy in the other.

"Night's benisons," said Cyrion. "Still hungry?"

Karuil gathered himself slowly.

"I heard you lay sick."

"It is sometimes possible to delay an attack, or forestall it. For the time being I am in no pain, and can see very clearly."

"Why are you here?"

"I saw Ysemid come to your tent."

"You feared for me?"

Cyrion was mildly astonished. "What other reason would I have?"

Karuil lapsed back on his cushions, putting down as he did so the wine cup, and reaching for a cup of sherbet. Cyrion stepped forward, took the cup, and courteously extended it. As he leaned close to Karuil, something happened that seemed to have to do with Cyrion's left hand. There was a dull lightning that ran from Karuil's throat to his sash. At the same instant the cup went flying in a spray of heavily scented juice, and Cyrion too, springing back, the knife bright in his grasp.

Karuil sat gaping. His robe gaped with him. Slashed from collar-bone to waist by Cyrion's blade, it hung open to display the gnarled and swarthy chest of a very strong and very old man. That, and one other thing. Above the heart were two black holes, jagged, deep, and utterly bloodless. Mortal wounds that had been cold a month or more.

If Cyrion was paler than he had been, was hard to tell. But very softly he commented on God in a way a priest might not have cared for.

Then the dead-live thing came at him, bounding with an agility it should not possess, and in its right hand, still sticky from sweets, Karuil's curved sword.

Cyrion was armed only with a knife. He ducked and came up with a bolster added to the itinerary. It met the first swooping advance of the sword and suffered from it. The second blow was more demanding yet, and cleaved the bolster almost in two.

As the larger blade stuck, clotted in silk, Cyrion lashed for Karuil's face with the knife. The sword dragged free, and Karuil jumped away—some reflex, the knife-play was a feint merely. Plainly, Karuil could not be wounded, or slain—both had already happened, and here he was, bouncing like a locust. But this, this was not Karuil.

The eyes of what had been a man flared, full of hate and a furious confusion. Cyrion was not meant to die quite yet, and the hour of his death was to be of Ysemid's choosing, so much Cyrion had gathered. Ysemid who was this thing's master—

Cyrion slid past the third sweep of the sword, casting the remains of the bolster. The pile of cushions was the last stage of his journey. Having achieved their eminence, gracefully avoiding as he did so the low-hung lamp, he turned again and made to the corpse-creature an unmistakable motion of encouragement. With a feverish growl, it plunged forward, the sword spurling in a web of torn silk. Cyrion watched it come. Then he moved like fire.

His hands found the bronze lamp and hurled it the length of its chain. A second more, and Cyrion dropped flat on the pillows. He seemed to have been smitten there, but the blow had not touched him and indeed was what he eluded. It passed over him instantly with a rasp of parted air, the sickle blade rushing through the empty space that should have been occupied by his body. Then came another noise: the inexorable muffled clang of bulky metal contacting, at speed, a human skull.

With a nasal grunt, the creature which had been Karuil was thrown backwards and went down. Cyrion in his turn was off the

pillows, and leapt after it. In less than a moment, he had prized the
great sword from the scrabbling long-nailed fingers. In half a
breath more, the sword swung upward and waited, shivering with
light, as a woman's voice said, quiet and harsh as a scraped bone:
"No. Do *not*—"

Cyrion did not lower the sword or look about. He looked only at
the glaring and now terrified eyes that still lived in Karuil's dead
face on the floor below him. The lamp had singed the hair of the
brows. If the flesh above them had lived, it might have been
bruised.

Just beyond Karuil, a drop of oil had fallen from the lamp and
burned sulkily. Not glancing, Cyrion put out his foot and quenched
it. Conversationally, he said, "Decapitation. One of the few deaths
a demon truly fears."

"Yes," whispered the voice in the doorway of the tent. "We are
demons, my brother and I. Remember, if you know of our kind,
our powers are greater by night and in dark places. Kill him, and
you have me to reckon with."

"Well," Cyrion answered gently, "it seems your brother has
slaughtered one I valued somewhat. This man whose body he now
uses like a glove. Perhaps I am not amenable to reason."

"Neither he nor I slew Karuil-Ysem. It was his son did that for
him, with a dagger, many days and nights before you came here. It
seems he sent for you, but you arrived too late. Hear the story,
before you judge it."

For a moment longer, Cyrion did not move. Then he lowered the
sword. Stepping away from the body of Karuil, he planted the
blade in a cushion, and standing by it took up the knife he had
dropped and sheathed it. Only then did he gaze across the tent.

The young woman who stood there, just within the closed flap of
the tent, had entered as silently as he, despite the costly sequins
sewn so thickly on her garments, and the jewels roped at her girdle.
Her unveiled face was seen to be very beautiful, and where the veil-
ing had slipped from her hair, its colour was the fierce peach-
golden common among female demons. Her long nails were
painted with gilt, however. She was Ysemid's third wife.

Karuil-who-was-not was now attempting to crawl to her. The
corpse appeared to be in sudden agony, and with a sharp intake of
her breath, the woman kneeled to help him.

"Yes," Cyrion observed. "An old man's body can be forced to the
flexibility of youth, but will suffer for it. I am fascinated so much

feeling remains in the nerves, and so much information in the brain. The sense of taste, also. For one who normally feeds on the exclusive diet of raw flesh and blood, the experience of second-hand sweetmeats must be novel."

The demon woman held the living corpse against her breast.

"I have heard tell of one who has your name," she said to Cyrion, with loathing.

"And I have heard of you," he returned graciously. "Or, of your kind."

"Yes. The nomads know us, and believe in our magic."

"And I was lessoned by nomads."

"You knew at once."

"Not at once." Cyrion seemed to look beyond her, into a void. But she did not make the mistake of thinking him unwary. "I suspected. Only a demon, it is said, has the spells to inhabit the dead and cause the flesh to animate."

"His own people reckon Karuil to be alive."

"They should note, when he embraces them, that he has no heartbeat."

"This was your warning?"

"This and other things. The borrowed brain yielded the memory to your brother that once I was, spiritually, the son of Karuil-Ysem —but the memory did not stretch to the correct area of occasion. Information was patchy, a threadbare traitor. This gave you away. There were other things. For one, Karuil had no liking for sugar and little for wine. With age, he might develop such greeds. But to trust the man he feared most to supply them? The Father of his People would not have been such a dolt."

"You owed Karuil filial love and desire vengeance," said the woman, staring at Cyrion through her rosy golden hair.

Cyrion stared back at her, bland again, innocent.

"Did I? Do I?"

She said, "Your vengeance and ours may be one. He has made slaves of us, this *Ysemid*." As she spoke the name, her painted claws raked at the floor.

"You mentioned a story. Tell it."

"Listen then. There is an ancient place far off in the desert, a ruined shrine. He came there, Ysemid. He was hunting, and seemed to have followed some beast to the well in the courtyard, but it was gone. Instead of going on himself, he drew water and drank. It was midday. My brother slept. I saw Ysemid, and I was roused by his handsomeness both to lust and to hunger. I put on myself the illusion of human rags, and went out to him, as a beggar, some pariah waif of the shrine. We spoke awhile, and then he offered me food if I would lie with him. I knew he had no food and sought to trick me, but I agreed gladly, for it served all my plan. We lay down together under the wall. . . ." The demoness bared her teeth in her rage. "I must inform you, he was not dressed in the clothing of the nomads, who are wary of us and wise. If he had been so, I should have shunned him. But he wore city garb—I thought him some merchant's son, easy prey. And when the sun should set and my brother wake—"

The sharp teeth were ground together. In her arms, the corpse which held her brother whispered its hate.

"Ysemid had an amulet," she said. "It was woven over by magic, for I had seen it, and thought it no more than a jewel. I remember, I meant to keep it as a plaything, when we were done with him. Then, when he stretched himself upon me, the thing touched my shoulder and *burned*. At once he pulled away, and then he laughed as if vastly amused. He spoke at last in the nomadic tongue. He said: "You are as I believed you to be." And he touched the amulet and uttered the words, and I was bound. Presently he had discovered my brother and bound him, also. I suppose now Ysemid had come hunting us rather than any animal. He required our kind. You comprehend the power of such an amulet? We might not move against him, and must obey him in all ways. Quickly, we learned his purpose."

A day after, the People of Karuil encamped some miles from the ruin. A genuine hunt was mounted, and Ysemid persuaded his father to ride with him. When dusk fell, the party sheltered at the shrine, and Ysemid took his father aside into the inner court, saying they should talk together for once. There had been many arguments between them. Among the nomads, the authority of any father was absolute, and of a king—paramount. Ysemid yearned to adopt urbane ways, and to make profit in the cities, using the wealth of the desert people as ballast. This Karuil would not allow, nor was he ever likely to alter his mind. Ysemid's options were limited. Either to fly with nothing—to rob the People would be to incite a dedicated pursuit with, even for a prince, stoning at the end of it—or to submit and live in the manner of his forebears until Karuil eventually died. And Karuil showed no sign of impending death. He was mighty and in excellent health, and might continue hale for a decade or more. To kill him was Ysemid's only hope, but to kill was to risk a hideous death penalty. Even those who followed Ysemid, his courtiers, would not have countenanced patricide.

It would appear Karuil-Ysem had guessed some circumvention of justice was devised, or why else had he sent for Cyrion? He did, nevertheless, walk into the inner court of the shrine alone with his son, and there Ysemid stabbed him, twice, to be sure. And there the demon, bound like his sister, had been required to use his magic, squeezing his own form, by fantastic demonic means, inside the fresh corpse of Karuil, before it should stiffen. They had begged, the demoness said, that rather than use this vile method, they might employ their spells of illusion to perpetrate the fraud. But Ysemid would have none of it. Illusion held too long might weaken, and was besides susceptible to revelation in countless ways.

In the morning it seemed the king had softened to his heir, and come to admit his view of things. Ysemid had performed his seduction of the People well, and rather than be suspiciously amazed, they were only glad at the change of heart, looking forward to the benefits of fat living, thinking their traditions could not be radically harmed or their strengths diffused. Like an omen to all this impending fortune, Ysemid had found a lovely beggar girl blooming like a golden rose in the shrine. He soon made her his wife.

Since that time, more than a month ago, the People of Karuil trod nearer and nearer to the cities. Ysemid lived more and more with city ways. There was chat of a palace close to Heshbel. Karuil, abruptly in this mild dotage of his, seemed resigned to the notion.

"And when all is as he wishes," said the demoness, licking her lips, "Ysemid will permit my brother to feign a peaceful death, and then escape the body before burial. Although we must set another spell on the flesh to prevent its instant disintegration. Me, he will divorce. But until that hour we must serve him. My brother samples sweets, by means of the human palate, which in his own form would choke him. But I, with whom Ysemid lay nightly—now consigned to another tent since he tires of me, as of a *mortal*—I yearn for the taste of his rent flesh and his smoking blood."

There was a silence. After which Cyrion asked, "The amulet is the sapphire in his ear?"

"*Yes*," she breathed.

"Could you not," he said, with apparent idleness, "have stolen it from him, on those nights when Ysemid slept by you?"

"It burns my kind and would char my fingers to the bone. Yet, if it had been possible, do you think I would have left it to him? But the gem is clasped through his ear and secured by three golden wires. I would have to wrench it out, and he would feel the wound at once. And if I had the amulet, still it would convey his sorcery, and I should be powerless as ever. Do you know nothing of the lore of such things?"

"You," said Cyrion, "tell me."

But this time it was the male demon, trapped in Karuil's body, who answered. In the dry borrowed voice, he said: "Unless Ysemid's own hand removes the jewel, and with his own hand the jewel is given into our keeping, the safeguards will not break, and we remain his slaves, and must follow every commandment he sets on us. Which he enjoys, being vicious. He loves to play, cat with rat. It is this way with certain men, uncleanly brutishness."

"Unlike your own clean and wholesome peccadilloes? From what you say, I can hardly see any way to come at him."

"You might coerce him to abandon the jewel to us," the demon woman insisted.

"I doubt that. Ysemid is of the people, despite his ambitions. If he is a sadist, he will be sensible to such matters. He will therefore prefer any torture I could inflict on him to the games your race would play. On the other hand, if I reveal his acts, either of you will be compelled to support his lies."

"This people understands such magics as his, and ours, exist."

"They also understand I am a foreigner, and that foreigners always lie."

The demon Karuil sat up.

"Go back, my sister. Ysemid may go to your tent and miss you."

She made a sound of derision, but still rose, her finery clinking now. It was likely the camp's guards had heard her pass them, though not seen. Being what she was, she could become less visible than the night itself.

"I will go back. And you," she said to Cyrion, "angel-hair with your sick beautiful eyes. You had best run away."

Cyrion drew the curved sword from the pillow and threw it down by the two of them.

"Oh, and I may."

The dawn, inverse of sunset, flowed from the east, set fire to the water of the oasis, and turned to electrum the sootless hair of Cyrion, as he was flung face-downward on the sand.

One of Ysemid's courtiers planted his foot on Cyrion's spine and dug in his heel. Another relieved the fallen man of his weapon belt. Yet others stood about smiling, a grim smile that had nothing whatever to do with jocularity.

"Turn him on his back." The authoritative tones of Ysemid himself. And Cyrion was wrenched up by electrum hair and black-robed arms and duly turned. He landed with a splash of dust, and Ysemid said: "Now strip him of the nomad's garment, the lion-skin he seeks to hide in, this jackal. Search for evidence of his crime."

Cyrion lay loosely as a doll, and quite expressionless, as these instructions were ungently carried out. Soon, the nomadic robe was gone, and the silk tunic after it, leaving him in the fashionable fitted breeches and soft leather boots of the Westerner—at which Ysemid's men ritualistically jeered.

"Oh, come now," said Cyrion, "when your lord lives at Heshbel, you also—"

—And was silenced by a blow across the head.

Aside from the burnished, lethal little knife, the clothing search had revealed a stoppered vial. This Ysemid showed about; to his favourites, to those who, hearing the commotion, had gathered by Cyrion's tent.

"You see this thing? This has been part of the witchcraft." He leaned down to Cyrion. "Its function?"

Cyrion looked at him, and not liking this look, Ysemid struck him again.

"*Answer*, jackal."

"The vial contains a drug."

"Which you would use in your death wishing."

"Which I would use to numb pain."

"Ah, yes. This aching of the head and blindness you pretend to. *Devil.*" Ysemid struck Cyrion more determinedly, and Cyrion closed his eyes, apparently bored.

Ysemid sprang upright. He held up the vial again. In his other hand was something else. Slowly, he displayed both objects, and a hush settled, dense as sand upon sand.

"You see?" Ysemid asked the People. "A little image made of wood, with a symbol upon it, graven *here*, that is the Father my father's name. We know the use to which such toys are put. This dung of the Arch-Demon, this spew of the Fiend, has come to us, aping friendship, seeking to settle some score with Karuil, our King. And if I had not found this item of witchcraft in the stranger's tent, who knows but Karuil might have died, and left us—fatherless."

Then, and only then, the soft, smooth growling. Cyrion did not look for it. Probably he knew how they would seem, like the lions for which they were so often called, black lions with eyes of black flame.

It was an unwieldy plot, but would serve. Cyrion was the alien, and aliens notoriously fared ill. Besides, here came the ultimate proof.

The name was murmured: *Karuil, Karuil.* Then the hush of impending murder descended once more. And in the hush, Karuil-Ysem's voice clear as the bite of a dagger.

"I have trusted a serpent, and almost, I have died of its venom. My son has saved my life. Take this viper and slay it, in the way we keep for the practitioner of evil magic." And, after this, the law-giving of Karuil-Ysem, real as when he had been alive: "I command it."

On the sand, Cyrion softly laughed. This time the blow they awarded him brought a respite of darkness.

The night of unconsciousness, however, also found a hurtful dawn. Thereafter the light came back and showed small mercy.

It was the custom of the nomads to tether a condemned felon at the centre of the campment for a day, and at dusk hygienically to take him a quarter of a mile from the tents to a death which, by then, he often wished for.

Cyrion, conscious or not, hung from his ropes and the post to which they bound him. All about, the tents, and the cool inks of the palm-shade, and cradled among them the glowing water, like spilled sky. But here, a patch of open sand, by noon white-hot, and a patch of sky above where the sun endlessly beat like a fiery dying heart. Now and then, of course, a shadow fell, refreshment, the prelude to unrefreshment. A stone was hurled—the blood soon dried in the heat—someone shouted, a pin scratched down his side, another was thrust under one of the nails of his ringed left hand—they would disdain to steal from him—a rain of kicks and slaps, dust tossed in his eyes, or rubbed between his lips. The nomads, who dwelled in a hard country, learned the trade of punishment well. That there was no worse Cyrion owed solely to the fact that he must be kept just sensible for death. So much he knew. Indeed, he guessed each act before it was performed against him. Some he foretold that had not yet come—

The thin rim of the cup, pushed out of the sick and pulsing haze against his lip, that alone surprised him.

"Drink," said a woman, close to his ear. "Quickly. Before they see what I do."

Cyrion wasted no time in inane queries. He drank the water, which she had known enough to warm before she gave it to him. Then he opened his eyes, straightened somewhat, and looked down at her through the long, long lashes mazed by thrown sand.

The demoness stood, exquisitely veiled, before him.

"Thank you," he said. "And now. Do you passionately release me?"

"If I did, he would kill me, too. He has you as he desires to have you. *Fool!*"

"Why then," Cyrion murmured, "waste the water?"

"Oh, beautiful flower," she mocked him, "to see you grow and burst your bonds." Cyrion's mouth curved faintly, and she said, "You have powers. Your skin is fair, but does not blister—"

"No. I have enough of the nomadic arts to save myself that inconvenience."

"The power of Will." She muttered, "Break *free. Kill* Ysemid."

"And be myself immediately killed by his loving court? That will happen at sunset, anyway."

"Dog of a coward."

"Gloriously lovely—" Cyrion paused— "astoundingly winsome —drinker of—"

"I will curse you," she interrupted. "We shall find your grave, and defile it."

"Alas."

"Die then," she said, and moved to go.

"One thing," he said, and she halted. "Will your brother, the King Karuil-Ysem, oversee my death?"

"He must. It is their law. You know this."

"Then," Cyrion sighed, slipping down again in his bonds, his head dropping forward, "follow him."

At once she was sizzlingly alert. She gripped his arm, pressing her claws into the naked flawless skin and the firm muscle beneath.

"Why? What is it?"

"For God's delightful sake," Cyrion whispered, "scratch or strike me. Five men are watching you."

She snarled her fury. "I shall see you die in your blood then, even if I may not drink it. That will appease my famishment."

To her increased rage he did not flinch as her nails scored over his breast. Then, concealing the glass cup, she ran.

When the first coolness sank down from the red-hot sunset sky, the bound man glanced up once, then lowered his gilded head again. The blessing of the cool was also the chime of the bell which sounded for his death.

With the shadows, came his executioners.

They dragged him, still roped, from the post, and hauled him after them, out of the encampment. The women, who had watched him with melting eyes before, now watched with hard flints, resembling those they had cast at him earlier. Though allowed to torment him, they were not allowed to see him die. No great odds. It was likely they could imagine how it would be. A fate decreed by custom, and somewhat nasty.

Most of the men went from the camp. They moved like a sinuous black herd, following their shepherd. Karuil-Ysem rode his horse, Ysemid striding by him, a proud son, revelling that he had rescued his king and his father from the assassin.

The first stars were embarking on the red air when they reached the chosen spot. It was the same as any other, merely the sand under the sunset.

The men formed a broad circle, to the centre of which Cyrion was conducted. Mostly, he walked. Sometimes he fell, and was helped to his feet by the fists and footwear of his captors. The post had also been brought and was rammed into the new sand, and the bonds again secured to it. Karuil sat his horse, looking on.

A wind blew over the desert. The sun was almost gone, and soon it would be night. And then night forever. But not quite yet.

Ysemid called, and torches were lit and placed along the circle. They would need to see what they did next, and the light was excellent.

Ysemid moved close. He stood looking at Cyrion's bowed head, and the sculpted torso that, despite all psychic art, had begun at last to flush along its pale gold with sunburn.

"Well," Ysemid said. His voice was quiet, private, for Cyrion only. "I trust you hear me, dainty house cat."

"I," Cyrion said, "hear you."

"Good, my house cat. Good."

"Have you never been told the story," Cyrion said—his own voice was a crumble of itself, yet audible, interesting; Ysemid listened attentively— "the story of the lynx who found himself among lions."

"Am I to be told it, little lynx? Soon told, I would think."

"Soon told. It seems the lynx explained to the lions that he was both a rare and a succulent animal, and that only the best of them was fit to devour him. At which the lions fell to disputing which was the best of them, and then to trial and combat. Being confident and ferocious, none of them survived. The moral of the story is, that the lynx was not eaten."

"But the moral of your story is that we shall not fight over you, but simply kill you."

Ysemid pressed closer still. In his ear the sapphire was like a drop spilled from the dusk.

"Do you see, fabulous swordsman?" said Ysemid. "Look at me and see me. I recall, my father spoke of you, not often, but tellingly. Look and see how we match with each other, now." And, growing impatient, Ysemid caught at Cyrion's jaw, and pulled his face up to confront him. There was something wrong, Ysemid beheld it at once. The face did not express its despair in the anticipated way, and the eyes—what was the matter with the eyes?—"*Look* at me," Ysemid repeated.

"I regret," Cyrion said, "I cannot."

Ysemid stared. Then he swore, with disbelieving pleasure.

"It is the truth then. This sickness of the vision—you have it now."

"I have it now."

"And how long will the affliction last?"

"An hour, perhaps a little longer."

"You may die blind, then."

"I hardly think it matters. And if you ever research the disease, you will learn that with the headache one sometimes wishes to be dead. You will be doing me a service."

"There is another service," Ysemid said. If Cyrion had been able to see him, he would have perceived that the prince shone now with a radiant joy. The sadistic, rather predictable game that had burgeoned in his mind was irresistible to him. "I have been told of your prowess as a swordsman. Over and over, told of it. And the scout reported to me your words as you were brought into the camp. What were they? It may prove difficult to fight a man I cannot see."

Eventually Cyrion said tonelessly, "By the codes of your own people, whatever else you do to me, you would spare me that."

"*My* people, cat-lynx-jackal. *Mine.* Not yours. And my father, not your father. And my wish, not your wish." Ysemid straightened. "I shall tell them you boasted to me that, unbound and armed, you could slay me. I shall tell them I must accept such a challenge. My valour is in question, and I must bring you to humiliation before you are slain in the proper manner. They will agree, and then witness how I outfight you, while you stumble up and down—like one blind."

"Any man standing in that ring is close enough to see, once it begins, I cannot fight for that very reason."

"Then I will send them farther off. I shall say you expect treachery. That you must be shown I can beat you unaided."

Quickly, Cyrion said, "And Karuil-Ysem also. Send him back with the others."

Ysemid frowned. He studied Cyrion's vacant face, its hateful glamour that even now was like a mask, the searching, hopeless eyes.

"Why? What have you fathomed? There is some trick you think you may play—" Ysemid nodded. "No. The old man shall come forward and watch. But only he. You will find, he will not try to help you. Or did you know that, and fear something else? You have only Ysemid to fear. Poor sick-eyes swordsman."

Ysemid turned and went to the human ring, shouting out at it. Cyrion must have heard some of the words, and the uncertain response, shortly swelling to assent. Then there were sounds, if not the sight, of the ring widening, drawing away. When the sounds stopped, one might judge the distance that had been added. If any in the surrounding ring had yearned to come to the rescue of a man in the circle's centre, it was doubtful they would reach him in time. But who would want such a thing? Only Karuil had dismounted and moved nearer, leaning on the shoulder of a young boy. Karuil who was a demon.

A knife cut through ropes, and Cyrion, losing their support, staggered forward. With a congratulatory curse, Ysemid steadied him, then pushed him away again. Something was insinuated into Cyrion's right hand. Familiar—a cross-hilted western sword.

As Cyrion raised it, awkwardly for perhaps the first time in its years with him, Ysemid came at him. The advance was leisurely, dancing, almost cloddish with its parody. The noise the sand made under this would give a clue even to one blinded—Cyrion swerved. His arm flung up and retracted, his sword glancing by under the other, clumsily. Like a drunkard, he finished the move by lunging aside. He fumbled at the darkening torch-fretted air with his free hand, trying to balance himself.

And now Ysemid entered swiftly. The sand responded with only the barest hiss at the upsurge. Cyrion heeded it, and spun away, almost falling. Ysemid's playful sword was cheated of him, by an inch. As Cyrion continued to give ground, uncertainly twisting his head to catch any sound from the sand which was his only friend, Ysemid began to stamp and kick about in it, silently laughing at Cyrion's bewildered dismay.

Suddenly, Cyrion came lurching after him. Ysemid side-stepped neatly, swirling his sword, then, enraged at such temerity, swung back to cut at Cyrion's left side. The blow should have hit home. Only Cyrion's present ungracefulness saved him, sending him into a sprawl before the blade reached him. Trying to rise, he almost put his hand on the curved steel, which would have sliced it to the bone. Some fluke saved him also from this, a shift of sand giving way, throwing him on his elbow, as the nomad's sword glided upward. The laugh was not quite silent now.

Finding himself with space to rise, seeming to mistrust it, Cyrion dove to his feet. Ysemid gazed at him, at the blond face now wide open and maddened, trying to read everything from the night which useless eyes would deny him. Ysemid's ecstasy was evident to any who could see. Then he lashed forward, deliberately missing the devastated figure before him, whirling the curved sword into a wheel of torchlight and metallic singing. Ludicrously, without cause, Cyrion ducked. Something in Ysemid overbrimmed. With a cry of pure orgasmic evil, Karuil's heir threw himself forward, knocking Cyrion once more to the sand. Even the cat will eventually sink its teeth in the spine of the mouse.

Kneeling over him, Ysemid had Cyrion by the hair, a left-handed grip, while the right hand, shortening its grasp on the blade, gathered itself for the initial wound of the death sentence: Castration.

Somewhere in the fume of sand between the two men, there lit two coals of icy fire, two stars—the torchglare on two brilliant eyes. And then a blade almost as bright came up with a wave of sand. A sword of fire, and it burned.

Ysemid found he had not completed the emasculating stroke. Stupidly perplexed, he peered down to seek the reason for failure.

And saw his own hand, severed just above the wrist and lying, bleeding and lost, under the edge of Cyrion's sword.

Before the scream could find its way through Ysemid's face, a ringed fist hammered upward into his jaw. Ysemid's teeth met in his tongue like an agonising vise. He slumped over into a roaring tawny darkness.

The next pain began far away, the awful pain in his earlobe—

Cyrion, having taken Ysemid's severed hand in his own, had clamped its fingers, tonglike, on the sapphire and ripped the amulet free. With a wicked twist, utilising the gold wires that had formerly held the jewel in Ysemid's ear, Cyrion bound it to the disinherited fingers. The operation had needed seconds. Now, gaining his feet without effort, Cyrion flung the bloody hand and its gem into the sand before Karuil-Ysem. Who bowed towards it, predatory, and next quite motionless.

From all sides the men of the People were running forward. Their wailing and the grin of their blades filled the night.

Cyrion, his voice dry and eroded, shouted at Karuil.

"Plucked from him by his own hand, and given you by his own hand. Pick it up, damn you, and use it."

But it was the boy on whom Karuil had leaned who crouched and caught up the hand and its prize. As the boy straightened, gold snaked under his hood. Face unpainted, and in purloined or illusory male attire, the demoness raised the piece of carcass to her lips, then paused.

"You are not blind then," she remarked to Cyrion.

"No. I shall be dead, however, in a few more moments."

"And we must save you by revealing the truth here and now?"

Cyrion shrugged. His eyes were clear and still. "Honour among slaves. If you would be so kind."

"For your beauty, then," she said. And beside her, Karuil-Ysem opened his mouth in a strangely terrifying yawn.

The first of the nomads were a handful of paces away when they checked. Through the yelling and the howl for retribution a high thin chord seemed to vibrate, and then all sound died. They stood in the attitude of those who grasped the night ways of the earth, respected and abhorred them. There was no fear, only the revulsion of total knowledge.

Karuil-Ysem, the Father of his People, had begun to split, as the robe had split from him under Cyrion's searching knife. Now skin and sinew parted, and the cloth of the garment fell intact from the bisecting cage of bones beneath. There was no bleeding. Within the dividing bag of the corpse there came a battling motion, a moan of anguish, and then the chrysalis of death was discarded absolutely. A naked and well-made man, physically even younger than Cyrion, bowed to the ground, holding his own body in his arms, his hair as black as the sky now was, and showering about him.

Cyrion spoke briefly to the People of Karuil-Ysem, as the demoness embraced her brother and clutched the bloody hand of the tyrant between them both, where both could see the spark of the vanquished jewel, and scent the warm gore. The story Cyrion told now was credited, and when he had finished, which was swiftly, the men were like statues about him, waiting, avoiding the demons with eyes and speech, prepared to listen only to the inevitable concluding words.

But Cyrion had waited also, for the stirring behind him in the sand, the tiny crying notes which informed them that Ysemid regained his senses.

"He bound demons," Cyrion said. "We know their pleasure. Perhaps a more fitting death than the lawful sentence, for this patricide. Leave him to them."

There was no given answer. Except the gradual turning away, even of Ysemid's court, those who had loved him, in tens and in scores, and then as if the whole night turned its back to depart, bearing the torches with it. The king's body they abandoned. There had been no choice. It had become one with the dust.

Cyrion heard the muttering of the demons over the hand and the gem and the honey to come. He too had turned. From the sand he drew the robe of Karuil-Ysem, and brushed from it, with quiet, unhurried strokes, the odourless sterile powder that had been a man.

Presently Cyrion put on the robe, and drew it closed under the belt of red leather in which his sword was now sheathed. He did not seem to pay attention, as he did this, to the weeping groans and entreaties, the shrilling upsoaring pipe of terror, nor to the climaxing shrieks of the condemned.

Under the ruthless cold of the gathering stars, Cyrion walked away.

He was a mile off before the shrieking ceased to be audible. That the shrieks were done did not, in any case, mean death had yet arrived.

Later, the infant moon arose, and seemed to embroider, over and over in the sand, the symbols of Karuil-Ysem's last message. Cyrion's clear-visioned eyes and brain, which no ailment of any sort had ever affected, yet followed these moon-mirages, sought them, lingered on them. Karuil had written thus:

*This comes to you by the hand of another people than mine, or yours, yet the man is my messenger. If you recall me, attend. I am threatened. There are troubles in me which are not the troubles of age. I have fallen prey to a hellish phantom which destroys my sight for an hour at a time, and ends in an enduring and grievous pain, covering half the head. My disciplines remain, and I evince no sign of this disease, but I think that one works on me, through a doll or some other witchcraft, to strike me with a bane unknown to me, and for which there is no cause, and no cure, unless you find one and bring it me. It is a fact, I suspect who is my enemy. He has given me to wonder by his sudden concern for my health, and, if it is true he practises on me, by his own randomness of skill, for it seems he looks for my ills, but does not know what form they should take.*

*I have a plan to be certain, and to bring him out.*

*You will, if you remember me, remember the sapphire amulet I had always about me beneath the breast of my robe, which could exert such sway over demons and similar spirits. You knew of this talisman, you and one other, a favourite wife who died, but who, I think now, passed on the knowledge. I mean purposely to lose this gem, and leave it where he may come on it, for only he is educated in how it may be used to set demons against me. Only he. I doubt if he will display it while I live, but should he find some way to kill or bind me, then he may flaunt it, a secret jest. So you will know.*

*I must inform you that if it is he who so hates me, then in my bitterness I will resign my life to him, and to God. Yet if it is to be so, and you ever in your soul, though not in blood, my son—*
AVENGE ME.

# MAGRITTE'S SECRET AGENT

**Y**OU ASKED ME ABOUT IT BEFORE, DIDN'T YOU—THE picture? And I never told you. But tonight, tonight I think I will. Why not? The wine was very nice, and there's still the other bottle. The autumn dusk is warm, clear, and beautiful, and the stars are blazing over the bay. It's so quiet that, when the tide starts to come back, we'll hear it. You're absolutely right. I'm obsessive about the sea. And that picture, the Magritte.

Of course, it's a print, nothing more, though that was quite difficult to obtain. I saw it first in a book, when I was eighteen or so. I felt a strangeness about it even then. Naturally, most of Magritte is bizarre. If you respond to him, you get special sensations, special inner stirrings over any or all of what he did, regardless even of whether you care for it or not. But this one—this one . . . He had a sort of game whereby he'd often call a picture by a name that had no connection—or no apparent connection—with its subject matter. The idea, I believe, was to throw out prior conception. I mean, generally you're told you're looking at a picture called *Basket of Apples*, and it's apples in a basket. But Magritte calls a painting *The Pleasure Principle*, and it's a man with a kind of white nova taking place where his head should be. Except that makes a sort of sense, doesn't it? Think of orgasm, for example, or someone who's crazy about Prokofiev, listening to the Third Piano Concerto. This picture, though. It's called *The Secret Agent*.

It's one of the strangest pictures in the world to me, partly because it's beautiful and it shocks, but the shock doesn't depend on revulsion or fear. There's another one, a real stinger—a fish lying on a beach, but it has the loins and legs of a girl: a mermaid but inverted. That has shock value all right, but it's different. This one . . . The head, neck, breast of a white horse, which is also a chess piece, which is also a girl. A girl's eye, and hair that's a mane, and yet still hair. And she—it—is lovely. She's in a room, by a window that faces out over heathland under a crescent moon, but she doesn't look at it. There are a few of the inevitable Magritte tricks —for example, the curtain hanging *outside* the window frame instead of in, that type of thing. But there's also this other thing. I don't know how I can quite explain it. I think I sensed it from the first. Or maybe I only read it into the picture afterwards. Or maybe it's just the idea of white horses and the foam that comes in on a breaker: white horses, or mythological Kelpies that can take the shape of a horse. Somehow, the window ought to show the sea, and it doesn't. It shows the land under the horned moon, not a trace of water anywhere. And her face that's a woman's, even though it's the face of a chess-piece horse. And the title. *The Secret Agent*, which maybe isn't meant to mean anything. And yet . . . Sometimes I wonder if Magritte—if he ever—

I was about twenty-three at the time, and it was before I'd got anything settled—my life, my ambitions, anything. I was rooming with a nominative aunt about five miles along the coast from here, at Ship Bay. I'd come out of art school without much hope of a job, and was using up my time working behind a lingerie counter in the local chain store, which, if you're female, is where any sort of diploma frequently gets you. I sorted packets of bras, stopped little kids putting the frilly 'nickers on their heads, and averted my eyes from gargantuan ladies who were jamming themselves into cubicles, corsets, and complementary heart attacks, in that order.

Thursday was cinema day at the Bay, when the movie palace showed its big matinee of the week. I don't know if there truly is a link between buyers of body linen and the matinee performance, but from two to four-thirty on Thursday afternoons you could count visitors to our department on two fingers or less.

A slender girl named Jill, ostentatiously braless, was haughtily pricing B-cups for those of us unlucky enough to require them. I was refolding trays of black lace slips, thinking about my own black, but quite laceless, depression, when sounds along the carpet told me one of our one or two non-film-buff customers had arrived. There was something a little odd about the sounds. Since Jill was trapped at the counter by her pricing activities, I felt safe to turn and look.

I got the guilty, nervous, flinching-away reaction one tends to on sight of a wheelchair. An oh-God-I-mustn't-let-them-think-I'm-staring feeling. Plus, of course, the unworthy survival-trait which manifests in the urge to stay uninvolved with anything that might need help, embarrass, or take time. Actually, there was someone with the wheelchair who had guided it to a stop. An escort normally makes it worse, since it implies total dependence. I was already looking away before I saw. Let's face it, what you do see is usually fairly bad. Paralysis, imbecility, encroaching death. I do know I'm most filthily in the wrong, and I thank God there are others who can think differently than I do.

You know how, when you're glancing from one thing to another, a sudden light or colour or movement snags the eye somewhere in between, you look away, then irresistibly back again. The visual centre has registered something ahead of the brain, and the message gets through so many seconds late. This is what happened as I glanced hurriedly aside from the wheelchair. I didn't know what had registered to make me look back, but I did. Then I found out.

In the chair was a young man—a boy—he looked about twenty. He was focusing somewhere ahead, or not focusing, it was a sort of blind look, but somehow there was no doubt he could see, or that he could think. The eyes are frequently the big giveaway when something has gone physically wrong. His eyes were clear, large, utterly contained, *containing*, like two cool cisterns. I didn't even see the colour of them, the construction and the content struck me so forcibly. Rather than an unseeing look, it was a seeing through —to something somewhere else. He had fair hair, a lot of it, and shining. The skin of his face had the sort of marvellous pale texture most men shave off when they rip the first razor blade through their stubble and the second upper dermis goes with it forever. He was slim and, if he had been standing, would have been tall. He had a rug over his knees like a geriatric. But his legs were long. You see, I've described him as analytically as I can, both his appearance and my reply to it. What it comes to is, he was beautiful. I fell in love with him, not in the carnal sense, but aesthetically, artistically. Dramatically. The fact that a woman was wheeling him about, helplessly, into a situation of women's underwear, made him also pathetic in the terms of pathos. He preserved a remote dignity even through this. Or not really; he was simply far away, not here at all.

The woman herself was just a woman. Stoutish, fawnish. I couldn't take her in. She was saying to Jill: "Should have been ready. I don't know why you don't deliver anymore like you used to."

And Jill was saying: "I'm sorry, maa-dum, we don't deliver things like this."

It was the sort of utterly futile conversation, redolent of dull, sullen frustration on both sides, so common at shop counters everywhere. I wondered if Jill had noticed the young man, but she didn't seem to have done so. She usually reacted swiftly to anything youngish and male and platitudinously in trousers, but presumably only when trousers included locomotive limbs inside them.

"Well, I can't stop," said the woman. She had a vague indeterminate Ship Bay accent, flat as the sands. "I really thought it would be ready by now."

"I'm sorry, maa-dum."

"I can't keep coming in. I haven't the time."

Jill stood and looked at her.

I felt blood swarm through my heart and head, which meant I was about to enter the arena, cease my purely observatory role.

"Perhaps we could take the lady's name and phone number," I said, walking over to the counter. "We could call her when her purchase arrives."

Jill glowered at me. This offer was a last resort, generally employed to placate only when a customer produced a carving knife.

I found a paper bag and a pen, and waited. When the woman didn't speak, I looked up. I was in first gear, unbalanced, and working hard to disguise it. So I still didn't see her, just a shape where her face was, the shadowy gleam of metal extending away from her hands, the more shattering gleam of his gilded bronze hair. (Did she wash it for him? Maybe he had simply broken his ankle or his knee. Maybe he was no longer there.)

I strove in vain towards the muddy aura of the woman. And she wouldn't meet me.

"If you'd just let me have your name," I said brightly, trying to enunciate like Olivier, which I do at my most desperate.

"There's no phone," she said. She could have been detailing a universal human condition.

"Well," I was offhand. "Your address. We could probably drop you a card or something." Jill made a noise, but couldn't summon the energy to tell us such a thing was never done. (Yes, he was still there. Perfectly still; perfect, still, a glimpse of long fingers lying on the rug.)

"Besmouth," said the woman, grudging me.

It was a silly name. It sounded like an antacid stomach preparation. What was he called, then? Billy Besmouth? Bonny Billy Besmouth, born broken, bundled babylike, bumped bodily by brassieres—

"I'm sorry?" She'd told me the address and I'd missed it. No I hadn't, I'd written it down.

"Nineteen Sea View Terrace, The Rise."

"Oh, yes. Just checking. Thank you."

The woman seemed to guess suddenly it was all a charade. She eased the brake off the chair and wheeled it abruptly away from us.

"What did you do that for?" said Jill. "We don't send cards. What d'you think we *aar?*"

I refrained from telling her. I asked instead what the woman had ordered. Jill showed me the book; it was one of a batlike collection of nylon-fur dressing gowns in cherry red.

At four-thirty, ten women and a male frillies-freak came in. By five-forty, when I left the store, I should have forgotten about Bonny Billy Besmouth, the wheelchair, the vellum skin, the eyes.

That evening I walked along the sands. It was autumn, getting chilly, but the afterglow lingered, and the sky above the town was made of green porcelain. The sea came in, scalloped, darkening, and streaked by the neons off the pier, till whooping untrustworthy voices along the shore drove me back to the promenade. When I was a kid, you could have strolled safely all night by the water. Or does it only seem that way? Once, when I was eight, I walked straight into the sea, and had to be dragged out, screaming at the scald of salt in my sinuses. I never managed to swim. It was as if I expected to know how without ever learning, as a fish does, and, when I failed, gave up in despair.

You could see The Rise from the promenade, a humped back flung up from the south side of the bay, with its terraced streets clinging onto it. He was up there somewhere. Not somewhere: 19, Sea View. Banal. I could walk it in half an hour. I went home and ate banal sausages, and watched banal TV.

On Saturday a box of furry bat-gowns came in, and one of them was cherry red.

"Look at this," I said to Jill.

She looked, as if into an open grave.

"Yes. Orrful."

"Don't you remember?"

Jill didn't remember.

Angela, who ran the department, was hung over from the night before, and was, besides, waiting for her extramarital relationship to call her. I showed her the dressing gown and she winced.

"If she's not on the phone, she's had it."

"I could drop it in to her," I lied ably. "I'm going to meet someone up on The Rise, at the pub. It isn't any trouble to me, and she has a crippled son."

"Poor cow," said Angela. She was touched by pity. Angela always struck me as a kind of Chaucerian character—fun-loving, warmhearted, raucously glamorous. She was, besides, making almost as much a mess of her life as I was of mine, with a head start on me of about ten years.

She organised everything, and the department did me the great favour of allowing me to become its errand-person. I suppose if the goods had been wild-silk erotica I might not have been allowed to take them from the building at all. But who was going to steal a bat-gown?

"You aar stew-pid," said Jill. "You should never volunteer to do anything like that. They'll have you at it all the time now."

At half past six, for Saturday was the store's late closing, I took the carrier and went out into the night, with my heart beating in slow hard concussions. I didn't know why, or properly what I was doing. The air smelled alcoholically of sea and frost.

I got on the yellow bus that went through The Rise.

I left the bus near the pub, whose broad lights followed me away down the slanting street. I imagined varieties of normal people in it, drinking gins and beer and low-calorie cola. Behind the windows of the houses I imagined dinners, TV, arguments. It had started to rain. What was I doing here? What did I anticipate? (*He opened the door, leaning on a crutch, last summer's tennis racket tucked pre-*

*dictively under the other arm. I stood beside his chair, brushing the*
*incense smoke from him, in a long queue at Lourdes.)* I thought
about his unspeaking farawayness. Maybe he wasn't crippled but
autistic. I could have been wrong about those strange containing
eyes. Anyway, she'd just look at me, grab the bag, shut the door.
She had paid for the garment months ago, when she ordered it. I
just had to give her the goods, collect her receipt. Afterwards I'd go
home, or at least to the place where I lived. I wouldn't even see
him. And what then? Nothing.

Sea View curved right around the bottom of The Rise. Behind its
railing the cliff lurched forward into the night and tumbled on the
sea. Number 19 was the farthest house down, the last in the terrace.
An odd, curly little alley ran off to the side of it, leading along the
downslope of the cliff and out of sight, probably to the beach. The
sound of the tide, coupled with the rain, was savage, close, and
immensely wet.

I pushed through the gate and walked up the short path. A dim
illumination came from the glass panels of the door. There was no
bell, just a knocker. I knocked and waited like the traveller in the
poem. Like him, it didn't seem I was going to get an answer—an
even more wretched end to my escapade than I had foreseen. I
hadn't considered the possibility of absence. Somehow I'd got the
notion Mrs. Besmouth–Antacid seldom went out. It must be difficult with him the way he was, whichever way that happened to be.
So why did I want to get caught up in it?

A minute more, and I turned with a feeling of letdown and relief.
I was halfway along the path when the front door opened.

"Hi, you," she said.

At this uninviting salute, I looked back. I didn't recognise her,
because I hadn't properly been able to see her on the previous occasion. A fizz of fawn hair, outlined by the inner light, stood round
her head like a martyr's crown. She was clad in a fiery apron.

"Mrs. Besmouth." I went towards her, extending the carrier bag
like meat offered to a wild dog.

"Besmouth, that's right. What is it?" She didn't know me at all.
I said the name of the store, a password, but she only blinked.

"You came in about your dressing gown, but it hadn't arrived. It
came today. I've got it here."

She looked at the bag.

"All right," she said. "What's the delivery charge?"

"No charge. I just thought I'd drop it in to you."

She went on looking at the bag. The rain went on falling.

"You live round here?" she demanded.

"No. The other end of the bay, actually."

"Long way for you to come," she said accusingly.

"Well . . . I had to come up to The Rise tonight. And it seemed a shame, the way you came in and just missed the delivery. Here, do take it, or the rain may get in the bag."

She extended her hand and took the carrier.

"It was kind of you," she said. Her voice was full of dislike because I'd forced her into a show of gratitude. "People don't usually bother nowadays."

"No, I know. But you said you hadn't got time to keep coming back, and I could see that, with—with your son—"

"Son," she interrupted. "So you know he's my son, do you?"

I felt hot with embarrassed fear.

"Well, whoever—"

"Haven't you got an umbrella?" she said.

"Er, no—"

"You're soaked," she said. I smiled foolishly, and her dislike reached its climax. "You'd better come in a minute."

"Oh no, really, that isn't—"

She stood aside in the doorway, and I slunk past her into the hall. The door banged to.

I experienced instant claustrophobia and a yearning to run, but it was too late now. The glow was murky. There was a faintly musty smell, not stale exactly, more like the odour of a long-closed box.

"This way."

We went by the stairs and a shut door, into a small back room, which in turn opened on a kitchen. There was a smokeless coal fire burning in an old brown fireplace. The curtains were drawn, even at the kitchen windows, which I could see through the doorway. A clock ticked, setting the scene as inexorably as in a radio play. It reminded me of my grandmother's house years before, except that in my grandmother's house you couldn't hear the sea. And then it came to me that I couldn't pick it up here, either. Maybe some freak meander of the cliff blocked off the sound, as it failed to in the street. . . .

I'd been looking for the wheelchair, and, not seeing it, had relaxed into an awful scared boredom. Then I registered the high-backed dark red chair, set facing the fire. I couldn't see him, and he was totally silent, yet I knew at once the chair was full of him. A type of electric charge went off under my heart. I felt quite horrible, as if I'd screamed with laughter at a funeral.

"Take your coat off," said Mrs. Besmouth. I protested feebly, trying not to gaze at the red chair. But she was used to managing those who could not help themselves, and she pulled the garment from me. "Sit down by the fire. I'm making a pot of tea."

I wondered why she was doing it, including me, offering her hospitality. She didn't want to—at least I didn't think she did. Maybe she was lonely. There appeared to be no Mr. Besmouth. The unmistakable spoor of the suburban male was everywhere absent.

To sit on the settee by the fire, I had to go round the chair. As I did so, he came into view. He was just as I recalled, even his position was unaltered. His hands rested loosely and beautifully on his knees. He watched the fire, or something beyond the fire. He was dressed neatly, as he had been in the shop. I wondered if she dressed him in these universal faded jeans, the dark pullover. Nondescript. The fire streamed down his hair and beaded the ends of his lashes.

"Hello," I said. I wanted to touch his shoulder quietly, but did not dare.

Immediately I spoke, she called from her kitchen.

"It's no good talking to him. Just leave him be, he'll be all right."

Admonished and intimidated, I sat down. The heavy anger was slow in coming. Whatever was wrong with him, this couldn't be the answer. My back to the kitchen, my feet still in their plastic boots which let in water, I sat and looked at him.

I hadn't made a mistake. He really was amazing. How could she have mothered anything like this? The looks must have been on the father's side. And where had the illness come from? And what was it? Could I ask her, in front of him?

He was so far away, not here in this room at all. But where was he? He didn't look—oh God, what word would do?—*deficient.* Leonardo da Vinci, staring through the face of one of his own half-finished, exquisite, lunar madonnas, staring through at some truth he was still seeking . . . that was the look. Not vacant. Not missing . . .

She came through with her pot of tea, the cups and sugar and milk.

"This is very kind of you," I said.

She grunted. She poured the tea in a cup and gave it to me. She had put sugar in without asking me, and I don't take sugar. The tea became a strange, alien, sickly brew, drunk for ritual. She poured tea into a mug, sugared it, and took it to the chair. I watched, breathing through my mouth. What would happen?

She took up his hand briskly and introduced the mug into it. I saw his long fingers grip the handle. His face did not change. With a remote gliding gesture, he brought the mug to his lips. He drank. We both, she and I, looked on, as if at the first man, drinking.

"That's right," she said.

She fetched her own cup and sat on the settee beside me. I didn't like to be so close to her, and yet we were now placed together, like an audience, before the profile of the red chair and the young man.

I wanted to question her, ask a hundred things. His name, his age. If we could get him to speak. If he were receiving any treatment, and for *what*, exactly. How I wanted to know that! It burned in me, my heart hammered, I was braised in racing waves of adrenaline.

But I asked her nothing like that.

You could not ask her these things, or I couldn't. And he was there, perhaps understanding—the ultimate constraint.

"It's very cosy here," I said. She grunted. "But I keep wondering why you can't hear the sea. Surely—"

"Yes," she said, "I don't get much time to go into the town centre. What with one thing and another."

That came over as weird. She belonged to a category of person who would do just that: skip an idea that had no interest for her and pass straight onto something that did. And yet what was it? She'd been a fraction too fast. But I was well out of my depth, and had been from the start.

"Surely," I said, "couldn't the council provide some sort of assistance? A home-help?"

"Don't want anything like that."

"But you'd be entitled—"

"I'm entitled to my peace and quiet."

"Well, yes—"

"Daniel," she said sharply, "drink your tea. Drink it. It'll get cold."

I jumped internally again, and again violently. She'd said his name. Not alliterative after all. Daniel . . . She'd also demonstrated he could hear, and respond to a direct order, for he was raising his mug again, drinking again.

"Now," she said to me, "if you've finished your tea, I'll have to ask you to go. I've his bath to see to, you understand."

I sat petrified, blurting some sort of apology. My momentary brush with the bizarre was over and done. I tried not to visualise, irresistibly, his slim, pale, probably flawless male body, naked in water. He would be utterly helpless, passive, and it frightened me.

I got up.

"Thank you," I said.

"No, it was good of you to bring the dressing gown."

I couldn't meet her eyes, and had not been able to do so at any time.

I wanted at least to say his name, before I went away. But I couldn't get it to my lips, my tongue wouldn't form it.

I was out of the room, in my coat, the door was opening. The rain had stopped. There wasn't even an excuse to linger. I stepped onto the path.

"Oh, well. Good-bye, Mrs. Besmouth."

Her face stayed shut, and then she shut the door too.

I walked quickly along Sea View Terrace, walking without having yet caught up to myself, an automaton. This was naturally an act, to convince Mrs. Antacid, and the unseen watchers in their houses, and the huge dark watcher of the night itself, that I knew precisely where I wanted to go now and had no more time to squander. After about half a minute, self-awareness put me wise, and I stopped dead. Then I did what I really felt compelled to do, still without understanding why. I reversed my direction, walked back along the terrace, and into the curling alley that ran down between Number 19 and the shoulder of the cliff.

I didn't have to go very far to see the truth of the amorphous thing I had somehow deductively fashioned already, in my mind. The back of Number 19, which would normally have looked towards the sea, was enclosed by an enormous brick wall. It was at least fourteen feet high; the topmost windows of the house were barely visible above it. I wondered how the council had been persuaded to permit such a wall. Maybe some consideration of sea-gales had come into it. . . . The next-door house, I now noticed for the first time, appeared empty, touched by mild dereliction. A humped black tree that looked like a deformed cypress grew in the garden there, a further barrier against open vistas. No lights were visible in either house, even where the preposterous wall allowed a glimpse of them.

I thought about prisons, while the excluded sea roared ferociously at the bottom of the alley.

I walked along the terrace again, and caught the bus home.

Sunday was cold and clear, and I went out with my camera, because there was too much pure-ice wind to sketch. The water was like mercury under colourless sunlight. That evening Angela had a party to which I had been invited. I drank too much, and a good-looking oaf called Ray mauled me about. I woke on Monday morning with the intense moral shame that results from the knowledge of truly wasted time.

Monday was my free day, or the day on which I performed my personal chores. I was loading the bag ready for the launderette when I remembered—the connection is elusive, but possibly Freudian—that I hadn't got the prepaid receipt back from Mrs. Besmouth. Not that it would matter too much. Such records tended to be scrappy, in Angela's department. I could leave it, and no one would die.

At eleven-thirty I was standing by the door of Number 19, the knocker knocked and my heart in my mouth.

I've always been obsessive. It's brought me some success and quite a lot of disillusion, not to mention definite hurt. But I'm used to the excitement and trauma of it, and even then I was; used to my heart in my mouth, the trembling in my hands, the deep breath I must take before I could speak.

The door opened on this occasion quite quickly. She stood in the pale hard sunlight. I was beginning to learn her face and its recalcitrant, seldom-varying expression. But she had on a different apron.

"Oh," she said, "it's you."

She'd expected me. She didn't exactly show it, she hadn't guessed what my excuse would be. But she'd known, just as I had, that I would come back.

"Look, I'm sorry to bother you," I said. "I forgot to ask you for the receipt."

"What receipt?"

"When you paid for the garment, they gave you a receipt. That one."

"I threw it away," she said.

"Oh. Oh well, never mind."

"I don't want to get you in trouble."

"No, it's all right. Really. I pulled air down into me like the drag of a cigarette or a reefer. "How's Daniel today?"

She looked at me, her face unchanging.

"He's all right."

"I hoped I hadn't—well—upset him. By being there," I said.

"He doesn't notice," she said. "He didn't notice you."

There was a tiny flash of spite when she said that. It really was there. Because of it, I knew she had fathomed me, perhaps from the beginning. Now was therefore the moment to retreat in good order.

"I was wondering," I said. "What you told me, that you find it difficult to make the time to get to the town centre."

"I do," she said.

"I have to go shopping there today. If there's anything you need, I could get it for you."

"Oh, no," she said swiftly. "There's local shops on The Rise."

"I don't mind," I said.

"I can manage."

"I'd really like to. It's no bother. For one thing," I added, "the local shops are all daylight robbers round here, aren't they?"

She faltered. Part of her wanted to slam the door in my face. The other part was nudging her: Go on, let this stupid girl fetch and carry for you, if she wants to.

"If you want to, there are a few things. I'll make you out a list."

"Yes, do."

"You'd better come in," she said, just like last time.

I followed her, and she left me to close the door, a sign of submission indeed. As we went into the back room, the adrenaline stopped coming, and I knew he wasn't there. There was something else, though. The lights were on, and the curtains were drawn across the windows. She saw me looking, but she said nothing. She began to write on a piece of paper.

I wandered to the red chair and rested my hands on the back of it.

"Daniel's upstairs," I said.

"That's right."

"But he's—he's well."

"He's all right. I don't get him up until dinnertime. He just has to sit anyway, when he's up."

"It must be difficult for you, lifting him."

"I manage. I have to."

"But—"

"It's no use going on about home-helps again," she said. "It's none of their business."

She meant mine, of course. I swallowed and said: "Was it an accident?" I'm rarely so blunt, and when I am, it somehow comes out rougher for disuse. She reacted obscurely, staring at me across the table.

"No, it wasn't. He's always been that way. He's got no strength in his lower limbs, he doesn't talk, and he doesn't understand much. His father was at sea, and he went off and left me before Daniel was born. He didn't marry me, either. So now you know everything, don't you?"

I took my hand off the chair.

"But somebody should—"

"No, they shouldn't."

"Couldn't he be helped—" I blurted.

"Oh, no," she said. "So if that's what you're after, you can get out now."

I was beginning to be terrified of her. I couldn't work it out if Daniel was officially beyond aid, and that was where her hatred sprang from, or if she had never attempted to have him aided—if she liked or needed or had just reasonlessly decided (God's will, My Cross) to let him rot alive. I didn't ask.

"I think you've got a lot to cope with," I said. "I can give you a hand, if you want to. I'd like to."

She nodded.

"Here's the list."

It was a long list, and after my boast I'd have to make sure I saved her money on the local shops. She walked into the kitchen and took a box out of the drawer. The kitchen windows were also curtained. She came back with a five-pound note I wasn't sure would be enough.

When I got out of the house, I was coldly sweating. If I had any sense I would now, having stuck myself with it, honourably do her shopping, hand it to her at the door, and get on my way. I wasn't any kind of a crusader, and, as one of life's more accomplished actors, even I could see I had blundered into the wrong play.

It was one o'clock before I'd finished her shopping. My own excursion to the launderette had been passed over, but her fiver had just lasted. The list was quite commonplace: washing powder, jam, flour, kitchen towels. I went into the pub opposite the store and had a gin and tonic. Nevertheless, I was shaking with nerves by the time I got back to Number 19. This was the last visit. This was it.

Gusts of white sunlight were blowing over the cliff. It was getting up rough in the bay, and the No Swimming notices had gone up.

She was a long while opening the door. When she did, she looked very odd, yellow-pale and tottery. Not as I'd come to anticipate. She was in her fifties and suddenly childlike, insubstantial.

"Come in," she said, and wandered away down the passage.

There's something unnerving about a big strong persona that abruptly shrinks pale and frail. It duly unnerved me—literally, in fact—and my nerves went away. Whatever had happened, I was in command.

I shut the door and followed her into the room. She was on the settee, sitting forward. Daniel still wasn't there. For the first time it occurred to me Daniel might be involved in this collapse, and I said quickly: "Something's wrong. What is it? Is it Daniel? Is he okay?"

She gave a feeble, contemptuous little laugh.

"Daniel's all right. I just had a bit of an accident. Silly thing, really, but it gave me a bit of a turn for a minute."

She lifted her left hand in which she was clutching a red and white handkerchief. Then I saw the red pattern was drying blood. I put the shopping on the table and approached cautiously.

"What have you done?"

"Just cut myself. Stupid. I was chopping up some veg for our dinner. Haven't done a thing like this since I was a girl."

I winced. Had she sliced her finger off and left it lying among the carrots? No, don't be a fool. Even she wouldn't be so quiescent if she had. Or would she?

"Let me see," I said, putting on my firm and knowledgeable act, which has once or twice kept people from the brink of panic when I was in a worse panic than they were. To my dismay, she let go the handkerchief and offered me her wound unresistingly.

It wasn't a pretty cut, but a cut was all it was, though deep enough almost to have touched the bone. I could see from her digital movements that nothing vital had been severed, and fingers will bleed profusely if you hit one of the blood vessels at the top.

"It's not too bad," I said. "I can bandage it up for you. Have you got some TCP?"

She told me where the things were in the kitchen, and I went to get them. The lights were still on, the curtains were still drawn. Through the thin plastic of the kitchen drapes I could detect only flat darkness. Maybe the prison wall around the garden kept daylight at bay.

I did a good amateur job on her finger. The bleeding had slackened off.

"I should get a doctor to have a look at it, if you're worried."

"I never use doctors," she predictably said.

"Well, a chemist then."

"It'll be all right. You've done it nicely. Just a bit of a shock." Her colour was coming back, what she had of it.

"Shall I make you a cup of tea?"

"That'd be nice."

I returned to the kitchen and put on the kettle. The tea apparatus sat all together on a tray, as if waiting. I looked at her fawn fizzy head over the settee back, and the soft coal-fire glows disturbing the room. It was always nighttime here, and always 1930.

The psychological aspect of her accident hadn't been lost on me. I supposed, always looking after someone, always independently alone, she'd abruptly given way to the subconscious urge to be in her turn looked after. She'd given me control. It frightened me.

The kettle started to boil, and I arranged the pot. I knew how she'd want her tea, nigrescently stewed and violently sweet. Her head elevated. She was on her feet. "I'll just go and check Daniel."

"I can do that, if you like," I said before I could hold my tongue.

"That's all right," she said. She went out, and I heard her go slowly up the stairs. Big and strong, how did she, even so, carry him down them?

I made the tea. I could hear nothing from upstairs. The vegetables lay scattered where she had left them, though the dangerous knife had been put from sight. On an impulse, I pulled aside a handful of kitchen curtain.

I wasn't surprised at what I saw. Somehow I must have worked it out, though not been aware I had. I let the curtain coil again into place, then carried the tea tray into the room. I set it down, went to the room's back window, and methodically inspected that, too. It was identical to the windows of the kitchen. Both had been boarded over outside with planks of wood behind the glass. Not a chink of light showed. It must have been one terrific gale that smashed these windows and necessitated such a barricade. Strange the boarding was still there, after she'd had the glass replaced.

I heard her coming down again, but she had given me control, however briefly. I'd caught the unmistakable scent of something that wants to lean, to confess. I was curious, or maybe it was the double gin catching up on me. Curiosity was going to master fear. I stayed looking at the boarding, and let her discover me at it when she came in.

I turned when she didn't say anything. She simply looked blankly at me and went to sit on the settee.

"Daniel's fine," she said. "He's got some of his books. Picture books. He can see the pictures, though he can't read the stories. You can go up and look at him, if you like."

That was a bribe. I went to the tea and started to pour it, spooning a mountain of sugar into her cup.

"You must be expecting a lot of bad weather, Mrs. Besmouth."

"Oh, yes?"

"Yes. The windows."

I didn't think she was going to say anything. Then she said: "They're boarded over upstairs too, on the one side."

"The side facing out to sea."

"That's right."

"Did you build the wall up, too?"

She said, without a trace of humour: "Oh, no. I got a man in to do that."

I gave her the tea, and she took it, and drank it straight down, and held the cup out to me.

"I could fancy another."

I repeated the actions with the tea. She took the second cup, but looked at it, not drinking. The clock ticked somnolently. The room felt hot and heavy and peculiarly still, out of place and time and light of sun or moon.

"You don't like the sea, do you?" I said. I sat on the arm of the red chair and watched her.

"Not much. Never did. This was my dad's house. When he died, I kept on here. Nowhere else to go." She raised her bandaged hand and stared at it. She looked very tired, very flaccid, as if she'd given up. "You know," she said, "I'd like a drop of something in this. Open that cupboard, will you? There's a bottle just inside."

I wondered if she were the proverbial secret drinker, but the bottle was alone and three-quarters full, quite a good whisky.

She drank some of the tea and held the cup so I could ruin the whisky by pouring it in. I poured, to the cup's brim.

"You have one," she said. She drank, and smacked her lips softly. "You've earned it. You've been a good little girl."

I poured the whisky neat into the other tealess cup and drank some, imagining it smiting the gin below with a clash of swords.

"I'll get merry," she said desolately. "I didn't have my dinner. The pie'll be spoiled. I turned the oven out."

"Shall I get you a sandwich?"

"No. But you can make one for Daniel, if you like."

"Yes," I said.

I got up and went into the kitchen. It was a relief to move away from her. Something was happening to Daniel's mother, something insidious and profound. She was accepting me, drawing me in. I could feel myself sinking in the quagmire.

As I made the sandwich from ingredients I came on more or less at random, she started to talk to me. It was a ramble of things, brought on by the relaxations of spilled blood and liquor, and the fact that there had seldom been anyone to talk *to*. As I buttered bread, sliced cheese and green cucumber, I learned how she had waited on and borne with a cantankerous father, nursed him, finally seen him off through the door in a box. I learned how she weighed meat behind the butcher's counter and did home sewing, and how she had been courted by a plain, stodgy young man, a plumber's assistant, and all she could come by in an era when it was essential to come by something. And how eventually he jilted her.

The whisky lay in a little warm pool across the floor of my mind. I began irresistibly to withdraw inside myself, comparing her hopeless life with mine, the deadly job leading nowhere, the loneliness. And all at once I saw a horrid thing, the horrid thing I had brought upon myself. Her position was not hereditary, and might be bestowed. By speaking freely, she was making her first moves. She was offering me, slyly, her mantle. The role of protectress, nurse, and mother, to Daniel.

I arranged the sandwich slowly on a plate. There was still time to run away. Lots of time.

"Just walking," I heard her say. "You didn't think about it then. Not like now. The sea was right out, and it was dark. I never saw him properly. They'd make a fuss about it now, all right. Rape. You didn't, then. I was that innocent. I didn't really know what he was doing. And then he let go and left me. He crawled off. I think he must have run along the edge of the sea, because I heard a splashing. And when the tide started to come in again, I got up and tidied myself, and I walked home."

I stood quite still in the kitchen, wide-eyed, listening, the sandwich on its plate in my hands.

"I didn't know I was pregnant. Thought I'd eaten something. The doctor put me right. He told me what he thought of me, too. Not in words, exactly, just his manner. Rotten old bugger. I went away to have the baby. Everybody knew, of course. When he was the way he was, they thought it was a punishment. They were like that round here, then. I lived off the allowance, and what I had put by, and I couldn't manage. And then, I used to steal things, what do you think of that? I never got found out. Just once, this woman stopped me. She said: I think you have a tin of beans in your bag. I had, too, and the bill. What a red face she got. She didn't tumble the other things I'd taken and hadn't paid for. Then I had a windfall. The old man I used to work for, the butcher, he died, and he left me something. That was a real surprise. A few thousand it was. And I put it in the Society, and I draw the interest."

I walked through into the room. She had had a refill from the bottle and was stirring sugar into it.

"Do you mean Daniel's father raped you?"

"Course that's what I mean."

"And you didn't know who it was?"

"No." She drank. She was smiling slightly and licked the sugar off her lips.

"I thought you said he was a sailor."

"I never. I said he was at sea. That's what I told people. My husband's at sea. I bought myself a ring and gave myself a different name. Besmouth. I saw it on an advertisement. Besmouth's Cheese Crackers." She laughed. "At sea," she repeated. "Or out of it. He was mother naked and wringing wet. I don't know where he'd left his clothes. Who'd believe you if you told them that?"

"Shall I take this up to Daniel?" I said.

She looked at me, and I didn't like her look, all whisky smile.

"Why not?" she said. She swallowed a belch primly. "That's where you've wanted to go all along, isn't it? 'How's Daniel?'" she mimicked me in an awful high soppy voice that was supposed to be mine, or mine the way she heard it. "'Is Daniel okay?' Couldn't stop looking at him, could you? Eyes all over him. But you won't get far. You can strip off and do the dance of the seven veils, and he won't notice."

My eyes started to water, a sure sign of revulsion. I felt I couldn't keep quiet, though my voice (high and soppy?) would tremble when I spoke.

"You're being very rude. I wanted to help."

"*Ohhh* yes," she said.

"The thing that worries me," I said, "is the way you coop him up. Don't you ever try to interest him in anything?" She laughed dirtily, and then did belch, patting her mouth as if in congratulation. "I think Daniel should be seen by a doctor. I'm sure there's some kind of therapy—"

She drank greedily, not taking any apparent notice of me.

I hurried out, clutching the sandwich plate, and went along the corridor and up the stairs, perching on two wobbly sticks. If I'd stayed with her much longer I, too, might have lost the use of my lower limbs.

Light came into the hall from the glass in the door, but going up, it grew progressively murkier.

It was a small house, and the landing, when I got to it, was barely wide enough to turn around on. There was the sort of afterthought of a cramped bathroom old houses have put in. It was to the back and through the open door; I could see curtains across the windows. They, too, must be boarded, as she had said—and in the bedroom which faced the back. A pathological hatred of the sea, ever since she had been raped into unwanted pregnancy beside it. If it were even true. . . . Did she hate Daniel, as well? Was that why she kept him as she did, clean, neat, fed, cared for, and deliberately devoid of joy, of soul—

There was a crisp little flick of paper, the virtually unmistakable sound of a page turning. It came from the room to my right: the front bedroom. There was a pane of light there too, falling past the angle of the half-closed door. I crossed to the door and pushed it wide.

He didn't glance up, just went on poring over the big slim book spread before him. He was sitting up in bed in spotless blue and white pyjamas. I had been beginning to visualise him as a child, but he was a man. He looked like some incredible convalescent prince, or an angel. The cold light from the window made glissandos over his hair. Outside, through the net, was the opposite side of the street, the houses, and the slope of the hill going up the other houses burgeoning on it. You couldn't even see the cliff. Perhaps this view might be more interesting to him than the sea. People would come and go, cars, dogs. But there was only weather in the street today, shards of it blowing about. The weather over the sea must be getting quite spectacular.

When she went out, how did she avoid the sea? She couldn't then, could she? I suddenly had an idea that somehow she had kept Daniel at all times from the sight of water. I imagined him, a sad, subnormal, beautiful little boy, sitting with his discarded toys—if he ever had any—on the floor of this house. And outside, five minutes walk away, the sand, the waves, the wind.

The room was warm, from a small electric heater fixed up in the wall, above his reach. Not even weather in this room.

He hadn't glanced up at me, though I'd come to the bedside. He just continued gazing at the book. It was a child's book, of course. It showed a princess leaning down from a tower with a pointed roof, and a knight below, not half so handsome as Daniel.

"I've brought you some lunch," I said. I felt self-conscious, vaguely ashamed, his mother drunk in the room downstairs and her secrets in my possession. How wonderful to look at the rapist must have been. Crawled away, she had said. Maybe he, too—

"Daniel," I said. I removed the book gently from his grasp and put the plate there instead.

How much of what she said to me about my own motives was actually the truth? There were just about a million things I wouldn't want to do for him, my aversion amounting to a phobia, to a state not of wouldn't but *couldn't*. Nor could I cope with this endless silent nonreaction. I'd try to make him react, I was trying to now. And maybe that was wrong, unkind—

Maybe I disliked and feared men so much I'd carried the theories of de Beauvoir and her like to an ultimate conclusion. I could only love what was male if it was also powerless, impotent, virtually inanimate. Not even love it. Be perversely aroused by it. The rape principle in reverse.

He wasn't eating, so I bent down and peered into his face, and for the first time I think he saw me. His luminous eyes moved and fixed on mine. They didn't seem completely focused, even so. But meeting them, I was conscious of a strange irony. Those eyes, which perhaps had never looked at the sea, held the sea inside them. *Were* the sea.

I shook myself mentally, remembering the whisky plummeting on the gin.

"Eat, Daniel," I said softly.

He grasped the sandwich plate with great serenity. He went on meeting my eyes, and mine, of course, filled abruptly and painfully with tears. Psychological symbolism: salt water.

I sat on the edge of the bed and stroked his hair. It felt like silk, as I'd known it did. His skin was so clear, the pores so astringently closed, that it was like a sort of silk, too. It didn't appear as if he had ever, so far, had to be shaved. Thank God. I didn't like the thought of her round him with a razor blade. I could even picture her producing her father's old cutthroat from somewhere and doing just that with it, another accident, with Daniel's neck.

You see my impulse, however. I didn't even attempt to deal with the hard practicality of supporting such a person as Daniel really was. I should have persuaded or coerced him to eat. Instead I sat and held him. He didn't respond, but he was quite relaxed. Something was going through my brain about supplying him with emotional food, affection, physical security, something she'd consistently omitted from his diet. I was trying to make life and human passion soak into him. To that height I aspired—and, viewed another way, to that depth I'd sunk.

I don't know when I'd have grown embarrassed, or bored, or merely too tired and cramped to go on perching there, maintaining my sentimental contact with him. I didn't have to make the decision. She walked in through the door and made it for me.

"Eat your sandwich, Daniel," she said as she entered. I hadn't heard her approach on this occasion, and I jerked away. Guilt, presumably. Some kind of guilt. But she ignored me and bore down on him from the bed's other side. She took his hand and put it down smack on the bread. "Eat up," she said. It was macabrely funny, somehow pure slapstick. But he immediately lifted the sandwich to his mouth. Presumably he'd recognised it as food by touch, but not sight.

She wasn't tight anymore. It had gone through her and away, like her dark tea through its strainer.

"I expect you want to get along," she said.

She was her old self, indeed. Graceless courtesies, platitudes. She might have told me nothing, accused me of nothing. We had been rifling each other's ids, but now it was done and might never have been. I didn't have enough fight left in me to try to rip the renewed façade away again. And besides, I doubt if I could have.

So I got along. What else?

Before I went back to my room, I stood on the promenade awhile, looking out to sea. It was in vast upheaval, coming in against the cliffs like breaking glasses and with a sound of torn atmosphere. Like a monstrous beast it ravened on the shore. A stupendous force seemed trying to burst from it, like anger, or love, or grief, orchestrated by Shostakovich and cunningly lit by an obscured blind sun.

I wished Daniel could have seen it. I couldn't imagine he would remain unmoved, though all about me people were scurrying to and fro, not sparing a glance.

When I reached my nominative aunt's, the voice of a dismal news broadcast drummed through the house and the odour of fried fish lurked like a ghost on the stairs.

The next day was Tuesday, and I went to work.

I dreamed about Daniel a lot during the next week. I could never quite recapture the substance of the dreams, their plot, except that they were to do with him and that they felt bad. I think they had boarded windows. Perhaps I dreamed she'd killed him, or that I had, and that the boards became a coffin.

Obviously I'd come to my senses, or come to avoid my senses. I had told myself the episode was finished with. Brooding about it, I detected only some perverted desire on my side, and a trap from hers. There was no one I could have discussed any of it with.

On Wednesday, a woman in a wheelchair rolled through lingerie on her way to the china department. Dizzy with fright, if it was fright, I watched the omen pass. She, Mrs. Besmouth, could get to me anytime. Here I was, vulnerably pinned to my counter like a butterfly on a board. But she didn't come in. Of course she didn't.

"Here," said Jill-sans-bra, "look what you've gone and done. You've priced all these eight-pound slips at six forty-five."

I'd sold one at six forty-five, too.

Thursday arrived, cinema day. A single customer came and went like a breeze from the cold wet street. There was a storm that night. A little ship, beating its way in from Calais, was swept over in the troughs, and there were three men missing, feared drowned. On Friday a calm dove-grey weather bloomed, and bubbles of lemonade sun lit the bay.

I thought about that window looking on the street. He should have seen the water, oh, he should have seen it, those bars of shining lead and the great cool topaz master bar that fell across them. That restless mass where men died and fish sprang. That other land that glowed and moved.

Saturday was pandemonium, as usual. Angela was cheerful. Her husband was in Scotland, and this evening the extramarital relationship was meeting her. Rather than yearn for aloneness together, they apparently deemed two no company at all.

"Come over the pub with us. Jill and Terry'll be there. And I know Ray will. He asked me if you were coming."

Viewed sober, a night of drinking followed by the inevitable Chinese nosh-up and the attentions of the writhing Ray was uninviting. But I, as all pariahs must be, was vaguely grateful for their toleration, vaguely pleased my act of participant was acceptable to them. It was also better than nothing, which was the only other alternative.

"It's nice here," said Jill, sipping her Bacardi and Coke.

They'd decided to go to a different pub, and I'd suggested the place on The Rise. It had a log fire, and they liked that, and horse brasses, and they liked sneering at those. Number 19, Sea View Terrace was less than a quarter of a mile away, but they didn't know about that, and wouldn't have cared if they had.

Lean, lithe Ray, far too tall for me, turned into a snake every time he flowed down towards me.

It was eight o'clock, and we were on the fourth round. I couldn't remember the extramarital relationship's name. Angela apparently couldn't either; to her he was "darling," "love," or in spritely yielding moments, "sir."

"Where we going to eat, then?" said Ray.

"The Hwong Fews's ever so nice," said Jill.

Terry was whispering a dirty joke to Angela, who screamed with laughter. "Listen to this—"

Very occasionally, between the spasms of noise from the bar, you could just hear the soft shattering boom of the ocean.

Angela said the punch line and we all laughed.

We got to the fifth round.

"If you put a bell on," Ray said to me, "I'll give you a ring sometime."

I was starting to withdraw rather than expand, the alternate phase of tipsiness. Drifting back into myself, away from the five people I was with. Out of the crowded public house. Astral projection, almost. Now I was on the street.

"You know, I could really fancy you," said Ray.

"You want to watch our Ray," said Angela.

Jill giggled and her jelly chest wobbled.

It was almost nine, and the sixth round. Jill had had an argument with Terry, and her eyes were damp. Terry, uneasy, stared into his beer.

"I think we should go and eat now," said the extramarital relationship.

"Yes, sir," said Angela.

"Have a good time," I said. My voice was slightly slurred. I was surprised by it, and by what it had just vocalised.

"Good time," joked Angela. "You're coming, too."

"Oh, no—didn't I say? I have to be somewhere else by nine."

"She just wants an excuse to be alone with me," said Ray. But he looked as amazed as the rest of them. Did I look amazed, too?

"But where are you going?" Angela demanded. "You said—"

"I'm sorry. I thought I told you. It's something I have to go to with the woman where I stay. I can't get out of it. We're sort of related."

"Oh, Jesus," said Ray.

"Oh, well, if you can't get out of it." Angela stared hard at me through her mascara.

I might be forfeiting my rights to their friendship, which was all I had. And why? To stagger, cross-eyed with vodka, to Daniel's house. To do and say what? Whatever it was, it was pointless. This had more point. Even Ray could be more use to me than Daniel.

But I couldn't hold myself in check any longer. I'd had five days of restraint. Vile liquor had let my personal animal out of its cage. What an animal it was! Burning, confident, exhilarated, and sure. If I didn't know exactly what its plans were, I still knew they would be glorious and great.

"Great," said Ray. "Well, if she's going, let's have another."

"I think I'll have a cream sherry," said Angela. "I feel like a change."

They had already excluded me, demonstrating I would not be missed. I stood on my feet, which no longer felt like mine.

"Thanks for the drinks," I said. I tried to look reluctant to be going, and they smiled at me, hardly trying at all, as if seeing me through panes of tinted glass.

It was black outside, where the street lights hadn't stained it; the sky looked clear beyond the glare, a vast roof. I walked on water.

Daniel's mother had been drunk when she told me about the rape. Truth in wine. So this maniac was presumably the true me.

The walk down the slope in the cold brittle air neither sobered me nor increased my inebriation. I simply began to learn how to move without a proper centre of balance. When I arrived, I hung on her gate a moment. The hall light mildly suffused the door panels. The upstairs room, which was his, looked dark.

I knocked. I seemed to have knocked on that door thirty times. Fifty. A hundred. Each time, like a clockwork mechanism, Mrs.

Besmouth opened it. Hello, I've come to see Daniel. Hello, I'm drunk and I've come to scare you. I've spoken to the police about your son, I've said you neglect him. I've come to tell you what I think of you. I've booked two seats on a plane, and I'm taking Daniel to Lourdes. I phoned the Pope, and he's meeting us there.

The door didn't open. I knocked twice more and leaned in the porch, practising my introductory gambits.

I'm really a famous artist in disguise, and all I want is to paint Daniel. As the young Apollo, I think. Only I couldn't find a lyre. (Liar.)

Only gradually did it come to me that the door stayed shut and gave every sign of remaining so. With the inebriate's hidebound immobility, I found this hard to assimilate. But presently it occurred to me that she might be inside, have guessed the identity of the caller, and was refusing to let me enter.

How long would the vodka stave off the cold? Ages, surely. I saw fur-clad Russians tossing it back neat amid snowdrifts, wolves howling in the background. I laughed sullenly and knocked once more. I'd just keep on and on, at intervals, until she gave in. Or would she? She'd had over fifty years of fighting, standing firm, being harassed and disappointed. She'd congealed into it, vitrified. I was comparatively new at the game.

After ten minutes I had a wild and terrifying notion that she might have left a spare key, cliché-fashion, under a flowerpot. I was crouching over my boots, feeling about on the paving round the step for the phantom flowerpot, when I heard a sound I scarcely knew but instantly identified. Glancing up, I beheld Mrs. Besmouth pushing the wheelchair into position outside her gate.

She had paused, looking at me, as blank as I had ever seen her. Daniel sat in the chair like a wonderful waxwork, or a strangely handsome Guy Fawkes dummy she had been out collecting money with for Firework Night.

She didn't comment on my posture; neither did I. I rose and confronted her. From a purely primitive viewpoint, I was between her and refuge.

"I didn't think I'd be seeing you again," she said.

"I didn't think you would, either."

"What do you want?"

It was, after all, more difficult to dispense with all constraint than the vodka had told me it would be.

"I happened to be up here," I said.

"You bloody little do-gooder, poking your nose in."

Her tone was flat. It was another sort of platitude and delivered without any feeling or spirit.

"I don't think," I said, enunciating pedantically, "I've ever done any good particularly. And last time, you decided my interest was solely prurient."

She pushed the gate, leaning over the chair, and I went forward and helped her. I held the gate and she came through, Daniel floating by below.

"You take him out at night," I said.

"He needs some fresh air."

"At night, so he won't see the water properly, if at all. How do you cope when you have to go out in daylight?"

As I said these preposterous things, I was already busy detecting, the local geography fresh in my mind, how such an evasion might be possible. Leave the house, backs to the sea, go up The Rise away from it, come around only at the top of the town where the houses and the blocks of flats exclude any street-level view. Then down into the town centre, where the ocean was only a distant surreal smudge in the valley between sky and promenade.

"The sea isn't anything," she said, wheeling him along the path, her way to the door clear now. "What's there to look at?"

"I thought he might like the sea."

"He doesn't."

"Has he ever been shown it?"

She came to the door and was taking a purse out of her coat pocket. As she fumbled for the key, the wheelchair rested by her, a little to one side of the porch. The brake was off.

The vodka shouted at me to do something. I was slow. It took me five whole seconds before I darted forward, thrust by her, grabbed the handles of the wheelchair, careered it around, and wheeled it madly back up the path and through the gate. She didn't try to stop me, or even shout; she simply stood there staring, the key in her hand. She didn't look nonplussed either—I somehow saw that. *I* was the startled one. Then I was going fast around the side of Number 19, driving the chair like a cart or a doll's pram into the curl of the alley that ran between cliff and wall to the beach. I'm not absolutely certain I remembered a live thing was in the chair. He was so still, so withdrawn. He really could have been some kind of doll.

But the alley was steep, steeper with the pendulum of man and chair and alcohol swinging ahead of me. As I braced against the momentum, I listened. I couldn't hear her coming after me. When I looked back, the top of the slope stayed empty. How odd. Instinctively I'd guessed she wouldn't lunge immediately into pursuit. I think she could have overcome me easily if she'd wanted to. As before, she had given over control of everything to me.

This time, I wasn't afraid.

Somewhere in the alley my head suddenly cleared, and all my senses, like a window going up. All that was left of my insanity was a grim, anguished determination not to be prevented. I must achieve the ocean. And that seemed very simple. The waves roared and hummed at me out of the invisible, unlit dark ahead. Walking down the alley was like walking into the primeval mouth of Noah's Flood.

The cliff rounded off like a castle bastion. The road on the left rose away. A concrete platform and steps went up, then just raw rock where a hut stood sentinel, purpose unknown. The beach appeared suddenly, a dull gleam of sand. The sea was all part of a black sky, until a soft white bomb of spray exploded out of it.

The street lamps didn't reach so far, and there were no fun-fair electrics to snag on the water. The sky was fairly clear, but with a thin intermittent race of clouds, and the nearest brightest stars and planets flashed on and off, pale grey and sapphire blue. A young crescent moon, too delicate to be out on such a cold fleeting night, tilted in the air, the only neon, but not even bleaching the sea.

"Look, Daniel," I murmured. "Look at the water."

All I could make out was the silken back of his head, the outline of his knees under the rug, the loosely lying artist's hands.

I'd reached the sand, and it was getting difficult to manoeuvre the wheelchair. The wheels were sinking. The long heels of my boots were sinking, too. A reasonable symbol, maybe.

I thrust the chair on by main force, and heard things grinding as the moist sand became clotted in them.

All at once the only way I could free my left foot was to pull my boot and leg up with both hands. When I tried the chair again, it wouldn't move anymore. I shoved a couple of times, wrenched a couple, but nothing happened, and I let go.

We were about ten feet from the ocean's edge, but the tide was going out, and soon the distance would be greater.

Walking on tiptoe to keep the sink-weight off my boot heels, I went around the chair to investigate Daniel's reaction. I don't know what I'd predicted. Something, patently.

But I wasn't prepared.

You've heard the words: *sea change*.

Daniel was changing. I don't mean in any supernatural way. Although it almost was, almost seemed so. Because he was coming alive.

The change had probably happened in the eyes first of all. Now they were focused. He was looking—really looking and seeing—at the water. His lips had parted, just slightly. The sea wind was blowing the hair back from his face, and this, too, lent it an aura of movement, animation, as though he was in the bow of a huge ship, her bladed prow cleaving the open sea, far from shore, no land in sight. . . . His hands had changed their shape. They were curiously flexed, arched, as if for the galvanic effort of lifting himself.

I crouched beside him, as I had crouched in front of the house searching for the make-believe spare key. I said phrases to him, quite meaningless, about the beauty of the ocean and how he must observe it. Meaningless, because he saw, he knew, he comprehended. There was genius in his face. But that's an interpretation. I think I'm trying to say possession, or atavism.

And all the while the astounding change went on, insidious now, barely explicable, yet continuing, mounting, like a series of waves running in through his blood, dazzling behind his eyes. He was alive—and *with* something. Yes, I think I do mean atavism. The gods of the sea were rising up in the void and empty spaces of Daniel, as maybe such gods are capable of rising in all of us, if terrified intellect didn't slam the door.

I knelt in the sand, growing silent, sharing it merely by being there beside him.

Then slowly, like a cinematic camera shot, my gaze detected something in the corner of vision. Automatically I adjusted the magical camera lens of the eye, the foreground blurring, the distant object springing into its dimensions. Mrs. Besmouth stood several yards off, at the limit of the beach. She seemed to be watching us, engrossed, yet not moving. Her hands were pressed together, rigidly; it resembled that exercise one can perform to tighten the pectoral muscles.

I got to my feet a second time. This time I ran towards her, floundering in the sand, deserting the wheelchair and its occupant, their backs to the shore, facing out to sea.

I panted as I ran, from more than the exertion. Her eyes also readjusted themselves as I blundered towards her, following me, but she gave no corresponding movement: a spectator only. As I came right up to her, I lost my footing and grabbed out to steady myself, and it was her arm I almost inadvertently caught. The frantic gesture—the same one I might have used to detain her if she had been running forward—triggered in me a whole series of responses suited to an act of aggression that had not in fact materialised.

"No!" I shouted. "Leave him alone! Don't you dare take him away. I won't let you—" And I raised my other hand, slapping at her shoulder ineffectually. I'm no fighter, I respect—or fear—the human body too much. To strike her breast or face would have appalled me. If we had really tussled, I think she could have killed me long before my survival reflexes dispensed with my inhibitions.

But she didn't kill me. She shook me off; I stumbled and fell on the thick cold cushion of the sand.

"I don't care what he does," she said. "Let him do what he wants." She smiled at me, a knowing, scornful smile. "You adopt him. You take care of him. I'll let you."

I felt panic, even though I disbelieved her. To this pass we had come, I had brought us, that she could threaten me with such things. Before I could find any words—they would have been inane, violent ones—her face lifted and her eyes went over my head, over the beach, back to the place where I'd left the chair.

She said: "I think I always expected it'd come. I think I always waited for it to happen. I'm sick and tired of it. I get no thanks. All the rest of them. They don't know when they're well off. When did I ever have anything? Go on, then. Go on."

I sat on the ground, for she'd knocked the strength from me. She didn't care, and I didn't care.

Someone ought to be with Daniel. Oh God, how were we going to get the wheelchair back across the sand? Perhaps we'd have to abandon it, carry him back between us. I'd have to pay for a new chair. I couldn't afford it, I—

I had been turning, just my head, and now I could see the wheelchair poised, an incongruous black cutout against the retreating breakers which still swam in and splintered on the lengthening beach. It was like a surrealist painting, I remember thinking that, the lost artifact, sigil of stasis, set by the wild night ocean, sigil of all things metamorphic. If the chair had been on fire, it could have been a Magritte.

Initially the movement didn't register. It seemed part of the insurge and retraction of the waves. A sort of pale glimmer, a gliding. Then the *weirdness* of it registered with me, and I realised it was Daniel. Somehow he had slipped from the chair, collapsed forward into the water, and, incredibly, the water was pulling him away with itself, away into the darkness.

I lurched up. I screamed something, a curse or a prayer or his name or nothing at all. I took two riotous running steps before she grasped me. It was a fierce hold, undeniable, made of iron. Oh, she was so strong. I should have guessed. She had been lifting and carrying a near grown man for several years. But I tried to go on rushing to the ocean, like those cartoon characters you see, held back by some article of elastic. And like them, when she wouldn't let go, I think I ran on the spot a moment, the sand cascading from under me.

"Daniel," I cried, "he's fallen in the water, the tide's dragging him out, can't you see—"

"I can see," she said. "You look and you'll see, too."

And her voice stopped me from moving, just as her grip had stopped my progression. All I could do then was look . . . so I looked.

We remained there, breathing, our bodies slotted together, like lovers, speechless, watching. We watched until the last pastel glimmer was extinguished. We watched until the sea had run far away into the throat of night. And after that we watched the ribbed sands, the plaster-cast the waves forever leave behind them. A few things had been stranded there—pebbles, weed, a broken bottle. But Daniel was gone, gone with the sea. Gone away into the throat of night and water.

"Best move the chair," she said at last, and let me go.

We walked together and hoisted the vacant wheelchair from the sand. We took it back across the beach, and at the foot of the alley we rested.

"I always knew," she said then. "I tried to stop it, but then I thought: Why try? What good is it?" Finally she said to me: "Frightened, are you?"

"Yes," I said, but it was a reflex.

"I'm glad," she said. "You silly little cow."

After that we hoisted the chair up the alley, to the gate of Number 19. She took it to the house, and inside, and shut the door without another word.

I walked to the bus stop, and when the lighted golden bus flew like a spaceship from the shadows, I got on it. I went home, or to the place where I lived. I recall I looked at everything with vague astonishment, but that was all. I didn't feel what had occurred, didn't recognise or accept it. That came days later, and when it did I put my fist through one of my nominative aunt's windows. The impulse came and was gone in a second. It was quite extraordinary. I didn't know I was going to, I simply did. My right hand, my painter's hand. I managed to say I'd tripped and fallen, and everything was a mistake. After the stitches came out, I packed my bags and went inland for a year. It was so physically painful for a while to manipulate a brush or palette knife, it became a discipline, a penance to do it. So I learned. So I became what now I am.

I never saw Mrs. Besmouth again. And no one, of course, ever again saw Daniel.

You see, a secret agent is one who masquerades, one who pretends to be what he or she is not. And, if successful, is indistinguishable from the society or group or affiliation into which he or she has been infiltrated. In the Magritte painting, you're shown the disguise, which is that of a human girl, but the actuality also, the creature within. And oddly, while she's more like a chess-piece horse than any human girl, her essence is of a girl, sheer girl—or rather, the sheer feminine principle, don't you think? Maybe I imagine it.

I heard some rumour or other at the time, just before the window incident. The atrocious Ray was supposed to have laced my drink. With what I don't know, nor do I truly credit it. It's too neat. It accounts for everything too well. But my own explanations then were exotic, to say the least. I became convinced at one point that Daniel had communicated with me telepathically, pleaded, coerced, engineered everything. I'd merely been a tool of his escape, like a file hidden in a cake. His mother had wanted it too. Afraid to let go, trying to let go. Letting go.

Obviously you think we murdered him, she and I. A helpless, retarded, crippled young man, drowned in Ship Bay one late autumn night, two women standing by in a horrific complicity, watching his satin head go under the black waters, not stirring to save him.

Now I ask myself, I often ask myself, if that's what took place. Maybe it did. Shall I tell you what I saw? I kept it till the end, *coup de grâce* or cherry, whichever you prefer.

It was a dark clear night, with not much illumination, that slender moon, those pulsing stars, a glint of phosphorus perhaps, gilding the sea. But naked, and so pale, so flawless, his body glowed with its own incandescence and his hair was water-fire, colourless and brilliant.

I don't know how he got free of his clothes. They *were* in the chair with the rug—jeans, trunks, pullover, shirt; no socks, I remember, and no shoes. I truly don't think he could walk, but somehow, as he slid forward those three or four yards into the sea, the waves must have aided him, drawing off his garments, sloughing them like a dead skin.

I saw him, just for a moment. His Apollo's head, modelled sleek with brine, shone from the breakers. He made a strong swimmer's movement. Naturally many victims of paralysis find sudden coordination of their limbs in the weightless medium of fluid. . . . Certainly Daniel was swimming, and certainly his movements were both spontaneous and voluntary.

And now I have the choice as to whether I tell you this or not. It's not that I'm afraid or nervous of telling you. I'm not even anxious as to whether or not you believe me. Perhaps I should be. But I shan't try to convince you. I'll state it once. Recollect, the story about Ray and the drinks may be true, or possibly the quirk was only in me, the desire for miracles in my world of Then, where nothing happened, nothing was rich or strange.

For half a minute I saw the shape of a man spearing fishlike through the water. And then came one of these deep lacunas when the outgoing tide abruptly collects itself, seems to swallow, pauses. And there in the trough, the beautiful leaping of something white as salt crystal, smoky green as glass. The hair rose on my head, just as they say it does. Not terror, but a feeling so close to it as to be untranslatable—a terror, yet without fear. I saw a shining horse, a stallion, with a mane like opals and unravelling foam, his forefeet raised, heraldic, his belly a carven bow, the curve of the moon, the rest a silken fish, a great greenish sheen of fish, like the tail of a dolphin, but scaled over in a waterfall of liquid armour, like a shower of silver coins. I saw it, and I knew it. And then it was gone.

The woman with me said nothing. She had barricaded her windows, built up her wall against such an advent. And I said nothing, because it is a dream we have, haven't we, the grossest of us, something that with childhood begins to perish: to tear the veil, to see. Just for a moment, a split second in all of life. And the split second was all I had, and it was enough. How could one bear more?

But I sometimes wonder if Magritte, whose pictures are so full of those clear moments of terror, but not fear, moment on moment on moment—I sometimes wonder—

Then again, when you look at the sea, or when I look at it, especially at night, anything at all seems possible.

# MEDRA

## I

**A**T THE HEART OF A DESERTED AND PARTLY RUINED CITY, an old hotel rose up eighty-nine storeys into the clear sunset air. The hotel was not necessarily the tallest structure left in the city. It had been a very modern metropolis; many of its buildings were of great height. But it had happened that several of the blocks surrounding the hotel plaza had fallen, for one reason or another. Now the tiered, white architecture, like a colossal wedding cake, was visible from almost any vantage of the city, and from miles away, across the dusty dry plains of the planet beyond, the hotel could be seen.

This planet's sunset took a number of hours, and was quite beautiful. The hotel seemed softened in the filmy, rosy light. Its garlands and sprays of ornamentation, long-blunted by the wind, had over the years become the nesting-places of large climbing lizards. During the hours of sunfall they would emerge, crawling up and down the stem of the building, past the empty windows behind which lay empty rooms. Their armour blinked gold, their gargoyle faces stared away over the vistas of the city whose tall abandoned blocks flashed goldenly back at them. The big lizards were not foolish enough to mistake these skyscrapers for anything alive. The only live thing, aside from themselves and occasional white skeletal birds which flew over, lived on the eighty-ninth floor. Sometimes the lizards saw the live thing moving about inside two layers of glass, and sometimes the throb of machineries, or music, ran down the limb of the hotel, so the stones trembled, and the lizards, clinging, trembled, listening with their fanlike swivelled ears.

Medra lived on the eighty-ninth floor. Through the glass portals she was frequently visible—a young Earth woman, by appearance, with coal-black hair that fell to her waist. She had a classical look, a look of calmness and restraint. Much of the day, and often for long intervals of the night, she would sit or lie perfectly still. She would not seem to move, not the flicker of a finger or quiver of an eyelid. It was just possible, after intense study, to see her breathing.

At such times, which actually occupied her on an average for perhaps twenty-seven hours in every thirty-six-hour diurnal-nocturnal planetary period, Medra—lying motionless—experienced curious mental states. She would, mentally, travel a multiplicity of geographies, physical and nonphysical, over mountains, under oceans, even across and among galaxies. Through the flaming peripheries of stars she had passed, and through the cold reaches of a space where the last worlds hung tiny as specks of moisture on the window-panes of her rooms. Endless varieties of creatures came and went on the paths of Medra's cerebral journeys. Creatures of landscape, waterscape, airscape, and of the gaplands between the suns. Cities and other tumuli evolved and disappeared as simply as the forests and cultivation which ran towards her and away. She had a sense that all these visions concerned and incorporated her. That she wove something into them, from herself, if she did not actually form them, and so was a part of her own weaving, and of them. She threaded them all with love, lacking any fear, and when they drifted behind her she knew a moment's pang of gentle loss. But solely for that moment. It was only when she "woke" that Medra felt a true bereavement.

Her eyes would open. She would look around her. She would presently get up and walk about her apartment, which the hotel mechanisms kept for her scrupulously.

All the rooms were comfortable, and two or three were elegant. A hot-house with stained-glass walls projected from one side of the building. Enormous plants bloomed and fruited. There was a bathroom with a sunken bath of marble, in which it was feasible to swim. The literature and music, the art and theatre of many worlds, were plenteously represented. At the touch of a button, food of exquisite quality—in its day, the hotel had been renowned through twenty solar systems—would be served to Medra from out of the depths below.

She herself never went downstairs. Years ago, now and then, she had done so. She had walked the dusty riverbeds of the streets, or, getting into one of the small hover-cars, gone gliding between the walls, past the blank windows, over the bridges—and back again. At night, she had sat eighty-nine floors down on the hotel's decorated porch, sipping coffee or sherbet. The planet's stars were lustrous and thickly scattered. Slaves to their generators, a few lights still quickened in the city when sunset faded. She did not trouble to pretend that any life went on in those distant lighted buildings. Sometimes one of the lizards would steal up to her. They were very cautious, despite their size. She caressed those that came close enough and would allow it. But the lizards did not need her, and "waking," she did not understand them.

In recent years she stayed at the top of her tower. There was no purpose in leaving her apartment. She accepted this.

But every so often, "waking," opening her eyes, sensing loss, she wept. She was alone and lonely. She felt the pain of it always, although always differently—sharp as a razor, insistent as a needle, dull as a healing bruise. "I'm alone," she said. Looking out from the balconied heights, she saw the lizards moving endlessly up and down. She saw the city and the dust haze far off which marked the plains beyond. The weaving of her dreams was her solace. But not enough.

"Alone," said Medra in a soft, tragic voice. She turned her back to the window.

And so missed a new golden spark that dazzled wildly over the sunset air, and the white feather of vapour which followed it down.

Jaxon landed his shuttle about half a mile from the city's outskirts. He emerged into the long sunset fully armed and, from force of habit, set the vessel's monitors on defensive. There was, almost certainly, nothing to defend against, out here. The planet had been thoroughly scanned by the mother-ship on the way in.

Jaxon began to stroll down to the city. He was an adventurer who would work for hire if the pay was good. What had tempted him to this outcast place, well-removed from the pioneer worlds and trade routes that generally supplied his living, was the connivance of a freelance captain whose ship now hung overhead. They had met in some dive on the rim of Lyra, Jaxon a figure of gold as he always was, but gold somewhat spoiled by the bloody nose and black eye gained at an adjacent fight.

"So thanks for saving my skin. What do you want?" The captain

showed him an old star-map and indicated a planet. "Why?" said
Jaxon. The captain explained. It was, at that juncture, only a story,
but stories sometimes led to facts. It would seem that a century
before, a machine of colossal energy had been secreted on this small
world. The planetary colony was promptly evacuated on the
excuse of unstabilised earthquake activity. A whole city was abandoned. No one went there anymore. Out of bounds and off the current maps, the planet had by now been overlooked, forgotten.
Only the story of the machine remained, and finally surfaced.

Very well, Jaxon would assume the captain wished that someone
(Jaxon) would investigate. What capacity did the hidden machine
have? There must be safeguards on it, which were? "It's presumably a war-machine. That's why it's been dumped. Whoever gets
hold of it will be able to call the shots." ("Oh, nice," said Jaxon
sarcastically, bleeding in his free drink.) "On the other hand, it may
be nothing. But we'd like to follow the rumour up, without sticking
our necks out too far."

"So you want to stick my neck out too far instead." The captain
detailed the fee. Jaxon thought about it. It was not until he was
aboard the ship that he asked again: "You still haven't given me
specific answers to my two specific questions. What does this
machine do? How's it protected?"

"All right. This is apocryphal, maybe. I heard it's an unraveller."
Which was the slang name for something that had been a nightmare
for decades, was condemned by all solar and galactic governments,
could not, in any case, exist.

Jaxon said, "By which we're talking about a Matter-Displace-
ment-Destructor?"

"Yes. And here's the punchline. Be ready to laugh. The only safe-
guard on the damn thing is one lone woman in a white hotel."

Legends abounded in space, birthed in bars and backlands, carried like seeds by the crazier shipping, planted in fertile minds, normally born to be nothing. But Jaxon, who had scented something
frenetic behind the deal, was ultimately granted the whole truth.
The freelance captain was a ruse. The entire run was government-
based, the mission—to find and destroy that machine, if it existed.
Anything else was a cover. A quasi-pirate on a joyride, a notorious
adventurer looking for computer treasure—that was all it was to
be. If the powers who had hidden the machine learned its fate and
made a fuss, the event must fail to become a galactic confrontation.
You didn't go to war because you'd been ripped off by a cat-
burglar.

"Alternatively, someone may pulverise the cat-burglar."

"Or it may all be nothing. Tall stories. Lies. A storm in a teacup."

"You ever seen a storm in a teacup?" asked Jaxon. "I did, once. A trick some character pulled in a bar one night. It made a hell of a mess of the bar."

As he entered the city, framed between the sky-touching pylons of the bridge, Jaxon saw the hotel.

He stood and looked at it, and thought about the idea of one woman guarding there an MDD chaos device that could literally claw the fabric of everything—planets, suns, space itself— apart. If any of it were so, she would have to be a robot, or robo-android. He had a scanner of his own, concealed in the plain gold ring he always wore. This would tell him exactly what she was, if she existed, from a distance of three hundred feet from the building.

One of the hover-cars swam by. Jaxon hailed it and got in. It carried him swiftly towards the eccentric old hotel. Two hundred feet away from its royal icing façade, Jaxon consulted the ring. It told him promptly the woman did indeed exist and, as expected, exactly what she was. Her name had been planet-registered in the past; it was Medra. She was not a robot, an android, or even (present analysis) biologically tampered with. She was a young woman. She had black springing hair, pale amber skin, dark amber eyes. She weighed— "Just wait," said Jaxon. "More important, what about implants?" But there were no implants. The car was now only thirty feet from the building, and rising smoothly as an elevator up the floors, sixty, sixty-nine, seventy— "Check again," said Jaxon. The lizards glared at him with bulging eyes as he passed them, but he had already checked those—there were over two thousand of them dwelling in and on the building. They were saurian, unaggressive, obliquely intelligent, harmless, and nonmechanic. A bird flew over, a couple of hundred feet up. "And check *that*," snapped Jaxon, scowling at the lizards. But it was only a bird.

Seventy-nine, eighty, eighty-nine— And the car stopped.

Jaxon beheld the woman called Medra. She was standing at a window, gazing out at him through a double thickness of glass. Her eyes were glorious, and wide.

Jaxon leaned forward, smiling, and mouthed: *Can I come in?*

He was made of gold. Golden skin, yellow-golden eyes, golden fleece of hair. The semi-uniform he wore was also of a tawny gleaming material. He seemed to blind what looked at him.

Medra retreated from the window and pressed the switch which let up the pressurised bubble over the balcony. The man stepped gracefully from the car to the balustrade and over. The bubble closed down again. Medra thought, should she leave him there, trapped and safe, an interesting specimen? But his presence was too powerful, and besides the inner glass was rather fragile and might be broken. She permitted the pane to rise, and golden Jaxon walked through into her room.

The selection of opening gambits was diverse. He had already decided what would be the most effective.

"Good evening," said Jaxon. "I gather the name by which you know yourself is Medra, M-E-D-R-A. Mine is usually Jaxon, J-A-X-O-N. I have been called other things. Your suite is charming. Is the service still good here? I'll bet it is. And the climate must be pleasant. How do you get on with the lizards?" He moved forward as he spoke. The woman did not back away. She met his eyes and waited. He paused when he was a couple of feet from her. "And the machine," he said, "where is that?"

She said, "Which machine? There are several."

"Now, you know which machine. Not the machine that makes the bed or tosses the salad or puts the music on. Not the city computer that keeps the cars running, or the generators that work the lights in the stores."

"There's nothing else," she said.

"Yes, there is. Or why are you here?"

"Why am I—?" She looked at him in astonishment.

All this time the ring was sending its tiny impulses through his skin, his finger joint, messages he had long ago learned to read quickly and imperceptibly. She is not lying. She is shocked by his arrival and so reacting unemotionally; presently emotion will break through. Her pulse ticks at this and this, rising now, faster. But she is not lying. (Brain-handled, then, not to know?) Possibly. Pulse rising, faster, and faster.

"—I'm here," she said, she gave a shaken little laugh, "because I stayed behind. That's all. The planet's core is unstable. We were told to leave. But I elected—to stay here. I was born here, you see. And all my family died here. My father was the architect who designed the hotel. I grew up in the hotel. When the ships lifted off I didn't go with them. There was nowhere else to go to. Nowhere else, no one else . . . How eccentric, to want to remain. But the earthquake activity—it's not so dangerous as they said. A few mild

tremors. The hotel is stabilised, although the other buildings sometimes— Only six months ago, one of the blocks across the plaza
collapsed—a column of dust going up for half an hour. I'm talking
too much," she said. "I haven't seen another human being for—I
can't remember—I suppose—ten years?" The last was a question,
as if he knew better than she and would tell her. She put her hands
over her eyes and began to fall very slowly forwards. Jaxon caught
her, and held her as she lay in his arms weeping. (No lies. Valid.
Emotional impulse verified: the ring stung and tickled its information through to him.) It was also a long time for him since he had
held any woman *this* way. He savoured it abstractedly, his
thoughts already tracking in other directions, after other deduc-
tions. As if in the distance he took pleasure in the warm scent of
her, the softness of her dark witch's hair; pleasure in comforting
her.

# II

There was time, all the time a world could give. For once, no one
and nothing urging him to hurry. The only necessity was to be
sure. And from the beginning he was sure enough, it was only a
matter of proving that sureness, being certain of a certainty. Aside
from the miniaturised gadgets he always carried with him, there
were his own well-tuned senses. Jaxon knew, inside ten minutes,
that there was nothing here remotely resembling the powerful technology of a fabled MDD. In other words, no key to nemesis. The
government ship continued to cruise and to scan far overhead,
tracking the hollows of the hills, the deep places underground, the
planet's natural penthouses and basements. And he, striding
through the city, riding through it in the ever-ready little cars,
picked up no resonance of anything.

Yet, there was something. Something strange, which did not fit.

Or was that only his excuse for remaining here a fraction longer?

The first evening, as the sunset began at last to dissolve in night,
she had said to him, "You're here, I don't know why. I don't understand you at all. But we'll have champagne. We'll open the ballroom." And when he grimaced with amusement she said, "Oh, be
kind to us. Be kind to the hotel. It's pining for a guest."

And it was true, the hotel came alive at the touch of switches. It
groomed and readied itself and put on a jewelry of lights. In the
ballroom they ate off the fine service, every plate, cup, napkin, and
knife printed and embossed with the hotel's blazon. They drank

from crystal goblets, and danced, on the crystal floor, the lazy sinuous contemporary dances of ten years ago, while music played down on them like a fountain. Sophisticated beyond his self-appointed station, Jaxon was not embarrassed or at a loss with any of this. Medra became a child again, or a very young girl. This had been her physical youth, which was happy, before—before the outsiders had come with their warnings, the death of the city, the going away of the ships and of everything.

But she was not a child. And though in her way she had the innocence of a very young girl, she was still a woman, moving against him when they danced, brushed by sequins from the lights. He was mostly accustomed to another kind of woman, hard, wise, sometimes even intellectual, the casual courtings, makings, and foregone departures amid the liquor-palaces he frequented on-planet, or in the great liners of deep space. This does not mean he had only ever known such women as these. There had been love affairs once or twice—that is, affairs of love. And Medra, her clever mind and her sweetness coming alive through the stimulus of this proximity—he was not immune to any of that. Nor to the obvious fact that, with a sort of primal cunning, she had trusted him, since she could do nothing else.

And for Medra? She fell in love with him the moment she saw him. It was inevitable, and she, recognising the cliché and the truth which underlay the cliché, and not being a fool, did not deny it.

After the first night, a first date, waited on and worshipped by the reborn glory of the hotel, they parted, went each to an allotted suite of rooms. As Jaxon revelled like a golden shark in the great bathroom, drew forth old brandies and elixirs from cabinets, eventually set up the miniaturised communicator and made contact with the ship, reporting nothing—as all this occurred, Medra lay on her bed, still clothed in her dancing dress, dreaming awake. The waking dream seemed superior to any other dream of stars and oceans and altitudes. The man who had entered her world—her planet, the planet of her awareness—he was now star, sun, ocean, and high sky-held peak. When she fell asleep, she merely slept, and in her sleep, dreamed of him.

Then the days began, extended warm days. Picnics in the ruins, where the dust made both carpet and parasol. Or lunches in the small number of restaurants which would respond, like the hotel, to a human request. Together they walked the city, explored its emptied libraries, occasionally finding some taped or crated masterpiece, which in the turmoil of evacuation had been overlooked.

In the stores, the mannequins, the solar cadillacs, had combined to form curious sculptures of mutation.

Jaxon accompanied her everywhere, testing, on the lookout, alert for anything that would indicate the presence of the item he sought, or had come seeking. But the other level of him was totally aware of Medra. She was no longer in the distance. Every day she moved nearer. The search had become a backdrop, a prelude.

Medra wandered through the abandoned city, refinding it. She was full of pity and nostalgia. She had come to realise she would be going away. Although nothing had been said, she knew that when he left he would take her with him.

The nights were warm, but with a cooler, more fragrant warmth. The lizards came into the lighted plaza before the hotel, staring, their ears raised and opened like odd flowers. They fed from Medra's hands, not because they needed to, but because they recognised her, and she offered them food. It was almost a tradition between them. They enjoyed, but did not require the adventure. Jaxon they avoided.

Medra and Jaxon patrolled the nighttime city. (A beacon, the hotel glowed from many vantages.) In other high places, the soft wind blowing between them and the star-encrusted dark, he would put his arm around her and she would lean on him. He told her something of his life. He told her things that generally he entrusted to no one. Black things. Things he accepted in himself but took no pride in. He was testing her again, seeing now how she would respond to these facts; she did not dismiss them, she did not grow horrified and shut them out. She was coming to understand him after all, through love. He knew she loved him. It was not a matter of indifference to him. It crossed his mind he would not leave her here when he left the planet. In some other place, less rarified than this one, they would be far better able, each of them, to judge what was between them.

In the end, one night, travelling together in the elevator up towards the top floors of the hotel, Jaxon told her this: "This business I had here is settled. I'm leaving tomorrow."

Although she knew he would not go without her, even so she thought in this instant that of course he would go without her.

"I shall turn out all the lights," she said simply. "As your ship takes you away, you'll see a shadow spread across the city."

"You can watch that too," he said. "There's plenty of room in a shuttle for both of us. Unless you want to bring any of those damn lizards along."

The ritual completed, they moved together, not anymore to comfort, or to dance. Not as a test. He kissed her, and she returned his kiss.

They reached the eighty-ninth floor, and went into her apartment. On the bed where she had slept, and wandered among galaxies, slept and dreamed of him, they made love. About the bright whirlwind of this act, the city stood still as a stopped clock. The hotel was just a pillar of fire, with fiery gargoyles hotly frozen on its sides, and one solitary nova burning on the eighty-ninth floor.

# III

A couple of hours before sunrise, Jaxon left his lover, Medra, sleeping. He returned to his rooms on the seventy-fourth floor and operated the communicator. He gave details to the mother-ship of his time of return. He told the government officer who manned the intercom that there would be a passenger on the shuttle. The officer was open-faced and noncommittal of tone, not discouraging. "She's the last of the colony," said Jaxon, reasonably, insidiously threatening. There would be no trouble over it. The story of the MDD had been run to ground and could be exploded. Spirits would be high, and Jaxon in favour. Maybe rich, for a short while. She would like that, the harmony money would produce for her, not the raw essentials of cash. . . .

Having switched off and dismantled the communicator into its compact travelling form, Jaxon lay back on his bed. He thought about the woman fifteen storeys above him, five minutes away. He thought about her as noncommittally and easily as the young man on the ship's bridge. But nevertheless, or perhaps sequentially, a wave of desire came in on him. Jaxon was about to leave the bed and go back to her, when he heard the door open and a whisper of silk. Medra had come to him.

She walked towards him slowly. Her face was very serious and composed. In the dimness of the one low lamp he had kept alight, her black hair gathered up the shadows and draped her with them. She was, no less than he, like a figure from a myth. No less than he. More so than he. And then he saw—with a start of adrenalin that brought him to his feet—that the one low lamp was shining *through* her.

"What," he said, putting his hand to the small gun by the bed— uselessly—"is going on? A real ghost, or just an inefficient hologram? Where are you really, Medra? If you *are* Medra."

"Yes," she said. The voice was exactly hers, the same voice which, a handful of hours ago, had answered his in passion and insistence. "I'm Medra. Truly Medra. Not a hologram. I must approximate. Will you countenance an astral projection—the subconscious, free of the body?"

"Oh, fine. And the body? Let's not forget that. I'm rather fond of your body, Medra. Where is it?"

"Upstairs. Asleep. Very deeply asleep. A form of ultra-sleep it's well used to."

"If you're playing some game, why not tell me the rules?"

"Yes, I know how dangerous you are. *I* know, better than I do, that is, my physical self. I'm sorry," the translucent image of Medra said to him, most politely. "It can only be done this way. Please listen. You'll find that you do grasp everything I say to you. On some level, you've known all the time. The inner mind is always stronger and more resilient than the thinking process we have, desperately, termed the brain."

He sat down on the bed again. He allowed her to go on. At some point, he let the gun slide from his hand.

Afterwards, for the brief while that he remembered, he seemed to have heard everything in her voice, a conversation or dialogue. It was not improbable that she had hypnotised him in some manner, an aid to his acceptance.

She understood (*she*, this essence of Medra), why he had come to the planet, and the nature of the machine he had been pursuing. The legend of an MDD was merely that. Such a device did not, anywhere, exist. However, the story had its roots in a fact far more ambivalent and interesting. The enormous structure of the universe, like any vast tapestry, rubbed and used and much plundered, had come with the centuries to contain particular areas of weakness. In such spots, the warp and woof began to fray, to come apart—*fundamentally.* Rather than a mechanical destruction which could be caused to engender calamity, the macrocosm itself, wearing thin, created calamity spontaneously. Of course, this giving way of atoms was a threat both local and, in the long term, all-encompassing. A running tear in such a fabric—there could be only one solution. That every rent be mended, and thereafter monitored, watchfully held together; for eternity, if need be. Or at least until the last sentient life of the physical universe was done with it.

"You must picture then," she said, "guardians. Those who will remain at their posts for all time, as time is known to us. Guardians who, by a vast mathematical and esoteric weaving, constantly repair and strengthen the tissue of cosmic life. No, they are not computers. What upholds a living thing must itself be *alive*. We are of many galactic races. We guard many gates. This planet is one such gate, and I am one such guardian."

"You're a woman, an Earth woman," he recalled saying.

"Yes. I was born here, in the Terran colony, the daughter of an architect who designed one of the most glamorous hotels in twenty systems. When they came—those who search out the guardians are also sentient creatures, of course—they discovered that my brain, my intellectual processes, were suitable for this task. So they trained me. Here is one more reality: extended to its full range, the mind of a human being is greater, more complex, capable of more astounding feats, than any mechanism mankind has or will ever design. *I* am the computer you searched for, Jaxon. Not a force of chaos, but a blueprint for renewal and safety. For this reason I remained, for this reason I always must remain. Those who were evacuated were given a memory, a whole table of excellent reasons for leaving. You, also, will be given a reason. I will give it to you. There'll be no regrets. Despite all the joy you've brought me."

"I didn't arrive here alone," he said. "The sky up there is full of suspicious characters who may not believe—"

"Yes. They'll believe whatever you tell them. I've seen to it they will."

"Good God. So what are you? A human machine, the slave of some—"

"No slave. In the beginning I was offered a choice. I chose—this. But also to forget, as you will forget."

"You're still a woman, not—"

"Both. And yes, in her forgetfulness, sometimes the woman despairs and is bitterly sad. 'Awake,' she doesn't know what she is. Only 'sleeping,' she knows. Always to know, to know when 'awake' carries implications of power I don't trust myself with. Occasional sadness is better."

"Perhaps I don't accept any of this."

"Yes," she said. "All of it. As always happens. Dear love, you're not the first to alleviate my physical loneliness. When the time is right, I call and I'm answered. Who do you think drew you here?"

He swore. She laughed.

She said, "Don't be appalled. This episode is full of charm and amusement. Thank you again, so very much. Good-bye."

And she was gone. Into the air. The opening of the door, the whisper of material, they had been reassurances, and a ploy. He told himself he had been tricked. His nerves rioted with an impression of traps and subterfuge, but then these instincts quietened and the sullen protests ceased. It must be as she had said, on some level he did know and had accepted. There had been a joke once, God's a woman—

He fell asleep, sitting on the bed.

Jaxon drove the shuttle up into the pure air of sunrise, then beyond the sunrise into the inky night of space. He left it all behind him, the planet, the city, the hotel, and the woman. He felt bad about leaving her, but he had foreseen the pit before his feet. Living as she had, she would be a little mad, and certainly more than a little dependent. There was no room in his life for that; he would not be able to deal with it. Her fey quality had delighted him, but it was no grounds for perpetuity. Eventually she would have clung and he would have sloughed her in anger. It might have been expressive anger at that, beyond a cruel word, a cruel blow, and the hospitals were makeshift in the areas he most frequented. She wasn't for him, and it was better to finish on a note of pathos than in that kind of mess. Ships came by, she had told him. Someone else would rescue her, or not.

"Which woman?" he said to the captain of the mother-ship. "Fine. She didn't want to leave after all. Come on, you got what you wanted, I did your work for you. Now elaborate on the fee."

He had left her sleeping. Her hair had spread across the pillows, black breakers and rivulets of hair. Eyes like dark red amber closed by two petals of lids. He thought of the façades of empty buildings, the glitter of meaningless lights, the lizards who did not talk to her. He thought of the hot-house of coloured glass. He had a memory of strange wild dreams she had mentioned to him, which took the place of life. She was a difficult woman, not a woman to be lived with, and if loved, only for a little while. *I am half sick of shadows,* she said to him now, in his mind's ear. But that was a line from some antique poem of Earth, wasn't it? Somehow he didn't believe the phantom words. Those shadows were very real for Medra.

In the deserted, partly ruined city, on the eighty-ninth floor of the white hotel, Medra wept.

She wept with a terrible hurt, with despair, in her anguish of loss. And with shame. For she had trusted and moved forward openly, without camouflage, and the blow had crashed against her, breaking her, crippling her—as it seemed to her—forever. She had been misled. Everything had contrived to mislead her. His smile, his words, gestures of politeness and lust, meaning nothing. Even her planet had deceived her. The way in which the sunlight fell on particular objects, the way music sounded. The leaves that towered in the hot-house had misled her with their scent. And she, she was guilty too. Hope is a punishable offence. The verdict is always death; one more death of the heart.

Medra wept.

Later she wandered her rooms. And she considered, with a practical regard, the means to her absolute death. There were medicines which would ensure a civilised exit. Or cruder implements. She could even die in agony, if she wished, as if to curse with her pain's savageness the one who had betrayed her.

But all violent measures require energy, and she felt herself drained. Her body, a bell, rang with misery. After a prolonged stasis of insomnia, there was no other refuge but sleep.

Medra slept.

She slept, and so . . . she *slept*. Down, down, deeper and deeper, further and further. The chains of her physical needs, her pulses, sighs, hormones, were left behind as the golden shards of the city had been left behind, and as she herself had been left, by one she had decided to love. Then her brain, fully cognisant, trained, motivated, keyed to vast concepts and extraordinary parallels, then her *brain* woke up.

Medra moved outwards now, like a sky-flying bird, her wings bearing her strongly. Into the vistas, into the sheens and shades, murmurs and orchestrations. She travelled through a multiplicity of geographies, over mountains, under oceans, galaxies—

Through the periphery of suns she passed, the cold reaches of space. She wove the tapestry and was the tapestry. The pictures filled her with happiness. The universe was her lover. Here, then, in the mystery, the weaver heard some far-off echo, diminishing. She thought, It must stay between the glass. She saw herself, part of a pattern, and elsewhere, random, her life. She said to it, kindly, You are my solace, but you are not enough. The stars flowed by her, and her brain fashioned their fires and was fashioned by them. She thought: But this—*this* is enough.

# NUNC DIMITTIS

THE VAMPIRE WAS OLD, AND NO LONGER BEAUTIFUL. IN
common with all living things, she had aged, though very
slowly, like the tall trees in the park. Slender and gaunt and
leafless, they stood out there, beyond the long windows,
rain-dashed in the grey morning. While she sat in her high-
backed chair in that corner of the room where the curtains of thick
yellow lace and the wine-coloured blinds kept every drop of daylight out. In the glimmer of the ornate oil-lamp, she had been reading. The lamp came from a Russian palace. The book had once
graced the library of a corrupt pope named, in his temporal existence, Roderigo Borgia. Now the Vampire's dry hands had fallen
upon the page. She sat in her black lace dress that was one hundred
and eighty years of age, far younger than she herself, and looked at
the old man, streaked by the shine of distant windows.

"You say you are tired, Vassu. I know how it is. To be so tired,
and unable to rest. It is a terrible thing."

"But, Princess," said the old man quietly, "it is more than this. I
am dying."

The Vampire stirred a little. The pale leaves of her hands rustled
on the page. She stared, with an almost childlike wonder.

"Dying? Can this be? You are sure?"

The old man, very clean and neat in his dark clothing, nodded
humbly.

"Yes, Princess."

"Oh, Vassu," she said, "are you glad?"

He seemed a little embarrassed. Finally he said:

"Forgive me, Princess, but I am very glad. Yes, very glad."

"I understand."

"Only," he said, "I am troubled for your sake."

"No, no," said the Vampire, with the fragile perfect courtesy of her class and kind. "No, it must not concern you. You have been a good servant. Far better than I might ever have hoped for. I am thankful, Vassu, for all your care of me. I shall miss you. But you have earned," she hesitated. She said, "You have more than earned your peace."

"But you," he said.

"I shall do very well. My requirements are small, now. The days when I was a huntress are gone, and the nights. Do you remember, Vassu?"

"I remember, Princess."

"When I was so hungry, and so relentless. And so lovely. My white face in a thousand ballroom mirrors. My silk slippers stained with dew. And my lovers waking in the cold morning, where I had left them. But now, I do not sleep, I am seldom hungry. I never lust. I never love. These are the comforts of old age. There is only one comfort that is denied to me. And who knows. One day, I too . . ." She smiled at him. Her teeth were beautiful, but almost even now, the exquisite points of the canines quite worn away. "Leave me when you must," she said. "I shall mourn you. I shall envy you. But I ask nothing more, my good and noble friend."

The old man bowed his head.

"I have," he said, "a few days, a handful of nights. There is something I wish to try to do in this time. I will try to find one who may take my place."

The Vampire stared at him again, now astonished. "But Vassu, my irreplaceable help—it is no longer possible."

"Yes. If I am swift."

"The world is not as it was," she said, with a grave and dreadful wisdom.

He lifted his head. More gravely, he answered:

"The world is as it has always been, Princess. Only our perceptions of it have grown more acute. Our knowledge less bearable."

She nodded.

"Yes, this must be so. How could the world have changed so terribly? It must be we who have changed."

He trimmed the lamp before he left her.

Outside, the rain dripped steadily from the trees.

The city, in the rain, was not unlike a forest. But the old man, who had been in many forests and many cities, had no special feeling for it. His feelings, his senses, were primed to other things.

Nevertheless, he was conscious of his bizarre and anachronistic effect, like that of a figure in some surrealist painting, walking the streets in clothes of a bygone era, aware he did not blend with his surroundings, nor render them homage of any kind. Yet even when, as sometimes happened, a gang of children or youths jeered and called after him the foul names he was familiar with in twenty languages, he neither cringed nor cared. He had no concern for such things. He had been so many places, seen so many sights; cities which burned or fell in ruin, the young who grew old, as he had, and who died, as now, at last, he too would die. This thought of death soothed him, comforted him, and brought with it a great sadness, a strange jealousy. He did not want to leave her. Of course he did not. The idea of her vulnerability in this harsh world, not new in its cruelty but ancient, though freshly recognised—it horrified him. This was the sadness. And the jealousy . . . that, because he must try to find another to take his place. And that other would come to be for her, as he had been.

The memories rose and sank in his brain like waking dreams all the time he moved about the streets. As he climbed the steps of museums and underpasses, he remembered other steps in other lands, of marble and fine stone. And looking out from high balconies, the city reduced to a map, he recollected the towers of cathedrals, the star-swept points of mountains. And then at last, as if turning over the pages of a book backwards, he reached the beginning.

There she stood, between two tall white graves, the château grounds behind her, everything silvered in the dusk before the dawn. She wore a ball dress, and a long white cloak. And even then, her hair was dressed in the fashion of a century ago; dark hair, like black flowers.

He had known for a year before that he would serve her. The moment he had heard them talk of her in the town. They were not afraid of her, but in awe. She did not prey upon her own people, as some of her line had done.

When he could get up, he went to her. He had kneeled, and stammered something; he was only sixteen, and she not much older. But she had simply looked at him quietly and said: "I know. You are welcome." The words had been in a language they seldom spoke together now. Yet always, when he recalled that meeting, she said them in that tongue, and with the same gentle inflection.

All about, in the small café where he had paused to sit and drink coffee, vague shapes came and went. Of no interest to him, no use to her. Throughout the morning there had been nothing to alert him. He would know. He would know, as he had known it of himself.

He rose, and left the café, and the waking dream walked with him. A lean black car slid by, and he recaptured a carriage carving through white snow—

A step brushed the pavement, perhaps twenty feet behind him. The old man did not hesitate. He stepped on, and into an alleyway that ran between the high buildings. The steps followed him; he could not hear them all, only one in seven, or eight. A little wire of tension began to draw taut within him, but he gave no sign. Water trickled along the brickwork beside him, and the noise of the city was lost.

Abruptly, a hand was on the back of his neck, a capable hand, warm and sure, not harming him yet, almost the touch of a lover.

"That's right, old man. Keep still. I'm not going to hurt you, not if you do what I say."

He stood, the warm and vital hand on his neck, and waited.

"All right," said the voice, which was masculine and young and with some other elusive quality to it. "Now let me have your wallet."

The old man spoke in a faltering tone, very foreign, very fearful. "I have—no wallet."

The hand changed its nature, gripped him, bit.

"Don't lie. I can hurt you. I don't want to, but I can. Give me whatever money you have.

"Yes," he faltered, "yes—yes—"

And slipped from the sure and merciless grip like water, spinning, gripping in turn, flinging away—there was a whirl of movement.

The old man's attacker slammed against the wet grey wall and rolled down it. He lay on the rainy debris of the alley floor, and stared up, too surprised to look surprised.

This had happened many times before. Several had supposed the old man an easy mark, but he had all the steely power of what he was. Even now, even dying, he was terrible in his strength. And yet, though it had happened often, now it was different. The tension had not gone away.

Swiftly, deliberately, the old man studied the young one.

Something struck home instantly. Even sprawled, the adversary was peculiarly graceful, the grace of enormous physical coordination. The touch of the hand, also, impervious and certain—there was strength here, too. And now the eyes. Yes, the eyes were steady, intelligent, and with a curious lambency, an innocence—

"Get up," the old man said. He had waited upon an aristocrat. He had become one himself, and sounded it. "Up. I will not hit you again."

The young man grinned, aware of the irony. The humour flitted through his eyes. In the dull light of the alley, they were the colour of leopards—not the eyes of leopards, but their *pelts.*

"Yes, and you could, couldn't you, granddad."

"My name," said the old man, "is Vasyelu Gorin. I am the father to none, and my nonexistent sons and daughters have no children. And you?"

"My name," said the young man, "is Snake."

The old man nodded. He did not really care about names, either.

"Get up, Snake. You attempted to rob me because you are poor, having no work and no wish for work. I will buy you food, now."

The young man continued to lie, as if at ease, on the ground.

"Why?"

"Because I want something from you."

"What? You're right. I'll do almost anything, if you pay me enough. So you can tell me."

The old man looked at the young man called Snake, and knew that all he said was a fact. Knew that here was one who had stolen and whored, and stolen again when the slack bodies slept, both male and female, exhausted by the sexual vampirism he had practised on them, drawing their misguided souls out through their pores as later he would draw the notes from purse and pocket. Yes, a vampire. Maybe a murderer, too. Very probably a murderer.

"If you will do anything," said the old man, "I need not tell you beforehand. You will do it anyway."

"Almost anything, is what I said."

"Advise me then," said Vasyelu Gorin, the servant of the Vampire, "what you will not do. I shall then refrain from asking it of you."

The young man laughed. In one fluid movement he came to his feet. When the old man walked on, he followed.

Testing him, the old man took Snake to an expensive restaurant, far up on the white hills of the city, where the glass geography nearly scratched the sky. Ignoring the mud on his dilapidated leather jacket, Snake became a flawless image of decorum, became what is always ultimately respected, one who does not care. The old man, who also did not care, appreciated this act, but knew it was nothing more. Snake had learned how to be a prince. But he was a gigolo with a closet full of skins to put on. Now and then the speckled leopard eyes, searching, wary, would give him away.

After the good food and the excellent wine, the cognac, the cigarettes taken from the silver box—Snake had stolen three, but, stylishly overt, had left them sticking like porcupine quills from his breast pocket—they went out again into the rain.

The dark was gathering, and Snake solicitously took the old man's arm. Vasyelu Gorin dislodged him, offended by the cheapness of the gesture after the acceptable one with the cigarettes.

"Don't you like me anymore?" said Snake. "I can go now, if you want. But you might pay for my wasted time."

"Stop that," said Vasyelu Gorin. "Come along."

Smiling, Snake came with him. They walked, between the glowing pyramids of stores, through shadowy tunnels, over the wet paving. When the thoroughfares folded away and the meadows of the great gardens began, Snake grew tense. The landscape was less familiar to him, obviously. This part of the forest was unknown.

Trees hung down from the air to the sides of the road.

"I could kill you here," said Snake. "Take your money, and run."

"You could try," said the old man, but he was becoming weary. He was no longer certain, and yet, he was sufficiently certain that his jealousy had assumed a tinge of hatred. If the young man were stupid enough to set on him, how simple it would be to break the columnar neck, like pale amber, between his fleshless hands. But then, she would know. She would know he had found for her, and destroyed the finding. And she would be generous, and he would leave her, aware he had failed her, too.

When the huge gates appeared, Snake made no comment. He

seemed, by then, to anticipate them. The old man went into the
park, moving quickly now, in order to outdistance his own feelings. Snake loped at his side.

Three windows were alight, high in the house. Her windows.
And as they came to the stair that led up, under its skeins of ivy,
into the porch, her pencil-thin shadow passed over the lights
above, like smoke, or a ghost.

"I thought you lived alone," said Snake. "I thought you were
lonely."

The old man did not answer anymore. He went up the stair and
opened the door. Snake came in behind him, and stood quite still,
until Vasyelu Gorin had found the lamp in the niche by the door,
and lit it. Unnatural stained glass flared in the door panels, and the
window-niches either side, owls and lotuses and far-off temples,
scrolled and luminous, oddly aloof.

Vasyelu began to walk towards the inner stair.

"Just a minute," said Snake. Vasyelu halted, saying nothing. "I'd
just like to know," said Snake, "how many of your friends are here,
and just what your friends are figuring to do, and how I fit into
their plans."

The old man sighed.

"There is one woman in the room above. I am taking you to see
her. She is a Princess. Her name is Darejan Draculas." He began to
ascend the stair.

Left in the dark, the visitor said softly:

"What?"

"You think you have heard the name. You are correct. But it is
another branch."

He heard only the first step as it touched the carpeted stair. With
a bound, the creature was upon him, the lamp was lifted from his
hand. Snake danced behind it, glittering and unreal.

"Dracula," he said.

"Draculas. Another branch."

"A vampire."

"Do you believe in such things?" said the old man. "You should,
living as you do, preying as you do."

"I never," said Snake, "pray."

"Prey," said the old man. "Prey upon. You cannot even speak
your own language. Give me the lamp, or shall I take it? The stair is
steep. You may be damaged, this time. Which will not be good for
any of your trades."

Snake made a little bow, and returned the lamp.

They continued up the carpeted hill of stair, and reached a landing and so a passage, and so her door.

The appurtenances of the house, even glimpsed in the erratic fleeting of the lamp, were very gracious. The old man was used to them, but Snake, perhaps, took note. Then again, like the size and importance of the park gates, the young thief might well have anticipated such elegance.

And there was no neglect, no dust, no air of decay, or, more tritely, of the grave. Women arrived regularly from the city to clean, under Vasyelu Gorin's stern command; flowers were even arranged in the salon for those occasions when the Princess came downstairs. Which was rarely, now. How tired she had grown. Not aged, but bored by life. The old man sighed again, and knocked upon her door.

Her response was given softly. Vasyelu Gorin saw, from the tail of his eye, the young man's reaction, his ears almost pricked, like a cat's.

"Wait here," Vasyelu said, and went into the room, shutting the door, leaving the other outside it in the dark.

The windows which had shone bright outside were black within. The candles burned, red and white as carnations.

The Vampire was seated before her little harpsichord. She had probably been playing it, its song so quiet it was seldom audible beyond her door. Long ago, nonetheless, he would have heard it. Long ago—

"Princess," he said, "I have brought someone with me."

He had not been sure what she would do, or say, confronted by the actuality. She might even remonstrate, grow angry, though he had not often seen her angry. But he saw now she had guessed, in some tangible way, that he would not return alone, and she had been preparing herself. As she rose to her feet, he beheld the red satin dress, the jewelled silver crucifix at her throat, the trickle of silver from her ears. On the thin hands, the great rings throbbed their sable colours. Her hair, which had never lost its blackness, abbreviated at her shoulders and waved in a fashion of only twenty years before, framed the starved bones of her face with a savage luxuriance. She was magnificent. Gaunt, elderly, her beauty lost, her heart dulled, yet—magnificent, wondrous.

He stared at her humbly, ready to weep because, for the half of one half moment, he had doubted.

"Yes," she said. She gave him the briefest smile, like a swift caress. "Then I will see him, Vassu."

Snake was seated cross-legged a short distance along the passage. He had discovered, in the dark, a slender Chinese vase of the *yang-ts'ai* palette, and held it between his hands, his chin resting on the brim.

"Shall I break this?" he asked.

Vasyelu ignored the remark. He indicated the opened door.

"You may go in now."

"May I? How excited you're making me."

Snake flowed upright. Still holding the vase, he went through into the Vampire's apartment. The old man came into the room after him, placing his black-garbed body, like a shadow, by the door, which he left now standing wide. The old man watched Snake.

Circling slightly, perhaps unconsciously, he had approached a third of the chamber's length towards the woman. Seeing him from the back, Vasyelu Gorin was able to observe all the play of tautening muscles along the spine, like those of something readying itself to spring, or to escape. Yet, not seeing the face, the eyes, was unsatisfactory. The old man shifted his position, edged shadowlike along the room's perimeter, until he had gained a better vantage.

"Good evening," the Vampire said to Snake. "Would you care to put down the vase? Or, if you prefer, smash it. Indecision can be distressing."

"Perhaps I'd prefer to keep the vase."

"Oh, then do so, by all means. But I suggest you allow Vasyelu to wrap it up for you, before you go. Or someone may rob you on the street."

Snake pivoted lightly, like a dancer, and put the vase on a side-table. Turning again, he smiled at her.

"There are so many valuable things here. What shall I take? What about the silver cross you're wearing?"

The Vampire also smiled.

"An heirloom. I am rather fond of it. I do not recommend you should try to take that."

Snake's eyes enlarged. He was naïve, amazed.

"But I thought, if I did what you wanted, if I made you happy—I could have whatever I liked. Wasn't that the bargain?"

"And how would you propose to make me happy?"

Snake went close to her; he prowled about her, very slowly. Disgusted, fascinated, the old man watched him. Snake stood behind her, leaning against her, his breath stirring the filaments of her hair. He slipped his left hand along her shoulder, sliding from the red satin to the dry uncoloured skin of her throat. Vasyelu remembered the touch of the hand, electric, and so sensitive, the fingers of an artist or a surgeon.

The Vampire never changed. She said:

"No. You will not make me happy, my child."

"Oh," Snake said into her ear. "You can't be certain. If you like, if you really like, I'll let you drink my blood."

The Vampire laughed. It was frightening. Something dormant yet intensely powerful seemed to come alive in her as she did so, like flame from a finished coal. The sound, the appalling life, shook the young man away from her. And for an instant, the old man saw fear in the leopard-yellow eyes, a fear as intrinsic to the being of Snake as to cause fear was intrinsic to the being of the Vampire.

And, still blazing with her power, she turned on him.

"What do you think I am," she said, "some senile hag greedy to rub her scaley flesh against your smoothness; some hag you can, being yourself without sanity or fastidiousness, corrupt with the phantoms, the left-overs of pleasure, and then murder, tearing the gems from her fingers with your teeth? Or I am a perverted hag, wanting to lick up your youth with your juices. Am I that? Come now," she said, her fire lowering itself, crackling with its amusement, with everything she held in check, her voice a long, long pin, skewering what she spoke to against the farther wall. "Come now. How can I be such a fiend, and wear the crucifix on my breast? My ancient, withered, fallen, empty breast. Come now. What's in a name?"

As the pin of her voice came out of him, the young man pushed himself away from the wall. For an instant there was an air of panic about him. He was accustomed to the characteristics of the world. Old men creeping through rainy alleys could not strike mighty blows with their iron hands. Women were moths that burnt, but did not burn, tones of tinsel and pleading, not razor blades.

Snake shuddered all over. And then his panic went away. Instinctively, he told something from the aura of the room itself. Living as he did, generally he had come to trust his instincts.

He slunk back to the woman, not close, this time, no nearer than two yards.

"Your man over there," he said, "he took me to a fancy restaurant. He got me drunk. I say things when I'm drunk I shouldn't say. You see? I'm a lout. I shouldn't be here in your nice house. I don't know how to talk to people like you. To a lady. You see? But I haven't any money. None. Ask him. I explained it all. I'll do anything for money. And the way I talk. Some of them like it. You see? It makes me sound dangerous. They like that. But it's just an act." Fawning on her, bending on her the groundless glory of his eyes, he had also retreated, was almost at the door.

The Vampire made no move. Like a marvellous waxwork she dominated the room, red and white and black, and the old man was only a shadow in a corner.

Snake darted about and bolted. In the blind lightlessness, he skimmed the passage, leapt out in space upon the stairs, touched, leapt, touched, reached the open area beyond. Some glint of star-shine revealed the stained-glass panes in the door. As it crashed open, he knew quite well that he had been let go. Then it slammed behind him and he pelted through ivy and down the outer steps, and across the hollow plain of tall wet trees.

So much, infallibly, his instincts had told him. Strangely, even as he came out of the gates upon the vacant road, and raced towards the heart of the city, they did not tell him he was free.

"Do you recollect," said the Vampire, "you asked me, at the very beginning, about the crucifix."

"I do recollect, Princess. It seemed odd to me, then. I did not understand, of course."

"And you," she said. "How would you have it, after—" She waited, then said, "After you leave me."

He rejoiced that his death would cause her a momentary pain. He could not help that, now. He had seen the fire wake in her, flash and scald in her, as it had not done for half a century, ignited by the presence of the thief, the gigolo, the parasite.

"He," said the old man, "is young and strong, and can dig some pit for me."

"And no ceremony?" She had overlooked his petulance, of course, and her tact made him ashamed.

"Just to lie quiet will be enough," he said, "but thank you, Princess, for your care. I do not suppose it will matter. Either there is nothing, or there is something so different I shall be astonished by it."

"Ah, my friend. Then you do not imagine yourself damned?"

"No," he said. "No, no." And all at once there was passion in his voice, one last fire of his own to offer her. "In the life you gave me, I was blessed."

She closed her eyes, and Vasyelu Gorin perceived he had wounded her with his love. And, no longer peevishly, but in the way of a lover, he was glad.

Next day, a little before three in the afternoon, Snake returned.

A wind was blowing, and seemed to have blown him to the door in a scurry of old brown leaves. His hair was also blown, and bright, his face wind-slapped to a ridiculous freshness. His eyes, however, were heavy, encircled, dulled. The eyes showed, as did nothing else about him, that he had spent the night, the forenoon, engaged in his second line of commerce. They might have drawn thick curtains and blown out the lights, but that would not have helped him. The senses of Snake were doubly acute in the dark, and he could see in the dark, like a lynx.

"Yes?" said the old man, looking at him blankly, as if at a tradesman.

"Yes," said Snake, and came by him into the house.

Vasyelu did not stop him. Of course not. He allowed the young man, and all his blown gleamingness and his wretched roué eyes, to stroll across to the doors of the salon, and walk through. Vasyelu followed.

The blinds, a sombre ivory colour, were down, and lamps had been lit; on a polished table hot-house flowers foamed from a jade bowl. A second door stood open on the small library, the soft glow of the lamps trembling over gold-worked spines, up and up, a torrent of static, priceless books.

Snake went into and around the library, and came out.

"I didn't take anything."

"Can you even read?" snapped Vasyelu Gorin, remembering when he could not, a wood-cutter's fifth son, an oaf and a sot, drinking his way or sleeping his way through a life without windows or vistas, a mere blackness of error and unrecognised boredom. Long ago. In that little town cobbled together under the forest. And the château with its starry lights, the carriages on the road, shining, the dark trees either side. And bowing in answer to a question, lifting a silver comfit box from a pocket as easily as he had lifted a coin the day before . . .

Snake sat down, leaning back relaxedly in the chair. He was not relaxed, the old man knew. What was he telling himself? That there was money here, eccentricity to be battened upon. That he could take her, the old woman, one way or another. There were always excuses that one could make to oneself.

When the Vampire entered the room, Snake, practised, a gigolo, came to his feet. And the Vampire was amused by him, gently now. She wore a bone-white frock that had been sent from Paris last year. She had never worn it before. Pinned at the neck was a black velvet rose with a single drop of dew shivering on a single petal: a pearl that had come from the crown jewels of a czar. Her tact, her peerless tact. *Naturally*, the pearl was saying, *this is why you have come back. Naturally. There is nothing to fear.*

Vasyelu Gorin left them. He returned later with the decanters and glasses. The cold supper had been laid out by people from the city who handled such things, paté and lobster and chicken, lemon slices cut like flowers, orange slices like suns, tomatoes that were anemones, and oceans of green lettuce, and cold, glittering ice. He decanted the wines. He arranged the silver coffee service, the boxes of different cigarettes. The winter night had settled by then against the house, and, roused by the brilliantly lighted rooms, a moth was dashing itself between the candles and the coloured fruits. The old man caught it in a crystal goblet, took it away, let it go into the darkness. For a hundred years and more, he had never killed anything.

Sometimes, he heard them laugh. The young man's laughter was at first too eloquent, too beautiful, too unreal. But then, it became ragged, boisterous; it became genuine.

The wind blew stonily. Vasyelu Gorin imagined the frail moth beating its wings against the huge wings of the wind, falling spent to the ground. It would be good to rest.

In the last half hour before dawn, she came quietly from the salon, and up the stair. The old man knew she had seen him as he waited in the shadows. That she did not look at him or call to him was her attempt to spare him this sudden sheen that was upon her, its direct and pitiless glare. So he glimpsed it obliquely, no more. Her straight pale figure ascending, slim and limpid as a girl's. Her eyes were young, full of a primal refinding, full of utter newness.

In the salon, Snake slept under his jacket on the long white couch, its brocaded cushions beneath his cheek. Would he, on waking, carefully examine his throat in a mirror?

The old man watched the young man sleeping. She had taught Vasyelu Gorin how to speak five languages, and how to read three others. She had allowed him to discover music, and art, history and the stars; profundity, mercy. He had found the closed tomb of life opened out on every side into unbelievable, inexpressible land-scapes. And yet, and yet. The journey must have its end. Worn out with ecstasy and experience, too tired anymore to laugh with joy. To rest was everything. To be still. Only she could continue, for only she could be eternally reborn. For Vasyelu, once had been enough.

He left the young man sleeping. Five hours later, Snake was noiselessly gone. He had taken all the cigarettes, but nothing else.

Snake sold the cigarettes quickly. At one of the cafés he sometimes frequented, he met with those who, sensing some change in his for-tunes, urged him to boast. Snake did not, remaining irritatingly reticent, vague. It was another patron. An old man who liked to give him things. Where did the old man live? Oh, a fine apartment, the north side of the city.

Some of the day, he walked.

A hunter, he distrusted the open veldt of daylight. There was too little cover, and equally too great cover for the things he stalked. In the afternoon, he sat in the gardens of a museum. Students came and went, seriously alone, or in groups riotously. Snake observed them. They were scarcely younger than he himself, yet to him, another species. Now and then a girl, catching his eye, might smile, or make an attempt to linger, to interest him. Snake did not respond. With the economic contempt of what he had become, he dismissed all such sexual encounters. Their allure, their youth, these were commodities valueless in others. They would not pay him.

The old woman, however, he did not dismiss. How old was she? Sixty, perhaps—no, much older. Ninety was more likely. And yet her face, her neck, her hands, were curiously smooth, unlined. At times, she might only have been fifty. And the dyed hair, which should have made her seem raddled, somehow enhanced the illu-sion of a young woman.

Yes, she fascinated him. Probably she had been an actress. Foreign, theatrical—rich. If she was prepared to keep him, thinking him mistakenly her pet cat, then he was willing, for a while. He could steal from her when she began to cloy and he decided to leave.

Yet, something in the uncomplexity of these thoughts disturbed him. The first time he had run away, he was unsure now from what. Not the vampire name, certainly, a stage name—*Draculas*—what else? But from something—some awareness of fate for which idea his vocabulary had no word, and no explanation. Driven once away, driven thereafter to return, since it was foolish not to. And she had known how to treat him. Gracefully, graciously. She would be honourable, for her kind always were. Used to spending money for what they wanted, they did not baulk at buying people, too. They had never forgotten flesh, also, had a price, since their roots were firmly locked in an era when there had been slaves.

But. But he would not, he told himself, go there tonight. No. It would be good she should not be able to rely on him. He might go tomorrow, or the next day, but not tonight.

The turning world lifted away from the sun, through a winter sunset, into darkness. Snake was glad to see the ending of the light, and false light instead spring up from the apartment blocks, the cafés.

He moved out onto the wide pavement of a street, and a man came and took his arm on the right side, another starting to walk by him on the left.

"Yes, this is the one, the one calls himself Snake."

"Are you?" the man who walked beside him asked.

"Of course it is," said the first man, squeezing his arm. "Didn't we have an exact description? Isn't he just the way he was described?"

"And the right place, too," agreed the other man, who did not hold him. "The right area."

The men wore neat nondescript clothing. Their faces were sallow and smiling, and fixed. This was a routine with which both were familiar. Snake did not know them, but he knew the touch, the accent, the smiling fixture of their masks. He had tensed. Now he let the tension melt away, so they should see and feel it had gone.

"What do you want?"

The man who held his arm only smiled.

The other man said, "Just to earn our living."

"Doing what?"

On either side the lighted street went by. Ahead, at the street's corner, a vacant lot opened where a broken wall lunged away into the shadows.

"It seems you upset someone," said the man who only walked. "Upset them badly."

"I upset a lot of people," Snake said.

"I'm sure you do. But some of them won't stand for it."

"Who was this? Perhaps I should see them."

"No. They don't want that. They don't want you to see any-body." The black turn was a few feet away.

"Perhaps I can put it right."

"No. That's what we've been paid to do."

"But if I don't know—" said Snake, and lurched against the man who held his arm, ramming his fist into the soft belly. The man let go of him and fell. Snake ran. He ran past the lot, into the brilliant glare of another street beyond, and was almost laughing when the thrown knife caught him in the back.

The lights turned over. Something hard and cold struck his chest, his face. Snake realised it was the pavement. There was a dim blurred noise, coming and going, perhaps a crowd gathering. Someone stood on his ribs and pulled the knife out of him and the pain began.

"Is that it?" a choked voice asked some way above him: the man he had punched in the stomach.

"It'll do nicely."

A new voice shouted. A car swam to the kerb and pulled up raucously. The car door slammed, and footsteps went over the cement. Behind him, Snake heard the two men walking briskly away.

Snake began to get up, and was surprised to find he was unable to.

"What happened?" someone asked, high, high above.

"I don't know."

A woman said softly, "Look, there's blood—"

Snake took no notice. After a moment he tried again to get up, and succeeded in getting to his knees. He had been hurt, that was all. He could feel the pain, no longer sharp, blurred, like the noise he could hear, coming and going. He opened his eyes. The light had faded, then came back in a long wave, then faded again. There seemed to be only five or six people standing around him. As he rose, the nearer shapes backed away.

"He shouldn't move," someone said urgently.

A hand touched his shoulder, fluttered off, like an insect.

The light faded into black, and the noise swept in like a tide, fill-ing his ears, dazing him. Something supported him, and he shook it from him—a wall—

"Come back, son," a man called. The lights burned up again, reminiscent of a cinema. He would be all right in a moment. He walked away from the small crowd, not looking at them. Respectfully, in awe, they let him go, and noted his blood trailing behind him along the pavement.

The French clock chimed sweetly in the salon; it was seven. Beyond the window, the park was black. It had begun to rain again.

The old man had been watching from the downstairs window for rather more than an hour. Sometimes, he would step restlessly away, circle the room, straighten a picture, pick up a petal discarded by the dying flowers. Then go back to the window, looking out at the trees, the rain, and the night.

Less than a minute after the chiming of the clock, a piece of the static darkness came away and began to move, very slowly, towards the house.

Vasyelu Gorin went out into the hall. As he did so, he glanced towards the stairway. The lamp at the stairhead was alight, and she stood there in its rays, her hands lying loosely at her sides, elegant as if weightless, her head raised.

"Princess?"

"Yes, I know. Please hurry, Vassu. I think there is scarcely any margin left."

The old man opened the door quickly. He sprang down the steps as lightly as a boy of eighteen. The black rain swept against his face, redolent of a thousand memories, and he ran through an orchard in Burgundy, across a hillside in Tuscany, along the path of a wild garden near St. Petersburg that was St. Petersburg no more, until he reached the body of a young man lying over the roots of a tree.

The old man bent down, and an eye opened palely in the dark and looked at him.

"Knifed me," said Snake. "Crawled all this way."

Vasyelu Gorin leaned in the rain to the grass of France, Italy, and Russia, and lifted Snake in his arms. The body lolled, heavy, not helping him. But it did not matter. How strong he was, he might marvel at it, as he stood, holding the young man across his breast, and turning, ran back towards the house.

"I don't know," Snake muttered, "don't know who sent them. Plenty would like to— How bad is it? I didn't think it was so bad."

The ivy drifted across Snake's face and he closed his eyes.

As Vasyelu entered the hall, the Vampire was already on the lowest stair. Vasyelu carried the dying man across to her, and laid him at her feet. Then Vasyelu turned to leave.

"Wait," she said.

"No, Princess. This is a private thing. Between the two of you, as once it was between us. I do not want to see it, Princess. I do not want to see it with another."

She looked at him, for a moment like a child, sorry to have distressed him, unwilling to give in. Then she nodded. "Go then, my dear."

He went away at once. So he did not witness it as she left the stair, and knelt beside Snake on the Turkish carpet newly coloured with blood. Yet, it seemed to him he heard the rustle her dress made, like thin crisp paper, and the whisper of the tiny dagger parting her flesh, and then the long still sigh.

He walked down through the house, into the clean and frigid modern kitchen full of electricity. There he sat, and remembered the forest above the town, the torches as the yelling aristocrats hunted him for his theft of the comfit box, the blows when they caught up with him. He remembered, with a painless unoppressed refinding, what it was like to begin to die in such a way, the confused anger, the coming and going of tangible things, long pulses of being alternating with deep valleys of nonbeing. And then the agonised impossible crawl, fingers in the earth itself, pulling him forward, legs sometimes able to assist, sometimes failing, passengers which must be dragged with the rest. In the graveyard at the edge of the estate, he ceased to move. He could go no farther. The soil was cold, and the white tombs, curious petrified vegetation over his head, seemed to suck the black sky into themselves, so they darkened, and the sky grew pale.

But as the sky was drained of its blood, the foretaste of day began to possess it. In less than an hour, the sun would rise.

He had heard her name, and known he would eventually come to serve her. The way in which he had known, both for himself and for the young man called Snake, had been in a presage of violent death.

All the while, searching through the city, there had been no one with that stigma upon him, that mark. Until, in the alley, the warm hand gripped his neck, until he looked into the leopard-coloured eyes. Then Vasyelu saw the mark, smelled the scent of it like singed bone.

How Snake, crippled by a mortal wound, bleeding and semi-aware, had brought himself such a distance, through the long streets hard as nails, through the mossy garden-land of the rich, through the colossal gates, over the watery night-tuned plain, so far, dying, the old man did not require to ask, or to be puzzled by. He, too, had done such a thing, more than two centuries ago. And there she had found him, between the tall white graves. When he could focus his vision again, he had looked and seen her, the most beautiful thing he ever set eyes upon. She had given him her blood. He had drunk the blood of Darejan Draculas, a princess, a vampire. Unique elixir, it had saved him. All wounds had healed. Death had dropped from him like a torn skin, and everything he had been —scavenger, thief, brawler, drunkard, and, for a certain number of coins, *whore*—each of these things had crumbled away. Standing up, he had trodden on them, left them behind. He had gone to her, and kneeled down as, a short while before, she had kneeled by him, cradling him, giving him the life of her silver veins.

And this, all this, was now for the other. Even her blood, it seemed, did not bestow immortality, only longevity, at last coming to a stop for Vasyelu Gorin. And so, many many decades from this night the other, too, would come to the same hiatus. Snake, too, would remember the waking moment, conscious another now endured the stupefied thrill of it, and all that would begin thereafter.

Finally, with a sort of guiltiness, the old man left the hygienic kitchen and went back towards the glow of the upper floor, stealing out into the shadow at the light's edge.

He understood that she would sense him there, untroubled by his presence—had she not been prepared to let him remain?

It was done.

Her dress was spread like an open rose, the young man lying against her, his eyes wide, gazing up at her. And she would be the most beautiful thing that he had ever seen. All about, invisible, the shed skins of his life, husks he would presently scuff uncaringly underfoot. And she?

The Vampire's head inclined towards Snake. The dark hair fell softly. Her face, powdered by the lampshine, was young, was full of vitality, serene vivacity, loveliness. Everything had come back to her. She was reborn.

Perhaps it was only an illusion.

The old man bowed his head, there in the shadows. The jealousy, the regret, were gone. In the end, his life with her had become only another skin that he must cast. He would have the peace that she might never have, and be glad of it. The young man would serve her, and she would be huntress once more, and dancer, a bright phantom gliding over the ballroom of the city, this city and others, and all the worlds of land and soul between.

Vasyelu Gorin stirred on the platform of his existence. He would depart now, or very soon; already he heard the murmur of the approaching train. It would be simple, this time, not like the other time at all. To go willingly, everything achieved, in order. Knowing she was safe.

There was even a faint colour in her cheeks, a blooming. Or maybe, that was just a trick of the lamp.

The old man waited until they had risen to their feet, and walked together quietly into the salon, before he came from the shadows and began to climb the stairs, hearing the silence, their silence, like that of new lovers.

At the head of the stair, beyond the lamp, the dark was gentle, soft as the Vampire's hair. Vasyelu walked forward into the dark without misgiving, tenderly.

How he had loved her.

# ODDS
# AGAINST
# THE GODS

NE YELLOW MORNING, ON THE ROSE-SANDED COAST OF
Skorm, three women of the religious sisterhood of
Donsar chanced on an abandoned female infant, and
accordingly adopted it into the fane. I was this hapless
child.

The life of the sisterhood, the Brides of Donsar, was simple, if perverse.

Continual ablutions, prayer, and self-chastisement were virtually the only occupations permitted them. For reading material the Brides might relax with the Manuscripts of Ardour—diaries of former initiates, detailing their ecstatically self-inflicted wounds, and love of their god. Suffering was the key to ultimate fulfillment in the fane. Thus, physical ills were reckoned to be help rather than hindrance—toothache, pains in the belly, or a broken limb were occasions for congratulation and rejoicing.

Donsar, a minor deity, manifested himself in the form of a small glowing light above the altar. In keeping with his general feebleness, the light was never particularly bright and sometimes flickered out altogether. Then all were summoned from whatever pastime they were at, washing, wounding, or wailing (or, less important, out of their beds), and commenced vociferous prayer and song until the light fluttered back to its original sickly intensity.

In this place I grew, and knowing nothing of myself, still my very blood and bones rebelled against such an immutable, futile existence.

They called me "Truth" so, at an early age, I asked:

"Who am I?"

"Why, a foundling, Truth, whom Donsar, in his illimitable mercy, conducted to our door."

"What then should I do?"

"Do? Why, spend the life Donsar has preserved in giving thanks to Donsar. What else, indeed?"

Indeed. What else?

At twelve, having been beaten vigorously by the Chief Bride for a spot of fish soup discovered on my robe, I ran away. I scrambled up slimy porcelain rocks and among green glass pools, and was eventually caught fast by the ankle in one of the numerous clasp traps laid out by the sisters for this purpose.

I was returned to the fane, the whip was produced, and I was once more corrected. The sisters began an anxious dialogue.

"Poor child. She has not suffered enough and consequently is unaware of the felicity of pain. All her teeth are sound and her limbs strong."

One or two offered to knock out a tooth or break a wrist for me, but these services the Chief Bride sternly refused on my behalf, saying such events were the will of Donsar and must not be anticipated.

"Perhaps the affliction lies in her hair," remarked one. "This orange shade cannot be healthful; it indicates passion and willfulness."

So they shaved my head and left me locked in my cell for three days, after which they found me much changed. In a delirium of anger and shame, I had formulated the only possible plan, which was to conform. From that day on I was most submissive, and found that by being circumspect and sly, I could achieve a great deal more than through open opposition.

By an adept use of chimney soot under my eyes, I could seem to have spent whole nights in prayer, when I had really slept, and applications of watered red ink—supposedly for use in writing a diary of contrition—could appear very like the marks of the whip to the dim-eyed sisters. I begged time to meditate alone in my cell on my sins and the redeeming glory of Donsar, in preference to the undoubted joy to be obtained by praying in unison with the sisters. These times I spent dreaming, or else scribbling poetry with the red ink. Inescapable rigours I submitted to, having no choice. I had in my mind a nebulous goal, which was my seventeenth birthday—or at least the seventeenth anniversary of that day I had been found. Something, I felt obscurely, would happen on that day to release me.

I wondered on occasion if the emanation of Donsar guessed my mind, but it did not seem to, which increased my spirit of defiance.

However, none of this was to be.

The very evening before my seventeenth anniversary came a dismal glaring of magenta resin in the courtyard, and seven or eight figures conducting another unfortunate to the insular doom of the fane.

It was habitual among the sisterhood—myself included—to be hugely curious about these new arrivals. The other Brides of Donsar welcomed them with cries of delight. I stared at them broodingly, thinking of their fate with ironic humour.

But this one, when her conductors had left her at the portal and retreated, walked with a graceful gliding motion into the stone hall.

*That vanity will soon be beaten out of you,* thought I bitterly and not without spite. Then her cloak was taken and she stood before the Chief Bride.

She was superlatively lovely.

Sulphurous yellow hair, lopped short at her shoulders, milk-white skin, ebony eyes. I took some time studying her, moving slowly behind the scuttling sisters. She seemed neither distressed nor joyful at the prospects before her. Even the cold refectory and uninteresting food evoked no symptoms of despair.

They called her Meekness.

It was the custom that a new initiate should spend the whole of her first night before the altar, observing and revering the light of Donsar. After Meekness had been despatched thence to take up her vigil, I approached the Chief Bride and begged to be permitted to watch too, alleging that I felt a spiritual need to bathe my psyche in the god's glow.

"Ah, Truth," murmured the Chief Bride sentimentally, "I remember well your turbulent childhood when I despaired for the equanimity of your soul." She patted my head. "Yes, go. My blessing on you. Acquaint our little sister Meekness with the true ecstasy of Donsar."

"Indeed I shall," I avowed earnestly.

In the sanctum of the fane a few tottering candles evolved a smoky subterranean light. The vague pulse of Donsar was just visible over the altar. I made out Meekness standing before it in an attitude of rapt attention.

"Greetings, sister," I said. "Tell me, what can have brought you to this disgusting pass?"

"Why," she said, looking at me out of her extraordinary eyes, "I thought all here to be devout."

"If I were concluded to be other than devout, I should have my skin ripped off by their whips, doubtless."

She appraised me slowly, and smiled.

"That would be a pity indeed," said she.

"If you are reluctant to reveal your history, at least grant me your name," said I.

"Why, Meekness."

"That is their name, not yours."

"At home I was called Lalmi," she amended, lowering her gaze, "and you?"

"I have no name, being an orphan of the accursed fane."

The emanation over the altar flickered.

"Oh, be still, you unoriginal phosphorescence," I reviled it. Lalmi gave a small cry of startlement and admiration. "One day that erroneous spark will go out, and then this temple of iniquity will sink in the sea," I blustered.

"Indeed," said Lalmi, "I can understand your anger. You are far too beautiful and unique to take to such a life."

I answered her that I was not alone in this.

"Ah, no, I am of small worth. There was a curse upon my house that at a certain season our palace would collapse in rubble unless its only daughter were given to a god. When the first cracks in the masonry appeared, it was thought advisable that I should go; as no particular god had been stipulated, and this fane was but a day's ride, it was here that I was delivered."

"Poor Lalmi. It seems we are both destined to atrophy in this unworthy pit."

So saying, I slipped my arm about her for purposes of comfort, which act she fortunately misconstrued.

All caution had escaped me, and Lalmi, in her excellent vagueness, never thought of it. Near dawn, we were interrupted by the shrill altercation of the Brides, who with their ritual torches had come on us, clasped in a manner as unsisterly as it was ardent.

What need to elaborate on the grisly drama which followed? Both of us were taken to the cold-larders and fettered there among the corpses of smoked fish. Certain sisters, examining my cell, came on poems hidden in my pallet, some of which related to Donsar in an inventive fashion.

Hearing the distant wailing and lamentation, Lalmi asked incuriously:

"I wonder how we shall be punished?"

"Since punishment is delicious to them, and they think deprivation the highest of joys, they will be hard put to devise a method," I said acidly. "Perhaps they will give us palatable food and a soft bed, and expect us to expire of misery."

The sisterhood, however, proved ultimately practical. We had dared physical pleasure, the most leaden of all the nine hundred and thirty-three sins set forth in the Manuscripts of Ardour, and, far worse, we had profaned the holy shrine. Nothing but unsanctified death, far from the bosom of Donsar, could be our lot.

After a day in the cold-larder, the Chief Bride came to us and read out our fate. It was to be a traditional doom, judging by the antiquity of the scroll. We were to be taken some miles up the coast to a certain infamous bay, there chained to the rock, and left for the sea monster which periodically emerged upon the shore.

I felt considerably disheartened at these tidings.

"Suppose," I postulated, "that the monster does not appear. Then we shall simply die of exposure to the elements and lack of nourishment—both of which will, of course, be delectable to us."

"Rest assured that the creature will come," averred the Chief Bride, "and that both of you will perish in a state of ungrace."

So saying, she turned her back, spoke an arcane curse, and left us. At midnight, silent sisters bore us into the upper courtyard, where six hooded men bound our hands together and mounted us on thin Skormish horses, and rode away with us into the dark. So I had escaped from the fane at last, but not in the manner I had foreseen.

It occurred to me that perhaps Donsar had had some part in my destiny after all. This thought inspired me to obstinacy rather than fear.

After an hour or so of our dreary ride, a horned moon rose and scattered pale motes on the sea below. We progressed along dismal cliffs, the water to our left hand, great promontories and escarpments lumbering to the right. What lay beyond these inland, I neither knew nor cared.

Our escort was obscure. Cloaked and hooded in black, with only slits cut to emit the glints of their eyes, they spoke neither to us nor to each other. If they were captors, executioners, or merely guides I did not know.

I turned to the rider on my left.

"Propound to me who or what you are, and why you do the bidding of the Brides of Donsar."

The rider answered in a deep emotionless voice.

"I am a felon, and have offended, in the Wastes of Sarro, a powerful goddess resembling a felder-cow, when, without thinking her more than she seemed, I attempted to extract milk from her udder. For this discourtesy I am forced to roam for seven years, hiring myself without fee to any religious order which might require my services. Those other five you see about you are similarly under the geas of various deities to do the same."

"Then you have no specific loyalty to Donsar," I hazarded. "Must you deliver this maiden and myself to death merely at the whim of the fane?"

"Certainly. And should you attempt flight, I, or one of my brother mercenaries, will cut you down immediately."

We presently reached a white terrace incised in the chalk which led down to the beach. Here patient Lalmi and I were lifted from the horses and invited courteously to proceed towards the scene of our extermination.

"We are entirely lost," I muttered.

"Indeed, so it would appear," said she, but I detected no great alarm. Only in love had she been ardent, in all else her sensibilities seemed masked in mist.

On the floor of the beach stood a hut built of mud-plastered stone, and encrusted with shells of various shapes, sizes, and lustre. Here our escort knocked, and out came a tall gaunt man with a lamp in his hand.

"Tush!" cried he, viewing Lalmi and myself with disfavour, "the land abounds in villainy. Have you brought these miscreant women for the Prince?"

"Just so," said one of the hooded men.

We were all conducted into the hut, which was larger than it appeared from without. Lalmi and I were tied to a post crusted with the caparisons of sand molluscs and other nacreous hardware. The six men and the hut-dweller, whose name they appeared to know to be Grunelt, sat at a stone table and drank out of iron cups.

"You are discourteous," I said, "to offer us no drink."

"You will soon be viands for fish," our host responded cheerfully. "No use in filling up your bellies for that."

After a while fatigue propelled me into a fitful doze, out of which I was roughly awakened in the first chilly intimation of dawn.

"Be swift now," encouraged Grunelt, "the Prince will come with the rising sun, and you must be ready to greet him."

"Who is this Prince you refer to?" Lalmi asked, showing some unexpected curiosity in this hour of our extremity.

"The Prince is the name I have designated the thing that comes from the sea."

The sands of the beach were lavender, the sea as opaque as jade, but on the eastern horizon hinted the first wan glow of day. Great manacles of gold depended from the rocks into which Lalmi and I were fastened with distressing precision. The six riders waited farther up the beach to see this part of the enterprise completed, then turned and took their leave.

"Dear Grunelt," I wheedled, "surely two of us are an unnecessary banquet for the monster, and may cause it some digestive trouble. Let my companion go. I assure you, she is innocent of all crime." These words were wrung from me partly because she was my first love and I valued her sweetness, partly out of a base desire to win her admiration in these last seconds, or else twist the murderer's heart, and tempt him to set us both at liberty.

But prosaic Grunelt only emitted yelps of mirth, and shortly, with a glance at the sky, departed to his shelter from which presently issued the sounds of drawn bolts.

The savage topaz disc of the sun now burst from the sea.

In its brilliant path came a turbulence of the waves, and, out of the turbulence, a silhouetted shape of unspeakable yet indefinite horror.

"The Prince!" cried Lalmi in a tone of unusual warmth. "It seems after all I shall be given to a god."

Thinking terror had driven her mad, I refrained from argument and gave myself over to desires that the end be swift.

Up the beach the thing came striding against the dazzle of the sky. It seemed to me eight or nine feet tall, a tangle of huge limbs, scalloped scales with seaweed hair. Sand splayed from its webbed toes, and it carried a fish-stink of the deep and primordial ocean with it. It struck with a huge paw at Lalmi's chains, which unlocked and cast her at once into its clutch. Paying no heed to me, it then turned and retraced its obscene progress towards the waves, carrying Lalmi in its embrace. I caught a last glimpse of her sulphurous hair as she flung her arms about its diluvian neck.

"My Prince!" she extolled it.

And for one wild moment it seemed I saw my first love carried into the sea, not by a monster but by a tall and magnificent man in a glittering armour of viridian scales, his green-gold hair hanging in moist ringlets down his powerful back. Then the water had closed over both their heads, and I had been deprived both of hallucination and lover altogether.


Soon Grunelt came slinking back, unchained me and replaced me in his shell hut. He seemed overfamiliar, but he set before me a bread-cake and a cup of watered wine which I gladly accepted.

"Regarding your earlier question," said Grunelt, "which was, if I recollect, whether the Prince could digest two maidens at once—I imagine you are now enlightened?"

"Imagine nothing," I said.

"Well, then. The Prince, if there be more than one, chooses whom he wishes, and takes her firstly. After an interval of one day he returns invariably for the other. If there be more, as occasionally happens in this wicked land, he will continue reappearances until all the victims have been removed."

"This seems a tidy arrangement. So I have but this one day before I join my unlucky friend."

"Just as you say. Nevertheless, we shall be merry in the interim, never fear."

"I am not inclined to merriment," I cautiously answered.

Grunelt leered.

"The yellow-haired girl was your leman, was she? Well, no matter. You shall be mine."

Whereupon Grunelt advanced upon me, licking his lips. However, I was not of his mind, and cried out warningly: "Beware of a jealous demon which guards me and will deprive you of life should you touch me."

Grunelt hesitated and considered.

"I am grateful for your council, but perhaps I shall be too quick for the demon, since it does not appear at this moment to be about your person."

"Alas, Grunelt, one erotic mannerism and the demon manifests itself out of the air."

"That being the case," said Grunelt, "I will return you to your chains. I cannot afford to feed and shelter criminals without some recompense."

"I see you do not properly understand, dear Grunelt," I temporised. "The demon is only active by day. At sunset it will depart upon other errands and leave me free to do as I wish. If you will be patient until dusk, we can then enjoy ourselves in whatever fashion you recommend."

Grunelt again licked his lips, and agreed to wait. "I, too, have a demon," he said presently, "though it operates in reverse of yours, being active only at night. It is greatly attracted to light, nevertheless, which it eats for sustenance. It smothered the candles and tore the wick out of the lamp on its arrival. Fortunately, once sated, I was able to impound it in a bottle of thick blue glass provided me for the purpose by a professional demon-catcher from the Wastes of Sarro."

"This is very interesting. Pray, where do you keep the bottle?"

"Securely locked in that stone chest. I am very careful of the key. The demon is particularly fond of gobbling animate light and aspires, I believe, to ingesting the moon, which, as you know, is a goddess composed of pure white flame. Should this calamity happen, the postsolar world would be plunged into eternal darkness."

I commended Grunelt on his good sense, plied him with his own wine, and so passed the day. Once or twice, when he fell briefly to snoring, I closely examined the locks of the stone chest, and snatched up one of the iron cups which I hid in my robe.

As the sun slid over the cliffs, Grunelt became vivacious.

"The moment is near when the demon departs," I said. "When I so tell you, you must avert your eyes, since it may make itself visible during egression and the sight of it is peculiarly horrible."

Grunelt complied nervously. Whereupon I uttered a warning and a dreadful shriek. Grunelt covered his face with his hands, and I, leaping across the hut, struck him vigorously several times on the head with the iron cup.

My jailor satisfactorily disposed of, I set about the locks of the stone chest with the same implement, and soon had all the drawers open.

In the lower section of the chest lay a welter of masculine clothing, not Grunelt's, but once the property of male wrong-doers who, as he had told me, being not to the taste of the monster, were pegged out naked on the flats and left for the returning tide and certain ferocious jellies that came with it. Here I found the black habit of a slender youth that fitted me not ill. Also, a long iron staff. Over all went a voluminous black cloak, whose hood I had fashioned to resemble those of the six riders, after which there was no knowing either me or my gender.

Grunelt had also accrued a small store of gold and gems, stolen from various victims, and this I took and stored in a bag at my hip. Finally I rummaged for the demon, and at last found a bottle of midnight-blue vitreous, which, held up to the single lamp I had lit, gave evidence of some inner agitation.

So, leaving the door of the hut unlocked, I set out, permitting Grunelt and the sea monster to resolve matters between them as they saw fit.

After a few hours on the cliff path, the sun rose, conquering the sea and the bastion faces with primrose flame.

I came upon an encampment of four or five travellers snoring round a fire with, in a pen, ten tawny damblepads, and a watchman fast asleep. I undid the wicket gate and led out the nearest beast—leaving the rest to stray—mounted, and encouraged it to a fast smooth loping, its leonine head pointed into the morning wind. It had a fine mane of coal-black curls to which I clung, for I rode it, perforce, without a bit, bridle, or saddle-cloth. There was no pursuit.

On the rest of my journey I saw no one and no thing, except for flocks of black sere-gulls screaming overhead.

I reached the fane at twilight and rapped on the door.

"Who is there?" trembled one of the sisters.

"I, who am an honest diviner, benighted on the north road and craving hospitality of the admirable Donsar," said I, putting on a low, hoarse voice.

After some murmuring, the door was opened and I was admitted. Thinking me a man, they hustled me to the tiny hostelry, where I secured my beast and obtained a bowl of fish soup and a meagre candle. In the wall was a grille through which I might question the Chief Bride, if I so wished, without polluting her face with my eyes. As I had thought, the old busybody came rustling up whether I desired her company or not, for she was avid for tattle.

"Pray enlighten me," said she, "what manner of diviner are you?"

"Why, madam, I divine cause, effect, and remedy. I have been trained in the School of the White Larch, and could tell you, at a need, why it is the sun rises, what results spring from such an occurrence, and how they may be remedied."

"Indeed, indeed. A great weight of knowledge for so green a youth," said she, with some asperity.

"By no means. My wisdom is not mine and I take no credit for it. The genius of an ancient sage possesses my body when I divine, and speaks through my mouth."

"Ah. That is commendable," said the Chief Bride.

After some further chat, I pleaded intense desire to commence my prayers to the god of the fane, and the Chief Bride, torn between vexation and piety, took her leave.

As soon as she was gone, I produced the blue glass bottle, carefully removed the stopper, and shook out the demon into the room. I saw nothing, but there came a rush of air and a frenzied cry, and at once the flame of my candle vanished. There followed some furious squeakings as the demon squeezed through the grille, followed by an advancing blackness throughout the fane. Leaving the hostelry for the court, I watched the progression of this dark until it was total. Then, from the direction of the sanctum came a loud unhuman scream and a flash of blue luminance. The demon, it seemed, had discovered the animate light of Donsar, and found it entirely digestible.

I hastened back to my room.

In the distance I heard wailing and weeping, succeeded by distracted chants and the monotonous rhythm of many whips. This continued for two hours.

Finally several footsteps came towards my grille, accompanied by guttering torchlight.

I lay down on the pallet and began to snore, but was soon woken from my feigned insensibility by the clamour of the sisters.

"Good sir," came the terrified voice of the Chief Bride at the grille, "are you awake?"

"So I believe," I said.

"You spoke of being a diviner of cause and remedy—we have a most urgent need of your help."

"I shall be delighted to assist you," said I, "naturally. However, I must first acquaint you with my fees."

There ensued some dismay among the sisters, but eventually the Chief Bride said sternly: "It grieves us to think that you should demand payment of the fane when it has treated you so hospitably. Surely, understanding that you serve the god should be reward in itself?"

"Without doubt it is, madam, but I am bound by the code of my profession to seek a fee, albeit with the greatest unwillingness. If I failed to do so, various rogues and villains in a similar line of business would accuse me of undercutting them, and have me expelled from my guild."

"Very well, whatever poor means we have shall be put at your disposal."

"Then tell me what is amiss," I said.

"Spirits of darkness extinguish our lamps," cried the Chief Bride, "and the god has abruptly withdrawn himself from the sanctum, and refuses to heed our prayers."

At that moment the demon, having partly digested its previous meal, rushed through the corridor and consumed the torches. The sisters screeched. In the darkness I applied the blue vitreous bottle to the grille, which when exerting its magic influence, the bloated elemental was presently sucked inside and stoppered.

"Well, well," I said. "This is grave, and requires some thought. The illustrious god Donsar has abandoned you and will not return, you say?"

I then told the sisters to gather up such valuables of the fane as they felt owing to me, and bring them to my door an hour after dawn, by which time, through cogitation and spell, I should have some idea of the origin of their predicament. Once they had gone snivelling away, I lay down and slept peacefully until sunrise.

At the appointed time I opened the door and found a pair of small candlesticks of antique silver and a miniature gold censer. These I put into various pockets of my cloak, well aware that no more of their clandestine wealth would be forthcoming.

Just then the Chief Bride made herself known at the grille.

"Have your deliberations borne fruit?" asked she.

"One moment while I activate my mentor." I then lapsed into a trance and fell like the dead onto the floor amid a clatter of candlesticks. Assuming a quavering voice, I declaimed as follows:

"The merciful god Donsar has been patient with his Brides a long while, forgiving their misinterpretations of his desires. But now, distressed by their continual transgressions, he has withdrawn to Limbo."

"What transgressions are these?" demanded the Chief Bride. "We have not left off prayer and the whip all night."

"Exactly so. The god does not wish to be worshipped in this manner, but in levity, merriment, and passions of the flesh. This, then, is the cause; the effect is as you see. The remedy is simple. Give yourselves over at once to carnality, song, strong drink, and libidinous exercise, and the god will return to you."

The Chief Bride uttered a scream of horror and fled from my presence, and soon began again the drone of prayers, the thrashing of whips.

Towards sunset, however, a great silence settled on the fane.

Walking in the court, in the afterglow, I was suddenly confronted by the Chief Bride.

"Good sir—all is as you have said. The god declines to return. Thus—" here she ripped open her robe— "I offer myself to you, as the first proof of our devotion to Donsar. Take me—I am yours!"

It is certain that the Chief Bride, aged and scrawny from deprivations, did not appeal to me, besides which, I had not the requisite equipment to fulfil her demand. I therefore bowed humbly and said: "Madam, I am greatly honoured, but, alas, I am under a vow of chastity and cannot therefore avail myself of your generous offer. Nevertheless, you have only to send word to the neighbouring villages and farms, and no doubt the local men will be delighted to accommodate you."

So it was that, within three hours, the desolate fane was ablaze with light, noisy with liquor and lust, the refectory crammed with roasting meats, and the cells with squeaking, panting sisters intent on propitiating Donsar.

To the accompaniment of these strident yet, as they would discover, ineffectual sights and sounds, I mounted my damblepad once again, and rode into the night.

Having escaped the Brides of Donsar, I, Truth, the orphan, had no plans. I was simply alert for such profit and pleasure as might be available to recompense for seventeen years spent in the thrall of a devoured god.

For a day or so I travelled aimlessly, taking a road inland, feeding from trees and bushes, and sleeping by night in deserted huts. All this while I saw not a soul, human or elemental.

One dusk, however, the road took me onto a desolate plain of rocks.

My mount soon began to evince unease, and I made out strings of red lights keeping watch along the ridges, while optimistic howlings reverberated in the near distance.

The damblepad and I sought refuge in a small cave next the road, and having piled up large stones at the entrance to deter eager visitors, I fell into a troubled sleep.

Just before dawn I woke with a start and stared about in alarm. All appeared peaceful—the stones undisturbed, the damblepad with its head on its paws, a dreaming expression in its eyes. Then I noticed how light my cloak had become and that the pouch with Grunelt's treasure lay flaccid on the ground. I consequently discovered that I had been robbed of all my wealth—gold, gems, candlesticks, and censer, even the blue glass bottle with the expedient demon in it.

I hastened to my barricade and stared out. I could not imagine a thief light-fingered enough to have been able to rob me, without either myself or the damblepad becoming aware of him. Nevertheless the eastern-facing surfaces of the plain were now varnished with sunrise, and I quickly discerned a tall agile figure picking a way over them. It appeared to be heading towards a line of marching stacks outlined on the pale purple of the western horizon, and, fearing I should lose the snatcher of my only recently acquired property, I pushed down the stones, leaped on the damblepad, and was quickly dashing in pursuit.

Rounding a spur of rock, I came upon the malefactor suddenly.

"Abandon flight, degenerate," I admonished him. "Your villainy has been noted. Kindly return to me those articles of mine you filched."

My quarry was revealed at that moment by the rising sun to be a slim yet muscular young man, dressed entirely in black, with a tanned and pensive countenance, slate-green eyes, crow-black hair far longer than my own, and a small sack strapped upon his back.

"Noble sir," said he, "for, despite your masked face and discourteous words, so much I will assume, let me assure you that I am innocent of this crime and have nothing of yours."

"What, then, is in your sack?"

"Certain personal possessions that I carry with me from a sense of nostalgia."

"That being so, you will hardly object to opening the said sack and letting me see for myself."

"Reluctantly, I must decline," said the young man, with an apologetic smile. "The sack holds nothing that could possibly interest you, besides which, I should find it distressing to set on display items of such an intimate emotional nature."

At this, I produced the iron staff, and directed it at him in an unsubtle manner.

"Now," I said, "let us reconsider this matter, bearing in mind that if you do not empty the sack, I shall stove in your skull."

"Hmm," he said, "I see your resourcefulness exceeds your years. Very well." And searching with lean fingers into the mouth of the sack, he drew out a metal rod some five inches long. "To begin," he said, "here is an artifact of ancient Minnoven, known as the Irresistible Transporter. I will demonstrate." At which he touched a nub on the rod, there came a dazzle of light all around me, and I found myself catapulted high into the air. Presently, painfully arriving at the base of a rock, stunned and debilitated, I dimly heard my adversary give a pleasant laugh, and noticed that he was now mounted on my damblepad.

"Pray do not trouble yourself to rise," he said. "After all your generosity, I should not dream of inconveniencing you further. I would not have taken your animal, but since you press me so forcibly, I can only accept with warm gratitude, and bid you an enjoyable journey."

So saying, and with a polite salute, my tormenter urged my beast to a fast lope and vanished among the stacks, leaving me writhing and helpless in the dust.

The sun had risen high before I was properly myself again, by which time I was consumed with hunger and thirst. Until now I had lived adequately off the land, but here on the plain no tree or bush grew, no stream ran, and the only shade came from the barren rocks.

I began to walk doggedly towards the west which had seemed to be the direction my attacker had taken. I became in due course very uncomfortable from the sun, and formulated curses with which to mutilate the thief as soon as I should find a seer able enough to effect them.

By afternoon the plain had become lost in low, featureless rock hills, and a line of mountains was faintly inscribed on the distant sky. I had begun to despair of remaining alive, for even if I should survive dehydration, the night would bring forth the wild beasts I had fled from before, and, in my weakness, I would be easily subdued.

Crossing the brow of a hill, I saw then a valley below, containing unexpectedly a square stone building with a beehive roof, and a gliding narrow river the colour of wine. With a glad cry, I staggered down at a run towards it, passed the beehive dwelling, and so came finally to the brink. I had long since removed my cloak in the heat of the day, and now when I cast it aside, a fold dropped in the ruby water. At once came a swirling of unseen presences, and in a second the garment had been dragged swiftly below the surface, to which rose presently small threads and particles. It occurred to me that had I plunged in face or hands to drink, I too would have been pulled bodily after and thereupon dismembered as the cloak had been. Thankful as I was at escaping such a fate, nevertheless the lack of water restored me to depression. Turning my back upon the maleficent river, I made my way towards the dwelling on its bank.

The entrance was barred by a stout door which, however, swung open at my touch.

Within was an amazing chamber, windowless, but lit up by floating lamps, and full of a disturbed and gaseous din. The entire space from wall to wall and high into the domed roof was entwined by silver tubes and crystalline pipes. Through the lower pipes bubbled a fierce red liquor, which grew by stages quieter and paler as it ascended to the channels in the ceiling. Alongside the tubing passed iron walkways, here and there marked by tall marble panels studded with knobs and ornamental silver levers. A flight of steps ran up one wall to a wooden gallery which circled the interior.

Bemused, I climbed the steps.

There, prostrate on a canopied and gorgeous bed, lay an old man with a white scarf bound about his skull, apparently oblivious. By the bed stood an open larder filled with cheeses, meats, pastries, and exotic fruit, and, in tall flagons, clear and wholesome water.

I crept closer, but no sooner had my hand closed on the nearest jar, than the old man shot up with a scream, and out from under the bed came tearing two hideous dogs of unnatural appearance and ferocity. These bore me to the floor, and crouched snarling at either side, surveying my vitals with meaningful deliberation.

"What, am I to have no peace?" inquired the old man.

"I beg your pardon, aged sir," said I. "To disturb your peace was not my intention. However, I feel I cannot make adequate recompense while stretched out thus, and if you will call off your dogs—"

"Call off my dogs! Ho Fangast, ho Bloodlover, keep good watch on the villain."

"I entreat you, sir," said I, "to be lenient. I am only a footsore, weary traveller, in desperate need of a sip or two of water."

"Very likely, and, mark my generosity, for two silver pieces I will give you an entire cup."

"This seems both just and thrifty on your part," said I, "but, alas, I have no money, since a rogue and cutthroat despoiled me of everything I had on the plain, and left me for dead."

"Such an event entitles you to my sympathy," said the old man, "but to nothing else. What you see about you is the ancient distillery of Sath Monnis, a town of repute and splendour some ten or eleven miles to the west. I, Trall the watchman, attend this elegant machinery, which converts the infested water of the river into healthful fluid, and then passes it by means of pumps and pipes into the cisterns of the aforementioned metropolis. This, as you will understand, is a responsible post, and due some remuneration and respect. My own drink I draw from a hidden tap and receive, naturally, gratis. However, since my wage from Sath Monnis is regrettably low, I am forced to extract payment from travellers. Still, I am not unreasonable. If you will watch the levers for three nights in my stead, I will waive the toll, and give you a cup of water on the fourth day."

"Good sir, if I pass three more days without drink, you may use the water to encourage flowers on my grave. If you will give me liquid and food now, I will then watch in your place with great attention."

"Your obstinacy displeases me," muttered the old man. "I do not watch here out of motives of altruism. Besides, you are the second vandal I have been subjected to today. Since the last—a black-haired fellow on a leonine beast—in some manner subdued my animals, thereafter robbing me and raining blows on my head besides, I am not inclined to further discourse. Either depart into the waterless hills, or remain to nourish the dogs."

"Neither of these alternatives conforms with my destiny," I said. "I will therefore muster strength and accept your first offer, namely, to watch three nights in your stead."

The old man assented testily, called off Fangfast and Bloodlover, to their great dejection, and took me about the iron walkways.

"On no account touch the levers or any other instrument," he instructed me, "but patrol the walks all night, with careful eye and ear."

He then retired to his couch, devoured a huge meal, quaffed water and wine, and fed the dogs. After which all three fell to snoring, and I was left to my task with empty belly and burning throat.

Nor were my spirits reinforced by knowing that the same felon who had put me in this pass had fared so much the better.

All night I slept on the comfortless iron. A little before dawn I rose and commenced experimenting with the marble panels. Those knobs which were outstanding, I depressed; those levers which angled towards the ceiling I pointed to the floor, and vice versa.

Soon came a strange dissonance in the tubes, while the light in the floating lamps dimmed and gradually went out.

In the dark I felt my way to the foot of the gallery steps, and hid myself behind the bannister.

At this point the perversity of the noises impinged on the old man's sleep. He woke above and began to screech and shout, and the dogs to whine and howl.

"Alas! Alas! The ruffian has ignored the watch and fled, and now disaster has prevailed!"

And shortly he came stumbling and groaning down the steps, and hobbled with shrill exclamations up the walkways in the blackness, the two dogs cowering at his heels. Judging this my only opportunity, I crept to the gallery, seized a stoppered water jar and some food, which I stowed in my sash, and then edged cautiously towards the doorway. When the crack of light appeared, the old man cried:

"There goes the malcontent—after him, Fangfast!"

But I got through and slammed the door shut, and took to my heels.

On the far slope of the valley, I looked back once, and saw the ruby river in boiling ferment, while gouts of steam belched from the beehive roof. I did not stay for more.

Some miles farther on, I sat in the shade of a solitary spear tree to eat my food, and drink the clear water.

In the distance I could now make out, with some clarity, the jagged heliotrope spires of the mountains. At the foot of these was a collection of pinnacles of a different sort which I concluded to be the towers of Sath Monnis, that reputable and splendid town whose cisterns I had no doubt poisoned.

Certainly, I thought, the accursed thief of my damblepad and other property has made for the town, therefore I must follow.

So I set out once again on the irksome trail.

On the outskirts of Sath Monnis I came upon cultivated fields of a pleasing yellow and green, groves of tall black poplars, and some marble statuary representing enormous heroic figures, before which wreaths of flowers, corn ears, pink grapes, and other flora had been laid. The town itself was of, to me, extraordinary construction. It consisted of countless marble bridges, each looping over and under the others, and connected by flights of steps. All the dwellings of Sath Monnis—some of which were exceedingly ramshackle—perched on these magnificent arches and swoops, while below ran a series of canals containing a wine-red water. I gave this some attention, for it could be nothing else than a continuation of the morbid river.

Walking the stately thoroughfares, I came upon a crowd of men and women, and forced by the press to halt, I was presently observer of a public execution. This took an original yet simple form. A band, apparently of soldiers, and dressed in brass with yellow cloaks, marched the five unfortunates to the perimeter of the bridge, persuaded them by urgent sword points to climb up on the parapet, and then pushed them off into the canal beneath. This action was greeted by a shout from the populace and some applause. In a moment or so, certain proofs of the execution appeared on the waters, after which the crowd cheerfully dispersed.

Curious, I fell into step beside a portly and well-dressed townsman, and inquired as to the misdemeanour the victims had committed.

"In Sath Monnis," he replied, "there is only one crime considered heinous enough to merit death. That is, to utter blasphemy against our gods."

"This is so in many places," I remarked, recalling the fane.

"And no doubt both wise and commendable," he answered. "I divine you are a stranger, young sir, and so I will take it on myself to acquaint you with the history of the town. All this magnificence you see about you was erected by our gods in the days of our ancestors. They it was who set up these wondrous bridges and excavated this imposing system of canals, they who perfected a distillery to supply us with delicious and health-giving springs, and also laid out pasture and field to provide our sustenance."

"You are undoubtedly most fortunate," I said.

"There is more," said my guide, with a benign smile. "In time of trouble we are assured our gods will come to our aid, and bring retribution upon any who harm us. In return, we have built a temple to their glory, and instigated a sacred guard—those in yellow cloaks—to protect their honour."

"I am most obliged for your assistance," I said. "Purely out of curiosity, might I ask if you would loan me a small sum until this evening, when I expect untold riches to be placed in my keeping."

My new-found friend became aloof.

"I regret I carry no money about me." And then, lowering his tone, "In addition, I should warn you that, while not a mortal offence, begging in a public place is generally penalised by amputation."

So saying, he hurried away.

For an hour or so I traipsed the streets, inquiring occasionally of passers-by if any had seen a green-eyed, black-haired fellow riding a damblepad. None had. It was now long past noon, and I was parched. Going to a round marble basin and tap, I attempted to drink, but a yellow-cloaked guard stepped smartly up and demanded payment, so I declined the water and went my way.

Finally, in an evil vein, I came upon a tall white building with a cupola of lemon glass. This I concluded to be the Temple of Sath Monnis, and went inside to implore some priest to send a vile curse upon my elusive assailant, for which work I was prepared to toil day and night for a month, such was my fury.

In the broad nave I made out a single yellow cloak turning over in his hands a small candlestick of antique silver. This I recognised very well as a piece of my fee from the Brides of Donsar. Sauntering to his side, I said:

"What a charming object. It drew my eyes at once."

"This exceeds mere prettiness," he avowed. "I bought it from a traveller who found it, while exploring the mountains, in the hoard of a sorceress. I have only to expose it to the next new moon and words will appear legibly on its sides, indicating the whereabouts of priceless hidden treasure in the earth. More: any maiden whose name I once inscribe in common ink on the metal will instantly be compelled by an insatiable lust to enjoy my person."

"A useful article, to be sure," I agreed, seized with a reluctant admiration for the villain who had robbed me. "No doubt it proved expensive."

"A matter of twenty gold coins—but, following the new moon, I shall soon recoup my losses." Then, fearing perhaps he had been too hasty in confiding all to me, he added: "I trust you recognise my claim to this item?"

I sternly assured him that I believed the true path of redemption lay through poverty and humbleness, and had no interest in such gew-gaws.

"However," I went on, "I would ask the whereabouts of the traveller who sold it you, for possibly he has other wares of more value to me—such as old books of prayers."

The yellow cloak then directed me to the Inn of the Bitten Quince, which lay some ten bridges distant, and which it took me until sunset to reach.

At the Bitten Quince all was merriment, eating, and drinking, which it grieved my heart to see. No sooner had I set my foot inside the door than the innkeeper came to my side.

"What may I offer you, young sir? Roast pork? Spiced dumplings? Fresh apricots? We stock four matchless wines produced from local vineyards—"

"My thanks. I am on business and require no refreshment," I said briskly, ignoring the lamentations of my inside.

Venomously I looked about, and soon noted the wretch I sought, on the gallery, at a secluded lamplit table, engaged in stuffing himself and gulping matchless wine at my expense.

Since I had been hooded on the plain and he had never seen my face, now revealed, I effected no further disguise, but mounted the gallery and approached him.

"Pardon my intrusion, sir, but it has come to my notice that you possess certain archaic relics which you are inclined to sell."

"This is conceivable," said he, and waved me to a chair.

There I sat, and watched him at his dinner with swimming eyes.

"Will you take some wine?" he courteously asked. I assented. "It is very strange," he said, "but it seems to me that we have met before."

"That is unlikely."

"Yes. Besides, I am positive I should have recalled you at once," he murmured warmly, filling my cup to the brim, "such a handsome face as yours being entirely memorable."

I thanked him, and begged to see his wares. Whereat, he drew the infamous sack from beneath his chair and set out one well-known silver candlestick, second of the pair, and the chain of the golden censer.

"Are you quite well?" he asked solicitously. "You have turned very pale."

"My pallor need not trouble you. But is this all? I heard that you had other goods. There was some mention of a container of incense, and a blue vitreous bottle. . . ."

"Alas, those I have already sold. But mark this candlestick, which has no fellow in the whole of the known world. . . . Permit me to inquire again if you are in the best of health?"

"My health is adequate, I thank you. Only tell me, is there not also a bag of jewels?"

The villain appeared surprised.

"It intrigues me to know how you discovered this, since I have told no one in the town."

"I have my sources of information, as is self-evident. Therefore, understand so much—these gems and bits of gold are more valuable to me, for reasons of sentiment, than any other treasure on the earth. Merely let me examine them to ascertain whether they are the store I seek. This proven, I will double, triple, quadruple, any value you may set on them, so anxious am I to be repossessed."

He raised his long brows and gave me a quizzical smile.

"Well, this being the case, and seeing your agitation, I should not dream of withholding them. Here," and from inside his shirt he drew a small pouch and emptied out the contents before me.

After a brief tally, I said, "It seems to me there are some garnet buttons missing."

"Just so. A certain lady on Eighth Bridge with whom I spent the afternoon took an unreasonable fancy to them and would settle for nothing else. Now, as to this praiseworthy intention of yours to quintuple the worth of the remainder—"

"One moment," I said, and, thrusting back my chair with a clatter, I leapt to my feet, and shouted in a loud and terrible voice:

"What? Do you dare assail my ears with such reprehensible filth? Blasphemy! Blasphemy! Summon the guard!"

There was instantaneous uproar throughout the inn. Townsfolk surged onto the gallery, some seizing my companion by the arms; others rushed into the night, clamouring for soldiers.

"We have him fast," declared the innkeeper. "What did the ingrate say?"

"I cannot repeat the foulness. He derided the gods of Sath Monnis, comparing them to pigs, goats, and I know not what besides—in addition, he has sold worthless talismans in the town, even aspiring to swindle a member of the Sacred Guard— I am speechless and faint with horror." Here I sank back into my chair and, with a desolate air, gathered up what was left of Grunelt's hoard, the censer chain, and the candlestick.

Only once did my adversary attempt to utter. Immediately several hands were clamped over his lips, in fear of some further obscenity, and he was shortly bound and gagged and hauled away into the night by the yellow guard.

The innkeeper commiserated with me and bemoaned his loss of revenue. I offered, in order to save him trouble, myself to take on the bedchamber and the dinner, and, I further assured him, since I had purchased the damblepad prior to the disturbance, also the stabling it would require. For these services I paid him in advance with a gold piece or two. He seemed curious about the censer chain and a small emerald discovered near the salt cellar. I explained that these were trifles of my own which I had produced in the line of business, before I discovered the vile nature of my client.

Then, having eaten and drunk my fill, I went above and sank on the first feather-soft mattress of my life.

I was rudely awoken in the hour after dawn by a hammering on my door. In answer to my inquiries, the hammerers announced themselves to be the Sacred Guard. I hastily arose, donned my male attire, and admitted the party, thinking I had been summoned as a witness.

However, the soldiers burst upon me and, to my intense vexation, contained my wrists with rope and unceremoniously conducted me downstairs, out of the inn and into the street.

"For what am I so shamefully misused?" I demanded.

"For grievous fraud," said one.

"What fraud is this? I have done nothing."

"The prisoner we arrested yesterday for profanity has laid a charge against you, to wit: that he bought certain items from you at great cost, which he then sold in good faith about the town, but which he has since discovered, by your own testimony, to be fakes and worthless."

"And do you take the word of a blasphemer against myself, who piously reported him?"

"It is the custom of Sath Monnis never to level any accusation against another unless it be true, since the penalty for falsehood is partial strangulation and removal of the tongue. Therefore all charges are instantly believed."

I reflected on this, and was moved, unwisely, to ask: "What then is the penalty for fraud?"

"Subtraction of the left foot and right hand."

Just then we reached a dismal portal, I was delivered into dank darkness, and the door securely fastened behind me.

Here I let forth such utterances as my mood inspired, but soon became aware of a low chuckling.

"Who or what is here? Your crimes must be foul indeed and your sorrows crushing, if you are able to derive such enjoyment from another's horrible distress."

"So they are," said a voice unpleasingly familiar and in a bantering tone. "However raw your fate, mine, as you may know, is both painful and conclusive. Therefore expect no condolence of mine, O traitorous youth."

"Traitorous! I at least delivered you to a doubtless well-deserved doom in order to recover my own property. What had you to gain by falsely incriminating me—save a sop for your deplorable spite?"

"I hoped that by bringing, as it seemed, another wrongdoer to justice, I should have my own sentence mitigated, but this, as it turned out, was not the case. By your outcry I perceive you are the young man I conversed with on the plain."

"You perceive clearly, and since that meeting my days have not been delightful, neither do I view the prospect before me with ecstasy. Probably there is little time left us, therefore acquaint me with your name that I may curse you more successfully."

"My name is Nazarn—but, before you commence your maledictions, let me suggest another pastime. Since we have both duped and brought the other to catastrophe, and are now approximately of equal score and desperation, let us pool our talents and effect a means of escape."

I considered this, and said, "Concerning my own abilities I modestly keep silent. What are yours? I seem to recollect an irresistible transporter. . . ."

"Of that, unfortunately, I was relieved at the door, also of the amulet which allowed me to lure the property of others from their clothing without the necessity of touch, or even proximity. However, I retain a certain intrinsic knack to charm into docility even the most nervous and savage of beasts."

"Since we are prisoners of men and not beasts this seems of small value. Nevertheless, you have resolved the mystery as to how you subdued the frenzied hounds of Trall the watchman. You put me to much trouble there, as in all else. Only by means of disrupting the machinery of distillation was I able to snatch a handful of fruit and a mouthful of water."

Nazarn, with courteous interest, asked details of this exploit. These I gave but concluded:

"I am greatly puzzled that the cisterns of Sath Monnis are still wholesome and the canals undisturbed."

"That is easily explained. The tubes run by circuitous routes beneath the earth to avoid the adamantine rock. Both pure and infested water, therefore, take a day and a half to reach the town. Thus," he added pensively, "the change will come about at noon, by my reckoning, which is, I am reminded, the time when all criminals receive justice in Sath Monnis."

"A method of deliverance springs to my mind," I said, "perhaps to yours also."

"Depend upon it."

"And may I also depend upon it that, having assisted you, I shall once more be deceived and abandoned to these barbarians?"

"I am wounded by your lack of trust. Now I have seen you fully, rest assured I intend to make you my companion for as long as it shall be mutually agreeable. Further, I protest, that had you revealed yourself on the plain," he added with some ardour, "I would not have treated you as I did."

So, setting aside enmity, we discussed a plan, until the onerous stride of the guard resounded on the bridge.

The door was suddenly thrown open, and we were prodded and pulled into the blinding sunlight of the street.

Here a great crowd had gathered, which followed us to the crest of the bridge with expectant faces.

"Hold!" cried Nazarn, "I have that to say you must attend, for fear of your lives."

At once the procession stopped, staring stupidly at this unforeseen audacity.

Up stalked a priest of the Temple in a yellow robe.

"You are permitted speech. Possibly you wish to repent your lunatic folly and ask pardon of the gods, before death and eternal damnation overwhelm you."

"Not so," cried Nazarn, "I fear nothing from the gods since I, and also the young man there, are messengers of the same. He and I

were sent to test the moral fibre of Sath Monnis, but have found
you all zealous to a fault, for which, be assured, our ethereal
masters will reward you."

"Silence, blasphemer!" roared the priest. "Is there no bottom to
the well of your iniquity?"

At which the yellow cloaks began to urge Nazarn to climb the
parapet, and I heard the sound of the Amputator sharpening his
knife for me.

Overhead the sun had reached its apex.

"Be warned!" I shouted, and there came another hush. "Maltreat
us and you will anger the gods, who will cause the canals to boil,
and the clear water of your springs to run like blood. Either release
us promptly, and with honour, or face the consequences."

As was to be expected, there was only a howl of fury for answer.

I was surprised to experience a pang at the sight of Nazarn forced
onto the parapet. *Now his calculations will, of course, prove mistaken*, thought I. But at that moment my accomplice gave a joyous
shout.

"Witness!" he thundered and pointed below.

A bubbling disagreeable sound filled the air. With yodels of
alarm, the crowd rushed to peer down from the bridge. The yodel-
ling turned to wailing and screaming, while out of a hundred doors
came pouring terrified men and women, shrieking of blood running
from the taps.

Nazarn and I found ourselves suddenly unbound, and besought
by townsfolk kneeling in the street.

"We shall depart to solitude," Nazarn declared bleakly, "and
attempt intercession. However, do not expect too much."

So we shouldered through the press and made our way to the
Bitten Quince, where all was in uproar since several guests, idling
late in the bath at the moment of metamorphosis, had abruptly
been dismembered.

"Whither and what now?" I asked.

"Since the corporation of the town bridges intimately parallels and incorporates that of the canals and cisterns, I fear Sath
Monnis will soon slump in rubble. Accordingly I propose instant
flight."

We led out the damblepad, both mounted it, for it was a sturdy
animal, and made all speed hence.

Beyond the town to the west lay a wood of spike trees. We
emerged from this upon the lower terraces of the mountains, in the

copper glare of a stormy late afternoon sun, and looked backwards at Sath Monnis.

There had been a curious rumbling underfoot as of violent subterranean rivers. Over the unlucky town there now hung a magenta pall from which burst occasional jets of smoke, steam, or debris.

"So much for religion," remarked Nazarn.

But I thought I made out something moving on the far horizon of the ruined fields. I pointed.

"What can that be?"

"That? But some trick of the light, fair and noble friend."

"To me, it has the appearance of several huge pale figures in motion."

"To me, also. There was some tale in Sath Monnis, was there not, that should any harm befall the people, her gods would seek vengeance on the culprits? But then, we do not know the form of these gods."

"In the poplar groves before the town I passed certain gigantic marble statues, at the feet of which offerings had been laid."

"Yes, I too seem to recall such a thing. Well. This beast has many swift miles in him yet. It would be a pity to waste such an excellent chance of exercise in fruitless chat."

So saying, we urged the damblepad to a furious gallop and rushed up the mountainside.

We and the beast bounded on over the crags until the sky grew like a pane of cobalt glass, set blazing with multicoloured stars. Behind us always followed a dim yet persistent thunder, that was oddly mindful of the fall of enormous and determined feet.

"I regret, friend Nazarn," I murmured at last, "that our animal is near collapse."

"Up there," said he, "shines an emerald lamp, generally the token of a seeress or witch. She may know some remedy for our plight."

We coaxed the damblepad to a last wild dash, and arrived on a twisted summit by a disreputable cot. The green lamp, nevertheless, burned over the leaning porch, and in answer to Nazarn's halloo, the door creaked open and the owner peered out.

Dramatically lit up by her magic light, she was revealed to be aged, toothless, and of surpassing unsightliness, though she turned on Nazarn and myself a look of unmistakable and optimistic libido.

"Well, well. And what can I do for two such handsome gentlemen?"

"Beauteous madam," Nazarn prudently addressed her, "certain lumps of limestone, hewn to resemble gods, are even now pursuing us, intent on our mutilation. In your wisdom, can you suggest how we might elude this unmerited fate?"

Thoughtfully tapping her warts, the beldame advanced to the edge of her eyrie, and looked out over the eastern ridges.

"Do you refer to those?" she inquired.

Nazarn and I stared across the bowl of night, and discerned some thirteen whitely-glowing giants, toiling with massive tread about two miles distant, yet coming nearer by the minute.

"Exactly so," complied Nazarn.

The seeress considered.

"It appears they follow blindly and without caution, intent only on their quarry. This being so, there is a certain thing I have may prove useful."

"Then, in the name of all things lovely—quantities of which you so exactly imitate—grant us this thing, or we are lost."

"You must understand," said the witch, "that nothing is to be got for nothing, for such a bargain would contravene the most ancient natural laws. I have in mind a particular exchange, but since the ground already trembles with the advancing nemesis, I fear we should not presently have the time for it. Therefore, I stipulate this: if my device protects you and you survive the giants, you must return at once to my abode, where we will discuss your duties further. Fail to do so, and I will send such perils and horrors against you as I can set hand to. Now. So much settled, tie these gernik feathers to your feet, run to that high spur, and leap off. The quality of the feathers will bear you safely to the opposite crag while, with luck, the marble beings will crash into the chasm between."

Nazarn and I did as we were bid, and the witch, mindful of our enemies, fled back into her hovel.

"Perhaps the hag mistakes the virtue of this plumage, and we also shall plunge to our deaths," I panted as we ran.

"If we remain, we shall be ground to bone-meal and mud by the gods of Sath Monnis, so much is certain," Nazarn shouted.

At which we reached the brink, and leapt.

Out rushed space, infinite and terrible, while overhead the pyrotechnic stars spun extravagantly. Beneath, an abyss of mouths, fangs, gorges, gaped to engulf us, but the miraculous feathers bore us up. We sailed the blue air and safely gained the star-gilded peak beyond. Meanwhile came the boom of the giants' feet, and rocks shook out from the mountain face and bounced away.

Shortly, a huge head, chalk white of countenance, blindly staring of eye, crested the peak we had vacated.

"Naturally, it is possible our pursuers, waxing inventive, might leap the gulf as we have done," muttered Nazarn.

Higher rose the monstrous head, and higher. Now a vast torso and knotted arms with upheld club. Next, powerful legs and feet, splashed red from the fall of Sath Monnis. Borne on these gargantuan limbs, the god advanced to the lip of the precipice. Glaring at us with its sightless gaze, it took one step into emptiness and tottered down into the dark below, whence presently burst a noisy shattering and a cloud of white dust.

Taking no heed of its fellow, and no more care, the second marble being soon perished similarly. After this, eleven more strode to the brink, unbalanced, descended, and exploded into powder.

A while later, the black silence of the night rebuilt itself.

I turned to my companion, who appeared to have lost his senses. When I touched his arm, he opened his eyes with a groan. I asked him, with some tenderness, if he had recovered from his faint.

"Faint?" he asked, amazed. "I, faint? Be enlightened. I was but resting after our exertions." So saying, he tottered to his feet.

A moment more, and we heard the witch's voice from the cot, calling in anticipatory tones for us to return to her. Receiving no reply, she presently emerged upon the other side of the chasm, her green lamp in her hand. Seeing us alive and whole, she beamed with joy, and beckoned ardently.

"Alas, fair madam," I said, "no longer are we in a position to repay you for your aid in the interesting fashion which you suggested."

"Come, come," said she, "do not be bashful. I have rubbed myself with the best toad's fat to be had, a most stimulating salve, you will agree."

"Exquisite lady," I persisted, "although we have escaped with our lives, the statue-gods, as they fell, each cursed us with a dreadful malady, none of which may be lifted from us by even the most powerful of sorcerers."

"Just so," added Nazarn decidedly.

The witch frowned.

"*Thirteen* maladies? Pray enumerate them."

"Trembling," I said, "twitching and itching."

"Vertigo," said Nazarn reeling, "lumbago, nausea, debility."

"Ah—!" broke in the witch.

"Deafness," I continued firmly, "short-sightedness."

"Headpains," expanded Nazarn, "nits—fits."

"And," I finished, "more agonising than all the rest: total impotence."

The witch sprang back with a squeal of wrath.

"Throw over my gernik feathers at once, and begone. Am I to waste time on castrates?"

The shoes thrown, the witch repossessed them, turned on her horny heel, and vanished again into her hovel, slamming the door, at which it tumbled off.

As we crouched that night among the mountains, Nazarn, his strength returned, made certain discoveries about me that surprised but did not necessarily displease him. These matters concluded satisfactorily, he at last inquired my name.

"My name is Truth," I told him. He gravely nodded, and courteously spoke of other things.

# A ROOM WITH A VIE

**T**HIS IS IT, THEN."

"Oh, yes."

"As you can see, it's in quite nice condition."

"Yes, it is."

"Clothes there, on the bed. Cutlery in the box. Basin. Cooker. The meter's the same as the one you had last year. And you saw the bathroom across the corridor."

"Yes. Thank you. It's all fine."

"Well, as I said. I was sorry we couldn't let you have your other room. But you didn't give us much notice. And right now, August, and such good weather, we're booked right up."

"I understand. It was kind of you to find me this room. I was lucky, wasn't I? The very last one."

"It's usually the last to go, this one."

"How odd. It's got such a lovely view of the sea and the bay."

"Well, I didn't mean there was anything wrong with the room."

"Of course not."

"Mr. Tinker always used to have this room. Every year, four months, June to September."

"Oh, yes."

"It was quite a shock last year, when his daughter rang to cancel. He died, just the night before he meant to take the train to come down. Heart attack. What a shame."

"Yes, it was."

"Well, I'll leave you to get settled in. You know where we are if you want anything."

"Thank you very much, Mrs. Rice."

Mr. Tinker, she thought, leaning on the closed door. *Tinker.* Like a dog, with one black ear. Here, Tinker! Don't be silly, she thought. It's just nerves. Arrival nerves. By-the-sea nerves. By-yourself nerves.

Caroline crossed to the window. She stared out at the esplanade where the brightly coloured summer people were walking about in the late afternoon sun. Beyond, the bay opened its arms to the sea. The little boats in the harbour lay stranded by an outgoing tide. The water was cornflower blue.

If David had been here, she would have told him that his eyes were exactly as blue as that sea, which wasn't at all the case. How many lies there had been between them. Even lies about eye colour. But she wasn't going to think of David. She had come here alone, as she had come here last season, to sketch, to paint, to meditate.

It was a pity, about not being able to have the other room. It had been larger, and the bathroom had been "contained" rather than shared and across the hall. But then she hadn't been going to take the holiday flat this year. She had been trying to patch things up with David. Until finally, all the patching had come undone, and she'd grasped at this remembered place in a panic—I must get *away.*

Caroline turned her back to the window. She glanced about. Yes. Of course it was quite all right. If anything, the view was better because the flat was higher up. As for the actual room, it was like all the rooms. Chintz curtains, cream walls, brown rugs, and jolly cushions. And Mr. Tinker had taken good care of it. There was only one cigarette burn in the table. And probably that wasn't Mr. Tinker at all. Somehow, she couldn't imagine Mr. Tinker doing a thing like that. It must be the result of the other tenants, those people who had accepted the room as their last choice.

Well now. Make up the bed, and then go out for a meal. No, she was too tired for that. She'd get sandwiches from the little café downstairs, perhaps some wine from the off-licence. It would be a chance to swallow some sea air. Those first breaths that always made her giddy and unsure, like too much oxygen.

She made the bed up carefully, as if for two. When she moved it

away from the wall to negotiate the sheets, she saw something
scratched in the cream plaster.

"Oh, Mr. Tinker, you naughty dog," she said aloud, and then
felt foolish.

Anyway, Mr. Tinker wouldn't do such a thing. Scratch with a
penknife, or even some of Mrs. Rice's loaned cutlery. Black ink had
been smeared into the scratches. Caroline peered down into the
gloom behind the bed. *A room with a view*, the scratching said.
Well, almost. Whoever it was had forgotten to put in the ultimate
*w*: *A room with a vie.* Either illiterate or careless. Or smitten with
guilt nine-tenths through.

She pushed the bed back again. She'd better tell the Rices sometime. God forbid they should suppose she was the vandal.

She was asleep when she heard the room breathing. She woke gradually, as if to a familiar and reassuring sound. Then, as gradually, a
confused fear stole upon her. Presently she located the breathing
sound as the noise of her own blood rhythm in her ears. Then, with
another shock of relief, as the sea. But, in the end, it was not the sea
either. It was the room, breathing.

A kind of itching void of pure terror sent her plunging upwards
from the bed. She scrabbled at the switch, and the bedside light
flared on. Blinded and gasping, she heard the sound seep away.

Out at sea, a ship mooed plaintively. She looked at the window
and began to detect stars over the water, and the pink lamps
glowing along the esplanade. The world was normal.

Too much wine after too much train travel. Nightmare.

She lay down. Though her eyes watered, she left the light on.

"I'm afraid so, Mrs. Rice. Someone's scratched and inked it on the
wall. A nostalgia freak: *A room with a view.*"

"Funny," said Mrs. Rice. She was a homely woman with jet
black gipsy hair that didn't seem to fit. "Of course, there's been two
or three had that room. No one for very long. Disgusting. Still, the
damage is done."

Caroline walked along the bay. The beach that spread from the
south side was packed with holidaymakers. Everyone was paired,
as if they meant to be ready for the ark. Some had a great luggage
of children as well. The gulls and the children screamed.

Caroline sat drawing, and the children raced screaming by. People stopped to ask her questions about the drawing. Some stared a long while over her shoulder. Some gave advice on perspective and subject matter. The glare of sun on the blue water hurt her eyes.

She put the sketchbook away. After lunch she'd go farther along, to Jaynes Bay, which she recollected had been very quiet last year. This year, it wasn't.

After about four o'clock, gangs of local youth began to gather on the esplanade and the beach. Their hair was greased, and their legs were like storks' legs in tight trousers. They whistled. They spoke in an impenetrable mumble which often flowered into four-letter words uttered in contrastingly clear diction.

There had been no gangs last year. The sun sank.

Caroline was still tired. She went along the esplanade to her block, up the steps to her room.

When she unlocked the door and stood on the threshold, for a moment—

What?

It was as if the pre-twilight amber that came into the room was slowly pulsing, throbbing. As if the walls, the floor, the ceiling were—

She switched on the overhead lamp.

"Mr. Tinker," she said firmly, "I'm not putting up with this."

"Pardon?" said a voice behind her.

Caroline's heart expanded with a sharp thud like a grenade exploding in her side. She spun around, and there stood a girl in jeans and a smock. Her hand was on the door of the shared bathroom. It was the previously unseen neighbour from down the hall.

"I'm sorry," said Caroline. "I must have been talking to myself."

The girl looked blank and unhelpful.

"I'm Mrs. Lacey," she said. She did not look lacy. Nor married. She looked about fourteen. "You've got number eight, then. How is it?"

Bloody nerve, Caroline thought.

"It's fine."

"They've had three in before you," said the fourteen-year-old Mrs. Lacey.

"All together?"

"Pardon? No. I meant three separate tenants. Nobody would stay. All kinds of trouble with that Mrs. Rice. Nobody would, though."

"Why ever not?" Caroline snapped.

"Too noisy or something. Or a smell. I can't remember."

Caroline stood in her doorway, her back to the room.

Fourteen-year-old Mrs. Lacey opened the bathroom door.

"At least we haven't clashed in the mornings," Caroline said.

"Oh, *we're* always up early on holiday," said young Mrs. Lacey pointedly. Somewhere down the hall, a child began to bang and quack like an insane automatic duck. A man's voice bawled: "Hurry up that piss, Brenda, will you?"

Brenda Lacey darted into the bathroom, and the bolt was shot.

Caroline entered her room. She slammed the door. She turned on the room, watching it.

There *was* a smell. It was very slight. A strange, faintly buttery smell. Not really unpleasant. Probably from the café below. She pushed up the window and breathed the sea.

As she leaned on the sill, breathing, she felt the room start breathing too.

She was six years old, and Auntie Sara was taking her to the park. Auntie Sara was very loving. Her fat warm arms were always reaching out to hold, to compress, to pinion against her fat warm bosom. Being hugged by Auntie Sara induced in six-year-old Caroline a sense of claustrophobia and primitive fright. Yet somehow she was aware that she had to be gentle with Auntie Sara and not wound her feelings. Auntie Sara couldn't have a little girl. So she had to share Caroline with Mummy.

And now they were in the park.

"There's Jenny," said Caroline. But of course Auntie Sara wouldn't want to let Caroline go to play with Jennifer. So Caroline pretended that Auntie Sara *would* let her go, and she ran very fast over the green grass towards Jenny. Then her foot caught in something. When she began to fall, for a moment it was exhilarating, like flying. But she hit the ground, stunning, bruising. She knew better than to cry, for in another moment Auntie Sara had reached her. "It doesn't hurt," said Caroline. But Auntie Sara took no notice. She crushed Caroline to her. Caroline was smothered on her breast, and the great round arms bound her like hot, faintly dairy-scented bolsters.

Caroline started to struggle. She pummelled, kicked, and shrieked.

It was dark, and she had not fallen in the grass after all. She was in bed in the room, and it was the room she was fighting. It was the room which was holding her close, squeezing her, hugging her. It was the room which had that faint cholesterol smell of fresh milk and butter. It was the room which was stroking and whispering.

But of course it couldn't be the damn room.

Caroline lay back exhausted, and the toils of her dream receded. Another nightmare. Switch on the light. Yes, that was it. Switch on the light and have a drink from the small traveller's bottle of gin she'd put ready in case she couldn't sleep.

"Christ." She shielded her eyes from the light.

Distantly, she heard a child crying—the offspring probably of young Mrs. unlacy Lacey along the hall. "God, I must have yelled," Caroline said aloud. Yelled and been heard. The unlacy Laceys were no doubt discussing her this very minute. The mad lazy slut in number eight.

The gin burned sweetly, going down.

This was stupid. The light—no, she'd have to leave the light on again.

Caroline looked at the walls. She could see them, very, very softly lifting, softly sinking. Don't be a fool. The smell was just discernible. It made her queasy. Too rich—yet, a human smell, a certain sort of human smell. Bovine, she concluded, exactly like poor childless Sara.

It was hot, even with the window open.

She drank halfway down the bottle and didn't care anymore.

"Mr. Tinker? Why ever are you interested in him?"

Mrs. Rice looked disapproving.

"I'm sorry. I'm not being ghoulish. It's just—well, it seemed such a shame, his dying like that. I suppose I've been brooding."

"Don't want to do that. You need company. Is your husband coming down at all, this year?"

"David? No, he can't get away right now."

"Pity."

"Yes. But about Mr. Tinker—"

"All right," said Mrs. Rice. "I don't see why I shouldn't tell you. He was a retired man. Don't know what line of work he'd been in, but not very well paid, I imagine. His wife was dead. He lived with his married daughter, and really I don't think it suited him, but there was no alternative. Then, four months of the year, he'd come here and take number eight. Done it for years. Used to get his meals out. Must have been quite expensive. But I think the daughter and

her husband paid for everything, you know, to get a bit of time on
their own. But he loved this place, Mr. Tinker did. He used to say
to me: 'Here I am home again, Mrs. Rice.' The room with his
daughter, I had the impression he didn't think of that as home at
all. But number eight. Well, he'd put his ornaments and books and
pieces round. My George even put a couple of nails in for him to
hang a picture or two. Why not? And number eight got quite cosy.
It really *was* Mr. Tinker's room in the end. My George said that's
why other tenants'd fight shy. They could feel it waiting for Mr.
Tinker to come back. But that's a lot of nonsense, and I can see I
shouldn't have said it."

"No. I think your husband was absolutely right. Poor old room.
It's going to be disappointed."

"Well, my George, you know, he's a bit of an idiot. The night
—the night we heard, he got properly upset, my George. He went
up to number eight, and opened the door and told it. I said to him,
you'll want me to hang black curtains in there next."

Beyond the fence, the headland dropped away in dry grass and the
feverish flowers of late summer to a blue sea ribbed with white.
North spread the curved claw of Jaynes Bay and the grey vertical of
the lighthouse. But the sketch pad and pencil case sat on the seat
beside Caroline.

She had attempted nothing. Even the novel lay closed. The first
page hadn't seemed to make sense. She kept reading the words
"home" and "Tinker" between the lines.

She understood she was afraid to return to the room. She had
walked along the headlands, telling herself that all the room had
wrong with it was sadness, a bereavement. That it wasn't waiting.
That it wasn't alive. And anyway, even sadness didn't happen to
rooms. If it did, it would have to get over that. Get used to being
just a holiday flat again, a space which people filled for a few
weeks, observed indifferently, cared nothing about, and then went
away from.

Which was all absurd because none of it was true.

Except, that she wasn't the only one to believe—

She wondered if David would have registered anything in the
room. Should she ring him and confide in him? Ask advice? No.
For God's sake, that was why she was imagining herself into this
state, wasn't it? So she could create a contact with him again. No.
David was out and out David would stay.

It was five o'clock. She packed her block and pencils into her bag and walked quickly along the grass verge above the fence.

She could walk into Kingscliff at this rate, and get a meal.

She wondered who the scared punster had been, the one who knew French. She'd got the joke by now. A room with a vie: a room with a *life*.

She reached Kingscliff and had a pleasantly unhealthy meal, with a pagoda of white ice cream and glacé cherries to follow. In the dusk the town was raucous and cheerful. Raspberry and yellow neons splashed and spat, and the motorbike gangs seemed suitable, almost friendly, *in situ*. Caroline strolled by the whelk stalls and across the car park, through an odour of frying doughnuts, chips, and fierce fish. She went to a cinema and watched a very bad and very pointless film with a sense of superiority and tolerance. When the film was over, she sat alone in a pub and drank vodka. Nobody accosted her or tried to pick her up. She was glad at first, but after the fourth vodka, rather sorry. She had to run to catch the last bus back. It was not until she stood on the esplanade, the bus vanishing, the pink lamps droning solemnly and the black water far below, that a real and undeniable terror came and twisted her stomach.

The café was still open, and she might have gone in there, but some of the greasy stork-legs she had seen previously were clustered about the counter. She was tight, and visualised sweeping amongst them, ignoring their adolescent nastiness. But presently she turned aside and into the block of holiday flats.

She dragged up the steps sluggishly. By the time she reached her door, her hands were trembling. She dropped her key and stifled a squeal as the short-time automatic hall light went out. Pressing the light button, she thought: Supposing it doesn't come on?

But the light did come on. She picked up her key, unlocked the door, and went determinedly inside the room, shutting the door behind her.

She experienced it instantly. It was like a vast indrawn sucking gasp.

"No," Caroline said to the room. Her hand fumbled the switch, and the room was lit.

Her heart was beating so very fast. That was, of course, what made the room also seem to pulse, as if its heart were also swiftly and greedily beating.

"Listen," Caroline said. "Oh, God, talking to a *room*. But I have to, don't I? Listen, you've got to stop this. Leave me alone!" she shouted at the room.

The room seemed to grow still.

She thought of the Laceys, and giggled.

She crossed to the window and opened it. The air was cool. Stars gleamed above the bay. She pulled the curtains to, and undressed. She washed, and brushed her teeth at the basin. She poured herself a gin.

She felt the room, all about her. Like an inheld breath, impossibly prolonged. She ignored that. She spoke to the room quietly.

"Naughty Mr. Tinker, to tinker with you, like this. Have to call you Sara now, shan't I? Like a great big womb. That's what she really wanted, you see. To squeeze me right through herself, pop me into her womb. I'd offer you a gin, but where the hell would you put it?"

Caroline shivered.

"No. This is truly silly."

She walked over to the cutlery box beside the baby cooker. She put in her hand and pulled out the vegetable knife. It had quite a vicious edge. George Rice had them frequently sharpened.

"See this," Caroline said to the room. "Just watch yourself."

When she lay down, the darkness whirled, carouselling her asleep.

In the womb, it was warm and dark, a warm blood dark. Rhythms came and went, came and went, placid and unending as the tides of the sea. The heart organ pumped with a soft deep noise like a muffled drum.

How comfortable and safe it was. But when am I to be born? Caroline wondered. Never, the womb told her, lapping her, cushioning her.

Caroline kicked out. She floated. She tried to seize hold of something, but the blood-warm cocoon was not to be seized.

"Let me go," said Caroline. "Auntie Sara, I'm all right. Let me go. I want to—please—"

Her eyes were wide, and she was sitting up in her holiday bed. She put out her hand spontaneously towards the light and touched the knife she had left beside it. The room breathed, regularly, deeply. Caroline moved her hand away from the light switch, and saw in the darkness.

"This is ridiculous," she said aloud.

The room breathed. She glanced at the window—she had left the curtains drawn over, and so could not focus on the esplanade beyond, or the bay: the outer world. The walls throbbed. She could *see* them. She was being calm now, and analytical, letting her eyes adjust, concentrating. The mammalian milky smell was heavy. Not precisely offensive, but naturally rather horrible, under these circumstances.

Very carefully, Caroline, still in darkness, slipped her feet out of the covers and stood up.

"All right," she said. "All right then."

She turned to the wall behind the bed. She reached across and laid her hand on it—

The *wall*. The wall was—*skin*. It was flesh. Live, pulsing, hot, moist—

It was—

The wall swelled under her touch. It adhered to her hand eagerly. The whole room writhed a little, surging towards her. It wanted—she knew it wanted—to clutch her to its breast.

Caroline ripped her hand from the flesh wall. Its rhythms were faster, and the cowlike smell much stronger. Caroline whimpered. She was flung backwards, and her fingers closed on the vegetable knife and she raised it.

Even as the knife plunged forwards, she knew it would skid or rebound from the plaster, probably slicing her. She knew all that, but could not help it. And then the knife thumped in, up to the handle. It was like stabbing into—into meat.

She jerked the knife away and free, and scalding fluid ran down her arm. I've cut myself after all. That's blood. But she felt nothing. And the room—

The room was screaming. She couldn't hear it, but the scream was all around her, hurting her ears. She had to stop the screaming. She thrust again with the knife. The blade was slippery. The impact was the same. Boneless meat. And the heated fluid, this time, splashed all over her. In the thick unlight, it looked black. She dabbed frantically at her arm, which had no wound. But in the wall—

She stabbed again. She ran to another wall and stabbed and hacked at it.

I'm dreaming, she thought. Christ, why can't I wake up?

The screaming was growing dim, losing power.

"Stop it!" she cried. The blade was so sticky now she had to use both hands to drive it home. There was something on the floor, spreading, that she slid on in her bare feet. She struck the wall with her fist, then with the knife. "Oh, Christ, please die," she said.

Like a butchered animal, the room shuddered, collapsed back upon itself, became silent and immobile.

Caroline sat in a chair. She was going to be sick, but then the sickness faded. I'm sitting here in a pool of blood.

She laughed and tears started to run from her eyes, which was the last thing she remembered.

When she woke it was very quiet. The tide must be far out, for even the sea did not sound. A crack of light came between the curtains.

What am I doing in this chair?

Caroline shifted, her mind blank and at peace.

Then she felt the utter emptiness that was in the room with her. The dreadful emptiness, occasioned only by the presence of the dead.

She froze. She stared at the crack of light. Then down.

"Oh, no," said Caroline. She raised her hands.

She wore black mittens. Her fingers were stuck together.

Now her gaze was racing over the room, not meaning to, trying to escape, but instead alighting on the black punctures, the streaks, the stripes along the wall, now on the black stains, the black splotches. Her own body was dappled, grotesquely mottled with black. She had one white toe left to her, on her right foot.

Woodenly, she managed to get up. She staggered to the curtains and hauled them open and turned back in the full flood of early sunlight, and saw everything over again. The gashes in the wall looked as if they had been accomplished with a drill or a pick. Flaked plaster was mingled with the—with the—blood. Except that it wasn't blood. Blood wasn't black.

Caroline turned away suddenly. She looked through the window, along the esplanade, pale and laved with morning. She looked at the bright sea, with the two or three fishing boats scattered on it, and the blueness beginning to flush sky and water. When she looked at these things, it was hard to believe in the room.

Perhaps most murderers were methodical in the aftermath. Perhaps they had to be.

She filled the basin again and again, washing herself, arms, body, feet. Even her hair had to be washed. The black had no particular texture. In the basin it diluted. It appeared like a superior kind of Parker fountain-pen ink.

She dressed herself in jeans and shirt, filled the largest saucepan with hot water and washing-up liquid. She began to scour the walls.

Soon her arms ached, and she was sweating the cold sweat of nervous debility. The black came off easily, but strange tangles of discolouration remained behind in the paint. Above, the holes did not ooze, they merely gaped. Inside each of them was chipped plaster and brick—not bone, muscle, or tissue. There was no feel of flesh anywhere.

Caroline murmured to herself. "When I've finished." It was quite matter-of-fact to say that, as if she were engaged in a normality. "When I've finished, I'll go and get some coffee downstairs. I won't tell Mrs. Rice about the holes. No, not yet. How can I explain them? I couldn't have caused that sort of hole with a knife. There's the floor to do yet. And I'd better wash the rugs. I'll do them in the bath when the ghastly Laceys go out at nine o'clock. When I've finished, I'll get some coffee. And I think I'll ring David. I really think I'll have to. When I finish."

She thought about ringing David. She couldn't guess what he'd say. What could *she* say, come to that? Her back ached now, and she felt sick, but she kept on with her work. Presently she heard energetic intimations of the Laceys visiting the bathroom, and the duck-child quacking happily.

She caught herself wondering why blood hadn't run when the nails were hammered in the walls for Mr. Tinker's pictures. But that was before the room really came to life, maybe. Or maybe the room had taken it in the spirit of beautification, like having one's ears pierced for gold earrings. Certainly the knife scratches had bled.

Caroline put down the cloth and went over to the basin and was sick.

Perhaps I'm pregnant, she thought, and all this is an hallucination of my fecundity.

David, I am pregnant, and I stabbed a room to death.

David.

David?

It was a boiling hot day, one of the last-fling days of the summer. Everything was blanched by the heat, apart from the apex of the blue sky and the core of the green-blue sea. Caroline wore a white dress. A quarter before each hour, she told herself she would ring David on the hour: ten o'clock, eleven, twelve. Then she would "forget." At one o'clock she rang him, and he was at lunch as she had known he would be, really.

Caroline went on the pier. She put money into little machines which whizzed and clattered. She ate a sandwich in a café. She walked along the sands, holding her shoes by the straps.

At half past four she felt compelled to return.

She had to speak to Mrs. Rice, about the holes in the walls.

And then again, perhaps she should go up to number eight first. It seemed possible that the dead room would somehow have righted itself. And then, too, there were the washed rugs drying over the bath that the unlaceys might come in and see. Caroline examined why she was so flippant and so cheerful. It was, of course, because she was afraid.

She went into the block, and abruptly she was trembling. As she climbed the steps, her legs melted horribly, and she wished she could crawl, pulling herself by her fingers.

As she came up to the landing, she beheld Mr. Lacey in the corridor. At least, she assumed it was Mr. Lacey. He was overweight and tanned a peachy gold by the sun. He stood glowering at her, blocking the way to her door. He's going to complain about the noise, she thought. She tried to smile, but no smile would oblige.

"I'm Mr. Lacey," he announced. "You met the wife the other day."

He sounded nervous rather than belligerent. When Caroline didn't speak, he went on, "My Brenda, you see. She noticed this funny smell from number eight. When you come along to the bathroom, you catch it. She was wondering if you'd left some meat out, forgotten it."

"No," said Caroline.

"Well, I reckoned you ought to be told," said Mr. Lacey.

"Yes, thank you."

"I mean, don't take this the wrong way, but we've got a kid. You can't be too careful."

"No. You can't."

"Well, then." He swung himself aside and moved a short way down the corridor towards the Lacey flat. Caroline went to her door. She knew he was watching her with his two shining Lacey piggy eyes. She turned and stared at him, her heart striking her side in huge bruising blows, until he grunted and went off.

Caroline stood before the door. She couldn't smell anything. No, there was nothing, nothing at all.

The stink came in a wave, out of nowhere. It smote her and she nearly reeled. It was foul, indescribably foul. And then it was gone.

Delicately, treading soft, Caroline stepped away from the door. She tiptoed to the head of the stairs. Then she ran.

But like someone drawn to the scene of an accident, she couldn't entirely vacate the area. She sat on the esplanade, watching.

The day went out over the town, and the dusk seeped from the sea. In the dusk, a police car came and drew up outside the block. Later, another.

It got dark. The lamps, the neons, and the stars glittered, and Caroline shuddered in her thin frock.

The stork-legs had gathered at the café. They pointed and jeered at the police cars. At the garden pavilion, a band was playing. Far out on the ocean, a great tanker passed, garlanded with lights.

At nine o'clock, Caroline found she had risen and was walking across the esplanade to the holiday block. She walked right through the crowd of stork-legs. "Got the time?" one of them yelled, but she paid no heed, didn't even flinch.

She went up the steps, and on the first flight she met two very young policemen.

"You can't come up here, miss."

"But I'm staying here," she said. Her mild voice, so reasonable, interested her. She missed what he asked next.

"I said, what number, miss."

"Number eight."

"Oh. Right. You'd better come up with me, then. You hang on here, Brian."

They climbed together, like old friends.

"What's the matter?" she questioned him, perversely.

"I'm not quite sure, miss."

They reached the landing.

All the way up from the landing below, the stench had been intensifying, solidifying. It was unique. Without ever having smelled such an odour before, instinctively and at once you knew it was the perfume of rottenness. Of decay and death.

Mrs. Rice stood in the corridor, her black hair in curlers, and she was absentmindedly crying. Another woman with a handkerchief to her nose patted Mrs. Rice's shoulder. Behind a shut door, a child

also cried, vehemently. Another noise came from the bathroom;
someone vomiting.

Caroline's door was wide open. A further two policemen were on
the threshold. They seemed to have no idea of how to proceed. One
was wiping his hands with a cloth, over and over.

Caroline gazed past them, into the room.

Putrescent lumps were coming away from the walls. The ceiling
dribbled and dripped. Yet one moment only was it like the flesh of
a corpse. Next moment, it was plaster, paint, and crumbling brick.
And then again, like flesh. And then again—

"Christ," one of the policemen said. He faced about at his
audience. He too was young. He stared at Caroline randomly.
"What are we supposed to do?"

Caroline breathed in the noxious air. She managed to smile at
last, kindly, inquiringly, trying to help.

"Bury it?"

# SIRRIAMNIS

I DO NOT THINK SHE IS QUIET. NO INDEED. IN THIS WORLD THERE are those things which come to be, and which cease to be, and men are of this kind, and beasts. And there are things also which do not come and go, but which remain. Like the weather, the skies, the waters, the land itself. Yet, deeper than these, there may be things which simply Are. What men call Spirit of Place, or The Dream, or other names, trying to find expression for what is not expressible, but which surely Is. These are civilised times. The seas are crowded by ships, the great libraries by books. Even a slave such as I am has been taught to read and write, for the benefit of my Master and his children. Yet I will use my civilised modern knowledge of writing to put this down, to tell of dark things and enduring things that have touched us, that continue with us, like a long shadow, though the substance is no more.

She too was a slave, and that is how we saw her first, in the slave-market near the harbour, at Crenthe. My Young Master, my Master's son, Lysias, was riding back from the harbour, and I behind him on my little donkey. The family has some interests in amber and dyes, and Lysias had been down to the dock to see what had come in, and to talk with some of the captains. He is a handsome young man, blond as Apollo, and with the easy gracious manner of the true nobleman, and a natural charm, capable of captivating anyone he has a mind to. His father lets him do much as he

pleases, for Lysias never yet did anything in the city to send trouble
or dishonour on the house. His friends are of the best, his pleasures
intellectual and athletic bring him credit, and if other pleasures are
indulged, then these are carried on with discretion and good taste.
A model son, and no harm in that. There are enough fathers in the
city with sound reason to curse fortune on this score. For myself,
the family has always been good to me. Generally, I am treated as
freeman more than slave. Being myself old and grizzled and childless, nor likely ever to get a child, having passed the age for such
inclinations, I admit I love my Master's boy, as if he were in part a
son of mine. And I, too, have taken a pride in him, from the day he
cut his first man's tooth, to the day he rode back from his first hunt,
a man indeed. And I know my Master says to someone, if ever
Lysias has done some extra thing of merit, as when he took the
prize for the chariot-racing, last spring, "Go tell old Tohmet. It
will please him."

As we went by the slave-market, then, the men were calling out
the virtues of the wares, as usual. Noise, and a smell of perfumes
and sweats washed round me, but I was figuring amber accounts on
my slate as I rode, and looked nowhere else. Until Lysias said
quietly to me: "Look, Toh. Look at that."

Then I looked. So I saw. About ten paces from us, Skiro, who
styles himself The Traveller, was selling off a troop of girls. They
were all shapes and sizes and complexions, and some I felt sorry
for, wilting and weeping in the hot sun. But foremost, as my eyes
came round to her, was one not like the others. I have seen the
blood now and then, and knew it before I remembered its name,
and first I took her for an Egyptian, though she was too little. For
she was short; she would stand no higher than my chin, and as I
later saw, the top of her head reached only to my Young Master's
heart, and only so far in high Samian sandal heels. But despite her
lack of stature, she was well-made, though not slender—her breasts
were full and her hips wide, yet her waist, made all the smaller by
its contrast, looked narrow as a stem. Like a sand-glass she was,
and her skin was olive, but very pale, and round her to her feet,
which were long and slim and pretty, poured thick-curling hair of
the bluest-black. The sort of hair which is called the Hyacinth, for
its blue tinting, and its little curls that resemble clustered petals.
Out of the hair looked a face of exquisite beauty that no man, even
an old man such as I, would not glance at a second time, and

maybe keep his eyes on her much longer. And in this face, two large eyes, staring away beyond us all, so for a moment I wondered if she were blind.

Skiro, The Traveller, noting Lysias had stopped, now began to bow and call winningly to him.

"Beautiful sir, come closer. Let me show you a rare wonder."

Lysias smiled, and half turned as if to ride on, and it seemed he could not. Abruptly he swung off his horse, threw the rein to me, and went over to where Skiro was grinning and nodding.

"Only touch her," said Skiro. "Her flesh is like a lily, her hair is like silk, her mouth—"

"Is like a rose. Yes, Skiro, I know," said Lysias good-naturedly. But he did put out one hand, gently—his courtesy extends to all—to smooth a strand of her hair.

"But if you would behold something wonderful," said Skiro, "look in her eyes."

"Seas to drown the senses?" hazarded Lysias.

"An enticing phrase. May I use it? But no, this is something unique. This is a mark of the gods. Bend close, and look."

So Lysias leaned near her, and looked at her eyes. And presently he exclaimed softly.

"Tohmet, come see this."

A child on the lookout for coins had run up, so I gave the reins to him, got off my donkey, and went over. It seemed a curious matter to make a business of, a woman's eyes, and again I pondered my notion of blindness.

When I was near enough, my Young Master stepped aside, and Skiro leeringly invited me. The girl stood quiet and still, but she blinked once, and I realised after all she could see me. When I put my face near hers, as I must to see the odd phenomenon, whatever it might be, I experienced a vague yet physical feeling I could neither locate nor put a name to, nor could I tell if it were pleasant or otherwise. Next instant, I found what Lysias had exclaimed over. Sometimes, I have seen strange marks in the eyes, frecklings, or differing colours, and once I knew a man in whose right eye the dark centre was cloven in two parts. But in the girl there was a stranger thing. For her eyes were both like two flowers of dark blue petals, raying out from the black centre. Nor was this an uncertain effect, but very clearly drawn. The coloured portion, which in all others I have ever seen, man or woman, is round, was in her, split, in each eye the same, into seven petallike segments. One must go close to see, but being close, it was not to be missed.

I straightened slowly, staring, and she staring back and through me and away beyond me, and the market, and beyond the world it almost seemed. And I knew in that moment I did not care for her eyes, or for her, and the feeling I felt at her nearness to me I did not like, either, and I stepped back three or four paces from her.

"Well, Toh. You're the scholar in our house. What does such a thing mean?"

My Young Master was obviously entranced. As I fumbled, Skiro replied: "It is the sign of Aphrodite, of Ishtar—the morning star, like a flower. The sign of Love."

Lysias laughed.

"Which means, you ask a high price."

"Sir, she is not merely lovely, but accomplished. She can play upon the Egyptian harp, the Lydian lyre."

"And does she sing, too?"

"That she does not do."

Something prompted me, and I said to Skiro:

"With my Master's permission, I'd ask you if she has a voice at all?"

Skiro faltered.

"Well, sir," he said to Lysias, appealingly, "she does not speak languages. She has no Greek, though she understands it. Her native tongue—"

"She's dumb," I said.

Skiro scowled at me.

"*Not* dumb," he said. He looked at the girl and said, "Utter, Sirriamnis, so the beautiful young lord, and his doubting slave, may hear you have a voice."

At that, she turned and looked at Lysias. Her lips, which were delicately shaped if rather thin, parted. She made at him a low, liquid crooning. She must have been schooled to it. It was the kind of sound a woman makes in bed. When she did it, the skin prickled on my neck and scalp, alerting me. But I beheld that Lysias was roused another way. He had never owned a woman before, but his father would certainly not disallow it, rather it was the tradition of the noble houses, for paid hetairas in such a port as Crenthe are not always of the best.

And I, why did I dislike her? Her odour was fresh and pleasing.

Even her breath was sweet. And yet my aversion was physical. Could it be, foolish old man, I had grown jealous of my Young Master's new interest?

I listened as Lysias haggled aristocratically over the price. He did not try very hard to beat Skiro down, for it would have been bad manners for a rich man to do so. In a few minutes it was settled, Skiro to expect payment by noon, my Master's house to take the girl in at sunset.

As we rode away up the street, Lysias was very silent. For myself, I made so many mistakes with my accounting that I gave over until we got home.

When the smoky redness of the sunset filled the house, and they began to light the lamps, one of Skiro's boys brought the slave to the gate. I watched her as she crossed the courtyard, and as she passed beneath the fig tree which grows there, its shadow turned her all a velvet black, and I shuddered and called myself an idiot.

That night, my Master, Lysias's father, had her in to play during dinner. We do not keep the Latin custom here, and the women of the house do not eat with the men, would think themselves insulted to be asked. The only female company during supper is that of a singer or dancer, although this is usually when there are guests and I am not present. Seated in the thick golden light of the lamps, the gold flying off the strings of the tall Egyptian harp with the well-wrought notes, her hair flooding about her, and dressed with white flowers, she was clearly an asset to the household. I could tell Lysias thought himself very cunning, and my Master was not displeased, saying things such as: "When Kaimon comes to dine, I will borrow her from you," and so on. Another time I would have been tickled, but not now. And when my Master turned to me, and said something about her beauty, I had to lie for wisdom's sake, a thing I have seldom had to do in this house.

I do not know if Lysias had already lain with her, but I do not think so. To snatch the sweet before supper would have had little propriety, and no finesse. But he went off early to sleep, and my Master chuckled, and called me to stay with him for a game of Jackal and Dog on the painted board.

"These young men, eh, Toh? The blood is hot. We must have some thoughts of marriage, next year, and it's a hard fact, there are few eligible girls bred to the looks of such as that Egyptian hussy."

"I think she may not be an Egyptian, sir."

"Is that so? Now you mention that, it comes to me the harp was not quite of the Egyptian fashion."

I considered the harp, when I should have been considering my first move of the game, and after a while it came to me there had been a bar across the lower body of the harp. It was more like the kinnor of the East—and then I remembered Skiro had mentioned Ishtar in his praises, the Semitic Venus.

"Where is she from then, Toh?" my Master asked me, when I had made my very poor pass with my jackal. "You can name races and a man's blood better than any other I ever knew."

"I am thinking of Assyria," I said. Yet that, too, was not exactly the geography I sensed in her lines, her aura, if you will.

"Assyrian? No wonder she will not talk. Their speech is like the hissing of snakes, the cackling of geese. She'll never get her tongue round honest Greek. They never can get it right."

We played on, and I lost. Nor was it from politeness.

After midnight, I walked out on the roof of the house in the cool. I could not sleep, or think of sleep. I looked at the stars, the dark buildings under me, the dark city, its lamps mostly out, and far away the wink of starlight and a thin moon on the sea. My eyes are still very good, though I have paid for my years in teeth.

My Young Master's window is away at the end of the courtyard, looking upon the fig tree and the marble cistern. I was a little embarrassed to find my eyes had strayed to that window. The hour was a late one. Most probably by now he had had his fill and put her out. He was to go hunting tomorrow, and would need to be awake before dawn. But some fixed, though unexplained, idea kept my eyes on the unlit slot of the window, and suddenly something moved there. My heart started, my tough old heart that is one of the soundest parts of me. At first I could not make out what it was at the window, and I had a weird fancy it was some sort of bird beating its wings up and down there. Then sense came to me, and I deciphered. Pushed through the slim holes of the ornamental grille were two forearms, two wrists, two hands. It could be none but she, the slave-girl Sirriamnis. Though wide-hipped, full-breasted, her ankles and her wrists were slender, and her hands narrow. What then were the motions she made, as if she signalled to someone out in the night? I looked swiftly beyond the west wall of the house. A wild garden grows there, about a ruined shrine which is no longer tended. Could it be some illicit lover lurked down there, looking for signals from the house? But no one stirred in the garden, or in the alley beyond. There was, else, only the sky she might make her gestures to, the sky and the young moon. When I had thought that, I grew uneasy, uneasy upon uneasiness. Girls who reverence Artemis are often dubious, since she prizes virginity and dislikes most mortal love, unless it be between woman and woman, man and man. But then I recalled Skiro's talk of Ishtar, who is also a goddess of moon and morning star, but is a voluptuary for all that.

The hands at the window went on and on, tirelessly dancing to the moon over the sea, as they had tirelessly skimmed the kinnor at supper. And the conviction began oddly to grow on me, that though her race was Semitic, its location was not in the East, or no longer, and the lunar deity she worshipped was not Ishtar, the Courtesan. And then, between one breath and another, it came to me, her origin and her blood. Her land lay over westward, on the African coast. The hub of her land was that trader city, Cartago, in the Latin tongue—Carthage, the port of blue-red dyes and ivory, proud genius of the seas, birthed out of the colonies of Tyre. And the goddess there, the Lady of the City, who ruled the moon and the morning star, ruled also darker things and older things, the daughter of that ancient god who drank the blood of small children, or else mouthed them in fire. Not Ishtar, but Tanit.

Her hands had stopped, as if she heard my thoughts. Perhaps, in some formless way, she did. I was glad she could not get her face by the iron lattice, which is there to prevent robbers. She could not get her face by it, and so see me, this Phoenician slave with her star-flower eyes, who worshipped the moon-witch and the darkness.

Next morning, I had some business to see to in the library, and was on my way there when I met young Mardian, who is Lysias's body-slave. Mardian is a handsome youth, of farm-stock, but with the eye-catching Persian strain in him, and more than half in love with his master; I believe he would die for Lysias if the need arose. But he has a free tongue, has Mardian, for, being beautiful, he has seldom had it checked. Stopping me between the pillars in the shade-walk, he said slyly:

"Lysias made fine music last night, with the Egyptian. And no, I did not listen, but saw the evidence with my eyes this morning."

"What evidence?" I demanded sternly.

Mardian laughed, and lowered his lashes like a girl.

"When I dressed him at sun-up for the hunt, I saw she had scored him all down the back, with her nails."

I told Mardian to keep such bawdy news to himself, and went to brood over the accounts amid the scrolls in the library. But having finished there, I could not rest, and wandered, listening closely to the gossip of the house. I know very well it is sometimes the fashion for lovers to mark each other, in the Eastern way, but I did not think it proper for a slave so to mark her lord, and I wondered he had let her, and not punished her. A slight punishment would have done, to be sure, but even small reprimands are spoken of, and all I heard of her, aside from Mardian's tale, was that she bided in the women's quarters, and that the other girls, those that had no household duties, were glad of her for she played music all day, and so entertained them—all but one who had a child at suck, and said the foreign melodies soured her milk. "But Kryse is envious of any new girl. And the Egyptian will be playing so she can dream of her home," said the cook, as he sliced oranges and livers for the evening meal. Every one of them now called her "the Egyptian," even my Master, who thought her Assyrian. Only I knew better.

Lysias came home from the hills in the afternoon, covered in dust and blood—the beast's, not his own, though I never like to see it, and many do not, for it is like an omen. He gave only a few words to me: "A bad day's work. Two dogs killed, Toh." He had lost none of his own, at least, for the three of them trotted in at his horse's heels, though their tails were down like wooden handles. Lysias called for the bath and went off to it, but presently, when I looked about for him in the shade-walk, where usually he is to be found with some of his friends at that time of day, when he is home, there he was not. And I did not really need Mardian, slipping by, to say to me, "You cannot discuss the price of amber with him now. He is with *her*."

I began now to be angry with myself. I could see Mardian was jealous of the slut, and I accused myself of something of the same kind. A powerful and unpleasant mood was growing on me, like the heaviness some feel before a storm. Come, old man, I thought. He will do as he wishes. She is new and she stirs him, and that is good, for he is young and strong, and would you have him otherwise? What does it matter if she acts moon-rites? In her country, that is religion, and perhaps it is to her credit that she is pious. But such musing did not comfort me. The memory of her hands at the window drove me, after a while, to the kitchen, which has a small walled courtyard, and in the wall a wicket gate which gives on the wild garden, and thus the alley.

To my surprise, I found one of the hounds there before me,

eagerly sniffing at the gate. It is the entrance to which traders come, and in the kitchen court sometimes there is slaughtering. I thought a piece of offal must have been dropped, and was astonished the dog wanted it, for they are well fed after hunting, and trained not to be greedy.

When I had the wicket open, however, the dog shot through like a spear, ignored the worn path in from the alley, and plunged among the dry tall grasses of the garden. With my sense of heaviness and dread absurdly increasing, I walked after the dog.

A low, broken wall bounds most of the garden. Tamarisk trees stand there, which some nights are strung with glowing necklets of fireflies. The shrine itself is little more than rubble, the plaster roof having fallen in more than a hundred years ago. The dog ran among the stones and the hedge of tamarisk and vanished. At that, I began to call to him, and he did not come out, though he is normally obedient. Then, when I, too, had come among the tamarisk shadow, I saw him again, pawing at a piece of stone, growling softly, his tongue lolling and spit running off it—and for a moment I checked, wondering if he had the madness, for there was surely nothing there. "Gently, Achilles," I said to him, as I came up. "Are you growing as stupid as I, and you a tenth my age?" And then I looked where Achilles pawed, and there was something there after all, of a sort.

The stone had a flat top, smoothed by weather, and it was drawn all over with a crowd of little signs. There were those which were like the crescent moon, and others by them that were circular as the moon at full. There were also stars of four, six, and seven points. And another sign, like a human figure with its arms outstretched. But in the centre of the stone was a handprint, a small, narrow hand, the thumb and the little finger stretched outwards in an unnatural way, the three middle fingers almost together: the print of a hand like the distorted form of a lotus. . . . These things were bizarre, and I did not care for them, but even less did I care for the ink she had used to write her symbols. It was brown now, as old blood always is. No astonishment then that the dog had snuffed at it, though his excitement still puzzled me. I had a vision of her as I stood there. I saw her stealing forth in the hour before dawn, after Lysias had sent her away. I saw her steal into the garden, passing through the tall grasses like a ghost in the twilight. The previous deity of the shrine would mean nothing to her, but that it had been holy ground, perhaps that might. Often there is something bloody to be found in a kitchen. She had dipped her hand in it before she went out, or caught some in a vessel and taken it with her. I did not relish such thoughts, and went back, calling the dog roughly. This time, he came.

When I came into the main courtyard, Mardian was sitting under the fig tree, burnishing Lysias's hunting spears. As soon as I saw Mardian, a horrible thought came to me, with no warning at all. I paused for several heartbeats, arguing with myself, gathering myself, before I could go up to him and say, "Mardian, do you recall what you told me of, this morning?"

"What did I tell you, Tohmet? That you are waxing fat? Was I so saucy as to say such a thing?"

"I will box your slim ear with my fat fist," I said, as a matter of course. Then: "You told me the slut had clawed her master's back."

"Oh ho," said Mardian, smiling his velvet smile, "so that spices you, does it?" Then he took in my face, and said, "What is it, Toh? I only joked. Why do you look sick?"

"Only tell me this," I said. "Had she drawn blood?"

"Blood? Yes, and to spare. And so had he. There was blood on the covers. She was a virgin, the Egyptian, and my Master the first to have her."

I dropped back when he said that, not sure if I was relieved, or if this made things darker. For she had surely used her own maiden's blood to paint the stone.

"Best go in, out of the sun, Tohmet," said Mardian.

Overhead, beyond the fig tree branches, beyond the lattice, there came a low wordless moan, a woman's sound. Both Mardian and I turned at it. He blushed and lowered his eyes. I went cold to my bones. I had heard the sound, or others like it, often enough. But I thought of the marks her hands had left, of the hands themselves thrust through the lattice, and I was afraid, with no true reason. But I knew I would rise early tomorrow, and the morrow after, every morrow if I must. I would wait in the kitchen yard. I would spy on her, if she returned that way, and certainly she would. I would find out her purpose, beyond paintings in blood. There would be one.

She did not make music that evening at supper, though my Master asked for her. Lysias turned and said something quietly to him, and my Master replied, "Sometimes a young man with his first female slave may be too lenient. She is not your wife, to earn this consideration." Lysias reddened, a thing he does not often do. I did not know if it was from anger or shame.

I did not sleep, even for three breaths, that night. When the dawn twilight began to come, I went out and waited in the kitchen yard, in the shadow of two walls' corners.

The world was very still in that place, though at the edges of my hearing I could make out the city astir below. Yet it seemed that here there was a lacuna where no sound came, or where no sound meant anything or had any power. And with the stillness and the grey-blue light, I began to feel a horrid icy dread, far worse than any dread I had felt the day before. I do not think I could have moved, either to follow her if she had come, or to run away. Then I noted the dawn star hanging like a blurred jewel, low down in the sky. And I commenced superfluously to pray for the sunrise, for the warmth and the light of day. It seemed to me, the Phoenician had summoned something from the night and from the twilight, and also from herself, something which had never touched this spot before. But now it had come there, walked there, *dwelled* there.

The sun did come up, at last, without my encouragement. Shivering, I went back into the house. I was angry with myself once more, and berated myself for an elderly child, falling into imagining things, and calling up horrors for himself. The girl was no magician, simply strange, as in some peoples it is racially usual to be strange. But I had no need to join her in her antics. I would keep an eye out for her, that was wise. But to creep round the chill corners of the house in the dawn, and sense coldness creeping from the ether, that was to become her accomplice.

But I did not get far with myself. And when I met with Mardian that day, I hastened by, nervous of what he might tell me, this time.

Many days went by then, many days, and their sistering nights. There is little to note of them. Perhaps no other but I could have seen any change in the house. Indeed, none but I seemed conscious of it. For the rest, they treated affairs separately, as they affected only themselves. The cook sulked that Lysias no longer ate heartily of his carefully prepared dishes. One of Lysias's closer companions, a very noble young man whose father is of high standing, came with his slave to inquire after Lysias's health, and Lysias sent him off with a courteous joke or two, but did not go with him. My Master, even, remarked, "I shall be glad when this Egyptian-Assyrian torch has burned itself out," but no more.

And the girls of the house were sorry that Lysias no longer flirted with them. And even his sisters had discreet, cruel words to trade about the slave-girl. In the women's quarters, the women had now apparently all grown jealous of her, nor did she play music for them anymore. The girl Kryse's baby was sick, and she had begun to mutter. An Egyptian trader who came to the house about this time, and from whom all the ladies of the house bought unguents and ornaments, remarked we should have trouble among the women soon, from that one bitter orange on the tree. For sure, *he* knew she was not of his people.

Then one morning Mardian was weeping in the shade-walk. Trying to conceal his tears in indignation, he blurted to me: "He beat me."

"Then you will have been negligent and deserved it," I said, though without much conviction, for in the matter of his master, Mardian is always diligent.

"No," he said now, "I had not deserved it. He was at his bath, and I saw the bitch had clawed him again. I said: 'I did not know you had gone hunting lions.' And he turned and struck me. And when he came from the bath, he beat me with the rod. Five blows. I shall be scarred forever."

He showed me the stripes, and they were light enough. His fine flesh would not be scarred at all. Yet having reassured him, I was myself perturbed. For Lysias had never before corrected any offence with the rod, though it is his right. And though Mardian had been insolent, I have overheard these two, who though master and slave are much of an age, exchange badinage of a rougher sort, when no other was by.

Perturbed then, not amazed. Indeed, not amazed, though I have no doubt my grey head grew more grey. Least of all did I like the way Lysias had become in himself. It was not that he was sick, nor that he looked sick, nor pale, nor that he became listless or tired swiftly; only his appetite seemed less, which in a young man generally so active was uncommon. No, it was nothing singular, or particular. And yet, something in his stride, which no longer had any spring to it. In his manner of reclining, of standing, even in such small things as these. . . . It seemed to me he moved now without the quick urgency of youth, as if all his eagerness had centred solely upon one object, and that was Sirriamnis. His eyes also were changed. They had begun to have a far-off look in them as if he gazed away into some other landscape, dimly seen beyond this one—*her* look, almost like blindness. I wondered he had come back sufficiently, from whatever weird country she was leading him to, that he should think to beat Mardian.

And then again, there was the sense of some other thing, some dark bloom upon the house, and only I felt it. Mostly at night it would steal upon me, and I would not let myself get up and walk about, knowing where my steps would lead me. I did not know what she did, or if she did anything at all, but if I should sleep, and I did not often sleep at that time, then I would dream of shadows. Shadows which slid down a wall into a courtyard, slid through the house, slid from the kitchen wicket into the garden of the ruined shrine. Curious, these shadows were, for they were very small, smaller by far than a woman, even a woman so little in stature as the Phoenician. And once or twice I think I dreamed of that old god who drank the blood of children, and I would see a moon-white hand, held awkwardly in the form of a lotus, and blood ran down its fingers to the wrist. And always there was foreboding in me, growing, day and night, like a vine of ivy, stifling me. Until that afternoon, following Mardian's beating, when, going in the library, I found Lysias there before me.

It had become a rule that, if he was at home, he would be with the woman in his chamber. He looked up and saw my expression before I could smooth it, and he laughed. For the moment of a moment, then, he was Lysias once more, and then the uncanny difference drew over him again, like a wave.

"It startles you to see me here, Toh. That says little for my studious nature."

"Excuse me, sir. I had thought—"

"Had thought I would be occupied. There are days when the gods insist on abstinence. I'm afraid my temper has been short today, and I beat poor Mardian. I do not think I marked him. It would be a pity if I had. He's as proud of his skin as a girl."

"No, sir, you have not marked him."

Lysias smiled, and we spoke of the dialogue in the scroll he was reading. All the while I was thinking: There is only one reason he would abstain from her. It is her woman's time. And this made me shiver, and I could not have said why, except for the dreams of blood and shadow, and the blood she had used to draw on the stone. It was not until suppertime, when I saw the moon come up over the hills beyond Crenthe, that I recollected it was at its first night of fullness—the same night she was purged of her fullness of female blood.

That evening at supper, I could eat little. My Master asked how I did, seeing me wave plates aside without selecting from them. I told some tale or other. Meanwhile, as I pecked and played with the food, my Young Master, for once, ate as heartily as if after a hunt.

Later, when I had taken myself to my bed, I lay and the thoughts came and went.

Eventually I rose as if I must, and went out quietly into the heart of the night. I could smell the scent of jasmine, of the day-burned walls cooling, and of the figs ripening on the tree. The stars shone, the moon had moved over towards the west, but her bloodless rays struck hard on everything, as if to suck the life from it. I had never been aware before of that nature of the moon's, which is like that of a cold, white sun. The sun's other self, perhaps, the sun of the dead. Such fancies I hid as I stole across the courtyard.

I went swiftly to the second yard, by the kitchen. I had awaited her there before, and she had not come. Yet tonight I knew that she would. How did I know? Because she was a worshipper of Tanit, that lady of dark things and of the darkness' eye, the moon, now at full. And because her condition kept her from my Young Master's bed, which left her free to wander the night as she willed. Logic therefore instructed me. Yet I think I would have gone to that place to wait, to feel of the night, if I had been blind and not seen the moon, if I had been deaf and did not know she was not to be with Lysias. It was my skin which saw, my bones which heard, and both quaked, yet I walked to the spot and stood there in the shadow between two walls' corners, still unsure if I should have the strength to follow her, or to fly from her—and presently, like a spirit, Sirriamnis passed.

It was like my dreams of her, though much darker than in my dreams. Her black hair mantled her, and some black cloak she had wrapped herself in. No sooner was she through the wicket than she slunk aside among the grasses and the tamarisks. And she vanished, blackness into blackness.

I, on stiff, numbed limbs, had set about following her, despite my fears. If she had turned about at any point, however, I cannot say what I should have done. But it did not seem likely. I had glimpsed something of her face as she went by me, and it was the face of one who is not wholly in the body, the face of the tranced, or the possessed. I had expected nothing else, though I had thought it horrible enough.

On her vanishing, I hesitated, then pressed on, through the tamarisks, reckoning to find her the far side of them and taking pains with my stealth. I ventured first to look out from among the boughs. There, not seven paces before me, stood the tumbled flat-topped stone where she had drawn. About stood others, none much higher than the back of a dog. Beyond was the ruined shrine, roofless and hollow. But nowhere in the vista could I discover the woman. There was no place for any grown creature to conceal itself, save they lay down on the ground, and even this would be poor cover, for the grasses were thinner here, and the moon itself pierced through and through them, like a blade through water. Truly, then, it seemed she had disappeared, a sorceress. And my chilled blood ran more lethargically, as if I were near to death.

And then—and then I saw a little quiver of movement in the grass. So, she crawled on her belly after all. What game was this, or did she know I spied on her, and seek to elude or confuse me?

Should I challenge her now, or keep still? Idle question. My tongue was swollen, my throat closed. And all the while the maddening sense of horror grew in me, and grew, and had no name.

And suddenly the eddy of motion flickered straight as invisible fire through the grass to the edge of the alley, and there it was gone. I did not see what made that rush, but certainly it was not the Phoenician. Some small night beast, it must be, or scavenging cat, perhaps. But she, *where then was Sirriamnis?*

Wretched in my dilemma, I hardly knew what I did. Nor do I properly recapture it now. But it seems I dragged myself away, groaning, I think, under my oppression and fright, and so into the courtyard where the fig tree grew. And there I crept into the shades of the branches, and sat on the rim of the marble cistern, trembling. I suppose I may have stayed a long while there, not knowing what I was at. I know that when the moon was lower, I heard a little noise, like a dry leaf blown about the court. And then, I suspect that I fathomed it, if not the heart, at least the manner of the spell, but I could not force myself to turn about and see.

When at long last I shifted myself, the courtyard, of course, was empty, save for the ultimate moonlight lying in shattered plates on the walls and in the lowest branches of the tree above.

I remember I thought, most clearly, This is not your business, Tohmet. Let it alone, whatever it should be. For it is stronger than you, and older even than you, old man. Old as the moon maybe, old as the night itself.

And thinking this, I felt myself give in, and a sort of relief came to me, as at a fever's breaking. I went back to my bed, and slept.

"Toh. There are black hairs on my Master's bed," said Mardian next afternoon.

I cursed him, being in a poor humour.

"Why tell me such a thing? They will be the woman's, will they not?"

"She was not with him. And these hairs are not hers, they are short and coarse. I did not dare say a word to him about it, for fear he'd beat me again."

"Why trouble *me?*"

Mardian came close. His face was pale and his dark eyes large and anxious.

"You do not like her, Toh. Or trust her. And—I think there is a bewitchment that has followed her. I woke in the night, in the outer room where I sleep, and there was something at the foot of my pallet, for I partly saw it—and then it was gone."

"A dream," I said.

"No dream. I smelled it."

"What smell then had this demon?" I demanded scornfully, tapping my stylus on my knee to show I had other tasks than to listen to his nightmares.

"A smell of the hills. Of grass and herbs and night."

"A smell of terror indeed."

"I heard its claws scrape on the floor."

"And its shape?"

"Small and crouching, like a frog—yet it had long straight horns. I would have cried out, but no sound would come. I could not move. When it was gone I lay awake an hour or more, rigid with fear, and thought I might die. It was an unnatural thing. It put stone on my limbs and my heart beat sluggishly. My mother told me once, before I was sold from the farm, of night things that come and go, that suck the strength from men, that eat their souls—"

I rose and shook my fist at him, and he fled.

And then I sank down, and saw night overlaid on day, the amber shadows turned to purple, the golden sun to a leprous whiteness. I thought of the Phoenician, and how she vanished among the tamarisks, of the grasses running as if with fire, of a noise like a dry leaf. . . .

I went to the kitchen. The cook was active with a goose, and feathers flew like foam. The cook was bursting with gossip, as ever. He soon spoke of Sirriamnis. "She sleeps all day through, the lazy slut, even when she has not been called to his bed. The women are afraid of her, and will not say why. They would like to harm her, but too scared of Lysias's anger to do it. Kryse's baby has a long scratch on its neck. Kryse mutters. The women blame the cat, but the cat has run away. We shall have trouble if she does not return. How will you fancy a nice plump mouse pie? I've heard in Rome it's a delicacy."

Lysias had gone riding with his friend, the noble young man who had called to inquire for him previously. Nor did Lysias come back at lamplighting, but was off at some supper in the friend's house. I thought this good. Yet I stayed abroad until midnight, and at midnight Lysias came home. Under the glare of the great moon, which again had risen in her pride, his face was pale as Mardian's. And when I rose to greet him, he went straight by me, unseeing, he who never passed without notice, and some kind word.

I had given it up, but not it seemed with my whole heart. I sat and worried over it as a dog at a bone. What was my life, old and used, the life of a slave, against that young shining vigorous life? His father had missed it. Did I, who dared think myself almost a father to him, did I mean to leave go the thread that might decide Lysias's fate?

An hour after, I had nerved myself enough, I went up silently into the lobby that opens on Lysias's sleeping room. There I woke up Mardian, nearly terrifying him from his wits.

"Hush, brat," said I. "I know you too scared to sleep, despite your snores, audible from the floor below. I've come to share the watch with you."

"It is you, Toh, who snore, not I," he said. But he had seized my hand. Awake, I saw he was indeed still afraid, and glad to have me by. But we could not light a lamp for fear of disturbance, and soon Mardian, regardless of his fears, or in some way because of them, fell asleep again. And so I let him slumber, for it seems old men require less of this balm than the young.

I sat alone, then, by the pallet on the floor, feeling a sort of horror at myself, and as cold as the marble. Quickly enough the moon slid sideways in through the lattice grille, and scattered patterns on the floor. I stared at these patterns, and it seemed to me I saw pictures in them, of white hands and lotuses. Then, my head nodded. I dozed in an icy druglike stupor, just as Mardian did, afraid, yet unable to resist the tide of sleep which somehow fastened on the tide of fear and came in with it.

In a while, I felt it pass like a breeze along the floor.

I felt, too, that it looked at me, and in some way I saw the light caught, low down, in its eyes, flat and colourless. And then it had gone by. My relief at its going was very great, for now I might sleep safe from harm. But then I dimly recalled where it would be proceeding—the chamber of my Young Master. The curtain rings whispered at just that instant, and I knew it had slipped by the curtain and was in the room with him. Ah, but it was no business of mine. For what were they to me, these lords of the house, I their slave, and considered less than a man, a clever animal that could do sums. . . . But then I heard him moan, just once, but frantic and deep, my boy, my Lysias, and I came alert as if I had been struck in the face. Those thoughts I had been having, they came from the enchantment, the air-borne night-borne poison of her spell. I shook them from me, and I got to my feet as if I raised myself through clinging mud, and I went towards the curtain as the little thing had done.

I have heard men say that to be often in great pain, as from an old wound, is in the end to grow accustomed to such pain, and thus, while suffering from it, to continue with other deeds in full concentration. And so it had come to be with me, I think. That dreadful clinging horror, which I had now felt so often, and which I felt at this hour as if my life's blood ran out of me, did not halt me, did not prevent my taking hold of the curtain and quietly stepping through. Nor did I flinch at standing there in the full glare of the moon's eye, a glare eased only by the window grille and the branches of the fig tree which came between yet could not stop the light from seeping through, like some deadly corrosive, into the room. And so I stood, unarmed by any weapon, as generally a slave will not be armed, or by any sorcery of my own. And this, in the white wild light, is what I saw.

Lysias lay out on the bed, naked and fine-made as any bronze of a sleeping youth, for sleep it seemed he did, though now and then he turned his head, and his hands clenched and loosened, yet he did not wake; it appeared only that he dreamed. Along his ribs was a thin dark glistening line like a narrow ribbon, but it was a narrow scratch some thin honed implement had made, a little blade, or a long claw, and it bled. At first, I took the heap of darkness for the bunching of the cover, or some trick of shadow, but it was neither of these, for all at once there came again that flat glowing of the two discs which were its eyes, and slowly, slowly, like the petals of a flower, I beheld the two straight horns rising upward until vertical upon its head.

I believe my heart did pause. To add fresh fear to the old was quite impossible, I seemed rather to disintegrate, to crumble, or maybe to petrify instead, as men did who faced the gorgon Medusa. And then—then my senses came back in a dazzling race, and I almost cursed aloud. For I saw, at last, what the thing was which was crouched on my Young Master's body. It was a hare.

Black as night, and smooth as velvet, its eyes gleaming soullessly and its two tall ears, that were not horns at all, raised up on its head to catch the sound of me. There was another sound, too. Very soft, a tiny modest mouthing sound, as of a child at suck. And at this sound, I froze again, and my eyes, which were already starting, strained wider.

I thought an instant that, having scratched him, the black hare drank from the trickling cut, milking Lysias of his blood. But quickly I saw the milking was of another order. Crouched against his groin, it had taken the organ of his manhood into its mouth, and worked on it, like some terrible uncanny harlot.

If I had kept motionless till then, if I had been petrified, now I gained a new layer of stone. The teeth of a hare, though square and uncarnivorous, are sharp as razors from the vegetation it must feed on. Now it mouthed him. But if it should bite—it would make a eunuch of him for sure, and most likely kill him too.

And so I must stand, and must oversee the foul, unnatural act, afraid to move either into the room or out of it. Though I would have wished to run forward and seize the monstrous beast and crush its neck in my hands. And so I stood, and so I watched, like the pimp who regards his whore and her customer from behind the screen, getting his delight by what is done by them. Though I had no delight in it. Rather I shook all over and nausea came in my throat, but I thrust it down, frightened even to retch lest I cause those two square fangs to close on what they fondled.

And for Lysias, in his charmed sleep, doubtless he dreamed of some wholesome pleasure. Presently his quickened breathing broke and his back arched upward from the bed. The hare, which had never taken its eyes from me, did not take them from me now, but I saw the swift movements of its throat.

As the spasm left him, Lysias fell back with a long sigh. I held my breath, waiting on what the beast would do now it had had its vampire's drink. I think I gave a quavering sob as the long mouth opened, letting go of him. The hare reared upward on its two hind limbs, and its round cold eyes seemed to flash, like two exploding moons, and then went black. Even as I staggered forward to grab for it, it sprang straight by me, and dashed through the curtain and was gone.

I did not wait for anything, not even to go to my Young Master—one glance had assured me he was unmaimed, indeed relaxed and peaceful now, and yet asleep. I stumbled out and through the lobby, not even calling to Mardian, for I did not reckon he could answer. I alone must pursue the demon, as before. For its name I knew well enough. It could be none other than Sirriamnis, and this her sorcery, which was transmogrification, the oldest and most sinister magic known to humankind. And that she had lapped his virility, his man's strength, this I knew also, for she had forced the vital fluid from him, which in the male creates the miracle of life, just as those fluids expended from the womb of the female are negative and waste.

Though far from young, I am sound in heart and wind, nor do my joints fail me. So I ran through the house and out into the court-yard, the way I knew the creature had gone. I knew also where it would be going next, in a sort of madness I knew it, recalling how Mardian, child of farm stock that he is, had noted the smell of open hills and night-blooming herbs. The hills beyond Crenthe, that was the way it would take, the way it must have gone firstly the night before, and returned to work its obscene will in the house.

I hesitated only once, to fetch two of the hunting dogs from their sleeping place. It never occurred to me, frantic as I was, that what I did was stupid and against the laws of men. I had no mind in me but the mind which would hunt her down before the sun came and made her back into what she was not, a woman I might not slay.

The dogs were eager. They had had hares now and then, and knew the scent gladly. Usually they will harken to my whistle, so I let them run ahead. Old Tohmet trotted behind, and I am sure my eyes were as hers had been, the look of one asleep or possessed.

It was very late that white night, the city closed and silent, save for the odd riot of a drinking house by the harbour, and the occa-sional solitary glimmer of a lamplit window, where someone kept awake from much sickness or much health.

The dogs' feet pattered on the stones or on the hard earth of the streets, and my sandalled feet padded soft as theirs. The quarry I no longer saw, but I knew she was before us, that bitch-beast, running under the auspice of Tanit's moon, to reach some haven in the hills. As I went, a strangely pragmatic brooding came over me, and I pondered Skiro, who called himself The Traveller, and if he knew that the girl might shape-change, or if she had not had the knack till her virginity was gone, or if she might resist the shape of the hare when she deemed it not expedient—but all this was theoretical to me. I cared only for my task as her executioner.

Over on Crenthe's east side, the wall is in bad repair, with many exits and entrances, but in these times of peace the rebuilding is slow, and slight watch is kept there. This would be the way she had taken, and the way I took with the dogs. Far off on a rise, a sentry leaned on a tree, and from the look of him he slept.

The moon was almost down now, and the hills, exactly before me, darkening, but the dawn star was up, and the dawn could not be so far behind her. I had come a great way, yet felt no weariness, such is the power of hatred in a man. But now I began to despair of our coming up with her before sunrise, such a fleet thing she had become.

But even a hare may tire. As we climbed through the coarse grass and the wild flowers of the hills, clouds rose in the west and blotted up the sinking moon. Suddenly the dogs began to whine and grunt, and all at once they launched themselves towards the top of the slope, frenzied as when the quarry first starts.

I was by now weary enough I could not, despite my hating strength, put on myself any extra burst of speed. But abruptly, against the dimly lightening eastern vault of sky, I saw something running in silhouette along the topmost slant of the hill. It was the hare, and after it the dogs went pelting, yipping, and snarling, their mouths stretched to rend.

I believe I, too, tried to run then, to reach them and see it done. And as I did my foot caught in a tussock of matted grass and I fell, hard and heavy, winding myself with my own brought-down bulk. As I sprawled there, it was all I could do to lift my head, but so I did. And so I witnessed the last event of that evil night, to which, if it were necessary, I would swear on the altar of any decent god.

The dogs were almost level with the hare, and knowing it, the beast leapt about. There was one moment then when I saw the hare, drawn black on the melting sky, the morning star above its long-eared head like a glistening dagger in the air. The dogs checked a second, as they will with anything at bay, but they slavered and I heard them growling. Then the growling changed to an awful whimpering noise, the kind a dog will give when he has been beaten, or torn in the hunt. Bewildered, yet I felt a sinking in my very soul. Next instant I learned that to the accustomed music of horror that hate had lulled, there could yet be added some new notes.

The hare rose up on its hind limbs, but having done as much, continued to rise up, and *continued.* I saw then a being which, if I must translate, was the interim condition of Sirriamnis's transmogrification, that state between beast and woman, and yet, too, was some other thing.

I think it had a woman's body, what I could see of it, and the long hair showered round it—yet it had a bestial face, still, though bloated up to human size, and the ears lifted from the head, and the hands were blunted paws, and from these sprayed the tremendous digging claws of the hare. While from its deformed mouth came, with its black tongue, a hideous hissing, quite unlike the hissing of snake or cat. The dogs cowered with their bellies flattened to the hill. For me, it was as if a million ants ran over my skin. My fear caused me to choke, and shortly I lost my senses.

The red sky of dawn was in my eyes and a leather flask of wine to my lips, when I recovered myself. It was none other than that guard I had taken to be asleep on the rise. Apparently wide awake he had seen me go by, and being speculative, when the dawn watch relieved him, he left his place and followed me, and found me on the hill, the two dogs cowering in the grass beside me. Of any other there was no sign.

"Up now, ancient one, if you are able," said my benefactor. He was a soldier, rough but not unkind, as the wine-flask showed. He had excellent eyesight too, and had spotted my slave-ring. "You never thought to run off, did you? You'd not get far on foot. And to take the dogs, too, that was a silly thing, was it not? You're a bit simple, I expect. Never mind it. I think I know your house," and he named it, and my Master. "He'll be just. Come along. I'll see you home. You're too full of years to be sleeping on the ground."

I did not disillusion him as to my wits. Indeed, I had been a veritable fool, and now I saw it. For sure, I was very shaken, too, and needed the support the young soldier gave me through the morning streets. He brought me direct to the gate, at which the dogs ran in on their own. But he would not have anything but that he should speak to my Master himself. Most respectfully, then, the soldier offered his tale, and handed me over to my Master like an idiot child, adding, "I am certain you'll be understanding, sir, for I'm sure he meant no harm."

My Master bore it all with equanimity, and even gifted the fellow with some money, which of course had been his hope all along. But when he had gone whistling back to his barracks, my Master set his hand on my shoulder and said: "Tohmet, are you such a fool indeed? You know the law better than I do, I should say. And to take the dogs— What were you thinking of? Did you mean to abscond?"

"No, sir." I had been puzzling all the way back what I should say to excuse myself, for I knew I could not, nor would I, tell him the fantastic truth of why I had gone out and what I had seen. That would have made him, civilised as he is, suppose me insane for sure.

"Come, Toh. If you've a reason, I will have it now."

I said, "A fox, or some other beast, had come down from the hills and was in the garden by the shrine. The dogs made a fuss, and I took a notion to let them out and see if they could catch it. Then they ran off and would not answer the whistle. And I, anxious they would be lost, went after them."

He frowned very long and hard at me, and then he said, "Well, I'll accept your word for that. But I never heard a dafter tale in all my life. I would think you out after woman, if you were younger and I did not know you better." Then he took a turn over the floor, and said with his back to me, "Here is the black part of it, Tohmet. That boy from the garrison knows the house and will spread the story. The household slaves will also catch the gossip from the one that let you in at the gate. I have no choice, this being the case, but to chastise you, or they may all be—taken with a notion. Do you see how it is, Tohmet?"

I could see how it was, and that my Master had no other course; also that he was sorry for it. But I had been unwise, and like many an unwise man, had brought trouble on more than myself.

I told him I understood the matter. He answered that he must use the whip on me, according to the law, and in the courtyard where they might all see, but that he would make it three stripes rather than the number which are customary in like circumstances.

In my boyhood I had been whipped now and then, and knew the process well enough not to relish making its acquaintance again.

But it was only justice, and besides being a good deal fatter now than then, the thong would have more padding to strike on.

Nevertheless, it was a nasty time I had of it, the three brief blows seeming to go on forever, and the pain, which grows worse as the numbing shocks of the blows themselves wear off, sickened me.

I felt my shame very keenly, too, to stand stripped to my drawers in the court—obese, elderly, and a clot—fit only to be whipped. I deserved no better.

Afterwards, my Master sent one of the women to see to my stripes, and a good job she made of her work, being gentle, and skilled with herbs. I was a little feverish, but I asked her, presently, if the black-haired slave was in the women's quarters. The girl answered with some surprise that certainly the Egyptian was in the house, and did I think that sly snake as addled as I to try sneaking off after foxes. It seemed Sirriamnis had made better speed home than I.

When the girl had gone, I lay on my belly, and I own I wept. It was weakness and pain, and it was anger, too. I knew well enough who was truly to blame for my beating, but I did not see how I could come near the witch anymore, to be rid of her.

I had the fever two days, but on the evening of the third, I was well enough to be sitting out in the shade-walk for the cool air. As I sat, Lysias came walking between the pillars and stopped when he saw me. His face was grey and his eyes were very bright, as if he had suffered my sickness with me.

"How are you, Toh?"

"I am well, sir."

"My father had no call to lash you," he said in a low and bitter voice.

"Every call, I regret, sir. He could hardly do otherwise."

"Nonsense, man. To take the whip to one of your years and standing in the house? Never. He was wrong, and I have told him so. There have been hot words between us."

I remonstrated, reminding him of the law, and his duty to his father. Yet I could hardly help being glad, too. All the while, my eyes roved about him. The nights of the moon's fullness were done, but I feared for him still as I never feared another thing all my life. Yet he looked as fine as ever he did, but for his pallor. As he went away I saw his eyes were moist, and my vanity was greatly uplifted by that, as it turned out with no cause. For when my nurse came to see to me an hour after, she brought a piece of news that almost set me fainting.

Soon after the noon meal, the Egyptian, as they still called her, and still do when they speak of her, had been overcome by a dreadful bout of vomiting. A physician was summoned, but his verdict came as no surprise. No one, judging by her symptoms, doubted she had been poisoned. Soon enough the facts emerged to light. The girl Kryse, who more than all others thought the Phoenician a sorceress, and feared some bane had been put on her child by the witch, had obtained particular cosmetics from the Egyptian trader who had earlier come to the house. And a portion of these cosmetics, which if swallowed are invariably lethal, she had crushed and dropped in Sirriamnis's food. At sunset, racked by ghastly contortions, and spewing blood, Sirriamnis had died.

My head spun, and I must have looked near death myself, for my nurse made a huge fuss. What I myself felt was a grim and burning joy. And with that, as I came to myself more, an urge to laugh. For I had laboured so mightily to be rid of her, and in the end it had taken only a woman's malice to see to it. And then I mused, and reasoned that maybe, since it was the shadow-magic of a female god, it would have needed another woman to accomplish the task, where a man must fail.

Lysias was not himself for a long while. He mourned his slave in private, yet as intensely as if she had been his lawful wife, the mother of his heir, one he loved as he loved himself. But he was young and healthy, and in the end they brought him round, his father and his friends, and he laughed and joked and chose spears for the hunt, and went to suppers and came home from them a little drunk, though not dishonourably so, and with flowers in his hair. And by the year's end, his father had seen to things, and Lysias was married.

She is a sweet child, his wife, with soft fair hair that falls to her waist when it is unbound, so he tells me. She loves and honours him, as a wife should, and he is very fond of her. But they have been wed well into the second year now, and still there are no children, and no promise of any.

It is general to blame the woman in such a pass. It might be the girl is barren, though her married sisters have each several sons to their credit. But, when I think of it, it is as if a cold wind blows by me, I smell the scent of the wild grass on the hills, and the three fading scars on my back flare up as if kissed with flame. I remember, nor shall I ever forget, what I saw in Lysias's sleeping chamber, the beast which crouched on him and did him that service of the harlot's, and which drank down his seed thirstily and to the last drop. It is a dream to haunt me, though only I know of it, the dream of the black hare, and the moon's blind white eye, and an eye which is a flower, and a flower which is a hand, and that mysterious goddess of the African coast, daughter to a god who only drank blood.

Nor is the house quite free of her. It is nothing I could put into words, as I have all the rest, nothing to which I could give a name. But sometimes, on the nights of the moon's fullness, or when the dawn star gathers itself in the east like a molten tear, then I would not be down by the wicket gate, nor in the courtyard by the fig tree. I keep to my bed, and though I invariably wake, I do not rise, I do not listen, I do not look, and I practise not to consider. But I do not think she is quiet, that goddess who has been invoked here. I cannot tell myself she is appeased.

Kryse was sold as a whore for what she had done, and her child kept here, for it is a boy. So she lost it, for all she had done to keep it with her. That was her punishment, and it was harsh. And I, for my part, was whipped, but I hazard it was not punishment enough for what I tried to do.

Maybe some night I will, after all, be drawn out into the darkness, and walk into that old garden and to the stone which Sirriamnis painted with her blood. I do not like to meditate upon such things, nor to believe in them. But there are matters so dark, so deep, so ancient, and so abiding, that believe them or not, still, they Are. And will Be, until the sun dies and only the moon is left in the sky, and that demon creature which surely is in all women, however gracious or kind, rises up to destroy us all.

# SOUTHERN LIGHTS

**R**IDING INTO THE SOUTH A YEAR AFTER SHE HAD LEFT IT, JAISEL
was aware of that strange disease of travellers—nostalgia
for the land she thought she remembered rather than the
land she had come back and found.

True, it was winter, the trees stripped, and black with a
sparse foliage of ravens. The heads of the mountains were seasoned
with snow. True, the pools were frozen, and the earth iron-hard,
and the people of the villages iron-hard to any not their kin, since
the cold time was no time to give anything away. Such a look and
feel to the South made it overly unwelcoming. And some things
had not changed, after all. The way those who saw her close
pointed, spat, or jeered. Those who saw her from a distance—her
slender mailed and wolfskin-folded lines atop the grey gelding, the
glint of the dagger, the sword, the short hair nearly pale as the ice
over the waters—those witnesses took her for a boy, or a young
renegade knight come home from some war. Altogether, what
should not have altered in the land had altered. What would have
been better altered had remained the same.

So she had ridden on, deeper and deeper into the Southern
uplands, higher and higher between the spearheads of the mountains. She had ridden beyond any landmark she recognised. As if
she foolishly searched for some new, refreshing place to heal the
ancient anger in her young heart. And coaxing the gelding up the
frigid cascading shale, or through the blue canyons where the birds

of winter wheeled and complained, she mocked herself for a fool, sensing her search, and its pointlessness. Eventually she recollected that platitude of the South: *All lights are friendly in the dark.* She resolved that the next community she came upon would provide her winter lodging, whether they or she liked it or not. Or, if she reached no habitation by sunset, she would turn back tomorrow and make for the valleys, and the cities beyond.

As the sun began to go, she was riding up an old road, and ahead of her the flank of a great mountain outcrop cut off any view beyond. Perversely—or superstitiously, perhaps—she had resolved to pass the outcrop and see what it hid. That done, for undoubtedly it hid nothing but further outcrops, mountains, the static vistas of winter country, she would turn back, and look for makeshift shelter where she could. The road had, of course, at some date led somewhere, but it had needed repairs a century or more. No one had come to repair it.

Near the top of the rise Jaisel paused, staring at the sunset, which the low temperature and the mountain air had given a wonderful clarity. A sullen gorgeous red of a peculiar depth ringed half the sky, soaking up into tawny amber and so, mysteriously unmixed, into a transparent violet. The sky was luminous and crystalline, darker at its apex than in the east. As its red blush began to fade, the stars opened their cold and blazing eyes from every quarter. Jaisel's throat tightened at the beauty spread so carelessly before her. She had missed beauty, maybe. The year had been harsh, like many years before it. It became too easy to forget the wonder that was the earth in the mere trouble of living.

Refocusing her eyes, one rather narrower than the other, Jaisel clucked to the gelding and urged him up the last quarter mile of incline. As they started, somewhere ahead a vague shudder of noise indicated a snow-slide from some peak, a disparaging note in the quiet. By the time they passed around the flank of the outcropping, the final whisper of the afterglow was gone.

Beyond the obstacle, the road ascended sheer for another mile. It ended, obscure in the twilight, at yet another irregular slab of rock. Jaisel looked at the slab with disfavour, for it offered nothing.

"Come, Grey," she murmured to the horse. "It's one more chilly bivouac for us, I am afraid. My apologies to you. When I got you, I seem to think I rashly promised you better."

The gelding twitched his ears and made a soft noise of licking at her. She had won the horse in a ferocious dice game with Northern thieves, three of whose number she had subsequently had to relieve of their lives when they tried to retrieve him a day later in a wood.

As Jaisel stroked her horse's neck, three yellow stars flashed out on the slab of rock ahead. Then, as she waited, countless others. In an eerie fascination, she sat and watched the progression of a strangely unanimous lamplighting. In another minute, there were many hundreds of gleams and glows flickering down at her, and then, with an equal appearance of strangeness, every one vanished. Or almost every one, for here and there a stranded point of ruddy colour still burned.

It was not hard to fathom. Shutters had been closed, wood where the flames had been concealed, heavy glass where they were still on show. Why the lamps had all virtually been lit in the same moment was apparent only to the people up ahead.

Whatever else, however, the irregular slab of rock was nothing less than the wall and top-roofs of a town, a town with hundreds of lights to suggest friendliness in the shimmering, creeping darkness.

Jaisel tapped the horse with her heels, and they rode quickly towards the lights.

The town had a gate, which was closed. But lamps also burned above in the unshuttered windows of the squat lookout tower. Jaisel rapped on the gate, and a man in haphazard leathers that might have been a uniform, or might not, peered out. He spotted, of course, the mail, the firefly of the single earring, the sword under the cloak. She told all that from his voice when he said,

"What do you want, sir?"

"To sit out here all night, naturally, and talk with you."

At which he must check, think to himself: *Not the voice of a man. It will be a boy.*

"I am not obliged to open the gate." Boys merited sterner tones. "You wish me to climb your wall?"

"Don't boast, young sir. Even if you could, your horse could not."

"How sadly true. Therefore, I suggest a silver coin passed from my hand to yours. Once I am inside the town."

"Tonight is Light of Angels Night. If you came to visit, you've come very late. The lamps have already been shown to heaven, and the merrymaking begun."

So. A parochial religious festival, the unified lamplighting was explained.

"If I am late, why delay me further?"

"You may be an outlaw or thief."

Jaisel sighed. *"Two* silver coins."

"Or a—"

"Two are my limit. There is all the night to house me, free of charge. Your town is not worth more than two silver coins, if worth those."

Seven minutes later, two coins thrown and caught, she was riding up the hilly street, hearing the gate thunk shut again behind her. The cold was pressing closer now, the stars vanishing as the lights had done, this time behind shutters of cloud. Despite her scornful words she was glad to have got in.

The houses were tall and timbered, and through chinks in their slats or behind their panes of sulky glass, the lamps beamed out a welcome, but none of them for her. Sometimes she caught a noise of music, or voices lifted in good cheer. Sometimes she glimpsed the gold-lit shadows of revellers, raising wine cups, garlands, or each other's hands as they danced. She began to feel inevitable melancholy and shook it off. Had she such a home, what would she be other than its servant, some fellow's wife or mother, slave and doll and drab. No. Better the free, cold darkness and to be alone. *Well, mistress,* she thought, *you have your wish.*

The street opened into a square, and Jaisel looked about her for the hostelry which, since she had not yet passed such a place, she had supposed might be here. But there was no hostelry and no hint of one. Only the houses leaning to each other around the square and up the hill ahead, and humping away down alleys on every side. At the square's centre was a well with a tall stone kerb, and as she gazed at it, the night fragmented.

Jaisel glanced up. The stars were falling in myriads. The winter's first sure snow was coming down.

She cursed gently, and withdrew against an overhanging wall. What now? Knock on some door, which would doubtless open and then sociably slam in her face. Turning her head in an involuntary scan of her surroundings, Jaisel saw someone coming towards her down the road from the hill.

As the figure came closer, it seemed muffled in the snow itself, a hooded mantle of white fur. Incongruous with this richness of attire were the two iron buckets the figure clasped, one in either hand. Destination was obviously the well. Jaisel went on waiting, allowing the snow-white creature to cross the square and reach the well, and raise the buckets to the kerb. As a gloved hand went up to loose the well's chain, Jaisel swung off the gelding. Leaving him to stamp and snort in the snow, she strode to the well. The fur-wrapped person was already looking at her, face a dim blurred triangle of darker whiteness in its hood. Probably startled, though it was difficult to tell through the snow, by the sudden manifestation of a stranger. Jaisel did not pause. She reached out to take over the operation of the bucket and chain.

"Let me help you," she said, leaving small option.

The chain had gone down the shaft and splashed through the ice below before the other answered in a light girl's voice, "Thank you, sir."

Jaisel forbore to comment, other than: "Oh, my pleasure, madam."

Nothing more was said, and she must haul the chain up again. She hauled.

"Inclement weather," said Jaisel.

"Indeed, yes."

"A cruel night for you to be out in."

Silence, and the first bucket filled. The chain went down again. Jaisel worked at it, and at the conversation.

"Surely," said Jaisel, "you have servants who would do this for you, lady."

"Oh, no," said the girl clad in fur, "my father will not have servants in the house. He says they interrupt his studies. And since we have no well in our yard—"

"He sent you out in the blizzard to fetch water," said Jaisel between amused rancor and angry, self-aware connivance. "Yet—" the second bucket was now full— "you shan't have the sorrow of carrying such a burden home. Permit me to escort you and act as porter."

"You are too kind, sir."

"Not at all."

Jaisel whistled, and the gelding came like a phantom over the square, obedient as a dog. Holding the buckets, Jaisel waited for the girl to precede her. Probably there would be hesitation, for this was all very improper, had Jaisel really been a man. Surprisingly enough, the girl did not hesitate very long. But after all, Jaisel had secured the water, and the cold of the night was argument enough.

"Come then," said the girl, "if you will be so good." And she turned and crossed the square, and began to go back up the street. Obedient as her horse, Jaisel trod after through the carpet of snow.

But five or six houses along, where a lamplit window threw a slim pane of yellow on the white, the fur girl turned suddenly, as if to take stock of Jaisel for the first time.

*And now she will see I am no man, and there will be new (old) questions to answer, while we both catch our deaths, or at least a sample of frostbite.*

But when she came level, and stared through the fluttering snow just as the girl stared at her, Jaisel tensed with a new and uneasy wariness. The girl was perhaps half a foot shorter than Jaisel, and plumper than Jaisel's swordlike self, and the girl's face, haloed by fur and by tendrils of long hair as flaxen fair as Jaisel's own, was extremely and disturbingly beautiful. Cameo pale skin that even the cold had not stung to any colour, save at the mouth, which was tawny-red as the sunset had been. The eyes and the brows were long and darkly marked, apparently by nature alone. The orbs of the eyes were black.

Jaisel found she had nothing to say, but noted the girl was looking her over with a shy immodesty, paying particular heed to dagger, sword, and mail.

"Are you a knight?" inquired the sunset mouth at last.

Jaisel swallowed.

"Surely you can see I am not."

"You are dressed as a knight, and armed like one, sir."

Jaisel raised one eyebrow, grew impatient with herself, and levelled it. Perhaps the weather and the wolfskin hid her more ably than usual.

"I'm no knight, but I surely *am* freezing to my own bones."

"Come, then," said the girl, as before, turning at once and moving on ahead again. They passed in another second away from the lighted window. Vague song came from within the house, but Jaisel paid it slight attention now. "Are you to stay at some dwelling hereabouts?" asked the fur girl in a moment.

"I've no lodging. I looked to find an inn—"

"There are no inns. I will inquire of my father if you may lodge with us, since you have been so courteous to me."

Jaisel did not have the skittishness in her to protest. She had been playing all along for such an invitation, but merely from opportunism; she did not have much hopes of its success in these circumstances. She could just picture the studious father firing up with wrath at his child's having been taken in by a virago who dared garb as a man. If he would not permit his solitude infringed by servants, how should he brook a guest, let alone one of Jaisel's blazon? Maybe there was an outhouse he would permit her to haunt for the night. Perhaps he would pity the horse if not the monster-woman who rode him. . . .

On the other hand, it was but too easy to follow the beautiful daughter home, even without the excuse of the two slopping buckets.

The first truly curious event of the evening took place a few minutes after. The house, tall and timbered like the others, although with no lights showing, presented to the street a thick wooden door, studded with iron. Straight by the door the girl went, and down an alley at the side of the house. Here, a high wall, already ermined, implied a garden. There was a low door set in the wall, with dead creepers twining above. The girl hesitated. Jaisel awaited the production of a key. Instead, the girl reached out and touched a strange iron thing hung on the door. There came the immediate sound of metal parts grinding together, a sharp click, and the door swung open.

Not speaking, the girl stepped through. Also not speaking, Jaisel followed. As she did so, she glanced at the metal thing, and saw it was a grinning, loathsome mask, rayed with wild hair. She knew at once, then, a pervasion of bored misgiving. It did not halt her. The horse also walked through the door, since no one denied him. But Jaisel had learned long ago that animals did not infallibly react against the presence of the occult.

The garden was small inside its high walls, which were massed by skeletal vines. In summer it would be luxuriant, plainly, but now it was forlorn in its powder of darkness and winter. In a corner, a stone statuette, that seemed of a woman, stood smothering in snow.

The garden door shut itself with a *clack*. Next instant, something whirred, and a nightingale burst into shrill song on the bough of a peach tree not a foot from Jaisel's head.

"God's Heart!" said Jaisel, reacting with deliberate vehemence, since she was alert now, and interested in answers.

"Do not flinch," said the girl, not looking back, still gliding on ahead of her. "It is only a mechanical toy of my father's making."

The second one, then, for the door had been the first.

They passed beneath a pergola and entered a stone yard. The automatic nightingale at once left off its music.

The girl in fur said, "You may bring your beast into the kitchen. There is nowhere else for him. We seldom use the room, though there are rushes down. The hearth above suffices for our needs, my father's and my own."

"And is your father," said Jaisel, "an alchemist?"

"Oh, a very great alchemist, I assure you."

"A sorcerer, would you say?"

"A man of science, versed in astrology, in the lore of plants and locomotive creatures, and wise in machineries." The latest door before them was ajar, and dull illumination seeped around it. "My father," said the fur girl, eddying through, "has invented marvels. He has made a ship which will fly through the air for one whole mile. A javelot cannon which would fire itself without the aid of a man. But he does not broadcast his genius. He experiments and creates solely for the sake of knowledge. Here he lives quietly, and I tend him. He is a great man. I am fortunate to have been born his daughter."

They were in a kitchen. Syrupy light entered from a stairway, showing a dead hearth and lack of all furniture. But, after the night, the room felt warm, and Jaisel shuddered.

"Come," repeated the girl, wafting over the kitchen rushes.

"Wait. If I'm to leave him here, I should see to my horse."

"Very well. Do so, then come up. I will tell my father of your arrival."

"Lady, your father may not be as inclined to generosity as you. Don't risk trouble for my sake."

The girl looked over her furry shoulder as she started up the stair. A delicate profile, one velour eye.

"And are you not worth a little trouble, then?"

Jaisel saw to her horse in an uncertain mood. The girl's final archness had somehow not accorded with the naïve simplicity that went before. Though finding it tiresome, Jaisel was prepared to be lenient with other women who sought to remain within the codes, and therefore the securities, of their lot. This was plainly a girl trained to serve the lordly male of the house, reverencing his superior intellect and rights without question, and probably quite happy in her fashion, for only doubt brought misery. And yet, despite her subservience, the girl seemed very sure of getting her way. Maybe, in his turn, the father patronisingly spoiled her. Certainly, no masculine voices bellowed in rage from within, no feminine screams or weeping arose. Only one sound was once dimly audible, a thickened noise, as of a heavy carpet dragged over some floor above. Jaisel paid it no special heed, as she finished with the gelding, and set food for him to eat.

Presently, as no one had come to bid her get out, she went after the girl.

The back stair continued on to the upper rooms of the house. A narrow landing gave on a doorway hung by a heavy curtain of red velvet. As she went by it, the hall of the house opened before her. Jaisel eyed the picture which confronted her.

The title *Alchemist* was not one she loved. Presumably, it had tinted her expectations of the scene she would have to enter. That the scene was so cheerful, so homely, so frankly charming, roused some insidious suspicion in her at once.

The fireplace, which was sunk into the wall, and surrounded by much carved stone, billowed golden-red with fire. On the flags before the hearth, catching its light, a silver pitcher stood, that might have wine warming in it. Tapestries, and metal-bound chests all about, caught also from this light, flaring and fading in harmony. The only lamp in the room was antique, a tall bronze stand, the pale cup dispensing the matchless pinkish glow of flame through alabaster. Between the lamp and the fire, an old man sat in a carved chair. His long grey hair was neatly combed, his long sombre gown immaculate and plain. An open book, the only token of his studies, rested on his lap, and his feet, in their embroidered shoes, were propped on a footstool of dull crimson velvet. By his feet, leaning on his knee, her white furs spilled about her on the floor, sat the alchemist's daughter, in a gown of darkest cramoisie and a stream of blondest hair.

"You are welcome, good sir," said the old man, at once.

*Am I? Let us see.*

Jaisel walked forward, and as she neared the fire, flung back the wolfskin cloak. A yard from him she said, "My name is Jaisel."

The old man nodded.

"Welcome, then, Jaisel. You sound to be a young man, as indeed my daughter tells me you are. When one is young, the world is an adventurous country. But it's a cold night to be adventuring in."

Jaisel looked at the alchemist closely, her heart drumming slow but hard. What was wrong here? She took in the elderly face with its fire-delineated fissures, and the two bright eyes.

"And may I," said Jaisel, "inquire your name?"

"A poor name, for a poor scholar. I am Parrivot. Ghisanne," he added, also revealing the name of his daughter, "Ghisanne, pour us some of the wine now. It should be warmed."

The girl rose instantly and went to do as he asked. While she saw to the wine, Jaisel watched the old man. His glittering, unblinking eyes had followed Ghisanne, very slowly. The fire struck against his eyeballs, and Jaisel started. The flame had passed straight through them; they appeared to dissolve. And so she saw they were not eyes at all, but extraordinary simulacra of glass. Before she could prevent herself, she had taken a step back. A clever alchemist indeed. Blind, no wonder he did not spy her a woman. But where had he lost his eyes . . . maybe better not to wonder. It seemed he did not wish her to know his debility, or why else don the replicates, why else pretend to read the book? But the fire had outwitted him.

The girl came to her with a silver wine cup with handles of ivory. Would this Ghisanne now tell her father his error? For sure, the girl could now see her own mistake in the matter of Jaisel. Her back to her father, Ghisanne smiled up at Jaisel. Very innocently, very wickedly, one black eye shut itself. A wink of complicity, no less.

Jaisel concluded herself in an odd household. But the fire warmed her, the horse was cared for, the wine smelled rare and was the colour of Ghisanne's gown. Possibly, such wine was poisoned, or drugged. And possibly the roof might fall, or God decide to end the world tonight. Speculation was a curse. Ghisanne had brought another chair to the fire. Jaisel sat in it, and drank with a sigh.

The dinner was simple. Bean soup and wheaten bread, and little cakes flavoured with honey. The girl ate little, but had prepared the food at the fire, as she had previously said she did. The soup kettle was hung from a hook, the bread and cakes already baked on a well-bleached stone. Jaisel, who many times had cooked less carefully at campfires, was intrigued by the girl's graceful dignity at her tasks. No doubt, the wine had a mellowing effect, combined with the warmth of the room. The old man, his glass eyes on Jaisel's face, or thereabouts, eyes now candidly real, now patently false, asked for news of outer lands. "I am a hermit, I fear. In these mountains, we know little of how the world goes on." Jaisel told him of current wars, which king ruled where, and the state of trade and lawlessness. In return, she asked about the local feast, the Light of Angels Night, though she was not remotely interested. Nor did the alchemist appear to be; he dismissed it with a word and a smile. Clearly, he himself did not celebrate, or allow Ghisanne to do so—no doubt wise. In some other house the girl might meet eligible young men eager to take her from her father's service into theirs. Strange that Parrivot let her out to draw water, but then that would be a necessity. Did he even know how beautiful his daughter was, or had he lost his sight before she grew to maturity?

Jaisel found it difficult to keep her own gaze from Ghisanne. There was a sort of endless fascination to each turn of that head, the waterfall of glistening hair, the supple waist and sculptured hands. Her skin was so pure it seemed almost possible to stare right through it at the blood, as one could stare at the flame through the lamp. It must be exquisite to touch. Jaisel found she had lost track of the old man's monotonous voice.

"—And, should you care to see, I'll demonstrate a few of them for your pleasure."

"My delight," said Jaisel, wondering what she had agreed to.

"Ghisanne. Go up and fetch my little ones to me."

"Yes, Father."

Mild irritation at his beneficent order-giving caused Jaisel to shift slightly in her chair. As she did so, the girl's eyes met hers. And again, peculiarly, Ghisanne winked. "I must humour him, poor blind old thing," this wink seemed to say. It unnerved Jaisel. Though she disliked the high-handedness demonstrated by most men, equally offensive to her, though more excusable, was the sly returning malice of women. Fed, warmed, wined, sheltered, accepted, the wry thought came suddenly to Jaisel: *I had rather be in the kitchen with my horse. I don't care for games.*

But Ghisanne had gone out through the red velvet curtain. Jaisel heard her first light step ascending, and then, directly overhead, there came again that other sound which Jaisel had formerly heard, at greater distance, from the kitchen. A sluggish, dragging *shift.* A moment's disorientation. She and Parrivot were here, the girl had only just started up the stair. Who, then, was above, to haul carpets or other furnishings about the floors?

Jaisel looked at Parrivot, who apparently had not heard the unpleasant noise. Deaf, too? Or was he accustomed to the sound?

Fetch down my little ones—whatever moved upstairs did not give an impression of littleness.

The sound suddenly came again, if anything more heavily and loudly than before.

"What," said Jaisel, "is that?"

The alchemist smiled at her. "You refer?"

"I refer to that recurrent dragging upstairs."

"Ah, that will be the snow settling on the roof. There's no danger, young sir. Our timbers are solid."

The explanation was so rational and so lucid, Jaisel discredited it at once. As when she had walked into the room and seen the pretty picture of father and daughter in the firelight, her hackles rose. With one deep breath she thrust off her sense of comfort and slight inebriation. Though her attitude and stance did not alter, she was now quite changed.

In another minute the alchemist's daughter came back into the room. She now appeared excited, and was carrying an oblong wooden box in her arms. This she set on Parrivot's knees, and his gnarled, nimble hands reached out to clasp and caress it. Next the lid went up, and folded back. The two hands slipped inside the box. The sightless eyes were bent downward, as if they saw, but the hands scrabbled around, searching. Jaisel was reminded of rats, and the fine hair stirred on her scalp. Rats in a box. And upstairs, what? Another rat, larger than was usual? Alchemists had a name for dark secrets, a name for all things bad. If she cared, she could recall the necromancer, Maudras, and those hellish powers which had even outlived him in the North. But this one, surely, was no Maudras, this reclusive, rather pathetic ancient.

The hands came out of the box. They held a figure some sixteen inches high. It was a knight, so real that for a moment Jaisel doubted her perceptions. Adorned in burnished mail, lace at his throat, his long curled hair hanging on his shoulders, and his cloak of sumptuous blue branded with a gold device.

Ghisanne clapped her hands.

"The knight! Make him fight, Father."

Parrivot chuckled. He put the knight on the extended open lid of the box, and tapped him on skull and spine. There came a dry creaking.

The knight raised his head, and his blue gem eyes met Jaisel's. His hand moved to the hilt of his sword—and for a preposterous second, Jaisel thought herself under challenge—then the jerky way

in which the sword was drawn destroyed the image. He bore the
sword to his lips nevertheless, kissed the cross-piece, and began to
move, with cranky stealth, upon a nonexistent adversary, the blade
cutting the air before him.

"Alas. He lacks oil, to his discredit and mine," remarked
Parrivot. The faint creaking had warned him, where vision could
not.

"But he is beautiful," said Ghisanne in rapturous tones. Despite
the wink, her emotion at this toy seemed feverish and genuine. "Is
he not wondrous, sir?"

"Very," said Jaisel. "I once saw figures on a clock, which moved
in a similar manner. But not so freely."

The knight spun round, and fell over the edge of the lid onto the
floor. Here, as if mortally wounded, he kicked feebly and slowly
waved his sword, gradually freezing back into immobility.

"Too much freedom may be unlucky," said Parrivot, as
Ghisanne hurried to retrieve the figure of the knight and put it back
into her father's hand.

"Father, the princess and the unicorn—" And Ghisanne plunged
her own hands into the box and drew out two smaller dolls. One
was a lady in an ornate headdress of gold wire and glass pearls, the
other a unicorn blond and white as Ghisanne herself, and with a
horn of silver. These two she set down meticulously, the unicorn at
one end of the lid, the lady at the other.

"Don't think I boast," said Parrivot. "But I reckon these a fraction more able than mere clockwork." This time he did not touch
the figures. He whistled, one short thin note.

As the whistle died, the unicorn lowered its head, as if to crop
pasturage. The princess turned, somewhat stiffly, and raised her
arms in their long sleeves. *And she sang.*

> *"All my sorcery is in my chastity,*
> *All my spell is in my piety.*
> *I may tame the savage unicorn*
> *By virtue only, who am woman born."*

Jaisel had not started, but she had now tensed visibly. Her slender hands lay white-knuckled on the arms of her chair. The voice of
the doll was squeaky, yet a voice it was. And now the princess
kneeled, and the unicorn raised its head and took a step towards
her. The kneeling, the step, were a little awkward, yet they had
been summoned by one single whistled note.

The princess sang another verse, which Jaisel did not hear, or at least, only the voice singing it. The unicorn approached and laid its head in the princess's lap.

"Is it not wonderful!" exclaimed Ghisanne, like a happy child.

"I am sure," said Parrivot, "our young guest has seen greater wonders than these on his travels."

"Seldom," Jaisel said. "But then, sir, these dolls work by means of witchcraft rather than mechanics."

Parrivot took the dolls and put them back in the box. Quite genially, he said:

"I prefer to call it science, young man. There is no huge blasphemy in tinkering with inanimate things. These little ones of mine do no harm, and may please. The enduring curse of God is, I have come to believe, only upon those experiments which deal with living flesh." As he said this, his smiling face sank in on itself. Jaisel beheld the marks of pain and long-cold fury washed to the surface of him, as if by a strong tide. It seemed he himself had committed such experiments, and felt himself accursed for them. She pitied him, and she distrusted him greatly, but she nodded.

"Your learning's beyond my shallow understanding, sir. If I spoke without courtesy, put it down to my tiredness, if you will. I've ridden more miles today than I care to remember."

"Then you must hurry to your bed," said Parrivot, his face growing benign again.

"I would not put you to such trouble."

"None, I assure you. There are several chambers upstairs, and Ghisanne has already lit candles and fire for you, and put a hot stone between the covers."

Jaisel got up. She bowed. She visualised, with some bitterness, the comfort of the bed and the miracle of sleep, neither of which she would allow herself in this house.

"Ghisanne. Take our guest to his chamber."

"Yes, Father."

Ghisanne glided towards the curtain, and Jaisel, saying an unctuous good night to the sorcerer, took up her wolfskin and went after.

They ascended the gloomy stair in silence. Above was a twisting passage, lit by a scatter of candles standing on chests which here and there lined it.

Ghisanne pushed open a door, and Jaisel glimpsed a brazier of live coals, a curtained bed, candleshine. As she walked in, Ghisanne ventured timidly, but determinedly, to follow.

"I must read to my father for a little," said Ghisanne. "Then he will go to his bed, which is in an annex leading from the hall."

Surprised to be offered this information, Jaisel turned to look at her. Ghisanne lowered her eyes.

"He is very kind to me," said Ghisanne. "I love and honour him dearly."

Jaisel repressed an urge to argue.

"But," murmured Ghisanne to the floor, "I am also very lonely."

Jaisel turned to stone, but to a stone whose blood thrummed.

"You will despise me," whispered Ghisanne, "but the moment I saw you in the light of the window—I think I have fallen in love with you. I know you cannot stay here, I know you will soon be gone—but—I entreat you—" Ghisanne raised her morning head, her midnight eyes. Her face was pale, passionate, and lovely. "Come to my bedchamber tonight. I will tap on your door after my father is abed. You should count a few minutes, then follow me. I will show you my door— Oh, for the love of heaven, grant what I ask, sweet sir!"

Jaisel winced. Clearly the conspiracy she had interpreted had been the wrong one, and she remained male, still.

"I thought," she said, "he was blind, not you, lady."

"Do not make a mock of me. I do love you, or I would not be so immodest as to petition you in this way, most handsome, handsome knight."

Jaisel took a breath. Slowly and carefully she said, "If you wish it, I'll come to your chamber. But I must stress first, I am no man. If it's a man you require, you will be sadly disillusioned."

Ghisanne's eyes were vast. She looked as if she were about to weep.

"I *love* you," she obstinately wailed.

"I am no *man.*"

"What does it matter? Love is love."

"So it seems," said Jaisel, uneasily.

Ghisanne flitted back into the passage, and beckoned. Jaisel cautiously pursued.

"There is my door. Allow me a short space after I tap, to prepare myself."

"Sweet, silly girl," Jaisel said. "What would your father say? He's a magician, and may yet turn me into a toad."

"You would make a very beautiful toad," opined Ghisanne.

Jaisel put out one hand to touch the flaxen storm of hair, but Ghisanne darted away.

"Not yet," she said coyly. "Do not mistake the door."

"I shall not. What is the other, by it?"

"My father's study. Do *not* enter there."

"Excellent advice."

Ghisanne whirled, and sped away down the passage. At the corner she turned, winked boldly again, and was gone.

Jaisel withdrew into her own chamber, her nerves taut as bowstrings. Just as she was closing the wooden door, she heard, louder than ever, the sinister heavy dragging sound that had alerted her below.

She shut the door and leaned on it.

Obviously, there was some fourth creature in the house, something of "living flesh" Parrivot had experimented with, in the way of his kind. A hybrid vileness, now kept, in apparent bizarre proximity to the bedchambers. In the sorcerer's study? Plainly, the girl did not fear it. Or pretended she did not. Men put up with rats, alchemists with monsters.

Jaisel touched the hilt of the sword on her hip, just as she breathed deeply of the cold night, viewing, as she did so, the long drop to the yard and the walled garden. In the white snow, the small and distant statue gleamed less whitely.

Jaisel touched the hilt of the sword on her hip, just as the clockwork knight had done.

It was rather more than an hour later that the tap came on the door. Jaisel, who had fallen to pacing up and down the room, grew motionless.

She had used the hour to think. Her thoughts had grown progressively less kind. She had been offered a romantic romp by a damsel who did not, it transpired, care if her partner were male or female, and in a room adjacent to the den, or prison, of God's Hosts knew what. And all this quite literally over the head of an unsociable mage, suddenly inclined to house a guest, who had ingenuously allowed this—unknown, male—guest to bed twenty paces from his cherished daughter. Jaisel had formed a series of conclusions, and, as she paced, had frequently warmed her swordfighter's hands.

Post tap, she squandered almost half of another hour before she stepped out into the corridor. The suspense, after all, should not be all on one side—hers.

In her right hand, unsuitable as it might be for a lover, she grasped the drawn sword; in her left, one of the candles so fortuitously left for her. Reaching the door that had been pointed out to

her as Ghisanne's chamber, she walked noiselessly by it. As noiselessly, she set her blade to the latch of the forbidden door, and
eased it up. There had been some chance it might be locked. She
had been prepared for violence. An acrobatic swordsmaster had
taught her tricks of lock-breaking, using obliquely angled blows of
the heels. But none of that proved necessary. The door gave way at
the latch's lifting. Jaisel stalked into the room, candle raised to
throw maximum light, sword glinting malevolently.

What she saw stopped her in the first stride.

She had expected to find the girl, likely in company with her
father. What followed, probably, would not have been ideal
behaviour between host and guest. But at least neither would it
have been unlooked for. For Jaisel had concluded that the girl,
rather than being intent on secret seduction, was a lure, well known
to, and doubtless instigated by, Parrivot. Somewhere in his upper
rooms lurked a misshapen beast, which might care for human flesh,
or human blood. Or simply the healthful exercise to be gained
when tearing a victim limb from limb. Why else had Jaisel been
welcomed in where even servants were not permitted, fed, wined,
lulled by toys, save for such a purpose?

Certainly, the girl had come into the town on the lookout for an
unwary citizen, the visit to the well an unbelievable excuse. For it
had occurred to Jaisel that the walled garden showed the results of
lavish summer watering, and that obligated a well to be on the
premises. Possibly hidden under that statuette.

The guest, won over, would respond to the unfailing appeal to
his vanity: I love you. Offered a night of sport with a pretty girl, an
innocent minx, how could he resist? As for the noises of the beast,
having no cause to distrust his affable benefactors, he would put it
down to snow on the roof, as intended. Ignoring the notion that in
fact it seemed to come from one of the rooms along the passage.

Jaisel had deduced that the monster dwelled in the room
Ghisanne had shown as hers. Crouched in darkness, it waited to
devour what hastened amorously in on it. The devilish father and
daughter would meanwhile attend, in an adjoining room, the clash
of sword on hide, conceivably swordproof, the shrieks of one
quartered alive, the slobberings of one which fed.

In the chamber which Jaisel had invaded, however, there was
neither monster nor daughter nor alchemist. There would have
been scant space for them. Five paces in, the whole area was taken
up by an enormous mechanism, incomprehensible. Rods of brass

ran up, and spirals of bronze coiled down. Wheels slowly turned, and pendulums bypassed each other. The rods were taller than a man, the spirals likewise. The wheels were from some giant's cart. The pendulums from his clock.

Jaisel stared, the sword drooping, the candle flickering. So much that moved, and yet was silent—even as she thought it, there rose out of the depth of the extraordinary engine a noise; large, awesome, and—by now—familiar. It was after all, then, no monster lugging its bulk about the floor, but something grating in the heart of this machine—perhaps ludicrously, as with the dolls, from want of oil.

As the noise died, another came from the passage.

Jaisel sprang round.

Framed by the doorway, she saw Parrivot, his arms weirdly outflung at her, blind eyes gleaming, all of him hideously half-lit by the candles on the chests, lurching towards her. As his lips parted, she anticipated a malign incantation, but all he cried at her were the words: "No—if you are here—do not touch. Beware."

Jaisel moved into the doorway of the room, sword idly swinging in his direction.

"Oh, I am always very wary, sir."

Parrivot halted. He said, pathetically, "Thank God for your safety. I could not hurry to you, I am blind."

"And reckoned me blind, too."

The other door, which truly led to Ghisanne's chamber after all, flew open. Out came Ghisanne in a cloud of nightgown, and hurried to the old man.

"Here I am, Father. Everything is well."

"No," he said. "I fear our guest's too clever for me."

"You knew she invited me," said Jaisel. "What was the purpose behind it?"

"A moment, sir," Parrivot said. He turned to the girl. "Ghisanne, go to bed now. As you said, everything is well."

Unprotesting, Ghisanne moved back to her door and passed through it with a dulcet, "Yes, Father." And as the door closed, one black eye winked at Jaisel.

Jaisel cursed.

"The favour of the truth, sorcerer."

"Yes. Well, then, be so good as to follow me downstairs. Due to my infirmity we must move hesitantly, but will arrive. Be patient. And be so kind, if you will, as to shut the door to the mechanism."

Jaisel did as he said, and walked after him, drawn sword still ready, though she set down the candle when they reentered the hall.

Parrivot tottered to his chair, and sat in it. Jaisel became very angry with his sorrowful, evil, well-meaning face.

"Sir, you may not see it, but I have honed steel in my hand. I can kill you one jot faster than you can spell me, I think."

"That might be a kindness."

Exasperated, she came and stood over him, where he could feel her shadow come between him and the heat of the hearth. He sighed, and said, "Hear then, cunning boy. You were to be part of an experiment of mine."

"So I guessed."

"It would not have hurt you. You might have been happy in it. You were to bed with Ghisanne, as she pledged you, that was all."

"You value your daughter highly, it seems."

"My daughter. I'll tell you of my daughter. She was everything to me. A flower, an angel. When my studies had seen me driven from the regard of my fellow creatures, when, in their damnable ignorance, they hated and shunned me, and I must live from their sight, then Ghisanne stayed at my side, to comfort and to care for me. A warm and living flame in my darkness. And then, she grew sick. I worked with my arts to aid her. I did things, unholy things. I was prepared to do anything indeed, if it would save her life. But rather than save her, my magic deformed her. At length, it killed her. She died on the night of the festival, the Light of Angels. But all the light died with her. Under that little statue in the garden, that is where she lies now, although that is not the first grave she had. And when I had laid her in that first grave, I did a terrible thing in my grief. Hazard? No? I put out my eyes which had seen the horror of her malformed corpse. I blinded myself."

Jaisel moved aside. She let the fire fall over him again, withdrawing even her shadow from touching him. But she waited, knowing there would be more.

"From my arts," he said, "I had means to heal my wounds, though not my sight. To begin with, I welcomed the void of nothing, which now was all I saw. What use was sight to me? What could I see anymore that would bring joy? The men and women who, if they ever came near me, would shun and hate me? The empty rooms where my daughter was not? But in the end, I wearied of it, that void. Then I made—no matter how, or with what help—a pair of magic optics, these you see now, and set them in my head. You think me blind, and so I am, but only to particular things. Such as yourself, or other worthy humans. All things sorcerous, with these eyes I can behold. I can read my books, I can conduct my science. I can even watch my performing dolls, since these are magical, too. It was from my researches with such dolls that I adopted a certain idea. And worked upon it, till it was perfection. For if a doll could sing, why should it not talk? And if talk, why not converse? And if converse, why not eat and drink and dance, and do all things mankind does, only more sweetly? Yes, perfection. You were to be the last test of that perfection. But I do not flatter you. Any traveller would have served. Served better, for you failed me."

"My abject apologies," Jaisel said. She shivered, knowing, disliking, what came next.

"I think you have your answer now," said Parrivot. "For, if I can see only magical things, then I will contrive as many as I am able, and if Ghisanne is dead, who is the damsel that asked you to her chamber? Let me swear to you, my daughter was ten times more lovely than the simulacrum I made of her. And I would have cut you in half before I let you lay one finger on her, if she had not been a doll."

Jaisel caught up her cloak and flung it over her shoulders.

"I was to prove, then, your doll seemed human in every situation, however intimate."

"As the creator, I'd have liked to know. She is so very real in other ways. I think she herself has come to believe she is real."

Jaisel had reached the curtain. She knew she would be allowed to leave, though her heart raced.

"Real?" she said. "Yes, real enough. In a world where most women are no better than dolls, a doll might pass as human. But one day, old man, *one* day—"

Rage choked her, though she was not sure it was rage. She thrust through the curtain, and ran down the stair.

In the kitchen, the horse moved at once to her, and she embraced his cool and living neck before leading him out, across the yard, the garden, and by the statue on the grave. The mechanical nightingale was silent, but the garden door opened to let her escape. In the street, she mounted. The snow was deep and still, the air was raw, but the sky had cleared. In the east a tinsel greyness had begun.

Lost in her thoughts, which were abstract yet dismal and veined by incoherent dread, she scarcely noticed the town that was to have been her wintering as she rode down through it. There was nothing to attract her attention. In the pale blackness of pre-dawn, not a breath rose from the houses. Blanket-spread in snow, weary after its revel of lights, it slept deep as some single thing. Not even a dog barked. There was not a ghost of movement, either, no cat on a roof, no solitary lamp left burning. The whole town was dumb, was dead, as if—

Jaisel reined in abruptly. She looked about.

Suddenly she urged her horse at the nearest house, towards the darkened glass of the windows. Through these windows, and others like them, as she entered the town, she had seen feasting, dancing mirth. Now she leaned close, peering in, and saw—and saw a tableau of motionless unlit figures, stuck in foolish attitudes, a cup raised high, a hand raised higher. She hurried the horse to the neighbouring house, and to the neighbour of that. Wherever she could look in, she did so. Each time she saw the same. Men shunned him, he had said. They had deserted the very town, it seemed, and Parrivot had filled all the houses with his toys, which he could see, and which were civil to him. Toys almost as fine as Ghisanne, toys that danced and drank and sang. Like figures on a clock. But now the clock had stopped.

They reached the square, where the well stood mantled in a white fur of snow, as the girl had been mantled in a white snow of fur.

Jaisel kicked the gelding harder than was her wont, and they ran for the gate . . .

. . . which stood open. And as they clattered through it, Jaisel looked and saw the man in leathers poised almost where she had left him on the street. His eyes were wide. Two silver coins shone in his palm. And snow piled thickly on his head and shoulders.

They flew down the road, Jaisel and the horse, and away from the gate of the town.

She swore she was sorry, as she kicked the gelding to go faster. Only when they reached the outcropping did she slow him, and then rein in again, appalled by their incautious gallop along the narrow mountain road.

One quarter of the sky was hollowing now, and turning to water and soon to light. Behind her, she heard the ominous sound of snow slipping from some mountain peak. Something in that sound made her uneasy, made her wish to look back, and yet, not wish to. As she had come towards the far side of the outcropping, on her arrival, she had heard that same dim boom of a snow-slip. It was a common enough noise in the winter uplands, she had not thought it might be anything else. And yet, now she imagined some mechanical signal, some sorcerous device of warning, buried in the road. She saw again the welcoming lights of the town bloom out like a garden of golden roses, as if at some cue.

Stiffly, Jaisel turned her head and looked behind her.

A mile back up the slope, where the slab of rock had been which was the town, was an empty vista of darkness and distance, swelling as the sky lightened and filled it in. Jaisel continued to look at it, and it complied by growing more and more visible as emptiness. Where the town had been, was *nothing*. And she considered the great mechanical engine in the alchemist's room above, the wheels, the pendulums, like the heart of some enormous clock.

She clicked her tongue to the horse, and let him make his own pace around the outcropping. However much she wished to be away, the road would be treacherous, particularly under the heavy snow. Stunned as she was, it was not until the sun rose that she saw the ground, the down-slopes of the mountains, were bare and dry.

Last night's snowstorm, it appeared, had been rather limited.

# TAMASTARA

**M**ISE EN SCÈNE

The sunset. It shocked him.

Natural things sometimes did startle Renard. It came from having spent so much time in stylised environments—not necessarily orderly, not predictable, but simplistic. Or else it came from spending so much time inside the world of his own skull.

The sun had almost vanished when there had been a sudden throwing open, as if of colossal doors. A blast of marigold light burst out like a wall of water from a broken dam. Everything flamed in it, and drowned. The shoulders of the ruin seemed made of molten honey, and from the jungle rose a swarm of parrots which dived upwards to their tenements among the carving. And then the light, the entire day, faded and went out, and in eighteen seconds there was darkness. Quietness came, too. The never-ending *clink-k-k* of a coppersmith bird miles off in the valleys below, which had driven him crazy all afternoon, fell silent at last. Only breezes and beasts moved now, rustling and breathing through the jungle forests on every side.

Renard had landed the ten-foot shuttle untidily between the temple roofs, then let the craft nose forward until hidden deep in the vegetation which sprang from them. From above, or beneath, it was invisible. He had also smashed the controls, anything that might be detected by sensors. Only heat-seeking devices were a threat now. But there were many warmth-radiating live things all about him on the surface of the Asian earth.

Further procedures were straightforward. He would stay put a few days, in case any of the others should reach him. Then move on to the border. But relentlessly, despite this lucidity, his mind shifted and went back, and he clenched his fists. The strato-station, weather control for half the northern states of the Azad, was a prize they had deemed worth gambling for. But they had failed. The violence, panic, and confusion of the aborted mission filled him again with wrath and fear. He had escaped with others of his party, the sirens wailing, the guards running with their guns. The life-shuttle had stalled in the lock as automatics tried to block the exit, but he had fought and cursed and screamed and torn the craft free as if by will alone. The lock had blown behind him, he heard it go, a dull soft boom of sound.

He shuddered and wrapped his arms about his thin body in the heat of night. Even when there had been success, he would be devilled in the aftermath by possibilities of calamity that had not occurred. This time, calamity was real. (Don't think of it then, Renard, if it bothers you. Make plans. Look about.) But it was black now, the temple had turned to ebony. The trees that rooted in the paving sighed, and up there they sighed too, where they stretched out through the roofs of the pavilions with the lacelike walls. Where the shuttle was hidden. Hansjosch had taken a shuttle, too, and been behind him, entering the lock. Had Hansjosch run clear before the pressure blew? Oh, God—and why say that, when he believed in no such thing—what a mess they had made of it. And after all, for what?

Something about the temple, eons old, had leaned on him harder than heat or cold or fear. The relentless note of the barbet, hammering out its eternal order of minute copper implements in the jungle, had tortured his ears like drops of scalding water. And the shock of sunset, an incendiary blast— There had always been doubts, always inevitable depressions after the great highs of anger and power. But these doubts were more terrible. For suddenly he could make no sense of any of it. The politics to which he had devoted his life, for which he had been prepared, in moments of extreme passion, to *give* his life—what had he done? Why? How did it happen that he had felt called on to do it? It was no use. No act of his had achieved anything. While every act was clothed in bloodshed, misery for the massed faceless peoples, that in setting out they had howled to liberate and save. But there was worse, far worse. For who was he, and what did it matter, these things he had courageously or stupidly or mistakenly done, or what became of him, as a result?

TAMAS

For a quarter of a century, the waters of Mother Ganges had not flowed beside the holy city; instead the *ghats* descended to a saffron marsh. Yet here still the pilgrims sought their ritual ablutions between the mud and reeds, in bubbling ponds like clear champagne. Sometimes, as the sun rose, they were distracted. Half a mile downstream from the marsh and the ancient suburbs, High Varanasi dawned visible, a cloud floating in the early sunlight, an island on long legs balanced over the river.

High Varanasi did not replicate the Islamic architecture of the old city. Upon its milky pillars, it had blossomed with the flowerlike shapes of India's morning kingdoms, made over again in the materials of her future. At sunrise the cloud-island shone. But after dark it glowed and glittered fantastically. Every night was *Diwali* for High Varanasi, a festival of lights up in the air.

Easy enough to access, it too had its pilgrims. As the Ganges served the dream of the soul, so the cloud-island served the spiritual intellect. More esoteric, less dependent on faith than on technology, High Varanasi was a sphere of secrets. Religion being the fount of ideals, it had also acted as a perfect camouflage against the prying generalised interest of more worldly regimes. There were several secrets here that went unknown by any, save those in need who blindly sought them. A kind of faith, then, after all.

When the young woman began to scream in High Varanasi of the secrets, a computer relay in the adjacent room thrummed with activity; and fell silent only as she did.

"You see, Controller," said the pandit.

The Controller said quietly, "She is *Kasha-Triy*?"

"Yes, by birth and also by caste."

"Warriors are the most prone we find, do we not? And sometimes the priestly *Brahma*. So far, the scholarly *Brahma* remain immune, to our knowledge."

"There was the young *Brahma*-born Slave who came to us."

"Quite so. I'd forgotten. But the Slaves are the saints-to-be. Distress is often adapted swiftly into learning for a Slave. Do I mistake, or did the Slave not extricate himself?"

"Exactly, Controller."

"But the *Kasha-Triy* will not be able to. We must *see* to fight, eh, my pandit?"

The pandit smiled. "She said to me today we only tortured her, for amusement."

"Well. She's been suffering some months. I think I should visit her now."

They went along the corridor together, walking slowly, two slender straight old men stepped from a *stupa*-carving. The eyes were very young in the old heads, the slow walk very limber.

At the door of the cubicle they announced themselves, and paused until let in.

It was a small room, open on one side to the stars of the warm night, and the starred lights below, and below that again, far, far down, the ghost-shimmer of the antique city on the river. The girl stood by her window. She said, "Have I performed enough for you, masters?"

"It's not unusual to feel bitterness," said the pandit. "Others have passed this way, in rage and terror, as you do."

"And what happened to them? It's a fine high window. Is suicide common?"

"Exchanging one act of darkness for another? We don't encourage it. Turn round, if you will. The Controller has come in with me."

The girl did turn. She stared at both of them. Her look of fear was absolute. Her eyes had it, her mouth, her hands, the line of her shoulders and her spine.

"The computer has all this while been working," said the Controller quietly. "Your match is now established."

The girl relaxed, but it was the toppling relaxation of another wave of fear, a different wave. Then, generative and spiritual *Kasha-Triy*, she stood up in the midst of the wave and said, "Tell me what I have to do. I'll do it. I'll do anything."

"I know," the Controller said serenely, with great compassion.

ENTR'ACTE

Renard woke because the barbet bird, like an infallible unnecessary alarm clock, had once more begun its coppersmithing in the jungle. *Clink-k-k; clink-k-k.* "Taisse-toi," Renard said aloud, and in Hindi, for the bird's benefit, "Be quiet." But the coppersmith paid no attention. Presently the man got to his feet, stiff from his sleep on the hard stone and the roots which pierced it. Light poured through this cell of the old temple. It showed faded red worshipful daubings on a phallus of yellow marble, and the blurred sweet limbs of stone dancers twining the columns. It showed also Renard himself, the tension of his features, brooding, unattractive, the long Frankish nose, the twisting mouth, and the beautiful eyes.

Someone seemed to be watching him. He had felt this sensation last night, after the sunset, writing here in his agony of doubts. But he had taken a reading from the small analyser his organisation supplied him. It was negative. No one watched. As for doubts, sleep eased all that. They would return, probably, with the dark. Or if he thought for too long.

He sat out in the sunshine and ate two slabs of the concentrated food from his shoulder-kit, then reached for the crumpled cigarettes. The rainwater in the handy cistern was full of creepers and scum, but he drank it, swallowing with it an antitoxicant capsule. A day or two now, that was all. Wait to see if Hansjosch had made it, or the others. They, but they alone, could trace him via the locater.

Later, he explored a little, the rambling stairways, the broken pavilions. The upper terraces reeked of the bats which hung inside the towers like ripe black fruit not to be plucked. The wholeness of the ruin troubled him, and eventually he lay out on a high open roof, absorbing the sun, smoking, listening to the ceaseless metal note of the bird. The sensation of being watched, which he supposed was guilt, did not abate.

TAL

Below on the *ghats* of the ancient city, the body of a Slave was being burned with great ceremony. The passing of a saint-to-be seldom went unmarked. The chants were robbed of force by distance, but great coils of smoke rose and fireworks exploded as the sky darkened. Who knew but that the next incarnation would bring fulfillment? The next incarnation. Whatever the caste, one looked forward, with joy and a certain consternation, and with hope, always with that.

"*Karma?*" the young woman said, standing beside him. The Controller turned to her gravely. "I mean," she said, "am I now paying the price for previous wrong-doing?"

"*Karma* isn't paid in suffering, but in *work*. Hard work, often. And sometimes indeed the labour involves pain. But pain, suffering, is the by-product, not the goal. The system of *Karma* promotes learning, never punishment."

"Then—"

"You are a musician," the Controller said.

"I *was*, before all this. . . ."

"Visualise *Karma* as a rhythmic musical cycle of the *raga*. A deed repeated, developed upon, so altered. Remember also that through a talent, one may often achieve whatever one needs to achieve, and pay whatever needs to be paid. While learning all one has set out to learn, in this life. Or, all that one is willing to learn. Time is endless. No lesson need be hurried, unless the need to hurry is itself integral."

"You're saying what's happened to me will stop?"

"Exactly. If you are brave enough."

"Yes. Most cowards must learn to be brave in the end."

"Your pandit took you to the main computer this afternoon. You've been shown where it is due to happen. You have viewed the apparatus involved. Also, I believe you were tutored in the forms you will need to adopt."

"*Well* tutored." The girl turned back to the visits of the city and the golden marsh that was the Ganges. Centuries ago, she had bathed in the flowing river. She was not a stranger to this place. "Then I know everything. But he doesn't know—doesn't credit—isn't—"

"*He?*"

She paused, thoughtfully. At last she said, "What is it the poet writes? To look into the fire and behold the dark star borne of the light, and the mirror which shows the face of a stranger."

A firework burst in the smoke below, like a fountain of sapphires, and left an afterimage of black veins.

"Come along," the Controller said, still very gentle, like an uncle she had once loved, long dead, long become, maybe, some other she did not know. "It is time, now."

Etat; Rajas

Just as it had awakened him before by staring up, the barbet in the forest woke him on this occasion by unaccountably ceasing. He opened his eyes to intense day sky with the temple towers leaning into it and the arms of trees reaching across it to clasp each other. Before he moved, intuitively, trained, Renard listened and took note. But nothing seemed very different. The shadows were longer, and the air heavier, the dust more peppery, with the approach of sunset. That was all. Then the coppersmith began again, so he cursed it and sat up. And so saw the girl sitting fifteen feet away.

Something happened then that was very strange. He said, stammering slightly because he was surprised at her arrival—noiseless, not waking him—"Oh, it's you."

*"Eh bien,"* she said. *"C'est moi."*

Only then, because she spoke in Eurofrench, the truly familiar reacting against the false, did he realise with a peculiar start that he did not know her at all.

What was it? Still half-asleep, so sure only his confrères could find him, he had assumed that therefore she was one of the women of his organisation, some girl he knew well and had often worked with, probably slept with, *that* familiar, *that* known.

Renard kept still now, save for the hand darting into his jacket, coming out with the little battery gun.

"Don't move," he said to the girl. "You know what this is? It fires electric volts. It can kill you. Do you understand?" He stared at her hard, but she said nothing. Perhaps he had frightened her too much to speak. "Just do as I tell you, you won't be hurt. How did you get up here?"

She smiled then, coldly. She was not afraid after all.

"How do you think?"

Her smile flattened out. She looked at him intently, but he could not really decipher the look.

"I have nothing to do with the government you are hiding from," she said. "Or with any government. I know, however, about your organisation. The taking of hostages, the destruction of property and life. In the name of freedom. Do I have that right? A terrorist." She spoke with an extraordinary loathing. He had listened to similar speeches, from the hysterical, the damned. But there was an extra emotion layered over her words, her voice, her whole body, as she spoke to him. He could not place it. But it bit into him. It followed and joined with his own previous thoughts so seamlessly, so pitilessly.

"Then I know what you think," he said.

"No. But you know I'm not armed. Your clever detection device has told you that. And I'm not here to harm you. And there are no police or soldiers down there, in the jungle." Involuntarily the gun twitched in his hand. "Also," she said, "you could fire directly at me, and not kill me. Not touch me."

He looked her over. He had heard of weapon-shields, deflective auras that could be switched on from a power-source in, say, a belt. But that was only rumour so far. There was no proof that they existed, or that she had one. She had, rather, the smug assurance of the insane. Which could explain everything. Some rich (yes, she looked rich) warp-brained technocrat of the Azad, joy-riding in an expensive silent hover-cruiser, coming on him by accident, wanting to play games.

She was also attractive, lovely in fact. That might have had something to do with the bizarre sense of recognition; the way all beautiful things tended to produce *déjà vu*. Her hair was blonde-white, but the rest of her was from a purely Eastern palette, rose-umber on the skin, liquid jet for the eyes.

"All right," he said eventually, "I believe you think you're safe with me. *I* think you are *mal de folle*. Why are you looking at me like that?"

"*Une folle*," she said, "as you say."

"Watch yourself," he said. "If you make me nervous, something bad may happen."

"I told you, you can't hurt me."

"You told me."

She sat relaxed, and perfect. Suddenly there was a feeling of tenderness so painfully within him, some memory or nostalgia that had no name, he could have wept. Not knowing what to do, he put the gun away. He stood up and said brusquely, "Show me where you left your vehicle."

"I didn't think we established I had one. Did we?"

"Then you walked from where?"

"Oh. Somewhere."

He went over to her, and leaning down he grabbed her arm and pulled her up. The touch of flesh and muscle was somehow astonishing. It was as if he had expected her to have no substance, to be made of paper or of light, a holograph of some sort. But she was actual. He could even smell faint perfume and the underlying scent of young skin, clean pale hair.

"Stop playing." He raised a hand to strike her, the last thing he wanted to do, and she laughed and suddenly tears brimmed out of her eyes. She said: "You make me ashamed."

When she said this, he too felt a kind of shame, so strong it amounted almost to nausea. He let her go, and they stood off from each other. It came to him abruptly that their expressions were now identical, breathing fast, their eyes full of tears. It confused him. He backed away a pace or two. "All right. Sit. Sit down." She seemed only to *decide* to obey him, to humour him, but not from fear. "Now you're with me," he said, "you must stay. There will be others coming."

"Yes," she said.

She seemed very certain. He wondered if despite her opening gambit, she was one of Hansjosch's couriers. But she must have told him by now. Unless Hansjosch-ji himself was playing some game. You could not be sure of Hansjosch.

Renard, too, sat down again. He took out the second-to-last cigarette and smoked it, watching her, thinking all the while she might try to run away, knowing somehow she would not. He had nothing to tie her with, but he would need to tie her, probably. Her dress was a mingled Euro-Asian style, of one of the new fabrics that did not tear. Perhaps her underclothes could be employed. He had roped plenty of women's ankles together by their ripped panties or brassieres.

"If you're good and quiet," he said, "we'll let you go when we move on."

"That's not your usual method," she said. She did not look at him now. She seemed appalled by him, sensitive to what she saw as his offensive villainy. (Like some sweetheart or sister he had let down.) It enraged him. She did not respond like any other he had ever come across, and again he thought of Hansjosch and some curious trick. "You kill," she said now, "normally. Frequently. *You* have killed frequently, in person, by hand. By other means. You needn't answer. I know a lot about you, Renard."

She knew his name, too. *That* was not possible, unless she came from Hansjosch. Then, she was safe, for all he did not understand. Safer than the one who had sent her, certainly. And yet, how had Hansjosch known Renard would bring the shuttle *here?* Even he, Renard, had chosen the ruin randomly. The locater must already have found him out, it was the only solution, and this emissary sent on ahead. (No—don't try to solve the mystery. Smoke, keep calm. Watch.)

"You're not very polite, *ma belle,*" he said. "You've been told my name. What do I call *you?*"

She raised her eyes and looked at him again. She was so beautiful it began to disturb him, not sex exactly, something else, like all of it—just beyond his comprehension. The French that had slipped back into his dialogue also surprised him. His native tongue; he had not used it aloud for years. His organisation kept to an argot all its own. In Asia you talked Hindi or Urdu, or English, or Franca-Rus. In these languages the cryptic messages and the threats were made, the orders given. Yes, he had killed. Yes, he had done all she said and mooted.

He shook himself. Come back. He must question *her*, not himself. Keep a grip on what he meant to do.

"No reply," he said. "What can it cost you, telling me your name?"

She might say, *I don't want you to speak my name, you filth.*

She said, "Tamastara."

He waited. That was all. An Indian name, genderless and poetic. He sensed she lied. It was not her name. And yet, from the way her eyes shaped themselves as she pronounced it, it meant . . . *something.*

"Dark star," he said.

"My name. Or yours."

He grinned. "Black hair, sallow skin. Shadow-with-the-knife; black heart. Why not? Is that what you mean?"

"No," she said.

The cigarette was long finished, and he tossed the butt away into the cistern. It occurred to him, stupidly, how in the far future it might be found, some scrap of symbolic tobacco or plastic filter. Evidence of modern man among the carvings of the temple's antiquity. He had a rushing feeling, as if the world moved differently, or time itself, and the passage of time were visible, audible, and tactile. He would be dead by then, when the piece of cigarette was found, dust, bones, rot. Finished. And then none of it would bother him at all.

He looked at the girl. She wouldn't believe that philosophy, of course. She would believe in the eternal inner life, in *Samsara*, the transmigration of the soul, and in herself as a particle going on and on. There had been one of the *Brahma*, once, under a palm-leaf umbrella on a riverbank. Renard had paused to listen. In a couple of decades the castes had altered, or been amplified. Uninterested, Renard had not fathomed how, only that things were freer among those who favoured the system. In sophisticated circles, there were no "unclean" anymore, that much he knew. And birth into caste was no longer predictable generation to generation. Warrior *Kasha-Triya* might be born of the Artisan class, for example, so

one heard. Scholars and Priests came from the households of Warriors and Slaves. And the Slaves themselves, often menials (where
machines had not ousted menials altogether), were held in esteem.
(On some street a young man sweeping up the orange peel, the
*Brahma* bowing as they passed.) There had been a Slave's crema-
tion he had seen—fireworks, cries of joy, and loud swinging—the
brotherhood of life, of man, continued forever. Liberty, equality,
eternity—

Why was he thinking of that nonsense? It was as if the girl made
him think of it, merely by her Indianity. In Casta, what was she?
Idly, he considered. A *Brahma?* No. A fighter: *Kasha-Triy.*

"*Kasha,*" he repeated. "That's your name."

"*Kasha,*" she repeated. "Your name, too."

Renard laughed, nastily. "Exclude me, if you please. I have no
caste."

"All have caste."

"Only if they believe so."

"It doesn't matter," she said, "if you believe it or not. It *is.*"

"Oh," he said, "and is Hansjosch-ji Casta, too?"

"Hansjosch and I have no connection. He didn't send me to you."

"He sent you. To irritate me, get on my nerves, and soften me
up. For something."

"I could very easily hate you," she said. "And that's funny,
Renard. But there's no time for joking. There's a limit, a radius, just
as trauma is limited. Less than three hours now."

"Yes, yes, talk on," he said. "I don't know what you're saying.
You don't know yourself. But I like to watch. Why don't you come
nearer? We could have some fun while we wait for him, for
Hansjosch who didn't send you."

There was a sudden sound. For a moment it meant nothing. Then
the sky split above them. Renard flung back his head and saw a
white scar all across the brassy blue. The second shuttle from the
strato-station, the shuttle Hansjosch had commandeered— Sweat
broke out all over Renard, and there was an acid taste in his mouth.
He stared at the girl again. "Now we'll see."

She had stood up. She looked frightened at long last. Scared of
Hansjosch? Well. They all were.

After about twenty seconds the tearing note came again, and the
white smoke pencilled over, fast and thin, a dark arrow-head leading it. It was closer now. The roots of the trees seemed to tremble,
and the stone walls. The craft was larger than Renard had thought.
It might carry three or four of the others. They had traced him

through the coded locator, which carried all their body signals like fingerprints. It seemed likely they would be coming down in the thinner scrub on the western side of the terraces.

"Renard."

He glanced over. The girl, Tamastara who was not, had moved nearer. She was very pale, ivory beneath the soft umber. Her blonde hair lay over one shoulder like a white bird's battle-wing.

"Don't worry. I'll tell him you did a good job on me. Pulped me. Made me dance and scream."

"*Pourquoi?*" she said. "Why? *Why?*" She did not mean Hansjosch or the landing.

"Leave me alone, you bitch." He turned his head, and she caught him a stinging blow across one cheekbone. He said, "I wanted to end the pain, a whole world of it—ambition, you concede."

"You resorted to murder to make the murder stop."

"Maybe. I don't know anymore. Yes. I murdered from ideals, from love—I was right, I was wrong. I'd do it again. Will do it. All of it."

"No," she said, "you will not."

The shuttle was making a third turn over the sky, much slower. It began to descend through its own three curdled rings of smoke, roaring. Then its motors choked out as the automatics came on. Trees wavered at the down-draught.

Renard swore at the girl.

"Am I real?" she said. "Do you see me?"

He switched to Hindi and spat the dirty words at her. She let him finish.

"*Çà et là,*" she said. She stood before him, her hair thrust back by the wind from the shuttle, her garments pressed over her body, like the muslin carving on the statues all around. She was so clear, the scent of her so exact, sweet, and the tingle of the blow on his face not yet subsided. Then she was gone.

He was alone.

There was nothing else in front of him but sky, the low sun, the ruin, the empty baking air. While behind him, when he turned, only the shuttle landed in the forest and the trees curtseyed as if afraid.

SAKTI

Just beyond the luminous bank of the computer, the pandit stirred.

"This is the cruelest portion," he said.

"No, that is still to come."

"But, to stand by, as she must."

"She knows. Was she not instructed? She understands the ethics of these things. Without this, she would go mad, or die. The worst is still before her, and she may survive it."

"Sometimes, Controller, as we know, they break on these rocks."

"The *Kasha-Triy* break most often. But the ego is feminine. This may be of assistance."

The pandit folded his hands. His face now was as calm and still as that of the Controller. Each of them had passed, a survivor, through these same waters and these precise rocks, long ago. They knew. Now they prepared, lessoned, guided others, utilising the mighty science which comprised this particular sector of High Varanasi, the intellect of the soul. Until finally, helpless, patient, they too waited, as all men wait, the outcome of destiny and Inescapable Choice.

## Coup d'État

The edges of the forest seemed to burn as the sun again began to set. Out of the burning, Hansjosch walked. There were two others behind him. Renard raised his hand in greeting, and one of the two, a man called Asok, waved back, then let his arm fall as if embarrassed. But Hansjosch was smiling. Thickset, with grizzled tawny hair, his face was vividly marked with brows, nose, eyes, and lips. There was one peculiarity, the third fingernail on the left hand was always painted black, a trademark of hidden significance. No one mentioned it, for he had once half killed a man of the party who did so. As a group leader Hansjosch was a hero, daring, inventive, and slippery. He was feared. Renard feared him.

The bird in the jungle had fallen quiet when the shuttle came over, and not resumed. The girl must have sprung that way, into the shrub and the roped lianas. But she had not. She had vanished, gone out like a light, directly in front of him. An hallucination, then. Or he himself was going mad. There was no space to think about it, Hansjosch thirty feet away, then twenty, ten, five.

"Well, Renard," said Hansjosch, smiling broadly now.

"Well. We got out."

"Yes," said Hansjosch.

Renard was shaking, which must be visible. The way the girl had disappeared, but also Hansjosch half a foot away. Renard tried to laugh. "When the lock blew I—" He saw a flicker, the enamelled black fingernail catching the sun. Then Hansjosch's fist slammed into the side of his jaw. Renard's head snapped back, his neck giving an agonising twang. He landed on the stone, dazed, dazzled by the light in his eyes, and Hansjosch loomed over him, and Asok and Baur craned behind.

"Why?" said Renard.

"Why?" Hansjosch kicked him delicately, not hurting him. "You ran."

"Everybody that could," Renard said; he began to stutter and started again, "everybody ran that could run, Hansjosch."

"Yes. But you. You got ahead of me. You fouled it for me, that exit. You nearly did for me, for us, Asok and me, and Baur."

"I didn't—know—"

"And the mission failed. Three of us died." He jerked his thumb up at the sinking sky. "Up there, in the weather station. And five or six with the guards. If they get a trial, how do you think it'll go for them, eh, Renard?"

Renard lay on the ground. Sweat rolled into his eyes. Behind Hansjosch Baur said sullenly, "So who is to blame? No one. Everyone."

Hansjosch smiled, not turning. He said to Baur: "Close your trap."

Baur shrugged and moved away. Renard saw him sit down against a vertical of carved masonry, looking off into the jungle while the stone nymphs gracefully gestured over his head.

"Are you going to let me get up?" Renard asked.

"Get up. Get on your knees."

Renard moved into a sitting position, all the time waiting for Hansjosch to knock him flat again, but Hansjosch did not.

Renard said, "I carried out my orders. I did nothing wrong. You can't say—"

"No, no." Hansjosch nodded. "It's all right. You did fine." He had stopped smiling. A look of earnest seriousness had come over his face. Suddenly he squatted down by Renard. "We all made mistakes up there. I admit even I, even Hansjosch-ji, made a mistake or two. But you see, Renard, your attitude isn't what it was, your resolve isn't firm enough. You argue, you have doubts. That's bad for the others. And when we go back, accounts have to be squared." Renard did not move now. Hansjosch said, "You see, someone has to carry the can of cream."

Baur was not looking. Asok stood with his eyes solemnly on Renard. As Renard stared back at him, Asok shrugged slightly. He was fatalistic. His eyes said, It could have been me. Next time, it may be me. "That's how it is, Renard," Asok said aloud. Then the embarrassment returned. Asok also turned and walked off.

"You mean," said Renard, "I take the blame for something."

"I mean you have to die," said Hansjosch. He was apologetic now.

Renard struggled to his feet, and Hansjosch was up like a tiger in front of him.

"*Die—kill* me—for *what*?" Renard screamed. He lashed out, but Hansjosch avoided him, politely.

"An example," said Hansjosch, explaining, reasonable.

Renard dodged by the heavier man. He started to run towards the forest, a blazing coil in his guts and his legs like rubber. Somehow he felt Baur and Asok would not stop him, and he still thought this when the volt from Baur's battery gun shocked against his thigh. The muscle went at once into spasm and he fell, yelling and mindless with pain, aware and not believing that this was the end.

## TAN: TAMAS TARA

The pandit sat before certain disciples in a garden high in High Varanasi. Those he spoke to might look at him, or beyond him into the frames of luminous sky where the stars were beginning to come shyly as young girls to a wedding. Away and below, the evening marsh of the Ganges lay still, gilded by a soft dying light.

"The reason for physical life?" the pandit said. "Insofar as it is understood, we are persuaded it is a means to growth. That is, a type of growing, of expanding in knowledge, which is not possible for the soul when in its incorporeal form. The soul, for example, is always happy and tranquil. Happiness and tranquillity, while being of great worth, in themselves are not perfect states." He bowed his head.

"Once," said the pandit, "there was a beautiful garden; ah, far more beautiful than this. It was a wonderful place. All who dwelled there moved and existed in a perpetually gentle though ecstatic condition. But it happened that now and then the Infinite walked in the garden, and on one occasion of His walking, certain of the inhabitants approached. 'Lord,' they said, 'we know that, for all the joy which is our lot, there is a greater joy we have never known, and beyond that greater joy, another greater, and so on, to the unlimited limits of eternal things, joy upon joy. But how are we ever to reach these marvels, for time is stationary here, as we are. Can it be joy greater than joy is to be come on only by standing quite motionless?' The Infinite smiled (for the gods are never without humour). He told those who had approached Him that indeed, there were roads that might be travelled whereby to reach the greater joys, and the joys greater than these. But the roads lay outside the garden, through arid deserts and savage forests, through darkness and sorrow and fear. And the gate to each was a gate of alarm and often of pain, as too was the gate at the road's end that returned them into the garden. Those who had asked the question turned to each other in surprise. They discussed the matter. At last, they said to the Infinite, 'Though it is pain and sorrow and a wilderness, yet we will take this adventure on. We cannot stand motionless. We must go forward. Let us try to learn the way.' The Infinite nodded. And so, bravely they went forth into the harsh and devastating lands beyond the garden. And there they toiled and strove, and flourished and suffered. They invented deeds and dramas for themselves and for others, and enacted them. They laughed and wept. At length their travelling garments and the shoes on their feet were worn out. They cast them off and returned, often with great misgiving, back through the gates of the beautiful garden. And there they cried out in pleasure, for they had mostly forgotten it in their wanderings, and all its refreshment and loveliness. Then the Infinite came walking, and He said, 'What have you learned?' And there was a babble of excited voices as they told Him. 'Good,' said the Infinite. 'Very good. But there is still much more to learn.' And to this, now knowing something of the business, they agreed." The pandit also smiled.

"In this way," the pandit said, "they come and go from the garden, seeking the world, this world and others, toiling and striving, flourishing and suffering, laughing and weeping. And all the while they learn. And all the while they move forward towards the greater joys; never standing motionless. And they are we."

Then for a time his disciples spoke to him and with him about the nature of suffering and weeping, and even of the nature of pleasure, and of laughter. And sometimes the discussion broke in laughter that rang down across the lawns, through the *dhak* trees and the mutant banana palms. Eventually they came to a debate upon *Karma*, of the deeds of one life which might influence the next, and thence to the modern notion of samsaranic trauma. It was rumoured that High Varanasi held a secret method of dealing with this ailment. The pandit did not deny or acquiesce. He did affirm that he was familiar with the poem of the Dark Star, the *Tamas Tara*.

"The comparison is a fair one," said the pandit. "Look at a strong light for a moment, then look away, and a dark patch, the after-image of the light, interferes briefly with vision. This is the dark star of the poet's imagery. The darkness fades swiftly from the eyes. But if the soul, the *atma*, has been exposed to some such strong glare, the resultant afterimage is not always eradicated so easily. The *tamas tara* which marks the *atma* is caused by the strong light of some terror or horror. Though unremembered memories of profound happiness may be retained in a similar way, delight never leaves raw tissue in its wake, unless seriously misinterpreted thereafter. The *tamas tara* is a scar—more accurately, a wound which has not closed. Free of the body, the soul of course understands all this. But on rebirth, when true vision is generally clouded by the flesh, and the *atma* translates itself in part as a function of the brain, the dark star may begin to bear upon the physical persona which does not remember it and sometimes cannot tolerate it. Sometimes, too, the darkness has lain dormant, then by accident the psychic memory is jogged. These are often the worst cases of all. For, while the expressions of samsaranic trauma are mostly mild—the dislike of a particular odour, an inexplicable phobia, a minor illness—now and then a grave disorder to disease may result, even madness. Here in the High City we employ counselling to dismiss, or at least to modify, the condition to controllable proportions. Consider, however, most men and women bear such scars. They are rarely if ever much inconvenienced by them. With so many lives behind us, we have each of us received many wounds. They fade."

"But suppose, master," one of the more wicked students said, "the wound is too deep, and counselling isn't enough?"

The pandit thought of the great computer. He thought of the musician, the ruined temple, the night blackness settling there like the wings of kites, as it had settled here with such kind wholeness.

"*Yaksha*," said the pandit, with some charm, "there is no necessity to demonstrate to you whether or not I can set a broken bone. At least, not until you have broken one."

SAMSARA; MORT

Renard lay on his back, as he had lain now for perhaps two hours. The others had brought with them means of binding, and he had been duly bound. The cords were wound tightly, like swaddling bands, around and around his body, containing all of him and allowing no part of him to move. Like a snake with a smashed spine, legless, armless, he had then been dragged and lodged against an angle of wall. The crooked position and the restriction of his limbs had caused evil rearing pains throughout his body, but mostly now all feeling was gone, save in the muscles hit by the volt, which ached on and on, steadily.

Hansjosch hung about, smoking, eating, poking around the site. So far he had done nothing further. When the darkness came he ordered the small fire lit in the middle of the roof, careless, where any low-flying aerial traffic could spot it. He was not nervous. He would leave Renard the fire, he said, when they went. To keep him company.

Since Renard was to die, to be an example, it was important that his remains be found, of course, by the government troops out searching.

Now Hansjosch came over to Renard and sat down a yard away.

"Not too uncomfortable, Renard? Heh? The circulation stops, then the pain stops. Until the rope comes off. By then you'll be dead. No problem."

"How?" Renard said, but his voice was a croak, the word just a noise. At first he had been so afraid, so startled, his bladder had given way inside the snake-case of cords. He had fought against the griping of his bowels which tried to do the same thing. God knew why. It hardly mattered, did it? Then terror grew leaden, and moved to other areas, a cerebral torture that made him want to cry. But somehow he stopped that too. Crying would not change Hansjosch's plan. Nothing would change it.

He had passed through a stage, as Asok and Baur made the fire, glancing at him sometimes, when he believed rescue might be solicited from them. He had asked Asok for a cigarette with this in mind. Asok had started forward, Baur had pulled him back. "One cigarette," said Renard. "Please."

"*Geen, frend,*" said Baur. Odd, how each native vernacular returned under stress. But there was apparently insufficient stress. Hansjosch ruled the men, and they had no intention of disobeying him, even in disgruntled disagreement. Renard himself had also acted in this way under Hansjosch's command. He knew how it was. It was useless.

"What?" Hansjosch now said, kindly, trying to be helpful. "Ah, you want to know how it will happen? Don't worry, *ami*. I'll see to everything."

A sadist, could it be that Hansjosch was only pretending, bluffing about the proposed murder in order to enjoy Renard's obvious terror? (No, stop dreaming. There's no escape, as you thought at first in this place. This is punishment, retribution. And you don't matter. A tiny insect crushed between two palms. Tell that to the heart, the brain. They fight on, they go on crying out—*let me live!*)

A new white pain shot through Renard's left leg, into his ribs, up through his skull, and he saw Hansjosch had secured some extra cord to his trussed body. The rope was slack, trailing away beyond the fire. Asok was working intently there in the shadow, and the new cord twitched. They were rigging something up.

"Yes," Hansjosch said. "You see? It's all in hand."

There was no point in begging Hansjosch. Renard had seen men beg from him before. Three years ago, forced to watch the spectacle for the first time, Renard had walked out of the room and vomited. A premonition, perhaps.

"Please," he whispered. He tried to keep quiet. "Please."

"Yes?" Hansjosch crowded him attentively.

Renard drew back his lips like a sick dog and spoke rapidly in French. Hansjosch followed most of it. He grunted, and buffeted his prisoner across the head, one-two-three— The fourth blow blotted everything out for a while, not for long, probably. When Renard came to, whatever the men had been arranging was complete. They stood close by, talking to Hansjosch, who suddenly ordered them off. Then they ran, towards the jungle and the large shuttle craft, not looking back. After the footfalls died, there was only the faint crackle of the fire and the noise of Hansjosch, whistling. There he stood, looking up at the stars, tweeting an aria from some popular opera. Presently he seemed to recall he must say farewell to Renard, and looked down at him.

"You see the rope, the rope that goes away over there? Moist-heat seeker fuse. That's it. The end's sitting in dry ice right now, but that's decaying fast. Then it'll come for your body heat. And when the spark inside the tube gets level—well, you know how it works. It should take about ten minutes, fifteen if you try not to sweat too hard. And so long as you don't snap the connection. You remember how the tubes are, once they're fixed? Remember that agent in the Hague, the one who cut the rope off his boss's wrist? Blew both of them out all the windows, huh?"

Hansjosch whistled another plaintive phrase. He took a few steps, turned, looked back. Sincerely, he said, "You were good. It was a pleasure working with you. I'll miss you. I should have dropped this on Baur. Now I'll have to put up with his belly-aching all the way to the border." He glanced at the sky. "With luck, someone might come looking and see the fire. Then you'll have company, going."

He stepped off the roof and downwards; the jungle rustled like harsh paper, and then there was the heavy pounding gallop of his retreat.

It seemed only seconds after that the shuttle roared to life. It rose without lights. A wind swept over, smelling of burned ions, and a blacker blackness that put out the stars, and then the stars and the silence returned.

In the silence there came a small dry *pop*. The noise cut through Renard's system like a jet of acid. Reflex caused him to lurch, and agony broke in his helpless pinioned body, and the sphincters of his sanity gave way as he gagged and howled in terror. But death was running towards him. There was no means of evasion. Even if there had been rescue, now it was too late. These devices of his organisation could not be detached or rendered harmless. There was nothing to do but to lie and wait for the explosion that would tear him open and hurl him free and bleeding and in fragments upwards and sideways, all about. Nothing but to lie and think of it and *know* it and wait for it to be— And again he rolled and cried out, and fell back. And again the silence of the night came in like water, although soon, soon, he would hear the little hissing sound of the spark searching towards him along the tube in the rope.

There was a seasick haze, sweat and fear, mixed with smoke, thick in his eyes. And something pale in the haze. And then the girl walked out of the dark, the haze, stepping over the deadly rope, and kneeled down beside him.

"Don't touch—" he shouted. "Don't touch the cord—"

"I won't," she said. The fire behind her, her pale hair was like a halo of white flame.

"You can't stop it," he said.

"I know."

"Then get out—go on, *run!* Five minutes and it reaches me. It's a *bomb*. You want to go too? Oh God, oh God," he cried. He screwed up his eyes so as not to see her, his ears alert radar bowls for the approach of death.

Her hand brushed his face, and he writhed away from it. She had not been real. (She isn't real.) Some figment of the mind. Or of dying.

But the hand returned, hard and cruel, gripping his face. He opened his eyes, and he saw *her* face, *her* eyes were also wild with terror, and yet she did not leave him. Her terror was held as she held him, cruel and hard, without pity. He could only stare at her.

"The river," she said. "The river flowed by and you sat on the *ghats*, listening to the teachers. Tell me you recall."

"Benares," he said. "Why—why—"

"Now there is High Varanasi," she said, hard as stone, her eyes like stone, her face, the one hand holding him. "Twenty-five years after tonight, the Ganges will have congealed to a golden swamp. But up in the air the secret machines are very busy."

"Get out," he muttered. "If you're really here—"

"Listen to me," she said, "there's only a little time."

"*I can hear the spark in the tube.*" He arched upwards inside the ropes, pushing against her. "Pain—"

"I know about the pain. And the explosion that will rip you apart. I know." She frowned at him. "You've reminded me in dreams every night, for half a year, over and over." As he slumped away, she leaned to him. "*Listen.* You—have only minutes. And I must make this work. But you are an atheist, Renard, aren't you? You call on God, but that is a child crying a stranger's name in the dark. The soul exists, Renard. Your soul. It goes on. Men live for-ever, they never die. Only the body dies." He laughed, coughing and retching at the same time, and she continued relentlessly, her eyes burning down into him. "Your body will die in four—three—minutes. In agony. But the agony was—will be swiftly over. Then the soul is liberated. I can't tell you anything of the liberation. That is the secret place beyond all secrets. We remember only when we return. I'm not your pandit. I'm not speaking of Heaven, or of *naravana*. Only of the body. Rebirth, Renard, do you understand? Rebirth will come after this death. A swift rebirth. But the trauma of this death will haunt you, the dark star, the scar on the soul, and the new life will be destroyed and wasted. Unless I can make you see—"

"Lives," he said. "Lives. *Get away.* Or you'll go with me."

"High Varanasi of the secrets has a secret machine. It can project the consciousness beyond place and through time, and with the consciousness an aspect of the body. Which appears quite physical.

It may be touched, as you have touched me, and itself touch, as I touch you. But it is *not* physical. Though I'm here, I am *not* here. The explosion that will kill you can't harm my body. I shall be with you, Renard, as you die."

"The fuse—the spark," he cried. He battled against her grasp and her look.

"Death," she said. "There is no death. Whatever the horror and despair and hurt, you will live. Why else have I come to tell you this?"

"Who sent you?" he said. His ears were filled by the firm loud hiss of the running fuse. He had no strength left, to right her or to be afraid. "What are you?"

"You knew me," she said.

And in that moment he heard the fuse meet his flesh, and sizzle, and stop in a hammer blow of nothing. And in the spaced moments of the nothing she said, "In the future you will be reborn. I travelled here through time. I am *you.*"

Then the blast came, the thunder, blindness, agony red and white and black, and the words were driven like scattered seeds before a whirlwind, away, away.

## Vedanta

The notes of a *bina* came in from the terrace, the little yellow *bina* the young woman had brought with her, as a child brings a favourite toy to hospital. There she stood now, playing mildly, occasionally altering the frets, the instrument resting left to right across her body, the rising sun gilding the wires and the strands of her blonde hair.

A golden oriole was making music, too, in the gardens below. Farther yet, the pilgrims would be wading in the holy marsh.

Religion and mysticism and teaching. These respected, ethereal things cloaked so much. In an era when repression of action and speech was not unknown, the soul was yet permitted its insubstantial course. In High Varanasi, this course had necessitated many wonders. But the great machines were nameless and unknown to the governments of the earth, who might, for example, see time travel as a thing of temporal power or weaponry, rather than as a means to heal astral wounds.

Presently the girl closed the *bina*'s sequence, and turned. She greeted the Controller civilly.

"Did you sleep well?" he asked.

"Oh, I *did*. For a week I have slept well. And for all the weeks of my life, I now anticipate sleeping well. It's over. A miracle. The wise computer of High Varanasi did all you promised it would."

"The computer is the servant of your need. It locates the past life, it enables you to reach and communicate with that life. But you yourself perform the miracle. You were cured of your malady only by you."

"Then I must have made him believe me— He—myself—must have accepted. . . . But why not? We recognised each other at once. He didn't understand why. I, of course, knew. He was as familiar as a lover. More familiar. And I can see, too, the strangeness, the way I was instructed to behave at first—these things would lend credence to what I told him later. While in such terror he would *want* to believe me. And then again, in the replaying of time, he didn't die alone. Though nothing fundamental might be altered, yet I shared that terrible death. As I've shared it so often in nightmares. But the nightmares have stopped. Perhaps the fault was in me as I am—but in reliving the trauma, second-hand at last—" she broke off. "Complexity doesn't matter, or explanation, does it? I died as Renard. But it's finished. Here I am—*myself*." She smiled. "Until the next life. What then, I wonder."

"The function of our system, as you know," said the Controller, "is to assist, but not to anticipate. For this reason we open the door only to past time."

In English she said, "'What's to come is still unsure.'" She nodded. "All I do know is that I shall receive a hypnotic this afternoon."

"In order that you can never, even inadvertently, betray us, or our technology. You will never forget, you may think and feel as you wish. But never again will you be able to speak of what has happened. This is unreasonable?"

"Oh, I'm more than willing. Anything to protect this place. Poor Renard," she said, gazing across the garden, "fighting in the wrong way against a regime that hasn't altered. Should *I* be fighting? Should I be humbled by him, by his struggle, while I'm playing my music, so easy and so safe? No," she said, answering herself, "that I did, and may do again. After that, it needs this. And besides, the *Kasha-Triy* are always in battle lines. The nature of the combat is all that changes." She looked serious and very young. The mark of *tamastara* lay behind her look, like the cicatrice of an ancient blow, long forgotten. The rest of her was fresh and new as if sprung from a chrysalis. The lesson was complete, the end of knowledge. But the end of knowledge is where knowledge begins. Suddenly, irrelevantly, she said, "He had beautiful eyes. And artist's hands that were never used for anything artistic." Then she lowered her gaze, and began again to bring life out of the yellow *bina* in smooth unbroken spirals.

It was not unusual for the physical component of the soul to fall in love with itself when glimpsed in another body. Renard, who had died in blood and anguish at the very age this young woman now was, had taken up again, through her, the adventure of search and growth. And she was exhilarated by her awareness of this, which seemed almost a benign possession. All that had been curtailed in execution, all that had been left unsaid, could now be resumed, vocalised, given expression, through the one he had become, and that one herself. The messages now were not written in incendiaries or theft or slaughter, but in long skeins of music, folding each into another. But the passionate fight went on, to reach the minds of men, to destroy obscurity and darkness, causing to flow between all life the current that all life contained and was a portion of.

But no profound melody drifted from the terrace. The golden oriole shut off its song as if affronted. A strange noise, a quarter-tone enactment of the French "Marseillaise," obtusely played on a *bina*, squealed over the garden in the risen sun.

Morning had come back to India.

# WHEN THE CLOCK STRIKES

**Y**ES, THE GREAT BALLROOM IS FILLED ONLY WITH DUST now. The slender columns of white marble and the slender columns of rose-red marble are woven together by cobwebs. The vivid frescoes, on which the Duke's treasury spent so much, are dimmed by the dust; the faces of the painted goddesses look grey. And the velvet curtains—touch them, they will crumble. Two hundred years now, since anyone danced in this place on the sea-green floor in the candle-gleam. Two hundred years since the wonderful clock struck for the very last time.

I thought you might care to examine the clock. It was considered exceptional in its day. The pedestal is ebony and the face fine porcelain. And these figures, which are of silver, would pass slowly about the circlet of the face. Each figure represents, you understand, an hour. And as the appropriate hours came level with this golden bell, they would strike it the correct number of times. All the figures are unique, as you see. Beginning at the first hour, they are, in this order, a girl-child, a dwarf, a maiden, a youth, a lady, and a knight. And here, notice, the figures grow older as the day declines: a queen and king for the seventh and eighth hours, and after these, an abbess and a magician, and next to last, a hag. But the very last is strangest of all. The twelfth figure; do you recognise him? It is Death. Yes, a most curious clock. It was reckoned a marvellous thing then. But it has not struck for two hundred years.

Possibly you have been told the story? No? Oh, but I am certain that you have heard it, in another form, perhaps.

However, as you have some while to wait for your carriage, I will recount the tale, if you wish.

I will start with what was said of the clock. In those years, this city was prosperous, a stronghold—not as you see it today. Much was made in the city that was ornamental and unusual. But the clock, on which the twelfth hour was Death, caused something of a stir. It was thought unlucky, foolhardy, to have such a clock. It began to be murmured, jokingly by some, by others in earnest, that one night when the clock struck the twelfth hour, Death would truly strike with it.

Now life has always been a chancy business, and it was more so then. The Great Plague had come but twenty years before and was not yet forgotten. Besides, in the Duke's court there was much intrigue, while enemies might be supposed to plot beyond the city walls, as happens even in our present age. But there was another thing.

It was rumoured that the Duke had obtained both his title and the city treacherously. Rumour declared that he had systematically destroyed those who had stood in line before him, the members of the princely house that formerly ruled here. He had accomplished the task slyly, hiring assassins talented with poisons and daggers. But rumour also declared that the Duke had not been sufficiently thorough. For though he had meant to rid himself of all that rival house, a single descendant remained, so obscure he had not traced her—for it was a woman.

Of course, such matters were not spoken of openly. Like the prophecy of the clock, it was a subject for the dark.

Nevertheless, I will tell you at once, there was such a descendant he had missed in his bloody work. And she was a woman. Royal and proud she was, and seething with bitter spite and a hunger for vengeance, and as bloody as the Duke, had he known it, in her own way.

For her safety and disguise, she had long ago wed a wealthy merchant in the city, and presently bore the man a daughter. The merchant, a dealer in silks, was respected, a good fellow but not wise. He rejoiced in his handsome and aristocratic wife. He never dreamed what she might be about when he was not with her. In fact, she had sworn allegiance to Satanas. In the dead of night she would go up into an old tower adjoining the merchant's house, and there she would say portions of the Black Mass, offer sacrifice, and thereafter practise witchcraft against the Duke. This witchery took a common form, the creation of a wax image and the maiming of the image that, by sympathy, the injuries inflicted on the wax be passed on to the living body of the victim. The woman was capable in what she did. The Duke fell sick. He lost the use of his limbs and was racked by excruciating pains from which he could get no relief. Thinking himself on the brink of death, the Duke named his sixteen-year-old son his heir. This son was dear to the Duke, as everyone knew, and be sure the woman knew it too. She intended sorcerously to murder the young man in his turn, preferably in his father's sight. Thus, she let the Duke linger in his agony, and commenced planning the fate of the prince.

Now all this while she had not been toiling alone. She had one helper. It was her own daughter, a maid of fourteen, that she had recruited to her service nearly as soon as the infant could walk. At six or seven, the child had been lisping the satanic rite along with her mother. At fourteen, you may imagine, the girl was well versed in the Black Arts, though she did not have her mother's natural genius for them.

Perhaps you would like me to describe the daughter at this point. It has a bearing on the story, for the girl was astonishingly beautiful. Her hair was the rich dark red of antique burnished copper, her eyes were the hue of the reddish-golden amber that traders bring from the East. When she walked, you would say she was dancing. But when she danced, a gate seemed to open in the world, and bright fire spangled inside it, but she was the fire.

The girl and her mother were close as gloves in a box. Their games in the old tower bound them closer. No doubt the woman believed herself clever to have got such a helpmate, but it proved her undoing.

It was in this manner. The silk merchant, who had never suspected his wife for an instant of anything, began to mistrust the daughter. She was not like other girls. Despite her great beauty, she professed no interest in marriage, and none in clothes or jewels. She preferred to read in the garden at the foot of the tower. Her mother had taught the girl her letters, though the merchant himself could read but poorly. And often the father peered at the books his daughter read, unable to make head or tail of them, yet somehow not liking them. One night very late, the silk merchant came home from a guild dinner in the city, and he saw a slim pale shadow gliding up the steps of the old tower, and he knew it for his child. On impulse, he followed her, but quietly. He had not considered any evil so far, and did not want to alarm her. At an angle of the stair, the lighted room above, he paused to spy and listen. He had something of a shock when he heard his wife's voice rise up in glad welcome. But what came next drained the blood from his heart. He crept away and went to his cellar for wine to stay himself. After the third glass he ran for neighbours and for the watch.

The woman and her daughter heard the shouts below and saw the torches in the garden. It was no use dissembling. The tower was littered with evidence of vile deeds, besides what the woman kept in a chest beneath her unknowing husband's bed. She understood it was all up with her, and she understood too how witchcraft was punished hereabouts. She snatched a knife from the altar.

The girl shrieked when she realised what her mother was at. The woman caught the girl by her red hair and shook her.

"Listen to me, my daughter," she cried, "and listen carefully, for the minutes are short. If you do as I tell you, you can escape their wrath and only I need die. And if you live I am satisfied, for you can carry on my labour after me. My vengeance I shall leave you, and my witchcraft to exact it by. Indeed, I promise you stronger powers than mine. I will beg my lord Satanas for it and he will not deny me, for he is just, in his fashion, and I have served him well. Now, will you attend?"

"I will," said the girl.

So the woman advised her, and swore her to the fellowship of Hell. And then the woman forced the knife into her own heart and dropped dead on the floor of the tower.

When the men burst in with their swords and staves and their torches and their madness, the girl was ready for them.

She stood blank-faced, blank-eyed, with her arms hanging at her sides. When one touched her, she dropped down at his feet.

"Surely she is innocent," this man said. She was lovely enough that it was hard to accuse her. Then her father went to her and took her hand and lifted her. At that the girl opened her eyes and she said, as if terrified: "How did I come here? I was in my chamber and sleeping—"

"The woman has bewitched her," her father said.

He desired very much that this be so. And when the girl clung to his hand and wept, he was certain of it. They showed her the body with the knife in it. The girl screamed and seemed to lose her senses totally.

She was put to bed. In the morning, a priest came and questioned her. She answered steadfastly. She remembered nothing, not even of the great books she had been observed reading. When they told her what was in them, she screamed again and apparently would have thrown herself from the narrow window, only the priest stopped her.

Finally, they brought her the holy cross in order that she might kiss it and prove herself blameless.

Then she knelt, and whispered softly, that nobody should hear but one—"Lord Satanas, protect thy handmaid." And either that gentleman has more power than he is credited with or else the symbols of God are only as holy as the men who deal in them, for she embraced the cross and it left her unscathed.

At that, the whole household thanked God. The whole household saving, of course, the woman's daughter. She had another to thank.

The woman's body was burnt, and the ashes put into unconsecrated ground beyond the city gates. Though they had discovered her to be a witch, they had not discovered the direction her witchcraft had selected. Nor did they find the wax image with its limbs all twisted and stuck through with needles. The girl had taken that up and concealed it. The Duke continued in his distress, but he did not die. Sometimes, in the dead of night, the girl would unearth the image from under a loose brick by the hearth, and gloat over it, but she did nothing else. Not yet. She was fourteen and the cloud of her mother's acts still hovered over her. She knew what she must do next.

The period of mourning ended.

"Daughter," said the silk merchant to her, "why do you not remove your black? The woman was malign and led you into wickedness. How long will you mourn her, who deserves no mourning?"

"Oh, my father," she said, "never think I regret my wretched mother. It is my own unwitting sin I mourn." And she grasped his hand and spilled her tears on it. "I would rather live in a convent," said she, "than mingle with proper folk. And I would seek a convent too, if it were not that I cannot bear to be parted from you."

Do you suppose she smiled secretly as she said this? One might suppose it. Presently she donned a robe of sackcloth and poured ashes over her red-copper hair. "It is my penance," she said, "I am glad to atone for my sins."

People forgot her beauty. She was at pains to obscure it. She slunk about like an aged woman, a rag pulled over her head, dirt smeared on her cheeks and brow. She elected to sleep in a cold cramped attic and sat all day by a smoky hearth in the kitchens. When someone came to her and begged her to wash her face and put on suitable clothes and sit in the rooms of the house, she smiled modestly, drawing the rag or a piece of hair over her face. "I swear," she said, "I am glad to be humble before God and men."

They reckoned her pious and they reckoned her simple. Two years passed. They mislaid her beauty altogether, and reckoned her ugly. They found it hard to call to mind who she was exactly, as she sat in the ashes, or shuffled unattended about the streets like a crone.

At the end of the second year, the silk merchant married again. It was inevitable, for he was not a man who liked to live alone.

On this occasion, his choice was a harmless widow. She already had two daughters, pretty in an unremarkable style. Perhaps the merchant hoped they would comfort him for what had gone before, this normal cheery wife and the two sweet, rather silly daughters, whose chief interests were clothes and weddings. Perhaps he hoped also that his deranged daughter might be drawn out by company. But that hope foundered. Not that the new mother did not try to be pleasant to the girl. And the new sisters, their hearts grieved by her condition, went to great lengths to enlist her friendship. They begged her to come from the kitchens or the attic. Failing in that, they sometimes ventured to join her, their fine silk dresses trailing on the greasy floor. They combed her hair, exclaiming, when some of the ash and dirt were removed, on its colour. But no sooner had they turned away, than the girl gathered up handfuls of soot and ash and rubbed them into her hair again. Now and then, the sisters attempted to interest their bizarre relative in a bracelet or a gown or a current song. They spoke to her of the young men they had seen at the suppers or the balls which were then given regularly by the rich families of the city. The girl ignored it all. If she ever said anything, it was to do with penance and humility. At last, as must happen, the sisters wearied of her, and left her alone. They had no cares and did not want to share in hers.

They came to resent her moping greyness, as indeed the merchant's second wife had already done.

"Can you do nothing with the girl?" she demanded of her husband. "People will say that I and my daughters are responsible for her condition and that I ill-treat the maid from jealousy of her dead mother."

"Now how could anyone say that," protested the merchant, "when you are famous as the epitome of generosity and kindness?"

Another year passed, and saw no huge difference in the household.

A difference there was, but not visible.

The girl who slouched in the corner of the hearth was seventeen. Under the filth and grime she was, impossibly, more beautiful, although no one could see it.

And there was one other invisible item—her power (which all this time she had nurtured, saying her prayers to Satanas in the black of midnight), her power was rising like a dark moon in her soul.

Three days after her seventeenth birthday, the girl straggled about the streets as she frequently did. A few noted her and muttered it was the merchant's ugly simple daughter and paid no more attention. Most did not know her at all. She had made herself appear one with the scores of impoverished flotsam which constantly roamed the city, beggars and starvelings. Just outside the city gates, these persons congregated in large numbers, slumped around fires of burning refuse, or else wandering to and fro in search of edible seeds, scraps, the miracle of a dropped coin. Here the girl now came, and began to wander about as they did. Dusk gathered and the shadows thickened. The girl sank to her knees in a patch of earth as if she had found something. Two or three of the beggars sneaked over to see if it were worth snatching from her—but the girl was only scrabbling in the empty soil. The beggars, making signs to each other that she was touched by God—mad—left her alone. But, very far from mad, the girl presently dug up a stoppered clay urn. In this urn were the ashes and charred bones of her mother. She had got a clue as to the location of the urn by devious questioning here and there. Her occult power had helped her to be sure of it.

In the twilight, padding along through the narrow streets and alleys of the city, the girl brought the urn homewards. In the garden at the foot of the old tower, gloom-wrapped, unwitnessed, she unstoppered the urn and buried the ashes freshly. She muttered certain unholy magics over the grave. Then she snapped off the sprig of a young hazel tree, and planted it in the newly turned ground.

I hazard you have begun to recognise the story by now. I see you suppose I tell it wrongly. Believe me, this is the truth of the matter. But if you would rather I left off the tale. . . .No doubt your carriage will soon be here— No? Very well. I shall continue.

I think I should speak of the Duke's son at this juncture. The prince was nineteen, able, intelligent, and of noble bearing. He was of that rather swarthy type of looks one finds here in the north, but tall and slim and clear-eyed. There is an ancient square where you may see a statue of him, but much eroded by two centuries, and the elements. After the city was sacked, no care was lavished on it.

The Duke treasured his son. He had constant delight in the sight of the young man and what he said and did. It was the only happiness the invalid had.

Then, one night, the Duke screamed out in his bed. Servants came running with candles. The Duke moaned that a sword was transfixing his heart, an inch at a time. The prince hurried into the chamber, but in that instant the Duke spasmed horribly and died. No mark was on his body. There had never been a mark to show what ailed him.

The prince wept. They were genuine tears. He had nothing to reproach his father with, everything to thank him for. Nevertheless, they brought the young man the seal-ring of the city, and he put it on.

It was winter, a cold blue-white weather with snow in the streets and countryside and a hard wizened sun that drove thin sharp blades of light through the sky, but gave no warmth. The Duke's funeral cortège passed slowly across the snow, the broad open chariots draped with black and silver, the black-plumed horses, the chanting priests with their glittering robes, their jewelled crucifixes and golden censers. Crowds lined the roadways to watch the spectacle. Among the beggar women stood a girl. No one noticed her. They did not glimpse the expression she veiled in her ragged scarf. She gazed at the bier pitilessly. As the young prince rode by in his sables, the seal-ring on his hand, the eyes of the girl burned through her ashy hair, like a red fox through grasses.

The Duke was buried in the mausoleum you can visit to this day, on the east side of the city. Several months elapsed. The prince put his grief from him, and took up the business of the city competently. Wise and courteous he was, but he rarely smiled. At nineteen his spirit seemed worn. You might think he guessed the destiny that hung over him.

The winter was a hard one, too. The snow had come, and having come was loath to withdraw. When at last the spring returned, flushing the hills with colour, it was no longer sensible to be sad.

The prince's name-day fell about this time. A great banquet was planned, a ball. There had been neither in the palace for nigh on three years, not since the Duke's fatal illness first claimed him. Now the royal doors were to be thrown open to all men of influence and their families. The prince was liberal, charming, and clever even in this. Aristocrat and rich trader were to mingle in the beautiful dining room, and in this very chamber, among the frescoes, the marbles, and the candelabra. Even a merchant's daughter, if the merchant were notable in the city, would get to dance on the sea-green floor, under the white eye of the fearful clock.

The clock. There was some renewed controversy about the clock. They did not dare speak to the young prince. He was a sceptic, as his father had been. But had not a death already occurred? Was the clock not a flying in the jaws of fate? For those disturbed by it, there was a dim writing in their minds, in the dust of the street or the pattern of blossoms. *When the clock strikes—* But people do not positively heed these warnings. Man is afraid of his fears. He ignores the shadow of the wolf thrown on the paving before him, saying: It is only a shadow.

The silk merchant received his invitation to the palace, and to be sure, thought nothing of the clock. His house had been thrown into uproar. The most luscious silks of his workshop were carried into the house and laid before the wife and her two daughters, who chirruped and squealed with excitement. The merchant stood smugly by, above it all yet pleased at being appreciated. "Oh, Father!" cried the two sisters, "may I have this one with the gold piping?" "Oh, Father, this one with the design of pineapples?" Later, a jeweller arrived and set out his trays. The merchant was generous. He wanted his women to look their best. It might be the night of their lives. Yet all the while, at the back of his mind, a little dark spot, itching, aching. He tried to ignore the spot, not scratch at it. His true daughter, the mad one. Nobody bothered to tell her about the invitation to the palace. They knew how she would react, mumbling in her hair about her sin and her penance, paddling her hands in the greasy ash to smear her face. Even the servants avoided her, as if she were just the cat seated by the fire. Less than the cat, for the cat saw to the mice— Just a block of stone. And yet, how fair she might have looked, decked in the pick of the merchant's wares, jewels at her throat. The prince himself could not have been unaware of her. And though marriage was impossible, other less holy, though equally honourable contracts might have been arranged to the benefit of all concerned. The merchant sighed. He had scratched the darkness after all. He attempted to comfort himself by watching the two sisters exult over their apparel. He refused to admit that the finery would somehow make them seem but more ordinary than they were by contrast.

The evening of the banquet arrived. The family set off. Most of the servants sidled after. The prince had distributed largesse in the city; oxen roasted in the squares and the wine was free by royal order.

The house grew sombre. In the deserted kitchen the fire went out.

By the hearth, a segment of gloom rose up.

The girl glanced around her, and she laughed softly and shook out her filthy hair. Of course, she knew as much as anyone, and more than most. This was to be her night, too.

A few minutes later she was in the garden beneath the old tower, standing over the young hazel tree which thrust up from the earth. It had become strong, the tree, despite the harsh winter. Now the girl nodded to it. She chanted under her breath. At length a pale light began to glow, far down near where the roots of the tree held to the ground. Out of the pale glow flew a thin black bird, which perched on the girl's shoulder. Together, the girl and the bird passed into the old tower. High up, a fire blazed that no one had lit. A tub steamed with scented water that no one had drawn. Shapes that were not real and barely seen flitted about. Rare perfumes, the rustle of garments, the glint of gems as yet invisible filled and did not fill the restless air.

Need I describe further? No. You will have seen paintings which depict the attendance upon a witch of her familiar demons. How one bathes her, another anoints her, another brings clothes and ornaments. Perhaps you do not credit such things in any case. Never mind that. I will tell you what happened in the courtyard before the palace.

Many carriages and chariots had driven through the square, avoiding the roasting oxen, the barrels of wine, the cheering drunken citizens, and so through the gates into the courtyard. Just before ten o'clock (the hour, if you recall the clock, of the magician) a solitary carriage drove through the square and into the court. The people in the square gawped at the carriage and pressed forward to see who would step out of it, this latecomer. It was a remarkable vehicle that looked to be fashioned of solid gold, all but the domed roof that was transparent flashing crystal. Six black horses drew it. The coachman and postillions were clad in crimson, and strangely masked as curious beasts and reptiles. One of these beast-men now hopped down and opened the door of the carriage. Out came a woman's figure in a cloak of white fur, and glided up the palace stair and in at the doors.

There was dancing in the ballroom. The whole chamber was bright and clamorous with music and the voices of men and women. There, between those two pillars, the prince sat in his chair, dark, courteous, seldom smiling. Here the musicians played, the deep-throated viol, the lively mandolin. And there the dancers moved up and down on the sea-green floor. But the music and the dancers had just paused. The figures on the clock were themselves in motion. The hour of the magician was about to strike.

As it struck, through the doorway came the figure in the fur cloak. And, as if they must, every eye turned to her.

For an instant she stood there, all white, as though she had brought the winter snow back with her. And then she loosed the cloak from her shoulders, it slipped away, and she was all fire.

She wore a gown of apricot brocade embroidered thickly with gold. Her sleeves and the bodice of her gown were slashed over ivory satin sewn with large rosy pearls. Pearls, too, were wound in her hair that was the shade of antique burnished copper. She was so beautiful that when the clock was still, nobody spoke. She was so beautiful it was hard to look at her for very long.

The prince got up from his chair. He did not know he had. Now he started out across the floor, between the dancers, who parted silently to let him through. He went towards the girl in the doorway as if she drew him by a chain.

The prince had hardly ever acted without considering first what he did. Now he did not consider. He bowed to the girl.

"Madam," he said. "You are welcome. Madam," he said. "Tell me who you are."

She smiled.

"My rank," she said. "Would you know that, my lord? It is similar to yours, or would be were I now mistress in my dead mother's palace. But, unfortunately, an unscrupulous man caused the downfall of our house."

"Misfortune indeed," said the prince. "Tell me your name. Let me right the wrong done you."

"You shall," said the girl. "Trust me, you shall. For my name, I would rather keep it a secret for the present. But you may call me, if you will, a pet name I have given myself—Ashella."

"Ashella . . . But I see no ash about you," said the prince, dazzled by her gleam, laughing a little, stiffly, for laughter was not his habit.

"Ash and cinders from a cold and bitter hearth," said she. But she smiled again. "Now everyone is staring at us, my lord, and the musicians are impatient to begin again. Out of all these ladies, can it be you will lead me in the dance?"

"As long as you will dance," he said. "You shall dance with me."

And that is how it was.

There were many dances, slow and fast, whirling measures and gentle ones. And here and there, the prince and the maiden were parted. Always then he looked eagerly after her, sparing no regard for the other girls whose hands lay in his. It was not like him, he was usually so careful. But the other young men who danced on that floor, who clasped her fingers or her narrow waist in the dance, also gazed after her when she was gone. She danced, as she appeared, like fire. Though if you had asked those young men whether they would rather tie her to themselves, as the prince did, they would have been at a loss. For it is not easy to keep pace with fire.

The hour of the hag struck on the clock.

The prince grew weary of dancing with the girl and losing her in the dance to others and refinding her and losing her again.

Behind the curtains there is a tall window in the east wall that opens on the terrace above the garden. He drew her out there, into the spring night. He gave an order, and small tables were brought with delicacies and sweets and wine. He sat by her, watching every gesture she made, as if he would paint her portrait afterwards.

In the ballroom, here, under the clock, the people murmured. But it was not quite the murmur you would expect, the scandalous murmur about a woman come from nowhere that the prince had

made so much of. At the periphery of the ballroom, the silk merchant sat, pale as a ghost, thinking of a ghost, the living ghost of his
true daughter. No one else recognised her. Only he. Some trick of
the heart had enabled him to know her. He said nothing of it. As
the step-sisters and wife gossiped with other wives and sisters, an
awful foreboding weighed him down, sent him cold and dumb.

And now it is almost midnight, the moment when the page of the
night turns over into day. Almost midnight, the hour when the
figure of Death strikes the golden bell of the clock. And what will
happen when the clock strikes? Your face announces that you
know. Be patient; let us see if you do.

"I am being foolish," said the prince to Ashella on the terrace. "But
perhaps I am entitled to be foolish, just once in my life. What are
you saying?" For the girl was speaking low beside him, and he
could not catch her words.

"I am saying a spell to bind you to me," she said.

"But I am already bound."

"Be bound then. Never go free."

"I do not wish it," he said. He kissed her hands and he said, "I do
not know you, but I will wed you. Is that proof your spell has
worked? I will wed you, and get back for you the rights you have
lost."

"If it were only so simple," said Ashella, smiling, smiling, "but
the debt is too cruel. Justice requires a harsher payment."

And then, in the ballroom, Death struck the first note on the
golden bell.

The girl smiled and she said,

"I curse you in my mother's name."

The second stroke.

"I curse you in my own name."

The third stroke.

"And in the name of those that your father slew."

The fourth stroke.

"And in the name of my Master, who rules the world."

As the fifth, the sixth, the seventh strokes pealed out, the prince
stood nonplussed. At the eighth and the ninth strokes, the strength
of the malediction seemed to curdle his blood. He shivered and his
brain writhed. At the tenth stroke, he saw a change in the loveliness
before him. She grew thinner, taller. At the eleventh stroke, he
beheld a thing in a ragged black cowl and robe. It grinned at him. It

was all grin below a triangle of sockets of nose and eyes. At the twelfth stroke, the prince saw Death and knew him.

In the ballroom, a hideous grinding noise, as the gears of the clock failed. Followed by a hollow booming, as the mechanism stopped entirely.

The conjuration of Death vanished from the terrace.

Only one thing was left behind. A woman's shoe. A shoe no woman could ever have danced in. It was made of glass.

Did you intend to protest about the shoe? Shall I finish the story, or would you rather I did not? It is not the ending you are familiar with. Yes, I perceive you understand that, now.

I will go quickly, then, for your carriage must soon be here. And there is not a great deal more to relate.

The prince lost his mind. Partly from what he had seen, partly from the spells the young witch had netted him in. He could think of nothing but the girl who had named herself Ashella. He raved that Death had borne her away but he would recover her from Death. She had left the glass shoe as token of her love. He must discover her with the aid of the shoe. Whomsoever the shoe fitted would be Ashella. For there was this added complication, that Death might hide her actual appearance. None had seen the girl before. She had disappeared like smoke. The one infallible test was the shoe. That was why she had left it for him.

His ministers would have reasoned with the prince, but he was past reason. His intellect had collapsed as totally as only a profound intellect can. A lunatic, he rode about the city. He struck out at those who argued with him. On a particular occasion, drawing a dagger, he killed, not apparently noticing what he did. His demand was explicit. Every woman, young or old, maid or married, must come forth from her home, must put her foot into the shoe of glass. They came. They had no choice. Some approached in terror, some weeping. Even the aged beggar women obliged, and they cackled, enjoying the sight of royalty gone mad. One alone did not come.

Now it is not illogical that out of the hundreds of women whose feet were put into the shoe, a single woman might have been found that the shoe fitted. But this did not happen. Nor did the situation alter, despite a lurid fable that some, tickled by the idea of wedding the prince, cut off their toes that the shoe might fit them. And if they did, it was to no avail, for still the shoe did not.

Is it really surprising? The shoe was sorcerous. It constantly changed itself, its shape, its size, in order that no foot, save one, could ever be got into it.

Summer spread across the land. The city took on its golden summer glaze, its fetid summer smell.

What had been a whisper of intrigue, swelled into a steady distant thunder. Plots were being hatched.

One day, the silk merchant was brought, trembling and grey of face, to the prince. The merchant's dumbness had broken. He had unburdened himself of his fear at confession, but the priest had not proved honest. In the dawn, men had knocked on the door of the merchant's house. Now he stumbled to the chair of the prince.

Both looked twice their years, but, if anything, the prince looked the elder. He did not lift his eyes. Over and over in his hands he turned the glass shoe.

The merchant, stumbling too in his speech, told the tale of his first wife and his daughter. He told everything, leaving out no detail. He did not even omit the end: that since the night of the banquet the girl had been absent from his house, taking nothing with her—save a young hazel from the garden beneath the tower.

The prince leapt from his chair.

His clothes were filthy and unkempt. His face was smeared with sweat and dust . . . it resembled, momentarily, another face.

Without guard or attendant, the prince ran through the city towards the merchant's house, and on the road, the intriguers waylaid and slew him. As he fell, the glass shoe dropped from his hands, and shattered in a thousand fragments.

There is little else worth mentioning.

Those who usurped the city were villains and not merely that, but fools. Within a year, external enemies were at the gates. A year more, and the city had been sacked, half burnt out, ruined. The manner in which you find it now, is somewhat better than it was then. And it is not now anything for a man to be proud of. As you were quick to note, many here earn a miserable existence by conducting visitors about the streets, the palace, showing them the dregs of the city's past.

Which was not a request, in fact, for you to give me money. Throw some from your carriage window if your conscience bothers you. My own wants are few.

No, I have no further news of the girl, Ashella, the witch. A devotee of Satanas, she has doubtless worked plentiful woe in the world. And a witch is long-lived. Even so, she will die eventually.

None escapes Death. Then you may pity her, if you like. Those who serve the gentleman below—who can guess what their final lot will be? But I am very sorry the story did not please you. It is not, maybe, a happy choice before a journey.

And there is your carriage at last.

What? Ah, no, I shall stay here in the ballroom where you came on me. I have often paused here through the years. It is the clock. It has a certain—what shall I call it—power, to draw me back.

I am not trying to unnerve you. Why should you suppose that? Because of my knowledge of the city, of the story? You think that I am implying that I myself am Death? Now you laugh. Yes, it is absurd. Observe the twelfth figure on the clock. Is he not as you have always heard Death described? And am I in the least like that twelfth figure?

Although, of course, the story was not as you have heard it, either.

# WOLFLAND

## I

WHEN THE SUMMONS ARRIVED FROM ANNA THE MATRIarch, Lisel did not wish to obey. The twilit winter had already come, and the great snows were down, spreading their aprons of shining ice, turning the trees to crystal candelabra. Lisel wanted to stay in the city, skating fur-clad on the frozen river beneath the torches, dancing till four in the morning, a vivid blonde in the flame-bright ballrooms, breaking hearts and not minding, lying late next day like a cat in her warm, soft bed. She did not want to go travelling several hours into the north to visit Anna the Matriarch.

Lisel's mother had been dead sixteen years, all Lisel's life. Her father had let her have her own way, in almost everything, for about the same length of time. But Anna the Matriarch, Lisel's maternal grandmother, was exceedingly rich. She lived thirty miles from the city, in a great wild château in the great wild forest.

A portrait of Anna as a young widow hung in the gallery of Lisel's father's house, a wicked-looking bone-pale person in a black dress, with rubies and diamonds at her throat, and in her ivory yellow hair. Even in her absence, Anna had always had a say in things. A recluse, she had still manipulated like a puppet-master from behind the curtain of the forest. Periodic instructions had been sent, pertaining to Lisel. The girl must be educated by this or that method. She must gain this or that accomplishment, read this or that book, favour this or that cologne or colour or jewel. The latter orders were always uncannily apposite and were often complemented by applicable—and sumptuous—gifts. The summons came in company with such. A swirling cloak of scarlet velvet leapt like a fire from its box to Lisel's hands. It was lined with albino fur, all but the hood, which was lined with the finest and heaviest red brocade. A clasp of gold joined the garment at the throat, the two portions, when closed, forming Anna's personal device, a many-petalled flower. Lisel had exclaimed with pleasure, embracing the cloak, picturing herself flying in it across the solid white river like a dangerous blood-red rose. Then the letter fell from its folds.

Lisel had never seen her grandmother, at least, not intelligently, for Anna had been in her proximity on one occasion only: the hour of her birth. Then, one glimpse had apparently sufficed. Anna had snatched it, and sped away from her son-in-law's house and the salubrious city in a demented black carriage. Now, as peremptory as then, she demanded that Lisel come to visit her before the week was out. Over thirty miles, into the uncivilised northern forest, to the strange mansion in the snow.

"Preposterous," said Lisel's father. "The woman is mad, as I've always suspected."

"I shan't go," said Lisel.

They both knew quite well that she would.

One day, every considerable thing her grandmother possessed would pass to Lisel, providing Lisel did not incur Anna's displeasure.

Half a week later, Lisel was on the northern road.

She sat amid cushions and rugs, in a high sled strung with silver bells, and drawn by a single black-satin horse. Before Lisel perched her driver, the whip in his hand, and a pistol at his belt, for the way north was not without its risks. There were, besides, three outriders, also equipped with whips, pistols, and knives, and muffled to the brows in fur. No female companion was in evidence. Anna had stipulated that it would be unnecessary and superfluous for her grandchild to burden herself with a maid.

But the whips had cracked, the horses had started off. The runners of the sled had smoothly hissed, sending up lacelike sprays of ice. Once clear of the city, the north road opened like a perfect skating floor of milky glass, dim-lit by the fragile winter sun smoking low on the horizon. The silver bells sang, and the fierce still air through which the horses dashed broke on Lisel's cheeks like the coldest champagne. Ablaze in her scarlet cloak, she was exhilarated and began to forget she had not wanted to come.

After about an hour, the forest marched up out of the ground and swiftly enveloped the road on all sides.

There was presently an insidious, but generally perceptible, change. Between the walls of the forest there gathered a new silence, a silence which was, if anything, *alive*, a personality which attended any humanly noisy passage with a cruel and resentful interest. Lisel stared up into the narrow lane of sky above. They might have been moving along the channel of a deep and partly frozen stream. When the drowned sun flashed through, splinters of light scattered and went out as if in water.

The tall pines in their pelts of snow seemed poised to lurch across the road.

The sled had been driving through the forest for perhaps another hour, when a wolf wailed somewhere amid the trees. Rather than break the silence of the place, the cry seemed born of the silence, a natural expression of the landscape's cold solitude and immensity.

The outriders touched the pistols in their belts, almost religiously, and the nearest of the three leaned to Lisel.

"Madame Anna's house isn't so far from here. In any case we have our guns, and these horses could race the wind."

"I'm not afraid," Lisel said haughtily. She glanced at the trees. "I've never seen a wolf. I should be interested to see one."

Made sullen by Lisel's pert reply, the outrider switched tactics. From trying to reassure her, he now ominously said: "Pray you don't, m'mselle. One wolf generally means a pack, and once the snow comes, they're hungry."

"As my father's servant, I would expect you to sacrifice yourself for me, of course," said Lisel. "A fine strong man like you should keep a pack of wolves busy long enough for the rest of us to escape."

The man scowled and spurred away from her.

Lisel smiled to herself. She was not at all afraid, not of the problematical wolves, not even of the eccentric grandmother she had never before seen. In a way, Lisel was looking forward to the meeting, now her annoyance at vacating the city had left her. There had been so many bizarre tales, so much hearsay. Lisel had even caught gossip concerning Anna's husband. He had been a handsome princely man, whose inclinations had not matched his appearance. Lisel's mother had been sent to the city to live with relations to avoid this monster's outbursts of perverse lust and savagery. He had allegedly died one night, mysteriously and luridly murdered on one of the forest tracks. This was not the history Lisel had got from her father, to be sure, but she had always partly credited the more extravagant version. After all, Anna the Matriarch was scarcely commonplace in her mode of life or her attitude to her granddaughter.

Yes, indeed, rather than apprehension, Lisel was beginning to entertain a faintly unholy glee in respect of the visit and the insights it might afford her.

A few minutes after the wolf had howled, the road took a sharp bend, and emerging around it, the party beheld an unexpected obstacle in the way. The driver of the sled cursed softly and drew hard on the reins, bringing the horse to a standstill. The outriders similarly halted. Each peered ahead to where, about twenty yards along the road, a great black carriage blotted the white snow.

A coachman sat immobile on the box of the black carriage, muffled in coal-black furs and almost indistinguishable from them. In forceful contrast, the carriage horses were blonds, and restless, tossing their necks, lifting their feet. A single creature stood on the track between the carriage and the sled. It was too small to be a man, too curiously proportioned to be simply a child.

"What's this?" demanded the third of Lisel's outriders, he who had spoken earlier of the wolves. It was an empty question, but had been a long time in finding a voice for all that.

"I think it is my grandmother's carriage come to meet me," declared Lisel brightly, though, for the first, she had felt a pang of apprehension.

This was not lessened when the dwarf came loping towards them, like a small misshapen furry dog, and reaching the sled, spoke to her, ignoring the others.

"You may leave your escort here and come with us."

Lisel was struck at once by the musical quality of his voice, while out of the shadow of his hood emerged the face of a fair and melancholy angel. As she stared at him, the men about her raised their objections.

"We're to go with m'mselle to her grandmother's house."

"You are not necessary," announced the beautiful dwarf, glancing at them with uninterest. "You are already on the Lady Anna's lands. The coachman and I are all the protection your mistress needs. The Lady Anna does not wish to receive you on her estate."

"What proof," snarled the third outrider, "that you're from Madame's château? Or that she told you to say such a thing. You could have come from any place, from hell itself most likely, and they crushed you in the door as you were coming out."

The riders and the driver laughed brutishly. The dwarf paid no attention to the insult. He drew from his glove one delicate, perfectly formed hand, and in it a folded letter. It was easy to recognise the Matriarch's sanguine wax and the imprint of the petalled flower. The riders brooded, and the dwarf held the letter towards Lisel. She accepted it with an uncanny but pronounced reluctance.

*Chère*, it said in its familiar, indeed its unmistakable, characters, *Why are you delaying the moment when I may look at you? Beautiful has already told you, I think, that your escort may go home. Anna is giving you her own escort, to guide you on the last laps of the journey. Come! Send the men away and step into the carriage.*

Lisel, reaching the word, or rather the name, Beautiful, had glanced involuntarily at the dwarf, oddly frightened at its horrid contrariness and its peculiar truth. A foreboding had clenched around her young heart, and, for a second, inexplicable terror. It was certainly a dreadful dilemma. She could refuse, and refuse thereby the goodwill, the gifts, the ultimate fortune her grandmother could bestow. Or she could brush aside her silly childish fears and walk boldly from the sled to the carriage. Surely, she had always known Madame Anna was an eccentric. Had it not been a source of intrigued curiosity but a few moments ago?

Lisel made her decision.

"Go home," she said regally to her father's servants. "My grandmother is wise and would hardly put me in danger."

The men grumbled, glaring at her, and as they did so, she got out of the sled and moved along the road towards the stationary and funereal carriage. As she came closer, she made out the flower device stamped in gilt on the door. Then the dwarf had darted ahead of her, seized the door, and was holding it wide, bowing to his knees, thus almost into the snow. A lock of pure golden hair spilled across his forehead.

Lisel entered the carriage and sat on the sombre cushions. Courageous prudence (or greed) had triumphed.

The door was shut. She felt the slight tremor as Beautiful leapt on the box beside the driver.

Morose and indecisive, the men her father had sent with her were still lingering on the ice between the trees as she was driven away.

She must have slept, dazed by the continuous rocking of the carriage, but all at once she was wide awake, clutching in alarm at the upholstery. What had roused her was a unique and awful choir. The cries of wolves.

Quite irresistibly she pressed against the window and stared out, impelled to look for what she did not, after all, wish to see. And what she saw was unreassuring.

A horde of wolves were running, not merely in pursuit, but actually alongside the carriage. Pale they were, a pale almost luminous-brownish shade, which made them seem phantasmal against the snow. Their small but jewellike eyes glinted, glowed, and burned. As they ran, their tongues lolling sideways from their mouths like those of huge hunting dogs, they seemed to smile up at her, and her heart turned over.

Why was it, she wondered, with panic-stricken anger, that the coach did not go faster and so outrun the pack? Why was it the brutes had been permitted to gain as much distance as they had? Could it be they had already plucked the coachman and the dwarf from the box and devoured them—she tried to recollect if, in her dozing, she had registered masculine shrieks of fear and agony— and that the horses plunged on? Imagination, grown detailed and pessimistic, soon dispensed with these images, replacing them with that of great pepper-coloured paws scratching on the frame of the coach, the grisly talons ripping at the door, at last a wolf's savage mask thrust through it, and her own frantic and pointless screaming, in the instants before her throat was silenced by the meeting of narrow yellow fangs.

Having run the gamut of her own premonition, Lisel sank back on the seat and yearned for a pistol, or at least a knife. A malicious streak in her lent her the extraordinary bravery of desiring to inflict as many hurts on her killers as she was able before they finished her. She also took space to curse Anna the Matriarch. How the wretched old woman would grieve and complain when the story reached her. The clean-picked bones of her granddaughter had been found a mere mile or so from her château, in the rags of a blood-red cloak; by the body a golden clasp, rejected as inedible. . . .

A heavy thud caused Lisel to leap to her feet, even in the galloping, bouncing carriage. There at the door, grinning in on her, the huge face of a wolf, which did not fall away. Dimly she realised it must impossibly be balancing itself on the running board of the carriage, its front paws raised and somehow keeping purchase on the door. With one sharp determined effort of its head, it might conceivably smash in the pane of the window. The glass would lacerate, and the scent of its own blood further inflame its starvation. The eyes of it, doused by the carriage's gloom, flared up in two sudden pupilless ovals of fire, like two little portholes into hell.

With a shrill howl, scarcely knowing what she did, Lisel flung herself at the closed door and the wolf the far side of it. Her eyes also blazed, her teeth also were bared, and her nails raised as if to claw. Her horror was such that she appeared ready to attack the wolf in its own primeval mode, and as her hands struck the glass against its face, the wolf shied and dropped away.

In that moment, Lisel heard the musical voice of the dwarf call out from the box, some wordless whoop, and a tall gate-post sprang by.

Lisel understood they had entered the grounds of the Matriarch's château. And, a moment later, learned, though did not understand, that the wolves had not followed them beyond the gateway.

## II

The Matriarch sat at the head of the long table. Her chair, like the table, was slender, carved, and intensely polished. The rest of the chairs, though similarly high-backed and angular, were plain and dull, including the chair to which Lisel had been conducted. Which increased Lisel's annoyance, the petty annoyance to which her more eloquent emotions of fright and rage had given way, on entering the domestic, if curious, atmosphere of the house. And Lisel must strive to conceal her ill-temper. It was difficult.

The château, ornate and swarthy under its pointings of snow, retained an air of decadent magnificence, which was increased within. Twin stairs flared from an immense great hall. A hearth, large as a room, and crow-hooded by its enormous mantel, roared with muffled firelight. There was scarcely a furnishing that was not at least two hundred years old, and many were much older. The very air seemed tinged by the sombre wood, the treacle darkness of the draperies, the old-gold gleams of picture frames, gilding, and tableware.

At the centre of it all sat Madame Anna, in her eighty-first year,

a weird apparition of improbable glamour. She appeared, from no more than a yard or so away, to be little over fifty. Her skin, though very dry, had scarcely any lines in it, and none of the pleatings and collapses Lisel generally associated with the elderly. Anna's hair had remained blonde, a fact Lisel was inclined to attribute to some preparation out of a bottle, yet she was not sure. The lady wore black as she had done in the portrait of her youth, a black starred over with astonishing jewels. But her nails were very long and discoloured, as were her teeth. These two incontrovertible proofs of old age gave Lisel a perverse satisfaction. Grandmother's eyes, on the other hand, were not so reassuring. Brilliant eyes, clear and very likely sharp-sighted, of a pallid silvery brown. Unnerving eyes, but Lisel did her best to stare them out, though when Anna spoke to her, Lisel now answered softly, ingratiatingly.

There had not, however, been much conversation, after the first clamour at the doorway:

"We were chased by wolves!" Lisel had cried. "Scores of them! Your coachman is a dolt who doesn't know enough to carry a pistol. I might have been killed."

"You were not," said Anna, imperiously standing in silhouette against the giant window of the hall, a stained glass of what appeared to be a hunting scene, done in murky reds and staring white.

"No thanks to your servants. You promised me an escort—the only reason I sent my father's men away."

"You had your escort."

Lisel had choked back another flood of sentences; she did not want to get on the wrong side of this strange relative. Nor had she liked the slight emphasis on the word "escort."

The handsome ghastly dwarf had gone forward into the hall, lifted the hem of Anna's long mantle, and kissed it. Anna had smoothed off his hood and caressed the bright hair beneath.

"Beautiful wasn't afraid," said Anna decidedly. "But, then, my people know the wolves will not harm them."

An ancient tale came back to Lisel in that moment. It concerned certain human denizens of the forests, who had power over wild beasts. It occurred to Lisel that mad old Anna liked to fancy herself a sorceress, and Lisel said fawningly: "I should have known I'd be safe. I'm sorry for my outburst, but I don't know the forest as you do. I was afraid."

In her allotted bedroom, a silver ewer and basin stood on a table. The embroideries on the canopied bed were faded but priceless.

Antique books stood in a case, catching the firelight, a vast yet random selection of the poetry and prose of many lands. From the bedchamber window, Lisel could look out across the clearing of the park, the white sweep of it occasionally broken by trees in their winter foliage of snow, or by the slash of the track which broke through the high wall. Beyond the wall, the forest pressed close under the heavy twilight of the sky. Lisel pondered with a grim irritation the open gateway. Wolves running, and the way to the château left wide at all times. She visualised mad Anna throwing chunks of raw meat to the wolves as another woman would toss bread to swans.

This unprepossessing notion returned to Lisel during the unusually early dinner, when she realised that Anna was receiving from her silent gliding servants various dishes of raw meats.

"I hope," said Anna, catching Lisel's eye, "my repast won't offend a delicate stomach. I have learned that the best way to keep my health is to eat the fruits of the earth in their intended state—so much goodness is wasted in cooking and garnishing."

Despite the reference to fruit, Anna touched none of the fruit or vegetables on the table. Nor did she drink any wine.

Lisel began again to be amused, if rather dubiously. Her own fare was excellent, and she ate it hungrily, admiring as she did so the crystal goblets and gold-handled knives which one day would be hers.

Presently a celebrated liqueur was served—to Lisel alone—and Anna rose on the black wings of her dress, waving her granddaughter to the fire. Beautiful, meanwhile, had crawled onto the stool of the tall piano and begun to play wildly despairing romances there, his elegant fingers darting over discoloured keys so like Anna's strong yet senile teeth.

"Well," said Anna, reseating herself in another carven throne before the cave of the hearth. "What do you think of us?"

"Think, Grandmère? Should I presume?"

"No. But you do."

"I think," said Lisel cautiously, "everything is very fine."

"And you are keenly aware, of course, the finery will eventually belong to you."

"Oh, Grandmère!" exclaimed Lisel, quite genuinely shocked by such frankness.

"Don't trouble yourself," said Anna. Her eyes caught the fire and became like the eyes of the wolf at the carriage window. "You expect to be my heiress. It's quite normal you should be making an inventory. I shan't last forever. Once I'm gone, presumably everything will be yours."

Despite herself, Lisel gave an involuntary shiver. A sudden plan of selling the château to be rid of it flitted through her thoughts, but she quickly put it aside, in case the Matriarch somehow read her mind.

"Don't speak like that, Grandmère. This is the first time I've met you, and you talk of dying."

"Did I? No, I did not. I spoke of *departure*. Nothing dies, it simply transmogrifies." Lisel watched politely this display of apparent piety. "As for my mansion," Anna went on, "you mustn't consider sale, you know." Lisel blanched—as she had feared, her mind had been read, or could it merely be that Anna found her predictable? "The château has stood on this land for many centuries. The old name for the spot, do you know that?"

"No, Grandmère."

"This, like the whole of the forest, was called the Wolfland. Because it was the wolves' country before ever men set foot on it with their piffling little roads and tracks, their carriages and foolish frightened walls. Wolfland. Their country then, and when the winter comes, their country once more."

"As I saw, Grandmère," said Lisel tartly.

"As you saw. You'll see and hear more of them while you're in my house. Their voices come and go like the wind, as they do. When that little idiot of a sun slips away and the night rises, you may hear scratching on the lower floor windows. I needn't tell you to stay indoors, need I?"

"Why do you let animals run in your park?" demanded Lisel.

"Because," said Anna, "the land is theirs by right."

The dwarf began to strike a polonaise from the piano. Anna clapped her hands, and the music ended. Anna beckoned, and Beautiful slid off the stool like a precocious child caught stickying the keys. He came to Anna, and she played with his hair. His face remained unreadable, yet his pellucid eyes swam dreamily to Lisel's face. She felt embarrassed by the scene, and at his glance was angered to find herself blushing.

"There was a time," said Anna, "when I did not rule this house. When a man ruled here."

"Grandpère," said Lisel, looking resolutely at the fire.

"*Grandpère*, yes. *Grandpère*." Her voice held the most awful scorn. "Grandpère believed it was a man's pleasure to beat his wife. You're young, but you should know, should be told. Every night, if I was not already sick from a beating, and sometimes when I was, I would hear his heavy drunken feet come stumbling to my door. At first I locked it, but I learned not to. What stood in his way he could always break. He was a strong man. A great legend of strength. I carry scars on my shoulders to this hour. One day I may show you."

Lisel gazed at Anna, caught between fascination and revulsion. "Why do I tell you?" Anna smiled. She had twisted Beautiful's gorgeous hair into a painful knot. Clearly it hurt him, but he made no sound, staring blindly at the ceiling. "I tell you, Lisel, because very soon your father will suggest to you that it is time you were wed. And however handsome or gracious the young man may seem to you that you choose, or that is chosen for you, however noble or marvellous or even docile he may seem, you have no way of being certain he will not turn out to be like your beloved grandpère. Do you know, he brought me peaches on our wedding night, all the way from the hot-houses of the city. Then he showed me the whip he had been hiding under the fruit. You see what it is to be a woman, Lisel. Is that what you want? The irrevocable marriage vow that binds you forever to a monster? And even if he is a good man, which is a rare beast indeed, you may die an agonising death in childbed, just as your mother did."

Lisel swallowed. A number of things went through her head now. A vague acknowledgement that, though she envisaged admiration, she had never wished to marry and therefore never considered it, and a starker awareness that she was being told improper things. She desired to learn more and dreaded to learn it. As she was struggling to find a rejoinder, Anna seemed to notice her own grip on the hair of the dwarf.

"Ah," she said, "forgive me. I did not mean to hurt you."

The words had an oddly sinister ring to them. Lisel suddenly guessed their origin, the brutish man rising from his act of depravity, of necessity still merely sketched by Lisel's innocence, whispering, gloatingly muttering: Forgive me. I did not mean to hurt.

"Beautiful," said Anna, "is the only man of any worth I've ever met. And my servants, of course, but I don't count them as men. Drink your liqueur."

"Yes, Grandmère," said Lisel, as she sipped, and slightly choked.

"Tomorrow," said Anna, "we must serve you something better.

A vintage indigenous to the château, made from a flower which grows here in the spring. For now," again she rose on her raven's wings; a hundred gems caught the light and went out, "for now, we keep early hours here, in the country."

"But, Grandmère," said Lisel, astounded, "it's scarcely sunset."

"In my house," said Anna, gently, "you will do as you are told, m'mselle."

And for once, Lisel did as she was told.

At first, of course, Lisel did not entertain a dream of sleep. She was used to staying awake till the early hours of the morning, rising at noon. She entered her bedroom, cast one scathing glance at the bed, and settled herself to read in a chair beside the bedroom fire. Luckily she had found a lurid novel amid the choice of books. By skimming over all passages of meditation, description, or philosophy, confining her attention to those portions which contained duels, rapes, black magic, and the firing squad, she had soon made great inroads on the work. Occasionally she would pause, and add another piece of wood to the fire. At such times she knew a medley of doubts concerning her grandmother. That the Matriarch could leave such a novel lying about openly where Lisel could get at it outraged the girl's propriety.

Eventually, two or three hours after the sun had gone and the windows blackened entirely behind the drapes, Lisel did fall asleep. The excitements of the journey and her medley of reactions to Madame Anna had worn her out.

She woke, as she had in the carriage, with a start of alarm. Her reason was the same one. Out in the winter forest of night sounded the awesome choir of the wolves. Their voices rose and fell, swelling, diminishing, resurging, like great icy waves of wind or water, breaking on the silence of the château.

Partly nude, a lovely maiden had been bound to a stake and the first torch applied, but Lisel no longer cared very much for her fate. Setting the book aside, she rose from the chair. The flames were low on the candles and the fire almost out. There was no clock, but it had the feel of midnight. Lisel went to the window and opened the drapes. Stepping through and pulling them fast closed again behind her, she gazed out into the glowing darkness of snow and night.

The wolf cries went on and on, thrilling her with a horrible disquiet, so she wondered how even mad Anna could ever have grown accustomed to them? Was this what had driven grandfather to brutishness and beatings? And, colder thought, the mysterious violent death he was supposed to have suffered—what more violent than to be torn apart by long pointed teeth under the pine trees?

Lisel quartered the night scene with her eyes, looking for shapes to fit the noises, and, as before, hoping not to find them.

There was decidedly something about wolves. Something beyond their reputation and the stories of the half-eaten bodies of little children with which nurses regularly scared their charges. Something to do with actual appearance, movement: the lean shadow manifesting from between the trunks of trees—the stuff of nightmare. And their howlings—! Yet, as it went on and on, Lisel became aware of a bizarre exhilaration, an almost-pleasure in the awful sounds which made the hair lift on her scalp and gooseflesh creep along her arms—the same sort of sensation as biting into a slice of lemon—

And then she saw it, a great pale wolf. It loped by directly beneath the window, and suddenly, to Lisel's horror, it raised its long head, and two fireworks flashed, which were its eyes meeting with hers. A primordial fear, worse even than in the carriage, turned Lisel's bones to liquid. She sank on her knees, and as she knelt there foolishly, as if in prayer, her chin on the sill, she beheld the wolf moving away across the park, seeming to dissolve into the gloom.

Gradually, then, the voices of the other wolves began to dull, eventually falling quiet.

Lisel got up, came back into the room, threw more wood on the fire and crouched there. It seemed odd to her that the wolf had run *away* from the château, but she was not sure why. Presumably it had ventured near in hopes of food, then, disappointed, withdrawn. That it had come from the spot directly by the hall's doors did not, could not, mean anything in particular. Then Lisel realised what had been so strange. She had seen the wolf in a faint radiance of light—but from where? The moon was almost full, but obscured behind the house. The drapes had been drawn across behind her, the light could not have fallen down from her own window. She was turning back unhappily to the window to investigate when she heard the unmistakable soft thud of a large door being carefully shut below her, in the château.

*The wolf had been in the house.* Anna's guest.

Lisel was petrified for a few moments, then a sort of fury came to

her rescue. How dared the old woman be so mad as all this and expect her civilised granddaughter to endure it? Brought to the wilds,
told improper tales, left improper literature to read, made unwilling party to the entertainment of savage beasts. Perhaps as a result
of the reading matter, Lisel saw her only course abruptly, and it
was escape. (She had already assumed Anna would not allow her
grandchild to depart until whatever lunatic game the old beldame
was playing was completed.) But if escape, then how? Though
there were carriage, horses, even coachman, all were Anna's. Lisel
did not have to ponder long, however. Her father's cynicism on the
lower classes had convinced her that anyone had his price. She
would bribe the coachman—her gold bracelets and her ruby eardrops—both previous gifts of Anna's, in fact. She could assure the
man of her father's protection and further valuables when they
reached the city. A vile thought came to her at that, that her father
might, after all, prove unsympathetic. Was she being stupid?
Should she turn a blind eye to Anna's wolfish foibles? If Anna
should disinherit her, as surely she would on Lisel's flight—

Assailed by doubts, Lisel paced the room. Soon she had added to
them. The coachman might snatch her bribe and still refuse to help
her. Or worse, drive her into the forest and violate her. Or—

The night slowed and flowed into the black valleys of early
morning. The moon crested the château and sank into the forest.
Lisel sat on the edge of the canopied bed, pleating and repleating
the folds of the scarlet cloak between her fingers. Her face was pale,
her blonde hair untidy, and her eyes enlarged. She looked every bit
as crazy as her grandmother.

Her decision was sudden, made with an awareness that she had
wasted much time. She flung the cloak round herself and started
up. She hurried to the bedroom door and softly, softly, opened it a
tiny crack.

All was black in the house, neither lamp nor candle visible anywhere. The sight, or rather lack of it, caused Lisel's heart to sink.
At the same instant, it indicated that the whole house was abed. Lisel's plan was a simple one. A passage led away from the great hall
to the kitchens and servants' quarters and ultimately to a courtyard
containing coachhouse and stables. Here the grooms and the coachman would sleep, and here too another gateway opened on the
park. These details she had either seen for herself as the carriage
was driven off on her arrival or deduced from the apparent structure of the château. Unsure of the hour, yet she felt dawn was ap-

proaching. If she could but reach the servants' quarters, she should be able to locate the courtyard. If the coachman proved a villain, she would have to use her wits. Threaten him or cajole him. Knowing very little of physical communion, it seemed better to Lisel in those moments, to lie down with a hairy peasant than to remain the Matriarch's captive. It was that time of night when humans are often prey to ominous or extravagant ideas of all sorts. She took up one of the low-burning candles. Closing the bedroom door behind her, Lisel stole forward into the black nothingness of unfamiliarity.

Even with the feeble light, she could barely see ten inches before her, and felt cautiously about with her free hand, dreading to collide with ornament or furniture and thereby rouse her enemies. The stray gleams, shot back at her from a mirror or a picture-frame, misled rather than aided her. At first her total concentration was taken up with her safe progress and her quest to find the head of the double stair. Presently, however, as she pressed on without mishap, secondary considerations began to steal in on her.

If it was difficult to proceed, how much more difficult it might be should she desire to retreat. She hoped there would be nothing to retreat from. But the ambience of the château, inspired by night and the limited candle, was growing more sinister by the second. Arches opened on drapes of black from which anything might spring. All about, the shadow furled, and she was one small target moving in it, lit as if on a stage.

She turned the passage and perceived the curve of the stair ahead and the dim hall below. The great stained window provided a grey illumination which elsewhere was absent. The stars bled on the snow outside and pierced the white panes. Or could it be the initial tinge of dawn?

Lisel paused, confronting once again the silliness of her simple plan of escape. Instinctively, she turned to look the way she had come, and the swiftness of the motion, or some complementary draught, quenched her candle. She stood marooned by this cliché, the phosphorescently discernible space before her, pitch-dark behind, and chose the path into the half-light as preferable.

She went down the stair delicately, as if descending into a ballroom. When she was twenty steps from the bottom, something moved in the thick drapes beside the outer doors. Lisel froze, feeling a shock like an electric volt passing through her vitals. In another second she knew from the uncanny littleness of the shape that it was Anna's dwarf who scuttled there. But before she divined what it was at, one leaf of the door began to swing heavily inwards.

Lisel felt no second shock of fear. She felt instead as if her soul drifted upward from her flesh.

Through the open door soaked the pale ghost-light that heralded sunrise, and with that, a scattering of fresh white snow. Lastly through the door, its long feet crushing both light and snow, glided the wolf she had seen beneath her window. It did not look real, it seemed to waver and to shine, yet, for any who had ever heard the name of wolf, or a single story of them, or the song of their voices, here stood that word, that story, that voice, personified.

The wolf raised its supernatural head, and once more it looked at the young girl.

The moment held no reason, no pity, and certainly no longer any hope of escape.

As the wolf began to pad noiselessly towards Lisel up the stair, she fled by the only route now possible to her. Into unconsciousness.

## III

She came to herself to find the face of a prince from a romance poised over hers. He was handsome enough to have kissed her awake, except that she knew immediately it was the dwarf.

"Get away from me!" she shrieked, and he moved aside.

She was in the bedchamber, lying on the canopied bed. She was not dead, she had not been eaten or had her throat torn out.

As if in response to her thoughts, the dwarf said musically to her: "You have had a nightmare, m'mselle." But she could tell from a faint expression somewhere between his eyes, that he did not truly expect her to believe such a feeble equivocation.

"There was a wolf," said Lisel, pulling herself into a sitting position, noting that she was still gowned and wearing the scarlet cloak. "A wolf which *you* let into the house."

"I?" The dwarf elegantly raised an eyebrow.

"You, you frog. Where is my grandmother? I demand to see her at once."

"The Lady Anna is resting. She sleeps late in the mornings."

"Wake her."

"Your pardon, m'mselle, but I take my orders from Madame." The dwarf bowed. "If you are recovered and hungry, a maid will bring *petit déjeuner* at once to your room, and hot water for bathing, when you are ready."

Lisel frowned. Her ordeal past, her anger paramount, she was still very hungry. An absurd notion came to her—*had* it all been a dream? No, she would not so doubt herself. Even though the wolf had not harmed her, it had been real. A household pet, then? She had heard of deranged monarchs who kept lions or tigers like cats. Why not a wolf kept like a dog?

"Bring me my breakfast," she snapped, and the dwarf bowed himself goldenly out.

All avenues of escape seemed closed, yet by day (for it was day, the tawny gloaming of winter) the phenomena of the darkness seemed far removed. Most of their terror had gone with them. With instinctive immature good sense, Lisel acknowledged that no hurt had come to her, that she was indeed being cherished.

She wished she had thought to reprimand the dwarf for his mention of intimate hot water and his presence in her bedroom. Recollections of unseemly novelettes led her to a swift examination of her apparel—unscathed. She rose and stood morosely by the fire, waiting for her breakfast, tapping her foot.

By the hour of noon, Lisel's impatience had reached its zenith with the sun. Of the two, only the sun's zenith was insignificant.

Lisel left the bedroom, flounced along the corridor, and came to the stairhead. Eerie memories of the previous night had trouble in remaining with her. Everything seemed to have become rather absurd, but this served only to increase her annoyance. Lisel went down the stair boldly. The fire was lit in the enormous hearth and blazing cheerfully. Lisel prowled about, gazing at the dubious stained glass, which she now saw did not portray a hunting scene at all, but some pagan subject of men metamorphosing into wolves.

At length a maid appeared. Lisel marched up to her.

"Kindly inform my grandmother that I am awaiting her in the hall."

The maid seemed struggling to repress a laugh, but she bobbed a curtsy and darted off. She did not come back, and neither did grandmother.

When a man entered bearing logs for the fire, Lisel said to him, "Put those down and take me at once to the coachman."

The man nodded and gestured her to follow him without a word of acquiescence or disagreement. Lisel, as she let herself be led through the back corridors and by the hub-bub of the huge stone kitchen, was struck by the incongruousness of her actions. No longer afraid, she felt foolish. She was carrying out her "plan" of the night before from sheer pique, nor did she have any greater hope of success. It was more as if some deeply hidden part of herself prompted her to flight, in spite of all resolutions, rationality, and desire. But it was rather like trying to walk on a numbed foot. She could manage to do it, but without feeling.

The coachhouse and stables bulked gloomily about the courtyard, where the snow had renewed itself in dazzling white drifts. The coachman stood in his black furs beside an iron brazier. One of the blond horses was being shod in an old-fashioned manner, the coachman overseeing the exercise. Seeking to ingratiate herself, Lisel spoke to the coachman in a silky voice.

"I remarked yesterday, how well you controlled the horses when the wolves came after the carriage."

The coachman did not answer, but hearing her voice, the horse sidled a little, rolling its eye at her.

"Suppose," said Lisel to the coachman, "I were to ask you if you would take me back to the city. What would you say?"

Nothing, apparently.

The brazier sizzled, and the hammer of the blacksmithing groom smacked the nails home into the horse's hoof. Lisel found the process disconcerting.

"You must understand," she said to the coachman, "my father would give you a great deal of money. He's unwell and wishes me to return. I received word this morning."

The coachman hulked there like a big black bear, and Lisel had the urge to bite him viciously.

"My grandmother," she announced, "would order you to obey me, but she is in bed."

"No, she is not," said the Matriarch at Lisel's back, and Lisel almost screamed. She shot around, and stared at the old woman, who stood about a foot away, imperious in her furs, jewels frostily blistering on her wrists.

"I wish," said Lisel, taking umbrage as her shield, "to go home at once."

"So I gather. But you can't, I regret."

"You mean to keep me prisoner?" blurted Lisel.

Grandmother laughed. The laugh was like fresh ice crackling under a steel skate. "Not at all. The road is snowed under and won't be clear for several days. I'm afraid you'll have to put up with us a while longer."

Lisel, in a turmoil she could not herself altogether fathom, had

her attention diverted by the behaviour of the horse. It was bris-
tling like a cat, tossing its head, dancing against the rope by which
the second groom was holding it.

Anna walked at once out into the yard and began to approach
the horse from the front. The horse instantly grew more agitated,
kicking up its heels, and neighing croupily. Lisel almost cried an
automatic warning, but restrained herself. Let the beldame get a
kicking; she deserved it. Rather to Lisel's chagrin, Anna reached the
horse without actually having her brains dashed out. She showed
not a moment's hesitation or doubt, placing her hand on its long
nose, eying it with an amused tenderness. She looked very cruel
and very indomitable.

"There now," said Anna to the horse, which, fallen quiet and
still, yet trembled feverishly. "You know you are used to me. You
know you were trained to endure me since you were a foal, as your
brothers are sometimes trained to endure fire."

The horse hung its head and shivered, cowed but noble.

Anna left it and strolled back through the snow. She came to
Lisel and took her arm.

"I'm afraid," said Anna, guiding them towards the château door,
"that they're never entirely at peace when I'm in the vicinity,
though they are good horses, and well-trained. They have borne
me long distances in the carriage."

"Do they fear you because you ill-treat them?" Lisel asked impet-
uously.

"Oh, not at all. They fear me because to them I smell of wolf."

Lisel bridled.

"Then do you think it wise to keep such a pet in the house?" she
flared.

Anna chuckled. It was not necessarily a merry sound.

"That's what you think, is it? What a little dunce you are, Lisel. *I*
am the beast you saw last night, and you had better get accustomed
to it. Grandmère is a werewolf."

The return walk through the domestic corridors into the hall was
notable for its silence. The dreadful Anna, her grip on the girl's arm
unabated, smiled thoughtfully to herself. Lisel was obviously also
deliberating inwardly. Her conclusions, however, continued to
lean to the deranged rather than the occult. Propitiation suggested
itself, as formerly, to be the answer. So, as they entered the hall,
casting their cloaks to a servant, Lisel brightly exclaimed:

"A werewolf, Grandmère. How interesting!"

"Dear me," said Anna, "what a child." She seated herself by the fire in one of her tall thrones. Beautiful had appeared. "Bring the liqueur and some biscuits," said Anna. "It's past the hour, but why should we be the slaves of custom?"

Lisel perched on a chair across the hearth, watching Anna guardedly.

"You are the interesting one," Anna now declared. "You look sulky rather than intimidated at being mured up here with one whom you wrongly suppose is a dangerous insane. No, *ma chère*, verily I'm not mad, but a transmogrifite. Every evening, once the sun sets, I become a wolf, and duly comport myself as a wolf does."

"You're going to eat me, then," snarled Lisel, irritated out of all attempts to placate.

"Eat you? Hardly necessary. The forest is bursting with game. I won't say I never tasted human meat, but I wouldn't stoop to devouring a blood relation. Enough is enough. Besides, I had the opportunity last night, don't you think, when you swooned away on the stairs not fifty feet from me. Of course, it was almost dawn, and I *had* dined, but to rip out your throat would have been the work only of a moment. Thereafter we might have stored you in the cold larder against a lean winter."

*"How dare you try to frighten me in this way!"* screamed Lisel in a paroxysm of rage.

Beautiful was coming back with a silver tray. On the tray rested a plate of biscuits and a decanter of the finest cut glass containing a golden drink.

"You note, Beautiful," said Madame Anna, "I like this wretched granddaughter of mine. She's very like me."

"Does that dwarf know you are a *werewolf?*" demanded Lisel, with baleful irony.

"Who else lets me in and out at night? But all my servants know, just as my other folk know, in the forest."

"You're disgusting," said Lisel.

"Tut, I shall disinherit you. Don't you want my fortune anymore?"

Beautiful set down the tray on a small table between them and began to pour the liqueur, smooth as honey, into two tiny crystal goblets.

Lisel watched. She remembered the nasty dishes of raw meat— part of Anna's game of werewolfery—and the drinking of water, but no wine. Lisel smirked, thinking she had caught the Matriarch out. She kept still and accepted the glass from Beautiful, who, while she remained seated, was a mere inch taller than she.

"I toast you," said Anna, raising her glass to Lisel. "Your health and your joy." She sipped. A strange look came into her strange eyes. "We have," she said, "a brief winter afternoon before us. There is just the time to tell you what you should be told."

"Why bother with me? I'm disinherited."

"Hardly. Taste the liqueur. You will enjoy it."

"I'm surprised that you did, Grandmère."

"Don't be," said Anna with asperity. "This wine is special to this place. We make it from a flower which grows here. A little yellow flower that comes in the spring, or sometimes, even in the winter. There is a difference then, of course. Do you recall the flower of my escutcheon? It is the self-same one."

Lisel sipped the liqueur. She had had a fleeting fancy it might be drugged or tampered with in some way, but both drinks had come from the decanter. Besides, what would be the point? The Matriarch valued an audience. The wine was pleasing, fragrant, and rather than sweet as Lisel had anticipated, tart. The flower which grew in winter was plainly another demented tale.

Relaxed, Lisel leant back in her chair. She gazed at the flames in the wide hearth. Her mad grandmother began to speak to her in a quiet, floating voice, and Lisel saw pictures form in the fire. Pictures of Anna, and of the château, and of darkness itself . . .

# IV

How young Anna looked. She was in her twenties. She wore a scarlet gown and a scarlet cloak lined with pale fur and heavy brocade. It resembled Lisel's cloak but had a different clasp. Snow melted on the shoulders of the cloak, and Anna held her slender hands to the fire on the hearth. Free of the hood, her hair, like marvellously tarnished ivory, was piled on her head, and there was a yellow flower in it. She wore ruby eardrops. She looked just like Lisel, or Lisel as she would become in six years or seven.

Someone called. It was more a roar than a call, as if a great beast came trampling into the château. He was a big man, dark, all darkness, his features hidden in a black beard, black hair—more, in a sort of swirling miasmic cloud, a kind of psychic smoke: Anna's hatred and fear. He bellowed for liquor, and a servant came running with a jug and cup. The man, Anna's husband, cuffed the servant aside, grabbing the jug as he did so. He strode to Anna, spun her about, grabbed her face in his hands as he had grabbed the jug. He leaned to her as if to kiss her, but he did not kiss, he merely stared. She had steeled herself not to shrink from him, so much was evident. His eyes, roving over her to find some overt trace of distaste or fright, suddenly found instead the yellow flower. He vented a powerful oath. His paw flung up and wrenched the flower free. He slung it in the fire and spat after it.

"You stupid bitch," he growled at her. "Where did you come on that?"

"It's only a flower."

"Not only a flower. Answer me, where? Or do I strike you?"

"Several of them are growing near the gate, beside the wall; and in the forest. I saw them when I was riding."

The man shouted again for his servant. He told him to take a fellow and go out. They must locate the flowers and burn them.

"Another superstition?" Anna asked. Her husband hit her across the head so she staggered and caught the mantel to steady herself.

"*Yes,*" he sneered, "another one. Now come upstairs."

Anna said, "Please excuse me, sir. I am not well today."

He said in a low and smiling voice:

"Do as I say, or you'll be worse."

The fire flared on the swirl of her bloody cloak as she moved to obey him.

And the image changed. There was a bedroom, fluttering with lamplight. Anna was perhaps thirty-five or -six, but she looked older. She lay in bed, soaked in sweat, uttering hoarse low cries or sometimes preventing herself from crying. She was in labour. The child was difficult. There were other women about the bed. One muttered to her neighbour that it was beyond her how the master had ever come to sire a child, since he got his pleasure another way, and the poor lady's body gave evidence of how. Then Anna screamed. Someone bent over her. There was a peculiar muttering among the women, as if they attended at some holy ceremony.

And another image came. Anna was seated in a shawl of gilded hair. She held a baby on her lap and was playing with it in an intense, quite silent way. As her hair shifted, traceries became momentarily visible over her bare shoulders and arms, horrible traceries left by a lash.

"Let me take the child," said a voice, and one of the women from the former scene appeared. She lifted the baby from Anna's lap, and Anna let the baby go, only holding her arms and hands in such a way that she touched it to the last second. The other woman was older than Anna, a peasant dressed smartly for service in the châ-teau. "You mustn't fret yourself," she said.

"But I can't suckle her," said Anna. "I wanted to."

"There's another can do that," said the woman. "Rest yourself. Rest while he is away." When she said "he" there could be no doubt of the one to whom she referred.

"Then, I'll rest," said Anna. She reclined on pillows, wincing slightly as her back made contact with the fine soft silk. "Tell me about the flowers again. The yellow flowers."

The woman showed her teeth as she rocked the baby. For an in-stant her face was just like a wolf's.

"You're not afraid," she said. "*He* is. But it's always been here. The wolf-magic. It's part of the Wolfland. Wherever wolves have been, you can find the wolf-magic. Somewhere. In a stream or a cave, or in a patch of ground. The château has it. That's why the flowers grow here. Yes, I'll tell you, then. It's simple. If any eat the flowers, then they receive the gift. It comes from the spirit, the wolfwoman, or maybe she's a goddess, an old goddess left over from the beginning of things, before Christ came to save us all. She has the head of a wolf and yellow hair. You swallow the flowers, and you call her, and she comes, and she gives it you. And then it's yours, till you die."

"And then what? Payment?" said Anna dreamily. "Hell?"

"Maybe."

The image faded gently. Suddenly there was another which was not gentle, a parody of the scene before. Staring light showed the bedchamber. The man, his shadow-face smouldering, clutched Anna's baby in his hands. The baby shrieked; he swung it to and fro as if to smash it on some handy piece of furniture. Anna stood in her nightdress. She held a whip out to him.

"Beat me," she said. "Please beat me. I want you to. Put down the child and beat me. It would be so easy to hurt her, and so soon over, she's so small. But I'm stronger. You can hurt me much more. See how vulnerable and afraid I am. Beat *me.*"

Then, with a snarl he tossed the child onto the bed where it lay wailing. He took the whip and caught Anna by her pale hair—

There was snow blowing like torn paper, everywhere. In the midst of it a servant woman, and a child perhaps a year old with soft dark hair, were seated in a carriage. Anna looked at them, then stepped away. A door slammed, horses broke into a gallop. Anna remained standing in the snowstorm.

No picture came. A man's voice thundered: "Where? Where did you send the thing? It's mine, I sired it. My property. *Where?*"

But the only reply he got was moans of pain. She would not tell him, and did not. He nearly killed her that time.

Now it is night, but a black night bleached with whiteness, for a full moon is up above the tops of the winter pines.

Anna is poised, motionless, in a glade of the wild northern forest. She wears the scarlet cloak, but the moon has drained its colour. The snow sparkles, the trees are umbrellas of diamond, sombre only at their undersides. The moon slaps the world with light. Anna has been singing, or chanting something, and though it can no longer be heard, the dew of it lies heavy over the ground. Something is drawn there, too, in the snow, a circle, and another shape inside it. A fire has been kindled nearby, but now it has burned low, and has a curious blueish tinge to it. All at once a wind begins to come through the forest. But it is not wind, not even storm. It is the soul of the forest, the spirit of the Wolfland.

Anna goes to her knees. She is afraid, but it is a new fear, an exulting fear. The stalks of the flowers whose heads she has eaten lie under her knees, and she raises her face like a dish to the moonlight.

The pines groan. They bend. Branches snap and snow showers down from them. The creature of the forest is coming, nearer and nearer. It is a huge single wing, or an enormous engine. Everything breaks and sways before it, even the moonlight, and darkness fills the glade. And out of the darkness Something whirls. It is difficult to see, to be sure—a glimpse of gold, two eyes like dots of lava seven feet in the air, a grey jaw, hung breasts which have hair growing on them, the long hand which is not a hand, lifting— And then every wolf in the forest seems to give tongue, and the darkness ebbs away.

Anna lies on her face. She is weeping. With terror. With—

It is night again, and the man of the house is coming home.

He swaggers, full of local beer, and eager to get to his wife. He was angry, a short while since, because his carriage, which was to have waited for him outside the inn, had mysteriously vanished. There will be men to curse and brutalise in the courtyard before he goes up to his beloved Anna, a prelude to his final acts with her. He finds her a challenge, his wife. She seems able to withstand so much, looking at him proudly with horror in her eyes. It would bore him to break her. He likes the fact he cannot, or thinks he does. And tonight he has some good news. One of the paid men has brought word of their child. She is discovered at last. She can be brought home to the château to her father's care. She is two years old now. Strong and healthy. Yes, good news indeed.

They had known better in the village than to tell him he should beware on the forest track. He is not anxious about wolves, the distance being less than a mile, and he has his pistol. Besides, he organised a wolf hunt last month and cleared quite a few of the brutes off his land. The area about the château has been silent for many nights. Even Anna went walking without a servant—though he had not approved of that and had taught her a lesson. (Sometimes it occurs to him that she enjoys his lessons as much as he enjoys delivering them, for she seems constantly to seek out new ways to vex him.)

He is about a quarter of a mile from the château now, and here a small clearing opens off on both sides of the track. It is the night after the full moon, and her disc, an almost perfect round, glares down on the clearing from the pine tops. Anna's husband dislikes the clearing. He had forgotten he would have to go through it, for generally he is mounted or in the carriage when he passes the spot. There is some old superstition about the place. He hates it, just as he hates the stinking yellow flowers that grew in it before he burned them out. Why does he hate them? The woman who nursed him told him something and it frightened him, long ago. Well, no matter. He walks more quickly.

How quiet it is, how still. The whole night like a pane of black-white silence. He can hardly hear his own noisy footfalls. There is a disturbance in the snow, over there, a mark like a circle.

Then he realises something is behind him. He is not sure how he realises, for it is quite soundless. He stops, and turns, and sees a great and ghostly wolf a few feet from him on the track.

In a way, it is almost a relief to see the wolf. It is alone, and it is a natural thing. Somehow he had half expected something unnatural. He draws his pistol, readies it, points it at the wolf. He is a fine shot. He already visualises lugging the bloody carcass, a trophy, into the house. He pulls the trigger.

A barren click. He is surprised. He tries again. Another click. It comes to him that his servant has emptied the chamber of bullets.

He sees a vision of the park gates a quarter of a mile away, and he turns immediately and runs towards them.

Ten seconds later a warm and living weight crashes against his back, and he falls screaming, screaming before the pain even begins. When the pain does begin, he is unable to scream for very long, but he does his best. The final thing he sees through the haze of his own blood, which has splashed up into his eyes, and the tears of agony and the enclosing of a most atrocious death, are the eyes of the wolf, gleaming coolly back at him. He knows they are the eyes of Anna. And that it is Anna who then tears out his throat.

The small crystal goblet slipped out of Lisel's hand, empty, and broke on the floor. Lisel started. Dazed, she looked away from the fire, to Anna the Matriarch.

Had Lisel been asleep and dreaming? What an unpleasant dream. Or had it been so unpleasant? Lisel became aware her teeth were clenched in spiteful gladness, as if on a bone. If Anna had told her the truth, that man—that *thing*—had deserved it all. To be betrayed by his servants, and by his wife, and to perish in the fangs of a wolf. A werewolf.

Grandmother and granddaughter confronted each other a second, with identical expressions of smiling and abstracted malice. Lisel suddenly flushed, smoothed her face, and looked down. There had been something in the drink after all.

"I don't think this at all nice," said Lisel.

"Nice isn't the word," Anna agreed. Beautiful reclined at her feet, and she stroked his hair. Across the big room, the stained-glass window was thickening richly to opacity. The sun must be near to going down.

"*If* it's the truth," said Lisel primly, "you will go to Hell."

"Oh? Don't you think me justified? He'd have killed your mother at the very least. *You* would never have been born."

Lisel reviewed this hypothetical omission. It carried some weight.

"You should have appealed for help."

"To whom? The marriage vow is a chain that may not be broken. If I had left him, he would have traced me, as he did the child. No law supports a wife. I could only kill him."

"I don't believe you killed him as you say you did."

"Don't you, m'mselle? Well, never mind. Once the sun has set, you'll see it happen before your eyes." Lisel stared and opened her mouth to remonstrate. Anna added gently: "And, I am afraid, not to myself alone."

Aside from all reasoning and the training of a short lifetime, Lisel felt the stranglehold of pure terror fasten on her. She rose and squealed: "What do you mean?"

"I mean," said Anna, "that the liqueur you drank is made from the same yellow flowers I ate to give me the power of transmogrification. I mean that the wolf-magic, once invoked, becomes hereditary, yet dormant. I mean that what the goddess of the Wolfland conveys must indeed be paid for at the hour of death—unless another will take up the gift."

Lisel, not properly understanding, not properly believing, began to shriek wildly. Anna came to her feet. She crossed to Lisel and shook the shrieks out of her, and when she was dumb, thrust her back in the chair.

"Now sit, fool, and be quiet. I've put nothing on you that was not already yours. Look in the mirror. Look at your hair and your eyes and your beautiful teeth. Haven't you always preferred the night to the day, staying up till the morning, lying abed till noon? Don't you love the cold forest? Doesn't the howl of the wolf thrill you through with fearful delight? And why else should the Wolfland accord you an escort, a pack of wolves running by you on the road. Do you think you'd have survived if you'd not been one of their kind, too?"

Lisel wept, stamping her foot. She could not have said at all what she felt. She tried to think of her father and the ballrooms of the city. She tried to consider if she credited magic.

"Now listen to me," snapped Anna, and Lisel muted her sobs just enough to catch the words. "Tonight is full moon, and the anniversary of that night, years ago, when I made my pact with the wolf goddess of the north. I have good cause to suspect I shan't live out this year. Therefore, tonight is the last chance I have to render you in my place into her charge. That frees me from her, do you see? Once you have swallowed the flowers, once she has acknowledged you, you belong to her. At death, I escape her sovereignty, which would otherwise bind me forever to the earth in wolf form, phantom form. A bargain: you save me. But you too can make your escape, when the time comes. Bear a child. You will be mistress here. You can command any man to serve you, and you're tolerable enough the service won't be unwilling. My own child, your mother, was not like me at all. I could not bring her to live with me, once I had the power. I was troubled as to how I should wean her to it. But she died, and in you I saw the mark from the first hour. You are fit to take my place. Your child can take yours."

"You're hateful!" shrieked Lisel. She had the wish to laugh.

But someone was flinging open the doors of the hall. The cinnamon light streamed through and fell into the fire and faded it. Another fire, like antique bronze, was quenching itself among the pines. The dying of the sun.

Anna moved towards the doors and straight out onto the snow. She stood a moment, tall and amazing on the peculiar sky. She seemed a figment of the land itself, and maybe she was.

"Come!" she barked. Then turned and walked away across the park.

All the servants seemed to have gathered like bats in the hall. They were silent, but they looked at Lisel. Her heart struck her over and over. She did not know what she felt or if she believed. Then a wolf sang in the forest. She lifted her head. She suddenly knew frost and running and black stillness, and a platinum moon, red feasts and wild hymnings, lovers with quicksilver eyes and the race of the ice wind and stars smashed under the hard soles of her four feet. A huge white ballroom opened before her, and the champagne of the air filled her mouth.

Beautiful had knelt and was kissing the hem of her red cloak. She patted his head absently, and the gathering of the servants sighed.

Presumably, as Anna's heiress, she might be expected to live on in the forest, in the château which would be hers. She could even visit the city, providing she was home by sunset.

The wolf howled again, filling her veins with lights, raising the hair along her scalp.

Lisel tossed her head. Of course, it was all a lot of nonsense.

She hastened out through the doors and over the winter park and followed her grandmother away into the Wolfland.

# WRITTEN IN WATER

T WAS A STILL SUMMER NIGHT, COLOURED THROUGH BY darkness. A snow-white star fell out of the sky and into the black field half a mile from the house. Ten minutes later, Jaina had walked from the house, through the fenced garden patch, the creaking gate, towards the place where the star had fallen. Presently, she was standing over a young man, lying tangled in a silver web, on the burned lap of the Earth.

"Who are you?" said Jaina. "What's happened to you? Can you talk? Can you tell me?"

The young man, who was very young, about twenty-two or -three, moved his slim young body, turning his face. He was wonderful to look at, so wonderful, Jaina needed to take a deep breath before she spoke to him again.

"I want to help you. Can you say anything?"

He opened a pair of eyes, like two windows opening on sunlight in the dark. His eyes were beautiful, and very golden. He said nothing, not even anything she could not understand. She looked at him, drinking in, intuitively, his beauty; knowing, also intuitively, that he had nothing to do either with her world, or her time.

"Where did you come from?" she said.

He looked back at her. He seemed to guess, and then to consider. Gravely, gracefully, he lifted one arm from the tangle of the web, and pointed at the sky.

He sat in her kitchen, at her table. She offered him medication, food, alcohol, and caffeine from a tall bronzed coffee pot. He shook his head, slowly. Semantically, some gestures were the same. Yet not the same. Even in the shaking of his head, she perceived he was alien. His hair was the colour of the coffee he refused. Coffee, with a few drops of milk in it, and a burnish like satin. His skin was pale. So pale, it too was barely humanly associable. She had an inspiration, and filled a glass with water. The water was pure, filtered through the faucet from the well in the courtyard, without chemicals or additives. Even so, it might poison him. He had not seemed hurt after all, merely stunned, shaken. He had walked to her house quietly, at her side, responding to her swift angular little gestures of beckoning and reception. Now she wanted to give him something.

She placed the glass before him. He looked at it, and took it up in two finely made, strong, articulate hands. They were the hands of a dancer, a musician. They had each only four fingers, one thumb, quite normal. He carried the glass to his mouth. She held her breath, wondering, waiting. He put the glass down carefully, and moved it, as carefully, away from him. He laid his arms across the table and his head upon his arms, and he wept.

Jaina stood staring at him. A single strand of silver, left adhering when he stripped himself of the web, lay across his arm, glittering as his shoulders shook. She listened to him crying, a young man's sobs, painful, tearing him. She approached him, and muttered: "What is it? What is it?" helplessly.

Of course, it was only grief. She put her hand on his shoulder, anxious, for he might flinch from her touch, or some inimical thing in their separate chemistries might damage both of them. But he did not flinch, and no flame burst out between her palm and the dark, apparently seamless clothing which he wore.

"Don't cry," she said. But she did not mean it. His distress afforded her an exquisite agony of empathic pain. She had not felt anything for a very long time. She stroked his hair gently. Perhaps some subtle radiation clung to him, some killer dust from a faraway star. She did not care. "Oh, don't cry, don't cry," she murmured, swimming in his tears.

She drove into the morning town in her ramshackle car, as usual not paying much attention to anything about her. Nor was her programme much changed. First, petrol from the self-service station, then a tour of the shops, going in and out of their uninviting façades: a tour of duty. In the large hypermarket at the edge of town, she made her way through the plastic and the cans, vaguely irritated, as always, by the soft mush of music, which came and went on a time switch, regardless of who wanted it, or no longer did. Once, she had seen a rat scuttle over the floor behind the frozen meat section. Jaina had done her best to ignore such evidence of neglect. She had walked out of the shop stiffly.

She had never liked people very much. They had always hurt her, or degraded her, always imposed on her in some way. Finally she had retreated into the old house, wanting to be alone, a hermitess. Her ultimate loneliness, deeper than any state she had actually imagined for herself, was almost like a judgement. She was thirty-five and, to herself, resembled a burned-out lamp. The dry leaf-brownness of her skin, the tindery quality of her hair, gave her but further evidence of this consuming. Alone, alone. She had been alone so long. And burned, a charred stick, incapable of moistures, fluidities. And yet, streams and oceans had moved in her, when the young man from outer space had sobbed with his arms on her table.

She supposed, wryly, that the normal human reaction to what had happened would be a desire to contact someone, inform someone of her miraculous find, her "Encounter." She only played with this idea, comparing it to her present circumstances. She felt, of course, no onus on her to act in a rational way. Besides, whom should she approach with her story, who would be likely to credit her? While she herself had no doubts.

But as she was turning on to the dirt road that led to the house, she became the prey of sudden insecurities. Perhaps the ultimate loneliness had told, she had gone insane, fantasising the falling star of the parachute, imagining the young man with eyes like golden sovereigns. Or, if it were true. . . .Possibly, virulent Terran germs, carried by herself, her touch, had already killed him. She pictured, irresistibly, Wells's Martians lying dead and decaying in their great machines, slain by the microbes of Earth.

Last night, when he had grown calm, or only tired, she had led him to her bedroom and shown him her bed. It was a narrow bed, what else, fit only for one. Past lovers had taught her that the single bed was to be hers, in spite of them, forever. But he had lain down there without a word. She had slept in the room below, in a straight-backed chair between the bureau and the TV set which did not work anymore. Waking at sunrise, with a shamed awareness of a new feeling, which was that of a child on Christmas morning, she had slunk to look at him asleep. And she was reminded of some poem she had read, long, long ago:

> How beautiful you look when sleeping; so beautiful
> It seems that you have gone away. . . .

She had left him there, afraid to disturb such completion, afraid to stand and feed parasitically on him. She had driven instead into town for extra supplies. She wanted to bring him things; food he might not eat, drink he might not drink. Even music, even books he could not assimilate.

But now—he might be gone, never have existed. Or he might be dead.

She spun the car to a complaining halt in the summer dust. She ran between the tall carboniferous trees, around the fence. Her heart was in her throat, congesting and blinding her.

The whole day lay out over the country in a white-hot film. She turned her head, trying to see through this film, as if underwater. The house looked silent, mummified. Empty. The land was the same, an erased tape. She glanced at the blackened field.

As she stumbled towards the house, her breathing harsh, he came out through the open door.

He carried the spade which she had used to turn the pitiful garden. He had been cleaning the spade; it looked bright and shiny. He leaned it on the porch and walked towards her. As she stared at him, taking oxygen in great gulps, he went by her, and began to lift things out of the car and carry them to the house.

"I thought you were dead," she said stupidly. She stood stupidly, her head stupidly hanging, feeling suddenly very sick and drained.

After a while she too walked slowly into the house. While he continued to fetch the boxes and tins into her kitchen like an errand boy, she sat at the table, where he had sat the night before. It occurred to her that she could have brought him fresh clothing from the stores in the town, but it would have embarrassed her slightly to choose things for him, even randomly off the peg in the hypermarket.

His intention had presumably been to work on her garden, some sort of repayment for her haphazard, inadequate hospitality. And for this work he had stripped bare to the waist. She was afraid to look at him. The torso, what was revealed of it, was also like a dancer's—supple, the musculature developed and flawless. She debated, in a dim terror of herself, if his human maleness extended to all regions of his body.

After a long time, he stopped bringing in the supplies, and took up the spade once more.

"Are you hungry?" she said to him. She showed him one of the cans. As previously, slow and quiet, he shook his head.

Perhaps he did not need to eat. Perhaps he would drink her blood. Her veins filled with fire, and she left the table, and went quickly upstairs. She should tell someone about him. If only she were able to. But she could not.

He was hers.

She lay in the bath, in the cool water, letting her washed wet hair float around her. She was Ophelia. Not swimming; drowning. A slender glass of greenish gin on five rocks of milky ice pulsed in her fingers to the rhythm of her heart.

Below, she heard the spade ring tirelessly on stone. She had struggled with the plot, raising a few beans, tomatoes, potatoes which blackened and a vine which died. But he would make her garden grow. Oh, yes.

She rested her head on the bath's porcelain rim, and laughed, trembling, the tips of her breasts breaking the water like buds.

She visualised a silver bud in the sky, blossoming into a huge and fiery ship. The ship came down on the black field. It had come for him, come to take him home. She held his hand and pleaded, in a language he did not comprehend, and a voice spoke to him out of the ship, in a language which he knew well. She clung to his ankle, and he pulled her through the scorched grass, not noticing her, as he ran towards the blazing port.

Why else had he wept? Somehow and somewhere, out beyond the moon, his inexplicable craft had foundered. Everything was lost to him. His vessel, his home, his world, his kind. Instead there was a bony house, a bony, dried-out hag, food he could not eat. A living death.

Jaina felt anger. She felt anger as she had not felt it for several months, hearing that spade ring on the indomitable rock under the soil. Still alone.

When the clock chimed six times that meant it was one-quarter past five, and Jaina came down the stairs of the house. She wore a dress like white tissue, and a marvellous scent out of a crystal bottle. She had seen herself in a mirror, brushing her face with delicate pastel dusts, and her eyes with cinnamon and charcoal.

She stood on the porch, feeling a butterfly lightness. She stretched up her hand to shield her eyes, the gesture of a heroine upon the veranda of a dream. He rested on the spade, watching her.

*See how I am*, she thought. *Please, please, see me, see me.*

She walked off the porch, across the garden. She went straight up to him. The sun in his eyes blinded her. She could not smile at him. She pointed to her breast.

"Jaina," she said. "I am *Jaina.*" She pointed to him. She did not touch him. "You?"

She had seen it done so frequently. In films. She had read it in books. Now he himself would smile slightly, uneasily touch his own chest and say, in some foreign otherworld tongue: *I am. . . .*

But he did not. He gazed at her, and once more he slowly shook his head. Suddenly, all the glorious pity and complementary grief she had felt through him before flooded back, overwhelming her. Could it be he did not know, could not remember, who he was? His name, his race, his planet? He had fallen out of the stars. He was amnesiac. Truly defenceless, then. Truly hers.

"Don't work anymore," she said. She took the spade from his hand, and let it drop on the upturned soil.

Again, she led him back to the house, still not touching him.

In the kitchen, she said to him, "You must try and tell me what food you need to eat. You really must."

He continued to watch her, if he actually saw her at all. She imagined him biting off her arm, and shivered. Perhaps he did not eat —she had considered that before. Not eat, not sleep—the illusion of sleep only a suspended state, induced to please her, or pacify her. She did not think he had used the bathroom. He did not seem to sweat. How odd he should have been able to shed tears.

She dismissed the idea of eating for herself, too. She poured herself another deep swamp of ice and gin. She sat on the porch and he sat beside her.

His eyes looked out across the country. Looking for escape? She could smell the strange sweatless, poreless, yet indefinably masculine scent of him. His extraordinary skin had taken on a water-colour glaze of sunburn.

The day flickered along the varied tops of the reddening horizon. Birds swirled over like a flight of miniature planes. When the first star appeared, she knew she would catch her breath in fear.

The valves of the sky loosened, and blueness poured into it. The sun had gone. He could not understand her, so she said to him: "I love you."

"I love you," she said. "I'm the last woman on Earth, and you're not even local talent. And I love you. I'm lonely," she said. And, unlike him, she cried quietly.

After a while, just as she would have wished him to if this had been a film, and she directing it, he put his arm about her, gently, gently. She lay against him, and he stroked her hair. She thought, with a strange ghostly sorrow: *He has learned such gestures from me.*

Of course, she did not love him, and of course she did. She was the last survivor, and he was also a survivor. Inevitably they must come together, find each other, love. She wished she was younger. She began to feel younger as his arm supported her, and his articulate fingers silked through and through her hair. In a low voice, although he could not understand, she began to tell him about the plague. How it had come, a whisper, the fall of a leaf far away. How it had swept over the world, its continents, its cities, like a sea. A sea of leaves, burning. A fire. They had not called it plague. The official name for it had been "Pandemic." At first, the radios had chattered with it, the glowing pools of the TVs had crackled with it. She had seen the hospitals packed like great antiseptic trays with racks of the dying. She had heard how silence came. At length, more than silence came. They burned the dead, or cremated them with burning chemicals. They evacuated the towns. Then "they" too ceased to organise anything. It was a selective disease. It killed men and women and children. It could not destroy the animals, the insects, the birds. Or Jaina.

At first, the first falling of the leaf, she had not believed. It was hard to believe that such an unstoppable engine had been started. The radio and the television set spoke of decaying cylinders in the sea, or satellites which corroded, letting go their cargoes of viruses, mistimed, on the Earth. Governments denied responsibility, and died denying it.

Jaina heard the tread of death draw near, and nearer. From disbelief, she came to fear. She stocked her hermitage, as she had always done, and crouched in new terror behind her door. As the radio turned dumb, and the TV spluttered and choked to blindness, Jaina stared from her porch, looking for a huge black shadow to descend across the land.

They burned a pile of the dead on a giant bonfire in the field, half a mile from the house. The ashes blew across the sunset. The sky was burning its dead, too.

A day later, Jaina found little fiery mottles over her skin. Her head throbbed, just as the walls were doing. She lay down with her terror, afraid to die. Then she did not care if she died. She wanted to die. Then she did not die at all.

A month later, she drove into the town. She found the emptiness of the evacuation and, two miles away, the marks of another enormous bonfire. And a mile beyond that, dead people lying out in the sun, turning to pillars of salt and white sticks of candy, and the fearless birds, immune, dropping like black rain on the place.

Jaina drove home, and became the last woman on Earth.

Her life was not so very different, she had been quite solitary for many years before the plague came.

She had sometimes mused as to why she had lived, but only in the silly, falsely modest way of any survivor. Everyone knew they could not die, hang the rest, they alone must come through. They had all been wrong, all but Jaina.

And then, one night, a snow-white star, the silver web of the alien parachute, a young man more beautiful than truth.

She told him everything as she lay against his shoulder. He might still be capable of dying, a Martian, susceptible to the plague virus. Or he might go away.

It was dark now. She lifted her mouth to his in the darkness. As she kissed him, she was unsure what he would do. He did not seem to react in any way. Would he make love to her, or want to, or was he able to? She slid her hands over his skin, like warm smooth stone. She loved him. But perhaps he was only a robot.

After a little while, she drew away, and left him seated on the porch. She went into the kitchen and threw the melted ice in her glass into the sink.

She climbed the stairs; she lay down on the narrow bed. Alone. Alone. But somehow even then, she sensed the irony was incomplete. And when he came into the room, she was not surprised. He leaned over her, silently, and his eyes shone in the darkness, like the eyes of a cat. She attempted to be afraid of him.

"Go away," she said.

But he stretched out beside her, very near, the bed so narrow. . . . As if he had learned now the etiquette of human lovemaking, reading its symbols from her mind.

"You're a robot, an android," she said. "Leave me alone."

He put his mouth over hers. She closed her eyes and saw a star, a nova. He was not a robot, he was a man, a beautiful man, and she loved him. . . .

Twenty million miles away, the clock chimed eight times. It was one-quarter past seven, on the first night of the world.

In the morning she baked bread, and brought him some, still warm. He held the bread cupped in his hands like a paralysed bird. She pointed to herself. "Please. Call me by my name. *Jaina.*"

She was sure she could make him grasp the meaning. She knew he had a voice. She had heard his tears, and, during their lovemaking, heard him groan. She would teach him to eat and drink, too. She would teach him everything.

He tilled the garden; he had found seedlings in the leaning shed and was planting them, until she came to him and led him to the ramshackle car. She drove him into town, then took him into the clothing stores, directing him, diffidently. In accordance with her instructions, he loaded the car. She had never seen him smile. She pondered if she ever would. He carried piled jeans with the same eternally dispassionate disinterest: still the errand boy.

During the afternoon she watched him in the garden. Her pulses raced, and she could think of nothing else but the play of muscles under his swiftly and mellifluously tanning skin. He hypnotised her. She fell asleep and dreamed of him.

She roused at a sound of light blows on metal. Alarmed, she walked out into the last gasps of the day, to find him behind the courtyard, hammering dents out of the battered car. She perceived he had changed a tyre she had not bothered with, though it was worn. She relaxed against the wall, brooding on him. He was going to be almost ludicrously useful. For some reason, the archaic word *help-meet* stole into her mind.

Over it all hung the smoke of premonition. He would be going away. Stranded, marooned, shipwrecked, the great liner would move out of the firmament, cruel as God, to rescue him.

She woke somewhere in the centre of the night, her lips against his spine, with a dreadful knowledge.

For a long while she lay immobile, then lifted herself onto one elbow. She stayed that way, looking at him, his feigned sleep, or the real unconsciousness which appeared to have claimed him. *It seems that you have gone away.* No. He would not be going anywhere.

His hair gleamed, his lashes lay in long brushstrokes on his cheeks. He was quiescent, limpid, as if poured from a jar. She touched his flank, coldly.

After a minute, she rose and went to the window, and looked out and upward into the vault of the night sky. A low blaring of hatred and contempt ran through her. *Where are you?* she thought. *Do you see? Are you laughing?*

She walked down the stairs and into the room where the dead TV sat in the dark. She opened a drawer in the bureau and took out a revolver. She loaded it carefully from the clip. She held it pointed before her as she went back up into the bedroom.

He did not wake up—or whatever simulation he contrived that passed for waking—until the hour before the dawn. She had sat there all the time, waiting for him, wanting him to open his eyes and see her, seated facing him, her hand resting on her knee, the revolver in her hand. Pointing now at him.

There was a chance he might not know what the gun was. Yet weapons, like certain semantic signs, would surely be instantly, instinctively recognisable. So she thought. As his eyes opened and fixed on the gun, she believed he knew perfectly well what it was, and that she had brought it there to kill him with.

His eyes grew very wide, but he did not move. He did not appear afraid, yet she considered he must be afraid. As afraid of her as she might have been expected to be of him, and yet had never been: the natural fear of an alien, xenophobia. She thought he could, after all, understand her words, had understood her from the beginning, her language, her loneliness. It would have been part of his instruction. Along with the lessons which had taught him how to work the land, change a tyre, make love, pretend to sleep. . . .About the same time, they must have inoculated him against the deadly plague virus, indeed all the viruses of Earth.

"Yes," she said. "I *am* going to kill you."

He only looked at her. She remembered how he had wept, out of dread of her, loathing and despair. Because he had known there would be no rescue for him. Neither rescue from her planet nor from herself. He had not fallen from a burning spacecraft into the world. The craft had been whole, and he had been dropped neatly out of it, at a designated hour, at a calculated altitude, his parachute unfolding, a preprogrammed cloud. Not shipwrecked, but despatched. Air mail. A present.

The great silent ship would not come seeking him. It had already come, and gone.

Why did they care so much? She could not fathom that. An interfering streak—was this the prerogative of gods? Altruistic benefactors, or simply playing with toys. Or it might be an experiment of some sort. They had not been able to prevent the plague, or had not wanted to—recall the Flood, Gomorrah—but when the plague had drawn away down its tidal drain, washing humanity with it, they had looked and seen Jaina wandering alone on the Earth, mistress of it, the last of her kind. So they had made for her a helpmate and companion. Presumably not made him in *their* extra-terrestrial image, whoever, whatever they omnipotently were, but in the image of a man.

She was uncertain what had triggered her final deduction. His acquiescence, the unlikely aptness of it all, the foolish coincidence of survivor flung down beside survivor, pat. Or was it the theatricality which had itself suggested puppet-masters to her subconscious: the last man and the last woman left to propagate continuance of a species. Or was it only her mistrust? All the wrongs she had, or imagined she had suffered, clamouring that this was no different from any other time. Someone still manipulated, still *imposed* on her.

"Well," she said softly, looking at him, it appeared to her, through the eye of the gun, "I seem to be missing a rib. Do I call you Adam? Or would it be *Eve?*" She clicked off the safety-catch. She trembled violently, though her voice was steady. "What about contraception, Adameve? Did they think I'd never heard of it, or used it? Did they think I'd risk having babies, with no hospitals, not even a vet in sight? At thirty-five years of age? When I dressed up for you, I dressed thoroughly, *all* of me. Just in case. Seems I was wise. I don't think even your specially designed seed is so potent it can negate my precautions. In the tank where they grew you, or the machine-shop where they built you, did they think of *that?* I don't want you," she whispered. "You cried like a child because they condemned you to live on my world, with me. Do you think I can forgive you that? Do you think I want you after that, now I *know?*"

She raised the gun and fired. She watched the sun go out in the windows of his eyes. His blood was red, quite normal.

Jaina walked across the burn-scar of the field. She pictured a huge wheel hanging over her, beyond and above the sky, pictured it no longer watching, already drawing inexorably away and away. She dragged the spade along the ground, as she had dragged his body. Now the spade had turned potatoes, and beans, and alien flesh.

She stood in the kitchen of the old house, and the darkness like space came and coloured the sky through. Jaina held her breath, held it and held it, as if the air had filled with water, closing over her head. For she knew. Long before it happened, she knew. She only let out her breath in a slow sigh, horribly flattered, as the second snow-white star fell out of the summer sky.

## A NOTE ON THE TYPE

*The text of this book was composed in the film version of Palatino, a typeface designed by the noted German typographer Hermann Zapf. Named after Giovanni Battista Palatino, a writing master of Renaissance Italy, Palatino was the earliest of Zapf's typefaces to be introduced to America. The first designs for this calligraphic-styled face were made in 1948, and complete fonts were issued between 1950 and 1952. Like all Zapf-designed typefaces, Palatino is beautifully balanced and exceedingly readable.*